Pat Manley
Father's Day, 1994
From Bob & Shirley

FOUR GREAT NOVELS OF THE WEST

FOUR GREAT NOVELS
OF THE WEST

SHANE by Jack Schaefer

BUGLES IN THE AFTERNOON
by Ernest Haycox

THE SEARCHERS by Alan LeMay

WARHORSE by John Cunningham

Edited by Marc Jaffe

WINGS BOOKS
New York • Avenel, New Jersey

The editor wishes to thank Michael Congdon of Don Congdon Associates, Inc. and Jon Tuska of the Golden West Literary Agency for invaluable research assistance in the preparation of this collection. His wife, Vivienne Jaffe, was equally invaluable as an editorial conscience and commentator.

This edition contains the complete and unabridged texts of the original editions. They have been completely reset for this volume.

This 1994 edition is published by Wings Books,
distributed by Outlet Book Company, Inc., a Random House Company,
40 Engelhard Avenue, Avenel, New Jersey 07001,
by arrangement with Marc Jaffe.

Random House
New York • Toronto • London • Sydney • Auckland

Printed and bound in the United States of America

Library of Congress Cataloging-in-Publication Data

Four great novels of the West / edited by Marc Jaffe
     p.   cm.
   Contents: Shane / J. Schaefer —Bugles in the afternoon / E. Haycox — The searchers / A. LeMay — Warhorse / J. Cunningham
    ISBN 0-517-10033-9
    1. Western stories. 2. American fiction—20th century.
 I. Jaffe, Marc.
 PS648.W4F68   1994
 813'.087408—dc20   93-36172
                                   CIP

8 7 6 5 4 3 2 1

CONTENTS

Introduction

The Western—
America's Popular Fiction

"When you call me that, smile." This danger-laden phrase, though not the first line of Owen Wister's *The Virginian*, may well stand as the "Call me Ishmael" of American popular fiction. Just as Melville's ambiguities suggest the dominant themes of much of the serious American literature that followed him, so did Wister's clear, unencumbered view of the good and the bad, of what makes a man's strength and weakness, of the glory of the great sweep of the western American landscape, describe the matrix of the twentieth-century form of American popular fiction known around the world as the "western."

Since 1902, when *The Virginian* was published, reader interest in the western novel has been cyclical, in a pattern difficult to relate to other prevailing currents of popular culture. In the 1920s, coming at a time when the country was looking for heroes, Zane Grey's myth-creating novels, such as *Spirit of the Border,* were often major bestsellers in hardcover, comparable to the Micheners and Clancys of the present. Eugene Manlove Rhodes, writing in the Wister tradition, William McLeod Raine, known for his elaborate prose, and B.M. Bower (Bertha M. hiding behind initials in those pre-Friedan days), were names to reckon with in the bookstores and were published by august entrepreneurs such as Harper & Bros. of New York and Houghton Mifflin, a Boston firm.

With the 1930s, and the development of an effective structure for the mass distribution of magazines, and (perhaps not coincidentally) with the impact of The Great Depression, came the Golden Age of so-called "pulp" fiction. Magazines of action and adventure, selling for a thin dime or a quarter, took over the newsstands as bare bosoms and bottoms did a generation later. And western fiction—as in *Dime Western, Ten Story Western* (for 15¢), *Fifteen Western Tales* (for 25¢), and *Western Short Stories*—dominated the shelves east and west of the Mississippi. Writers, learning their craft and often their very subject matter as they wrote, poured (or pounded) out the words by the penny. Names like William R. Cox, Walt Coburn, Wayne D. Overholser, Tom Blackburn, and Nelson C. Nye, sold magazines by the hundreds of thousands: and at the top of the mountain of words was the multi-named and multi-plotting Frederick Faust, who as Max Brand symbolized the best in western pulp fiction.

As the '30s wore on the nation's ears became thoroughly glued to the mahogany box. Though radio's evening hours may well have been dominated by family humor of the Benny, Burns, and Allen variety, the after-school audience did have its taste of the West, with the Lone Ranger and Tonto, signalled by the oddly appropriate strains of Rossini's warhorse, *William Tell Overture.*

While Saturday eyes were most often drawn to the movie screen, entertainment in print still managed to maintain a powerful hold. The "general interest" magazine grew into a major force, and the *Saturday Evening Post* and *Collier's* reached millions of readers each week, numbers hard to believe in these electronic '80s and '90s. As these magazines climbed in circulation, western fiction rose with them to a new plateau of style, sophistication, and content as it reached a wider and more demanding audience.

Even more demanding were the editorial standards of the magazines themselves. The best of the pulp writers moved up to the "slicks" (a term derived from paper quality, not business practices) and the guardians at the gate were editors like the famed Erd Brandt and his co-worker Stuart Rose at the *Saturday Evening Post,* and Kenneth Littauer and later Knox Burger at *Collier's.* The editor's task, not only to discover talent, but to nurture and guide it—sometimes with a forceful hand—has never been better exemplified than in this period of the development of popular western fiction. The pulp magazine story depended for success essentially on its treatment of action, with a leavening of freshness of setting and plot. Brandt and his colleagues urged writers toward a more serious attention to historical accuracy, to a more careful and sensitive evocation of place, and to the details of the lifestyle of the plains and mountains, the ranches, military posts, and towns of the post-Civil War American West. Most important, one finds in both short stories and full-length novels (which normally appeared in serial form in both the *Post* and *Collier's*) a newfound concentration on character development and the emotional depth of human conflict. Novels by Ernest Haycox and Alex LeMay, two of the three brightest stars in this "slick" firmament, appear in this volume. The third, Luke Short (the pen name of Frederick Dilley Glidden) went on to become the bestselling western writer of the paperback world of the late 1940s and '50s. These three, and a few others, set standards of quality which have been exceeded by only a very few in the decades since they flourished.

The fortunes of the general interest magazines such as the *Saturday Evening Post* and *Collier's,* much less the pulps, began to wane as the 1950s wore on. Not so the fortunes of the popular western novel, which quickly found a new home between paper covers. The reading audience created by the mass magazines had no difficulty transferring its allegiance to the mass-distributed paperbacks, pleasantly priced at 25¢ to 35¢ or even 50¢; and the names on the covers were familiar. The western became a staple of this new world of publishing and reading.

What happened to the message of content and quality in the western, as the reading medium changed? At one end, the pulp tradition flowed on in its stream of fast pace and action. To this reader, at least, "shoot 'em up," a common phrase in the editorial jargon of the West, is not necessarily a term of opprobrium. There is good and bad at all levels and varieties of popular culture, as there are in all varieties of what we call literary culture. The good is not easy to spot, but it's there: good "pulp" writing, along with purity of action, is shot through with purity of intention. The good pulp writer, whether or not he worked at the effect, had that extra spark of energy which is derived both from real creativity and a sense of conviction that one's work has value beyond the financial; and that spark leaps across the gap to the reader.

If there was room for the old pulp writers in paperbacks, the tradition of Haycox, LeMay, and Short was carried on as well, fostered by another group of editors, notably Mrs. Ian (Betty) Ballantine, whose list at Ballantine Books was probably the most consistently high in quality of any publisher, hardcover or soft. Other enthusiasts for the genre were Saul David, who brought Louis L'Amour to Bantam Books; Austin Olney who brought Oregonian Bill Gulick, Clay Fisher (Will Henry under another name), and Jack Schaefer to the afore-mentioned Houghton Mifflin; and Knox Burger who was still on the scene, having shed slick paper for newsprint in paper covers at Fawcett's Gold Medal Books and then Dell First Editions. These sharp-eyed and sometimes even sharper-pencilled professionals encouraged talent, old and young. They challenged writers to even higher standards of historical accuracy or local color (as required), sophistication of style, and attention to the complexities of human motivation and character. The result was popular fiction at its very best.

Were these novels something new under the "western" sun? Not really. There were still good guys and bad; gunfire splitting the night; the wide, open spaces. Something new was added, however, a much harder look at the line between the truth and the myth of the West. Will Henry, perhaps the best of his time, wrote the watershed novel about the Indian wars of the West in his version of the tragic saga of Chief Joseph and the Nez Perce, *Where the Sun Now Stands*. Jack Schaefer, eastern-born but western to the bone, wrote *Shane*, a coming-of-age novel. Elmore Leonard wrote *Hombre*, in which the half-breed hero forces the dark undercurrent of racism right to the surface, conflicting with fellow characters, and stirring the reader. Elmer Kelton wrote about cowboys so well that in his words you can feel the heat of the branding iron and smell the prairie oysters sizzling in the pan.

Now here comes the irony. While the quality goes up at both ends of the western literary spectrum, the reader population, contrary to the rising census figures, begins to level off and even slide down. In the mass paperback world, the title which may have sold three hundred thousand copies in the early 1950s, sells half that many ten or twelve years later; by the mid-seventies, initial printings might be seventy-five thousand or less. Westerns fare no better in hardcover; bookstore sales fade away almost to zero, leaving only the modest library market to sustain the persevering publisher of whom, by the 1980s, only two or three remain.

Who or what killed—or, perhaps better, wounded—the western? The reasons are varied, some subtle, some obvious and, in any case, quite difficult to put under the harsh light of culturo-sociological analysis. A generation of readers dying off? TV-watching? Movement of reader population from quiet rural to jazzy city life? All these are factors, but without even pseudo-scientific proof let's just accept the conclusion that there are downward slides in the never-ending up- and -down cycle of popular taste. Even now, in the '90s, westerns are still being written, the official western writers' organization, the Western Writers of America, grows and thrives, new titles are, despite the odds, being published. We old-timers are just living through a drought. And believe it or not, though many wells are dry, the rare, lush green of a desert spring shows up on the horizon from time to time; and at least once in these post '50s years, a kind of miracle happens.

Do miracles really happen in publishing? "Sleepers" may just happen—the books that find the huge unexpected audience, defying all fears and doubts, discovered the hard way by normally cautious publishers. But publishing miracles just don't happen. They are made; and no account of the recent history of the western, no matter how brief, can avoid mention of the miracle of Louis L'Amour. The ingredients of the miracle are not mysterious. They include a writer with great innate storytelling ability and a powerful ego to go with a powerful presence and physique; a writer with an honest drive to communicate a passion for a land and history he knew and loved. Combine this writer with a publisher whose sense of what the total marketing of paperback books—publicity, promotion, distribution—was all about in the 1970s and '80s. The result is a publishing phenomenon, the making of a celebrity author, the sale of millions of books in paperback and hardcovers, in stores and through the mails, not to speak of audiotapes, films, and TV series. This is a business phenomenon worth study, perhaps, but our concern here is with the world of western popular fiction. What comes through most strongly is that, even in lean times, the basic elements of the western story have a powerful attraction for the American reader in search of entertainment, a sense of linkage with the American past, however tenuous, and an identification with a value system both simple and satisfying.

Whither the western, as it comes out of a low period, L'Amour notwithstanding? The visual media have led the way, as they must. From the huge (and surprising to the filmmakers) success of *Lonesome Dove* and *Unforgiven* on the small and large screens, to the countless replays of "B"-picture westerns on the 2:00 a.m. shift on television, the western still holds its magic. As for print, it will without doubt be a matter of changing form, not content. By the turn of the century, if not before, the print will appear on screens as well as on paper. Some enterprising editor will no doubt create the first "hyper-western"—a text enhanced by explanatory images and sounds for reproduction via CD-ROM or another such mechanism. You'll see the difference between the trail of a shod and unshod horse's hoof as the marshal follows the man in the black hat; you'll hear the hoot of an owl; you'll follow the herd north on an early map of the Chisholm Trail. The book, however, will still be the book, hardcover and paperback, perhaps made available in new ways—in new, as well as the familiar, kinds of bookstores. Most important, one would hope that a new young Louis L'Amour or Luke Short is sweating over a typewriter, a word-processing computer, or even a long yellow pad, creating new stories based on old themes, for a waiting audience.

While we wait, there could be no better place to settle in than with the four great novels in this volume. They have been chosen from among the score of more generally accepted—by writers and literary experts of the genre—as the best westerns ever written. Further, they have been chosen as representatives of broad subject areas which have formed the background of hundreds, perhaps thousands, of short stories and novels over the years.

In *Bugles in the Afternoon,* Ernest Haycox wrote what is arguably the best popular novel about the U.S. Cavalry in the West in the 1870s and 1880s. More specifically, this is a story of the Seventh Cavalry during the time leading up to and then including the Battle of the Little Bighorn. Haycox, as other writers have, before and since, intersperses historical and fictional characters and events in a many-stranded plot. There are surprises here, one being the significant presence of women on the scene, women who are faced with real problems of love and survival as well as seduction and sentiment. Further, Haycox has, in a masterly stroke, devised a successful novel of Custer's Seventh without the presence of Custer himself. The principal action is seen from the point of view of Custer's subordinates, Reno and Benteen, and the suspense builds as we wait for Custer to appear; he never does. Custer and his men die offstage. So this is a novel about cavalry life and death, not about that now-mythic figure George Armstrong Custer. It is a novel of enlisted men and officers—and their women. It is a novel about sweat and saddle-leather, courage and cowardice. It is an imaginative military adventure, but one which rings loudly of the truth.

Ernest Haycox's broad canvas of history gives way to Jack Schaefer's sharp focus on a family ranch and a struggle for survival against savage odds in his classic *Shane.* The novel is unique among westerns in that, over the years, it has become a staple on high school and even many elementary school reading lists. And with good reason, for it is the emotional conflict within a family, and the maturing of a young boy, that form the core of a narrative which, in other respects, has only traditional elements of the western story, i.e., the lone stranger trying to live down a violent past, the powerful landowner trying to drive out the small rancher, the unrelenting and ruthless hired gun. Moral questions are raised along the way. What is the nature of manhood? Must we meet violence with violence? What are the limits to a wife's temptations? We may or may not agree with the author's resolution of these issues, but it is their presence which makes *Shane* a permanent fixture on the literary landscape.

Alan LeMay's *The Searchers* shares with *Shane* a classic simplicity of structure. Yet it is unusual, perhaps even unique, in the genre in that the story itself is spun out over a long period of time. A crime is committed—the kidnapping of a young white girl by Indians after a bloody raid on a homestead on the plains. The crime must be avenged, the girl found; and it is one man's years-long mission to accomplish this end. The power of the novel rests on a solid foundation of a strong literary style common to the best of historical fiction. This is the raw frontier as it *must* have been, in its sights, sounds and smells, its loneliness and danger. Only in such a land could such an unrelenting search take place—men sacrificing livelihood and even love to pursue a trail grown dim.

In *Warhorse,* finally, the trail is far from dim. The trail *is* the story, for John Cunningham has chosen, like his peers in this volume, to build his narrative around a myth-making event of our western past: not a mano-a-mano gunfight, not a cavalry-Indian battle, not a girl spirited away by savages, but a cattle drive. The great journey, an odyssey if you will, is typical of classic stories of all peoples down through the ages, and when the Chisholm Trail was marked out in nineteenth-century America, yet another aspect of this nation's myth fell into place. The harsh conflict between father and son in *Warhorse* not only gives depth and shape to this novel, it creates a resonance with a world of popular literature reaching back to the Bible and up through the Greeks to our own day.

Read on!

Marc Jaffe
Berlin, New York
December, 1993

SHANE

by
Jack Schaefer

TO CARL
for my first son
my first book

JACK SCHAEFER, a writer all his life, was born in 1907, the son of a lawyer (on whom the character of Shane was based) in Cleveland, Ohio. An English major at Oberlin College, he then studied at Columbia University before becoming a reporter in Norfolk, Virginia, Baltimore, Maryland, and New Haven, Connecticut, between 1930 and 1949.

Shane, by far his most popular novel, was also his first, written, he has said, "for relaxation" while working as a newspaper reporter. First published as a three-part serial in *Argosy* magazine in 1946, it was brought out three years later in hardcover by Houghton Mifflin Company, which remained his publisher throughout his career. Amazingly, Schaefer had never travelled west of his native Ohio and hadn't read westerns other than Zane Grey and Owen Wister. He attributed his success in the genre to his study of the classics as a literature major, his experience on newspapers, and his fascination with western history. His hallmark was thorough research and historical accuracy.

After *Shane* came four other books set in the West, before he ever got there. It wasn't until 1954, when an editor paid his way out West to write a series of articles, that he got his first look. A year later, he and his family moved to Santa Fe where they lived for over twenty-five years.

His 1953 novel, *The Canyon*, about a Cheyenne Indian before the arrival of the white man, was his personal favorite of the six novels, two story collections, two juvenile books, and five works of non-fiction he wrote. One other of his books, *Monte Walsh*, is regarded by many as the best novel about cowboy life ever written. Schaefer's gradual disenchantment with mankind as he saw the West being destroyed by developers led him to reflect, "Today I couldn't put Shane on the side of the homesteaders, because they were destroying the West. But I couldn't really put him on the side of the ranchers, either, because they were no better. If I had to today, I couldn't write the book."

Jack Schaefer died in 1991 at 83, of congestive heart failure, leaving relatives including his second wife, eleven grandchildren and five great-grandchildren.

1

He rode into our valley in the summer of '89. I was a kid then, barely topping the backboard of father's old chuck-wagon. I was on the upper rail of our small corral, soaking in the late afternoon sun, when I saw him far down the road where it swung into the valley from the open plain beyond.

In that clear Wyoming air I could see him plainly, though he was still several miles away. There seemed nothing remarkable about him, just another stray horseman riding up the road toward the cluster of frame buildings that was our town. Then I saw a pair of cowhands, loping past him, stop and stare after him with a curious intentness.

He came steadily on, straight through the town without slackening pace, until he reached the fork a half-mile below our place. One branch turned left across the river ford and on to Luke Fletcher's big spread. The other bore ahead along the right bank where we homesteaders had pegged our claims in a row up the valley. He hesitated briefly, studying the choice, and moved again steadily on our side.

As he came near, what impressed me first was his clothes. He wore dark trousers of some serge material tucked into tall boots and held at the waist by a wide belt, both of a soft black leather tooled in intricate design. A coat of the same dark material as the trousers was neatly folded and strapped to his saddle-roll. His shirt was finespun linen, rich brown in color. The handkerchief knotted loosely around his throat was black silk. His hat was not the familiar Stetson, not the familiar gray or muddy tan. It was a plain black, soft in texture, unlike any hat I had ever seen, with a creased crown and a wide curling brim swept down in front to shield the face.

All trace of newness was long since gone from these things. The dust of distance was beaten into them. They were worn and stained and several neat patches showed on the shirt. Yet a kind of magnificence remained and with it a hint of men and manners alien to my limited boy's experience.

Then I forgot the clothes in the impact of the man himself. He was not much above medium height, almost slight in build. He would have looked frail along-side father's square, solid bulk. But even I could read the endurance in the lines of that dark figure and the quiet power in its effortless, unthinking adjustment to every movement of the tired horse.

He was clean-shaven and his face was lean and hard and burned from high forehead to firm, tapering chin. His eyes seemed hooded in the shadow of the hat's brim. He came closer, and I could see that this was because the brows were drawn in a frown of fixed and habitual alertness. Beneath them the eyes were endlessly searching from side to side and forward, checking off every item in view, missing nothing. As I noticed this, a sudden chill, I could not have told why, struck through me there in the warm and open sun.

He rode easily, relaxed in the saddle, leaning his weight lazily into the stirrups. Yet even in this easiness was a suggestion of tension. It was the easiness of a coiled spring, of a trap set.

He drew rein not twenty feet from me. His glance hit me, dismissed me, flicked over our place. This was not much, if you were thinking in terms of size and scope. But what there was was good. You could trust father for that. The corral, big enough for about thirty head if you crowded them in, was railed right to true sunk posts. The pasture behind, taking in nearly half of our claim, was fenced tight. The barn was small, but it was solid, and we were raising a loft at one end for the alfalfa growing green in the north forty. We had a fair-sized field in potatoes that year and father was trying a new corn he had sent all the way to Washington for and they were showing properly in weedless rows.

Behind the house, mother's kitchen garden was a brave sight. The house itself was three rooms—two really, the big kitchen where we spent most of our time indoors and the bedroom beside it. My little lean-to room was added back of the kitchen. Father was planning, when he could get around to it, to build mother the parlor she wanted.

We had wooden floors and a nice porch across the front. The house was painted too, white with green trim, rare thing in all that region, to remind her, mother said when she made father do it, of her native New England. Even rarer, the roof was shingled. I knew what that meant. I had helped father split those shingles. Few places so spruce and well worked could be found so deep in the Territory in those days.

The stranger took it all in, sitting there easily in the saddle. I saw his eyes slow on the flowers mother had planted by the porch steps, then come to rest on our shiny new pump and the trough beside it. They shifted back to me, and again, without knowing why, I felt that sudden chill. But his voice was gentle and he spoke like a man schooled in patience.

"I'd appreciate a chance at the pump for myself and the horse."

I was trying to frame a reply and choking on it, when I realized that he was not speaking to me but past me. Father had come up behind me and was leaning against the gate to the corral.

"Use all the water you want, stranger."

Father and I watched him dismount in a single flowing tilt of his body and lead the horse over to the trough. He pumped it almost full and let the horse sink its nose in the cool water before he picked up the dipper for himself.

He took off his hat and slapped the dust out of it and hung it on a corner of the trough. With his hands he brushed the dust from his clothes. With a piece of rag pulled from his saddle-roll he carefully wiped his boots. He untied the handkerchief from around his neck and rolled his sleeves and dipped his arms in the trough, rubbing thoroughly and splashing water over his face. He shook his hands dry and used the handkerchief to remove the last drops from his face. Taking a comb from his shirt pocket, he smoothed back his long dark hair. All his movements were deft and sure, and with a quick precision he flipped down his sleeves, reknotted the handkerchief, and picked up his hat.

Then, holding it in his hand, he spun about and strode directly toward the house. He bent low and snapped the stem of one of mother's petunias and tucked this into the hatband. In another moment the hat was on his head, brim swept down in swift, unconscious gesture, and he was swinging gracefully into the saddle and starting toward the road.

I was fascinated. None of the men I knew were proud like that about their appearance. In that short time the kind of magnificence I had noticed had emerged into plainer view. It was in the very air of him. Everything about him showed the effects of long use and hard use, but showed too the strength of quality and competence. There was no chill on me now. Already I was imagining myself in hat and belt and boots like those.

He stopped the horse and looked down at us. He was refreshed and I would have sworn the tiny wrinkles around his eyes were what with him would be a smile. His eyes were not restless when he looked at you like this. They were still and steady and you knew the man's whole attention was concentrated on you even in the casual glance.

"Thank you," he said in his gentle voice and was turning into the road, back to us, before father spoke in his slow, deliberate way.

"Don't be in such a hurry, stranger."

I had to hold tight to the rail or I would have fallen backwards into the corral. At the first sound of father's voice, the man and the horse, like a single being, had wheeled to face us, the man's eyes boring at father, bright and deep in the shadow of the hat's brim. I was shivering, struck through once more. Something intangible and cold and terrifying was there in the air between us.

I stared in wonder as father and the stranger looked at each other a long moment, measuring each other in an unspoken fraternity of adult knowledge beyond my reach. Then the warm sunlight was flooding over us, for father was smiling and he was speaking with the drawling emphasis that meant he had made up his mind.

"I said don't be in such a hurry, stranger. Food will be on the table soon and you can bed down here tonight."

The stranger nodded quietly as if he too had made up his mind. "That's mighty thoughtful of you," he said and swung down and came toward us, leading his horse. Father slipped into step beside him and we all headed for the barn.

"My name's Starrett," said father, "Joe Starrett. This here," waving at me, "is Robert MacPherson Starrett. Too much name for a boy. I make it Bob."

The stranger nodded again. "Call me Shane," he said. Then to me: "Bob it is. You were watching me for quite a spell coming up the road."

It was not a question. It was a simple statement. "Yes . . ." I stammered. "Yes. I was."

"Right," he said. "I like that. A man who watches what's going on around him will make his mark."

A man who watches . . . For all his dark appearance and lean, hard look, this Shane knew what would please a boy. The glow of it held me as he took care of his horse, and I fussed around, hanging up his saddle, forking over some hay, getting in his way and my own in my eagerness. He let me slip the bridle off and the horse, bigger and more powerful than I had thought now that I was close beside it, put its head down patiently for me and stood quietly while I helped him curry away the caked dust. Only once did he stop me. That was when I reached for his saddle-roll to put it to one side. In the instant my fingers touched it, he was taking it from me and he put it on a shelf with a finality that indicated no interference.

When the three of us went up to the house, mother was waiting and four places were set at the table. "I saw you through the window," she said and came to shake our visitor's hand. She was a slender, lively woman with a fair complexion even our weather never seemed to affect and a mass of light brown hair she wore piled high to bring her, she used to say, closer to father's size.

"Marian," father said, "I'd like you to meet Mr. Shane."

"Good evening, ma'am," said our visitor. He took her hand and bowed over it. Mother stepped back and, to my surprise, dropped in a dainty curtsy. I had never seen her do that before. She was an unpredictable woman. Father and I would have painted the house three times over and in rainbow colors to please her.

"And a good evening to you, Mr. Shane. If Joe hadn't called you back, I would have done it myself. You'd never find a decent meal up the valley."

She was proud of her cooking, was mother. That was one thing she learned back home, she would often say, that was of some use out in this raw land. As long as she could still prepare a proper dinner, she would tell father when things were not going right, she knew she was still civilized and there was hope of getting ahead. Then she would tighten her lips and whisk together her special most delicious biscuits and father would watch her bustling about and eat them to the last little crumb and stand up and wipe his eyes and stretch his big frame and stomp out to his always unfinished work like daring anything to stop him now.

We sat down to supper and a good one. Mother's eyes sparkled as our visitor kept pace with father and me. Then we all leaned back and while I listened the talk ran on almost like old friends around a familiar table. But I could sense that it was following a pattern. Father was trying, with mother helping and both of them avoiding direct questions, to get hold of facts about this Shane and he was dodging at every turn. He was aware of their purpose and not in the least annoyed by it. He was mild and courteous and spoke readily enough. But always he put them off with words that gave no real information.

He must have been riding many days, for he was full of news from towns along his back trail as far as Cheyenne and even Dodge City and others beyond

I had never heard of before. But he had no news about himself. His past was fenced as tightly as our pasture. All they could learn was that he was riding through, taking each day as it came, with nothing particular in mind except maybe seeing a part of the country he had not been in before.

Afterwards mother washed the dishes and I dried and the two men sat on the porch, their voices carrying through the open door. Our visitor was guiding the conversation now and in no time at all he had father talking about his own plans. That was no trick. Father was ever one to argue his ideas whenever he could find a listener. This time he was going strong.

"Yes, Shane, the boys I used to ride with don't see it yet. They will some day. The open range can't last forever. The fence lines are closing in. Running cattle in big lots is good business only for the top ranchers and it's really a poor business at that. Poor in terms of the resources going into it. Too much space for too little results. It's certain to be crowded out."

"Well, now," said Shane, "that's mighty interesting. I've been hearing the same quite a lot lately and from men with pretty clear heads. Maybe there's something to it."

"By Godfrey, there's plenty to it. Listen to me, Shane. The thing to do is pick your spot, get your land, your own land. Put in enough crops to carry you and make your money play with a small herd, not all horns and bone, but bred for meat and fenced in and fed right. I haven't been at it long, but already I've raised stock that averages three hundred pounds more than that long-legged stuff Fletcher runs on the other side of the river and it's better beef, and that's only a beginning.

"Sure, his outfit sprawls over most of this valley and it looks big. But he's got range rights on a lot more acres than he has cows and he won't even have those acres as more homesteaders move in. His way is wasteful. Too much land for what he gets out of it. He can't see that. He thinks we small fellows are nothing but nuisances."

"You are," said Shane mildly. "From his point of view, you are."

"Yes, I guess you're right. I'll have to admit that. Those of us here now would make it tough for him if he wanted to use the range behind us on this side of the river as he used to. Altogether we cut some pretty good slices out of it. Worse still, we block off part of the river, shut the range off from the water. He's been grumbling about that off and on ever since we've been here. He's worried that more of us will keep coming and settle on the other side too, and then he will be in a fix."

The dishes were done and I was edging to the door. Mother nailed me as she usually did and shunted me off to bed. After she had left me in my little back room and went to join the men on the porch, I tried to catch more of the words. The voices were too low. Then I must have dozed, for with a start I realized that father and mother were again in the kitchen. By now, I gathered, our visitor was out in the barn in the bunk father had built there for the hired man who had been with us for a few weeks in the spring.

"Wasn't it peculiar," I heard mother say, "how he wouldn't talk about himself?"

"Peculiar?" said father. "Well, yes. In a way."

"Everything about him is peculiar." Mother sounded as if she was stirred up and interested. "I never saw a man quite like him before."

"You wouldn't have. Not where you come from. He's a special brand we sometimes get out here in the grass country. I've come across a few. A bad one's poison. A good one's straight grain clear through."

"How can you be so sure about him? Why, he wouldn't even tell where he was raised."

"Born back east a ways would be my guess. And pretty far south. Tennessee maybe. But he's been around plenty."

"I like him." Mother's voice was serious. "He's so nice and polite and sort of gentle. Not like most men I've met out here. But there's something about him. Something underneath the gentleness . . . Something . . ." Her voice trailed away.

"Mysterious?" suggested father.

"Yes, of course. Mysterious. But more than that. Dangerous."

"He's dangerous all right." Father said it in a musing way. Then he chuckled. "But not to us, my dear." And then he said what seemed to me a curious thing. "In fact, I don't think you ever had a safer man in your house."

2

In the morning I slept late and stumbled into the kitchen to find father and our visitor working their way through piles of mother's flapjacks. She smiled at me from over by the stove. Father slapped my rump by way of greeting. Our visitor nodded at me gravely over his heaped-up plate.

"Good morning, Bob. You'd better dig in fast or I'll do away with your share too. There's magic in your mother's cooking. Eat enough of these flannel cakes and you'll grow a bigger man than your father."

"Flannel cakes! Did you hear that, Joe?" Mother came whisking over to tousle father's hair. "You must be right. Tennessee or some such place. I never heard them called that out here."

Our visitor looked up at her. "A good guess, ma'am. Mighty close to the mark. But you had a husband to help you. My folks came out of Mississippi and settled in Arkansas. Me, though—I was fiddle-footed and left home at fifteen. Haven't had anything worth being called a real flannel cake since." He put his hands on the table edge and leaned back and the little wrinkles at the corners of his eyes were plainer and deeper. "That is, ma'am, till now."

Mother gave what in a girl I would have called a giggle. "If I'm any judge of men," she said, "that means more." And she whisked back to the stove.

That was how it was often in our house, kind of jolly and warm with good feeling. It needed to be this morning because there was a cool grayness in the air and before I had even begun to slow on my second plate of flapjacks the wind was rushing down the valley with the rain of one of our sudden summer storms following fast.

Our visitor had finished his breakfast. He had eaten so many flapjacks that I had begun to wonder whether he really would cut into my share. Now he turned to look out the window and his lips tightened. But he pushed back from the table and started to rise. Mother's voice held him to his chair.

"You'll not be traveling in any such weather. Wait a bit and it'll clear. These rains don't last long. I've another pot of coffee on the stove."

Father was getting his pipe going. He kept his eyes carefully on the smoke drifting upward. "Marian's right. Only she doesn't go far enough. These rains are short. But they sure mess up the road. It's new. Hasn't settled much yet. Mighty soggy when wet. Won't be fit for traveling till it drains. You better stay over till tomorrow."

Our visitor stared down at his empty plate as if it was the most important object in the whole room. You could see he liked the idea. Yet he seemed somehow worried about it.

"Yes," said father. "That's the sensible dodge. That horse of yours was pretty much beat last night. If I was a horse doctor now, I'd order a day's rest right off. Darned if I don't think the same prescription would do me good too. You stick here the day and I'll follow it. I'd like to take you around, show you what I'm doing with the place."

He looked pleadingly at mother. She was surprised and good reason. Father was usually so set on working every possible minute to catch up on his plans that she would have a tussle making him ease some once a week out of respect for the Sabbath. In bad weather like this he usually would fidget and stomp about the house as if he thought it was a personal insult to him, a trick to keep him from being out and doing things. And here he was talking of a whole day's rest. She was puzzled. But she played right up.

"You'd be doing us a favor, Mr. Shane. We don't get many visitors from outside the valley. It'd be real nice to have you stay. And besides—" She crinkled her nose at him the way she did when she would be teasing father into some new scheme of hers. "And besides—I've been waiting for an excuse to try a deep-dish apple pie I've heard tell of. It would just be wasted on these other two. They eat everything in sight and don't rightly know good from poor."

He was looking up, straight at her. She shook a finger at him. "And another thing. I'm fair bubbling with questions about what the women are wearing back in civilization. You know, hats and such. You're the kind of man would notice them. You're not getting away till you've told me."

Shane sat back in his chair. A faint quizzical expression softened the lean ridges of his face. "Ma'am, I'm not positive I appreciate how you've pegged me. No one else ever wrote me down an expert on ladies' millinery." He reached out and pushed his cup across the table toward her. "You said something about more coffee. But I draw the line on more flannel cakes. I'm plumb full. I'm starting in to conserve space for that pie."

"You'd better!" Father was mighty pleased about something. "When Marian puts her mind to cooking, she makes a man forget he's got any limits to his appetite. Only don't you go giving her fancy notions of new hats so she'll be sending off to the mail-order house and throwing my money away on silly frippery. She's got a hat."

Mother did not even notice that. She knew father was just talking. She knew that whenever she wanted anything real much and said so, father would bust himself trying to get it for her. She whisked over to the table with the coffee pot, poured a fresh round, then set it down within easy reach and sat down herself.

I thought that business about hats was only a joke she made up to help father persuade our visitor to stay. But she began almost at once, pestering him to describe the ladies he had seen in Cheyenne and other towns where the new styles might be. He sat there, easy and friendly, telling her how they were wearing wide floppy-brimmed bonnets with lots of flowers in front on top and slits in the brims for scarves to come through and be tied in bows under their chins.

Talk like that seemed foolish to me to be coming from a grown man. Yet this Shane was not bothered at all. And father listened as if he thought it was all right, only not very interesting. He watched them most of the time in a good-natured quiet, trying every so often to break in with his own talk about crops and steers and giving up and trying again and giving up again with a smiling shake of his head at those two. And the rain outside was a far distance away and meaningless because the friendly feeling in our kitchen was enough to warm all our world.

Then Shane was telling about the annual stock show at Dodge City and father was interested and excited, and it was mother who said: "Look, the sun's shining."

It was, so clear and sweet you wanted to run out and breathe the brilliant freshness. Father must have felt that way because he jumped up and fairly shouted, "Come on, Shane. I'll show you what this hop-scotch climate does to my alfalfa. You can almost see the stuff growing."

Shane was only a step behind him, but I beat them to the door. Mother followed and stood watching awhile on the porch as we three started out, picking our path around the puddles and the taller clumps of grass bright with the raindrops. We covered the whole place pretty thoroughly, father talking all the time, more enthusiastic about his plans than he had been for many weeks. He really hit his stride when we were behind the barn where we could have a good view of our little herd spreading out through the pasture. Then he stopped short. He had noticed that Shane was not paying much attention. He was quiet as could be for a moment when he saw that Shane was looking at the stump.

That was the one bad spot on our place. It stuck out like an old scarred sore in the cleared space back of the barn—a big old stump, all jagged across the top, the legacy of some great tree that must have died long before we came into the valley and finally been snapped by a heavy windstorm. It was big enough, I used to think, so that if it was smooth on top you could have served supper to a good-sized family on it.

But you could not have done that because you could not have got them close around it. The huge old roots humped out in every direction, some as big about as my waist, pushing out and twisting down into the ground like they would hold there to eternity and past.

Father had been working at it off and on, gnawing at the roots with an axe, ever since he finished poling the corral. The going was slow, even for him. The wood was so hard that he could not sink the blade much more than a quarter inch at a time. I guess it had been an old burr oak. Not many of those grew that far up in the Territory, but the ones that did grew big and hard. Ironwood we called it.

Father had tried burning brushpiles against it. That old stump just jeered at fire. The scorching seemed to make the wood harder than ever. So he was fighting his way around root by root. He never thought he had much time to spare on it. The rare occasions he was real mad about something he would stomp out there and chew into another root.

He went over to the stump now and kicked the nearest root, a smart kick, the way he did every time he passed it. "Yes," he said. "That's the millstone round my neck. That's the one fool thing about this place I haven't licked yet. But I will. There's no wood ever grew can stand up to a man that's got the strength and the will to keep hammering at it."

He stared at the stump like it might be a person sprouting in front of him. "You know, Shane, I've been feuding with this thing so long I've worked up a spot of affection for it. It's tough. I can admire toughness. The right kind."

He was running on again, full of words and sort of happy to be letting them out, when he noticed again that Shane was not paying much attention, was listening to some sound in the distance. Sure enough, a horse was coming up the road.

Father and I turned with him to look toward town. In a moment we saw it as it cleared the grove of trees and tall bushes about a quarter-mile away, a high-necked sorrel drawing a light buckboard wagon. The mud was splattering from its hooves, but not bad, and it was stepping free and easy. Shane glanced sideways at father.

"Not fit for traveling," he said softly. "Starrett, you're poor shakes as a liar." Then his attention was on the wagon and he was tense and alert, studying the man upright on the swaying seat.

Father simply chuckled at Shane's remark. "That's Jake Ledyard's outfit," he said, taking the lead toward our lane. "I thought maybe he'd get up this way this week. Hope he has that cultivator I've been wanting."

Ledyard was a small, thin-featured man, a peddler or trader who came through every couple of months with things you could not get at the general store in town. He would pack in his stock on a mule-team freighter driven by an old, white-haired Negro who acted like he was afraid even to speak without permission. Ledyard would make deliveries in his buckboard, claiming a hard bargain always and picking up orders for articles to bring on the next trip. I did not like him, and not just because he said nice things about me he did not mean for father's benefit. He smiled too much and there was no real friendliness in it.

By the time we were beside the porch, he had swung the horse into our lane and was pulling it to a stop. He jumped down, calling greetings. Father went to meet him. Shane stayed by the porch, leaning against the end post.

"It's here," said Ledyard. "The beauty I told you about." He yanked away the canvas covering from the body of the wagon and the sun was bright on a shiny new seven-pronged cultivator lying on its side on the floor boards. "That's the best buy I've toted this haul."

"Hm-m-m-m," said father. "You've hit it right. That's what I've been wanting. But when you start chattering about a best buy that always means big money. What's the tariff?"

"Well, now." Ledyard was slow with his reply. "It cost me more than I figured when we was talking last time. You might think it a bit steep. I don't. Not for a new beauty like that there. You'll make up the difference in no time with the work you'll save with that. Handles so easy even the boy here will be using it before long."

"Pin it down," said father. "I've asked you a question."

Ledyard was quick now. "Tell you what. I'll shave the price, take a loss to please a good customer. I'll let you have it for a hundred and ten."

I was startled to hear Shane's voice cutting in, quiet and even and plain. "Let you have it? I reckon he will. There was one like that in a store in Cheyenne. List price sixty dollars."

Ledyard shifted part way around. For the first time he looked closely at our visitor. The surface smile left his face. His voice held an ugly undertone. "Did anyone ask you to push in on this?"

"No," said Shane, quietly and evenly as before. "I reckon no one did." He was still leaning against the post. He did not move and he did not say anything more. Ledyard turned to father, speaking rapidly.

"Forget what he says, Starrett. I've spotted him now. Heard of him half a dozen times along the road up here. No one knows him. No one can figure him. I think I can. Just a stray wandering through, probably chased out of some town and hunting cover. I'm surprised you'd let him hang around."

"You might be surprised at a lot of things," said father, beginning to bite off his words. "Now give it to me straight on the price."

"It's what I said. A hundred and ten. Heck, I'll be out money on the deal anyway, so I'll shave it to a hundred if that'll make you feel any better." Ledyard hesitated, watching father. "Maybe he did see something in Cheyenne. But he's mixed up. Must have been one of those little makes—flimsy and barely half the size. That might match his price."

Father did not say anything. He was looking at Ledyard in a steady, unwavering way. He had not even glanced at Shane. You might have believed he had not even heard what Shane had said. But his lips were folding in to a tight line like he was thinking what was not pleasant to think. Ledyard waited and father did not say anything and the climbing anger in Ledyard broke free.

"Starrett! Are you going to stand there and let that—that tramp nobody knows about call me a liar? Are you going to take his word over mine? Look at him! Look at his clothes! He's just a cheap, tinhorn—"

Ledyard stopped, choking on whatever it was he had meant to say. He fell back a step with a sudden fear showing in his face. I knew why even as I turned my head to see Shane. That same chill I had felt the day before, intangible and terrifying, was in the air again. Shane was no longer leaning against the porch post. He was standing erect, his hands clenched at his sides, his eyes boring at Ledyard, his whole body alert and alive in the leaping instant.

You felt without knowing how that each teetering second could bring a burst of indescribable deadliness. Then the tension passed, fading in the empty silence. Shane's eyes lost their sharp focus on Ledyard and it seemed to me that reflected in them was some pain deep within him.

Father had pivoted so that he could see the two of them in the one sweep. He swung back to Ledyard alone.

"Yes, Ledyard, I'm taking his word. He's my guest. He's here at my invitation. But that's not the reason." Father straightened a little and his head went up and he gazed into the distance beyond the river. "I can figure men for myself. I'll take his word on anything he wants to say any day of the year."

Father's head came down and his voice was flat and final. "Sixty is the price. Add ten for a fair profit, even though you probably got it wholesale. Another ten for hauling it here. That tallies to eighty. Take that or leave that. Whatever you do, snap to it and get off my land."

Ledyard stared down at his hands, rubbing them together as if he were cold. "Where's your money?" he said.

Father went into the house, into the bedroom where he kept our money in a little leather bag on the closet shelf. He came back with the crumpled bills. All this while Shane stood there, not moving, his face hard, his eyes following father with a strange wildness in them that I could not understand.

Ledyard helped father heave the cultivator to the ground, then jumped to the wagon seat and drove off like he was glad to get away from our place. Father and I turned from watching him into the road. We looked around for Shane and he was not in sight. Father shook his head in wonderment. "Now where do you suppose—" he was saying, when we saw Shane coming out of the barn.

He was carrying an axe, the one father used for heavy kindling. He went directly around the corner of the building. We stared after him and we were still staring when we heard it, the clear ringing sound of steel biting into wood.

I never could have explained what that sound did to me. It struck through me as no single sound had ever done before. With it ran a warmth that erased at once and forever the feeling of sudden chill terror that our visitor had evoked in me. There were sharp hidden hardnesses in him. But these were not for us. He was dangerous as mother had said. But not to us as father too had said. And he was no longer a stranger. He was a man like father in whom a boy could believe in the simple knowing that what was beyond comprehension was still clean and solid and right.

I looked up at father to try to see what he was thinking, but he was starting toward the barn with strides so long that I had to run to stay close behind him. We went around the far corner and there was Shane squared away at the biggest uncut root of that big old stump. He was swinging the axe in steady rhythm. He was chewing into that root with bites almost as deep as father could drive.

Father halted, legs wide, hands on hips. "Now lookahere," he began, "there's no call for you—"

Shane broke his rhythm just long enough to level a straight look at us. "A man has to pay his debts," he said and was again swinging the axe. He was really slicing into that root.

He seemed so desperate in his determination that I had to speak. "You don't owe us anything," I said. "Lots of times we have folks in for meals and—"

Father's hand was on my shoulder. "No, Bob. He doesn't mean meals." Father was smiling, but he was having to blink several times together and I would have sworn that his eyes were misty. He stood in silence now, not moving, watching Shane.

It was something worth seeing. When father worked on that old stump, that was worth seeing too. He could handle an axe mighty well and what impressed you was the strength and will of him making it behave and fight for him against the tough old wood. This was different. What impressed you as Shane found what he was up against and settled to it was the easy way the power in him poured smoothly into each stroke. The man and the axe seemed to be partners in the work. The blade would sink into the parallel grooves almost as if it knew itself what to do and the chips from between would come out in firm and thin little blocks.

Father watched him and I watched the two of them and time passed over us, and then the axe sliced through the last strip and the root was cut. I was sure that Shane would stop. But he stepped right around to the next root and squared away again and the blade sank in once more.

As it hit this second root, father winced like it had hit him. Then he stiffened and looked away from Shane and stared at the old stump. He began to fidget, throwing his weight from one foot to the other. In a short while more he was walking around inspecting the stump from different angles as if it was something he had never seen before. Finally he gave the nearest root a kick and hurried away. In a moment he was back with the other axe, the big double-bladed one that I could hardly heft from the ground.

He picked a root on the opposite side from Shane. He was not angry the way he usually was when he confronted one of those roots. There was a kind of serene and contented look on his face. He whirled that big axe as if it was only a kid's tool. The striking blade sank in maybe a whole half-inch. At the sound Shane straightened on his side. Their eyes met over the top of the stump and held and neither one of them said a word. Then they swung up their axes and both of them said plenty to that old stump.

 **3**

It was exciting at first watching them. They were hitting a fast pace, making the chips dance. I thought maybe each one would cut through a root now and stop. But Shane finished his and looked over at father working steadily away and with a grim little smile pulling at his mouth he moved on to another root. A few moments later father smashed through his with a blow that sent the axe head into the ground beneath. He wrestled with the handle to yank the head loose and he too tackled another root without even waiting to wipe off the dirt. This began to look like a long session, so I started to wander away. Just as I headed around the corner of the barn, mother came past the corner.

She was the freshest, prettiest thing I had ever seen. She had taken her hat and stripped the old ribbon from it and fixed it as Shane had told her. Some of the flowers by the house were in a small bouquet in front. She had cut slits in the brim and the sash from her best dress came around the crown and through the slits and was tied in a perky bow under her chin. She was stepping along daintily, mighty proud of herself.

She went up close to the stump. Those two choppers were so busy and intent that even if they were aware she was there they did not really notice her.

"Well," she said, "aren't you going to look at me?"

They both stopped and they both stared at her.

"Have I got it right?" she asked Shane. "Is this the way they do it?"

"Yes, ma'am," he said. "About like that. Only their brims are wider." And he swung back to his root.

"Joe Starrett," said mother, "aren't you at least going to tell me whether you like me in this hat?"

"Lookahere, Marian," said father, "you know darned well that whether you have a hat on or whether you don't have a hat on, you're the nicest thing to me that ever happened on God's green earth. Now stop bothering us. Can't you see we're busy?" And he swung back to his root.

Mother's face was a deep pink. She pulled the bow out and the hat from her head. She held it swinging from her hand by the sash ends. Her hair was mussed and she was really mad.

"Humph," she said. "This is a funny kind of resting you're doing today."

Father set the axe head on the ground and leaned on the handle. "Maybe it seems funny to you, Marian. But this is the best resting I've had for about as long as I can remember."

"Humph," said mother again. "You'll have to quit your resting for a while

19

anyhow and do what I suppose you'll call work. Dinner's hot on the stove and waiting to be served."

She flounced around and went straight back to the house. We all tagged her in and to an uncomfortable meal. Mother always believed you should be decent and polite at mealtime, particularly with company. She was polite enough now. She was being special sweet, talking enough for the whole table of us without once saying a word about her hat lying where she had thrown it on the chair by the stove. The trouble was that she was too polite. She was trying too hard to be sweet.

As far as you could tell, though, the two men were not worried by her at all. They listened absently to her talk, chiming in when she asked them direct questions, but otherwise keeping quiet. Their minds were on that old stump and whatever it was that old stump had come to mean to them and they were in a hurry to get at it again.

After they had gone out and I had been helping mother with the dishes awhile, she began humming low under her breath and I knew she was not mad any more. She was too curious and puzzled to have room for anything else.

"What went on out there, Bob?" she asked me. "What got into those two?"

I did not rightly know. All I could do was try to tell her about Ledyard and how our visitor had called him on the cultivator. I must have used the wrong words, because, when I told her about Ledyard talking mean and the way Shane acted, she got all flushed and excited.

"What do you say, Bob? You were afraid of him? He frightened you? Your father would never let him do that."

"I wasn't frightened of him," I said, struggling to make her see the difference. "I was—well, I was just frightened. I was scared of whatever it was that might happen."

She reached out and rumpled my hair. "I think I understand," she said softly. "He's made me feel a little that way too." She went to the window and stared toward the barn. The steady rhythm of double blows, so together they sounded almost as one, was faint yet clear in the kitchen. "I hope Joe knows what he's doing," she murmured to herself. Then she turned to me. "Skip along out, Bob. I'll finish myself."

It was no fun watching them now. They had eased down to a slow, dogged pace. Father sent me once for the hone, so they could sharpen the blades, and again for a spade so he could clear the dirt away from the lowest roots, and I realized he might keep me running as long as I was handy. I slipped off by myself to see how mother's garden was doing after the rain and maybe add to the population in the box of worms I was collecting for when I would go fishing with the boys in town.

I took my time about it. I played pretty far afield. But no matter where I went, always I could hear that chopping in the distance. You could not help beginning to feel tired just to hear it, to think how they were working and staying at it.

Along the middle of the afternoon, I wandered into the barn. There was mother by the rear stall, up on a box peering through the little window above it. She hopped down as soon as she heard me and put a finger to her lips.

"I declare," she whispered. "In some ways those two aren't even as old as you are, Bob. Just the same—" She frowned at me in such a funny, confiding manner that I felt all warm inside. "Don't you dare tell them I said so. But there's something splendid in the battle they're giving that old monster." She went past me and toward the house with such a brisk air that I followed to see what she was going to do.

She whisked about the kitchen and in almost no time at all she had a pan of biscuits in the oven. While they were baking, she took her hat and carefully sewed the old ribbon into its old place. "Humph," she said, more to herself than to me. "You'd think I'd learn. This isn't Dodge City. This isn't even a whistle stop. It's Joe Starrett's farm. It's where I'm proud to be."

Out came the biscuits. She piled as many as she could on a plate, popping one of the leftovers into her mouth and giving me the rest. She picked up the plate and marched with it out behind the barn. She stepped over the cut roots and set the plate on a fairly smooth spot on top of the stump. She looked at the two men, first one and then the other. "You're a pair of fools," she said. "But there's no law against me being a fool too." Without looking at either of them again, she marched away, her head high, back toward the house.

The two of them stared after her till she was out of sight. They turned to stare at the biscuits. Father gave a deep sigh, so deep it seemed to come all the way from his heavy work shoes. There was nothing sad or sorrowful about it. There was just something in him too big to be held tight in comfort. He let his axe fall to the ground. He leaned forward and separated the biscuits into two piles beside the plate, counting them even. One was left on the plate. He set this by itself on the stump. He took up his axe and reached it out and let it drop gently on the lone biscuit exactly in the middle. He rested the axe against the stump and took the two halves of the biscuit and put one on each pile.

He did not say a word to Shane. He pitched into one pile and Shane did into the other, and the two of them faced each other over the last uncut roots, munching at those biscuits as if eating them was the most serious business they had ever done.

Father finished his pile and dabbled his fingers on the plate for the last crumbs. He straightened and stretched his arms high and wide. He seemed to stretch and stretch until he was a tremendous tower of strength reaching up into the late afternoon sun. He swooped suddenly to grab the plate and toss it to me. Still in the same movement he seized the axe and swung it in a great arc into the root he was working on. Quick as he was, Shane was right with him, and together they were talking again to that old stump.

I took the plate in to mother. She was peeling apples in the kitchen, humming gaily to herself. "The woodbox, Bob," she said, and went on humming. I carried in stove-lengths till the box would not hold any more. Then I slipped out before she might think of more chores.

I tried to keep myself busy down by the river skipping flat stones across the current all muddy still from the rain. I was able to for a while. But that steady chopping had a peculiar fascination. It was always pulling me toward the barn. I simply could not grasp how they could stick at it hour after hour. It made no sense to me, why they should work so when routing out that old stump was not really so important. I was wavering in front of the barn, when I noticed that the chopping was different. Only one axe was working.

I hurried around back. Shane was still swinging, cutting into the last root. Father was using the spade, was digging under one side of the stump, bringing the dirt out between the cut roots. As I watched, he laid the spade aside and put his shoulder to the stump. He heaved against it. Sweat started to pour down his face. There was a little sucking sound and the stump moved ever so slightly.

That did it. Of a sudden I was so excited that I could hear my own blood pounding past my eardrums. I wanted to dash to that stump and push it and feel it move. Only I knew father would think I was in the way.

Shane finished the root and came to help him. Together they heaved against the stump. It angled up nearly a whole inch. You could begin to see an open space in the dirt where it was ripping loose. But as soon as they released the pressure, it fell back.

Again and again they heaved at it. Each time it would angle up a bit farther. Each time it would fall back. They had it up once about a foot and a half, and that was the limit. They could not get past it.

They stopped, breathing hard, mighty streaked now from the sweat rivulets down their faces. Father peered underneath as best he could. "Must be a tap-root," he said. That was the one time either of them had spoken to the other, as far as I knew, the whole afternoon through. Father did not say anything more. And Shane said nothing. He just picked up his axe and looked at father and waited.

Father began to shake his head. There was some unspoken thought between them that bothered him. He looked down at his own big hands and slowly the fingers curled until they were clenched into big fists. Then his head stopped shaking and he stood taller and he drew a deep breath. He turned and backed in between two cut root ends, pressing against the stump. He pushed his feet into the ground for firm footholds. He bent his knees and slid his shoulders down the stump and wrapped his big hands around the root ends. Slowly he began to straighten. Slowly that huge old stump began to rise. Up it came, inch by inch, until the side was all the way up to the limit they had reached before.

Shane stooped to peer under. He poked his axe into the opening and I heard it strike wood. But the only way he could get in position to swing the axe into the opening was to drop on his right knee and extend his left leg and thigh into the opening and lean his weight on them. Then he could bring the axe sweeping in at a low angle close to the ground.

He flashed one quick glance at father beside and behind him, eyes closed, muscles locked in that great sustained effort, and he dropped into position with the whole terrible weight of the stump poised above nearly half of his body and sent the axe sweeping under in swift powerful strokes.

Suddenly father seemed to slip. Only he had not slipped. He had straightened even further. The stump had leaped up a few more inches. Shane jumped out and up and tossed his axe aside. He grabbed one of the root ends and helped father ease the stump down. They both were blowing like they had run a long way. But they would not stay more than a minute before they were heaving again at the stump. It came up more easily now and the dirt was tearing loose all around it.

I ran to the house fast as I could. I dashed into the kitchen and took hold of mother's hand. "Hurry!" I yelled. "You've got to come!" She did not seem to want to come at first and I pulled her. "You've got to see it! They're getting it out!" Then she was excited as I was and was running right with me.

They had the stump way up at a high angle. They were down in the hole, one on each side of it, pushing up and forward with hands flat on the under part reared before them higher than their heads. You would have thought the stump was ready to topple over clear of its ancient foundation. But there it stuck. They could not quite push it the final inches.

Mother watched them battling with it. "Joe," she called, "why don't you use some sense? Hitch up the team. Horses will have it out in no time at all."

Father braced himself to hold the stump still. He turned his head to look at her. "Horses!" he shouted. All the pent silence of the two of them that long afternoon through was being shattered in the one wonderful shout. "Horses! Great jumping Jehoshaphat! No! We started this with manpower and, by Godfrey, we'll finish it with manpower!"

He turned his head to face the stump once more and dropped it lower between his humped shoulders. Shane, opposite him, stiffened, and together they pushed in a fresh assault. The stump quivered and swayed a little—and hung fixed at its crazy high angle.

Father grunted in exasperation. You could see the strength building up in his legs and broad shoulders and big corded arms. His side of the upturned stump rocked forward and Shane's side moved back and the whole stump trembled like it would twist down and into the hole on them at a grotesque new angle.

I wanted to shout a warning. But I could not speak, for Shane had thrown his head in a quick sideways gesture to fling his hair from falling over his face and I had caught a glimpse of his eyes. They were aflame with a concentrated cold fire. Not another separate discernible movement did he make. It was all of him, the whole man, pulsing in the one incredible surge of power. You could fairly feel the fierce energy suddenly burning in him, pouring through him in the single coordinated drive. His side of the stump rocked forward even with father's and the whole mass of the stump tore loose from the last hold and toppled away to sprawl in ungainly defeat beyond them.

Father climbed slowly out of the hole. He walked to the stump and placed a hand on the rounded bole and patted it like it was an old friend and he was perhaps a little sorry for it. Shane was with him, across from him, laying a hand gently on the old hard wood. They both looked up and their eyes met and held as they had so long ago in the morning hours.

The silence should have been complete. It was not because someone was shouting, a high-pitched, wordless shout. I realized that the voice was mine and I closed my mouth. The silence was clean and wholesome, and this was one of the things you could never forget whatever time might do to you in the furrowing of the years, an old stump on its side with root ends making a strange pattern against the glow of the sun sinking behind the far mountains and two men looking over it into each other's eyes.

I thought they should join the hands so close on the bole of the stump. I thought they should at least say something to each other. They stood quiet and motionless. At last father turned and came toward mother. He was so tired that the weariness showed in his walk. But there was no weariness in his voice. "Marian," he said, "I'm rested now. I don't believe any man since the world began was ever more rested."

Shane too was coming toward us. He too spoke only to mother. "Ma'am, I've learned something today. Being a farmer has more to it than I ever thought. Now I'm about ready for some of that pie."

Mother had been watching them in a wide-eyed wonder. At his last words she let out a positive wail. "Oh-h-h—you—you—men! You made me forget about it! It's probably all burned!" And she was running for the house so fast she was tripping over her skirt.

The pie was burned all right. We could smell it when we were in front of the house and the men were scrubbing themselves at the pump-trough. Mother had the door open to let the kitchen air out. The noises from inside sounded as if she might be throwing things around. Kettles were banging and dishes were clattering. When we went in, we saw why. She had the table set and was putting supper on it and she was grabbing the things from their places and putting them down on the table with solid thumps. She would not look at one of us.

We sat down and waited for her to join us. She put her back to us and stood by the low shelf near the stove staring at her big pie tin and the burned stuff in it. Finally father spoke kind of sharply. "Lookahere, Marian. Aren't you ever going to sit down?"

She whirled and glared at him. I thought maybe she had been crying. But there were no tears on her face. It was dry and pinched-looking and there was no color in it. Her voice was sharp like father's. "I was planning to have a deep-dish apple pie. Well, I will. None of your silly man foolishness is going to stop me."

She swept up the big tin and went out the door with it. We heard her on the steps, and a few seconds later the rattle of the cover of the garbage pail. We heard her on the steps again. She came in and went to the side bench where the dishpan was and began to scrub the pie tin. The way she acted, we might not have been in the room.

Father's face was getting red. He picked up his fork to begin eating and let it drop with a little clatter. He squirmed on his chair and kept taking quick side looks at her. She finished scrubbing the tin and went to the apple barrel and filled her wooden bowl with fat round ones. She sat by the stove and started peeling them. Father fished in a pocket and pulled out his old jackknife. He moved over to her, stepping softly. He reached out for an apple to help her.

She did not look up. But her voice caught him like she had flicked him with a whip. "Joe Starrett, don't you dare touch a one of these apples."

He was sheepish as he returned to his chair. Then he was downright mad. He grabbed his knife and fork and dug into the food on his plate, taking big bites and chewing vigorously. There was nothing for our visitor and me to do but follow his example. Maybe it was a good supper. I could not tell. The food was only something to put in your mouth. And when we finished, there was nothing to do but wait because mother was sitting by the stove, arms folded, staring at the wall, waiting herself for her pie to bake.

We three watched her in a quiet so tight that it hurt. We could not help it. We would try to look away and always our eyes would turn back to her. She did not appear to notice us. You might have said she had forgotten we were there.

She had not forgotten because as soon as she sensed that the pie was done, she lifted it out, cut four wide pieces, and put them on plates. The first two she set in front of the two men. The third one she set down for me. The last one she laid at her own place and she sat down in her own chair at the table. Her voice was still sharp.

"I'm sorry to keep you men waiting so long. Your pie is ready now."

Father inspected his portion like he was afraid of it. He needed to make a real effort to take his fork and lift a piece. He chewed on it and swallowed and he flipped his eyes sidewise at mother and back again quickly to look across the table at Shane. "That's prime pie," he said.

Shane raised a piece on his fork. He considered it closely. He put it in his mouth and chewed on it gravely. "Yes," he said. The quizzical expression on his face was so plain you could not possibly miss it. "Yes. That's the best bit of stump I ever tasted."

What could a silly remark like that mean? I had not time to wonder, for father and mother were acting so queer. They both stared at Shane and their mouths were sagging open. Then father snapped his shut and he chuckled and chuckled till he was swaying in his chair.

"By Godfrey, Marian, he's right. You've done it, too."

Mother stared from one to the other of them. Her pinched look faded and her cheeks were flushed and her eyes were soft and warm as they should be, and she was laughing so that the tears came. And all of us were pitching into that pie, and the one thing wrong in the whole world was that there was not enough of it.

 4

The sun was already well up the sky when I awakened the next morning. I had been a long time getting to sleep because my mind was full of the day's excitement and shifting moods. I could not straighten out in my mind the way the grown folks had behaved, the way things that did not really matter so much had become so important to them.

I had lain in my bed thinking of our visitor out in the bunk in the barn. It scarce seemed possible that he was the same man I had first seen, stern and chilling in his dark solitude, riding up our road. Something in father, something not of words or of actions but of the essential substance of the human spirit, had reached out and spoken to him and he had replied to it and had unlocked a part of himself to us. He was far off and unapproachable at times even when he was right there with you. Yet somehow he was closer, too, than my uncle, mother's brother, had been when he visited us the summer before.

I had been thinking, too, of the effect he had on father and mother. They were more alive, more vibrant, like they wanted to show more what they were, when they were with him. I could appreciate that because I felt the same way myself. But it puzzled me that a man so deep and vital in his own being, so ready to respond to father, should be riding a lone trail out of a closed and guarded past.

I realized with a jolt how late it was. The door to my little room was closed. Mother must have closed it so I could sleep undisturbed. I was frantic that the others might have finished breakfast and that our visitor was gone and I had missed him. I pulled on my clothes, not even bothering with buttons, and ran to the door.

They were still at the table. Father was fussing with his pipe. Mother and Shane were working on a last round of coffee. All three of them were subdued and quiet. They stared at me as I burst out of my room.

"My heavens," said mother. "You came in here like something was after you. What's the matter?"

"I just thought," I blurted out, nodding at our visitor, "that maybe he had ridden off and forgotten me."

Shane shook his head slightly, looking straight at me. "I wouldn't forget you, Bob." He pulled himself up a little in his chair. He turned to mother and his voice took on a bantering tone. "And I wouldn't forget your cooking, ma'am. If you begin having a special lot of people passing by at mealtimes, that'll be because a grateful man has been boasting of your flannel cakes all along the road."

"Now there's an idea," struck in father as if he was glad to find something safe to talk about. "We'll turn this place into a boarding house. Marian'll fill folks full of her meals and I'll fill my pockets full of their money. That hits me as a mighty convenient arrangement."

Mother sniffed at him. But she was pleased at their talk and she was smiling as they kept on playing with the idea while she stirred me up my breakfast. She came right back at them, threatening to take father at his word and make him spend all his time peeling potatoes and washing dishes. They were enjoying themselves even though I could feel a bit of constraint behind the easy joshing. It was remarkable, too, how natural it was to have this Shane sitting there and joining in almost like he was a member of the family. There was none of the awkwardness some visitors always brought with them. You did feel you ought to be on your good behavior with him, a mite extra careful about your manners and your speech. But not stiffly so. Just quiet and friendly about it.

He stood up at last and I knew he was going to ride away from us and I wanted desperately to stop him. Father did it for me.

"You certainly are a man for being in a hurry. Sit down, Shane. I've a question to ask you."

Father was suddenly very serious. Shane, standing there, was as suddenly withdrawn into a distant alertness. But he dropped back into his chair.

Father looked directly at him. "Are you running away from anything?"

Shane stared at the plate in front of him for a long moment. It seemed to me that a shade of sadness passed over him. Then he raised his eyes and looked directly at father.

"No. I'm not running away from anything. Not in the way you mean."

"Good." Father stooped forward and stabbed at the table with a forefinger for emphasis. "Look, Shane. I'm not a rancher. Now you've seen my place, you know that. I'm a farmer. Something of a stockman, maybe. But really a farmer. That's what I decided to be when I quit punching cattle for another man's money. That's what I want to be and I'm proud of it. I've made a fair start. This outfit isn't as big as I hope to have it some day. But there's more work here already than one man can handle if it's to be done right. The young fellow I had ran out on me after he tangled with a couple of Fletcher's boys in town one day." Father was talking fast and he paused to draw breath.

Shane had been watching him intently. He moved his head to look out the window over the valley to the mountains marching along the horizon. "It's always the same," he murmured. He was sort of talking to himself. "The old ways die hard." He looked at mother and then at me, and as his eyes came back to father he seemed to have decided something that had been troubling him. "So Fletcher's crowding you," he said gently.

Father snorted. "I don't crowd easy. But I've got a job to do here and it's too big for one man, even for me. And none of the strays that drift up this way are worth a darn."

"Yes?" Shane said. His eyes were crinkling again, and he was one of us again and waiting.

"Will you stick here awhile and help me get things in shape for the winter?"

Shane rose to his feet. He loomed up taller across the table than I had thought him. "I never figured to be a farmer, Starrett. I would have laughed at the notion a few days ago. All the same, you've hired yourself a hand." He and father were looking at each other in a way that showed they were saying things words could never cover. Shane snapped it by swinging toward mother. "And I'll rate your cooking, ma'am, wages enough."

Father slapped his hands on his knees. "You'll get good wages and you'll earn 'em. First off, now, why don't you drop into town and get some work clothes. Try Sam Grafton's store. Tell him to put it on my bill."

Shane was already at the door. "I'll buy my own," he said, and was gone.

Father was so pleased he could not sit still. He jumped up and whirled mother around. "Marian, the sun's shining mighty bright at last. We've got ourselves a man."

"But, Joe, are you sure what you're doing? What kind of work can a man like that do? Oh, I know he stood right up to you with that stump. But that was something special. He's been used to good living and plenty of money. You can tell that. He said himself he doesn't know anything about farming."

"Neither did I when I started here. What a man knows isn't important. It's what he is that counts. I'll bet you that one was a cowpuncher when he was younger and a tophand too. Anything he does will be done right. You watch. In a week he'll be making even me hump or he'll be bossing the place."

"Perhaps."

"No perhapsing about it. Did you notice how he took it when I told him about Fletcher's boys and young Morley? That's what fetched him. He knows I'm in a spot and he's not the man to leave me there. Nobody'll push him around or scare him away. He's my kind of a man."

"Why, Joe Starrett. He isn't like you at all. He's smaller and he looks different and his clothes are different and he talks different. I know he's lived different."

"Huh?" Father was surprised. "I wasn't talking about things like that."

Shane came back with a pair of dungaree pants, a flannel shirt, stout work shoes, and a good, serviceable Stetson. He disappeared into the barn and emerged a few moments later in his new clothes, leading his horse unsaddled. At the pasture gate he slipped off the halter, turned the horse in with a hearty slap, and tossed the halter to me.

"Take care of a horse, Bob, and it will take care of you. This one now has brought me better than a thousand miles in the last few weeks." And he was striding away to join father, who was ditching the field out past the growing corn where the ground was rich but marshy and would not be worth much till it was properly drained. I watched him swinging through the rows of young corn, no longer a dark stranger but part of the place, a farmer like father and me.

Only he was not a farmer and never really could be. It was not three days before you saw that he could stay right beside father in any kind of work. Show him what needed to be done and he could do it, and like as not would figure out a better way of getting it done. He never shirked the meanest task. He was ever ready to take the hard end of any chore. Yet you always felt in some indefinable fashion that he was a man apart.

There were times when he would stop and look off at the mountains and then down at himself and any tool he happened to have in his hands as if in wry amusement at what he was doing. You had no impression that he thought himself too good for the work or did not like it. He was just different. He was shaped in some firm forging of past circumstance for other things.

For all his slim build he was plenty rugged. His slenderness could fool you at first. But when you saw him close in action, you saw that he was solid, compact, that there was no waste weight on his frame just as there was no waste effort in his smooth, flowing motion. What he lacked alongside father in size and strength, he made up in quickness of movement, in instinctive coordination of mind and muscle, and in that sudden fierce energy that had burned in him when the old stump tried to topple back on him. Mostly this last slept in him, not needed while he went easily through the day's routine. But when a call came, it could flame forward with a driving intensity that never failed to frighten me.

I would be frightened, as I had tried to explain to mother, not at Shane himself, but at the suggestion it always gave me of things in the human equation beyond my comprehension. At such times there would be a concentration in him, a singleness of dedication to the instant need, that seemed to me at once wonderful and disturbing. And then he would be again the quiet, steady man who shared with father my boy's allegiance.

I was beginning to feel my oats about then, proud of myself for being able to lick Ollie Johnson at the next place down the road. Fighting, boy style, was much in my mind.

Once, when father and I were alone, I asked him: "Could you beat Shane? In a fight, I mean."

"Son, that's a tough question. If I had to, I might do it. But, by Godfrey, I'd hate to try it. Some men just plain have dynamite inside them, and he's one. I'll tell you, though, I've never met a man I'd rather have more on my side in any kind of trouble."

I could understand that and it satisfied me. But there were things about Shane I could not understand. When he came in to the first meal after he agreed to stay on with us, he went to the chair that had always been father's and stood beside it waiting for the rest of us to take the other places. Mother was surprised and somewhat annoyed. She started to say something. Father quieted her with a warning glance. He walked to the chair across from Shane and sat down like this was the right and natural spot for him and afterwards he and Shane always used these same places.

I could not see any reason for the shift until the first time one of our homestead neighbors knocked on the door while we were eating and came straight on in as most of them usually did. Then I suddenly realized that Shane was sitting opposite the door where he could directly confront anyone coming through it. I could see that was the way he wanted it to be. But I could not understand why he wanted it that way.

In the evenings after supper when he was talking lazily with us, he would never sit by a window. Out on the porch he would always face the road. He liked to have a wall behind him and not just to lean against. No matter where he was, away from the table, before sitting down he would swing his chair into position, back to the nearest wall, not making any show, simply putting it there and bending into it in one easy motion. He did not even seem to be aware that this was unusual. It was part of his fixed alertness. He always wanted to know everything happening around him.

This alertness could be noted, too, in the watch he kept, without appearing to make any special effort, on every approach to our place. He knew first when anyone was moving along the road and he would stop whatever he was doing to study carefully any passing rider.

We often had company in the evenings, for the other homesteaders regarded father as their leader and would drop in to discuss their affairs with him. They were interesting men in their own fashions, a various assortment. But Shane was not anxious to meet people. He would share little in their talk. With us he spoke freely enough. We were, in some subtle way, his folks. Though we had taken him in, you had the feeling that he had adopted us. But with others he was reserved; courteous and soft-spoken, yet withdrawn beyond a line of his own making.

These things puzzled me and not me alone. The people in town and those who rode or drove in pretty regularly were all curious about him. It was a wonder how quickly everyone in the valley, and even on the ranches out in the open country, knew that he was working with father.

They were not sure they liked having him in their neighborhood. Ledyard had told some tall tale about what happened at our place that made them stare sharply at Shane whenever they had a chance. But they must have had their own measure of Ledyard, for they did not take his story too straight. They just could not really make up their minds about Shane and it seemed to worry them.

More than once, when I was with Ollie Johnson on the way to our favorite fishing hole the other side of town, I heard men arguing about him in front of Mr. Grafton's store. "He's like one of these here slow-burning fuses," I heard an old mule-skinner say one day. "Quiet and no sputtering. So quiet you forget it's burning. Then it sets off one heck of a blow-off of trouble when it touches powder. That's him. And there's been trouble brewing in this valley for a long spell now. Maybe it'll be good when it comes. Maybe it'll be bad. You just can't tell." And that puzzled me too.

What puzzled me most, though, was something it took me nearly two weeks to appreciate. And yet it was the most striking thing of all. Shane carried no gun.

In those days guns were as familiar all through the Territory as boots and saddles. They were not used much in the valley except for occasional hunting. But they were always in evidence. Most men did not feel fully dressed without one.

We homesteaders went in mostly for rifles and shotguns when we had any shooting to do. A pistol slapping on the hip was a nuisance for a farmer. Still every man had his cartridge belt and holstered Colt to be worn when he was not working or loafing around the house. Father buckled his on whenever he rode off on any trip, even just into town, as much out of habit, I guess, as anything else.

But this Shane never carried a gun. And that was a peculiar thing because he had a gun.

I saw it once. I saw it when I was alone in the barn one day and I spotted his saddle-roll lying on his bunk. Usually he kept it carefully put away underneath. He must have forgotten it this time, for it was there in the open by the pillow. I reached to sort of feel it—and I felt the gun inside. No one was near, so I unfastened the straps and unrolled the blankets. There it was, the most beautiful-looking weapon I ever saw. Beautiful and deadly-looking.

The holster and filled cartridge belt were of the same soft black leather as the boots tucked under the bunk, tooled in the same intricate design. I knew enough to know that the gun was a single-action Colt, the same model as the Regular Army issue that was the favorite of all men in those days and that oldtimers used to say was the finest pistol ever made.

This was the same model. But this was no Army gun. It was black, almost blue black, with the darkness not in any enamel but in the metal itself. The grip was clear on the outer curve, shaped to the fingers on the inner curve, and two ivory plates were set into it with exquisite skill, one on each side.

The smooth invitation of it tempted your grasp. I took hold and pulled the gun out of the holster. It came so easily that I could hardly believe it was there in my hand. Heavy like father's, it was somehow much easier to handle. You held it up to aiming level and it seemed to balance itself into your hand.

It was clean and polished and oiled. The empty cylinder, when I released the catch and flicked it, spun swiftly and noiselessly. I was surprised to see that the front sight was gone, the barrel smooth right down to the end, and that the hammer had been filed to a sharp point.

Why should a man do that to a gun? Why should a man with a gun like that refuse to wear it and show it off? And then, staring at that dark and deadly efficiency, I was again suddenly chilled, and I quickly put everything back exactly as before and hurried out into the sun.

The first chance I tried to tell father about it. "Father," I said, all excited, "do you know what Shane has rolled up in his blankets?"

"Probably a gun."

"But—but how did you know? Have you seen it?"

"No. That's what he would have."

I was all mixed up. "Well, why doesn't he ever carry it? Do you suppose maybe it's because he doesn't know how to use it very well?"

Father chuckled like I had made a joke. "Son, I wouldn't be surprised if he could take that gun and shoot the buttons off your shirt with you awearing it and all you'd feel would be a breeze."

"Gosh agorry! Why does he keep it hidden in the barn then?"

"I don't know. Not exactly."

"Why don't you ask him?"

Father looked straight at me, very serious. "That's one question I'll never ask him. And don't you ever say anything to him about it. There are some things you don't ask a man. Not if you respect him. He's entitled to stake his claim to what he considers private to himself alone. But you can take my word for it, Bob, that when a man like Shane doesn't want to tote a gun you can bet your shirt, buttons and all, he's got a mighty good reason."

That was that. I was still mixed up. But whenever father gave you his word on something, there was nothing more to be said. He never did that except when he knew he was right. I started to wander off.

"Bob."

"Yes, father."

"Listen to me, son. Don't get to liking Shane too much."

"Why not? Is there anything wrong with him?"

"No-o-o-o. There's nothing wrong about Shane. Nothing you could put that way. There's more right about him than most any man you're ever likely to meet. But—" Father was throwing around for what to say. "But he's fiddle-footed. Remember. He said so himself. He'll be moving on one of these days and then you'll be all upset if you get to liking him too much."

That was not what father really meant. But that was what he wanted me to think. So I did not ask any more questions.

5

The weeks went rocking past, and soon it did not seem possible that there ever had been a time when Shane was not with us. He and father worked together more like partners than boss and hired man. The amount they could get through in a day was a marvel. The ditching father had reckoned would take him most of the summer was done in less than a month. The loft was finished and the first cutting of alfalfa stowed away.

We would have enough fodder to carry a few more young steers through the winter for fattening next summer, so father rode out of the valley and all the way to the ranch where he worked once and came back herding a half-dozen more. He was gone two days. He came back to find that Shane, while he was gone, had knocked out the end of the corral and posted a new section making it half again as big.

"Now we can really get going next year," Shane said as father sat on his horse staring at the corral like he could not quite believe what he saw. "We ought to get enough hay off that new field to help us carry forty head."

"Oho!" said father. "So we can get going. And we ought to get enough hay." He was pleased as could be because he was scowling at Shane the way he did at me when he was tickled silly over something I had done and did not want to let on that he was. He jumped off his horse and hurried up to the house where mother was standing on the porch.

"Marian," he demanded right off, waving at the corral, "whose idea was that?"

"Well-l-l," she said, "Shane suggested it." Then she added slyly, "But I told him to go ahead."

"That's right." Shane had come up beside him. "She rode me like she had spurs to get it done by today. Kind of a present. It's your wedding anniversary."

"Well, I'll be darned," said father. "So it is." He stared foolishly at one and then the other of them. With Shane there watching, he hopped on the porch and gave mother a kiss. I was embarrassed for him and I turned away—and hopped about a foot myself.

"Hey! Those steers are running away!"

The grown folks had forgotten about them. All six were wandering up the road, straggling and separating. Shane, that soft-spoken man, let out a whoop you might have heard halfway to town and ran to father's horse, putting his hands on the saddle and vaulting into it. He fairly lifted the horse into a gallop in one leap and that old cowpony of father's lit out after those steers like this was fun. By the time father reached the corral gate, Shane had the runaways in a compact bunch and padding back at a trot. He dropped them through the gateway neat as pie.

He was tall and straight in the saddle the few seconds it took father to close the gate. He and the horse were blowing a bit and both of them were perky and proud.

"It's been ten years," he said, "since I did anything like that."

Father grinned at him. "Shane, if I didn't know better, I'd say you were a faker. There's still a lot of kid in you."

The first real smile I had seen yet flashed across Shane's face. "Maybe. Maybe there is at that."

I think that was the happiest summer of my life.

The only shadow over our valley, the recurrent trouble between Fletcher and us homesteaders, seemed to have faded away. Fletcher himself was gone most of those months. He had gone to Fort Bennett in Dakota and even on East to Washington, so we heard, trying to get a contract to supply beef to the Indian agent at Standing Rock, the big Sioux reservation over beyond the Black Hills. Except for his foreman, Morgan, and several surly older men, his hands were young, easy-going cowboys who made a lot of noise in town once in a while but rarely did any harm and even then only in high spirits. We liked them—when Fletcher was not there driving them into harassing us in constant shrewd ways. Now, with him away, they kept to the other side of the river and did not bother us. Sometimes, riding in sight on the other bank, they might even wave to us in their rollicking fashion.

Until Shane came, they had been my heroes. Father, of course, was special all to himself. There could never be anyone quite to match him. I wanted to be like him, just as he was. But first I wanted, as he had done, to ride the range, to have my own string of ponies and take part in an all-brand round-up and in a big cattle drive and dash into strange towns with just such a rollicking crew and with a season's pay jingling in my pockets.

Now I was not so sure. I wanted more and more to be like Shane, like the man I imagined he was in the past fenced off so securely. I had to imagine most of it. He would never speak of it, not in any way at all. Even his name remained mysterious. Just Shane. Nothing else. We never knew whether that was his first name or last name or, indeed, any name that came from his family. "Call me Shane," he said, and that was all he ever said. But I conjured up all manner of adventures for him, not tied to any particular time or place, seeing him as a slim and dark and dashing figure coolly passing through perils that would overcome a lesser man.

I would listen in what was closely akin to worship while my two men, father and Shane, argued long and amiably about the cattle business. They would wrangle over methods of feeding and bringing steers up to top weight. But they were agreed that controlled breeding was better than open range running and that improvement of stock was needed even if that meant spending big money on imported bulls. And they would speculate about the chances of a railroad spur ever reaching the valley, so you could ship direct without thinning good meat off your cattle driving them to market.

It was plain that Shane was beginning to enjoy living with us and working the place. Little by little the tension in him was fading out. He was still alert and watchful, instinct with that unfailing awareness of everything about him. I came to realize that this was inherent in him, not learned or acquired, simply a part of his natural being. But the sharp extra edge of conscious alertness, almost of expectancy of some unknown trouble always waiting, was wearing away.

Yet why was he sometimes so strange and stricken in his own secret bitterness? Like the time I was playing with a gun Mr. Grafton gave me, an old frontier model Colt with a cracked barrel someone had turned in at the store.

I had rigged a holster out of a torn chunk of oilcloth and a belt of rope. I was stalking around near the barn, whirling every few steps to pick off a skulking Indian, when I saw Shane watching me from the barn door. I stopped short, thinking of that beautiful gun under his bunk and afraid he would make fun of me and my sorry old broken pistol. Instead he looked gravely at me.

"How many you knocked over so far, Bob?"

Could I ever repay the man? My gun was a shining new weapon, my hand steady as a rock as I drew a bead on another one.

"That makes seven."

"Indians or timber wolves?"

"Indians. Big ones."

"Better leave a few for the other scouts," he said gently. "It wouldn't do to make them jealous. And look here, Bob. You're not doing that quite right."

He sat down on an upturned crate and beckoned me over. "Your holster's too low. Don't let it drag full arm's length. Have it just below the hip, so the grip is about halfway between your wrist and elbow when the arm's hanging limp. You can take the gun then as your hand's coming up and there's still room to clear the holster without having to lift the gun too high."

"Gosh agorry! Is that the way the real gunfighters do?"

A queer light flickered in his eyes and was gone. "No. Not all of them. Most have their own tricks. One likes a shoulder holster; another packs his gun in his pants belt. Some carry two guns, but that's a show-off stunt and a waste of weight. One's enough, if you know how to use it. I've even seen a man have a tight holster with an open end and fastened on a little swivel to the belt. He didn't have to pull the gun then. Just swung up the barrel and blazed away from the hip. That's mighty fast for close work and a big target. But it's not certain past ten or fifteen paces and no good at all for putting your shot right where you want it. The way I'm telling you is as good as any and better than most. And another thing—"

He reached and took the gun. Suddenly, as for the first time, I was aware of his hands. They were broad and strong, but not heavy and fleshy like father's. The fingers were long and square on the ends. It was funny how, touching the gun, the hands seemed to have an intelligence all their own, a sure movement that needed no guidance of thought.

His right hand closed around the grip and you knew at once it was doing what it had been created for. He hefted the old gun, letting it lie loosely in the hand. Then the fingers tightened and the thumb toyed with the hammer, testing the play of it.

While I gaped at him, he tossed it swiftly in the air and caught it in his left hand and in the instant of catching, it nestled snugly into this hand too. He tossed it again, high this time and spinning end over end, and as it came down, his right hand flicked forward and took it. The forefinger slipped through the trigger guard and the gun spun, coming up into firing position in the one un-broken motion. With him that old pistol seemed alive, not an inanimate and rusting metal object, but an extension of the man himself.

"If it's speed you're after, Bob, don't split the move into parts. Don't pull, cock, aim, and fire. Slip back the hammer as you bring the gun up and squeeze the trigger the second it's up level."

"How do you aim it, then? How do you get a sight on it?"

"No need to. Learn to hold it so the barrel's right in line with the fingers if they were out straight. You won't have to waste time bringing it high to take a sight. Just point it, low and quick and easy, like pointing a finger."

Like pointing a finger. As the words came, he was doing it. The old gun was bearing on some target over by the corral and the hammer was clicking at the empty cylinder. Then the hand around the gun whitened and the fingers slowly opened and the gun fell to the ground. The hand sank to his side, stiff and awkward. He raised his head and the mouth was a bitter gash in his face. His eyes were fastened on the mountains climbing in the distance.

"Shane! Shane! What's the matter?"

He did not hear me. He was back somewhere along the dark trail of the past.

He took a deep breath, and I could see the effort run through him as he dragged himself into the present and a realization of a boy staring at him. He beckoned to me to pick up the gun. When I did he leaned forward and spoke earnestly.

"Listen, Bob. A gun is just a tool. No better and no worse than any other tool, a shovel—or an axe or a saddle or a stove or anything. Think of it always that way. A gun is as good—and as bad—as the man who carries it. Remember that."

He stood up and strode off into the fields and I knew he wanted to be alone. I remembered what he said all right, tucked away unforgettably in my mind. But in those days I remembered more the way he handled the gun and the advice he gave me about using it. I would practice with it and think of the time when I could have one that would really shoot.

And then the summer was over. School began again and the days were growing shorter and the first cutting edge of cold was creeping down from the mountains.

More than the summer was over. The season of friendship in our valley was fading with the sun's warmth. Fletcher was back and he had his contract. He was talking in town that he would need the whole range again. The homesteaders would have to go.

He was a reasonable man, he was saying in his smooth way, and he would pay a fair price for any improvements they had put in. But we knew what Luke Fletcher would call a fair price. And we had no intention of leaving. The land was ours by right of settlement, guaranteed by the government. Only we knew, too, how faraway the government was from our valley way up there in the Territory.

The nearest marshal was a good hundred miles away. We did not even have a sheriff in our town. There never had been any reason for one. When folks had any lawing to do, they would head for Sheridan, nearly a full day's ride away. Our town was small, not even organized as a town. It was growing, but it was still not much more than a roadside settlement.

The first people there were three or four miners who had come prospecting after the blow-up of the Big Horn Mining Association about twenty years before, and had found gold traces leading to a moderate vein in the jutting rocks that partially closed off the valley where it edged into the plain. You could not have called it a strike, for others that followed were soon disappointed. Those first few, however, had done fairly well and had brought in their families and a number of helpers.

Then a stage and freighting line had picked the site for a relay post. That meant a place where you could get drinks as well as horses, and before long the cowboys from the ranches out on the plain and Fletcher's spread in the valley were drifting in of an evening. With us homesteaders coming now, one or two more almost every season, the town was taking shape. Already there were several stores, a harness and blacksmith shop, and nearly a dozen houses. Just the year before, the men had put together a one-room schoolhouse.

Sam Grafton's place was the biggest. He had a general store with several rooms for living quarters back of it in one half of his rambling building, a saloon with a long bar and tables for cards and the like in the other half. Upstairs he had some rooms he rented to stray drummers or anyone else stranded overnight. He acted as our postmaster, an elderly man, a close bargainer but honest in all his dealings. Sometimes he served as a sort of magistrate in minor disputes. His wife was dead. His daughter Jane kept house for him and was our schoolteacher when school was in session.

Even if we had had a sheriff, he would have been Fletcher's man. Fletcher was the power in the valley in those days. We homesteaders had been around only a few years and the other people still thought of us as there by his sufferance. He had been running cattle through the whole valley at the time the miners arrived, having bought or bulldozed out the few small ranchers there ahead of him. A series of bad years working up to the dry summer and terrible winter of '86 had cut his herds about the time the first of the homesteaders moved in and he had not objected too much. But now there were seven of us in all and the number rising each year.

It was a certain thing, father used to say, that the town would grow and swing our way. Mr. Grafton knew that too, I guess, but he was a careful man who never let thoughts about the future interfere with present business. The others were the kind to veer with the prevailing wind. Fletcher was the big man in the valley, so they looked up to him and tolerated us. Led to it, they probably would have helped him run us out. With him out of the way, they would just as willingly accept us. And Fletcher was back, with a contract in his pocket, wanting his full range again.

There was a hurried counsel in our house soon as the news was around. Our neighbor toward town, Lew Johnson, who heard it in Grafton's store, spread the word and arrived first. He was followed by Henry Shipstead, who had the place next to him, the closest to town. These two had been the original homesteaders, staking out their hundred and eighties two years before the drought and riding out Fletcher's annoyance until the cut in his herds gave him other worries. They were solid, dependable men, old-line farmers who had come West from Iowa.

You could not say quite as much for the rest, straggling in at intervals. James Lewis and Ed Howells were two middle-aged cowhands who had grown dissatisfied and tagged father into the valley, coming pretty much on his example.

Lacking his energy and drive, they had not done too well and could be easily discouraged.

Frank Torrey from farther up the valley was a nervous, fidgety man with a querulous wife and a string of dirty kids growing longer every year. He was always talking about pulling up stakes and heading for California. But he had a stubborn streak in him, and he was always saying, too, that he'd be darned if he'd make tracks just because some big-hatted rancher wanted him to.

Ernie Wright, who had the last stand up the valley butting out into the range still used by Fletcher, was probably the weakest of the lot. Not in any physical way. He was a husky, likable man, so dark-complected that there were rumors he was part Indian. He was always singing and telling tall stories. But he would be off hunting when he should be working and he had a quick temper that would trap him into doing fool things without taking thought.

He was as serious as the rest of them that night. Mr. Grafton had said that this time Fletcher meant business. His contract called for all the beef he could drive in the next five years and he was determined to push the chance to the limit.

"But what can he do?" asked Frank Torrey. "The land's ours as long as we live on it and we get title in three years. Some of you fellows have already proved up."

"He won't really make trouble," chimed in James Lewis. "Fletcher's never been the shooting kind. He's a good talker, but talk can't hurt us." Several of the others nodded. Johnson and Shipstead did not seem to be so sure. Father had not said anything yet and they all looked at him.

"Jim's right," he admitted. "Fletcher hasn't ever let his boys get careless thataway. Not yet anyhow. That ain't saying he wouldn't, if there wasn't any other way. There's a hard streak in him. But he won't get real tough for a while. I don't figure he'll start moving cattle in now till spring. My guess is he'll try putting pressure on us this fall and winter, see if he can wear us down. He'll probably start right here. He doesn't like any of us. But he doesn't like me most."

"That's true." Ed Howells was expressing the unspoken verdict that father was their leader. "How do you figure he'll go about it?"

"My guess on that," father said—drawling now and smiling a grim little smile like he knew he was holding a good hole card in a tight game—"my guess on that is that he'll begin by trying to convince Shane here that it isn't healthy to be working with me."

"You mean the way he—" began Ernie Wright.

"Yes." Father cut him short. "I mean the way he did with young Morley."

I was peeping around the door of my little room. I saw Shane sitting off to one side, listening quietly as he had been right along. He did not seem the least bit surprised. He did not seem the least bit interested in finding out what had happened to young Morley. I knew what had. I had seen Morley come back from town, bruised and a beaten man, and gather his things and curse father for hiring him and ride away without once looking back.

Yet Shane sat there quietly as if what had happened to Morley had nothing to do with him. He simply did not care what it was. And then I understood why. It was because he was not Morley. He was Shane.

Father was right. In some strange fashion the feeling was abroad that Shane was a marked man. Attention was on him as a sort of symbol. By taking him on father had accepted in a way a challenge from the big ranch across the river. What had happened to Morley had been a warning and father had deliberately answered it. The long unpleasantness was sharpened now after the summer lull. The issue in our valley was plain and would in time have to be pushed to a showdown. If Shane could be driven out, there would be a break in the homestead ranks, a defeat going beyond the loss of a man into the realm of prestige and morale. It could be the crack in the dam that weakens the whole structure and finally lets through the flood.

The people in town were more curious than ever, not now so much about Shane's past as about what he might do if Fletcher tried any move against him. They would stop me and ask me questions when I was hurrying to and from school. I knew that father would not want me to say anything and I pretended that I did not know what they were talking about. But I used to watch Shane closely myself and wonder how all the slow-climbing tenseness in our valley could be so focused on one man and he seem to be so indifferent to it.

For of course he was aware of it. He never missed anything. Yet he went about his work as usual, smiling frequently now at me, bantering mother at mealtimes in his courteous manner, arguing amiably as before with father on plans for next year. The only thing that was different was that there appeared to be a lot of new activity across the river. It was surprising how often Fletcher's cowboys were finding jobs to do within view of our place.

Then one afternoon, when we were stowing away the second and last cutting of hay, one fork of the big tongs we were using to haul it up to the loft broke loose. "Have to get it welded in town," father said in disgust and began to hitch up the team.

Shane stared over the river where a cowboy was riding lazily back and forth by a bunch of cattle. "I'll take it in," he said.

Father looked at Shane and he looked across the way and he grinned. "All right. It's as good a time as any." He slapped down the final buckle and started for the house. "Just a minute and I'll be ready."

"Take it easy, Joe." Shane's voice was gentle, but it stopped father in his tracks. "I said I'll take it in."

Father whirled to face him. "Darn it all, man. Do you think I'd let you go alone? Suppose they—" He bit down on his own words. He wiped a hand slowly across his face and he said what I had never heard him say to any man. "I'm sorry," he said. "I should have known better." He stood there silently watching as Shane gathered up the reins and jumped to the wagon seat.

I was afraid father would stop me, so I waited till Shane was driving out of the lane. I ducked behind the barn, around the end of the corral, and hopped into the wagon going past. As I did, I saw the cowboy across the river spin his horse and ride rapidly off in the direction of the ranchhouse.

Shane saw it, too, and it seemed to give him a grim amusement. He reached backwards and hauled me over the seat and sat me beside him.

"You Starretts like to mix into things." For a moment I thought he might send me back. Instead he grinned at me. "I'll buy you a jackknife when we hit town."

He did, a dandy big one with two blades and a corkscrew. After we left the tongs with the blacksmith and found the welding would take nearly an hour, I squatted on the steps on the long porch across the front of Grafton's building, busy whittling, while Shane stepped into the saloon side and ordered a drink. Will Atkey, Grafton's thin, sad-faced clerk and bartender, was behind the bar and several other men were loafing at one of the tables.

It was only a few moments before two cowboys came galloping down the road. They slowed to a walk about fifty yards off and with a show of nonchalance ambled the rest of the way to Grafton's, dismounting and looping their reins over the r⸱ı in front. One of them I had seen often, a young fellow everyone called Chris, who had worked with Fletcher several years and was known for a gay manner and reckless courage. The other was new to me, a sallow, pinch-cheek man, not much older, who looked like he had crowded a lot of hard living into his years. He must have been one of the new hands Fletcher had been bringing into the valley since he got his contract.

They paid no attention to me. They stepped softly up on the porch and to the window of the saloon part of the building. As they peered through, Chris nodded and jerked his head toward the inside. The new man stiffened. He leaned closer for a better look. Abruptly he turned clear about and came right down past me and went over to his horse.

Chris was startled and hurried after him. They were both so intent they did not realize I was there. The new man was lifting the reins back over his horse's head when Chris caught his arm.

"What the—?"

"I'm leaving."

"Huh? I don't get it."

"I'm leaving. Now. For good."

"Hey, listen. Do you know that guy?"

"I didn't say that. There ain't nobody can claim I said that. I'm leaving, that's all. You can tell Fletcher. This is a heck of a country up here anyhow."

Chris was getting mad. "I might have known," he said. "Scared, eh. Yellow."

Color rushed into the new man's sallow face. But he climbed on his horse and swung out from the rail. "You can call it that," he said flatly and started down the road, out of town, out of the valley.

Chris was standing still by the rail, shaking his head in wonderment. "Well," he said to himself, "I'll brace him myself." He stalked up on the porch, into the saloon.

I dashed into the store side, over to the opening between the two big rooms. I crouched on a box just inside the store where I could hear everything and see most of the other room. It was long and fairly wide. The bar curved out from the opening and ran all the way along the inner wall to the back wall, which closed off a room Grafton used as an office. There was a row of windows on the far side, too high for anyone to look in from outside. A small stairway behind them led up to a sort of balcony across the back with doors opening into several little rooms.

Shane was leaning easily with one arm on the bar, his drink in his other hand, when Chris came to perhaps six feet away and called for a whiskey bottle and a glass. Chris pretended he did not notice Shane at first and bobbed his head in greeting to the men at the table. They were a pair of mule-skinners who made regular trips into the valley freighting in goods for Grafton and the other shops. I could have sworn that Shane, studying Chris in his effortless way, was somehow disappointed.

Chris waited until he had his whiskey and had gulped a stiff shot. Then he deliberately looked Shane over like he had just spotted him.

"Hello, farmer," he said. He said it as if he did not like farmers.

Shane regarded him with grave attention. "Speaking to me?" he asked mildly and finished his drink.

"Heck, there ain't nobody else standing there. Here, have a drink of this." Chris shoved his bottle along the bar. Shane poured himself a generous slug and raised it to his lips.

"I'll be darned," flipped Chris. "So you drink whiskey."

Shane tossed off the rest in his glass and set it down. "I've had better," he said, as friendly as could be. "But this will do."

Chris slapped his leather chaps with a loud smack. He turned to take in the other men. "Did you hear that? This farmer drinks whiskey! I didn't think these plow-pushing dirt-grubbers drank anything stronger than soda pop!"

"Some of us do," said Shane, friendly as before. Then he was no longer friendly and his voice was like winter frost. "You've had your fun and it's mighty young fun. Now run home and tell Fletcher to send a grown-up man next time." He turned away and sang out to Will Atkey. "Do you have any soda pop? I'd like a bottle."

Will hesitated, looked kind of funny, and scuttled past me into the store room. He came back right away with a bottle of the pop Grafton kept there for us school kids. Chris was standing quiet, not so much mad, I would have said, as puzzled. It was as though they were playing some queer game and he was not sure of the next move. He sucked on his lower lip for a while. Then he snapped his mouth and began to look elaborately around the room, sniffing loudly.

"Hey, Will!" he called. "What's been happening in here? It smells. That ain't no clean cattleman smell. That's plain dirty barnyard." He stared at Shane. "You, farmer. What are you and Starrett raising out there? Pigs?"

Shane was just taking hold of the bottle Will had fetched him. His hand closed on it and the knuckles showed white. He moved slowly, almost unwillingly, to face Chris. Every line of his body was as taut as stretched whipcord, was alive and somehow rich with an immense eagerness. There was that fierce concentration in him, filling him, blazing in his eyes. In that moment there was nothing in the room for him but that mocking man only a few feet away.

The big room was so quiet the stillness fairly hurt. Chris stepped back involuntarily, one pace, two, then pulled up erect. And still nothing happened. The lean muscles along the sides of Shane's jaw were ridged like rock.

Then the breath, pent in him, broke the stillness with a soft sound as it left his lungs. He looked away from Chris, past him, over the tops of the swinging doors beyond, over the roof of the shed across the road, on into the distance where the mountains loomed in their own unending loneliness. Quietly he walked, the bottle forgotten in his hand, so close by Chris as almost to brush him yet apparently not even seeing him, through the doors and was gone.

I heard a sigh of relief near me. Mr. Grafton had come up from somewhere behind me. He was watching Chris with a strange, ironic quirk at his mouth corners. Chris was trying not to look pleased with himself. But he swaggered as he went to the doors and peered over them.

"You saw it, Will," he called over his shoulder. "He walked out on me." Chris pushed up his hat and rolled back on his heels and laughed. "With a bottle of soda pop too!" He was still laughing as he went out and we heard him ride away.

"That boy's a fool," Mr. Grafton muttered.

Will Atkey came sidling over to Mr. Grafton. "I never pegged Shane for a play like that," he said.

"He was afraid, Will."

"Yeah. That's what was so funny. I would've guessed he could take Chris."

Mr. Grafton looked at Will as he did often, like he was a little sorry for him. "No, Will. He wasn't afraid of Chris. He was afraid of himself." Mr. Grafton was thoughtful and perhaps sad too. "There's trouble ahead, Will. The worst trouble we've ever had."

He noticed me, realizing my presence. "Better skip along, Bob, and find your friend. Do you think he got that bottle for himself?"

True enough, Shane had it waiting for me at the blacksmith shop. Cherry pop, the kind I favored most. But I could not enjoy it much. Shane was so silent and stern. He had slipped back into the dark mood that was on him when he first came riding up our road. I did not dare say anything. Only once did he speak to me and I knew he did not expect me to understand or to answer.

"Why should a man be smashed because he has courage and does what he's told? Life's a dirty business, Bob. I could like that boy." And he turned inward again to his own thoughts and stayed the same until we had loaded the tongs in the wagon and were well started home. Then the closer we came, the more cheerful he was. By the time we swung in toward the barn, he was the way I wanted him again, crinkling his eyes at me and gravely joshing me about the Indians I would scalp with my new knife.

Father popped out the barn door so quick you could tell he had been itching for us to return. He was busting with curiosity, but he would not come straight out with a question to Shane. He tackled me instead.

"See any of your cowboy heroes in town?"

Shane cut in ahead of me. "One of Fletcher's crew chased us in to pay his respects."

"No," I said, proud of my information. "There was two of them."

"Two?" Shane said it. Father was the one who was not surprised. "What did the other one do?"

"He went up on the porch and looked in the window where you were and came right back down and rode off."

"Back to the ranch?"

"The other way. He said he was leaving for good."

Father and Shane looked at each other. Father was smiling. "One down and you didn't even know it. What did you do to the other?"

"Nothing. He passed a few remarks about farmers. I went back to the blacksmith shop."

Father repeated it, spacing the words like there might be meanings between them. "You—went—back—to—the—blacksmith—shop."

I was worried that he must be thinking what Will Atkey did. Then I knew nothing like that had even entered his head. He switched to me. "Who was it?"

"It was Chris."

Father was smiling again. He had not been there but he had the whole thing clear. "Fletcher was right to send two. Young ones like Chris need to hunt in pairs or they might get hurt." He chuckled in a sort of wry amusement. "Chris must have been considerable surprised when the other fellow skipped. And more when you walked out. It was too bad the other one didn't stick around."

"Yes," Shane said, "it was."

The way he said it sobered father. "I hadn't thought of that. Chris is just cocky enough to take it wrong. That can make things plenty unpleasant."

"Yes," Shane said again, "it can."

It was just as father and Shane had said. The story Chris told was common knowledge all through the valley before the sun set the next day and the story grew in the telling. Fletcher had an advantage now and he was quick to push it. He and his foreman, Morgan, a broad slab of a man with flattened face and head small in proportion to great sloping shoulders, were shrewd at things like this and they kept their men primed to rowel us homesteaders at every chance.

They took to using the upper ford, up above Ernie Wright's stand, and riding down the road past our places every time they had an excuse for going to town.

They would go by slowly, looking everything over with insolent interest and passing remarks for our benefit.

The same week, maybe three days later, a covey of them came riding by while father was putting a new hinge on the corral gate. They acted like they were too busy staring over our land to see him there close.

"Wonder where Starrett keeps the critters," said one of them. "I don't see a pig in sight."

"But I can smell 'em!" shouted another one. With that they all began to laugh and whoop and holler and went tearing off, kicking up a lot of dust and leaving father with a tightness around his mouth that was not there before.

They were impartial with attentions like that. They would hand them out anywhere along the line an opportunity offered. But they liked best to catch father within earshot and burn him with their sarcasm.

It was crude. It was coarse. I thought it silly for grown men to act that way. But it was effective. Shane, as self-sufficient as the mountains, could ignore it. Father, while it galled him, could keep it from getting him. The other homesteaders, though, could not help being irritated and showing they felt insulted. It roughed their nerves and made them angry and restless. They did not know Shane as father and I did. They were not sure there might not be some truth in the big talk Chris was making.

Things became so bad they could not go into Grafton's store without someone singing out for soda pop. And wherever they went, the conversation nearby always snuck around somehow to pigs. You could sense the contempt building up in town, in people who used to be neutral, not taking sides.

The effect showed, too, in the attitude our neighbors now had toward Shane. They were constrained when they called to see father and Shane was there. They resented that he was linked to them. And as a result their opinion of father was changing.

That was what finally drove Shane. He did not mind what they thought of him. Since his session with Chris he seemed to have won a kind of inner peace. He was as alert and watchful as ever, but there was a serenity in him that had erased entirely the old tension. I think he did not care what anyone anywhere thought of him. Except us, his folks. And he knew that with us he was one of us, unchangeable and always.

But he did care what they thought of father. He was standing silently on the porch the night Ernie Wright and Henry Shipstead were arguing with father in the kitchen.

"I can't stomach much more," Ernie Wright was saying. "You know the trouble I've had with those blasted cowboys cutting my fence. Today a couple of them rode over and helped me repair a piece. Helped me! Waited till we were through, then said Fletcher didn't want any of my pigs getting loose and mixing with his cattle. My pigs! There ain't a pig in this whole valley and they know it. I'm sick of the word."

Father made it worse by chuckling. Grim, maybe, yet still a chuckle. "Sounds like one of Morgan's ideas. He's smart. Mean, but—"

Henry Shipstead would not let him finish. "This is nothing to laugh at, Joe. You least of all. Darn it, man, I'm beginning to doubt your judgment. None of us can keep our heads up around here any more. Just a while ago I was in Grafton's and Chris was there blowing high about your Shane must be thirsty because he's so scared he hasn't been in town lately for his soda pop."

Both of them were hammering at father now. He was sitting back, saying nothing, his face clouding.

"You can't dodge it, Joe." This was Wright. "Your man's responsible. You can try explaining all night, but you can't change the facts. Chris braced him for a fight and he ducked out—and left us stuck with those stinking pigs."

"You know as well as I do what Fletcher's doing," growled Henry Shipstead. "He's pushing us with this and he won't let up till one of us gets enough and makes a fool play and starts something so he can move in and finish it."

"Fool play or not," said Ernie Wright. "I've had all I can take. The next time one of those—"

Father stopped him with a hand up for silence. "Listen. What's that?"

It was a horse, picking up speed and tearing down our lane into the road. Father was at the door in a single jump, peering out.

The others were close behind him. "Shane?"

Father nodded. He was muttering under his breath. As I watched from the doorway of my little room, I could see that his eyes were bright and dancing. He was calling Shane names, cursing him, softly, fluently. He came back to his chair and grinned at the other two. "That's Shane," he told them and the words meant more than they seemed to say. "All we can do now is wait."

They were a silent crew waiting. Mother got up from her sewing in the bedroom where she had been listening as she always did and came into the kitchen and made up a pot of coffee and they all sat there sipping at the hot stuff and waiting.

It could not have been much more than twenty minutes before we heard the horse again, coming swiftly and slewing around to make the lane without slowing. There were quick steps on the porch and Shane stood in the doorway. He was breathing strongly and his face was hard. His mouth was a thin line in the bleakness of his face and his eyes were deep and dark. He looked at Shipstead and Wright and he made no effort to hide the disgust in his voice.

"Your pigs are dead and buried."

As his gaze shifted to father, his face softened. But the voice was still bitter. "There's another one down. Chris won't be bothering anybody for quite a spell." He turned and disappeared and we could hear him leading the horse into the barn.

In the quiet following, hoofbeats like an echo sounded in the distance. They swelled louder and this second horse galloped into our lane and pulled to a stop. Ed Howells jumped to the porch and hurried in.

"Where's Shane?"

"Out in the barn," father said.

"Did he tell you what happened?"

"Not much," father said mildly. "Something about burying pigs."

Ed Howells slumped into a chair. He seemed a bit dazed. The words came out of him slowly at first as he tried to make the others grasp just how he felt. "I never saw anything like it," he said, and he told about it.

He had been in Grafton's store buying a few things, not caring about going into the saloon because Chris and Red Marlin, another of Fletcher's cowboys, had hands in the evening poker game, when he noticed how still the place was. He went over to sneak a look and there was Shane just moving to the bar, cool and easy as if the room was empty and he the only one in it. Neither Chris nor Red Marlin was saying a word, though you might have thought this was a good chance for them to cut loose with some of their raw sarcasm. One look at Shane was enough to tell why. He was cool and easy, right enough. But there was a curious kind of smooth flow to his movements that made you realize without being conscious of thinking about it that being quiet was a mighty sensible way to be at the moment.

"Two bottles of soda pop," he called to Will Atkey. He leaned his back to the bar and looked the poker game over with what seemed a friendly interest while Will fetched the bottles from the store. Not another person even twitched a muscle. They were all watching him and wondering what the play was. He took the two bottles and walked to the table and set them down, reaching over to put one in front of Chris.

"The last time I was in here you bought me a drink. Now it's my turn."

The words sort of lingered in the stillness. He got the impression, Ed Howells said, that Shane meant just what the words said. He wanted to buy Chris a drink. He wanted Chris to take that bottle and grin at him and drink with him.

You could have heard a bug crawl, I guess, while Chris carefully laid down the cards in his right hand and stretched it to the bottle. He lifted it in a sudden jerk and flung it across the table at Shane.

So fast Shane moved, Ed Howells said, that the bottle was still in the air when he had dodged, lunged forward, grabbed Chris by the shirtfront and hauled him right out of his chair and over the table. As Chris struggled to get his feet under him, Shane let go the shirt and slapped him, sharp and stinging, three times, the hand flicking back and forth so quick you could hardly see it, the slaps sounding like pistol shots.

Shane stepped back and Chris stood swaying a little and shaking his head to clear it. He was a game one and mad down to his boots. He plunged in, fists smashing, and Shane let him come, slipping inside the flailing arms and jolting a powerful blow low into his stomach. As Chris gasped and his head came down, Shane brought his right hand up, open, and with the heel of it caught Chris full on the mouth, snapping his head back and raking up over the nose and eyes.

The force of it knocked Chris off balance and he staggered badly. His lips were crushed. Blood was dripping over them from his battered nose. His eyes were red and watery and he was having trouble seeing with them. His face, Ed Howells said, and shook a little as he said it, looked like a horse had stomped it. But he drove in again, swinging wildly.

Shane ducked under, caught one of the flying wrists, twisted the arm to lock it and keep it from bending, and swung his shoulder into the armpit. He yanked hard on the wrist and Chris went up and over him. As the body hurtled over, Shane kept hold of the arm and wrenched it sideways and let the weight bear on it and you could hear the bone crack as Chris crashed to the floor.

A long sobbing sigh came from Chris and that died away and there was not a sound in the room. Shane never looked at the crumpled figure. He was straight and deadly and still. Every line of him was alive and eager. But he stood motionless. Only his eyes shifted to search the faces of the others at the table. They stopped on Red Marlin and Red seemed to dwindle lower in his chair.

"Perhaps," Shane said softly, and the very softness of his voice sent shivers through Ed Howells, "perhaps you have something to say about soda pop or pigs."

Red Marlin sat quiet like he was trying not even to breathe. Tiny drops of sweat appeared on his forehead. He was frightened, maybe for the first time in his life, and the others knew it and he knew they knew and he did not care. And none of them blamed him at all.

Then, as they watched, the fire in Shane smouldered down and out. He seemed to withdraw back within himself. He forgot them all and turned toward Chris unconscious on the floor, and a sort of sadness, Ed Howells said, crept over him and held him. He bent and scooped the sprawling figure up in his arms and carried it to one of the other tables. Gently he set it down, the legs falling limp over the edge. He crossed to the bar and took the rag Will used to wipe it and returned to the table and tenderly cleared the blood from the face. He felt carefully along the broken arm and nodded to himself at what he felt.

All this while no one said a word. Not a one of them would have interfered with that man for a year's top wages. He spoke and his voice rang across the room at Red Marlin. "You'd better tote him home and get that arm fixed. Take right good care of him. He has the makings of a good man." Then he forgot them all again and looked at Chris and went on speaking as if to that limp figure that could not hear him. "There's only one thing really wrong with you. You're young. That's the one thing time can always cure."

The thought hurt him and he strode to the swinging doors and through them into the night. That was what Ed Howells told. "The whole business," he finished, "didn't take five minutes. It was maybe thirty seconds from the time he grabbed holt of Chris till Chris was out cold on the floor. In my opinion that Shane is the most dangerous man I've ever seen. I'm glad he's working for Joe here and not for Fletcher."

Father leveled a triumphant look at Henry Shipstead. "So I've made a mistake, have I?"

Before anyone else could push in a word, mother was speaking. I was surprised, because she was upset and her voice was a little shrill. "I wouldn't be too sure about that, Joe Starrett. I think you've made a bad mistake."

"Marian, what's got into you?"

"Look what you've done just because you got him to stay on here and get mixed up in this trouble with Fletcher!"

Father was edging toward being peeved himself. "Women never do understand these things. Lookahere, Marian. Chris will be all right. He's young and he's healthy. Soon as that arm is mended, he'll be in as good shape as he ever was."

"Oh, Joe, can't you see what I'm talking about? I don't mean what you've done to Chris. I mean what you've done to Shane."

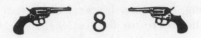 8

This time mother was right. Shane was changed. He tried to keep things as they had been with us and on the surface nothing was different. But he had lost the serenity that had seeped into him through the summer. He would no longer sit around and talk with us as much as he had. He was restless with some far hidden desperation.

At times, when it rode him worst, he would wander alone about our place, and this was the one thing that seemed to soothe him. I used to see him, when he thought no one was watching, run his hands along the rails of the corral he had fastened, test with a tug the posts he had set, pace out past the barn looking up at the bulging loft and stride out where the tall corn was standing in big shocks to dig his hands in the loose soil and lift some of it and let it run through his fingers.

He would lean on the pasture fence and study our little herd like it meant more to him than lazy steers to be fattened for market. Sometimes he would whistle softly, and his horse, filled out now so you could see the quality of him and moving with a quiet sureness and power that made you think of Shane himself, would trot to the fence and nuzzle at him.

Often he would disappear from the house in the early evening after supper. More than once, the dishes done, when I managed to slip past mother, I found him far back in the pasture alone with the horse. He would be standing there, one arm on the smooth arch of the horse's neck, the fingers gently rubbing around the ears, and he would be looking out over our land where the last light of the sun, now out of sight, would be flaring up the far side of the mountains, capping them with a deep glow and leaving a mystic gloaming in the valley.

Some of the assurance that was in him when he came was gone now. He seemed to feel that he needed to justify himself, even to me, to a boy tagging his heels.

"Could you teach me," I asked him, "to throw somebody the way you threw Chris?"

He waited so long I thought he would not answer. "A man doesn't learn things like that," he said at last. "You know them and that's all." Then he was talking rapidly to me, as close to pleading as he could ever come. "I tried. You can see that, can't you, Bob? I let him ride me and I gave him his chance. A man can keep his self-respect without having to cram it down another man's throat. Surely you can see that, Bob?"

I could not see it. What he was trying to explain to me was beyond my comprehension then. And I could think of nothing to say.

"I left it up to him. He didn't have to jump me that second time. He could have called it off without crawling. IIe could have if he was man enough. Can't you see that, Bob?"

And still I could not. But I said I could. He was so earnest and he wanted me to so badly. It was a long, long time before I did see it and then I was a man myself and Shane was not there for me to tell. . . .

I was not sure whether father and mother were aware of the change in him. They did not talk about it, not while I was around anyway. But one afternoon I overheard something that showed mother knew.

I had hurried home from school and put on my old clothes and started out to see what father and Shane were doing in the cornfield, when I thought of a trick that had worked several times. Mother was firm set against eating between meals. That was a silly notion. I had my mind set on the cookies she kept in a tin box on a shelf by the stove. She was settled on the porch with a batch of potatoes to peel, so I slipped up to the back of the house, through the window of my little room, and tiptoed into the kitchen. Just as I was carefully putting a chair under the shelf, I heard her call to Shane.

He must have come to the barn on some errand, for he was there by the porch in only a moment. I peered out the front window and saw him standing close in, his hat in his hand, his face tilted up slightly to look at her leaning forward in her chair.

"I've been wanting to talk to you when Joe wasn't around."

"Yes, Marian." He called her that the same as father did, familiar yet respectful, just as he always regarded her with a tenderness in his eyes he had for no one else.

"You've been worrying, haven't you, about what may happen in this Fletcher business? You thought it would just be a case of not letting him scare you away and of helping us through a hard time. You didn't know it would come to what it has. And now you're worried about what you might do if there's any more fighting."

"You're a discerning woman, Marian."

"You've been worrying about something else too."

"You're a mighty discerning woman, Marian."

"And you've been thinking that maybe you'll be moving on."

"And how did you know that?"

"Because it's what you ought to do. For your own sake. But I'm asking you not to." Mother was intense and serious, as lovely there with the light striking through her hair as I had ever seen her. "Don't go, Shane. Joe needs you. More than ever now. More than he would ever say."

"And you?" Shane's lips barely moved and I was not sure of the words.

Mother hesitated. Then her head went up. "Yes. It's only fair to say it. I need you too."

"So-o-o," he said softly, the words lingering on his lips. He considered her gravely. "Do you know what you're asking, Marian?"

"I know. And I know that you're the man to stand up to it. In some ways it would be easier for me, too, if you rode out of this valley and never came back. But we can't let Joe down. I'm counting on you not ever to make me do that. Because you've got to stay, Shane, no matter how hard it is for us. Joe can't keep this place without you. He can't buck Fletcher alone."

Shane was silent, and it seemed to me that he was troubled and hard pressed in his mind. Mother was talking straight to him, slow and feeling for the words, and her voice was beginning to tremble.

"It would just about kill Joe to lose this place. He's too old to start in again somewhere else. Oh, we would get along and might even do real well. After all, he's Joe Starrett. He's all man and he can do what has to be done. But he promised me this place when we were married. He had it in his mind for all the first years. He did two men's work to get the extra money for the things we would need. When Bob was big enough to walk and help some and he could leave us, he came on here and filed his claim and built this house with his own hands, and when he brought us here it was home. Nothing else would ever be the same."

Shane drew a deep breath and let it ease out slowly. He smiled at her and yet, somehow, as I watched him, my heart ached for him. "Joe should be proud of a wife like you. Don't fret any more, Marian. You'll not lose this place."

Mother dropped back in her chair. Her face, the side I could see from the window, was radiant. Then, woman like, she was talking against herself. "But that Fletcher is a mean and tricky man. Are you sure it will work out all right?"

Shane was already starting toward the barn. He stopped and turned to look at her again. "I said you won't lose this place." You knew he was right because of the way he said it and because he said it.

9

Another period of peace had settled over our valley. Since the night Shane rode into town, Fletcher's cowboys had quit using the road past the homesteads. They were not annoying us at all and only once in a while was there a rider in view across the river. They had a good excuse to let us be. They were busy fixing the ranch buildings and poling a big new corral in preparation for the spring drive of new cattle Fletcher was planning.

Just the same, I noticed that father was as watchful as Shane now. The two of them worked always together. They did not split any more to do separate jobs in different parts of the farm. They worked together, rode into town together when anything was needed. And father took to wearing his gun all the time, even in the fields. He strapped it on after breakfast the first morning following the fight with Chris, and I saw him catch Shane's eye with a questioning glance as he buckled the belt. But Shane shook his head and father nodded, accepting the decision, and they went out together without saying a word.

Those were beautiful fall days, clear and stirring, with the coolness in the air just enough to set one atingling, not yet mounting to the bitter cold that soon would come sweeping down out of the mountains. It did not seem possible that in such a harvest season, giving a lift to the spirit to match the well-being of the body, violence could flare so suddenly and swiftly.

Saturday evenings all of us would pile into the light work wagon, father and mother on the seat, Shane and I swinging legs at the rear, and go into town. It was the break in routine we looked forward to all week.

There was always a bustle in Grafton's store with people we knew coming and going. Mother would lay in her supplies for the week ahead, taking a long time about it and chatting with the womenfolk. She and the wives of the other homesteaders were great ones for swapping recipes and this was their bartering ground. Father would give Mr. Grafton his order for what he wanted and go direct for the mail. He was always getting catalogues of farm equipment and pamphlets from Washington. He would flip through their pages and skim through any letters, then settle on a barrel and spread out his newspaper. But like as not he would soon be bogged down in an argument with almost any man handy about the best crops for the Territory and it would be Shane who would really work his way into the newspaper.

I used to explore the store, filling myself with crackers from the open barrel at the end of the main counter, playing hide and seek with Mr. Grafton's big and knowing old cat that was a whiz of a mouser. Many a time, turning up boxes, I chased out fat furry ones for her to pounce on. If mother was in the right mood, I would have a bag of candy in my pocket.

This time we had a special reason for staying longer than usual, a reason I did not like. Our schoolteacher, Jane Grafton, had made me take a note home to mother asking her to stop in for a talk. About me. I never was too smart at formal schooling to begin with. Being all excited over the doings at the big ranch and what they might mean to us had not helped any. Miss Grafton, I guess, just sort of endured me under the best of conditions. But what tipped her into being downright annoyed and writing to mother was the weather. No one could expect a boy with any spirit in him to be shut up in a schoolroom in weather like we had been having. Twice that week I had persuaded Ollie Johnson to sneak away with me after the lunch hour to see if the fish were still biting in our favorite pool below town.

Mother finished the last item on her list, looked around at me, sighed a little, and stiffened her shoulders. I knew she was going to the living quarters behind the store and talk to Miss Grafton. I squirmed and pretended I did not notice her. Only a few people were left in the store, though the saloon in the adjoining big room was doing fair business. She went over to where father was leafing through a catalogue and tapped him.

"Come along, Joe. You should hear this, too. I declare, that boy is getting too big for me to handle."

Father glanced quickly over the store and paused, listening to the voices from the next room. We had not seen any of Fletcher's men all evening and he seemed satisfied. He looked at Shane, who was folding the newspaper.

"This won't take long. We'll be out in a moment."

As they passed through the door at the rear of the store, Shane strolled to the saloon opening. He took in the whole room in his easy, alert way and stepped inside. I followed. But I was supposed not ever to go in there, so I stopped at the entrance. Shane was at the bar, joshing Will Atkey with a grave face that he didn't think he'd have soda pop tonight. It was a scattered group in the room, most of them from around town and familiar to me by sight at least. Those close to Shane moved a little away, eyeing him curiously. He did not appear to notice.

He picked up his drink and savored it, one elbow on the bar, not shoving himself forward into the room's companionship and not withdrawing either, just ready to be friendly if anyone wanted that and unfriendly if anyone wanted that too.

I was letting my eyes wander about, trying to tag names to faces, when I saw that one of the swinging doors was partly open and Red Marlin was peeking in. Shane saw it too. But he could not see that more men were out on the porch, for they were close by the building wall and on the store side. I could sense them through the window near me, hulking shapes in the darkness. I was so frightened I could scarcely move.

But I had to. I had to go against mother's rule. I scrambled into the saloon and to Shane and I gasped: "Shane! There's a lot of them out front!"

I was too late. Red Marlin was inside and the others were hurrying in and fanning out to close off the store opening. Morgan was one of them, his flat face sour and determined, his huge shoulders almost filling the doorway as he came through. Behind him was the cowboy they called Curly because of his shock of unruly hair. He was stupid and slow-moving, but he was thick and powerful, and he had worked in harness with Chris for several years. Two others followed them, new men to me, with the tough, experienced look of old herd hands.

There was still the back office with its outside door opening on a side stoop and the rear alley. My knees were shaking and I tugged at Shane and tried to say something about it. He stopped me with a sharp gesture. His face was clear, his eyes bright. He was somehow happy, not in the pleased and laughing way, but happy that the waiting was over and what had been ahead was here and seen and realized and he was ready for it. He put one hand on my head and rocked it gently, the fingers feeling through my hair.

"Bobby boy, would you have me run away?"

Love for that man raced through me and the warmth ran down and stiffened my legs and I was so proud of being there with him that I could not keep the tears from my eyes. I could see the rightness of it and I was ready to do as he told me when he said: "Get out of here, Bob. This isn't going to be pretty."

But I would go no farther than my perch just inside the store where I could watch most of the big room. I was so bound in the moment that I did not even think of running for father.

✧   ✧   ✧

Morgan was in the lead now with his men spread out behind him. He came about half the way to Shane and stopped. The room was quiet except for the shuffling of feet as the men by the bar and the nearest tables hastened over to the far wall and some of them ducked out the front doors. Neither Shane nor Morgan gave any attention to them. They had attention only for each other. They did not look aside even when Mr. Grafton, who could smell trouble in his place from any distance, stalked in from the store, planting his feet down firmly, and pushed past Will Atkey behind the bar. He had a resigned expression on his face and he reached under the counter, his hands reappearing with a short-barreled shotgun. He laid it before him on the bar and he said in a dry, disgusted voice: "There will be no gunplay, gentlemen. And all damages will be paid for."

Morgan nodded curtly, not taking his eyes from Shane. He came closer and stopped again little more than an arm's length away. His head was thrust forward. His big fists were clenched at his sides.

"No one messes up one of my boys and gets away with it. We're riding you out of this valley on a rail, Shane. We're going to rough you a bit and ride you out and you'll stay out."

"So you have it all planned," Shane said softly. Even as he was speaking, he was moving. He flowed into action so swift you could hardly believe what was happening. He scooped up his half-filled glass from the bar, whipped it and its contents into Morgan's face, and when Morgan's hands came up reaching or striking for him, he grasped the wrists and flung himself backwards, dragging Morgan with him. His body rolled to meet the floor and his legs doubled and his feet, catching Morgan just below the belt, sent him flying on and over to fall flat in a grotesque spraddle and slide along the boards in a tangle of chairs and a table.

The other four were on Shane in a rush. As they came, he whirled to his hands and knees and leaped up and behind the nearest table, tipping it in a strong heave among them. They scattered, dodging, and he stepped, fast and light, around the end and drove into the tail man, one of the new men, now nearest to him. He took the blows at him straight on to get in close and I saw his knee surge up and into the man's groin. A high scream was literally torn from the man and he collapsed to the floor and dragged himself toward the doors.

Morgan was on his feet, wavering, rubbing a hand across his face, staring hard as if trying to focus again on the room about him. The other three were battering at Shane, seeking to box him between them. They were piling blows into him, crowding in. Through that blur of movement he was weaving, quick and confident. It was incredible, but they could not hurt him. You could see the blows hit, hear the solid chunk of knuckles on flesh. But they had no effect. They seemed only to feed that fierce energy. He moved like a flame among them. He would burst out of the mêlée and whirl and plunge back, the one man actually pressing the three. He had picked the second new man and was driving always directly at him.

Curly, slow and clumsy, grunting in exasperation, grabbed at Shane to grapple with him and hold down his arms. Shane dropped one shoulder and as Curly hugged tighter brought it up under his jaw with a jolt that knocked him loose and away.

They were wary now and none too eager to let him get close to any one of them. Then Red Marlin came at him from one side, forcing him to turn that way, and at the same time the second new man did a strange thing. He jumped high in the air, like a jack rabbit in a spy hop, and lashed out viciously with one boot at Shane's head. Shane saw it coming, but could not avoid it, so he rolled his head with the kick, taking it along the side. It shook him badly. But it did not block the instant response. His hands shot up and seized the foot and the man crashed down to land on the small of his back. As he hit, Shane twisted the whole leg and threw his weight on it. The man buckled on the floor like a snake when you hit it and groaned sharply and hitched himself away, the leg dragging, the fight gone out of him.

But the swing to bend down on the leg had put Shane's back to Curly and the big man was plowing at him. Curly's arms clamped around him, pinning his arms to his body. Red Marlin leaped to help and the two of them had Shane caught tight between them.

"Hold him!" That was Morgan, coming forward with the hate plain in his eyes. Even then, Shane would have broke away. He stomped one heavy work shoe, heel edged and with all the strength he could get in quick leverage, on Curly's near foot. As Curly winced and pulled it back and was unsteady, Shane strained with his whole body in a powerful arch and you could see their arms slipping and loosening. Morgan, circling in, saw it too. He swept a bottle off the bar and brought it smashing down from behind on Shane's head.

Shane slumped and would have fallen if they had not been holding him. Then, as Morgan stepped around in front of him and watched, the vitality pumped through him and his head came up.

"Hold him!" Morgan said again. He deliberately flung a huge fist to Shane's face. Shane tried to jerk aside and the fist missed the jaw, tearing along the cheek, the heavy ring on one finger slicing deep. Morgan pulled back for another blow. He never made it.

Nothing, I would have said, could have drawn my attention from those men. But I heard a kind of choking sob beside me and it was queer and yet familiar and it turned me instantly.

Father was there in the entranceway!

He was big and terrible and he was looking across the overturned table and scattered chairs at Shane, at the dark purplish bruise along the side of Shane's head and the blood running down his cheek. I had never seen father like this. He was past anger. He was filled with a fury that was shaking him almost beyond endurance.

I never thought he could move so fast. He was on them before they even knew he was in the room. He hurtled into Morgan with ruthless force, sending that huge man reeling across the room. He reached out one broad hand and grabbed Curly by the shoulder and you could see the fingers sink into the flesh. He took hold of Curly's belt with the other hand and ripped him loose from Shane and his own shirt shredded down the back and the great muscles there knotted and bulged as he lifted Curly right up over his head and hurled the threshing body from him. Curly spun through the air, his limbs waving wildly, and crashed on the top of a table way over by the wall. It cracked under him, collapsing in splintered pieces, and the man and the wreckage smacked against the wall. Curly tried to rise, pushing himself with hands on the floor, and fell back and was still.

Shane must have exploded into action the second father yanked Curly away, for now there was another noise. It was Red Marlin, his face contorted, flung against the bar and catching at it to keep himself from falling. He staggered and caught his balance and ran for the front doorway. His flight was frantic, head-long. He tore through the swinging doors without slowing to push them. They flapped with a swishing sound and my eyes shifted quickly to Shane, for he was laughing.

He was standing there, straight and superb, the blood on his face bright like a badge, and he was laughing.

It was a soft laugh, soft and gentle, not in amusement at Red Marlin or any single thing, but in the joy of being alive and released from long discipline and answering the urge in mind and body. The lithe power in him, so different from father's sheer strength, was singing in every fiber of him.

Morgan was in the rear corner, his face clouded and uncertain. Father, his fury eased by the mighty effort of throwing Curly, had looked around to watch Red Marlin's run and now was starting toward Morgan. Shane's voice stopped him.

"Wait, Joe. The man's mine." He was at father's side and he put a hand on father's arm. "You'd better get them out of here." He nodded in my direction and I noticed with surprise that mother was near and watching. She must have followed father and have been there all this while. Her lips were parted. Her eyes were glowing, looking at the whole room, not at anyone or anything in particular, but at the whole room.

Father was disappointed. "Morgan's more my size," he said, grumbling fashion. He was not worried about Shane. He was thinking of an excuse to take Morgan himself. But he went no further. He looked at the men over by the wall. "This is Shane's play. If a one of you tries to interfere, he'll have me to reckon with." His tone showed that he was not mad at them, that he was not even really warning them. He was simply making the play plain. Then he came to us and looked down at mother. "You wait out at the wagon. Marian. Morgan's had this coming to him for quite a long time now and it's not for a woman to see."

Mother shook her head without moving her eyes now from Shane. "No, Joe. He's one of us. I'll see this through." And the three of us stayed there together and that was right, for he was Shane.

*   *   *

He advanced toward Morgan, as flowing and graceful as the old mouser in the store. He had forgotten us and the battered men on the floor and those withdrawn by the wall and Mr. Grafton and Will Atkey crouched behind the bar. His whole being was concentrated on the big man before him.

Morgan was taller, half again as broad, with a long reputation as a bullying fighter in the valley. But he did not like this and he was desperate. He knew better than to wait. He rushed at Shane to overwhelm the smaller man with his weight. Shane faded from in front of him and as Morgan went past hooked a sharp blow to his stomach and another to the side of his jaw. They were short and quick, flicking in so fast they were just a blur of movement. Yet each time at the instant of impact Morgan's big frame shook and halted in its rush for a fraction of a second before the momentum carried him forward. Again and again he rushed, driving his big fists ahead. Always Shane slipped away, sending in those swift hard punches.

Breathing heavily, Morgan stopped, grasping the futility of straight fighting. He plunged at Shane now, arms wide, trying to get hold of him and wrestle him down. Shane was ready and let him come without dodging, disregarding the arms stretching to encircle him. He brought up his right hand, open, just as Ed Howells had told us, and the force of Morgan's own lunge as the hand met his mouth and raked upwards snapped back his head and sent him staggering.

Morgan's face was puffy and red-mottled. He bellowed some insane sound and swung up a chair. Holding it in front of him, legs forward, he rushed again at Shane, who sidestepped neatly. Morgan was expecting this and halted suddenly, swinging the chair in a swift arc to strike Shane with it full on the side. The chair shattered and Shane faltered, and then, queerly for a man usually so sure on his feet, he seemed to slip and fall to the floor.

Forgetting all caution. Morgan dove at him—and Shane's legs bent and he caught Morgan on his heavy work shoes and sent him flying back and against the bar with a crash that shook the whole length of it.

Shane was up and leaping at Morgan as if there had been springs under him there on the floor. His left hand, palm out, smacked against Morgan's forehead, pushing the head back, and his right fist drove straight to Morgan's throat. You could see the agony twist the man's face and the fear widen his eyes. And Shane, using his right fist now like a club and lining his whole body behind it, struck him on the neck below and back of the ear. It made a sickening, dull sound and Morgan's eyes rolled white and he went limp all over, sagging slowly and forward to the floor.

10

In the hush that followed Morgan's fall, the big barroom was so quiet again that the rustle of Will Atkey straightening from below the bar level was loud and clear and Will stopped moving, embarrassed and a little frightened.

Shane looked neither at him nor at any of the other men staring from the wall. He looked only at us, at father and mother and me, and it seemed to me that it hurt him to see us there.

He breathed deeply and his chest filled and he held it, held it long and achingly, and released it slowly and sighing. Suddenly you were impressed by the fact that he was quiet, that he was quiet, that he was still. You saw how battered and bloody he was. In the moments before you saw only the splendor of movement, the flowing brute beauty of line and power in action. The man, you felt, was tireless and indestructible. Now that he was still and the fire in him banked and subsided, you saw, and in the seeing remembered, that he had taken bitter punishment.

His shirt collar was dark and sodden. Blood was soaking into it, and this came only in part from the cut on his cheek. More was oozing from the matted hair where Morgan's bottle had hit. Unconsciously he put up one hand and it came away smeared and sticky. He regarded it grimly and wiped it clean on his shirt. He swayed slightly and when he started toward us, his feet dragged and he almost fell forward.

One of the townsmen, Mr. Weir, a friendly man who kept the stage post, pushed out from the wall, clucking sympathy, as though to help him. Shane pulled himself erect. His eyes blazed refusal. Straight and superb, not a tremor in him, he came to us and you knew that the spirit in him would sustain him thus alone for the farthest distance and forever.

But there was no need. The one man in our valley, the one man, I believe, in all the world whose help he would take, not to whom he would turn but whose help he would take, was there and ready. Father stepped to meet him and put out a big arm reaching for his shoulders. "All right, Joe," Shane said, so softly I doubt whether the others in the room heard. His eyes closed and he leaned against father's arm, his body relaxing and his head dropping sideways. Father bent and fitted his other arm under Shane's knees and picked him up like he did me when I stayed up too late and got all drowsy and had to be carried to bed.

Father held Shane in his arms and looked over him at Mr. Grafton. "I'd consider it a favor, Sam, if you'd figure the damage and put it on my bill."

For a man strict about bills and keen for a bargain, Mr. Grafton surprised me. "I'm marking this to Fletcher's account. I'm seeing that he pays."

Mr. Weir surprised me even more. He spoke promptly and he was emphatic about it. "Listen to me, Starrett. It's about time this town worked up a little pride. Maybe it's time, too, we got to be more neighborly with you homesteaders. I'll take a collection to cover this. I've been ashamed of myself ever since it started tonight, standing here and letting five of them jump that man of yours."

Father was pleased. But he knew what he wanted to do. "That's mighty nice of you, Weir. But this ain't your fight. I wouldn't worry, was I you, about keeping out of it." He looked down at Shane and the pride was plain busting out of him. "Matter of fact, I'd say the odds tonight, without me butting in, too, was mighty close to even." He looked again at Mr. Grafton. "Fletcher ain't getting in on this with a nickel. I'm paying." He tossed back his head. "No, by Godfrey! We're paying. Me and Shane."

He went to the swinging doors, turning sideways to push them open. Mother took my hand and we followed. She always knew when to talk and when not to talk, and she said no word while we watched father lift Shane to the wagon seat, climb beside him, hoist him to sitting position with one arm around him and take the reins in the other hand. Will Atkey trotted out with our things and stowed them away. Mother and I perched on the back of the wagon, father chirruped to the team, and we were started home.

There was not a sound for quite a stretch except the clop of hooves and the little creakings of the wheels. Then I heard a chuckle up front. It was Shane. The cool air was reviving him and he was sitting straight, swaying with the wagon's motion.

"What did you do with the thick one, Joe? I was busy with the redhead."

"Oh, I just kind of tucked him out of the way." Father wanted to let it go at that. Not mother.

"He picked him up like—like a bag of potatoes and threw him clear across the room." She did not say it to Shane, not to any person. She said it to the night, to the sweet darkness around us, and her eyes were shining in the starlight.

We turned in at our place and father shooed the rest of us into the house while he unhitched the team. In the kitchen mother set some water to heat on the stove and chased me to bed. Her back was barely to me after she tucked me in before I was peering around the door jamb. She got several clean rags, took the water from the stove, and went to work on Shane's head. She was tender as could be, crooning like to herself under her breath the while. It pained him plenty as the warm water soaked into the gash under the matted hair and as she washed the clotted blood from his cheek. But it seemed to pain her more, for her hand shook at the worst moments, and she was the one who flinched while he sat there quietly and smiled reassuringly at her.

Father came in and sat by the stove, watching them. He pulled out his pipe and made a very careful business of packing it and lighting it.

She finished. Shane would not let her try a bandage. "This air is the best medicine," he said. She had to be content with cleaning the cuts thoroughly and making certain all bleeding had stopped. Then it was father's turn.

"Get that shirt off, Joe. It's torn all down the back. Let me see what I can do with it." Before he could rise, she had changed her mind. "No. We'll keep it just like it is. To remember tonight by. You were magnificent, Joe, tearing that man away and—"

"Shucks," said father. "I was just peeved. Him holding Shane so Morgan could pound him."

"And you, Shane." Mother was in the middle of the kitchen, looking from one to the other. "You were magnificent, too. Morgan was so big and horrible and yet he didn't have even a chance. You were so cool and quick and—and dangerous and—"

"A woman shouldn't have to see things like that." Shane interrupted her, and he meant it. But she was talking right ahead.

"You think I shouldn't because it's brutal and nasty and not just fighting to see who is better at it, but mean and vicious and to win by any way, but to win. Of course it is. But you didn't start it. You didn't want to do it. Not until they made you anyway. You did it because you had to."

Her voice was climbing and she was looking back and forth and losing control of herself. "Did ever a woman have two such men?" And she turned from them and reached out blindly for a chair and sank into it and dropped her face into her hands and the tears came.

The two men stared at her and then at each other in that adult knowledge beyond my understanding. Shane rose and stepped over by mother. He put a hand gently on her head and I felt again his fingers in my hair and the affection flooding through me. He walked quietly out the door and into the night.

Father drew on his pipe. It was out and absently he lit it. He rose and went to the door and out on the porch. I could see him there dimly in the darkness, gazing across the river.

Gradually mother's sobs died down. She raised her head and wiped away the tears.

"Joe."

He turned and started in and waited then by the door. She stood up. She stretched her hands toward him and he was there and had her in his arms.

"Do you think I don't know, Marian?"

"But you don't. Not really. You can't. Because I don't know myself."

Father was staring over her head at the kitchen wall, not seeing anything there. "Don't fret yourself, Marian. I'm man enough to know a better when his trail meets mine. Whatever happens will be all right."

"Oh, Joe . . . Joe! Kiss me. Hold me tight and don't ever let go."

11

What happened in our kitchen that night was beyond me in those days. But it did not worry me because father had said it would be all right, and how could anyone, knowing him, doubt that he would make it so.

And we were not bothered by Fletcher's men any more at all. There might not have been a big ranch on the other side of the river, sprawling up the valley and over on our side above Ernie Wright's place, for all you could tell from our house. They left us strictly alone and were hardly ever seen now even in town. Fletcher himself, I heard from kids at school, was gone again. He went on the stage to Cheyenne and maybe farther, and nobody seemed to know why he went.

Yet father and Shane were more wary than they had been before. They stayed even closer together and they spent no more time than they had to in the fields. There was no more talking on the porch in the evenings, though the nights were so cool and lovely they called you to be out and under the winking stars. We kept to the house, and father insisted on having the lamps well shaded and he polished his rifle and hung it, ready loaded, on a couple of nails by the kitchen door.

All this caution failed to make sense to me. So at dinner about a week later I asked: "Is there something new that's wrong? That stuff about Fletcher is finished, isn't it?"

"Finished?" said Shane, looking at me over his coffee cup. "Bobby boy, it's only begun."

"That's right," said father. "Fletcher's gone too far to back out now. It's a case of now or never with him. If he can make us run, he'll be setting pretty for a long stretch. If he can't, it'll be only a matter o' time before he's shoved smack out of this valley. There's three or four of the men who looked through here last year ready right now to sharpen stakes and move in soon as they think it's safe. I'll bet Fletcher feels he got aholt of a bear by the tail and it'd be nice to be able to let go."

"Why doesn't he do something, then?" I asked. "Seems to me mighty quiet around here lately."

"Seems to you, eh?" said father. "Seems to me you're mighty young to be doing much seemsing. Don't you worry, son. Fletcher is fixing to do something. The grass that grows under his feet won't feed any cow. I'd be easier in my mind if I knew what he's up to."

"You see, Bob"—Shane was speaking to me the way I liked, as if maybe I was a man and could understand all he said—"by talking big and playing it rough,

60

Fletcher has made this a straight win or lose deal. It's the same as if he'd kicked loose a stone that starts a rockslide and all he can do is hope to ride it down and hit bottom safe. Maybe he doesn't realize that yet. I think he does. And don't let things being quiet fool you. When there's noise, you know where to look and what's happening. When things are quiet, you've got to be most careful."

Mother sighed. She was looking at Shane's cheek where the cut was healing into a scar like a thin line running back from near the mouth corner. "I suppose you two are right. But does there have to be any more fighting?"

"Like the other night?" asked father. "No, Marian, I don't think so. Fletcher knows better now."

"He knows better," Shane said, "because he knows it won't work. If he's the man I think he is, he's known that since the first time he sicced Chris on me. I doubt that was his move the other night. That was Morgan's. Fletcher'll be watching for some way that has more finesse—and will be more final."

"Hm-m-m," said father, a little surprised. "Some legal trick, eh?"

"Could be. If he can find one. If not—" Shane shrugged and gazed out the window. "There are other ways. You can't call a man like Fletcher on things like that. Depends on how far he's willing to go. But whatever he does, once he's ready, he'll do it speedy and sure."

"Hm-m-m," said father again. "Now you put it thataway, I see you're right. That's Fletcher's way. Bet you've bumped against someone like him before." When Shane did not answer, just kept staring out the window, he went on. "Wish I could be as patient about it as you. I don't like this waiting."

But we did not have to wait long. It was the next day, a Friday, when we were finishing supper, that Lew Johnson and Henry Shipstead brought us the news. Fletcher was back and he had not come back alone. There was another man with him.

Lew Johnson saw them as they got off the stage. He had a good chance to look the stranger over while they waited in front of the post for horses to be brought in from the ranch. Since it was beginning to get dark, he had not been able to make out the stranger's face too well. The light striking through the post window, however, was enough for him to see what kind of man he was.

He was tall, rather broad in the shoulders and slim in the waist. He carried himself with a sort of swagger. He had a mustache that he favored and his eyes, when Johnson saw them reflecting the light from the window, were cold and had a glitter that bothered Johnson.

This stranger was something of a dude about his clothes. Still, that did not mean anything. When he turned, the coat he wore matching his pants flapped open and Johnson could see what had been half-hidden before. He was carrying two guns, big capable forty-fives, in holsters hung fairly low and forward. Those holsters were pegged down at the tips with thin straps fastened around the man's legs. Johnson said he saw the tiny buckles when the light flashed on them.

Wilson was the man's name. That was what Fletcher called him when a cowboy rode up leading a couple of horses. A funny other name. Stark. Stark Wilson. And that was not all.

Lew Johnson was worried and went into Grafton's to find Will Atkey, who always knew more than anyone else about people apt to be coming along the road because he was constantly picking up information from the talk of men drifting in to the bar. Will would not believe it at first when Johnson told him the name. What would he be doing up here, Will kept saying. Then Will blurted out that this Wilson was a bad one, a killer. He was a gunfighter said to be just as good with either hand and as fast on the draw as the best of them. He came to Cheyenne from Kansas, Will claimed he had heard, with a reputation for killing three men there and nobody knew how many more down in the southwest territories where he used to be.

Lew Johnson was rattling on, adding details as he could think of them. Henry Shipstead was slumped in a chair by the stove. Father was frowning at his pipe, absently fishing in a pocket for a match. It was Shane who shut off Johnson with a suddenness that startled the rest of us. His voice was sharp and clear and it seemed to crackle in the air. You could feel him taking charge of that room and all of us in it.

"When did they hit town?"

"Last night."

"And you waited till now to tell it!" There was disgust in Shane's voice. "You're a farmer all right, Johnson. That's all you ever will be." He whirled on father. "Quick, Joe. Which one has the hottest head? Which one's the easiest to prod into being a fool? Torrey is it? Or Wright?"

"Ernie Wright," father said slowly.

"Get moving, Johnson. Get out there on your horse and make it to Wright's in a hurry. Bring him here. Pick up Torrey, too. But get Wright first."

"He'll have to go into town for that," Henry Shipstead said heavily. "We passed them both down the road riding in."

Shane jumped to his feet. Lew Johnson was shuffling reluctantly toward the door. Shane brushed him aside. He strode to the door himself, yanked it open, started out. He stopped, leaning forward and listening.

"Heck, man," Henry Shipstead was grumbling, "what's your hurry? We told them about Wilson. They'll stop here on their way back." His voice ceased. All of us could hear it now, a horse pounding up the road at full gallop.

Shane turned back into the room. "There's your answer," he said bitterly. He swung the nearest chair to the wall and sat down. The fire blazing in him a moment before was gone. He was withdrawn into his own thoughts, and they were dark and not pleasant.

We heard the horse sliding to a stop out front. The sound was so plain you could fairly see the forelegs bracing and the hooves digging into the ground. Frank Torrey burst into the doorway. His hat was gone, his hair blowing wild. His chest heaved like he had been running as hard as the horse. He put his hands on the doorposts to hold himself steady and his voice was a hoarse whisper, though he was trying to shout across the room at father.

"Ernie's shot! They've killed him!"

The words jerked us to our feet and we stood staring. All but Shane. He did not move. You might have thought he was not even interested in what Torrey had said.

Father was the one who took hold of the scene. "Come in, Frank," he said quietly. "I take it we're too late to help Ernie now. Sit down and talk and don't leave anything out." He led Frank Torrey to a chair and pushed him into it. He closed the door and returned to his own chair. He looked older and tired.

It took Frank Torrey quite a while to pull himself together and tell his story straight. He was frightened. The fear was bedded deep in him and he was ashamed of himself for it.

He and Ernie Wright, he told us, had been to the stage office asking for a parcel Ernie was expecting. They dropped into Grafton's for a freshener before starting back. Since things had been so quiet lately, they were not thinking of any trouble even though Fletcher and the new man, Stark Wilson, were in the poker game at the big table. But Fletcher and Wilson must have been watching for a chance like that. They chucked in their hands and came over to the bar.

Fletcher was nice and polite as could be, nodding to Torrey and singling out Ernie for talk. He said he was sorry about it, but he really needed the land Ernie had filed on. It was the right place to put up winter windshelters for the new herd he was bringing in soon. He knew Ernie had not proved up on it yet. Just the same, he was willing to pay a fair price.

"I'll give you three hundred dollars," he said, "and that's more than the lumber in your buildings will be worth to me."

Ernie had more than that of his money in the place already. He had turned Fletcher down three or four times before. He was mad, the way he always was when Fletcher started his smooth talk.

"No," he said shortly. "I'm not selling. Not now or ever."

Fletcher shrugged like he had done all he could and slipped a quick nod at Stark Wilson. This Wilson was half-smiling at Ernie. But his eyes, Frank Torrey said, had nothing like a smile in them.

"I'd change my mind if I were you," he said to Ernie. "That is, if you have a mind to change."

"Keep out of this," snapped Ernie. "It's none of your business."

"I see you haven't heard," Wilson said softly. "I'm Mr. Fletcher's new business agent. I'm handling his business affairs for him. His business with stubborn jackasses like you." Then he said what showed Fletcher had coaxed him to it. "You're a fool, Wright. But what can you expect from a breed?"

"That's a lie!" shouted Ernie. "My mother wasn't no Indian!"

"Why, you crossbred squatter," Wilson said, quick and sharp, "are you telling me I'm wrong?"

"I'm telling you you're a liar!"

The silence that shut down over the saloon was so complete, Frank Torrey told us, that he could hear the ticking of the old alarm clock on the shelf behind the bar. Even Ernie, in the second his voice stopped, saw what he had done. But he was mad clear through and he glared at Wilson, his eyes reckless.

"So-o-o-o," said Wilson, satisfied now and stretching out the word with ominous softness. He flipped back his coat on the right side in front and the holster there was free with the gun grip ready for his hand.

"You'll back that, Wright. Or you'll crawl out of here on your belly."

Ernie moved out a step from the bar, his arms stiff at his sides. The anger in him held him erect as he beat down the terror tearing at him. He knew what this meant, but he met it straight. His hand was firm on his gun and pulling up when Wilson's first bullet hit him and staggered him. The second spun him halfway around and a faint froth appeared on his lips and all expression died from his face and he sagged to the floor.

While Frank Torrey was talking, Jim Lewis and a few minutes later Ed Howells had come in. Bad news travels fast and they seemed to know something was wrong. Perhaps they had heard that frantic galloping, the sound carrying far in the still night air. They were all in our kitchen now and they were more shaken and sober than I had ever seen them.

I was pressed close to mother, grateful for her arms around me. I noticed that she had little attention for the other men. She was watching Shane, bitter and silent across the room.

"So that's it," father said grimly. "We'll have to face it. We sell and at his price or he slips the leash on his hired killer. Did Wilson make a move toward you, Frank?"

"He looked at me." Simply recalling that made Torrey shiver through. "He looked at me and he said, 'Too bad, isn't it, mister, that Wright didn't change his mind?' "

"Then what?"

"I got out of there quick as I could and came here."

Jim Lewis had been fidgeting on his seat, more nervous every minute. Now he jumped up, almost shouting. "But darn it, Joe! A man can't just go around shooting people!"

"Shut up, Jim," growled Henry Shipstead. "Don't you see the setup? Wilson badgered Ernie into getting himself in a spot where he had to go for his gun. Wilson can claim he shot in self-defense. He'll try the same thing on each of us."

"That's right, Jim," put in Lew Johnson. "Even if we tried to get a marshal in here, he couldn't hold Wilson. It was an even break and the faster man won is the way most people will figure it and plenty of them saw it. A marshal couldn't get here in time anyway."

"But we've got to stop it!" Lewis was really shouting now. "What chance have any of us got against Wilson? We're not gunmen. We're just a bunch of old cowhands and farmers. Call it anything you want. I call it murder."

"Yes!"

The word sliced through the room. Shane was up and his face was hard with the rock ridges running along his jaw. "Yes. It's murder. Trick it out as self-defense or with fancy words about an even break for a fair draw and it's still murder." He looked at father and the pain was deep in his eyes. But there was only contempt in his voice as he turned to the others.

"You five can crawl back in your burrows. You don't have to worry—yet. If the time comes, you can always sell and run. Fletcher won't bother with the likes of you now. He's going the limit and he knows the game. He picked Wright to make the play plain. That's done. Now he'll head straight for the one real man in this valley, the man who's held you here and will go on trying to hold you and keep for you what's yours as long as there's life in him. He's standing between you and Fletcher and Wilson this minute and you ought to be thankful that once in a while this country turns out a man like Joe Starrett."

And a man like Shane. . . . Were those words only in my mind or did I hear mother whisper them? She was looking at him and then at father and she was both frightened and proud at once. Father was fumbling with his pipe, packing it and making a fuss with it like it needed his whole attention.

The others stirred uneasily. They were reassured by what Shane said and yet shamed that they should be. And they did not like the way he said it.

"You seem to know a lot about that kind of dirty business," Ed Howells said, with maybe an edge of malice to his voice.

"I do."

Shane let the words lie there, plain and short and ugly. His face was stern and behind the hard front of his features was a sadness that fought to break through. But he stared levelly at Howells and it was the other man who dropped his eyes and turned away.

Father had his pipe going. "Maybe it's a lucky break for the rest of us," he said mildly, "that Shane here has been around a bit. He can call the cards for us plain. Ernie might still be alive, Johnson, if you had had the sense to tell us about Wilson right off. It's a good thing Ernie wasn't a family man." He turned to Shane. "How do you rate Fletcher now he's shown his hand?"

You could see that the chance to do something, even just to talk at the problem pressing us, eased the bitterness in Shane.

"He'll move in on Wright's place first thing tomorrow. He'll have a lot of men busy on this side of the river from now on, probably push some cattle around behind the homesteads, to keep the pressure plain on all of you. How quick he'll try you, Joe, depends on how he reads you. If he thinks you might crack, he'll wait and let knowing what happened to Wright work on you. If he really knows you, he'll not wait more than a day or two to make sure you've had time to think it over and then he'll grab the first chance to throw Wilson at you. He'll want it, like with Wright, in a public place where there'll be plenty of witnesses. If you don't give him a chance, he'll try to make one."

"Hm-m-m," father said soberly. "I was sure you'd give it to me straight and that rings right." He pulled on his pipe for a moment. "I reckon, boys, this will be a matter of waiting for the next few days. There's no immediate danger right off anyway. Grafton will take care of Ernie's body tonight. We can meet in town in the morning to fix him a funeral. After that, we'd better stay out of town and stick close to home as much as possible. I'd suggest you all study on this and drop in again tomorrow night. Maybe we can figure out something. I'd like to see how the town's taking it before I make up my mind on anything."

They were ready to leave it at that. They were ready to leave it to father. They were decent men and good neighbors. But not a one of them, were the decision his, would have stood up to Fletcher now. They would stay as long as father was there. With him gone, Fletcher would have things his way. That was how they felt as they muttered their goodnights and bunched out to scatter up and down the road.

Father stood in the doorway and watched them go. When he came back to his chair, he walked slowly and he seemed haggard and worn. "Somebody will have to go to Ernie's place tomorrow," he said, "and gather up his things. He's got relatives somewhere in Iowa."

"No." There was finality in Shane's tone. "You'll not go near the place. Fletcher might be counting on that. Grafton can do it."

"But Ernie was my friend," father said simply.

"Ernie's past friendship. Your debt is to the living."

Father looked at Shane and this brought him again into the immediate moment and cheered him. He nodded assent and turned to mother, who was hurrying to argue with him.

"Don't you see, Joe? If you can stay away from any place where you might meet Fletcher and—and that Wilson, things will work out. He can't keep a man like Wilson in this little valley forever."

She was talking rapidly and I knew why. She was not really trying to convince father as much as she was trying to convince herself. Father knew it, too.

"No, Marian. A man can't crawl into a hole somewhere and hide like a rabbit. Not if he has any pride."

"All right, then. But can't you keep quiet and not let him ride you and drive you into any fight?"

"That won't work either." Father was grim, but he was better and facing up to it. "A man can stand for a lot of pushing if he has to. 'Specially when he has his reasons." His glance shifted briefly to me. "But there are some things a man can't take. Not if he's to go on living with himself."

I was startled as Shane suddenly sucked in his breath with a long breaking intake. He was battling something within him, that old hidden desperation, and his eyes were dark and tormented against the paleness of his face. He seemed unable to look at us. He strode to the door and went out. We heard his footsteps fading toward the barn.

I was startled now at father. His breath, too, was coming in long, broken sweeps. He was up and pacing back and forth. When he swung on mother and his voice battered at her, almost fierce in its intensity, I realized that he knew about the change in Shane and that the knowing had been cankering in him all the past weeks.

"That's the one thing I can't stand, Marian. What we're doing to him. What happens to me doesn't matter too much. I talk big and I don't belittle myself. But my weight in any kind of a scale won't match his and I know it. If I understood him then as I do now, I'd never have got him to stay on here. But I didn't figure Fletcher would go this far. Shane won his fight before ever he came riding into this valley. It's been tough enough on him already. Should we let him lose just because of us? Fletcher can have his way. We'll sell out and move on."

I was not thinking. I was only feeling. For some strange reason I was feeling Shane's fingers in my hair, gently rocking my head. I could not help what I was saying, shouting across the room. "Father! Shane wouldn't run away! He wouldn't run away from anything!"

Father stopped pacing, his eyes narrowed in surprise. He stared at me without really seeing me. He was listening to mother.

"Bob's right, Joe. We can't let Shane down." It was queer, hearing her say the same thing to father she had said to Shane, the same thing with only the name different, "He'd never forgive us if we ran away from this. That's what we'd be doing. This isn't just a case of bucking Fletcher any more. It isn't just a case of keeping a piece of ground Fletcher wants for his range. We've got to be the kind of people Shane thinks we are. Bob's right. He wouldn't run away from anything like that. And that's the reason we can't."

"Lookahere, Marian, you don't think I want to do any running? No. You know me better than that. It'd go against everything in me. But what's my fool pride and this place and any plans we've had alongside of a man like that?"

"I know, Joe. But you don't see far enough." They were both talking earnestly, not breaking in, hearing each other out and sort of groping to put their meaning plain. "I can't really explain it, Joe. But I just know that we're bound up in something bigger than any one of us, and that running away is the one thing that would be worse than whatever might happen to us. There wouldn't be anything real ahead for us, any of us, maybe even for Bob, all the rest of our lives."

"Humph," said father. "Torrey could do it. And Johnson. All the rest of them. And it wouldn't bother them too much."

"Joe! Joe Starrett! Are you trying to make me mad? I'm not talking about them. I'm talking about us."

"Hm-m-m," said father softly, musing like to himself. "The salt would be gone. There just wouldn't be any flavor. There wouldn't be much meaning left."

"Oh, Joe! Joe! That's what I've been trying to say. And I know this will work out some way. I don't know how. But it will, if we face it and stand up to it and have faith in each other. It'll work out. Because it's got to."

"That's a woman's reason, Marian. But you're part right anyway. We'll play this game through. It'll need careful watching and close figuring. But maybe we can wait Fletcher out and make him overplay his hand. The town won't take much to this Wilson deal. Men like that fellow Weir have minds of their own."

Father was more cheerful now that he was beginning to get his thoughts straightened out. He and mother talked low in the kitchen for a long time after they sent me to bed, and I lay in my little room and saw through the window the stars wheeling distantly in the far outer darkness until I fell asleep at last.

12

The morning sun brightened our house and everything in the world outside. We had a good breakfast, father and Shane taking their time because they had routed out early to get the chores done and were waiting to go to town. They saddled up presently and rode off, and I moped in front of the house, not able to settle to any kind of playing.

After she bustled through the dishes, mother saw me standing and staring down the road and called me to the porch. She got our tattered old parchesi board and she kept me humping to beat her. She was a grand one for games like that. She would be as excited as a kid, squealing at the big numbers and doubles and counting proudly out loud as she moved her markers ahead.

When I had won three games running, she put the board away and brought out two fat apples and my favorite of the books she had from the time she taught school. Munching on her apple, she read to me and before I knew it the shadows were mighty short and she had to skip in to get dinner and father and Shane were riding up to the barn.

They came in while she was putting the food on the table. We sat down and it was almost like a holiday, not just because it was not a work day, but because the grown folks were talking lightly, were determined not to let this Fletcher business spoil our good times. Father was pleased at what had happened in town.

"Yes, sir," he was saying as we were finishing dinner. "Ernie had a right good funeral. He would have appreciated it. Grafton made a nice speech and, by Godfrey, I believe he meant it. That fellow Weir had his clerk put together a really fine coffin. Wouldn't take a cent for it. And Sims over at the mine is knocking out a good stone. He wouldn't take a cent either. I was surprised at the crowd, too. Not a good word for Fletcher among them. And there must have been thirty people there."

"Thirty-four," said Shane. "I counted 'em. They weren't just paying their respects to Wright, Marian. That wouldn't have brought in some of those I checked. They were showing their opinion of a certain man named Starrett, who made a pretty fair speech himself. This husband of yours is becoming quite a respected citizen in these parts. Soon as the town gets grown up and organized, he's likely to start going places. Give him time and he'll be mayor."

Mother caught her breath with a little sob. "Give . . . him . . . time," she said slowly. She looked at Shane and there was panic in her eyes. The lightness was gone and before anyone could say more, we heard the horses turning into our yard.

I dashed to the window to peer out. It struck me strange that Shane, usually so alert, was not there ahead of me. Instead he pushed back his chair and spoke gently, still sitting in it. "That will be Fletcher, Joe. He's heard how the town is taking this and knows he has to move fast. You take it easy. He's playing against time now, but he won't push anything here."

Father nodded at Shane and went to the door. He had taken off his gunbelt when he came in and now passed it to lift the rifle from its nails on the wall. Holding it in his right hand, barrel down, he opened the door and stepped out on the porch, clear to the front edge. Shane followed quietly and leaned in the doorway, relaxed and watchful. Mother was beside me at the window, staring out, crumpling her apron in her hand.

There were four of them, Fletcher and Wilson in the lead, two cowboys tagging. They had pulled up about twenty feet from the porch. This was the first time I had seen Fletcher for nearly a year. He was a tall man who must once have been a handsome figure in the fine clothes he always wore and with his arrogant air and his finely chiseled face set off by his short-cropped black beard and brilliant eyes. Now a heaviness was setting in about his features and a fatty softness was beginning to show in his body. His face had a shrewd cast and a kind of reckless determination was on him that I did not remember ever noticing before.

Stark Wilson, for all the dude look Frank Torrey had mentioned, seemed lean and fit. He was sitting idly in his saddle, but the pose did not fool you. He was wearing no coat and the two guns were swinging free. He was sure of himself, serene and deadly. The curl of his lip beneath his mustache was a combination of confidence in himself and contempt for us.

Fletcher was smiling and affable. He was certain he held the cards and was going to deal them as he wanted. "Sorry to bother you, Starrett, so soon after that unfortunate affair last night. I wish it could have been avoided. I really do. Shooting is so unnecessary in these things, if only people would show sense. But Wright never should have called Mr. Wilson here a liar. That was a mistake."

"It was," father said curtly. "But then Ernie always did believe in telling the truth." I could see Wilson stiffen and his lips tighten. Father did not look at him. "Speak your piece, Fletcher, and get off my land."

Fletcher was still smiling. "There's no call for us to quarrel, Starrett. What's done is done. Let's hope there's no need for anything like it to be done again. You've worked cattle on a big ranch and you can understand my position. I'll be wanting all the range I can get from now on. Even without that, I can't let a bunch of nesters keep coming in here and choke me off from my water rights."

"We've been over that before," father said. "You know where I stand. If you have more to say, speak up and be done with it."

"All right, Starrett. Here's my proposition. I like the way you do things. You've got some queer notions about the cattle business, but when you tackle a job, you take hold and do it thoroughly. You and that man of yours are a combination I could use. I want you on my side of the fence. I'm getting rid of Morgan and I want you to take over as foreman. From what I hear your man would make one heck of a driving trail boss. The spot's his. Since you've proved up on this place, I'll buy it from you. If you want to go on living here, that can be arranged. If you want to play around with that little herd of yours, that can be arranged too. But I want you working for me."

Father was surprised. He had not expected anything quite like this. He spoke softly to Shane behind him. He did not turn or look away from Fletcher, but his voice carried clearly.

"Can I call the turn for you, Shane?"

"Yes, Joe." Shane's voice was just as soft, but it, too, carried clearly and there was a little note of pride in it.

Father stood taller there on the edge of the porch. He stared straight at Fletcher. "And the others," he said slowly. "Johnson, Shipstead, and the rest. What about them?"

"They'll have to go."

Father did not hesitate. "No."

"I'll give you a thousand dollars for this place as it stands and that's my top offer."

"No."

The fury in Fletcher broke over his face and he started to turn in the saddle toward Wilson. He caught himself and forced again that shrewd smile. "There's no percentage in being hasty, Starrett. I'll boost the ante to twelve hundred. That's a lot better than what might happen if you stick to being stubborn. I'll not take an answer now. I'll give you till tonight to think it over. I'll be waiting at Grafton's to hear you talk sense."

He swung his horse and started away. The two cowboys turned to join him by the road. Wilson did not follow at once. He leaned forward in his saddle and drove a sneering look at father.

"Yes, Starrett. Think it over. You wouldn't like someone else to be enjoying this place of yours—and that woman there in the window."

He was lifting his reins with one hand to pull his horse around and suddenly he dropped them and froze to attention. It must have been what he saw in father's face. We could not see it, mother and I, because father's back was to us. But we could see his hand tightening on the rifle at his side.

"Don't, Joe!"

Shane was beside father. He slipped past, moving smooth and steady, down the steps and over to one side to come at Wilson on his right hand and stop not six feet from him. Wilson was puzzled and his right hand twitched and then was still as Shane stopped and as he saw that Shane carried no gun.

Shane looked up at him and Shane's voice flicked in a whiplash of contempt. "You talk like a man because of that flashy hardware you're wearing. Strip it away and you'd shrivel down to boy size."

The very daring of it held Wilson motionless for an instant and father's voice cut into it. "Shane! Stop it!"

The blackness faded from Wilson's face. He smiled grimly at Shane. "You do need someone to look after you." He whirled his horse and put it to a run to join Fletcher and the others in the road.

It was only then that I realized mother was gripping my shoulders so that they hurt. She dropped on a chair and held me to her. We could hear father and Shane on the porch.

"He'd have drilled you, Joe, before you could have brought the gun up and pumped in a shell."

"But you, you crazy fool!" Father was covering his feelings with a show of exasperation. "You'd have made him plug you just so I'd have a chance to get him."

Mother jumped up. She pushed me aside. She flared at them from the doorway. "And both of you would have acted like fools just because he said that about me. I'll have you two know that if it's got to be done, I can take being insulted just as much as you can."

Peering around her, I saw them gaping at her in astonishment. "But, Marian," father objected mildly, coming to her. "What better reason could a man have?"

"Yes," said Shane gently. "What better reason?" He was not looking just at mother. He was looking at the two of them.

13

I do not know how long they would have stood there on the porch in the warmth of that moment. I shattered it by asking what seemed to me a simple question until after I had asked it and the significance hit me.

"Father, what are you going to tell Fletcher tonight?"

There was no answer. There was no need for one. I guess I was growing up. I knew what he would tell Fletcher. I knew what he would say. I knew, too, that because he was father he would have to go to Grafton's and say it. And I understood why they could no longer bear to look at one another, and the breeze blowing in from the sun-washed fields was suddenly so chill and cheerless.

They did not look at each other. They did not say a word to each other. Yet somehow I realized that they were closer together in the stillness there on the porch than they had ever been. They knew themselves and each of them knew that the other grasped the situation whole. They knew that Fletcher had dealt himself a winning hand, had caught father in the one play that he could not avoid because he would not avoid it. They knew that talk is meaningless when a common knowledge is already there. The silence bound them as no words ever could.

Father sat on the top porch step. He took out his pipe and drew on it as the match flamed and fixed his eyes on the horizon, on the mountains far across the river. Shane took the chair I had used for the games with mother. He swung it to the house wall and bent into it in that familiar unconscious gesture and he, too, looked into the distance. Mother turned into the kitchen and went about clearing the table as if she was not really aware of what she was doing. I helped her with the dishes and the old joy of sharing with her in the work was gone and there was no sound in the kitchen except the drip of the water and the chink of dish on dish.

When we were done, she went to father. She sat beside him on the step, her hand on the wood between them, and his covered hers and the moments merged in the slow, dwindling procession of time.

Loneliness gripped me. I wandered through the house, finding nothing there to do, and out on the porch and past those three and to the barn. I searched around and found an old shovel handle and started to whittle me a play saber with my knife. I had been thinking of this for days. Now the idea held no interest. The wood curls dropped to the barn floor, and after a while I let the shovel handle drop among them. Everything that had happened before seemed far off, almost like another existence. All that mattered was the length of the shadows creeping across the yard as the sun drove down the afternoon sky.

I took a hoe and went into mother's garden where the ground was caked around the turnips, the only things left unharvested. But there was scant work in me. I kept at it for a couple of rows, then the hoe dropped and I let it lie. I went to the front of the house, and there they were sitting, just as before.

I sat on the step below father and mother, between them, and their legs on each side of me made it seem better. I felt father's hand on my head.

"This is kind of tough on you, Bob." He could talk to me because I was only a kid. He was really talking to himself.

"I can't see the full finish. But I can see this. Wilson down and there'll be an end to it. Fletcher'll be done. The town will see to that. I can't beat Wilson on the draw. But there's strength enough in this clumsy body of mine to keep me on my feet till I get him, too." Mother stirred and was still, and his voice went on. "Things could be worse. It helps a man to know that if anything happens to him, his family will be in better hands than his own."

There was a sharp sound behind us on the porch. Shane had risen so swiftly that his chair had knocked against the wall. His hands were clenched tightly and his arms were quivering. His face was pale with the effort shaking him. He was desperate with an inner torment, his eyes tortured by thoughts that he could not escape, and the marks were obvious on him and he did not care. He strode to the steps, down past us and around the corner of the house.

Mother was up and after him, running headlong. She stopped abruptly at the house corner, clutching at the wood, panting and irresolute. Slowly she came back, her hands outstretched as if to keep from falling. She sank again on the step, close against father, and he gathered her to him with one great arm.

The silence spread and filled the whole valley and the shadows crept across the yard. They touched the road and began to merge in the deeper shading that meant the sun was dipping below the mountains far behind the house. Mother straightened, and as she stood up, father rose, too. He took hold of her two arms and held her in front of him. "I'm counting on you, Marian, to help him win again. You can do it, if anyone can." He smiled a strange little sad smile and he loomed up there above me the biggest man in all the world. "No supper for me now, Marian. A cup of your coffee is all I want." They passed through the doorway together.

Where was Shane? I hurried toward the barn. I was almost to it when I saw him out by the pasture. He was staring over it and the grazing steers at the great lonely mountains tipped with the gold of the sun now rushing down behind them. As I watched, he stretched his arms up, the fingers reaching to their utmost limits, grasping and grasping, it seemed, at the glory glowing in the sky.

He whirled and came straight back, striding with long steady steps, his head held high. There was some subtle, new, unchangeable certainty in him. He came close and I saw that his face was quiet and untroubled and that little lights danced in his eyes.

"Skip into the house, Bobby boy. Put on a smile. Everything is going to be all right." He was past me, without slowing, swinging into the barn.

But I could not go into the house. And I did not dare follow him, not after he had told me to go. A wild excitement was building up in me while I waited by the porch, watching the barn door.

The minutes ticked past and the twilight deepened and a patch of light sprang from the house as the lamp in the kitchen was lit. And still I waited. Then he was coming swiftly toward me and I stared and stared and broke and ran into the house with the blood pounding in my head.

"Father! Father! Shane's got his gun!"

He was close back of me. Father and mother barely had time to look up from the table before he was framed in the doorway. He was dressed as he was that first day when he rode into our lives, in that dark and worn magnificence from the black hat with its wide curling brim to the soft black boots. But what caught your eye was the single flash of white, the outer ivory plate on the grip of the gun, showing sharp and distinct against the dark material of the trousers. The tooled cartridge belt nestled around him, riding above the hip on the left, sweeping down on the right to hold the holster snug along the thigh, just as he had said, the gun handle about halfway between the wrist and elbow of his right arm hanging there relaxed and ready.

Belt and holster and gun . . . . These were not things he was wearing or carrying. They were part of him, part of the man, of the full sum of the integral forces that were Shane. You could see now that for the first time this man who had been living with us, who was one of us, was complete, was himself in the final effect of his being.

Now that he was no longer in his crude work clothes, he seemed again slender, almost slight, as he did that first day. The change was more than that. What had been seeming iron was again steel. The slenderness was that of a tempered blade and a razor edge was there. Slim and dark in the doorway, he seemed somehow to fill the whole frame.

This was not our Shane. And yet it was. I remembered Ed Howell's saying that this was the most dangerous man he had ever seen. I remembered in the same rush that father had said he was the safest man we ever had in our house. I realized that both were right and that this, this at last, was Shane.

He was in the room now and he was speaking to them both in that bantering tone he used to have only for mother. "A fine pair of parents you are. Haven't even fed Bob yet. Stack him full of a good supper. Yourselves, too. I have a little business to tend to in town."

Father was looking fixedly at him. The sudden hope that had sprung in his face had as quickly gone. "No, Shane. It won't do. Even your thinking of it is the finest thing any man ever did for me. But I won't let you. It's my stand. Fletcher's making his play against me. There's no dodging. It's my business."

"There's where you're wrong, Joe," Shane said gently. "This is my business. My kind of business. I've had fun being a farmer. You've shown me new meaning in the word, and I'm proud that for a while maybe I qualified. But there are a few things a farmer can't handle."

The strain of the long afternoon was telling on father. He pushed up from the table. "Shane, be sensible. Don't make it harder for me. You can't do this."

Shane stepped near, to the side of the table, facing father across a corner. "Easy does it, Joe. I'm making this my business."

"No. I won't let you. Suppose you do put Wilson out of the way. That won't finish anything. It'll only even the score and swing things back worse than ever. Think what it'll mean to you. And where will it leave me? I couldn't hold my head up around here any more. They'd say I ducked and they'd be right. You can't do it and that's that."

"No?" Shane's voice was even more gentle, but it had a quiet, inflexible quality that had never been there before. "There's no man living can tell me what I can't do. Not even you, Joe. You forget there is still a way."

He was talking to hold father's attention. As he spoke the gun was in his hand and before father could move he swung it, swift and sharp, so the barrel lined flush along the side of father's head, back of the temple, above the ear. Strength was in the blow and it thudded dully on the bone and father folded over the table and as it tipped with his weight slid toward the floor. Shane's arm was under him before he hit and Shane pivoted father's loose body up and into his chair and righted the table while the coffee cups rattled on the floor boards. Father's head lolled back and Shane caught it and eased it and the big shoulders forward till they rested on the table, the face down and cradled in the limp arms.

Shane stood erect and looked across the table at mother. She had not moved since he appeared in the doorway, not even when father fell and the table teetered under her hands on its edge. She was watching Shane, her throat curving in a lovely proud line, her eyes wide with a sweet warmth shining in them.

Darkness had shut down over the valley as they looked at each other across the table and the only light now was from the lamp swinging ever so slightly above them, circling them with its steady glow. They were alone in a moment that was all their own. Yet, when they spoke, it was of father.

"I was afraid," Shane murmured, "that he would take it that way. He couldn't do otherwise and be Joe Starrett."

"I know."

"He'll rest easy and come out maybe a little groggy but all right. Tell him, Marian. Tell him no man need be ashamed of being beat by Shane."

The name sounded queer like that, the man speaking of himself. It was the closest he ever came to boasting. And then you understood that there was not the least hint of a boast. He was stating a fact, simple and elemental as the power that dwelled in him.

"I know," she said again. "I don't need to tell him. He knows, too." She was rising, earnest and intent. "But there is something else I must know. We have battered down words that might have been spoken between us and that was as it should be. But I have a right to know now. I am part of this, too. And what I do depends on what you tell me now. Are you doing this just for me?"

Shane hesitated for a long, long moment. "No, Marian." His gaze seemed to widen and encompass us all, mother and the still figure of father and me huddled on a chair by the window, and somehow the room and the house and the whole place. Then he was looking only at mother and she was all that he could see.

"No, Marian. Could I separate you in my mind and afterwards be a man?"

He pulled his eyes from her and stared into the night beyond the open door. His face hardened, his thoughts leaping to what lay ahead in town. So quiet and easy you were scarce aware that he was moving, he was gone into the outer darkness.

14

Nothing could have kept me there in the house that night. My mind held nothing but the driving desire to follow Shane. I waited, hardly daring to breathe, while mother watched him go. I waited until she turned to father, bending over him, then I slipped around the doorpost out to the porch. I thought for a moment she had noticed me, but I could not be sure and she did not call to me. I went softly down the steps and into the freedom of the night.

Shane was nowhere in sight. I stayed in the darker shadows, looking about, and at last I saw him emerging once more from the barn. The moon was rising low over the mountains, a clean, bright crescent. Its light was enough for me to see him plainly in outline. He was carrying his saddle and a sudden pain stabbed through me as I saw that with it was his saddle-roll. He went toward the pasture gate, not slow, not fast, just firm and steady. There was a catlike certainty in his every movement, a silent, inevitable deadliness. I heard him, there by the gate, give his low whistle and the horse came out of the shadows at the far end of the pasture, its hooves making no noise in the deep grass, a dark and powerful shape etched in the moonlight drifting across the field straight to the man.

I knew what I would have to do. I crept along the corral fence, keeping tight to it, until I reached the road. As soon as I was around the corner of the corral with it and the barn between me and the pasture, I started to run as rapidly as I could toward town, my feet plumping softly in the thick dust of the road. I walked this every school day and it had never seemed long before. Now the distance stretched ahead, lengthening in my mind as if to mock me.

I could not let him see me. I kept looking back over my shoulder as I ran. When I saw him swinging into the road, I was well past Johnson's, almost past Shipstead's, striking into the last open stretch to the edge of town. I scurried to the side of the road and behind a clump of bullberry bushes. Panting to get my breath, I crouched there and waited for him to pass. The hoofbeats swelled in my ears, mingled with the pounding beat of my own blood. In my imagination he was galloping furiously and I was positive he was already rushing past me. But when I parted the bushes and pushed forward to peer out, he was moving at a moderate pace and was only almost abreast of me.

He was tall and terrible there in the road, looming up gigantic in the mystic half-light. He was the man I saw that first day, a stranger, dark and forbidding, forging his lone way out of an unknown past in the utter loneliness of his own immovable and instinctive defiance. He was the symbol of all the dim, formless imaginings of danger and terror in the untested realm of human potentialities beyond my understanding. The impact of the menace that marked him was like a physical blow.

I could not help it. I cried out and stumbled and fell. He was off his horse and over me before I could right myself, picking me up, his grasp strong and reassuring. I looked at him, tearful and afraid, and the fear faded from me. He was no stranger. That was some trick of the shadows. He was Shane. He was shaking me gently and smiling at me.

"Bobby boy, this is no time for you to be out. Skip along home and help your mother. I told you everything would be all right."

He let go of me and turned slowly, gazing out across the far sweep of the valley silvered in the moon's glow. "Look at it, Bob. Hold it in your mind like this. It's a lovely land, Bob. A good place to be a boy and grow straight inside as a man should."

My gaze followed his, and I saw our valley as though for the first time and the emotion in me was more than I could stand. I choked and reached out for him and he was not there.

He was rising into the saddle and the two shapes, the man and the horse, became one and moved down the road toward the yellow squares that were the patches of light from the windows of Grafton's building a quarter of a mile away. I wavered a moment, but the call was too strong. I started after him, running frantically in the middle of the road.

Whether he heard me or not, he kept right on. There were several men on the long porch of the building by the saloon doors. Red Marlin's hair made him easy to spot. They were scanning the road intently. As Shane hit the panel of light from the near big front window, the store window, they stiffened to attention. Red Marlin, a startled expression on his face, dived quickly through the doors.

Shane stopped, not by the rail but by the steps on the store side. When he dismounted, he did not slip the reins over the horse's head as the cowboys always did. He left them looped over the pommel of the saddle and the horse seemed to know what this meant. It stood motionless, close by the steps, head up, waiting, ready for whatever swift need.

Shane went along the porch and halted briefly, fronting the two men still there.

"Where's Fletcher?"

They looked at each other and at Shane. One of them started to speak. "He doesn't want—" Shane's voice stopped him. It slapped at them, low and with an edge that cut right into your mind. "Where's Fletcher?"

One of them jerked a hand toward the doors and then, as they moved to shift out of his way, his voice caught them.

"Get inside. Go clear to the bar before you turn."

They stared at him and stirred uneasily and swung together to push through the doors. As the doors came back, Shane grabbed them, one with each hand, and pulled them out and wide open and he disappeared between them.

Clumsy and tripping in my haste, I scrambled up the steps and into the store. Sam Grafton and Mr. Weir were the only persons there and they were both hurrying to the entrance to the saloon, so intent that they failed to notice me. They stopped in the opening. I crept behind them to my familiar perch on my box where I could see past them.

The big room was crowded. Almost everyone who could be seen regularly around town was there, everyone but our homestead neighbors. There were many others who were new to me. They were lined up elbow to elbow nearly the entire length of the bar. The tables were full and more men were lounging along the far wall. The big round poker table at the back between the stairway to the little balcony and the door to Grafton's office was littered with glasses and chips. It seemed strange, for all the men standing, that there should be an empty chair at the far curve of the table. Someone must have been in that chair, because chips were at the place and a half-smoked cigar, a wisp of smoke curling up from it, was by them on the table.

Red Marlin was leaning against the back wall, behind the chair. As I looked, he saw the smoke and appeared to start a little. With a careful show of casualness he slid into the chair and picked up the cigar.

A haze of thinning smoke was by the ceiling over them all, floating in involved streamers around the hanging lamps. This was Grafton's saloon in the flush of a banner evening's business. But something was wrong, was missing. The hum of activity, the whirr of voices, that should have risen from the scene, been part of it, was stilled in a hush more impressive than any noise could be. The attention of everyone in the room, like a single sense, was centered on that dark figure just inside the swinging doors, back to them and touching them.

This was the Shane of the adventures I had dreamed for him, cool and competent, facing that room full of men in the simple solitude of his own invincible completeness.

His eyes searched the room. They halted on a man sitting at a small table in the front corner with his hat on low over his forehead. With a thump of surprise I recognized it was Stark Wilson and he was studying Shane with a puzzled look on his face. Shane's eyes swept on, checking off each person. They stopped again on a figure over by the wall and the beginnings of a smile showed in them and he nodded almost imperceptibly. It was Chris, tall and lanky, his arm in a sling, and as he caught the nod he flushed a little and shifted his weight from one foot to the other. Then he straightened his shoulders and over his face came a slow smile, warm and friendly, the smile of a man who knows his own mind at last.

But Shane's eyes were already moving on. They narrowed as they rested on Red Marlin. Then they jumped to Will Atkey trying to make himself small behind the bar.

"Where's Fletcher?"

Will fumbled with the cloth in his hands. "I—I don't know. He was here awhile ago." Frightened at the sound of his own voice in the stillness, Will dropped the cloth, started to stoop for it, and checked himself, putting his hands to the inside rim of the bar to hold himself steady.

Shane tilted his head slightly so his eyes could clear his hatbrim. He was scanning the balcony across the rear of the room. It was empty and the doors there were closed. He stepped forward, disregarding the men by the bar, and walked quietly past them the long length of the room. He went through the doorway to Grafton's office and into the semi-darkness beyond.

And still the hush held. Then he was in the office doorway again and his eyes bored toward Red Marlin.

"Where's Fletcher?"

The silence was taut and unendurable. It had to break. The sound was that of Stark Wilson coming to his feet in the far front corner. His voice, lazy and insolent, floated down the room.

"Where's Starrett?"

While the words yet seemed to hang in the air, Shane was moving toward the front of the room. But Wilson was moving, too. He was crossing toward the swinging doors and he took his stand just to the left of them, a few feet out from the wall. The position gave him command of the wide aisle running back between the bar and the tables and Shane coming forward in it.

Shane stopped about three quarters of the way forward, about five yards from Wilson. He cocked his head for one quick sidewise glance again at the balcony and then he was looking only at Wilson. He did not like the setup.

Wilson had the front wall and he was left in the open of the room. He understood the fact, assessed it, accepted it.

They faced each other in the aisle and the men along the bar jostled one
another in their hurry to get to the opposite side of the room. A reckless arrogance was on Wilson, certain of himself and his control of the situation. He was
not one to miss the significance of the slim deadliness that was Shane. But even
now, I think, he did not believe that anyone in our valley would deliberately
stand up to him.

"Where's Starrett?" he said once more, still mocking Shane but making it this
time a real question.

The words went past Shane as if they had not been spoken. "I had a few
things to say to Fletcher," he said gently. "That can wait. You're a pushing man,
Wilson, so I reckon I had better accommodate you."

Wilson's face sobered and his eyes glinted coldly. "I've no quarrel with you,"
he said flatly, "even if you are Starrett's man. Walk out of here without any fuss
and I'll let you go. It's Starrett I want."

"What you want, Wilson, and what you'll get are two different things. Your
killing days are done."

Wilson had it now. You could see him grasp the meaning. This quiet man was
pushing him just as he had pushed Ernie Wright. As he measured Shane, it was
not to his liking. Something that was not fear but a kind of wondering and
baffled reluctance showed in his face. And then there was no escape, for that
gentle voice was pegging him to the immediate and implacable moment.

"I'm waiting, Wilson. Do I have to crowd you into slapping leather?"

Time stopped and there was nothing in all the world but two men looking
into eternity in each other's eyes. And the room rocked in the sudden blur of
action indistinct in its incredible swiftness and the roar of their guns was a
single sustained blast. And Shane stood, solid on his feet as a rooted oak, and
Wilson swayed, his right arm hanging useless, blood beginning to show in a
small stream from under the sleeve over the hand, the gun slipping from the
numbing fingers.

He backed against the wall, a bitter disbelief twisting his features. His left
arm hooked and the second gun was showing and Shane's bullet smashed into
his chest and his knees buckled, sliding him slowly down the wall till the lifeless
weight of the body toppled it sideways to the floor.

Shane gazed across the space between and he seemed to have forgotten all
else as he let his gun ease into the holster. "I gave him his chance," he murmured out of the depths of a great sadness. But the words had no meaning for
me, because I noticed on the dark brown of his shirt, low and just above the
belt to one side of the buckle, the darker spot gradually widening. Then others
noticed, too, and there was a stir in the air and the room was coming to life.

Voices were starting, but no one focused on them. They were snapped short
by the roar of a shot from the rear of the room. A wind seemed to whip Shane's
shirt at the shoulder and the glass of the front window beyond shattered near
the bottom.

Then I saw it.

It was mine alone. The others were turning to stare at the back of the room.

My eyes were fixed on Shane and I saw it. I saw the whole man move, all of him, in the single flashing instant. I saw the head lead and the body swing and the driving power of the legs beneath. I saw the arm leap and the hand take the gun in the lightning sweep. I saw the barrel line up like—like a finger pointing —and the flame spurt even as the man himself was still in motion.

And there on the balcony Fletcher, impaled in the act of aiming for a second shot, rocked on his heels and fell back into the open doorway behind him. He clawed at the jambs and pulled himself forward. He staggered to the rail and tried to raise the gun. But the strength was draining out of him and he collapsed over the rail, jarring it loose and falling with it.

Across the stunned and barren silence of the room Shane's voice seemed to come from a great distance. "I expect that finishes it," he said. Unconsciously, without looking down, he broke out the cylinder of his gun and reloaded it. The stain on his shirt was bigger now, spreading fanlike above the belt, but he did not appear to know or care. Only his movements were slow, retarded by an unutterable weariness. The hands were sure and steady, but they moved slowly and the gun dropped into the holster of its own weight.

He backed with dragging steps toward the swinging doors until his shoulders touched them. The light in his eyes was unsteady like the flickering of a candle guttering toward darkness. And then, as he stood there, a strange thing happened.

How could one describe it, the change that came over him? Out of the mysterious resources of his will the vitality came. It came creeping, a tide of strength that crept through him and fought and shook off the weakness. It shone in his eyes and they were alive again and alert. It welled up in him, sending that familiar power surging through him again until it was singing again in every vibrant line of him.

He faced that room full of men and read them all with the one sweeping glance and spoke to them in that gentle voice with that quiet, inflexible quality.

"I'll be riding on now. And there's not a one of you that will follow."

He turned his back on them in the indifference of absolute knowledge they would do as he said. Straight and superb, he was silhouetted against the doors and the patch of night above them. The next moment they were closing with a soft swish of sound.

The room was crowded with action now. Men were clustering around the bodies of Wilson and Fletcher, pressing to the bar, talking excitedly. Not a one of them, though, approached too close to the doors. There was a cleared space by the doorway as if someone had drawn a line marking it off.

I did not care what they were doing or what they were saying. I had to get to Shane. I had to get to him in time. I had to know, and he was the only one who could ever tell me.

I dashed out the store door and I was in time. He was on his horse, already starting away from the steps.

"Shane," I whispered desperately, loud as I dared without the men inside hearing me. "Oh, Shane!"

He heard me and reined around and I hurried to him, standing by a stirrup and looking up.

"Bobby! Bobby boy! What are you doing here?"

"I've been here all along," I blurted out. "You've got to tell me. Was that Wilson—"

He knew what was troubling me. He always knew. "Wilson," he said, "was mighty fast. As fast as I've ever seen."

"I don't care," I said, the tears starting. "I don't care if he was the fastest that ever was. He'd never have been able to shoot you, would he? You'd have got him straight, wouldn't you—if you had been in practice?"

He hesitated a moment. He gazed down at me and into me and he knew. He knew what goes on in a boy's mind and what can help him stay clean inside through the muddled, dirtied years of growing up.

"Sure. Sure, Bob. He'd never even have cleared the holster."

He started to bend down toward me, his hand reaching for my head. But the pain struck him like a whiplash and the hand jumped to his shirt front by the belt, pressing hard, and he reeled a little in the saddle.

The ache in me was more than I could bear. I stared dumbly at him, and because I was just a boy and helpless I turned away and hid my face against the firm, warm flank of the horse.

"Bob."

"Yes, Shane."

"A man is what he is, Bob, and there's no breaking the mold. I tried that and I've lost. But I reckon it was in the cards from the moment I saw a freckled kid on a rail up the road there and a real man behind him, the kind that could back him for the chance another kid never had."

"But—but, Shane, you—"

"There's no going back from a killing, Bob. Right or wrong, the brand sticks and there's no going back. It's up to you now. Go home to your mother and father. Grow strong and straight and take care of them. Both of them."

"Yes, Shane."

"There's only one thing more I can do for them now."

I felt the horse move away from me. Shane was looking down the road and on to the open plain and the horse was obeying the silent command of the reins. He was riding away and I knew that no word or thought could hold him. The big horse, patient and powerful, was already settling into the steady pace that had brought him into our valley, and the two, the man and the horse, were a single dark shape in the road as they passed beyond the reach of the light from the windows.

I strained my eyes after him, and then in the moonlight I could make out the inalienable outline of his figure receding into the distance. Lost in my loneliness, I watched him go, out of town, far down the road where it curved out to the level country beyond the valley. There were men on the porch behind me, but I was aware only of that dark shape growing small and indistinct along the far reach of the road. A cloud passed over the moon and he merged into the general shadow and I could not see him and the cloud passed on and the road was a plain thin ribbon to the horizon and he was gone.

I stumbled back to fall on the steps, my head in my arms to hide the tears. The voices of the men around me were meaningless noises in a bleak and empty world. It was Mr. Weir who took me home.

 15

Father and mother were in the kitchen, almost as I had left them. Mother had hitched her chair close to father's. He was sitting up, his face tired and haggard, the ugly red mark standing out plain along the side of his head. They did not come to meet us. They sat still and watched us move into the doorway.

They did not even scold me. Mother reached and pulled me to her and let me crawl into her lap as I had not done for three years or more. Father just stared at Mr. Weir. He could not trust himself to speak first.

"Your troubles are over, Starrett."

Father nodded. "You've come to tell me," he said wearily, "that he killed Wilson before they got him. I know. He was Shane."

"Wilson," said Mr. Weir. "And Fletcher."

Father started. "Fletcher, too? By Godfrey, yes. He would do it right." Then father sighed and ran a finger along the bruise on his head. "He let me know this was one thing he wanted to handle by himself. I can tell you, Weir, waiting here is the hardest job I ever had."

Mr. Weir looked at the bruise. "I thought so. Listen, Starrett. There's not a man in town doesn't know you didn't stay here of your own will. And there's darn few that aren't glad it was Shane came into the saloon tonight."

The words broke from me. "You should have seen him, father. He was—he was—" I could not find it at first. "He was—beautiful, father. And Wilson wouldn't even have hit him if he'd been in practice. He told me so."

"He told you!" The table was banging over as father drove to his feet. He grabbed Mr. Weir by the coat front. "My God, man! Why didn't you tell me? He's alive?"

"Yes," said Mr. Weir. "He's alive all right. Wilson got to him. But no bullet can kill that man." A puzzled, faraway sort of look flitted across Mr. Weir's face. "Sometimes I wonder whether anything ever could."

Father was shaking him. "Where is he?"

"He's gone," said Mr. Weir. "He's gone, alone and unfollowed as he wanted it. Out of the valley and no one knows where."

Father's hands dropped. He slumped again into his chair. He picked up his pipe and it broke in his fingers. He let the pieces fall and stared at them on the floor. He was still staring at them when new footsteps sounded on the porch and a man pushed into our kitchen.

It was Chris. His right arm was tight in the sling, his eyes unnaturally bright and the color high in his face. In his left hand he was carrying a bottle, a bottle of red cherry soda pop. He came straight in and righted the table with the hand holding the bottle. He smacked the bottle on the top boards and seemed startled at the noise he made. He was embarrassed and he was having trouble with his voice. But he spoke up firmly.

"I brought that for Bob. I'm a poor substitute, Starrett. But as soon as this arm's healed, I'm asking you to let me work for you."

Father's face twisted and his lips moved, but no words came. Mother was the one who said it. "Shane would like that, Chris."

And still father said nothing. What Chris and Mr. Weir saw as they looked at him must have shown them that nothing they could do or say would help at all. They turned and went out together, walking with long, quick steps.

Mother and I sat there watching father. There was nothing we could do either. This was something he had to wrestle alone. He was so still that he seemed even to have stopped breathing. Then a sudden restlessness hit him and he was up and pacing aimlessly about. He glared at the walls as if they stifled him and strode out the door into the yard. We heard his steps around the house and heading into the fields and then we could hear nothing.

I do not know how long we sat there. I know that the wick in the lamp burned low and sputtered awhile and went out and the darkness was a relief and a comfort. At last mother rose, still holding me, the big boy bulk of me, in her arms. I was surprised at the strength in her. She was holding me tightly to her and she carried me into my little room and helped me undress in the dim shadows of the moonlight through the window. She tucked me in and sat on the edge of the bed, and then, only then, she whispered to me: "Now, Bob. Tell me everything. Just as you saw it happen."

I told her, and when I was done, all she said in a soft little murmur was "Thank you." She looked out the window and murmured the words again and they were not for me and she was still looking out over the land to the great gray mountains when finally I fell asleep.

She must have been there the whole night through, for when I woke with a start, the first streaks of dawn were showing through the window and the bed was warm where she had been. The movement of her leaving must have wakened me. I crept out of bed and peeked into the kitchen. She was standing in the open outside doorway.

I fumbled into my clothes and tiptoed through the kitchen to her. She took my hand and I clung to hers and it was right that we should be together and that together we should go find father.

We found him out by the corral, by the far end where Shane had added to it. The sun was beginning to rise through the cleft in the mountains across the river, not the brilliant glory of midday but the fresh and renewed reddish radiance of early morning. Father's arms were folded on the top rail, his head bowed on them. When he turned to face us, he leaned back against the rail as if he needed the support. His eyes were rimmed and a little wild.

"Marian, I'm sick of the sight of this valley and all that's in it. If I tried to stay here now, my heart wouldn't be in it any more. I know it's hard on you and the boy, but we'll have to pull up stakes and move on. Montana, maybe. I've heard there's good land for the claiming up that way."

Mother heard him through. She had let go my hand and stood erect, so angry that her eyes snapped and her chin quivered. But she heard him through.

"Joe! Joe Starrett!" Her voice fairly crackled and was rich with emotion that was more than anger. "So you'd run out on Shane just when he's really here to stay?"

"But, Marian. You don't understand. He's gone."

"He's not gone. He's here, in this place, in this place he gave us. He's all around us and in us, and he always will be."

She ran to the tall corner post, to the one Shane had set. She beat at it with her hands. "Here, Joe. Quick. Take hold. Pull it down."

Father stared at her in amazement. But he did as she said. No one could have denied her in that moment. He took hold of the post and pulled at it. He shook his head and braced his feet and strained at it with all his strength. The big muscles of his shoulders and back knotted and bulged till I thought this shirt, too, would shred. Creakings ran along the rails and the post moved ever so slightly and the ground at the base showed little cracks fanning out. But the rails held and the post stood.

Father turned from it, beads of sweat breaking on his face, a light creeping up his drawn cheeks.

"See, Joe. See what I mean. We have roots here now that we can never tear loose."

And the morning was in father's face, shining in his eyes, giving him new color and hope and understanding.

16

I guess that is all there is to tell. The folks in town and the kids at school liked to talk about Shane, to spin tales and speculate about him. I never did. Those nights at Grafton's became legends in the valley and countless details were added as they grew and spread just as the town, too, grew and spread up the river banks. But I never bothered, no matter how strange the tales became in the constant retelling. He belonged to me, to father and mother and me, and nothing could ever spoil that.

For mother was right. He was there. He was there in our place and in us. Whenever I needed him, he was there. I could close my eyes and he would be with me and I would see him plain and hear again that gentle voice.

I would think of him in each of the moments that revealed him to me. I would think of him most vividly in that single flashing instant when he whirled to shoot Fletcher on the balcony at Grafton's saloon. I would see again the power and grace of a coordinate force beautiful beyond comprehension. I would see the man and the weapon wedded in the one indivisible deadliness. I would see the man and the tool, a good man and a good tool, doing what had to be done.

And always my mind would go back at the last to that moment when I saw him from the bushes by the roadside just on the edge of town. I would see him there in the road, tall and terrible in the moonlight, going down to kill or be killed, and stopping to help a stumbling boy and to look out over the land, the lovely land, where that boy had a chance to live out his boyhood and grow straight inside as a man should.

And when I would hear the men in town talking among themselves and trying to pin him down to a definite past, I would smile quietly to myself. For a time they inclined to the notion, spurred by the talk of a passing stranger, that he was a certain Shannon who was famous as a gunman and gambler way down in Arkansas and Texas and dropped from sight without anyone knowing why or where. When that notion dwindled, others followed, pieced together in turn from scraps of information gleaned from stray travelers. But when they talked like that, I simply smiled because I knew he could have been none of these.

He was the man who rode into our little valley out of the heart of the great glowing West and when his work was done rode back whence he had come and he was Shane.

BUGLES
IN THE
AFTERNOON

by
Ernest Haycox

CONTENTS

ERNEST HAYCOX was born in Portland, Oregon, in 1899. He spent his boyhood in logging camps, shingle mills, on ranches and in numerous small towns, attending almost a dozen elementary schools. Haycox began service with the National Guard at the age of 16, going to Mexico and then to France in World War I. After a year as a commercial fisherman in Alaska, Haycox returned to Portland to attend college, and began writing fiction while still an undergraduate.

After graduation and a short stint as a reporter for *The Oregonian*, Haycox travelled to New York to break into the magazine market. On the way, he met the woman who was to become his wife, and while there, he met his first editor, F.E. Beachwell at *Western Story*. Settling in Portland, where he would spend the remainder of his life, Haycox began writing stories set in the Oregon that he knew intimately. His stories were published in pulp magazines such as *Western Story, The Frontier, Adventure, Short Stories* and *West,* and later in *Collier's* and the *Saturday Evening Post*. He was also published by Doubleday, Houghton Mifflin, and Little, Brown in hardcover.

Bugles in the Afternoon was the first of his works to be published in the *Saturday Evening Post*. Of the view popular at the time, that Custer was a misguided hero, Haycox remarked, "This whole Custer thing is not in the hands of scholars. It is in the hands of partisans who started with a conviction and thereafter spent years hunting for facts to justify their view."

Haycox, who was so steeped in western history he couldn't sit through a western film without being pained by its inaccuracies, was a writer who left a profound legacy of western characters, stories and dark and menacing magic in his prose. He died, at the age of 51, in 1950.

☆ 1 ☆

That Bright Day—That Far Land

The town had a name but no shape, no street, no core. It was simply five buildings, flung without thought upon the dusty prairie at the eastern edge of Dakota, and these stood gaunt and hard-angled against the last of day's streaming sunlight. The railroad, which gave the town a single pulse beat once a day, came as a black ribbon out of emptiness, touched this Corapolis with hurried indifference, and moved away into equal emptiness. The five buildings were alone in a gray-yellow space which ran outward in all directions, so empty that the tiring eye never saw where earth ended and sky began. There were no trees in this world, no accents, no relieving interruptions; nothing but the gray soil rolling on and a short brown grass turned crisp and now ready to fade when winter temperatures touched it.

The train—a wood-burning engine and three coaches—had paused and had gone, leaving one woman and one man on the cinders in front of the depot shed; the woman fair and round-bodied and slightly smiling at the land as if it pleased her. Beside her stood a collection of trunks and valises.

Nobody walked abroad, nobody met the train. These two were alone, facing the mute buildings whose western window panes burned yellow in the sunlight. From this cinder platform ran a sinuous pathway through the short grass to a frame building, two stories high, three hundred feet away; in front of the building were a wagon and a team and a pair of saddled ponies. Far out on the prairie a gauzy spiral of dust signaled the passage of riders, inbound or outbound. The man, somewhat farther down the platform, took his view of the town, looked at the woman and her luggage, and moved forward.

"That," he said, pointing toward the two-story building, "is probably the hotel. I presume you are going there. I'll take your light luggage."

She was not more than twenty-five, he thought; she had gray eyes and a pleasantly expressive mouth and her glance, turned upon him, was self-possessed. She smiled and said: "Thank you," and when he took up her valises and turned to the winding pathway she followed him without comment.

There had been a sharp and bright and full sun all day. Now it settled westward and seemed to melt into a shapeless bed of gold flame as it touched the far-away mountains; with its passage the air at once chilled and small streaks of breeze came out of the north with the smell of hard weather. Winter crouched yonder on the rim of the horizon and one day or one night, in the space of an hour, would turn this land black and bitter, shriveling every living thing exposed to it. He knew this land, or land like it; and the feeling of again being in it expanded his tissues and sharpened his zest for living. Yet for all its goodness it was like a smiling and beautiful woman, whose lavish warmth and generosity sprang up from those same strongly primitive sources which could make her cruel.

The wall of the hotel had a door and a set of windows opening up the dusty earth; and a single railroad tie lay before the door to serve as a step. The man paused to permit the girl to go before him into the place; and then followed. There was a narrow hall and a steep stairway splitting the building into equal halves. To the right of the hall a broad doorway opened into a saloon; another doorway on the left led to a ladies' parlor and office. He followed the girl into the parlor and set down the suitcases, waiting back while she signed the register. The hotelkeeper was a neat and large and taciturn woman. She said, "Together or separate?" When she found out, she said to the girl: "You can take Number Three." As the man stepped up to the register, she watched him a moment, estimating him; and then gave the girl another quick inspection.

He signed his name in a steady-slanting motion, *Kern Shafter,* and his pen momentarily hesitated and then continued, *Cincinnati, O.* It was a slight flaw in his certainty, at once noticed by the hotel woman; her glance held him a longer moment, not so much with interest or suspicion but with a cold steadiness. He laid the pen down, at the same time reading the name of the girl written directly above his own. It was: *Josephine Russell, Bismarck, D.T.*

"You take Seven," said the hotel woman to Shafter. She spoke to both of them with an inclusive glance. "If you're northbound on the stage, it's at half-past four in the mornin'. We serve breakfast at four."

Josephine Russell said: "May I have the key to my room?"

"They were carried away in people's pockets a long time ago. If you shut your door it will stay shut. If you're afraid, prop a chair against the inside knob." She added in a small, grim tone: "You needn't be afraid. I don't stand for anything in this house. You'll have to carry your own luggage. I've got no man handy. Not that men are very handy."

Shafter turned to the valises and carried them up the stairs and waited for the girl to go ahead of him. She led the way down the hall and stepped inside Number Three. She walked across the room to the window and turned to watch him, one last flare of sunlight coming through her window, running over the curve of her shoulders, deepening her breasts. She had removed her hat and he observed that her hair was a dense black; even so she seemed fair of complexion to him. Perhaps it was the way her lips were shaped against her face or the way her eyes held their smiling.

"I appreciate your help," she said. "Do you think my trunk will be safe on the station platform until morning?"

"I'll bring it to the hotel," he said, and went away.

She remained where she was a moment, her head slightly tilted as she watched the doorway, idly thinking of him. He had worn a cravat which looked as though it might have been the present of some woman. His clothes were excellent clothes for this part of the land, and smiling came easily to him. Yet his hands, she recalled, were very brown; and the palms were square and thick. She swung about and observed that the sun had gone, leaving the land with a strange, thin, glass-colored light. The horsemen out on the prairie were seemingly no nearer now than they had been fifteen minutes before.

But all of it pleased her: the raw running of the earth, the great empty arc of the sky, the smells rendered out by the warm day and the curt bite of approaching winter, this sprawled little town that served as a rendezvous for homesteaders and cow hands and drifters fifty miles roundabout, the sound of men's voices in the saloon below; for Josephine Russell was a western girl returned from a trip east, and this West eased her with its familiar things. She hummed a little song as she took the grime of coach travel from her and prepared herself for supper; she stood awhile, watching the last glow of the disappeared sun fade in the high sky. Suddenly, then, the prairie all around her was dark and the shapes of the town's other buildings were sharp-edged shadows in the swift night. She turned down the stairs to the dining room.

There was no door to shut out the barroom and she looked directly into it when she reached the foot of the stairs, noticing that Shafter now sat at a poker table with four other men. He had removed his coat for comfort and sat back in his chair with a long cigar burning between his lips. He seemed cheerful, he seemed content . . .

At four the next morning she came half asleep down the stairs and saw him again, at the same table and in the same chair, finishing up an all-night game. Later, she watched him come into the dining room. He had quickly shaved and, although he showed the lack of sleep, he had the same air of being pleased with everything around him. She smiled at him when he looked toward her, and got his smile back. He had a kind of ease with him, as though he had settled the question of himself and his future, had arrived at a decision and had shrugged off many of the worries or the ambitions that made other men exhaust themselves. His hair was black and bushy and his face was of the long, thick-boned sort, browned by weather and showing the small seams of experience around his eyes. He had quick eyes which looked about him and saw the people and the situations which surrounded him; and it was this kind of watchfulness which inclined her to the belief that he was either western, or had long been in the West. All western men had that same awareness of their surroundings.

The breakfast was bacon and hot cakes and fried potatoes and bitter coffee. Afterwards she walked to the waiting stage in time to see Shafter lift her luggage into the boot. He said to her: "I never saw a stage that wouldn't go off without somebody's luggage. I put a trunk and three valises up there. Is that all?"

"Yes," she said, and stepped into the coach. A pair of young men came aboard and sat on the opposite seat, facing her; a huge man entered, sized up the seating capacity and squeezed himself beside her. Shafter was last, throwing away the unsmoked end of a cigar as he came. He had a long overcoat on his arm and as soon as he took a place between the two younger men he opened the coat and laid it over her lap.

"It will be cold for an hour or so," he said.

Daylight flowed over the land in gray, chill waves; the smell of dust lay rank and still upon the earth and all sounds had a brittleness in the air. The brake rod struck sharp against the metal bracket and the driver's hearty cursing put the four horses in motion. They lumbered across the baked earth, leather braces groaning; they turned the hotel's corner with the cry of one townsman coming up from behind: "Don't forget to tell Mike I'll be there tomorrow night!" Suddenly the town disappeared and they were rolling onward, with the coach wheels lifting and dripping an acrid dust.

The coach swayed and shuddered as it struck deeper depressions and the impact went through the five passengers closely crowded on the two seats. The big man sat with his hands on his knees, his bulk spilling against Josephine Russell. He made some small effort to pull himself together but found it impossible; and sat still, a horsy smell flowing from his clothes. He turned his head and grinned at her. "These rigs sure never were made for an ord'nary-size man."

She smiled at him, saying nothing. The smile encouraged him and he said: "I shot buff'lo here five years ago. Ain't none on this side of the Mizzoura any more."

Early morning's dullness was on them. Josephine Russell had, woman fashion, settled herself to endure discomfort as gracefully as possible. The two younger men, each pushed into his corner, looked vacantly out upon the land, while Kern Shafter planted his feet solidly on the coach floor and, using the two men on either side of him as supports, fell promptly asleep.

Josephine Russell passed time's monotony by letting herself be curious about him. He knew how to relax completely in odd circumstances and had dropped asleep almost at once, his chin touching his chest, the long full line of his mouth softening. The wrinkles at the edge of his temples disappeared when his eyes were closed and the squareness of his upper body went away. She had noticed earlier that when he stood still he carried himself at a balance, which was something civilians didn't often do. He was slightly under six feet; he had big hands and heavy legs. In a country that somehow impelled men to grow sweeping mustaches, burnsides, imperials or Dundrearies, he had remained clean-shaven; and he showed some kind of taste in his clothes and appearance. In the West such a thing was noticeable. He had fine manners with women and he knew how to be easy and smooth with them. That was noticeable, too. Her eyes narrowed slightly on him as she thought that this perhaps explained his reason for being out here; men who came west nearly always had reasons, some of which were gallant and some of which were sordid.

Time dragged on and the day grew warm. Sunlight struck through the coach window, burning on Shafter's face. He was instantly awake at that hot touch, motionless but with his eyes fully open. He looked at the coat still on Josephine's lap, and bent forward and took it and stowed it in a roll beneath his feet; and fell asleep again. The four horses went on at a walk, at a run, at a walk, each change of pace producing its agreeable break and its new discomforts. The wheels lifted the dust in ropy, dripping sheets and this dust traveled as a pall over and around the coach, setting up a landmark that could be seen miles distant; its gauze clouds rolled inside the coach, laying its fine film on every-thing, and crept into nostril and lung. The morning's coolness was absorbed by the first full rush of sunlight; a dust-stale heat began to collect.

The big man, cramped in the corner of the seat, rolled his eyes around him and, by a series of cautious and self-conscious movements of his arm, burrowed into his pocket and found a cigar. He lighted it and dragged deeply on the smoke, his face growing bland and happier at once. Clouds of smoke spread through the coach and the big man made an ineffectual effort with his hand to sweep them away from Josephine.

The first smell of it woke Shafter at once. He opened his eyes and watched the big man steadily. The big man felt the weight of the glance but avoided it by looking out the window; he sighed heavily, he clenched the cigar between his teeth, he rolled it around his mouth, he took three rapid drags on it, and then irritably stared at Shafter. He held the glance with some defiance, but at last he pitched the cigar out of the window, whereupon Shafter again fell asleep.

At noon the coach, struggling against the endlessness of space, dipped into a coulee and drew before a drab, squat building which sat in a yard littered by tin cans and empty bottles. The passengers moved painfully from their confine-ment, ate dinner and returned reluctantly to their seats. The big man climbed beside the driver, replacing a slim, wild-haired youth who took his seat inside with a glowering silence. Coach and horses struggled up the coulee's side, faced the rolling sea of grass again, and resumed the steady march. The overhead sun pressed upon the coach, building up a trapped, sulky heat inside; and the dust began to drift up through the cracked floorboards in small, twining eddies. Shafter noticed how the dust touched and clung to the girl's hair; and noticed how the sun played against her face, against the gentle crease of her lips. Hu-mor lived there, even in this discomfort. She had been looking through the window, but felt his glance and met it coolly, now not smiling.

He turned his glance, staring upon the land and the land's gray-brown mo-notony. Haze came down on the far edges of the world but in that haze indis-tinct shapes moved—the only motion to be seen anywhere. He watched those shapes for half an hour and noticed them gradually drift in. Presently he knew what they were and his eyelids came closer together and a different expression reached his face. The driver's voice drifted down through the squealing and the coarse grinding noise of wheels and straps and double tree chains. "Always about here." But the coach's speed neither increased nor decreased.

It was a file of young Indians, slanting forward through the western sunlight on little patch-colored ponies. The Indians rode with a spraddled, keeling mo-tion, their bronze-bare legs shining in the sun. Some of them were breech-clouted only and some wore white man's trousers and white man's shirts dropped outside; a hundred yards from the stage they wheeled and ran abreast of it, the little ponies controlled by single braided rawhide lines attached to their lower jaws. One Indian slowly drew an arrow back in his bow, aimed it, made an imaginary shot, and relaxed the bow; he flung up one finger derisively, whereupon the whole party wheeled and raced away. The driver's voice came down again, windy and relieved. "Agency bucks, but you never know whut they're up to."

Josephine Russell's face was steady and sharp and hardened, but she said nothing. She looked at Shafter.

He said: "Indian kids, just playing at trouble. Nothing to fear."

The sullen young man with the mop of wild hair had remained rigidly drawn together during the affair. Now he relaxed and spoke. "You live in this country?"

"No."

"Then you don't know. There's always trouble. Meet those kids where they thought they had a chance and it would of been different."

"No use worrying about things that don't happen."

The youngster was inclined to be intolerant of this apparent greenhorn, and the presence of a woman made him accent his own frontier wisdom. "If you'd seen what I seen out here—people scalped and whole families with their heads busted in—you wouldn't be so easy about it."

"If it had been spring or summer," said Shafter, "I would have been worried. But winter's coming. These Indians will be on the reservation, eating government beef. They will be good Indians, until spring comes again."

The youngster disliked his point of view being overthrown and he gave Shafter a hard, scowling glance and was evidently tempted to set him in his proper place by a few bolder words. Shafter took the lad's beetling glance and held it, and presently the lad reconsidered his intentions and only said, "If you'd seen what I seen," and reached into his pocket, producing a plug of tobacco from which he chewed an enormous lump and pouched it against one cheek.

Occasionally the stage rolled down the side of the coulee, struck rocky bottom with painful impact and tilted upward, throwing the passengers violently around the seats. The heat clung on with the westering sun and the dust was a screen through which the passengers viewed each other with blurred vision. It dampered normal breathing; it coated the faces of all and presently these faces turned oil-slick and this wetness grew gray and streaky as it formed small rivulets across the dust. The smell of the coach became rank with the odors of bodies rendering out their moisture and the confinement turned from discomfort to actual pain. Shafter noticed that Josephine Russell had taken firm control of herself, pressing back her feelings, and from this he realized she was feeling the ordeal. Now and then, aware of her bedraggled appearance, she pressed her handkerchief against her face.

The road had swung directly into the blast of the low burning sun and therefore it was a surprise when the stage wheeled to a stop before a raw and ungainly house standing alone in all this emptiness. The driver got down, grunting as his feet struck, he called back "Night stop," and walked away. A man moved from the house toward the horses, and one by one the weary passengers lifted themselves from the vehicle and tried their cramped legs. Shafter stood by, giving the girl a hand down. For a moment he supported her, seeing a faintness come to her face; she touched him with both arms, she held him a little while and then, embarrassed, she stepped away. Shafter climbed to the boot of the coach and sorted amongst the luggage. "Which will you need for overnight?"

"The small gray one," she said.

He found it and brought it down. He stood a moment, surveying the house; he looked to an upper window and saw a woman there, staring out upon the coach. He gave the girl a quick side glance and noticed she had not seen the woman; a short and darker expression crossed his face and he led the way over the packed yard to the door. Three great hounds lifted up and growled at him but a voice—a woman's sharp voice—came out of the house, cowing them.

Josephine Russell murmured: "Are there nothing but women hotelkeepers in eastern Dakota?" She had made a more deliberate appraisal of the place and now she gave Shafter a sober glance. "Is it all right?"

"It will have to be," he said.

A woman met them in the half light of the long front room; a woman once young, and still not old in point of years. She stood back, ample-bosomed and careless of dress; her eyes were ready for Shafter and had warmth for him, but they turned cool and watchful when they swung to the girl. There was a moment—a long and unsure moment—while she studied them. Shafter said in a short voice: "You have a room for this lady?"

"Take the one at the top of the stairs. On the left."

He followed Josephine up the stairs. She stopped before a door and looked back at him a moment, and then opened the door and stepped into the room and stood in the center of it, looking on without expression at the room's furniture, at the rough blankets on the bed. He put down her suitcase and went to the window; he pried it open and looked out, and turned back to her. Her glance came over to him and he saw a slight flicker of embarrassment, calm and self-possessed as she was.

He said: "A hell of a place."

She shrugged her shoulders. "But the only place." Then she said: "Are you going to be around here tonight?"

"Yes," he said. He looked at the door when he left the room and saw that there was no key; he closed the door and walked down the stairs. The woman who ran this doubtful desert shelter stood nearby, waiting for him.

He said: "Is that room all right?"

She shrugged her shoulders. "Yes. But I don't ask the genteel to come here."

"This is a stage stop, isn't it?"

"Let it stop some other place," she said. Then she laughed, and her lips were full and heavy and red. "But there's no other place. Do you want a room?"

He said, "No," and color came to him and he turned out to the porch. He walked around the house, sizing it up, its windows blanked out by drawn green roller shades, its paintless angles, its unloveliness. There was an outside stairway running up the east wall, on which he laid a moment's attention; behind the house was another porch, and water and basin. He washed here and beat the dust from his clothes, and resumed his circle of the house. The sun dropped in a silent crash of light and, coming from an apparent nowhere, riders shaped themselves against the sudden twilight. He sat on the porch steps, watching them reach the yard, wheel and step off; all men stamped by their trade, booted and spurred and dusty and scorched by the sun, turned dry by the heat and hollow-hungry, careless and nervous of eye, watching everything and nothing. There was a bar farther back in the house and out of it lights presently rose, and the sound of men talking—and of women talking. He got up and crossed the main room. He paused at the doorway of the bar and had his look at the women; he moved to the bar and took his drink, and stood with his elbows on the bar until he heard the dinner triangle banging. Then he went on to the dining-room door and waited for Josephine.

She came down the stairs and paused to look around; when her eyes found him he saw the relieved lightening of her face. She came up to him, smiling a little, and went into the dining room with him. He saw her glance touch the dozen men at the table and coolly take in the woman at its head—and the two other women also present. She knew them at once, he realized; it was the faintest break on her face, soon covered. After that she took her place and she never looked at them again.

The big plates and platters came circling around, were emptied and carried away by a China boy to be refilled. One man, already drunk, talked steadily; but otherwise the crowd was silent and hungry and ate without conversation. Small talk was a custom of the East; out here men resented making a ceremony out of a meal and wasted no time on it. Ten minutes after they had entered the room, most of the men had finished, and had gone on to the bar; in a little while the rest of the group had deserted the table, leaving Shafter and Josephine to themselves. She sipped at her coffee, tired but relaxed. Through his cigar smoke he watched the lamplight shining against the gray of her eyes, he observed the sweetness and the humor restlessly living in her lip corners. She caught his glance and held it, thoughtfully considering him, making her own silent observations concerning him. Racket began to spread from the saloon and a woman's voice grew strident. The girl shrugged her shoulders and rose from the table.

He followed her back to the big front room and he observed that she stopped at the stairs and looked toward the second floor with an expression of distaste. Suddenly she wheeled toward him and took his arm and they went out of the house and strolled along the vague road. A sickle moon lay far down in the sky, turned butter yellow by the haze in the air, and the stars were great woolly-crystal masses overhead. Sharp-scented dust rose beneath their feet, the fragrance of the earth was strong—the harsh and vigorous emanations of the earth itself. He felt the girl's body sway as she walked; he felt the warmth of her body, the warmth of her thoughts. The desert ran blackly away, formless and mysterious, and far out on the flats a coyote called.

"Do you know this country?" she asked.

"I know the West," he said. "I put in some time in the Southwest."

"Do you like it?"

"It's better than what I've had lately."

They went half a mile onward, slowly pacing; and turned back. The lights of the house gushed from a dozen windows—the only light and the only warmth in all this empty stretch of space; and the sound of laughter, sharply shrill, rode in the little wind.

She said: "What is your name?"

"Kern Shafter. I regret that you have to stay here tonight."

She didn't answer that until they had reached the porch. Then she murmured: "It will do," and passed into the house. At the foot of the stairs she turned to him and asked a question she had asked once before. "You'll be here?"

"Yes," he said. "Good night."

She nodded her head slightly by way of answer, and climbed the stairs.

After she had gone into her room Shafter left the house and went to the coach standing in the yard. He climbed to the boot and found his valise and took out a revolver. He sat on the top of the coach and hefted the gun idly in his palm, feeling its familiar weight, its accustomed and comfortable reality. He thrust it inside his trouser band and lay back to smoke out his cigar while the depth of night increased. The moon's light had no effect on the blind blackness; this yard, touched by house lights, was an island in all the surrounding emptiness. The stars sharply glistened and the scented wind lifted; and mystery closed down and loneliness moved in, with its questions and its far wonder. He sat still, brooding over things behind him, over old injuries still burning and old memories still sweet. When he had thought of them and had felt the heat of them, he closed his mind upon them; and yet, like the leaks in a dam gate, there were apertures in his will and his resolution, through which little seepages of memory still came. He stretched out full length, feeling the goodness of the wind and the ease that came to him. Looking at the sky, he seemed to grow longer and broader, and the space inside him was less crowded. He thought: "I have made one right decision," and felt the peace of knowing it.

With the night also came the quick chill of winter not far away; the starglow had its frigid glitter, the far unseen distance had its threat of storm. Other riders came out of the night, dropped off before the house and moved in, to add to the growing noise. Shafter dropped from the coach and returned to the main room. He found a pair of chairs and drew them together, sitting on one and laying his feet on the other. The big woman who ran the place found him here, so placed that he had a view of the stairs and the doorway of the room directly above.

She stopped before him, smiling down. She lifted his hat and threw it aside and, still with her half smile, ran one finger along the edge of his head. "Your woman will be all right."

"Not mine," he said.

"I guess," she said, "you wouldn't have much trouble with a woman, if you wished. I know your kind."

"No," he said, "you don't."

"Don't tell me what I don't know," she said, half sharp with him. But her brief smile came back as she continued to watch him. "You don't need to curl up like a hound in front of her door. It will get noisy, but nothing will happen."

"Nothing will," he agreed.

"You plan to stay here all night? Right here?"

"Yes."

She ceased to smile. She spoke in a soft, jeering, faintly envious tone. "That's romantic, isn't it? You fool." Suddenly she dropped a hand on his stomach, on the shape of the revolver beneath his coat. "I wouldn't flourish that thing around here. There's a couple men in the bar who could shoot that diamond ring off your finger without scratching your skin."

"Ah," he said, and grinned, "tough ones."

She was puzzled at his reaction. Her lips indecisively loosened while she watched him. He lay back on his chair, a quiet man who didn't seem to care about many things, who didn't give himself away. He dressed well and she knew, without giving it a thought, that he was far above her and perhaps had only a scorn for her. She hated men like that, even more than she hated the rough ones who came here to this house with their appetites; she hated them with a hard desire to use her claws on them—the fashionable, cool ones—and pull them down to her. But she didn't find herself hating this man. It was as she had said before to him: he had a way that women liked and an appeal that women would answer. But he didn't seem to care.

She started to touch him again but checked the gesture. "My God," she murmured, "this is a lonely place. Sometimes . . . If you're crazy enough to sit here all night I'll bring you a blanket later. Maybe some hot coffee."

"I'll be here," he said. She had swung away, but she checked and turned, her eyes scanning him with a small break of hope. Hard living had begun to etch its lines along her face, yet she still was a pretty woman in a loose, heavy, physical way. Carefulness of dress would have done much for her, but she had forgotten to care. She shrugged her shoulders and walked into the saloon, which grew increasingly noisy.

Josephine's room was ceiled with rough lumber whose edges never quite lay together. There was a single window, with a green roller shade discolored by sun and inbeating rain. A lighted lamp stood on a table made up of fragments of boxes which once had contained canned goods; above the table a blemished mirror hung askew. The bed was a four-poster made of solid mahogany, the possible derelict of some wagon train passing through, and on it lay lumpy quilts and a pillow without a slip. The floor had once been covered with a lead-colored paint, but this now had largely broken away so that it was a kind of leprous gray and brown.

Josephine stood in the middle of the room, remembering the people downstairs and hearing the noise which now came up in growing stridency; particularly she heard the voices of the women. She shrugged her shoulders and walked to the bed, pulling back the quilt to explore the two blue army blankets which served as sheets. She bent, looking closely at the blankets; she peeled back the blankets and studied the mattress. She bent still farther down, running a finger along its stitched edge. "At least there are no bedbugs," she thought, and got ready for bed.

She propped the room's lone chair against the doorknob, turned out the light and stood a moment at the window, watching the yard. She saw a man lying on top of the coach, smoking a cigar, and though it was intensely black beyond the range of house lights, she thought she recognized the shape of Shafter's shoulders. The thought of him, vagrant and curious and slightly warm, held her still for a little while; then she crept into bed.

There were men in the adjoining rooms, their lights coming through the warped joining of the wall boards, their voices quite plain as they exchanged stories, each worse than the one before. She rested, still and wide awake, listening to a fight begin and go through the house in grunting, crashing, falling echoes. Some man yelled out his cursing and a gun exploded and a woman screamed; afterwards a man rushed into the night and presently rode away at a dead run. Near midnight someone came slowly up the stairs, his body making a weight on the flimsy wood. He crawled along the hall, his hands scraping the wall. He touched the knob of the door and stopped, and she heard the knob turn and the door give; after that, she heard another traveler come lightly up the steps. One soft word was said and a sharp blow struck, sending one of the men against the wall. Presently that one fell down the stairs in a tumbling, rocketing fashion. The man who had so lightly come upward now went down with the same soft footfalls. Josephine thought: "He's watching out for me," and thought of Shafter, again with relief. Little by little some kind of order crept into this wild house as its inmates fell asleep, and its guests rode away.

<h2 style="text-align:center">☆ 2 ☆</h2>

<h1 style="text-align:center">West of the River</h1>

At one o'clock, Shafter left his seat at the foot of the stairs and went into the barroom. Everybody had gone except one drunk stretched dead to the world across the pool table, and one gloomy houseman cleaning up the debris. Shafter got a glass of whiskey and carried it to a table and sat down; the woman who seemed to run this place came up from some other quarter of the house and took a chair across from him. The flame of her vitality obviously burned low, for she sat with her elbows on the table, supporting her head, staring at the table's green felt top. She murmured:—

"Hard way to make a living, isn't it?"

He said nothing and presently his silence made her lift her glance to him. He smiled at her and pushed his drink over the table. She looked at it a long while, all the brightness faded out of her. "No," she murmured, "I hate the sight of it." She looked up at the barman. "Go get us some coffee, Bill." Then she noticed the drunk on the pool table and a raspiness came to her voice. "Roll that dumb beast off there before he digs his spurs into a thousand dollars' worth of woodwork."

The barkeep was a taciturn and a literal man. He moved to the table, put both arms under the sleeping drunk and gave him a short shove. The drunk fell loosely, striking in sections, at the knees and then at the shoulders. His head slammed hard on the floor and his mouth flew open. He rolled slightly, threshed his arms, and ceased to move. Bill went on toward the back of the house.

"Look at him," said the woman in bitter disgust, pointing to the drunk. "That's a man. That's what they all look like. He'll sober up, eat breakfast and go away. But he'll be back in a couple days. That's what I've got to make my living from."

He said: "Feel this way every night?"

"Every night."

"Time to move on then."

"One place is no better than another," she said, and looked at him with a small revival of interest. When she realized he had been steadily watching her, she pulled herself straight and ran her hands lightly over her hair. "Do I look as bad as I feel?"

"What's your name?"

"May," she said. "There's another May here, but she's Straight-Edge May."

"All women are beautiful, May."

"You fool," she murmured, "don't talk like that. You don't mean it. Even if you did mean it, it would get a woman like me to thinking about things she shouldn't any more." But his words had lifted her; they had revived her spirits. "You've knocked around, haven't you?"

"Yes."

"Running from something."

He showed her his smile again, that easy and careless smile which changed him, which took the darkness out of him. He had sympathy for her but he let it show in his eyes rather than spend words on it. He sat with her and took her as she was. "Everybody runs from something, May. Or runs after something."

"In trouble?"

"No. I don't have to watch what's behind me."

"You've never had to come to places like this for your fun, either," she said, judging him with her wealth of man-knowledge. "Your kind uses theater tickets and bonbons, and back rooms at fashionable restaurants."

For the second time this night, she caught him off guard, causing him to flush. "May," he said. "Let's talk about the weather."

She regarded him closely, amused that she could embarrass him but also puzzled by it; embarrassment was a rare thing in a man and somewhat beyond her limits of experience. She shrugged her shoulders. "I guess I don't know much about your kind. I only met one like you. That was a long time ago. If I knew where he was now I'd write him a letter and let him know just how I turned out after he got through with me." A small tinge of bitterness got into her voice. "Maybe it would make him add something extra on the collection plate next time he went to church."

"How do you know he goes to church, May?"

"It's fashionable for his kind to marry somebody respectable and go to church, and buy his way into heaven. No doubt, when he gets sentimental, he sometimes thinks, 'I wonder where she is now.' Not that he's sorry. His kind of man is proud of one good sinful memory. As for the woman, she can just look out for herself." She bent toward him and showed him an old, old anger. "I don't like your kind of men." But as soon as she said it, her mouth softened. "But I like you. I guess that explains how I got here."

Bill came in with two cups of coffee, black and hot and rank, and moved back to his dismal chores. Shafter dumped his whiskey into the coffee and drank it slowly. He was loose in the chair, he was thoroughly at rest, enjoying the small tastes and sounds and colors around him. She thought to herself, as she studied him: "I'd figure him a genteel bum, except that he threw George Dixon down the stairs." That made her speak up. "You're too quick for your own good. Dixon didn't mean to go into the lady's room. He was just drunk."

"There is only one way to handle Dixons," he said.

"He may come back," she said. "He's a mean one."

"If you hit Dixons hard," he said, "they don't come back. If you hit them soft, they do."

She said: "You uncover yourself just a little bit at a time. You get different as you go. Is there anything I can do for you?"

He looked at her with a greater attention. "How's that, May?"

"Do you need a stake? I've got plenty of money."

He didn't immediately answer and he didn't smile at her again. He finished his coffee, and rose. Her glance remained on him.

"Didn't hurt your feelings, did I?" she wanted to know.

He shook his head. "No, May, you made me feel fine. But I don't need it."

She followed him from the barroom to the front room. "You don't need to stay down here any more. Take the room across the hall from your lady."

He turned on her, looking down, the quietness of his eyes and the expression in them giving her goodness. She wanted to touch him, to reach up and lay her fingers through his black hair; she wanted to come close upon him and lift her mouth for him. But she stood back, a realist who knew that for him she was a vessel long since drained empty; it was the first time in many years she had felt that way about a man.

"Why did you offer me the grubstake, May?"

"People can always hope," she said. "Maybe you would have taken it. Maybe you would have stayed."

He moved to the stairs and turned back there, one hand lying heavy-spread on the railing. "Remember what I told you," he said. "All women are beautiful."

She shook her head, darkened by what she wanted and couldn't have. "If you wish to be kind, never say that to a woman like me." She watched him all the way up the stairs.

And she was at the foot of the stairs at five in the morning when, following breakfast, he turned out of the house. She had taken pains with her hair; she had pressed away the lines about her eyes with cold towels, and she had put on the dress she used for trips to Fargo. But she didn't speak to him as he went by, for he had Josephine with him, and she knew exactly what her station was. After they had gone out, she moved to the porch, watching the stage swing around in the yard. She saw him bend and look through the window at her; and she stood still and watched the stage roll away through its dust and become at last a point in the distance.

The man who had been capsized from the table the night before now moved out of the house in painful slowness. He stopped beside her, puzzled as to the soreness of his bones. "By God," he said, "it must of been a big night. Somebody ride a horse through the barroom, May? I been stepped on, all over."

"No," she said. "You just fell down."

"Must of been from the roof," he murmured and went on to his horse. He groaned when he went into the saddle; he turned and waved a hand. "See you soon, May."

She still watched the stage, but she said, with a piece of a smile: "All right, Tom. Be good and come again."

The coach ran along the twin ruts of the road, outward upon the prairie, under the rising flood of clear and brilliant sunshine. For the space of half an hour, the world stood bathed in morning's freshness, in its coolness, in its bright cleansing light; and for that half hour the horizons were sharp lines in the distance. Then the coolness went away and the faint fog began to rise and the enveloping dust settled within the coach and the monotony of the ride gripped them again. Three of the passengers had dropped off at the night station, leaving only the heavy man, Josephine and Shafter inside. Shafter propped his shoulders in the corner of the coach, braced his feet on the floor and fell asleep.

When he awoke, there was a series of small, ragged up-and-down black strokes against the emptiness and the horses had smelled their destination and were now running freely without the urging of the driver; somewhat later the stage moved into the mouth of Fargo's main street, passed a row of rawboarded houses to either side, turned a corner and stopped at a depot shed standing beside a single track.

The driver got down, shouting, "Fargo, and yore train's in sight," and went up to the boot, throwing down the luggage without regard for the contents. Shafter stepped out and gave Josephine a hand; he found her luggage and piled it near the track, standing back to light a cigar. The train had come out of the east, its progress singing forward on the rails and its whistle hoarsely warning the town. Townsmen strolled up to break the day's tedium and to touch again for an instant that East out of which they had come; to catch, in the train's steamy bustle, the feeling of motion and excitement and freedom which had impelled most of them to come west but which they had lost as soon as they had taken root here.

Josephine turned to Shafter and regarded him with soberness. "You have been kind. If I should not see you again, let me wish you all good luck."

"I'll be on the train."

"Bismarck?" asked Josephine, and showed him a remote pleasure with her eyes.

He nodded instead of speaking; for the engine coasted by with its bell steadily clanging and its exhausts ejaculating gusts of steam. Two baggage cars and five coaches growled to a jerky stop, and passengers looked curiously through the grimed car windows; and an army captain stepped to the runway and began a vigorous constitutional, his cap slanted rakishly on a head of long, bright red hair. The conductor stood on the runway and shouted, "Fargo—Fargo, twenty minutes for lunch!"

Passengers now descended and ran for the lunchroom sitting at the edge of the platform. Josephine meanwhile turned to the train, whereupon Shafter gave her an arm up the nearest coach platform, collected her luggage and carried it into the car. He stowed his own valise on an empty seat and left the train, crossing to the lunchroom. Some of the passengers had seated themselves along a table, before a row of dishes prepared for hasty service; and other passengers, unable to find seats, reached over the heads of the fortunate ones and improvised sandwiches for themselves. Shafter noticed a pile of lunch boxes made up, took two of them, paid the bill and returned to Josephine.

"You never know when these trains get where they're going," he said, leaving a lunch box with her.

He returned to his own seat and began on his meal. The engine bell had begun to sound again and the conductor stood on the runway, crying "Bo-o-o-ard," to summon passengers from the lunchroom. The engine released its brakes and gave a first hard *chuff*, sending a preliminary quiver through the coaches. The train slid forward, gathering speed, while a woman on the train began to scream as a last man rushed from the lunchroom, sprinted along the runway and caught the grab rails of the last coach. The gathered townsmen cheered this extra touch of melodrama, and the engine whistled its throaty farewell as it gathered speed, and the vacuum of its passage lifted eddies of dust and paper on the tracks. It left behind the smell of steam and coal smoke and warm lubricating oil; it left behind the memory of liveliness and motion and it left behind, in the heart of more than one townsman, the half-formed decision to pull up his roots again, as he had before, and move into that bright West whose unknown distances held perpetual promise of fortune and adventure.

The coaches, castoffs of other lines in the East, swayed with the not yet thoroughly settled grade of this new railroad, stretched taut on their couplings, and slammed together when the engine slightly abated speed. Cinders pelted the windows and smoke streamed back the length of the train; and the engine whistle laid out its hoarse notice upon the land. Here and there a siding ran briefly beside the main line and here and there a yellow section shanty stood lonely in the sun. Out in the distance an occasional antelope band, startled from grazing, fled away in beautiful smoothness. Once in a great while Shafter saw a ranch house or a rider, or cattle. Propping his feet on the opposite seat, he fell asleep, and later woke to find the train stopping at a town that was four little shanties facing the tracks; and slept again until he heard the conductor cry, "Bismarck!"

The town's gray out-sheds and slovenly shanties and corrals slid forward and its main street appeared—one long row of saloons, stores, livery barns and freighter sheds crowded side by side, unevenly joined and roughly thrown together. The train stopped, heads bobbed beside the car windows and presently people came in to search for friends. Shafter picked up his valise and left the coach.

The sun was down and coolness already began to move over the earth. There had been rain in Bismarck, turning the yellow dust gray and slick, and coating the boots of the gathered crowd. An army ambulance stood near the track, held by a cavalry corporal, and a pair of ladies crossed to it and were whirled away. Josephine Russell meanwhile descended, walked to a gray-haired man and kissed him. The gray-haired man took her luggage and turned off, but for a moment Josephine Russell paused to look back at Shafter. Impulse moved her to him.

"I wish you luck," she said.

"I'll remember your wish," he answered and lifted his hat to her and watched her walk on. She was an alert, happy woman; she had presented him with that fair and serene face which he most admired, and as he looked at her retreating shape he had his slight regret—the regret of a man who sees beauty and grace disappear.

The cars were now empty, the engine had been uncoupled and moved on; for this was the farthest west of the railroad, in this year of 1875. Beyond Bismarck was the yellow Missouri, and beyond the Missouri lay the unknown lands of the Sioux where, intermittently for ten years, little columns and detachments of the army had marched and fought, had won and had been defeated. Shafter lifted his valise and moved toward a wagon wherein sat a driver. He spoke to the driver:—

"Where's Fort Abraham Lincoln?"

The driver pointed a finger southwesterly. "Along that road, four miles to the Point. Ferry there." Then he said: "Get in."

Shafter dumped his valise into the wagon's bed and took a place beside the driver who now set his team down the street at a trot. At the end of the street the road moved in dog-leg fashion up and down and around little folds of earth, past an occasional house, past Indians riding head down and indifferent, their toes pointed outward, their shoulders stooped. The team kept up an easy mincing trot, making a little melody of harness chains, and so covered four miles, coming then to a highland upon which sat a collection of houses sitting apart and facing all directions. Beyond this highland the terrain rolled into bottom lands and reached the Missouri. Beyond the river stood the fort on its bluff, its line of houses square and trim and formidable. The driver slammed on his brakes as the wagon descended the grade to the ferry dock; and pointed at the houses to either hand.

"If you got money to spend, don't come here. This is the Point. It's off the military reservation. It is a bad place, my friend." He let go the brakes and the wagon rolled to the deck of a river steamer, once glamorous but now converted to something little better than a scow with steam; on the pilot house a gilded sign gave its name, THE UNION. The name was its only substantial part, for when the lines were cast off the ancient engines shook the boat in all its frames. They surged forward through the near shore's back eddy, came upon the middle channel and were seized by a current that lay deceptively beneath this murky river's surface. The *Union* shuddered throughout, paused and lost steerage way. It skewed across the current, fell five hundred yards downriver, and reached slack water on the far side; with its engines racking its ancient frame, it worked slowly upstream and nosed into the slip. The wagoner released his brakes, whipped his team into a run and went up the grade to the top of the bluff. When he reached it he sat back and blew out a breath.

"Damn boat someday is goin' to keep going right on down to Yankton. Or blow up."

The walls of this fort were formed by the back edges of barracks, storehouses, officers' quarters and stables, all these facing a great parade ground running a thousand feet or better in each direction. The teamster drew before the guardhouse post, said "Commissary," and was waved in.

"You know where the adjutant's office might be?" asked Shafter.

"Down there by the end of the quartermaster building."

"Thanks for the ride," offered Shafter and dropped off with his valise. He went along the east side of the parade ground, traveling on a board walk which skirted troop quarters; and as he passed these long barracks he heard the clatter of dishes coming up from the mess hall in the rear of each barrack. This was supper time, the sun just dropping below the ridge to the west of the fort; and the ceremony of retreat was not far away, for orderlies were now cutting out of the stable area, leading horses across the parade to Officers' Row. He had just reached the doorway of the adjutant's office when the trumpeter at the guard gate blew first call.

He stepped inside in time to see a huge, tall first lieutenant clap on a dress helmet with its plume, thrust the chin strap into place and hook up his sword. Dundreary whiskers grew in silken luxury along his jowls, out of which showed a big-fleshed mouth, a solid nose and a pair of darkly sharp eyes. He looked at Shafter. He said, "Yes?" and started for the door. "Yes?"

"I'll wait until the lieutenant returns from retreat," said Shafter.

The lieutenant said, "Very well," and flung himself through the door, followed by a sergeant major empurpled with years of weather and hard living. A corporal remained behind in the office, his arm hanging from a sling.

Shafter watched five cavalry companies file out from the stables to the parade ground. The hark of officers came sharp through the still air. "Column right! Left into line! Com-m-pany, halt!" Horsemen trotted briskly here and there, lifting quick puffs of dust from the hard parade. One by one, the five companies came into regimental front, each company mounted on horses of matched color, each company's guidon colorfully waving from the pole affixed in the stirrup socket of the guidon corporal's stirrup. For a moment the regiment remained still, each trooper sitting with a grooved ease in his McClellan, legs well down and back arched, saber hanging on loosened sling to left side, carbine suspended from belt swivel to right, dress helmet cowled down to the level of his eyes. Thus the Seventh sat in disciplined, impassive form—a long double rank of dark, largely mustached faces—homely, burned faces, Irish faces, seasoned and youthful faces, faces of solid value and faces of wildness—all pointed frontward to the company commander and to the adjutant now taking his report. Presently, the adjutant wheeled his horse, trotted it fifty feet forward and came to a halt before a slim shape poised lithe and watchful on his mount.

Even at this distance Shafter recognized the commanding officer—that long, bushy fall of almost golden hair which even the cowling of the dress helmet could not conceal, that sweeping tawny dragoon's mustache which sharpened the bony, hawkish nose and accented the depth of eye sockets, that sinuous and muscularly restless body now held in momentary restraint against its own incessant rebellion. There sat the man who was a living legend, the least-disciplined and poorest scholar of his West Point class of 1861; whose wild charges and consuming love of naked action had turned him into a major general by brevet at the age of twenty-five and who was, in the shrunken peacetime army, Lieutenant Colonel of the Seventh Cavalry and its commander by virtue of the absence of Colonel Sturgis. Everybody in America knew the face of the man; it was a household familiarity, the thin lips half concealed by the waterfall mustache, the hungry boniness of the jaw, the blue inset eyes seeking attention, seeking any audacity to prove the right to attention.

Custer's arm answered the adjutant's salute, with a swift nervous jerk. A word was spoken. The band burst into a quick march, still stationary on the right of the line. The officers of the regiment rode slowly front and center, formed a rank and moved upon the commanding officer. Shafter heard the brittle crack of an officer's voice halt them. He watched them salute Custer, and receive his return salute, after which they took place behind him. Suddenly now the band swung around and marched down the front of the regiment, in full tune, and wheeled and marched back. Silence came completely; all the shapes upon this parade turned still as the massed buglers tossed up their trumpets and sounded retreat. Hard upon the heels of the last trumpet note the little brass cannon at the foot of the flagpole boomed out, its echo rocketing into the western ridge and out across the Missouri. The flag began to descend and the band struck up a national air. Shafter pulled his heels together and removed his hat; he stood balanced, facing the flag as it slid down the pole toward the trooper waiting to receive it. In the ensuing quiet, Custer's strident voice carried the length and breadth of the parade.

"Pass in review!"

The first sergeants, now commanding the companies, wheeled about, harking their stiff calls. The band broke into a march tune, the regimental front broke like a fan and came into platoon column; it turned the corners of the parade and passed before the commanding officer with hard dust smoking up around it. Down at the far end of the parade ground, each company pulled away toward its own stable. The ceremony was done.

Out by the flagstaff the officers surrendered their horses and moved idly along the walk toward their quarters. The adjutant took his last orders and departed. An orderly galloped forward to take Custer's horse, but the general swung his mount and flung it headlong across the parade, wheeled and raced it back. Arriving before his quarters he sprang to the ground, tossed over the reins and stamped up the porch of his house; it had been one sudden outburst of energy which could no longer be dammed up.

Shafter meanwhile stepped back into the adjutant's office. Presently the adjutant came in, slightly sweating; he removed his dress hat and laid it on a desk, he unbuckled his saber and hung it to a peg on the wall and, having done this, he looked at Shafter.

"Well, sir."

"I should like to enlist in this regiment," said Shafter.

"Where are you from?"

"Ohio."

"How was it you did not enlist at the nearest recruiting service?"

"I prefer to pick my regiment."

"That involved considerable train fare," observed the adjutant, and took time to consider Shafter with a very cool eye. "Normally we are recruited from Jefferson Barracks. Still, we can enlist you." He turned to the corporal with the bad arm. "Get an enlistment form, Jackson. Get a doctor's blank, too."

Jackson searched another desk for the required forms and the adjutant lowered his rather massive frame into a chair and considered the work on his desk. The corporal sat down at another desk and beckoned Shafter before him. "Name?" he said, and began to take Shafter's history. "Recent address? Next of kin?"

"No next of kin."

"Closest friend, then."

"None," said Shafter.

The corporal leaned back and chewed his pen a moment, looking at Shafter. The adjutant raised his head to consider this new recruit. "Are you that alone in this world?" he asked, with some skepticism. But he nodded at the corporal and murmured, "Let it go." Both the corporal and the lieutenant, Shafter realized, were thinking the same thing: that he was another drifter running from a past. These regiments on the border had many such men; it was an old story.

"Birthplace, parents' names? Age, weight, color of hair and eyes? Height? Distinguishing marks?" The clerk rattled off the inquiries and scrawled them down. It grew late and he was impatient to be free—to join the poker game at troop barrack, to meet a woman across the river at the Point, to sleep—or perhaps simply to sit idle and dream of the comfort and the freedom of civilian life. Shafter quietly supplied the answers required of him, thinking of that same civilian life with no regrets and no particular warmth. Insofar as he had a home, this army post would satisfy him completely; the uniform would be the answer to his wants. He heard men come into the adjutant's office behind him. He heard the adjutant say:—

"It is slightly late, Doctor. But could you examine this man for enlistment?"

"Yes."

Shafter turned and saw the doctor, standing by the adjutant's desk. But his eyes lingered on the man only a moment; for there was another officer now in the room, a captain looking out from beneath the rim of his dress helmet at Shafter, with a keen attention. He was a heavy, stocky man with a broad practical face, with a heavy sand-colored mustache guarding his upper mouth. It was a serviceable, unemotional Irish countenance, a face disciplined by duty and routine and largely beyond the whims of excitement. Shafter looked back at him gravely. The doctor said, "Step in the room," pointing to a doorway back of the adjutant, "and strip."

He followed Shafter, he waited, his mind obviously on other things. He took a mechanical survey of Shafter's naked frame and pointed to the thick whitened welt of a scar that made a foot-long crescent on Shafter's left flank, above the hip "What was that?"

"Saber cut."

"Ah," said the doctor, and made his tapping inspection of Shafter's chest. "How old?"

"Thirty-two."

The doctor completed the rest of his routine in silence and motioned for Shafter to resume his clothes, meanwhile himself leaving the room. He sat down at the edge of the adjutant's desk, completing the physical form. "He'll do physically," he said to the adjutant.

The captain still remained in the room. Now he said: "I'll take that man."

The adjutant grinned. "You want everything for A Company, Moylan."

"I'm down to fifty-three men," said Captain Moylan.

"You're no worse off than the other companies."

"I'd like to have him, Cooke," said Captain Moylan, pressing the point.

The adjutant looked at the enlistment blank placed on his desk by the corporal. The corporal had gone. Cooke read through it. "He came all the way out here to enlist. You're buying a pig in the poke. Probably he's using the uniform to hide."

"He's had service before," said the doctor. "Saber scar."

Cooke said: "Jackson forgot to ask that question. It doesn't show here."

"Do I get him?" asked Moylan.

"You can have him, but the other company commanders will charge me with partiality."

"One more thing," said Moylan. "Let me swear him in."

Both Cooke and the doctor showed some degree of surprise. Cooke was on the point of asking a question, but at that moment Shafter, having dressed, returned to the office and took stand in front of the adjutant's desk. Cooke now gave Shafter a more thorough glance, noting his posture, his drawn-together carriage, his composed silence. Cooke said:—

"Do you leave any felonies behind you?"

"No," said Shafter.

"Have you had prior service?"

Shafter's answer came after a small pause, noticeable to all of them. "Yes," he said.

"What organization?"

The small delay was again noticeable. "Fourteenth Ohio."

"That would be the Civil War," said Cooke.

"Yes."

"What was the quality of your discharge?"

"Honorably mustered out, end of war."

Cooke nodded. He took a little brown volume of army regulations from a pile on the desk, searched through it and found a page. He handed the open book to Captain Moylan. Shafter turned to face the captain and, without being requested, raised his right hand. Moylan looked at the page and began the oath: "Do you solemnly swear . . ."

When it was done with, Moylan gravely listened to Shafter's "I do," watched his face a considerable moment, and tossed the book of regulations on the table. "Very well," he softly said. "You are now a private in the Seventh Cavalry, attached to A Company. Follow me over to barracks."

"Yes, sir," said Shafter, and moved out of the office behind Moylan. Cooke sat with his chin propped in one massive, meaty hand, watching the two go. "That was odd, Porter. Something there, I fancy."

"He's no raw Irishman off the boat," commented Porter. "He smells like a broken-down gentleman to me."

"I didn't seem to catch the broken-down part. If he is a gentleman, may God help him. We've got a few of them. They're very forlorn souls. Well." He rose and made a halfhearted gesture of creating some sort of neatness on his desk. "A little game tonight?"

"I've been invited to dance the opening set at D Company's ball," said Porter. "I'll meet you later."

Out on the baked parade ground, Shafter fell in step with Moylan, to the left and slightly behind the captain. First twilight had come to the land, the low hills to the west of the fort turning dark and edged against the sky, the great endless prairie to the east slowly foreshortening, as night crept over it. A guard relief detachment went scuffing by, the sergeant saluting Moylan as he passed. Moylan returned it absent-mindedly. He spoke to Shafter without turning his head.

"This was considerable of a surprise, Kern."

"I hadn't realized you were with the Seventh."

"I'm damned glad to see you. Often thought of you, It has been a long time since Winchester and Cumberland Gap. I don't suppose you expected to see old Myles Moylan as a captain of cavalry. It has been a hard route. I was sergeant major in this outfit before I got my commission. Coming up through the ranks is not the easy way to do it."

"God bless you," said Shafter. "I can think of nothing better."

"I asked Cooke to attach you to my company," said Moylan. "I didn't say why. You didn't wish me to say why, did you?"

"No."

"It was a hard, hard thing," murmured Moylan. "I have never ceased to feel anger over it. Have you done anything about it?"

"Nothing to be done."

Moylan walked a full twenty feet before speaking again; and his words were troubled. "The strangeness of it does not stop with my being here and you being here. It is more than that. I wish I could have had the chance of speaking to you quietly before you took the oath. I think you wouldn't have stayed. Garnett is here. Or did you know that, and come to hunt him especially out?"

"I didn't know it," said Shafter, and said nothing more. He walked steadily beside Moylan, his chin dropped, expression drained from his face.

Moylan said: "He is first lieutenant of L. That is why I had Cooke assign you to my company. It would have been highly unpleasant for you to have served under him."

"It is strange how a thing never ends," said Shafter.

Moylan stepped to the porch of a barrack at the south end of the parade; a first sergeant sat there with a pipe in his mouth; he came to his feet and

snatched the pipe from his mouth. "Hines," said Moylan, "this recruit is assigned to A. Take care of him."

"Yes, sir," said the sergeant. Moylan swung off, going at a steady, fast pace
down the walk, into the gathering twilight. The first sergeant gave Shafter a
considerable stare. "What's your name?"

"Shafter."

"Well, then, Shafter, come with me," said Hines.

The barracks was a building thirty feet wide and better than a hundred long,
with peeled logs standing upright as supports and a floor of rammed earth. A
continuous row of double-decked bunks ran down the walls. At the foot of each
bunk was a small locker for each man's effects and a rack for sabers and gear
and carbines and other equipment. At the far end of the building was a little
office over the door of which was a painted sign, ORDERLY ROOM. A door led
back into what seemed a mess hall. Meanwhile the sergeant strode along the
bunk row, past men already asleep, past men lying awake on their blankets, past
a table where men sat at a poker game and looked up at Shafter with an
indifferent interest. The first sergeant stopped at a bunk. "This," he said, "is
yours. Do I have to teach you to ride and handle a gun and mind your orders
or—" and he studied Shafter with a closer eye—"is it that you've had service
before?"

"Yes," said Shafter.

"Cavalry?"

"Yes."

"Alcott," called Hines, and drew another sergeant across the room with a
waggle of his hand. "Take this man—Shafter's his name—and give him an outfit."

"Come along," said Alcott and towed him into a dark little cubbyhole of a
quartermaster's supply room. The sergeant did a moment's measuring on
Shafter with his eyes, then turned to his shelves and began to toss pieces of
uniform over his shoulder.

Twenty minutes later Shafter emerged with an outfit stacked from his outspread arms to his chin—underwear, socks, field boots and garrison shoes, blue
pants and blue blouse and two blue wool shirts, campaign hat, forage cap and
dress helmet with plume, saber and saber sling, carbine with its sling, Colt
revolver, Springfield carbine, ammunition, cartridge belt, canteen, mess outfit,
intrenching tools, saddle bags, housewife kit, bridle, lariat and hobbles and
picket pin, a razor, a silvered mirror, a cake of soap, a comb, two blankets, a
straw tick, a box of shoe polish and a dauber, an overcoat, a rubber poncho with
a hole through its center, a pair of wool gloves, a bacon can, currycomb and
brush, and a pair of collar ornaments with cross-saber, the regimental number 7
above and the troop letter A below.

He laid these things on his bunk, took up his tick and left the room, headed
for the stables. A hard-packed area lay between them and the rear of the barrack hall, used for troop assembly; beyond the stables stood the edge of the
bluff which dropped to the Missouri now blackly running on into the night with
a soft rustle of its silted waters. Beyond the river winked the lights of the Point
and over the water at this moment slid the *Union* with a panting *chow-chow* of

its engines. Shafter found the straw stack and knelt to fill his tick; he heard the casual stamping of the horses and smelled the rankness of horses—and the night came blackly down upon him and from afar drifted the rolling tune of the band, made beautiful by the distance, by the night, by the shining of the stars. When he had finished his chore he returned to the barrack hall, laid the tick on the bunk and made his bed. He took off his civilian suit and pulled on the army pants and shirt; he rolled up his civilian clothes and stood a moment looking at them, and had his long, backward thoughts. He turned around, speaking down the barrack hall.

"Anybody getting a discharge soon?"

"Yes," said a trooper, and sat up from his bunk. "I'm leavin' next week."

"How big are you?"

"Five-ten, one hundred and sixty."

Shafter rolled the suit into a ball and threw it at the man on the bunk. "The tailor can pull in the trouser legs and cinch up the coat. It's yours. When you get to New York, walk into the Netherlands House, and tell the headwaiter who wore those clothes last. You'll get a free meal out of it."

The guardhouse trumpet drew the slow notes of tattoo across the silence of the night, softly and beautifully. Shafter got a cigar from his luggage on the cot. He lighted it and strolled in his stocking feet to the barrack porch. Across the thousand-foot parade ground the lights of Officers' Row were pleasantly shining and somewhere about the fort the regimental band still was playing dance music. Out from Number One Post at the guardhouse came the sentry's call: "Nine o'clock—all's well," and the call was picked up, post by post, until it ran all around the fort. He thrust his hands into the pockets of the pants, feeling the roughness of them; they had the smell of the storehouse on them and they were stiff. But they covered him and they brought back to him recollections of the years gone, and all those recollections were satisfying. It was like coming home; nothing was strange. The voices of the men within the barrack, the sight of the carbines racked together, the sabers hanging at the foot of the bunks—all this was familiar. It was a way of living which, once surrendered, he now embraced again.

The darkness was a complete, moonless dark. Beyond Officers' Row lay the low, curved silhouette of the western ridge, over which a soft wind came with its scent of winter, with its scent of farther wildness. Out there, far out, lay a country as mysterious as the heart of Africa. Across it, during the past ten years, occasional military expeditions had traveled, had fought, had won and lost—but never had penetrated the core of it. That was Sioux land, the last refuge of a race which had given ground before the promises, the threats and the treacheries of the white man's frontier; and now had vowed to retreat no farther. Out there Sioux tepees made their rows and clusters along the Powder, the Yellowstone, the Tongue and the Rosebud; and along a stream which the Indians called the Greasy Grass but which was known to white men as the Little Bighorn.

The Ritual of Acceptance

"Abbott!"
"Yo!"
"Allen!"
"Yo!"
"Benzen!"
"Here!"

This was at five-thirty in the morning, the company assembled unarmed and dismounted behind its barrack to answer roll call. A mist lay hard upon the Missouri, hiding the water, but holding in suspension all the river's rich, dank and racy smells, and day's first light pressed down upon the mist from above. The troop stood glumly double-ranked in the chill air. The sergeant's nose was a reddening thermometer of both his temperature and his disposition. Upon completion of roll call, he made an about-face and rendered his slowly precise salute to the sharp-visaged young second lieutenant waiting by.

"Present or accounted for, sir."

The lieutenant acknowledged the salute and thus, having fulfilled regulations, walked away. Hines turned back upon the troop, morning-sour and professionally cranky. "I never saw a filthier yard, nor a dirtier barrack. After breakfast you'll all turn out for police on it. Mind me, you have been doin' too much soldierin' on your bunks. Corp'ril King and squad, wood detail. Costain, duty at the orderly room, Melish, Duker and Straub, kitchen. Sergeant McDermott, Corp'ril Roy, Privates Bean, Ryneerson, Hoch and Muldoon, guard duty to-night." He thought a moment and thereafter opened his roster book again. "By order of this date, Private Shafter appointed sergeant. Dismiss."

The heavy smell of coffee came reeking out of the mess-hall wing as they broke up and ran back to barrack. All down the parade sounded the brisk mess call. Day broke through the mist, sparkling against the dew-beaded grass. Shafter got his mess outfit from his bunk, crossed to the hall, and joined the forming line. A private with a vein-netted face and a pair of flushed eyes overhung with a solid lacework of stiff black brows came up behind him, growling. "A sergeant," he said, "does nawt eat with us common ones. You belong at the head o' the line."

"I'll wait until I sew the stripes on," said Shafter and gave this new one a thoughtful appraisal. The man had muscular shoulders; he was full of bone and meat, but his belly was round and liquor had softened him. On his sleeve was a faded spot where, not long before, sergeant stripes had been.

"The rank came easy, did it not?" said the man, accenting his insolence.

116

"As easy as yours went away," said Shafter.

"I worked for mine," said the man. "Four years. I licked nobody's boots for 'em. I gave 'em up because it was me own wish."

"So that you could breathe freer into a whiskey bottle," said Shafter.

"You've got a tongue, I do observe," said the man. He lifted his voice a little and half the line of men heard this. "To be a sergeant is not a matter of tongue in this outfit, bucky. It is a matter of knuckles. Do you know what I think? I think you'll not last long."

The line moved up, passing before the cook's table where a pair of troopers served out breakfast from kitchen kettles. Shafter got his oatmeal, his bacon and biscuits and held out his cup for coffee. The trooper handling the pot let his hand waver a little so that the coffee spilled over, scalding Shafter's hand; and then the trooper gave him a blank stare. Shafter looked back at him, a little light dancing gray-bright in his eyes, and passed on to a long table. That was the way it would be in this troop; he was untested, and suddenly a sergeant—made so by Captain Moylan out of memory of incidents long ago. Moylan must have known that he put his new sergeant in a hard position.

Hines passed by and dropped a brusque word. "Come to the orderly room."

In a little while Shafter followed him into the small room at the end of the barracks. Hines was at his desk. He said, "Shut the damned door," and waited until it was done. "I'm too old a man to remark upon my company commander's choices. You've been in the army before?"

"Yes."

"Moylan knew you somewhere?"

"Let's let that slide," said Shafter.

Hines was displeased, and his stare was like the slap of his heavy hand. "It is his choice to make, but it is me that has to keep the company runnin' like a company should run. There is somethin' here which the company will not like, and I cannot put my hand upon any man to stop him from givin' you the roll of his eye. I will not have this outfit go sour because of the advancement of a rooky to sergeant. So, then, you must lick somebody to show what you've got. It will be the one that was sergeant and got broke for tryin' to lap up all the whiskey in Bismarck. That's Donovan."

Shafter remembered the meaty one with the round belly. "He's opened the door already."

"See that you walk right through that door," said Hines. "You must give him a hell of a beating, or you'll never draw any water in this outfit as a noncom. If he should give you the beatin'—and it is my bet that he'll do just that—there is but one thing for you to do. You will turn in your stripes."

Shafter stood easy in front of the first sergeant, smiling a little. "You have got a fine collection of savages for a company, Sergeant. I shall tame one of them for you."

"So," said Hines and was not impressed. Four hashmarks on his sleeve testified his service; in the rounds of his eyes lay an iron, taciturn wisdom. The army had made and shaped him until he was all that the army stood for, a solid, short-tempered and thoroughly valuable man. "You talk like a damned gentleman. Get your stripes sewed on. At stable call you will be assigned a horse.

Afternoon you will hitch up the light wagon and go to Bismarck to do errands for the captain and his lady. You will stay until the train comes in, pick up the first lieutenant of this company, who arrives from St. Paul—the Lieutenant Smith."

"Who is the officer that took roll call this morning?"

"That one is Varnum. He has some knowledge of Indians, which God knows we'll need when they break out again next spring."

Stable call came sharp upon the parade ground, pulling Shafter from the orderly room. The fog had lifted and bright sunshine slanted out of the east; he was assigned his horse, and his stall, and spent time grooming the horse. Sick call came, and first call for drill; at nine o'clock the sharp-faced Lieutenant Varnum took the company out upon the parade. Heat lay like a thinned film in the windless air, only suggesting what it had been a few short months before, but the fine dust rose beneath the hoofs of the turning horses as the five companies, each on a section of the parade, went through their close-order maneuvers, wheeling in column, fours left, fours right, left into line, walk, trot, gallop; the horses, old in the business, automatically responding, crowding upon each other, grunting, precisely coming about. At eleven-thirty recall sounded; and mess call came at noon. Afterwards, Shafter hitched up the light wagon to a pair of horses and, with a shopping list from Mrs. Moylan in his pocket, drove through Lincoln's guard gate—past the post gardens and hospital and band quarters, past the barracks of the regimental noncommissioned staff, past bakery and officers' club and civilian quarters and post trader's store—and so came to the ferry.

Over the river, he drove through the Point which lay exhausted after its night's excesses, and followed the straggling road into Bismarck. As soon as he arrived there he did the shopping for Mrs. Moylan; after that he hunted up a tailor and sat in his underclothes for an hour, reading an old copy of the *New York Tribune* while the tailor cut his uniform to better size, sewed on the sergeant's chevrons and the yellow noncom strip down each trouser leg.

He still had an hour to spend before train time; and walked the length of Bismarck's street, the sun's warmth going through his heavy blue blouse and bringing out its woolly smell; he turned and strolled back and, in front of the town's big grocery store, he came upon Josephine Russell. She halted at once, showing surprise; she tipped her head as she studied him.

"So that is why you came west?"

"Yes."

She said: "I think you've worn the uniform before. I thought that when I saw you standing in front of the depot at Corapolis."

She carried a basket of groceries, and she had a roll of checked red-and-white oilcloth under her arm. Shafter relieved her of these bundles. "Where can I carry these for you?"

"You're on duty, aren't you?"

"Waiting for the train to come in."

They moved down the street, side by side. She wore a light dress, and she had no hat, and she seemed fairer to him than before; her gray eyes were calm and pleased in the way they looked at him. Her lips held their steady hint of a smile.

"It's good to see you," he said.

She gave him a quick side glance, slightly speculative, her eyes gently narrowing. Her lips made a softly pursed line and afterwards she walked on in silence, looking before her. This day the town was crowded. Half a dozen punchers came up the walk, shoulder to shoulder, thrown slightly forward by the high heels of their riding boots—all sharp-eyed, roughly dressed men, and all keenly alive. They broke aside to let Josephine pass, and eyed her with surreptitious admiration. Indians sat against a stable wall, dourly indifferent. Up from a warehouse at the lower end of town moved a caravan of ox-drawn wagons crowded to the canvas tops with freight, headed outward from the railroad into that southward distance which ran three hundred miles to Yankton without the break of a town or settlement, except for the dreary little army posts or steamboat landings along the Missouri.

A man sat on the steps of a barbershop with a carbine and calmly shot between the traffic at a target over near the railroad tracks; and drew up his gun to let Josephine and Shafter pass by. At the foot of the street Josephine turned the corner of a feed store and moved back upon the prairie to a house standing somewhat removed from the town. A picket fence surrounded it, but otherwise it was without ornament, shade or grass.

Josephine opened the gate and led Shafter to the porch, there relieving him of the packages. She dropped them inside the house door and turned back. "If you must wait somewhere, it might be just as comfortable waiting here. Sit down."

There were a chair and a rocker on the porch, both made of merchandise packing boxes. Josephine took the chair and Shafter settled himself in the rocker and let his long legs sprawl before him. The gesture brought an instant smile and comment from the girl. "You have a wonderful gift of just going loose all over whenever you can."

"I got that from the army. A man learns, when he's on long marches, to make the short stops count."

"The uniform changes you entirely. My first judgment of you was a great deal different." Her glance turned thoughtful. "In civilian clothes you seemed a somewhat skeptical man, perhaps accustomed to the good things of life."

He showed some embarrassment at the remark. He said: "I guess that's true."

She realized she had struck something in him which was vulnerable; he had a sensitive spot, and she was sorry she had touched it and changed the subject. "You were lucky to get a uniform that fitted you."

"I had the tailor work on it," he said. "Well, whatever I was, I still am. You can't change a man by clothes. But I have wanted to get back into the uniform for ten years. I remembered that when I was a soldier last time I had about as much complete peace of mind, as much personal contentment, as I ever had. That's why I came back. I do not require much comfort and I do not need many possessions. What I need, I guess, is to be with plain and honest men."

"Men can be plain and honest outside the army."

"Then," he said, "it must be something else the uniform has that I have needed. At any rate, I feel at home, which is something I have not felt for a long time."

"Adventure?" she murmured. "The sound of bugles?"

He shook his head. "I went through four years of the Civil War. I heard a lot of bugles blowing for the charge. I saw a lot of men fall, a lot of good friends die. That's the other side of adventure. I am no longer a young man dreaming of gallantry in action."

She bent a little in the chair, smiling and curious. "You make yourself a greater puzzle to me, Sergeant." Then she rose and went into the house. He reached into his blouse for a cigar, and lighted it and relaxed wholly in the rocker. The afternoon was warm, all of summer's scorch gone out of it. The deep haze of summer, this far west, had lightened, so that the prairie was a tawny floor, running immeasurably away into the distance. The railroad line marched eastward, marked by the single row of telegraph poles; and in that direction was the smudge of the afternoon train coming on. Josephine Russell came back with a tall glass of milk and handed it to him.

"How long have you lived out here?" he asked.

"Two years. We have always been moving up on the edge of the frontier. I suppose in two or three years more we'll be out there in Montana somewhere. My father has that store—where you saw me. But he is restless, and more so since my mother died."

"You like it here?"

"I like whatever place I am." A more sober expression came to her face. "It was nice to visit the East, though. I don't know when I shall see it again."

The train flung its long warning whistle forward from the distance, reminding Shafter of his duty. He rose with reluctance and stood easy-balanced on his feet, looking down at her with his expression of personal interest, and he repeated what he had said earlier: "It is good to see you again."

"The post can be a very lonely place. Are you sure it won't bore you?"

"I don't need much in the way of distraction."

She said: "This house is open, if you feel like visiting."

He nodded, he said: "I shall do that," and walked back toward town. She watched him go, his shoulders cut against the sunlight, his long frame swinging. She had known, as soon as she saw him in uniform, that the sergeant's stripes did not represent what he once had been. Somewhere in the past he had been a man with a career, had met disaster, and had stepped away from the wreckage with a shrug of his shoulder. She had guessed that much about him two days before, and was more certain of it now. There was, she thought, a woman somewhere involved. Reluctantly she lifted her guard against him. "I should not," she murmured, "be very much interested in him," and continued to watch him until he swung around the corner of a building and disappeared.

Shafter drove the small wagon to the station and arrived just as the train did. He watched the passengers come out, saw only one army officer, and walked toward him. Lieutenant Algernon Smith was a dark, chunky-shouldered man with a bushy black cavalry mustache, heavy black brows, a solid chin and sharp eyes. He took Shafter's salute.

"Sergeant Shafter, sir. I am to drive you to the post."

The lieutenant said. "You're new?"

"I enlisted yesterday, sir."

"Rapid promotion," said the lieutenant enigmatically and nothing more. He had a small portmanteau which he flung into the wagon when he reached it, and stepped up to the seat, folding his arms across his chest like an artilleryman riding a caisson. Shafter ran the team out of town and down the rutty road. Past the Point he saw the ferry ready to cast off, whereupon he whipped the team into a dead run down the incline and put it aboard with a sudden shock of brakes. Lieutenant Smith grabbed the edge of the seat to prevent falling out, and gave Shafter the benefit of his dry voice: "I guess you have dash enough for cavalry service."

Once inside the guard gate, Shafter drove over the parade to Officers' Row, let off the lieutenant and went on to Captain Moylan's quarters. He carried the packages to the back door, delivered them to the captain's striker, and returned the wagon and team to stables. It was past five o'clock then, afternoon stable call having occurred while he was gone; therefore he curried his horse and walked into the barrack. As soon as he reached his bunk he saw that it had been ripped apart. His box of cigars, which he had placed beneath the tick, now lay in sight, its lid open and the cigars gone.

The men of the troop sat around the barrack, waiting mess call, cleaning up equipment for retreat, or lying back on their bunks. Donovan, he noticed, was at one of the tables, playing a game of solitaire. Donovan was smoking a cigar and, to make the point clearer, Donovan had a row of cigars lying on the table before him. A scar-mouthed trooper stood by, thinly grinning and watching Shafter from the evil corners of his eyes. It was a published thing in the barrack room; everybody knew what was happening, and waited for the rest of it to happen.

Shafter turned to the table and stood beside it, looking down on the red surface of Donovan's neck. The ex-sergeant kept on with his solitaire, aware of Shafter's presence but ignoring it. He had his feet planted squarely on the floor, beneath the table; he had his forearms lightly braced on the table's top so that one warning would bring him roaring up to his feet.

"Donovan," said Shafter, easy and plain, "where do we have this fight?"

"Behind the stables," said Donovan with equal calmness. "Tinney, have a cigar. They're good ones, picked by a gentleman lately come among us to dodge a warrant. I guess we have smoked the gentleman out." He slapped a hand down on the table so hard that the cards jumped and he leaned back and shouted out a heavy laughter at his own joke.

The scar-mouthed trooper grinned and reached for a cigar. He was not entirely sure of his act, however, and cast a sly glance at Shafter. He held his hand on the cigar, dividing his attention between the two men, and for a moment he seemed to debate on which side of this coming fight the power lay—and safety for him. Presently he decided the question in Donovan's favor, picked up the cigar and turned away. In the background Shafter saw the other troopers watching, interested and speculative. It was a break in the dull day, a flash of violence feeding their hungry appetites.

"I'll be behind the stables after tattoo," said Shafter. "Better smoke those things up now, Donovan. You'll be sick of cigars later."

Donovan continued imperturbably with his playing. He said to the room at large, "Listen to the gentleman's words carefully, boys. The gentleman is a sergeant. He is an educated sergeant, sent among us heathens to bring us knowledge."

Supper was over and retreat gone by; twilight came, layer on layer, with its sharpening chill. Along the quadrangle, lights splashed their yellow lanes out of doorways, poured their fan-shaped patterns through dusty windows. A patrol, half a company in strength, came in from the western distance and moved with jaded temper across the parade, equipment clinking in the dark. Shafter strolled along the barracks walk with his cigar, hearing the talk of men come out in drawling eddies, in sudden bursts of laughter, in sharpness, in murmuring. A guard detail tramped briskly by, an officer crossed the parade at full-out gallop; and somewhere a deep voice yelled: "Flynn—hey, Flynn!"

The stars were up, turned brilliant by the cold air, and for a moment Shafter stopped to watch them. Other troopers moved by him, some with idleness and some hurrying to reach the ferry and the gaudy dens beyond the river at the Point. Across the parade, General Custer's house was filled with light and officers and their ladies strolled toward it, the quick and gay voices of these people coming over the long stretch of ground in softened cadence. He listened a moment to those tones of warmth and he stood still with his eyes half closed, and then swung on with the idle current of troopers, moving past the guard gate toward the post trader's store.

He turned about before he reached it, remembering that he had a date with Donovan after tattoo, and he paced back through the outthrown lights of the guardhouse, indifferently noticing an officer appear from the guardhouse, and swung toward Officer's Row at a quick and nervous pace. Twenty feet onward, he heard the officer's stride cease and he heard the officer call at him:—

"Hold up there."

He had not seen the officer's face, but a ruffling chill ran along his back and a strange tight spasm went through his belly as he swung. The officer stood waiting twenty feet away, his face obscured by the shadows; and then the officer murmured in a long, odd voice: "Come here, Sergeant."

Shafter moved up, watching the other man's face take on shape and form— and identity. When he was ten feet removed, he discovered whom he faced and a feeling greater than any feeling he had known for years broke through him and shook him from top to bottom. He came to a stand and remembered he was in uniform, and made his salute.

The lieutenant did not return the salute. He looked upon Shafter with a face exceedingly sharpened by astonishment, by the shock of past memories, by the rousing of old rages and evils. He had no motion in him at that moment, he had only one thought, and this escaped him with a slicing-sharp expelling of wind.

"How in God's name did you get here?"

Shafter could think of but one answer, and made it: "It's a small world, Mr. Garnett. A very small world to a man trying to escape his conscience."

"Your conscience?" said Lieutenant Edward Christian Garnett.

"Yours," said Shafter.

The lieutenant stood still and began to curse Shafter with a softly terrible voice. He pulled up his high shoulders, he straightened his long body and he used his words as he would have used a whip, to cut, to disfigure, to destroy. The guard patrol swung around the corner of the quadrangle and passed close at hand, stopping the lieutenant's voice for a little while, and in this silence Shafter saw the man's pale wedge of a face—so handsome and tempting a face to women—show its hard evil, its unforgiving and brutal blackness. This was Garnett, formed like an aristocrat out of a French novel, with dark round eyes well recessed in their sockets, with a head of dark hair that broke along his forehead in a dashing wave, and a gallant mustache trimmed above a full, thick-centered mouth. He had the whitest of teeth; he had a smile, Shafter remembered, which could charm a woman and capture her without effort. He was a man with the obsession of conquest—the conquest of a woman; he had the predatory instincts of a tiger and no morals, no scruples, no decencies. He had touched nothing that he had not destroyed, so that all along his career was the wreckage of his passing. He was, Shafter bitterly knew, an inner rottenness covered by a uniform, and cloaked by a kind of gallantry which passed for courage.

The patrol passed on. Garnett said, sharply: "See to it that you are not in this fort tomorrow."

"What are you afraid of, Mr. Garnett?"

"Damn you," said Garnett, "speak to me properly."

"Then let us start right. Return the salute I offered you. You were always a slovenly soldier."

Garnett stared at him. "I could prefer charges against you, Shafter."

"Do you want to open the record of the past, Mr. Garnett?" murmured Shafter.

"And how could you open it?" answered Garnett, thinly malicious. "Your word against mine? Who would take it?"

"Captain Moylan is also here," said Shafter. "As a gentleman, I suppose he has kept his knowledge of you to himself. How would you like the ladies of the post to know of the events of your past? It would interfere with your prowling. I think you will never prefer charges against me."

Garnett stepped nearer him. "Listen to me. I have got a hundred ways of getting at you. Believe me, I'll use them all. I'll break your damned back and I'll break your heart. Before I'm through with you, you'll crawl over the hill one dark night and never come back."

"You are a dog, Mr. Garnett," said Shafter.

Garnett lifted a hand and hit him one cracking blow across the face with his open palm. The effect of it roared through Shafter's head; he stepped away and then he stepped forward, to find Garnett backed four paces from him and holding a drawn revolver on him. "Go ahead," Garnett softly murmured. "You are in a hard regiment, Shafter, with damned little mercy shown on insubordination. The colonel would have you shot, as he has had others shot before you."

Over by the guardhouse, the bugler softly breathed into his instrument, readying his lips for tattoo. Shafter waited out the dismal silence, pulling his impulses back into safe place, and spoke to this man he both despised and hated more than any other person upon earth. "I did not know you were here," he said. "Probably I would not have come if I had known it. Still, I'm here. Here I shall stay. And now that you have used your hands on me, I'll tell you something: One way or another, I'll destroy you."

Lieutenant Garnett held the gun on him, watching him with strict attention. He said, "You may go now, Sergeant."

They were alone in the darkness, thus facing. Shafter thought of this, knowing that he had the advantage. By daylight he could not pass the strict line which divided him from Garnett; by daylight Garnett could make him dance. But there would always be times when he might catch this man on even terms; for Garnett would take no chances on his own blemished reputation being published at this post. So Shafter stood his ground and gave Garnett a taste of what would come.

"Put up the revolver and turn about and march away. I think Moylan would relish the opportunity of exposing you."

Garnett cursed him again, in his whispering wicked way. Tattoo broke over the parade, drowning out the sound of Garnett's voice; but he watched the lieutenant's lips form their blasphemies and then close thinly together. The lieutenant holstered his gun, swung and went toward Custer's quarters at a long-reaching pace.

He left behind him a man who, once turned bitter against the world, had mastered his bitterness; and suddenly now was bitter again. He left behind him an enemy of dangerous shape, a man tempered and toughened by a war, knowing its trickeries, its subterfuges, its brutal modes of combat. All that knowledge Shafter had subdued and put aside during the ten following years, but it returned to him as he turned back toward A Company's barrack with tattoo's last notes falling away in softened, melancholy loveliness across the parade and across the dark yonder earth. Nine-o'clock call began to run from post to post as he rounded the barrack and moved through the dark space between barrack and stable. He cut about the stable and found A Company's men waiting in the blackness, all ranked along the river bluff. He saw a shape lift from the earth and heard the shape say:—

"What kept you? Now where's that lantern?"

It was Donovan speaking. He stood heavy-shouldered in the dark, stripped to his shirt, with his paunch spilling over the belt of his trousers. A man moved up and pulled a blanket away from a lantern, so that its light danced in yellow crystals upon the night. Donovan clapped his meaty hands together and held them dropped before him, grinning at Shafter. He was a confident old hand, facing another routine battle; and the battle was life to him, so that he gave no thought to hurt or to injury or to scars. There was no real anger in the man, Shafter understood; Donovan had only used his sarcasm and his ridicule as a weapon to produce the fight he needed as much as he needed food. "Take off your blouse—take off your shirt. I'll have no advantage. I need none."

It was a full ten degrees colder than on the previous night, and a wind played out of the north as an idle warning. Stripping off blouse and shirt, Shafter studied Donovan's bullet-round head, the blunt bevel of his shoulders, the softening pads of fat which lay along his upper arm. The man's coolness, the man's complete calm warned him; this Donovan had been a professional somewhere and thought of his opponent as only another green, awkward one to be pounded down and added to his list. He saw Donovan winking at the dark shape of the crowd.

"If the gentleman is ready," said Donovan with his ridiculing tone, "let's be off to the fair."

He waited no longer. He took a striding, squatty plunge forward, his left fist feinting, his right thundering out. Shafter came in, caught that right-armed blow on his elbow and threw it aside. He hit Donovan hard in the belly; he felt his fist sink into the doughlike fat. He heard Donovan's blast of expelled wind; he shifted his hips as Donovan tried to ram a knee into his crotch; he trapped both of Donovan's arms under his elbows and he rode around a circle as Donovan used his strength to pull free. He let go, hooked a punch against Donovan's kidney and moved away.

Donovan shook his head. Donovan's mouth was open, sucking wind. Donovan's face was rouge red. He gave an impatient cry, his narrowed eyes showing a crimson, sly fury as they studied Shafter. He stood still. He stamped the ground with one foot, shuffled forward and feinted with his body, luring Shafter in. He dropped his arms, opening himself wide, and rushed forward again with his head down, growling strange things under his breath; he was suddenly hard to hit. Shafter tried for the man's belly, missed, and then, before he could swing clear, he was thrown back on his heel and knocked to the ground by a savage punch he had never seen. He rolled and saw Donovan's legs striding forward; he seized Donovan's foot and turned with it and brought the man down. The ex-sergeant struck hard, and the fall drew its grunt, and after that Donovan was a fat ball of fury, reaching and striking and kicking.

Shafter flung himself away, stood up and watched Donovan rise. He hit the Irishman, left and right hand, in the belly and brought Donovan's guard down. He saw his opening, stepped in and sledged Donovan at the side of the neck. He got two hard blows in before Donovan reached for him and tied him up. He went loose, letting Donovan pay out his strength in the struggle.

Donovan cried, "You damned leech, stand out and fight it!" He used all his muscles and heaved Shafter clear, and raised a hand to brush his sweaty face. Shafter slid in, driving for the man's belly, and saw the sick look that came to Donovan's mouth. Donovan reached for him but Shafter whirled aside, found his chance, and hit him in the kidney again. The man's softness was crawling up on him; he had his mouth sprung wide and his eyes were not clear. Helplessness seemed to come to him, for he shook his head and let his arms drop. Shafter started in, but feinted back as Donovan, playing possum, came to life and struck out in long-reaching left and right blows. He missed and now, off balance, stumbled forward. Shafter caught him with a short, up-cutting blow beneath the chin. Donovan sighed; the power went out of him and he fell slowly and cumbersomely to the dust, his face striking.

The light bobbed up and down in Tinney's hands. Tinney said, "For God's sakes Donovan, quit foolin'!" He ran forward and tickled Donovan with the toe of his boot; he bent nearer and straightened back, to say in a dull astonishment: "He's out."

"Water bucket," said Shafter.

Somebody went running back to the stable while Tinney helplessly circled Donovan with the lantern. "Donovan—hey, Donovan," he pleaded. Troopers formed a fascinated, silent circle. Shafter said, "Tinney, how did you like that cigar?" and watched Tinney's head spring up. Tinney opened his scar-shaped mouth to speak, found nothing to say and slowly backed off. The messenger ran in from the stable and flung a full bucket of water on Donovan's naked torso. The Irishman, half-wakened by it, made a wild swing and got to his hands and knees. He shook his head and looked up. He saw Shafter. He ran a hand over his face to slash the water away. "I got licked?" he said.

"You should quit smoking, Donovan," said Shafter. "Cigars are bad on the wind."

Donovan pulled himself to his feet. He said, "What fool dumped the bucket on me? Because a man is on his knees is nothin'." Then he said curiously, "Was I out?"

"Dead out," said Shafter.

"Then I got licked," said Donovan in a practical voice. He studied Shafter at some length, without resentment. He put out his hand. "That's the end of it," he said. "I never bear a grudge."

Shafter took Donovan's hand, whereupon Donovan thought of something and swung around, pointing a finger at the men of A Company. "When I'm licked, I'm licked. But don't none of you lads think you can do better than me. Don't none of you get fresh with me. I'm still man enough to lick the lot of you. Another thing—if you back-talk the professor here, I'll beat your ears down. You hear?"

He started for the barracks, his head dropped in weariness. Shafter came up to him and laid an arm on his shoulder, so that the two went on through the dark. Donovan murmured: "I'll buy the cigars, bucko. You're all right. If you can lick me, you can wear the stripes. I'd like to see the man that can take 'em off you."

"Donovan," said Shafter. "One night soon we'll take a few of the lads and drop over the river. A little drinking will do no harm."

"Ah," said Donovan, "you're my kind. But if I'd lay off the whiskey you'd never of had me. Professor, this is a damned good outfit."

Shafter moved through the barrack room, putting on his shirt as he walked; he continued on to the porch which confronted the parade and he stood there and felt the ache of his bruises, the loosening aftereffect of the fight. But he knew he had ceased to be an outsider. He had joined the company; he could tell that by the way the men looked at him. This was why he had joined—to be one of a company of men. To be with them and a part of them; remembering away back, he knew that it was in this closeness he had been happiest. Maybe it was discipline or maybe it was service, or maybe it was the feeling of a man as he rode with other men, joined in the roughness, in the brawling and in the fighting, in the lust and evil and in the honesty and the faithfulness that bound them all together. He stood still, coming close to the reason, but never quite grasping the tangible form of it. As he searched himself, going down into the strange places where lived those prime hungers which made him a man, he remembered what things had been important to him in the past, and what things he had missed in civilian life. They were little things, but all of them strong—the sweat that started out of his pores and stung his eyes, the heavy dust rising up from a marching column, the wind against his face when he rode through some early March morning with the fog lifting out of the lowlands of the Wilderness; the rain beating hard upon him until the smell of his uniform was woolly and rank; the pure pleasure that had come to him when, dried and exhausted, he dropped to his belly beside a sluggish branch in Virginia and drank the brackish water until he could hold no more; the evening shadows with the campfires glittering through them and the sound of tired voices coming from afar; the stretch of his leg muscles as he lifted in the saddle for a run; and the wicked satisfaction that came of taking a blow and giving one; and the comfort of the earth as he lay against it—and the calm dark mystery of the heavens as he looked up to them. Each was a little thing, but each one fashioned and formed him and fed him and made life full.

A trooper came out of the barrack and stood silently by; he was a young lad, tall but still not wholly filled out with man's muscles. He had light hair and a fair face and he smiled in an engaging way when Shafter looked at him. He was not more than eighteen. He said wistfully: "I wish I knew how to fight. I mean, well enough to take care of myself."

"It will come," said Shafter.

"Funny thing," said the boy, "I never had a fight."

"It may be you can get through the next forty years without one," said Shafter. "I hope you do."

"A man's got to fight sometime," said the boy.

"Don't look for one—don't give it a thought," said Shafter. "Wait until it comes—and perhaps it will never come." He fell silent, noting the boy's puzzled face. What he had said seemed a contradiction to the lad; and so he quietly added: "Men are not dogs to be growling at each other."

"Well, I suppose so," said the youngster and, still puzzled, moved down the parade toward the south; in that direction, beyond the quartermaster quarters, lay Suds Row, which was a line of houses occupied by married sergeants whose wives were troop laundresses. He heard the boy whistle a little as he moved into the darkness.

Shafter returned to his bunk and pulled off his uniform. Donovan walked out of the washroom, stripped naked. He tapped his paunch, turned red by the punches Shafter had put there. He was grinning. "A good fight, bucko." The first sergeant came out of the orderly room and paused to look at these two.

"What happened to your belly, Donovan?"

"I fell on a picket pin," said Donovan, and grinned again.

Hines said "I'll have to send a detail out to pull up all these picket pins which the men of this troop keep stumblin' over." He showed Shafter a sardonic humor and passed on, grumbling at a group of poker players. "Break up that. Taps is comin'." He left the barrack and went at an old soldier's steady, established pace through the dark, along the side of the quartermaster department and the commissary building; he turned down Officers' Row and stopped and tapped on the door of Captain Moylan's house. When the captain came out, he rendered his slow, grooved salute and said: "He licked Donovan, sir."

"So," said Moylan, and was pleased. "It will be all right."

"It will be better than I thought," agreed Hines. "Now, can he soldier?"

"As good as you or I, Hines."

"Let us not be givin' him too much credit," said Hines. "If the man is half as good as either of us, Captain, he is an angel."

"You'll see," said Moylan.

☆ 4 ☆

On Officers' Row

Lieutenant Garnett moved rapidly over the parade toward Officers' Row, preoccupied and scowling, with the shock of the meeting still affecting him, with fear still a sharp sensation in him. As he came before General Custer's house, he paused to pull himself straight, to compose the expression on his face and to make a few quick jerks at the tail of his coat. Once more in trim, he crossed the porch with his cap removed and tucked in the crook of his left arm.

Mrs. Custer met him, touched his elbow and led him forward to the crowd arranged in groups around the room. She was a demure woman, quietly charming and with a light and softhearted manner of meeting people. She said: "I believe you know everybody, except perhaps our very young and very pretty guest from Bismarck."

She paused before Josephine Russell, who was seated on the piano stool. Lieutenant Garnett's back sprung into a tenser arch, like a race horse waiting the drop of the barrier; his deep-set and slightly mournful eyes saw the girl's prettiness and the hunting instinct in him rose and fashioned a flashing smile, and all the proper gestures of gallantry; he made a show in his uniform—the long straight sweep of his trousers with their broad yellow stripes, the tight brass-buttoned coat above which lay the white wing collar and black cravat. He had a long wedge of a face with an olive pallor which no amount of sun changed and this, against the intense blackness of his wavy hair, made him an extremely striking man.

"Josephine," said Mrs. Custer, "let me present Mr. Garnett. This is Josephine Russell." And then, because Mrs. Custer had a motherly instinct for the men of the command, and loved to make matches, she added with her air of bright and gentle interest, "Mr. Garnett is so wedded to his profession that I fear he has never had time for ladies."

Lieutenant Garnett gave Mrs. Custer a quick glance, suspecting irony; but he saw only a very human pleasure on the face of the commanding officer's wife and so turned and made his distinguished bow. "I must warn you, Miss Russell. There are many bachelors and you will be rushed."

"Ah," said Mrs. Custer, "all the eligible bachelors of the post have rushed her."

"I propose to join their ranks immediately," said Garnett.

Josephine acknowledged the compliment with a smile; she sat with her hands on her lap, pleasantly reposed. Her hair lay darkly back on top of her head, exposing the small and dainty ears with their pearl pendants. She had a soft roundness to her bosom, and she had a reserve in her eyes; and the shadow of strength and intensity behind her smiling greatly intrigued the lieutenant. She said: "The gallantry of the Seventh is well known, Mr. Garnett."

Mrs. Custer went away and for a little while the lieutenant tried his best wares on Josephine, idly but deceptively probing and drawing her out, testing the metal in her, searching for some entry through her vanity, her weaknesses, her romantic notions or her pride. He was a clever man and presently when the general's brother, Captain Tom Custer, came up—a slim, restless man with a boyish and daredevil face topped by lank light hair—the lieutenant passed on to pay his respects to the other officers and their ladies. The general was in a corner, having some sort of tactical discussion with Major Reno and Captain Weir of D Company and the tawny Yates who was commander of F. Garnett left that weighty circle to itself, said a few words to Algernon Smith and Mrs. Smith, joined in with Calhoun and Edgerly for a moment—the latter as handsome a man as himself—and so, punctiliously leaving his word and his smile from person to person, he came finally to Major Barrows and his lady, the major being here on tour of duty from the inspector general's department.

The major was on the small and lean side, leaf brown and quiet of face, very soft of voice and with a taciturn cast to his eyes. A small mustache and imperial gave a tempered sharpness to an otherwise gentle set of features, and his manner in addressing Garnett had a kind of formal courtesy. "Good evening, Mr. Garnett. A pleasant evening."

"Pleasant, but there's a chill in it. Winter's coming."

"Always does," said Major Barrows, inflecting a most commonplace remark with his dryness.

Garnett, usually extraordinarily attentive to the ladies, talked on with the major for a full minute or more before turning his head and looking down at Mrs. Barrows; and then gave her a smile and a word, nothing more. She looked up at him, a woman somewhat younger than her husband, still of feature and with only her eyes showing much expression. She sat back in the chair, her head rested against it so that her throat revealed its ivory lines. Her lids dropped and for a moment her lashes touched as she watched this man— darkly, indifferently, strangely.

The major divided an inexpressive glance between them and then thought to say: "You have met, have you not?"

The major's wife smiled slightly. "Of course. Two or three times."

"My memory for things social has grown rusty," apologized the major. He sought his coat for a cigar, cast a glance at the general and his party and made a little bow to be excused, going over to join that discussion. Garnett thrust his arms across his chest, matching the depthless inspection of the woman with one of his own. In the little pocket of her throat he saw her heart beating and he knew he had stirred her. He had met her at a party like this only a month before, had smiled at her; he had sat beside her at Major Tilford's dinner slightly later, studying her silence and her indifference until he knew what it was. This was his third meeting and he understood what his method was to be with her; it was to be dark and somber, with soft words carrying more in tone than in meaning. The major's wife, he guessed was a lonely woman with un-spent emotions.

"Do you enjoy it here?" he asked.

"Yes," she said, and continued to watch him out of her half-closed eyes. It was a challenge to be met and he murmured: "Of what are you thinking?"

"Many things."

"Have you walked through these shadows, late at night, by yourself?"

"Yes. Often."

"I know what you have felt. I know what you have thought," he said.

"Do you?" she asked. Her eyes grew wider and a slight warmth escaped her control and showed on her lips. He watched her suppress it, he heard practical-ness return to her voice: "You are gallant, Mr. Garnett."

He had interested her but, like a wise campaigner, he did not overdo his pressing; he nodded and turned back to join Calhoun and Edgerly who stood before Josephine. Presently the talk of the older officers interested him and he drifted that way. Weir was speaking:—

"It is absurd to suppose that the Sioux, having had their best country in the Black Hills opened up to the white miner, will not brood upon it. We have respected no treaty we ever made with them. They know we never will. What good is a treaty, solemnly made in Washington, when a month later five hundred white men cross the deadline? The prospector, the emigrant and the squatter have a hunger for gold and land that we cannot stop by treaty. We have spent two years trying to run the whites out of country which we have promised shall be the Indian's. It is an impossible job. The Indian knows we will continue to back him westward until we have pushed him into the ocean. All the Sioux leaders see it. They will make a stand. Of course there will be a campaign next year."

"If so," said Custer, "we shall decisively defeat them."

"I wish," said Weir, "I were as optimistic. All this summer the traders have been freighting repeating rifles up the Missouri, trading for fur. Winchesters and Henrys. They are better arms in many ways than ours. Did I tell you that last week when I took out my company for target practice one third of all our carbines jammed after the fifth shot."

"Tell your recruits to keep the breech mechanism clean."

"That is not the trouble. These cartridges have got a lot of soft base metal in them. The cartridge expands quickly and sticks in the breech. The extractor tears through the rim of the shell—and there's a gun you've got to hack at with a pocket knife."

"Major," said Custer to Barrows, "I wish you'd stress things like that in your report to the department. I have written so many critical letters that I'm regarded as a dangerous and undisciplined officer. I am heartsick at the things I see which I cannot improve. Things which lead a very slimy trail right back to Washington."

Mrs. Custer overheard him and gave him a wifely side glance. But the general, impetuous in any kind of attack, used his words as he would have used a saber. "The post-trader situation is rotten. It is corrupt, it is venal. The prices charged by the post trader here are outrageous. Do you know what his excuse is? It is that his expenses in getting the job were so enormous that he must recoup himself. Why were they enormous? Because there are gentlemen in Washington who sell these post-traderships to the highest bidder. How can such a situation exist? Because there exists a corrupt ring in Washington, so protected by extremely high-placed officials that they cannot be touched."

The group of officers appeared mildly embarrassed. Major Barrows cast his reserved, taciturn glance at the general. "That is a risky thing for an army officer to say, Custer."

"I don't give a continental," said the general. "I personally know of a brother of one official—one of the highest in our land—" he checked himself, looked about the group with his bony, flushed face, and plunged on—"in fact the brother of the very highest public official of our land, who is receiving financial reward for using his indirect influence in assisting civilians to receive these post-traderships from the Department of Interior."

"Custer," said Major Barrows, "no army officer who wishes for a successful career can afford to question civil authority in Washington."

"I shall be in Washington soon," said Custer. "I shall mention the evil as I see it."

Mrs. Custer moved forward and lightly laid her hand on her husband's arm. "You must not ignore the rest of your guests," she said, smiling the dangerous subject away.

Custer immediately grew gentle at her touch. His sharp blue eyes sent a dancing glance around the room and saw his brother, Captain Tom Custer, seated alone in a rear corner of the room, hands over his stomach as he caught a bit of sleep.

"All right, Libby," he told his wife, "I'll be mealy-mouthed." But his eyes returned to the figure of Tom Custer and an edged grin formed beneath the tawny fall of his mustache; he made a signal at Lieutenant Edgerly, who came immediately near. He whispered something in Edgerly's ear. The lieutenant left the room at once.

Major Barrows said: "How certain are you of a spring campaign?"

"Wholly certain," said Captain Weir. "Nothing will stop the Sioux from defending their ground, if we push at them."

"How do you know you'll get orders to push at them?" asked Barrows.

Garnett had meanwhile drifted away and now was again in the corner with Mrs. Barrows. The major slightly changed his stand so that he saw them without turning his head greatly; he watched them as they talked, he watched his wife's face.

Weir said: "People on the frontier want to move west. They see the Indians barring their way. So they shoot a few Indians and then the Indians shoot them. That creates an incident. People here then cry to Congress and Congress puts pressure upon the War Department. We shall be sent out."

Major Reno had not spoken thus far. He was a stocky, rumpled figure, round and sallow of face with black hair pressed down upon his head and a pair of round recessed eyes, darkly circled. He seemed not wholly a part of the group; he seemed outside of it. But he said now: "It will not be a summer's jaunt. We shall face formidable resistance."

"Oh, pshaw," said Custer. "I know Indians. They will see us, and break. The question will not be one of fighting them. The question will be can we reach them soon enough to surround them before they break into little bands and disappear. I can take this regiment and handle the situation entirely."

"Your regiment," said Barrows, "has an average muster of sixty-four men per company. Full strength, you might take eight hundred men into the field. A third of those are apt to be recruits. It is not an extraordinary show of strength."

The general said, with his dogmatic certainty: "The Seventh can whip any collection of Indians on the plains," and turned to meet Edgerly, who had returned with a hank of clothesline. The general looked at his brother Tom, still snoozing in the chair, and chuckled as he took the line. He walked along the edge of the wall; he got down on his hands and knees and crept forward until he was behind Tom Custer's chair. Crouched there, he looped the clothesline around Tom Custer's boot at the instep, made a slip knot and softly drew it tight; then he crawled to a rear window, standing open to the night, and made the other end of the clothesline fast to the window's latch.

Edgerly had meanwhile brought in the guard trumpeter. The general tiptoed to the front of the room and whispered to the trumpeter; he went around to the other officers and softly spoke to them—with Majors Reno and Barrows alone standing indifferent and puzzled in the group. Edgerly closed the front door and the trumpeter retreated into the general's study. The rest of the officers had risen and were waiting Custer's signal.

Suddenly he cut his hand sharply down through the air, the trumpeter blasted boots and saddles into the room and the officers began to rush pell-mell for the door, shouting: "Sioux! Edgerly, get to your troop! They're attacking the back side! My God, they're coming down the hill by the hundreds!"

Custer yelled, "Where's my hat? Reno, take the first troops assembled— Weir—" Somebody yanked open the front door and rushed out, shouting back: "Hurry up!" and hard after that a gun cracked through the night.

Tom Custer came up from his chair in one bound, roused out of his peaceful catnap. Reacting with an old soldier's pure impulse, he made a headlong rush for the door. Three steps took him to the end of the clothesline, which snapped tight and cut his legs from beneath him. He fell in one flat, long-bodied crash, face flat on the floor.

Everybody yelled in terrific delight and even Reno permitted himself a smile. General Custer staggered to the nearest wall and laid himself against it, laughing so uncontrollably that tears rolled along his face. Mrs. Custer, in all this pandemonium, stood still and smiled her gentle smile while Tom Custer, the holder of two Congressional medals of honor, sat up in the middle of the floor and unhooked the clothesline from his boot. He shook his head, staring at all the convulsed shapes around him; he pointed a finger at the general and shook his head, and began to grin. "That was a frivolous kind of amusement. I damned near shook out my teeth."

The general drew a handkerchief from his pocket and wiped away his ribald tears. Major Barrows looked at his wife, who rose; and the two made their expressions of pleasure and departed. Edgerly brought around a rig for Josephine. Gradually the rest of the visitors said good night and went away until the general and his wife were alone.

Mrs. Custer moved upstairs, leaving the general to a restless back-and-forth pacing. He had his hands clasped behind him and now and then stopped to rearrange some object on the table, to change the location of a chair, to lift or lower one of the frayed window shades; and then resumed his nervous traveling. Presently he passed through the doorless arch into a room whose walls were crowded with animal heads, guns and Indian relics. Two large pictures looked down upon his desk; one was of McClellan—to whom he gave a loyalty he seldom gave any other man—and one was of himself in his flamboyant uniform. He sat down and picked up a pen, and sighed his dislike for the chore before him. But physical energy nagged at him and so in a moment he resumed the article he was writing on frontier life for an eastern magazine, sending the pen across the page in a rapid plunging scrawl.

He worked for an hour, tense and aggressive in this thing as he was in all things and abruptly stopped and sat back, listening to the faint scratches of sound coming through the lonely house. Taps blew and the guard call went around. He fidgeted in the chair and lifted his voice: "Libby!"

She descended the stairs, wrapped in an old blue robe, her hair done back for the night and her eyes sleepy. "Libby," he said, "how can I write if you're not around?"

She smiled at him and settled in a chair, all curled in it, and watched him as he read what he had written; she watched his face, her eyes soft and affectionate, and when he had finished she said: "That's very good, Autie."

"Is it?" he asked, like a small boy, anxious for praise. "Is it any good?"

"Nothing you put your hand to is not good."

"Then," he said, "I shall send it, though the Lord knows why they should want to pay me two hundred dollars for it. It will help out on our next trip east, old lady."

"Yes," she said, absent-mindedly. Her thoughts were elsewhere; they revealed a half fear on her face. "Autie—all this talk of a campaign next summer —do you think it will come?"

"I expect so."

"Then I hope winter never passes," she said, suddenly intense.

"Libby," he said, "you were a little cool toward Reno tonight."

"It is not in my heart to be nice to anybody who is not your friend."

"Still, he's an officer of this regiment. We must show no favorites. We must be the same to all."

"I'll try," she murmured.

He smiled at her and rose and went around to her. He lifted her out of the chair and carried her around the rooms, her small protests coming against his chest: "Autie—let me down. Autie—"

"Blow out the lamps," he said, and lowered her by the tables while she blew; and in the darkness he carried her up the stairs. "Autie," she murmured, "I'm too old a woman for such romantic foolishness."

"You are a child," said he.

Major Barrows moved slowly down the walk with his wife, silent as he usually was, preoccupied by his own reflections. Margaret Barrows did not disturb them for she was engaged in thoughts of her own, and so the two reached the house assigned to them. The major lighted the lamp and stood a moment by it, his taciturn eyes observing the willow shape of his wife as she moved about the room, the luminous gravity of her face, the shining in her eyes.

"Pleasant evening," he said.

"Yes."

"Custer was indiscreet. He always is. Nothing saves him but a reputation for dash. That will not save him forever, unless he grows humbler than he is now."

She moved toward him and watched him with that strange expression which always deeply disturbed him; for he was not a stupid man and he knew the depths of his wife's nature, and struggled in his own way to satisfy the rich, racy current of vitality within her. But the stiffness of his nature was a hard thing to change, so that he knew he could not satisfy the romantic side of her character. It troubled him that she stood here now and wanted only some little display of ordinary affection, some word that would please her; and the best he could contrive was a stolid, "I think I'll finish my smoke on the porch. You're a beautiful woman, Margaret. I was conscious of that tonight." He bent forward and kissed her and straightened. She stood a moment longer, permitting him to see the iron control come to her again, and he knew he had failed. She said: "Good night," and went into the bedroom.

The major walked to the porch and sat down, hooking his feet to the rail; there to brood over the fragrance of his cigar. Lieutenant Smith and his wife strolled past, on the way to their own quarters. Mrs. Smith's musical voice came to him. "Good night, Major."

He said, "Good night," and watched the two move through the shadows. They were a well-matched couple, a very gay and companionable woman and a very handsome man; after several years of married life they were still close to each other. Some marriages were like that, he thought, in which the dispositions, the tastes and hungers of two people were so perfectly matched that the union was indestructible. It was an uncommon thing, and a beautiful thing to see, and it made him keenly feel his own failure. Life was mostly humdrum, drudgery and tedious hours stretched end on end; for him that was well enough but for his wife it was a kind of suffocation against which she fought. She needed brightness and drama and moments when her cry for beauty would be answered. He thought: "If I could play the gallant part, if I could go to her as a swashbuckling man and sweep her up and arouse her and stir her all through—" But he shook his head, knowing he was not that kind of man; even if he tried to play the part it would not come off. Some men were born for one thing, some for another. As he sat there thinking of this and knowing his wife's terrible need for some kind of release, he felt a tragic unhappiness for her.

Lieutenant Smith and his wife moved into their quarters and made ready for bed. Smith said: "That was strong meat Custer was serving up—that talk about graft and scandal. All true, every word of it, but he's on dangerous ground talking about it."

"He loves dangerous ground," said his wife. She sat on a chair scarred by repeated ownerships and changes of station, before a bureau made of scrap lumber by some trooper of the command. There was a mirror one foot square on the wall and into this she looked as she took down her hair. It was another threadbare room to match all the threadbare rooms along Officers' Row, with a dull neutral wallpaper pasted against the uneven walls. The floor was bare boards painted brown and at the windows hung those same green sun-cracked shades which were to be seen in all the quarters. One austere army rule covered these habitations: No house should be better than another house and no family was to have more comforts than another family. Therefore all quarters were shabby and mean and without grace, except as the small pocketbook of the officer could improve them. In the East these houses would have been tenements belonging near the railroad track.

"So he does," said Smith. He pulled off his shoes, removed his shirt, and sat back to enjoy a last fragment of his cigar.

"I never cease to think of that," said Mrs. Smith.

"What?"

"All of you—forty officers and eight hundred men—are in the hands of one impulsive commander. When he courts danger for himself, he courts it for you."

"That's the way of soldiering. You're old enough a campaigner by now to know it couldn't be otherwise."

"I'm old enough a campaigner to know that no commander has the right to take risks for the fun of it, or for personal glory, or for newspaper stories back east, or to show his enemies what a great soldier he is."

He looked at his wife with some surprise. "How long have you been thinking these things?"

"A long while."

"You shouldn't harbor them in your head. It's been a long stretch for you out here in this dreary nowhere. I should have sent you east last fall."

She looked at him, disturbed yet affectionate. "You know we couldn't afford it. If we could have, I wouldn't have gone without you. What fun would that be?"

"Well," he said, "it would have been nearer possible last year than now."

"Are we broke?"

He grinned, taking it an easy way. "Just more broke than usual. That last change of station set us back a lot in railroad fare." He thought about it a long interval, then sighed and said, "Maybe someday the government will be generous enough to pay for the transportation of an officer's wife when she follows her husband from post to post." Then he added, "Not that I'm complaining. We have had good times. We're healthy. We sleep well. We have few worries."

"And when you die," said Mrs. Smith with a touch of irony, "the government will even be generous enough to bury you without expense."

"Ah, now," he said, and grinned, "you get that out of your head, old girl."

She was not a woman to complain and not a woman to fret with him or to add to his worries; yet tonight a good many small things seemed to collect in her mind and make her restless.

"I heard the general speak of a campaign next spring. Is it that certain?"

"Looks so. Government has been sending expeditions out there year after year without results. The Sioux grow more discontented. The settlers become more insistent on opening the country. We've been hearing that government intends to order all Sioux back to their reservations permanently. The Sioux will not comply. I think we shall see a big campaign, intended to end the question once and for all."

She sat still, thinking of his words; and her face darkened and he saw worry he had not seen before. It made him say again, very regretfully: "I wish I'd sent you back east for a vacation."

"No," she said, "it isn't that. I can't help thinking of the general's temper. He would throw this regiment away, all in a moment of recklessness."

"He would be at the head of it when he threw it," Smith gently reminded her.

"I believe," she said, "you'd appreciate a campaign full of fighting."

He gave that a moment's consideration and arrived at his basic belief in the matter. "After a winter of garrison confinement, I'm always glad to be riding out. But after a summer of eating dust I'm always glad to come back. No, I think I prefer easy ways to hard ones. But that's scarcely the point, is it? The government has trained me to take the hard ways. We're not in the hands of Custer, old girl. We're all in the hands of our country."

She shrugged her shoulders and went to bed. Smith finished his cigar and walked through the house in his nightgown, blowing out the lights; and came beside his wife. He put his arm around her. "You're a little blue tonight."

"I wish," she whispered, "I knew what was troubling me. It is there, but I can't name it. Sometimes it is a lump in my stomach."

"Maybe we'd better have Porter give you a looking-over."

"You idiot," she said, "you know I'm healthy as a horse," and moved against him.

After leaving Shafter, the young trooper—Frank Lovelace—walked into the night, his desires setting a compass course toward Suds Row. He thought of

Shafter in youth's instinctively admiring way. He was greatly impressed by the sergeant's coolness and quietness under strain and he wistfully wished that he might have the same kind of qualities. His age made him dream of great things; and his vivid imagination placed him in the sergeant's shoes, so that he saw himself equally cool and brave and triumphant. This was the world he made for himself, but he was young and therefore he was unsure, not knowing his capacities and secretly doubting himself.

He turned into Suds Row and passed along the row of small houses occupied by the married sergeants. He had been walking rapidly; now he dropped to a slow saunter and began to whistle. When he passed the house of Mary Mulrane, he gave the lighted window a swift sidewise glance and saw Mary's father, old Mulrane who was a sergeant major, bowed over a paper on the table. Young Lovelace continued his stroll to the end of the row and stood a moment listening to the Missouri lap at the base of the bluff. He turned back. Mulrane's door had opened, letting out a bright gush of light; it closed again and he felt dispirited. But when he came abreast the house he found Mary waiting.

He turned in and saw her face pale in the shadows; he touched her with his hand and he drew her smile. He stood still, a wonder and a wanting rushing through him and setting off the purest and most violent kind of flame, and he drew a long sigh and thought of nothing to say. He saw the way she held up her head and he thought he might kiss her; but he never had kissed her and he didn't want her to think the wrong thing about him. She waited, watching him, the smile steady on her face. Presently she came from the wall and slipped her hand into his hand and walked back down the row beside him.

He said: "It's cold tonight. Aren't you cold?"

"No. I'm not cold at all."

"I should think you would be."

"It's pretty tonight."

"Yes," he said. "The darkness just kind of stretches away. Like it was moving." They came to the edge of the bluff and he reached down and got a chunk of earth; he threw it and waited, and long afterwards heard it strike the river. He said: "The river's always going somewhere. I wish I could get in a rowboat and just drift. Next week, Yankton. Then St. Louis. Then New Orleans."

She didn't answer him and he felt her somehow draw away from him. She didn't stir, but she wasn't as near him as she had been. He could feel it distinctly. Then she said: "Do you want to go that bad?"

"Oh," he said, "it isn't that. I'd just like to be doing something. I'd like to see the country."

"The girls in the South," she said, "are supposed to be very pretty."

"I wasn't thinking of that," he answered at once. "I'd like—" But he didn't know what it was. It was something formless; it pushed at him and it pulled at him, it filled him up.

"You're funny," she murmured.

He looked at her and saw her smiling again. She was near him, she was watching him closely. He said: "It's tough to just stand around when everything is happening everywhere. I've got three more years to serve. When I get out, what'll I be? Nothing at all."

She murmured: "I think you're something."

He looked at her, his pulse beating faster. He waited a long while, on the edge of what he wanted; he felt himself shoved toward it but he knew he never would take the chance of making her think he was another easy trooper. She made a little motion with her head and she looked away from him a moment and took his hand again, standing still. "I get lonely too, sometimes," she said, and turned her face toward him. Suddenly a kind of terror went through him for what he knew he was about to do, but he couldn't help it. He put one arm around her and saw that she didn't draw back. Her face was still near him and just below him. He put both arms around her and kissed her. He was trembling, he was hot, he was cold. He squeezed her until a sigh came out of her; he felt the heat and the urgent sweetness of her mouth and it astonished him to realize she held him as tightly as he held her. He felt her fingers at the back of his neck.

She stepped away, looked at him a moment; she dropped her head against his chest and continued to hold him. He heard her murmur: "Did you mean that, Frank? It wasn't just something you'd do to any girl if you got the chance?"

"Oh, no," he said, shocked.

"I'm glad. I wouldn't let anybody else do it."

They heard Mulrane calling in his thick Irish voice: "Mary," and turned to see the sergeant blocked against the light of his open door. Mary Mulrane softly laughed and seized young Lovelace's hand and walked up the street with him. Young Lovelace felt the sergeant's hard eyes on him, and was embarrassed. But Mary held his hand so that her father could see it.

"Going out like that;" said Mulrane, "in a cold night without a coat. Where is your mind awanderin'?"

"It isn't cold," said Mary.

"Ah," said the sergeant, "it isn't cold, is it?" And he grunted something under his breath. "You come in. And you, Lovelace, you had better get back before you're picked up by the rounds. Taps will be blowin'."

"Yes," said Lovelace and started up the street. He had gone a few feet when he heard Mary murmur something. In another few feet the sergeant's voice came after him. "Come to Sunday supper, Lovelace."

"Thanks," said Lovelace, and went on. The earth came up and struck his boots; but it was soft—the earth was—and it seemed to roll and sink with his weight. The air was fine and cold and full of fine smells and the night's sky sparkled with its diamond stars. He could not breathe enough; he could not feel enough. Taps broke as he entered the barrack. Tinney saw him and Tinney gave him an evil grin. "Pickin' up your washin' again? I saw Purple down that way tonight. Maybe he was pickin' up his laundry too."

Lovelace said, "Ah," and turned to his bunk. But after the lights were out he lay on the bunk and was racked by doubt, by a deep hate of Tinney and Purple. He thought: "I've got to learn to fight." He lay still and suffered.

Rehearsal for a Tragedy

At six o'clock in the morning Lieutenant Algernon Smith led twenty men of A Company out upon the parade, joined a platoon of L Company waiting there under Garnett, and made a motion of his hand which put the combined column across the parade. The troopers moved two by two through the guardhouse gate, rode up the slope of the ridge east of the post and came to its crest, facing the desert's long western reach, now a-smolder with the tan and ashy colors of fresh sunlight.

Shafter rode as right guide at the head of the column, Smith beside him. Adjoining the lieutenant was the civilian guide, a tall and very thin man wearing a sloppy blue serge coat and a hat scorched by many campfires and discolored by many a dip into wayside creeks. His name was Bannack Bill and he had a gaunt neck up and down which an Adam's apple slid like a loose chestnut; his calico eyes, half hidden behind dropped lids, never ceased to search the landscape.

Early morning glumness held the troopers silent; they rode half awake, slumped on their McClellans, gradually taking on life as the sun warmed them and the steady riding loosened their muscles. All this was familiar country, and the ride was just one more scout detail flung out daily to keep an eye on the Sioux, who moved in mercurial restlessness over the land. East of the river the Indians lived in sulky peace and paid their visits to Bismarck, sitting in motionless rows along the sidewalk. East of the river they were a subjugated race. But west of the river they were a free and intractable people, at peace if it pleased them and at war if it pleased them, made haughty and insolent by the memory of the many evils done them by white people, made proud by the recollection of their vanishing freedom, made warlike by nature. They came into the post to hold council with the general and the pipe was smoked and presents passed and gestures of friendship made; but at night these same warriors waited in the darkness outside the guard line to cut down whatever foolish trooper strayed beyond the limit of safety. East of the river a man might sleep at night in safety but west of the river was only an uneasy peace maintained by the threat of guns —Indians and soldiers facing each other with the knowledge that the penned-up flood of hatred and vengeance grew stronger and stronger behind its barrier.

Bannack Bill made a little gesture and rode wide of the column, staring toward the ground as he traveled. He came back. "Small party headin' south. Half a dozen bucks. Dozen kids and women. Four travwaws."

Algernon Smith turned to Shafter. "You're new. Maybe you don't know what we're doing."

"No sir."

"Keeping watch on these people. Never know what they might do. Maybe they'd strike against the fort some night to drive off stock. Maybe they might try to raid the guard lines. The only way we can guess their state of mind is to watch the trails they make—to see if they're collecting any place in a big bunch, which is always indication of something in the wind. Unusual activity is a good sign that they're disturbed. Right now it is customary for them to collect from summer villages and go down to the Agency for the winter. If they go down in big numbers we can guess they're going to cause us no trouble until spring. If they stay away from the Agency we can expect something." A little later the lieutenant added: "Of course there are many villages, farther west, who never come in. They're beyond our reach."

The middle of the morning, some thirteen miles from the fort, the column came upon little hills and bluffs bordering the meandering course of Heart River. At this time of the year the river had receded to a small creek, over which the command passed easily, wound through willow and cottonwood and filed through a series of gullies. A ridge ran to either side of the column, shutting off the farther view of the land. Lieutenant Smith scanned it with a moment's professional interest, turned and made a motion of his hand which was sufficient to send a pair of troopers forward to act as points for the column, to send another pair galloping up the side of the left ridge—and a third pair toward the summit of the right ridge.

Bannack Bill meanwhile had found himself another interesting set of tracks and pursued them forward at a trot, his light body jiggling up and down on the saddle. Lieutenant Garnett, hitherto riding halfway down the column, now came forward to travel beside Smith.

"Usual course this time, Smith?"

"Unless we run into something that draws us aside."

Shafter sat easy in the saddle, pleased as he had not been pleased for ten years. Behind him were the usual sounds of troopers in motion, the squeezing sibilance of leather, the off-key clinking of metal gear and the slap of canteens, the murmuring play of talk among the men, the sudden chuffing of a horse. He turned and saw the column stretch two and two behind him in blue-figure line, the men so dark of face that their eyes seemed to glitter; it was a tough, raw-boned line—like a sinuous whip being dragged across the country. Carbines lay athwart each man's pommel; the yellow seam of each noncom's pants leg made a splash of color. He saw Donovan's round raw face slowly grin and Donovan's eyelid slowly wink; he settled himself frontward again and he thought: "A damned fine life I have been missing." Around him eddied the odor of dust and the odor of his horse—and the smell of his own body rendering up its warmth. All of it was good.

Smith said: "Tell flankers and point men to get farther ahead," and sent off the trumpeter with the message. The trumpeter's name was Kane and he was a round and ruddy-faced boy who had creased the front brim of his cavalry hat upward so that it gave him a dash; he left the column like a gunshot, flinging his horse into an instant run, body swinging on the saddle. Directly in rear of Shafter, Corporal Bierss and a private by the name of Jordan were rolling out the tempting juices of one obscene story and another, each man matching story for story. Donovan, overhearing this, called forward to Bierss. "Lad, you talk too big. You don't know that many women."

"I meet 'em quick—I get rid of 'em quick."

"Like Kimono Lizzie in the Big Bend House," said Donovan.

The column liked that and laughed at it, though the laughter didn't trouble Bierss. He said amiably: "She wasn't no lady, so I left."

"By the second-story window," said Donovan.

"It was too much trouble walkin' back down the stairs," said Bierss.

"Just so," jeered Donovan. "There was a sergeant from D Company comin' up the stairs, him havin' a better track on Lizzie."

That did disturb Bierss, who said: "The hell with any sergeant from D. I wouldn't walk a foot from none of that crowd. And he didn't have no better track than I had."

"Whut'd you jump out the window for then?"

Bierss thought rapidly and came out with a virtuous answer. "I wouldn't compromise a lady."

A shout of laughter exploded and rolled down the column and came echoing back. The effect of it pleased Bierss, who grinned beneath his ragged dragoon mustaches and shook his shoulders into squarer shape. The two officers rode on in self-enforced isolation, hearing it all but ignoring it. The column came up from a long ravine and faced a desert studded with glacial rocks. Ahead of them stretched a bumpier country, and still farther ahead the misshapen outline of badlands showed through the thin fall haze.

The point scouts had gone forward, the flankers were working off to a greater distance, and the civilian guide was two miles in advance, just now entering a scattered fringe of trees which marked a creek flowing from the northwest. Smith shook his head. "Bill's too old a hand to be doing that. He might get jumped before we could reach him."

"Old ones get careless," said Garnett.

"Damned seldom," said Smith. "That's why they live to be old."

He had not sent out advance scouts to survey the previous crossing. But they were now thirty miles from the fort, and in deeper Indian land, wherefore he watched the two point men as they moved cautiously upon the timber before them and presently turned his head to Shafter. "Take six men and go up there."

Shafter half swung in his saddle. He made a motion that pulled the three nearest sets of twos away from the column, and set his horse to the gallop across the ground. He had Corporal Bierss with him and Bierss still held on with his stories:—

"So I saw she was lookin' at me with somethin' in her eyes and I knew all I had to do was . . ."

Shafter watched the two point men fade into the timber; when he got within a hundred feet of it he waggled a hand to left and right, bringing his six men into skirmish line. All these troopers knew their business and spread farther and farther apart as they approached the timber, and so went into it, threshing carefully through. They crossed a creek, breasted a loose thicket and reached the top of a small bluff. Shafter stopped here, waiting for the main command to come up. They dismounted and crouched down to break the riding monotony, and Bierss took time to catch a smoke. "You been at this kind of business before, Sarge?"

"Yes."

"I thought so. Ever in the South?"

"Yes."

"The girls down there," said Bierss dreamily, "have got skin the color of cream."

"Beautiful faces," agreed Shafter.

"Wasn't talking about their faces," said Bierss.

The main column splashed over the creek, came grunting up the side of the bluff. The advance group went to the saddle and fell in at the head of the column. Smith swung it left, climbing again to the crest of a ridge wherefrom he might see the roundabout pockets and ravines; the flankers in the distance were rising and falling across this rough ground like small boats in a heavy seaswell. Smith grunted and shaded his eyes against the western sun, looking at the small figure of the guide who, two miles forward, now turned his horse and rode a steady circle in signal. Smith said "Gallop," and put the troop to a run.

The troop whirled down the ridge, the horses grunting as they pitched across the uneven ground, accouterments banging and slapping down. The civilian guide waited sedately, and pointed to the south, whereupon Smith brought the column to a halt with a downthrust of his hand. He looked back at the strung-out column. He called testily: "Stop that sleeping on your elbows. Close up— close up! Sergeant McDermott, what are you back there for?" Then he looked ahead once more in the direction which had drawn the guide's interest.

Off there, now showing on a ridge, now lost in a depression, Shafter saw a column moving beneath the shape of its own dust—a long string of ponies and riders and travois; and over the distance he heard Indian dogs barking.

"Biggest one yet," said the guide. "Fifty lodges in that outfit."

Garnett said, with a show of eagerness: "Let's go have a look."

Smith was a cooler and more reflective man, with considerable experience in frontier campaigning. He considered Garnett's wish, and rejected it. "As long as they're heading for the Agency there's no point in our stopping them. They might misjudge our intentions as we rode up, and prepare for a fight. One shot by a careless buck would start trouble which nobody wants or intends."

"I hate like hell to let them think we're avoiding them," grumbled Garnett.

"That's scarcely the point," Smith said dryly, and put the column forward at its former pace and in its day-long direction. This march carried them along the ridge, so that they were in plain sight, and gradually as they moved west they had a better view of the long Indian column as it wound through and around and over the depressions and hummocks of the land. The head of the column passed out of sight on the yonder side of a ridge, but a group of warriors came streaming back on their ponies, stopped at the end of their column and stood watchfully there, faced against the cavalry. Presently, as the tail of the column dropped over the ridge, this rear-guard wheeled and went scudding away—a thin yell of defiance floating back.

"That's all right—that's all right," grumbled Garnett. "We'll take care of that someday."

"Possible," said Smith, still dry-toned, and gestured the command forward.

The sun's violent flame rolled back like sea waves across butte and ridge and far-scattered clumps of timber; into that yellow flare the column rode with growing weariness and longer silences. At six o'clock Smith rose in his stirrups to have a look before him; at six-thirty the command had camped in a grove beside another small creek, the horses standing on picket, the guards posted, the campfires burning and the smell of coffee and bacon drifting in a chilling air. Men went beating along the earth with sticks, routing out rattlesnakes, and the sun sank and twilight fell full-handed upon the earth—and then the stars were all a-shine across infinity's pure space and the campfires became round, dull spots in the black. Shafter rolled in his blanket, settled his head on the saddle and for a few drowsy moments listened to the murmuring around him. The creek left a smooth, undulating tone behind as it ran north and the smell of the half-dead fires drifted against Shafter's face to remind him of a thousand bivouacs, and so to revive one by one the tangled memories of his past. Weariness played through his bones—the wonderful luxury of physical looseness rolling all along his body; and his cares and strange involved wanderings went away, taking him back to the pure simplicity of being one tired man sleeping near other tired men.

There were no trumpet calls on scout patrol. Men stirred out of sleep and saw daylight crack through the eastern blackness; and sat up to put on their hats, their blouses and their boots, thus rising full-dressed. One trooper gave a springing shout and jumped aside and began to swear; he got a stick and beat the life out of a rattlesnake which, drawn by warmth, had spent part of the night curled against his blanket. A water detail took the horses down to the creek, vanishing in the damp fog. Fires sprang up, rich yellow in the half light, and the smell of coffee and bacon pungently spread. An hour before sunrise the company moved out, silent and cold and morose.

The way now was southwest as the column began to make its curve upon the land and strike homeward; but the guide said, "I'll look yander a bit," and rode straight into the west. Somewhere near the tail end of the column a trooper began to sing and was stopped by half a dozen grumbling voices. A bleak chill lay in the still air, its thin edge cutting against face and hand; the breath of the horses laid little puffs of visible moisture against the light. Sunrise broke tawny in the east, bright but heatless, and the sleazy fog lying over the earth vanished. The horses' hoofs struck and rattled along scattered rock brought down by glaciers tens of thousands of years before, and little patches of alkali showed on the ground, and clouds of small black birds wheeled up and went away in wheeling billows.

Far ahead of them the guide came into view on a ridge and circled his horse as he had done the preceding night. Smith watched the guide a long while but forbore to push the troop into a gallop because of the rocky underfooting. He swung the column to higher ground and then, clearing the gravel, simply waved his hand overhead; the column burst into a steady run, with the lieutenant's glance now and then going back to see how the formation was. His voice laid down a growling insistence.

"Keep up—keep up. Dooly, handle your horse." Garnett had come abreast of Smith again, but the senior lieutenant gave him a tough look and said: "Ride back." Garnett dropped to the rear. The lieutenant, Shafter decided, was that kind of officer who kept his amiability and charm for the social hours; on duty he was a brusque man attending strictly to business and determined that others under him should attend to theirs.

The column followed Bannack Bill downgrade toward a thin fringe of willows scattered along a creek. There was something scattered on the ground which, upon a steady inspection, had to Shafter a familiar attitude; he had seen many men thus, arms crooked carelessly, bodies lying in the disheveled posture of death. The guide waited near by and said nothing when Smith halted the column. There were three men stripped naked, two of them apparently beyond middle age and a young one. This was not entirely a matter of certainty, for they had all been scalped, their heads cracked in and their bodies mutilated. Each man had half a dozen arrows thrust into him.

"Look like prospectors coming back from the Black Hills," commented Smith. "Ever see them before, Bill?"

"Can't recognize 'em."

"Not dead long. They've not swollen much."

"Sometime yesterday afternoon," said the guide. He got down from his piebald horse and had a look around the ground. "They hadn't started a fire and so I guess they were just makin' camp."

There wasn't much to show the story for there was nothing left except the bodies. Horses, equipment and supplies had been carried off. One white trail showed where a warrior had dumped the prospector's flour and, a few yards from the scene, a muslin bag of beans lay spilled on the ground.

"It was that party we passed yesterday late," said Bannack Bill.

"How sure are you of it?" asked Smith.

"A party of bucks would of sculped these fellers and let it go like that. That knife work was done by squaws and the arrers prob'ly by kids practisin' up on their shootin'. You'll find them scalps with that party."

"We'll go see," said Smith.

He led the column to the creek and let it water, and then swung back into the southwest, moving at a walk through the rough gravel-strewn valley. They traveled steadily, passing over small ridges and into other small lands of level grass, and through broken formations and areas of upheaval. Near eleven o'clock they cut the trail of the large party bound south for the reservation and came upon an old Indian lying alone in the half-warm sun. He rose to his elbows and looked at them with a bitter-black glance out of his shrunken, disease-ravaged face, half expecting death at the hands of the troopers; and fell back on his side, not caring. The troop passed on.

Smith spoke to Shafter. "You've had campaign service?"

"Yes sir."

"How much?"

"Four years and a half."

"Any against Indians?"

"Half a year against the Comanches down in the Nations."

"I like to know how far I can depend on my sergeants," said Smith briefly, and fell silent. He had followed the Indian trail directly for an hour when he left it and moved over a hill to the west and set his troop into a gallop along a sandy valley. They went this way, walking and running, until the sun tipped over the line and started down; and then the lieutenant stopped the command for half an hour's nooning. When he moved the column on again it was straight to the south in a line that roughly paralleled the course of the Indian band. Around two o'clock he called Garnett forward.

"Take Shafter and the first ten troopers and scout to the left. Don't expose yourself. My desire is to come in ahead of the Sioux and catch them before they can set themselves for trouble. If you sight them, send back a messenger and wait for me to come up."

Garnett nodded his head and started away with his detachment. Smith's voice came after him, sharply inquisitive. "Do you thoroughly understand you are not to precipitate any action of your own if you sight them?"

"Yes," said Garnett, and rode on.

Shafter moved beside the lieutenant, jarred out of his calm, suddenly heated by his anger and his contempt and his savage distrust of Garnett. He ignored the lieutenant as they slanted up the side of the valley's east ridge, zigzagging around rock shoulders, following old deer and antelope trails. Looking back he saw the rest of the command streaming directly south, kicking up a heavy pall of dust. A hundred feet short of the ridge's crest, Garnett stopped his detachment and nodded at Shafter.

"Climb up there on foot and see what's beyond."

There was still some distance that might have been covered on horse, relieving that much foot labor, but Shafter got out of the saddle, handed over his reins to Corporal Bierss and climbed upward over the spongy soil, his boots sliding back on the slick, summer-cured grass. The climb made him reach for wind and he knew this was Garnett's idea of hazing him. Near the crest of the ridge he flattened down, removed his hat and looked over. There was a succession of low, choppy ridges before him, and no sight of Indians. He turned and gestured the command forward, and got into his saddle when it came.

Garnett led his detachment down the far side of the ridge at a quartering run, crossed through a series of little pockets and started up the side of another ridge. Halfway to the top he spoke to Shafter again. "Scout ahead on foot. Make it faster. We're losing time."

Shafter dropped to the ground, catching a puzzled stare from Bierss; he moved up the slope, digging his heels against the turf, and flattened and looked over the high ground into a small cross ravine which led from the valley in which the main column moved to the one where the Sioux were presumably traveling. He saw nothing and once more signaled up the detachment. Garnett, when he arrived, said:—

"You ride ahead. Half a mile. When you come near the summit of these rolls of ground, go up afoot and have a look. You'll have to move fast to keep ahead of us."

Shafter got on his saddle and started away. Garnett's sudden-loud voice turned him. "Did you hear what I told you?"

"Yes sir," said Shafter.

"Then speak up when I give you an order," said Garnett.

"Yes sir," said Shafter and swung off. He dropped down into the canyon and slanted up another slope until he got within ten feet of its summit, and went the rest of the way afoot. A plateau lay before him, badly broken into gullies, dappled with small knobs and minor pinnacles, and beyond that there seemed to be a drop-off into a definite valley. He stopped long enough to signal the detachment forward and proceeded into the rough terrain.

There was no clear view of any of this for more than three hundred yards in any direction and therefore he kept a sharp watch around him, realizing that it was likely the Indian party might have its own scouts out. Garnett, he guessed, had thought of the same thing in sending him forward alone. The lieutenant had a fixed hatred of him.

He passed around a knob and looked back in time to see the detachment rise to the crest behind him. He waved at it and dipped into a gully, followed it to a butte and circled the butte; and thus he veered and tacked his way forward until he reached what seemed to be the final ridge on the plateau. He crawled the last few yards and looked over the crest into a plain running eastward toward the Missouri. Out there, close by the base of the plateau, the Indian band moved sedately southward, enveloped in its own dust.

He made his way leisurely down the hill and lay back on the ground until the detachment came up. Garnett rode his horse almost on top of him. Shafter rose slowly, and enjoying the black flash of temper he saw leap into Garnett's eyes. "Over the ridge, just below us," he said and swung to the saddle.

Garnett said: "Maybe we should have brought a bed for you," and wheeled the column away. Shafter turned to look back at Bierss; he saw Bierss grinning, and he winked at Bierss, knowing that the lieutenant also saw this from the corner of his eyes. They ran along the foot of the ridge, turned a corner of an intervening butte, and discovered Smith riding upgrade from the west with the rest of the command. Garnett lifted in his saddle and made a wheeling gesture with his arm, pointing east. Smith acknowledged it but made no effort to hurry his command on the slope of the hill; therefore Garnett halted his group and waited. There was a quarter-hour delay, but Garnett held his men tight in their saddles, giving them no chance to dismount. He sat still, completely ignoring the command.

Smith came up and said: "Whereabouts?"

"Over the ridge."

"Garnett," said Smith, "you should know enough to rest your men when you have the chance." He led the column forward, staying beneath the shelter of the ridge and following it across the plateau until it pinched out. When they broke over the summit of the plateau they were within five hundred feet of the Sioux, face-on with them. Smith trotted his column forward. He turned in the saddle to speak back to the troopers. "No false motions now," he said. "Wait for my commands." He spoke in a lower tone to Garnett. "We shall ferret out the warriors who did the killing. I propose to take them back to Lincoln."

"Like hunting for a piece of coal in the cellar on a black night without a match."

"There are ways of doing it," said Smith. "Hold yourself ready to do what I say. When I swing side to side in the saddle, drift the column into a skirmish line very slowly."

"Very well," murmured Garnett, a touch of irritation in his voice. Smith heard that and gave his junior officer a sharp glance: "I don't want any damned notions of gallantry or dash to upset this job." The column of Sioux was immediately before him and he flung up his hand to halt the troopers. He said to Shafter and to Bannack Bill, "Come with me," and rode forward.

A line of warriors milled out from the rear of the long Indian column, racing forward, low-bent and weaving on their ponies. The older men in the forefront of the procession ranked themselves and sat still. Smith stopped in front of them and murmured to Bannack Bill:—

"Tell them I'm glad to see them and hope they have had a good summer. Tell them I presume they're going to the Agency for winter. Tell them we're pleased to have them come in, that the meat is fat at the Agency. Tell them any compliment you happen to think of for about two minutes. I want to watch these young bucks while you're talking."

Bannack Bill began to speak, using his hands to cut sign across the air. The leading Sioux, all old men with faces bronzed and chiseled by weather and years, listened. They were wholly still except for their eyes, which lay on Bill as he spoke, and darted covert glances at the lieutenant, and struck shrewdly farther out to the waiting troopers. The younger men of the band had drifted forward, forming a scattered semicircle.

Shafter murmured: "There's a fresh scalp hanging to the arrow pouch of that pug-nosed lad out on the left."

"Very good, Sergeant," said Smith coolly. "That's what we're looking for."

"You'll probably find the blankets and the clothes among the squaws."

"Ever try to handle a squaw?" said Smith, dryly. "We'll leave those dusky beauties alone."

Bannack Bill finished his interpreting and sat idle in the saddle. All the old men remained silent, thereby lending dignity to the parley. A good deal later one of them straightened on his horse and spoke in the guttural, abrupt Sioux tongue.

Bill said: "He says he's very happy to see the government soldiers. They are his friends. He is their friend. All Sioux are friends of all whites. All whites should be friends of the Sioux, though sometimes they are not. He says he is on his way to the Agency and is glad to hear the beef is fat. Most years, he says, it is very poor and the Indians starve. Why is that, he asks."

"Don't tell him I said so, Bill," said Smith, "but there isn't any answer to that question. There are as many white thieves as red ones and probably he's dead right. Tell him I'm happy to see him in such good health, tell him things like that for a couple more minutes."

"By God," said Bill, "I can only invent about so many lies. Anyhow, these old codgers know what you're up to."

"How do they know?"

"You got here too fast from where they saw you last."

"Tell him we're all happy," said Smith.

Shafter said: "The lad next to the lad with the scalp has got a gold watch and chain wrapped around his neck."

"Two out of three will do nicely," said Smith. "You've got a good eye, Sergeant." He eased himself in the saddle, rolling from side to side, which was his signal to Garnett a hundred feet behind him. The old Sioux men watched him in beady interest, their glances flicking back to the troopers now idly deploying into skirmish line. The young bucks saw it as well and stirred uneasily, drifting their ponies back and forth.

"Bill," said Smith, "tell him we're happy over everything but the murder of the three white men. Ask him if he knows of that evil thing."

Bannack Bill murmured: "You sure you're ready to start the fireworks?"

"Let it start," said Smith. He waited until Bannack Bill began speaking; then he turned his head and gave Shafter the kind of glance which not only delved for toughness in another man, but mirrored his own essentially hard spirit. "We need a display of decision here, Sergeant. It has to be done quietly, but without any show of hesitation. When I give the word, ride over and bring out those two bucks. I shall back you up."

Shafter said, "Yes sir," and felt the continuing force of Smith's glance. The lieutenant was aware of the risk involved in so brisk a show of power, for the warriors in this band were all well-armed and they could muster as much strength as the detachment. Meanwhile Bannack Bill said his say and waited for reply. It was not long in coming. The old spokesman of the Sioux straightened himself, pointed to the earth, to the sky and to the four cardinal points, no doubt invoking all the gods he knew about to attest his sincerity, and launched into speech.

"Winding himself up," murmured Smith and impassively listened. When the old one had finished, Bannack Bill paused a moment to summarize what he had heard, and proceeded to translate it freehand.

"The old codger decorates his damned lie as follows: His heart is pure, his mouth is wide open to truth, his soul is hurt to think the lieutenant would think that Red Owl's band would hurt a white man. Not one of his people touched a hair on those three prospectors. He has seen many bad things done by the whites but he's ready to forgive and forget and would share his blanket with any white man to show he means it. He says likewise it is gettin' late and he's got forty miles more to go before reachin' the Agency. The nights are growin' chilly and some of his old ones are hungry. Which is a way of sayin' to us that it is time to quit the foolin' around."

Smith nodded, meeting the old warrior's eyes. They were eyes of black liquid, full of pride and complete confidence—and touched with shrewd scheming as they stared back at the lieutenant. Smith said: "Tell him I'm glad to hear of his peaceful intentions. Ask him this: If he knew that some of his young men had killed the prospectors, would he bring them to the fort as a sign of his good will?"

Bannack Bill asked it. Out on the wings of the crowd the young bucks grew increasingly restive and there was a murmuring among them. The old one placed a hand on his heart and briefly answered the question. Bannack Bill said: "He says he would bring in his own son if his son had done it."

"Go get them, Sergeant," murmured Smith, not turning his head. He stared at the old one. "Tell him I believe his word to be true. Tell him he has no doubt been deceived by his own young men, for we see the scalp and we see the watch. Tell him we take him at his word and will carry the two young men back to the fort with us."

Bannack Bill hesitated, casting a bland stare at Smith. "I hope you got the best cards in this game, Lieutenant."

"Tell him," said Smith.

Shafter had meanwhile turned and now rode directly and unhurriedly to the left, passing along the ranks of the younger warriors. They sat still, staring back at him with their haughty faces, with the snake-twining of insolence in their eyes. He came to the warrior who had the fresh scalp hanging from his quiver and to the warrior with the watch wrapped by its chain around his neck. He stopped, looking at the scalp and at the watch. Suddenly other bucks crowded close to these two and grasped their carbines and lifted them suggestively and a steady, thick stream of Sioux words went back and forth along the line, growing sharper, growing more excited.

Shafter heard Bannack Bill say: "He says there must be a mistake. That is an old scalp, from many years ago. The watch was a present."

"Tell him we shall take the two warriors to Lincoln. If he speaks the truth we shall release them."

Shafter pulled his .44 and laid it on the buck with the scalp. He pointed his finger at that one, and at the other one. He made a gesture of command. These two sat dead still and stared back, animosity burning brightly in them; but the younger men began to push around them to make a screen that Shafter could not get through and, seeing this, he shoved his horse forward and swung it and laid the muzzle of his gun against the ribs of the warrior with the scalp. He pushed on the muzzle. He said: "Move out." A sudden crying freshened about him. He heard the clicking of carbine hammers and he watched the young bucks drift in to trap him. One buck swung his arm toward his revolver. Shafter laid the gun on him at once and stopped him, and pulled the weapon back to his original target. He heard Smith coolly say: "Ask him if a chief swallows his words as soon as they are spoken."

Bannack Bill repeated it to Red Owl and Red Owl sat still thoughtfully. Back in the column the women were beginning to lift their shrill voices, the savage intent of their words scraping Shafter's nerves and inciting the young warriors to greater violence. One brave flung his carbine around and took a steady aim on Shafter. Then Red Owl's voice came out quickly and spoke three words that settled the question, for the two wanted warriors moved out of the group, Shafter behind them. They rode straight toward the waiting cavalry, never turning their heads.

Smith said crisply: "Tell Red Owl I'm pleased he keeps his word," and wheeled back to the detachment. He called to it, "Hold your places," and swung to watch the Indian band take up its forward motion. The old ones rode by in stony silence but the bucks, fermenting with rage, dashed back and forth along the cavalry line, shrilly crying, flinging up their guns in provocation. They wheeled and charged at the troopers, sliding down from their ponies in beautiful displays of horsemanship, coming full tilt against the troopers' outspread line, and wheeling away with a derisive shouting.

"Hold steady," said Smith.

Garnett watched the Sioux with the clearest kind of desire on his wedge-shaped face. He spoke in strong enough tone for his words to carry through the troopers. "It would be better to kill them now than wait until next year when they may kill us."

"Garnett," said Lieutenant Smith, "there's women and children in that group."

"They're worse than the men."

"Never mind," said Smith.

The procession went slowly by, the squaws all shouting at the troopers and some of them crying wildly. The travois dragged up dust and the young warriors suddenly drove the Sioux horse-herd through the deployed troopers. This was a moment of danger and Smith saw it and called sharply again: "Hold tight," and watched the scene with the sharpest attention until horses and Sioux had passed on. Then he said: "Column of twos—forward—walk." The troopers came in, resuming formation. Smith settled himself taciturnly at the head of the group.

"It was a question in my mind how we'd come out," murmured Bannack Bill.

"They had their women and kids along," said Smith. "That kept them from fighting." He turned to Shafter, who rode with the two captive Sioux. "Very good, Sergeant," he said, and pointed the column due east. He was disposed to let the silence continue, being naturally a blunt man who seldom saw the necessity of extended conversation. But Bannack Bill, who knew a good deal about Indians, had the recent scene still in his mind. "Something else to make them hate us. You know how an Indian hates, Smith? It is like one of these fires that burns in a coal bed out there on the Bad Lands. Goes down underneath and smokes and gets hotter. It just never goes out. One day it breaks into the open —the damnedest blaze you ever saw."

"That may come," admitted Smith.

"Sure it's comin'. These Sioux have been pushed back as fur as they'll push. They're right now on the last of their huntin' land. Last buff'lo is there. Last freedom is there. They have made up their minds to go no further. I know."

"If I were a Sioux," said Smith, "I'd feel the same way. We can only hope that the authority in Washington will see the point and let the Sioux alone."

"The authority in Washington," stated Bannack Bill, "will order the Seventh out for a campaign when spring comes. I been here a long time on the frontier. It is the same old story."

Smith rode a long distance in silence; he was a soldierly shape, he was that kind of officer whose presence reassured the command, practical and assured and humane, with the habit of decision and the knowledge of men well-blended in him. A dozen years of soldiering had seasoned him, taught him rough-and-tumble, swiftness of action; it had taught him the distinction between caution and daring. West Point and the campaign field had made of him an excellent sample of that type of officer and gentleman which the army regarded as its ideal.

Now and then his thoughts laid a temporary shadow across his face; now and then he shook his head as his thinking took him to impassable ground. Presently he shrugged his shoulders. "You're right," he said. "There will be a campaign. Well, it is one of those things over which a soldier has no control, and never will. We do what we are told to do, and presently we shall be told to subjugate the Indians. The fault is higher up." Then he corrected that. "Still, the men higher up are not free agents either. Something pushes them on, whether they like it or not. It goes back to one race against another race. The white man's idea against the red man's idea. If the situation were reversed, the Indians would be doing to us what we are now trying to do to them. White men have fought each other since the beginning of time. Red men have fought each other. Now the races fight. Well, we're in the hands of history, and history is a cruel thing."

"Lieutenant," said Bannack Bill, "just remember one thing when you're campaignin'. Every man in Red Owl's band has got the memory of you and me and the sergeant here burned deep in his head. He would know us next week, next month, next year. And he has got his notions of what he'll do when he meets us. Finger by finger and joint by joint and one chunk of flesh after another. Remember that next summer and take damned good care you don't fall in their hands."

"Things sometimes drift on for years," said Smith. "Nothing happens. Just reveille and retreat, summer and winter. Sort of a holiday in a man's life. Then a cloud gathers and you smell bad weather. You feel it in your bones, as I have been feeling it for months. Never tell me there isn't such a thing as a sixth sense. Well then, the storm breaks. When it is over, you look around and you see a lot of faces missing. That's the hard thing—to recall all those men who once were beside you on the firing line, and now are gone."

"It is coming," said Bannack Bill.

Smith lifted his shoulders and reclaimed his practical manner. "Never pays to speculate upon the future."

It was then three o'clock. At ten, the command reached the guard gate at Fort Lincoln, answered the challenge and passed in. Taps ran the cold air as Shafter stepped wearily from his saddle.

☆ 6 ☆

The Ride to Rice

Colder weather squeezed the land; a thin crust formed on water buckets and barrels and the ground showed crazed frost patterns. Troopers turned out for morning roll call in overcoats and Berlin mittens. Sergeant Hines's voice had a more brittle snap to it and his nose, which was an adequate weather vane, made a scarlet point in the gray dawn. After he had announced the details for the day he said: "Shafter, harness up the light wagon and report to commanding officer's house. Take along a couple blankets, your carbine and fifty rounds of ammunition. Dismiss."

Shafter had his breakfast, hitched the team and rolled over the parade through a woolly fog, through a stillness that was unlike any other stillness. The sun lay somewhere above this fog, without heat enough to dispel it or to break the steady cold. He rolled before Custer's house and stepped to the porch as Custer came out with Mrs. Custer and Josephine Russell.

Shafter saluted and noticed the general's sharp eyes go around the horizon. Custer said: "Not quite time for a blizzard, but it will be cold. Are you dressed warm enough?"

"I'm stuffed and padded," said Josephine.

"Sergeant," said Custer, "drive Miss Russell to Fort Rice, remain overnight, and bring her back. Be sure you leave Rice soon enough to make the fort before sundown." Custer gave the girl a hand to the seat of the light wagon, saw to it that a blanket was folded over her legs, and meanwhile cast a professional eye on the carbine lying under the seat. Mrs. Custer called from the porch: "Give my love to Mrs. Benteen and the other ladies and say I hope to see them soon." Shafter sent the team over the parade at a willing trot, passed commissary and quartermaster buildings, rolled down Laundress Row, and set out upon the road which ran south beside the swinging loops of the river toward Fort Rice twenty miles away. The morning-fresh team went spanking along.

He had not seen Josephine for a week, and experienced a good deal of pleasure at her presence. "I have been wondering how you were."

"So have I," she said. "I grew rather curious to see how the experiment was turning out."

"What experiment?"

"Your coming back to an old trade. Other men have tried it and seldom found it satisfactory."

"Do you think I'll regret it?"

"You seemed a different sort of person. I mean—accustomed to better circumstances than you are in now." She paused, opening the subject for him.

152

When he refused the opening she calmly qualified her observation. "It didn't seem to me that you would deliberately accept so rough a life."

"Not as rough as it looks," he commented. "It is a very good life in fact."

"I know something of soldiers," she said. "I have heard them talk and I have seen them drunk."

"Both the genteel and the common get drunk."

She sat straight, looking before her for a few thoughtful moments. "I suppose I was rude."

"No," he said. "Not rude. You don't know my kind of people."

"Those are not your kind of people," she said, now on firm ground again. "That is why you are such a puzzle to me."

"When did you bother to think of me at all?"

"Why," she said, as though surprised that he should doubt her interest, "don't you know any woman is intrigued by contradictions? You are a contradiction. I wanted to go visit Mrs. Benteen—and I suggested to Mrs. Custer that you were undoubtedly a good driver."

He turned, smiling, to her and watched her smile answer him. The cold day rouged her cheeks and sparkled in her eyes. She had a beautifully fashioned face, all its features generous and capable of robust emotion, all of them graceful. She was a girl with a great degree of vitality and imagination, these things held under careful restraint. He saw the hint of her will, or of her pride, in the corners of her eyes and lips.

"I am flattered," he said.

"Under pressure," she said, with quick humor, "you do rise to gallantry. Do you know—I think your thoughts of women are sometimes less than generous."

He said, very seriously: "I hope I've never shown it to you."

"It is only a guess," she said and at once changed the subject. "A beautiful day."

The fog had closed in, bringing the horizons close upon them. It was colder than it had been, with grayer shadows lying upon the dull earth. To the left of them the Missouri ran between its crumbling banks, to the right lay a strip of moderately level country, this running up to a low ridge; and this ridge marched southward a matter of miles and dwindled away into a general plain. They came, late in the morning, to a narrow wooden bridge over the Little Heart, which trembled to their passage; they followed the road's rutty course steadily southward, steam beginning to rise from the winter-thick wool of the horses. At intervals during the morning a courier ran full speed by them and later they overtook a slow-laboring freight outfit bound southward from Bismarck. Near eleven o'clock the Bismarck-Black Hills stage came out of the lonely land to the southwest, pitching on its fore and aft straps.

"I have never liked the sharp line between officers and men," Josephine suddenly said.

She had been following some line of thought; and this was its conclusion. He tried to guess what the thought had been but failed. He said: "A regiment is a machine built for violent action. Men make up the parts of the machine—and each part has to perform its particular chore. There's no time to argue about it when a fight starts; so it has to be settled a long time beforehand. Every man must understand his place."

She said, in a lightly speculative voice: "I should not think you'd be happy in your place."

"Why not?"

"You've had a higher place."

He smiled a little. "You're an indiscreet woman."

"Perhaps," she said calmly. "After all, a woman has two privileges. To be inconsistent and to be indiscreet."

He said, now grown sober, "I have had both qualities used on me. It has made me wonder what a man's privileges are."

"To walk away when he grows weary of it," she said promptly. "That's what you did, didn't you?"

She hit hard when she chose to. He looked at her and saw her half-smile temper the cool realism of her thinking.

"Many men have walked away," he admitted. "But few men ever walked away whole. They left some of themselves behind. The ability to trust, maybe. Faith. The first idealism they had. The wonderful dream of youth. Love is supposed to be the core of a woman, it is supposed to be the entire meaning of her life. The philosophers, at least, say so. A man is supposed to have many interests, of which love is only one. So the wreck of a love is supposed to leave a woman bankrupt, whereas it is presumed that a man easily mends his heart and hunts for another love. That is entirely a fiction of the philosophers."

"Are you quite sure?" she asked, gentle with her voice.

"It is the woman who mends her heart and finds another love," he said. "She knows she's got to do it, if she's to get along with the business of living. So she does it. She's far more realistic than the man. She gets her balance back and moves forward. Very frequently he doesn't."

"It was as I thought," she murmured. "You are skeptical regarding women."

"Yes," he said. "I am."

Her answer to that was extremely soft. "I am so sorry."

"Why should you be?"

"It leaves you so little."

"There is still the world of men for a man to be comfortable in."

Fort Rice came through the fog, a blur and then a square shape huddled against the earth. He slapped the team into a trot and looked at her and saw that she was quietly studying him; and he caught an expression on her face that was wholly mature and far-thinking. She said: "This has been a nice trip, Sergeant. At least I have relieved you from drill, haven't I?"

"Yes," he said, and drove into Rice as mess call sounded. Mrs. Benteen, a tall and tired-appearing woman, came to the porch of one of the half-dozen homely houses to greet Josephine. Shafter took the girl's portmanteau into the house, came back and drove the rig around to the stables and put up the horses. He had no particular mess assignment and therefore hunted up a sergeant and got permission to attach himself to H Company. After noon meal he took a stroll around the post.

It was only a shabby collection of buildings, made of warped cottonwood lumber, closely surrounded by a stockade of logs set upright in the ground and capped at each corner by a small bastion from which sentries might view the roundabout country at night. All the ground was worn smooth of vegetation and all the quarters were paintless, their walls warped apart by the reaction of sun and rain. Thus shabby and forlorn, Fort Rice commanded the Missouri's bluff, exposed to the full rigors of winter wind and to summer's brutal heat. For the people of this post there were no diversions, no entertainment, no break in a dull and confined life. East and west of them stretched an empty land. Forty miles to the south lay the Agency, twenty miles northward were Lincoln and Bismarck—too far away for a casual ride.

He sat on the barracks porch, watching the two skeleton companies drill briefly in the afternoon; and later he made a circle outside the post. There was a cemetery lying slightly beyond the post on a small knoll with little mounds slowly losing identity as weather faded them back to the blank anonymity of the gray earth. In a short while the very mark of these people would be gone—they who had been round-formed and fair, their bodies taut with hunger, their lips red and warm and all their dreams making them great. For a short while they had lived, had voice and motion and were set apart from other living things; they left footprints upon the earth and their hands formed objects which were dear to them, but now the shifting sands filled in the crevices which marked the oblong spot where they lay and the same wind which once had blown its fragrance against them now blew where they were not. They had occupied space beneath the sky and above the earth; that space was now empty. Somewhere, somebody still remembered the touch of these people, but in time that remembrance would grow fainter until at last there would be no living thing that knew them—and the great void of time would have absorbed them into its nothingness.

He thought of this and it was a gesture of rebellion which made him draw his boot along the edge of one fading grave, to sharpen its outline and thus postpone that inevitable oblivion; and he turned and made his circuit of the post, coming upon the crumbling bluff of the river. A wooden incline led down the side of the bluff, upon which stood a wooden platform with wheels, and a keg. To the machine was attached a pair of ropes by which the keg was run to the river for its cargo of water and drawn up. He stood awhile, smoking a cigar and watching the later afternoon grow gray. The strange fog held on, thickening and rolling forward until the river became a silver blur beneath the woolly overcast. A wind came up with its keen cold.

After supper and after retreat, he sat awhile in H Company's barrack-room, watching men sit taciturnly at poker tables, watching them lie back on their bunks. A big-bellied cast-iron stove slowly grew red and tobacco smoke rolled in sleazy layers through the room, through which the barrels of the carbines played a dull blue gleaming. One trooper squatted on his bunk, plucking a sad tune from a guitar, while two other troopers stood close by and tried to make a harmony from the tune. Out of the washroom stalked a lean-flanked cavalryman, naked entirely, with a pure white skin which ran up to a sun-blackened collar line. The wind had risen and sang a soft song at the barrack eaves and men lifted their heads, shrewdly listening to that warning. Gun oil and dressed leather and men's bodies and the horse-impregnated uniforms made a heavy male odor in the room.

"Who's goin' to be mail sergeant this winter?" asked somebody.

A corporal sitting by had an answer. "John Tunis took his discharge this week. They're breakin' in a new man at Lincoln."

"What's that?" asked Shafter.

"Always a sergeant detached to carry mail in the winter when the railroad stops runnin'. Lincoln to Fargo and back, twice a month. A team and a sleigh. Tunis was the only one who could make his way through a blizzard."

Shafter moved from the barracks, into the windy blackness. Lights glistened along the cramped parade and the bastions at each corner of the stockade stood lonesome against the shadows. There was a party in Benteen's quarters, all lights gleaming cheerfully upon the cold world. Through the shadeless windows he saw the officers and ladies of the post gathered, with Josephine surrounded by young lieutenants. He pulled on his cigar, and was surprised that he stood here. "I am well past sentimental longings," he thought. But he stood fast, and observed her carefully. One of the lieutenants drew laughter from her—from this self-contained girl who was so careful of her inner riches; she lifted her head and he had a full view of her face, changed by the laughter, and he said to himself: "She's damned attractive," and for a moment he felt a small thread of loneliness, of outsideness and was reminded of many things in his past. Turning away, he returned to the barracks, coming suddenly upon a scene.

Men sat motionless on the bunks looking toward the end of the big room; and those at the tables had suddenly quit their games. The first sergeant of H, a leather-lean man with four hashmarks across his sleeve, stood in the middle of the room and faced a man at the far end. He was speaking in a cool, persuasive voice to that one. "Put it down, Stampfer. When you're drunk you've got no business handling a gun—and you're damned drunk now."

The trooper at the end of the room had placed his back against the wall. He was short and chunky, with a wildness burning in his eyes and a mass of hair half fallen down over his forehead. His mouth opened and closed and opened again; and then he said with a drunk-mad distinctness: "I am going to kill you!" He brought up the carbine in his hand. He patted it with one hand. "The only friend I've got in the whole damned world. It don't sneak around behind me. It don't steal things out of my bunk. It don't take my rights away."

"Now," said the first sergeant in a most practical voice, "what's the good of shootin' me, Stampfer? You want to be hung?"

"I'm smarter than that," said Stampfer. "I'll leave one bullet for myself."

"You're makin' a damn fool out of yourself in front of the lads," said the first sergeant. "Put the gun down."

"Sure," said Stampfer. "All of you think I'm a damned fool. Don't think I don't know that. I seen you laugh behind me. I hear what you say about me. I'm nothin' but a dog around here!" His voice went up-pitch, uncontrolled and half screaming. "I hate the lot of you. I could kill you all and beat your brains out! That's for you, Beckett—and I'm goin' to kill you first! Then I'm goin' out to hunt the officers of this troop—the dirty slave drivers. I'm goin' to kill Benteen and I'm goin' to put a slug right through Gibson's guts." He shouted it out. "I've had enough of it—from all of you—from this stinking hell hole—from these bastard officers that look at us like we was scum and give us the butt end of their tongues whenever they please! You can cringe! You can stick it out when they drive you like cattle through the heat! You can stand guard duty this winter when it's so cold your fingers rot off! That's fine—that's fine! I won't— not me!"

He stopped in quivering exhaustion. He lifted the gun half to his shoulder and fired at Sergeant Beckett, who never moved a muscle. The sound slammed through quarters and one man, crouched on a bunk near Stampfer, now flung himself forward. Stampfer swung the muzzle of the gun and caught the trooper on the side of the head, dropping him senseless to the floor. Suddenly the whole half end of the barrack rose and rushed at him. Stampfer swept the gun before him like a scythe; a second trooper went down, but a third one ducked in and caught the gun. After that H Company went to work.

Stampfer was against the wall and the liquor's madness had added strength to his heavy frame. He took these men as they came to him, breaking his knuckles against them, plunging his feet into their bellies. He caught them at the arms and butted his head sharp under the chins; he slashed his fingers across their faces and drew blood. He was struck, and struck again until sight left him, but he stood on his feet and fought as a blind and senseless brute would fight. One man got a strangle hold on him, was carried around and around and flung off; another trooper tackled him at the waist and had his face smashed by Stampfer's up-driving knee. All this carried the fight away from the wall toward the center of the room. Suddenly Sergeant Beckett drew his revolver, made a quick pace forward and cracked the barrel across Stampfer's skull. Stampfer went down, no more motion in him.

He left wreckage behind him, two men knocked completely out, one man kneeling dazed on the floor with a broken nose, and half a dozen others nursing lesser injuries. The sergeant stood still, staring at Stampfer and cursing him. "Two months since the last spell. I have warned you boys to offer him no booze."

"He had a bottle. It was full half an hour ago. It's empty now."

"Dump him on his bunk and tie him to it," said Beckett. He saw somebody coming in the door, turned about and yelled, "Attention." He stood stiff before the entering officer, who was Captain Benteen.

Benteen said in a querulous, rasping voice: "What's this?"

"Stampfer again."

Benteen was an officer of long service. He had a thatch of snow-white hair, a round stubborn face and a mouth made for acid comment. Benteen was a cranky realist and a disciplinarian; he wasted no sympathy on Stampfer. "Did you lay him out?"

"Cold enough."

Benteen looked at the carbine on the floor. "Was that his shot I heard?"

"It was so."

The captain saw the two men lying unconscious. "Badly hurt?"

"Just knocked out," said the sergeant. "They'll come around."

"Sergeant," said Benteen, "next time he draws a gun on any man of this company, shoot him. You have that as an order from me. Now tomorrow when he comes to you with his regrets, make up a pack for him with seventy pounds of bricks in it. He'll march around this post with that until he falls down."

"Yes sir," said the sergeant.

Benteen gave the troop a harsh stare and turned from the room. Outside at the moment taps ran the post and the sentries were calling. The trooper with a smashed face rose with his lips redly smeared. He clapped a hand to his mouth, swearing. "He broke one of me front teeth with his damned knee, Sarge!"

The sergeant went to the man. He said gruffly, "Hold up your head," and used his fingers to pull back the man's bruised lips as he would have opened the mouth of a horse. He looked at the tooth sharply snapped off and he murmured: "You'll have a hell of a toothache if that thing stays in. It has got to come out. I'll get my pliers."

He went to the man who had made the first jump at Stampfer; he bent down, and rose up. "Neely," he said softly, "go fetch the surgeon."

☆ 7 ☆

Of Many Incidents

At one o'clock Shafter brought the light wagon before Captain Benteen's door, gave Josephine a lift to the seat and stood by while Benteen arranged the robe around her with an old man's motions of gallantry. The captain looked at the sky a moment, suspecting the weather. "Sergeant," he said, "waste no time in returning to Lincoln. Do you know what an oncoming blizzard smells like? Do you know the signs?"

"Yes sir."

"If bad weather blows up before you reach the Little Heart River bridge, turn back to this post. If you should be unable to return, take cover in the bridge. It has served such purpose before."

"You mustn't worry," said Josephine. "I have been out in many a storm."

There was a wind, and the wind ruffled the captain's white mane when he removed his garrison cap. He gave the girl a hard smile. "A blizzard is not a storm. A blizzard is the world upside down. It is the wind gone mad and the world drowned out. It will drive the breath from your lungs and the heat from your body. When the blizzard blows it brings on a fury that will pound the reason from your head. Nothing stands against it—nothing at all. You know that. However, I am merely cautioning you against a remote possibility. If I thought a storm likely I should not permit you to return to Lincoln. I think it is too early in the winter. But don't waste time, Sergeant."

"It has been most pleasant," said Josephine. "I shall tell the Custers how kind you were."

Benteen gave the girl an oblique glance. "Convey our regards to the general and his lady," he said and turned away. It had not been an effusive message.

Shafter rolled through the guard gate at a trot, facing a gray plain upon which the winter fog pressed and thickened and was churned by the stiff wind moving out of the north. It was colder than the day before and the sun was a thin refraction of light above the overcast. Summer and fall had departed from the plains in the space of thirty-six hours and the smell of the air was raw, almost dangerous. Shafter was smiling. "What is amusing?" asked Josephine.

"Benteen's reluctant courtesy to Custer."

"It was rather wryly given. I noticed it."

"Have you heard the story?"

"Not all of it."

"About seven years ago the Seventh had a battle down on the Washita in the dead of winter and wiped out Black Kettle's band of Cheyennes. It was somewhat of a fight and a small detachment under Major Elliot wandered off and didn't come back. Custer considered himself in a tight fix—other bands being in the neighborhood—and spent a couple days getting his regiment and supply train together before looking for Elliot. He found Elliot and nineteen men dead. Benteen considered Custer had exhibited complete callousness in the matter and wrote a letter about it to the newspapers. It was quite an affair. Benteen despises Custer. If you consider the man's face you can see he would be capable of a good robust hate."

"The regiment seems a very close and agreeable family."

"You can't put a group of men—and their wives—together over a period of years without having animosities. This regiment has its factions. The general is an extremely dashing man, very proud of his abilities. You will remember he was a boy general in the Civil War. He hasn't forgotten it and neither have some other officers who are serving under him, twenty years older than he is. Some of them feel he has too much dash and too little judgment. Others would follow him into point-blank artillery fire if he ordered it."

"I admire him," said Josephine. "Very much."

"He is either loved or hated. He commands no lesser feelings in men."

"How do you feel about him?"

He gave her an easy, half-smiling glance. "I shall reserve my judgment until I serve my first campaign under him."

She said, very soberly, "Are you that sure there will be fighting?"

"Yes," he said, "I'm very sure there will be."

He rode along in silence, not thinking seriously of very much but simply sitting by while the day touched him with its fingers. The damp fog moved over his face like soft fine bristles and a smell, slightly rank and rotten, came from the nearby river. High up beyond the overcast was the subdued murmuring of geese, scudding delayed before the onset of winter.

"Sergeant," she said, "I'm glad to be riding back with you."

When he turned he saw that she was smiling at him and then he remembered how blunt she had been with him the day before; and was struck by the change. She had drawn the curtain of reserve away and seemed to like him and seemed to wish to be liked by him. She had a teasing expression of gaity in her eyes; she had a provocative challenge in them—and all this made her a more complex and unfathomable woman, and a more striking woman.

"I appreciate the honor," he said. "It was different yesterday."

"Ah," she said, and didn't bother to explain the change. "Isn't it a wonderful day?"

"When you feel good," he said, "any day is good."

"It is the country," she said. "It makes you spread out inside. It makes you giddy. It even makes you reckless. It is easy to cry or laugh here. Or to love, or kill."

"Killing and loving are close together sometimes."

They rolled on over the prairie, jarred steadily by the dry-baked ruts. There was a sound ahead of them, of riders moving fast through the thickening mists, and presently a lithe little officer sitting forward on his horse like a jockey darted out of the haze with a file of six troopers behind him; they fled by, one shout dropping from them, and faded into the haze again.

He remembered, suddenly, that she had fallen long silent and turned to see darkness on her face. She said: "That was a strange remark. It came out of experience."

"Yes."

She looked at him as she had the previous afternoon—judging him. "You should not permit your experiences to sour you."

"Yes," he said, "it is a nice day."

She was wholly mature at the moment, alert enough to understand the undercurrent between them, to fathom his desire to push her away from his secret. She said: "That was a rebuff wasn't it, Sergeant?"

"There is no real gallantry in me."

She thought of it, and watched him with a half-lidded attention. She was very cool, and very frank with her eyes. "It was unnecessary to warn me. You see, Sergeant, I was brought up to believe that each person must stand the consequences of his own actions. I never could expect sympathy from my people when I hurt myself doing some foolish thing. So, if I do a foolish thing now, I shall not cry. You needn't worry."

"What is the foolish thing?"

"I have decided I like you."

He gave her a half-embarrassed and half-astonished glance, whereupon her soberness unexpectedly left her and she put a hand lightly on his arm and laughed. She had a way of laughing that was extremely attractive, her chin tilting up and her lips curving in pretty lines. A small dimple appeared at the left of her mouth and light danced in her eyes.

He said brusquely, "You're a damned strange woman."

"The simplest kind of a woman. There is no complexity to a woman until a man puts it there."

He shook his head and let the talk drop, but he thought about it through the long stretch of following silence. The Little Heart bridge shaped up through the fog murk. They passed it and dropped their booming echoes behind; the horses, sensing home, stepped briskly through the chilling wind.

"Have a nice visit?" he asked.

"Yes. All officers of this regiment are gallant. There was one young lad newly from West Point—the colonel's son. Sturgis. It is confusing. Do you suppose Colonel Sturgis will ever return to take the command from Custer?"

"I doubt it. The War Department seems to regard it as Custer's command. He's been in charge of it for ten years or so—except for a season when he was courtmartialed and deprived of authority."

"What was his transgression?"

"Rode a hundred miles to see his wife—and wore out his escort troopers getting there. All this without permission to leave his post."

"It was a romantic gesture," she murmured.

"It was something he would have arrested one of his own officers for doing. He is a man with violent swings of temper. Inconsistent and unpredictable. You can never know for a certainty what he'll do next. That's been his history. Steadfastness is not one of his virtues."

She said unexpectedly: "Did I see you strolling through the dark last night, past Captain Benteen's quarters?"

"Yes."

"Smoking your cigar. I understand a cigar and a woman go together in a man's mind. Was there a woman in your mind?"

"I wondered," he said, "if you were enjoying yourself."

"I was also thinking of you," she murmured.

He looked at her and noticed the sweetness of her expression and was greatly troubled. He had started out with this girl pretty much as a stranger; and found himself now somehow engaged in her emotions. It threw him back on his honor, and he searched himself carefully, wondering if he had given her encouragement. He thought: "She's old enough to know her mind, she knows what she's doing." But he was uneasy with the responsibility which lay with him. It bore hard against him, the more he thought of it, the farther he silently traveled, until he came to his abrupt conclusion. "It will have to be settled," he thought.

He stopped the team and wrapped the reins around the brake bar, turning to her. Her eyes lifted to him, narrowed and watchful, but she made no motion when he bent and put his arms around her; for a small moment he hesitated, looking carefully at her lips and the expression in her glance, and saw nothing but the layered darkness in her eyes. He bent down and kissed her, and held the kiss longer than he intended, and drew away. She had made no gesture and no sound; she had put no resistance against him. But now she said, in a curt, precise voice: "I think I heard the general say we should be home by suppertime."

He sent the team on at a faster clip, much more uncertain than he had been. He thought with some self-disgust: "There is no such thing as a study of women. Nothing is to be learned from them. A man gains no permanent wisdom." It was then past the middle of the afternoon, and the sky turning gray; at five o'clock he passed through Lincoln's south gate, and drew before Custer's house. He got down to give her a hand, and felt the weight of her body momentarily spring against his arm. She had a light perfume that drifted to him—a sudden, disturbing fragrance. He started back around the horses and was halted by her clear, sharp voice:—

"One moment, Sergeant."

He turned and watched her come forward. She was on guard, she was cool and quite self-assured, and smiling. It was not a soft smile, not tender or indulgent; it came out to him as the reflection of tumult and stirred emotions.

"You meant to frighten me away, didn't you?"

"To show you that your knowledge of me was incomplete. You must not take men at face value."

He saw the fire and the intensity within her, the swift feelings under hard control. "I think you'll find it was a dangerous subterfuge, Sergeant," she said evenly.

He lifted his cap as she turned away; he climbed to the seat and drove the rig through the sweeping wind, back to stable quarters. He unharnessed and stalled the horses and backed the wagon into its proper place. Having missed stable call, he groomed his own horse in the gathering dusk. But all this while he remembered the taste of her lips and her fragrance and the stillness of her body, neither accepting nor rejecting him. That got into him and suddenly he realized she had broken through his barrier. Afterwards, walking back to quarters, he recalled her voice as she had said: "You'll find it a dangerous subterfuge," and wondered at her meaning.

He reached the barracks with all this churning through his head, and heard first call for drill rocketing down the parade. "It comes early tonight," he said to Hines.

"For the rest of the winter it will be before supper."

He stood retreat and for a while the ceremony took the girl out of his head. There was this power in the trumpets and in the music of the band, in the old grooved ritual of arms, in the voice of the adjutant calling all across the parade's distance, in the somber, stilled ranks of the men and in the pageantry of troopers wheeling by the commanding officer and the bright flash of gold epaulet and the swords tossed gallantly up. It was a thing that was in his blood and bones, not so much because of its color but because of all that it meant in the way of men faithfully standing together—of hard and proud men, of evil ones, of young ones and old ones—all for the moment surrendering what they individually were to become something greater than they could ever individually be. That was it, he thought; that was the thing that brought peace to him, and comfort—this faith in a symbol, in an idea. He rode back to stables in a better frame of mind, but at supper table the recollection of the afternoon scenes recurred and turned him irritable. Afterwards he lighted up a cigar and moved around the big room, as undecided as he had been for many weeks. Sergeant McDermott and Corporal Bierss had started a poker game. McDermott said, "Sit down, Shafter."

Shafter took a chair and waited for his cards. He saw Donovan at the far end of the room with half a dozen other troopers, all of them talking over something. Donovan saw him and came over. Donovan murmured: "This is a good night to get wet, Professor. How you feelin'?"

"Any night's a good night," said Shafter. "Where you goin'?"

"There's a place across the river called the Stud Horse," said Donovan. "Bierss here knows it's a lively spot. A little fun, Professor?"

"Let the man alone," said Sergeant McDermott. "He's just about to catch up on his arithmetic."

"A lad from L dropped word there'd be a group of his boys over there," said Donovan. "It was a kind of an invitation. He said if we had the guts to drop in—"

McDermott and Bierss showed immediate interest. McDermott said: "Why didn't you say that to begin with? You comin', Shafter?"

Shafter got up, still undecided. Maybe, he thought, this was the way to knock his troubles out of his head, maybe it wasn't. But this was his troop and the lads had let him into it; he was one of the crowd. "I had a notion to go into Bismarck," he said. "How long can you keep that fight on ice?"

"It won't get started until the police patrol clears out, after tattoo."

"I'll be there," said Shafter.

McDermott and Bierss and Donovan went into a close study. McDermott said: "Last time we got licked. We didn't take the best scrappers along. Get Rusk and O'Mallan and Carter. Get . . . ."

Troopers drifted forward. Lovelace came up and heard what was in the making. He said: "I'll go, too."

McDermott looked at him, critical but not unkind. "You ain't had much experience in this business, son. Barroom fightin' is a science. You'd get your head knocked off before you turned around. L Company will bring along its best scrappers."

Lovelace revealed embarrassment. He held his place and he repeated his wish. "How am I going to learn if I don't start sometime? Let me go along, Sarge."

Shafter studied the boy a moment, knowing exactly what lay in Lovelace's mind. Presently Shafter said to McDermott: "Take Lovelace, Mac."

McDermott shrugged his shoulders. "All right. You get a couple of boats and take 'em over to the other shore, son."

"What are the boats for?" asked Shafter. "There's a ferry."

"It will be after taps," said McDermott, "so we can't come back on the ferry. Who's guard on Number Six Post at ten o'clock?"

"Don't know," said Donovan.

"I'll go see the sergeant of the guard," said McDermott. "Last time there was a green lad who didn't know much about soldierin'. He might have caused us trouble."

Shafter turned away, but he heard McDermott's voice call after him: "We ain't ever had enough foxy scrappers to cope with that outfit. By God, it will be a different tune tonight. You be there sure, Professor."

"Sure," said Shafter. He put on his overcoat and stepped into the raw, steady wind. Beyond the guard gate he caught a late-traveling ambulance, crossed the wind-chopped river and so rode into Bismarck.

Earlier that afternoon Major Barrows' wife rode out of the post on a dark bay horse and swung toward the ferry at the same time Lieutenant Garnett came trotting off the old Fort McKean road with half a platoon behind him. He saw her and lifted his hat and smiled. Afterwards, inside the post, he nodded at one of the troopers. "Purple, report to me at my quarters." He surrendered his horse and strode over the parade to bachelors' quarters at his usual pacing gate, every inch of his frame taut and soldierly. He was thinking of Mrs. Barrows in his aggressive way when he moved into the frame house at the end of Officers' Row and entered his own particular room. He was still appraising her as he washed up and groomed himself before his mirror. He thought: "Lonesome as hell, and ready for a little flirting." He corrected himself on that. "Not the precise flirting type, I think. Probably trying to be honest with a husband who is somewhat of a fool in his handling of her."

Purple presently tapped on the door and came in and stood by with a half-respectful, half-knowing interest. Jack Purple was the lieutenant's striker, doing the necessary valet chores, running the usual errands and, on occasion, executing chores which were scarcely routine. He had followed the lieutenant through two enlistments, being transferred at his instance from one outfit to another so that he might serve Garnett. He was in many respects a cheaper edition of the lieutenant, as base and as fundamentally predatory, but lacking Garnett's covering veneer. He was a lean man with a sharp face in whose crevices a kind of handsomeness dwelled in company with a poorly reined boldness. He imitated the lieutenant's long hair-cut, the lieutenant's fastidiousness of dress and in his way he tried to copy the lieutenant's dash. An apt and willing pupil, he had learned many of Garnett's methods with women and after eight years of association he knew more of the lieutenant's secrets than any other man, so that the relation between them was a thing compounded of servility, trust, and contempt. Bound together as they were, they had no illusions, and each man secretly harbored his opinion of the other.

"Purple," said Garnett, "keep my boots in a better state. Your private affairs have made you forgetful."

"The lieutenant knows," said Purple with a veiled grin, "that I have nothing new to trouble me."

"You're lying," said Garnett. "I know about that girl on Laundress Row."

Purple showed concern. "My God, Lieutenant, you ain't got your eyes on her, have you?"

"No, but she's going with a boy in A Company."

"Oh, him," said Purple with indifference. "Lovelace is his name. A dummy."

"Never take a woman away from a man who's liable to cripple you, Purple. You never see me doing that, do you?"

"I'll take care of him."

"That's your affair. Now listen to me. I want a man in this outfit soundly whipped. I wanted him busted up."

"Lieutenant," said Purple, "some things I can do, some I can't do."

"Not you," said Garnett. "Get Conboy to do it. Just drop the word to Conboy that you can get him a hundred dollars if he does a first-rate job."

"It will be first-rate if Conboy does it," said Purple. "Who you wastin' that money on?"

"The new sergeant in A Company. Shafter."

"The one that licked Donovan?"

"Did he?" said Garnett and looked displeased.

"He did," said Purple and stood still, trying to remember where Shafter had cut Garnett's past trail. "But it shouldn't be much for Conboy. Conboy licked Donovan twice. This Shafter won't reach him at all."

"Go see Conboy," said Garnett. "Keep my name out of it of course."

"The man's a sergeant. How could he be after any woman you wanted? Was it a long time ago, Lieutenant?"

"Get out of here," said Garnett. "Bring my horse around."

He pulled on his overcoat, buttoned it and snugged his shoulders into it until the cloth lay smooth; he gave his hair a last brushing at the edges and took care to adjust his garrison cap; and he stood a moment before the mirror, watching his face. "She will play the deep game," he thought. "She will want me to play it." He went out to his horse and swung up with a last word for Purple. "See Conboy right away," he said, and broke into a gallop across the parade, through the guard gate and along the ferry road. Mrs. Barrows waited at the slip for the ferry now nosing in; she turned her head when she heard Garnett approaching.

He lifted his cap to her, not smiling; he had the exact expression on his face he wished her to see—a repressed look which came from stirred feelings, a gentleman of honor hard-drawn to a woman but holding himself in. He noticed the violet coloring of her eyes and he closely watched the small change around her lips. These little fugitive shifts on a woman's face, the varying sounds of a woman's voice, the small gestures or phrases half spoken—these were things on which he always laid much emphasis. He was not certain, but he thought he made an effect on her.

"To Bismarck?"

She nodded and put her horse across the staging to the boat. She rode through to the boat's far end, Garnett following. "My destination also. Do you wish to dismount?"

"No."

He made nothing of her brevity. It was a thing to be read either way. She was, in his own expert judgment, a fully formed and beautiful woman, an instrument of many strings, awaiting somebody's touch.

"Winter's here."

"Yes," she said. Then, as though conscious that her sparing conversation might be rude, she gave him a full glance, murmuring: "Now the light goes out until spring. I dread it."

"There's still a train back," he pointed out.

"An officer's wife has no business living apart from her husband."

"I understand that," he said.

"Do you?" she softly said.

For all his assurance he was halted by the remark; he made nothing of it and saw no lead for him. He thought with impatience: "Have I misjudged this woman?" He tried a few idle phrases, and was answered with equally idle phrases as the boat labored with the current, reached the eastern shore and dropped its plank. The two moved upgrade to the forking of the road—one branch going through the Point, the other swinging wide of the place and running along the bluff. He said:—

"Shall we take the roundabout road?"

She gave him an odd glance. She said, "I don't believe in avoiding realities, Mr. Garnett. The Point can't be ignored by circling it." But she looked behind her at the east side of the river, which at this distance was covered by the day's thin fog; then her eyes touched him, the excitement in them quite distinct. "But if you wish," she said in a quicker, shallower voice, and turned to the side road.

He felt a quick elation. She had made a decision and had indirectly told him why she had made it. They moved up the road to the top of the bluff and came in another quarter hour to the scar of the railroad right-of-way being built west of Bismarck and now abandoned for winter. They rode along the right-of-way until, by her gesture, they swung into the flat prairie. Presently they were two figures riding along in the mist. "I like it better this way."

"Strange," he said. "I should think you'd like to stick to lights and comfort. I should not think you'd enjoy lonely places."

"Lonely people for lonely places," she said.

"I recognized the loneliness in you."

"I suspect you are rather clever at reading people, Mr. Garnett. Have you been wasting your time reading me?"

"Yes. Is it a waste of time?"

"Better if it were."

"It is a damned hard thing," he said, his voice rough and edged.

"What is?"

"To see a woman—to know that woman is your kind of a woman. Dreaming the same kind of dreams. Ready to laugh at the same things, to feel the same loves, the same passions. To lie awake at night—"

"Mr. Garnett," she murmured in the softest of voices. He looked down and saw her hands tightly gripping the pommel; he saw hurt and hard restraint on her face. He had struck her emotions forcibly and he knew this was the moment he had waited for. "Wait," he said, and stopped his horse and got down. He came beside her, looking up; the things he felt were hot enough and real enough at this moment to show upon him and the woman saw them as she stared at him and struggled with herself. "No," she murmured, "get back on your horse."

"Come down," he said, and touched her. He felt her body trembling as she hung to the pommel, he noticed a weakening in her, he recognized something almost like terror on her face; and then that broke and she crossed the deadline she had set herself, and suddenly put out her arms and came down to him. He had her in his arms and his mouth upon her and he held her like that over the lengthening moments, feeling surrender soften her. When she pulled her lips away she was silently crying, even as she clung to him; she dropped her head and laid it against his chest.

"I knew this was coming," she whispered. "I knew it at the Custers'. I sat there and could look ahead and see all of it. You're not a good man, Mr. Garnett. I know that."

He said: "I am very much in love with you."

She lifted her head and showed him her bitter glance. "You needn't lie. It isn't necessary."

Her realism had not left her and this threw him off balance and made his next words ridiculous even in his own ears. "Do you think I'd touch you if I didn't have the deepest kind of feelings—"

"Yes," she said, "you would. I know you—and now I think you know me. You have studied me rather carefully haven't you? Help me up, please."

He gave her a hand to the side saddle, flushing at the position in which he had been placed. She made him seem awkward and amateurish and that was to him an unforgivable thing. He got to his own saddle and quickly attempted to get the scene back within his control. "Mrs. Barrows," he said, "if you believe that about me I shall certainly not come near you again."

She stared into the thickening, graying mist of the afternoon and then she turned and gave him a glance which revealed the fatalism in her. "Yes, you will. And you know also that when you come, I'll be where you want me. That is the way it will be, Edward. We both know what we are and we both know there is no help for us. I'm going back to the fort. Don't come with me."

She turned her horse and started away, then checked around and rode back to him. Her voice softened and her face showed a more tender side of her character. Her eyes searched him and seemed to have hope in him. "Edward," she murmured, "we can be better people. Let's try to be."

He gave her a dark, rash look. He said, "I want you. I've got to have you."

Her voice lifted to a sudden passionate appeal. "Let me alone!"

"No," he said, "I can't. I want you and I know you want me. That's enough isn't it? What else matters at all? I can't play a hypocritical part. Neither can you. There's too much in both of us."

She watched him a long moment, her shoulders dropping and the softness going from her face—the odd glow of beauty dying. A long sigh escaped from her. "All right, Edward," she whispered. "All right," and turned from him.

He watched her grow smaller and dimmer in the rapid-falling twilight, and at last vanish. He had a twinge of conscience, not at his conquest of her, but in permitting her to return home alone. He had done better than he expected; he had caught her sooner than he believed possible, and now said to himself: "A ripe peach ready to drop from the tree." As soon as he said it, he thought differently of her, he valued his triumph less highly, and he had another cynical thought: "From what she said I don't suppose I'm the first man to come along." Even so, he was thinking of when he should next see her, and of what he would say. With this in his mind to excite him, he pointed his horse southeastward, hearing the fort's sunset gun send its echo up along the river's canyon in rocketing waves. At late dusk he arrived in Bismarck, stabled his horse and went into the restaurant frequently patronized by the post's unattached officers. He discovered Edgerly in the back of the place.

"Got tired of the food at Bachelor Hall?" asked Garnett.

"Been tired of it for years," said Edgerly.

"You should do as I do—get yourself invited more often to married quarters for your meals."

"I've been a star boarder at every table in the garrison," said Edgerly. "A man can push his luck just so far. Then he becomes a damned bore."

"Maybe our salvation," said Garnett, "lies in marriage."

"That," said Edgerly, "is a damned bizarre suggestion, coming from you."

Garnett accepted the remark with a grin, but he felt the pointed edge of it. He envied Edgerly's magnificent stature and was jealous of Edgerly's thoroughly masculine appearance. The man was as handsome as hell and was the cynosure of many a woman's eyes. While he ordered and ate, he turned Edgerly's remark over in his head, possessing a Beau Brummel's sensitiveness to the opinions of other men; and he wondered if he had acquired a reputation among his brother officers of which he was not aware. The thought inevitably brought along its companion worry: Had any part of his past caught up with him? There were only two men in the post—Captain Moylan and Shafter—who knew his reputation and both these men, being gentlemen of their own standards, would keep silent; a gentleman, he thought with a return of cynicism, was a man who suppressed his natural desires for fear of what people would say.

"You came in here looking rather pleased," observed Edgerly. "Had luck?"

"Luck?" said Garnett and felt himself betray a certain embarrassment. Edgerly had a sharp pair of eyes and it seemed to him that Edgerly now watched him with something more than casual curiosity. "Just the winter air vitalizing me, I suppose." He lighted a cigar with his coffee, taking such ease as could be found in the restaurant's drab atmosphere. The place had become crowded with the odd assortment of rough frontier types—cowhands, railroad men, gamblers and freighters. A buxom and floridly handsome woman swept into the place, wearing a vivid mauve dress fitted snug at bosom and hips; she took a table and she called out in her hearty voice: "Hurry it up, Charley," and cast a speculative glance at the two officers.

"Shall we take in the opera?" suggested Garnett sardonically.

"The girls at the Wave put on a pretty good show," said Edgerly. "Rough but diverting. However, I think I'll go back to the post and spend the evening with Upton's *Tactics*."

"Scarcely answers the problems of a Sioux campaign," said Garnett. "Upton conceives of a cavalry as a solid force meeting a solid enemy. The Sioux simply do not subscribe to the doctrine of staying in one place or in sufficient force to be met and defeated. It is like charging a cloud of dust."

"The answer is," suggested Edgerly, "for the cavalry to in turn do the same thing. Make rapid night marches, hide by day, split and come together."

"That would be practical if we had no wagon train, no luggage, no such impediments as saddles, intrenching tools and so on. The Anglo-Saxon horse soldier is a cumbersome object moving along at five miles an hour. The element of surprise is not in him unless he is fighting equally cumbersome opposition. If you attempt to split forces in front of the Sioux the result is that the Sioux see it and destroy each force separately."

Edgerly said: "It depends a great deal on the commander."

"Our commanders are still fighting the Civil War—mass against mass. They come out here with a total lack of information regarding Indians."

"Scarcely true of Custer."

"Edgerly," said Garnett, "doesn't it strike you a little odd to hear him say that one white solider can match ten Indians? Do you believe that? I don't. I believe it to be the kind of reasoning which may lead us into difficulty."

"You sound like Benteen," said Edgerly. "I had not known you were a Benteen adherent."

"No," said Garnett, "I have not aligned myself."

"For my part," said Edgerly, "I believe the regiment will acquit itself with credit when the campaign comes. Did you hear Custer is presently leaving for the East on vacation?"

The two rose, paid their bill and went out—a pair of tall and extremely distinguished-appearing men drawing the covertly admiring glance of the buxom woman at the table. They stepped into a street turned robust and lively by Saturday night's traffic. The gush of Bismarck's lamps played upon the street's moisture-clodded dust and cappers stood before the gaming houses, each with his patter and his urgent invitation. A line of soldiers were spread along a shooting gallery's arcade, the twenty-two-caliber rifle bullets clanging on the metal targets. Edgerly paused a moment to look on, and to make his observation. "That's something we could stand more of in the regiment. We've got too many recruits who are indifferent shots." Half a dozen cowhands whirled through the night's darkness, primed for excitement, and sending their high sudden shouting into the clamor; the town marshal paced taciturnly by on his steady rounds and a tall, white-mustached man came down the street side by side with Josephine Russell.

Edgerly paused before them and lifted his hat, smiling. He shook hands with the elderly man and he made a gallant bow before Josephine, who said: "Nighthawking, gentlemen?"

"A couple of soldiers on the prowl," agreed Edgerly and then, remembering that Garnett had not previously met Josephine's father, made the introduction.

Garnett made his bow and accepted Russell's hand. The girl's presence straightened him like a cold shock and placed him on his best and most charming manner. He observed the girl's casual glance, and met it, and his fast mind began to hunt for the usual signs that would give him a proper lead. He held her attention until she swung her glance to Edgerly.

Russell said: "You've had a cold ride over from the fort, and mighty little entertainment to be had here to pay for it. Happy to have you both join us at our house for a cup of coffee."

Edgerly said, "I should be back at the post, but I shall accept, in order to give Garnett here a view into one of the few civilized homes in this territory."

"You must be thinking of our new plush chair," said Josephine. Edgerly made a move to drop beside her and was forestalled by Garnett who smoothly turned and took her arm. She gave Garnett an amused glance and then again diverted her attention to Edgerly.

"How was the last scout?"

"No excitement. None at all. The Sioux are all coming in willingly for a winter of free beef at the Agency."

"Don't you folks be deceived," said Russell. "There's more things brewing than you're familiar with. I talk to the traders and teamsters. They catch what's going on."

"What's going on?" asked Edgerly.

"The Sioux have got plenty of guns and plenty of shells and plenty of horses. They been visiting, band to band, all this fall. Sitting Bull's been around talking to Gall and Two Moons and Crazy Horse and the other chiefs. It is unusual for Indians to make plans that way. Each band most always goes it alone."

"What are they talking about?"

"You'd never get a Sioux, not even a renegade Sioux, to tell you that."

Edgerly spoke soberly: "Let it be, if they want to fight it out next spring. We shall settle the Indian question once and for all."

Mr. Russell gave the lieutenant an old man's glance of reserved knowledge. "The army's said that for ten years, and it has tried. It has nothing yet to show for its campaigning." But then his courtesy made him smooth over the reflection. "Let's not discuss politics. Coffee will be good after this cold wind. Early winter coming."

☆ 8 ☆

At the Stud Horse

Shafter came into Bismarck half an hour later and entered the nearest saloon; he strolled along the filled tables, he watched the faro rig and he tried a dollar on the roulette wheel. One of A's troopers, a Dutchman by the name of Kanser, sat at the blackjack table, having luck. Kanser looked up at him, pointed to his pile and said: "Sit in, Sarge. I'll bank you. I'm lucky." Shafter shook his head and passed on out of the saloon into the gathering wind. He had reached the far end of the street before he quite realized where he was bound, and then he shrugged his shoulders and continued on across the empty area toward Josephine Russell's. Suddenly he knew that she had been in his mind ever since he had dropped her at the Custer house. He had the clearest picture of her smile, the strongest recollection of her voice. He was going back to her, he told himself, to straighten out a misunderstanding. He had meant nothing by the kiss; he wanted her to know that.

He wasn't aware of visitors until he had knocked; and then it was too late to turn back, for Josephine opened the door at once and seemed pleased to see him. She took his arm, saying, "Come in out of the cold," and drew him through the door. As soon as he got inside he saw Edgerly and Garnett.

He stood still and his thorough knowledge of the gulf that separated officer and enlisted man made him realize the embarrassment of his position, even though he was on the neutral ground of a civilian house. Edgerly was faintly smiling the smile of a man who looked upon an awkward situation with some puzzlement; and he was quick to say, "Good evening, Sergeant."

"Good evening, sir," said Shafter. He was at the moment watching Garnett's eyes display a malice and a thin pleasure, and the sight of that heated him physically and hatred of Garnett was a force that kicked him in his stomach. He thought rapidly of one means or another by which he might gracefully retire from a situation which was as painful to his hosts and to Edgerly as to himself.

The girl understood this as well as he did. She saw the whole scene quite clearly, Shafter's stony attitude of attention in front of his superior officers, Edgerly's gentlemanly effort to break the restraint with his friendly smile, and the satisfaction visible on Garnett's face. She said to Shafter in a soft and hurried voice: "Wouldn't you like to have a cup of coffee?"

He said: "I've had supper."

Edgerly meanwhile had done his quick thinking. Now he said: "Did you find the horse I sent you after?"

"Yes sir," said Shafter.

"That's fine, Sergeant. Where was he?"

"Beyond the Point."

"Take him back to the fort for me, Sergeant," suggested Edgerly, and gave Shafter his repressed grin.

Shafter turned out of the house at once. The girl followed him, closing the door. He had stepped from the porch when her voice stopped and turned him. He stood still, watching her move forward. "I'm very sorry," she murmured. "I suppose it was my fault. If I hadn't invited you inside you wouldn't have been placed in an uncomfortable situation. But it would have seemed very rude if I hadn't asked you in, wouldn't it? You wouldn't have known the reason and you would have thought me without any manners at all."

"It doesn't matter," he said.

But she shook her head as she watched him. "I'm afraid it does. You're quite angry."

"No," he said. "I have no privilege to be angry. Good night."

He was down the steps when she stopped him again. "Just a moment," she said and turned into the house. Presently she came out with a heavy coat wrapped around her. She took his arm, not saying anything, and she walked with him back through the windy darkness toward Bismarck's street. When they reached the foot of the street he stopped and faced her. "That was nice of you."

She said: "I hate that military distinction between officers and men. I really hate it."

"It can't be otherwise," he said.

"Edgerly was very thoughtful."

"The man is a gentleman by instinct."

"There's something very bitter between you and the other one—Garnett. I think that's what made you most angry."

He looked at her and was ashamed of the trouble he had caused her. He said: "I apologize for bringing any of my feelings into your house. You shouldn't give it another thought. I had no right to come to you."

She chose her words with a good deal of care. "I have my own rules of right and wrong. You must let me feel the way I wish to feel about it."

He smiled down at her somewhat in his old and easy way, but she knew he was inwardly rankling and then she was completely convinced that her prior judgment of him was correct. Had he never been of a higher grade than a sergeant he would have accepted the scene in her house without a second thought and automatically would have made his departure. But he had felt embarrassment, even though he knew the rules of the game; he had made his exit as gracefully as possible, to save her feelings as well as his own. He had once been something better, and perhaps the memory of that was the thing that had most hurt him.

"You have a gentle heart," he said. "Do you wish me to see you back to the house?"

"No. Come to supper Wednesday night."

She thought he meant to refuse, for he stood silent as he considered it. Then she saw his smile come again. "That will be something to look forward to," he said and lifted his hat to her and went up the street.

She stood a moment, watching him stride away, sharing his embarrassment and made angry at the scene which had produced it. Presently she shrugged her shoulders and moved back toward the house. "Some of it I don't understand," she thought. "Some of it came from the other officer—from Garnett."

At the south end of the street Shafter hailed a freighter moving out of town and climbed aboard, to sit in heavy silence beside a taciturn driver whose sole remark was "Hyah Lily, hyah, Don!" The blackness of the night closed in and the fog broke like a fine rain against them, very cold. "Damn him," Shafter thought, "he's moved into another home, to stalk another woman." There was no feeling as bad as the one which that knowledge brought; it whetted his temper dangerously, it brought up from the past small pieces of memory one by one and revived a story he had never been able wholly to forget. "He'll spoil her if he can, knowing I know her. God damn him!" He slammed the palm of a hand hard down on the seat from thinking of it, drawing the teamster's slanted glance. "No mosquitoes this time of year," said the driver.

Three quarters of an hour later the lights of the Point began to make crystal blooms through the fog and by degrees the sound of music moved forward. They passed a building strongly lighted and skirted others one by one. "Which is the Stud Horse?" asked Shafter.

The driver pointed with his arm. Then he said: "Been there before?"

"No."

"Then you're a fool for goin' near it."

Shafter said, "That may be," and dropped into a road slowly turning to mud beneath the wheels of the steady-passing wagons. When he reached the door of the Stud Horse he noticed a few troopers hanging back in the darkness, grouped together. Passing through he came upon a room the approximate size of A Company's quarters, with its bar running the full length of one wall, with the customary grouping of poker tables and other gambling layouts. There was a small floor for dancing and a raised platform at one end on which sat a piano, and a pianist in a velveteen jacket, an accordion player and a fiddler. There was additionally on the platform a rawboned girl singing a song about a soldier lad who would hear no more bugles to the muted accompaniment of the violin. Fragments of the song came through a considerable racket, for the place was well occupied by soldiers from the post, and this was the latter part of the evening so that the fun had gotten moderately rough. He saw Lovelace standing at the bar and walked toward him. The youngster gave him a look and murmured: "The crowd's been waitin' for you. They're in the back room."

Lovelace's hair was as yellow as a girl's and he had a nice pair of eyes. A glass of whiskey stood before him on the bar, so far untouched; he moved it between his hands with short restless gestures and he seemed nervous.

"I'd let that stuff alone until later," said Shafter.

"I wish this was over with," said the lad. "But we got to wait until the patrol comes through. L Company's outside. I saw 'em awhile ago."

"You been in this kind of fighting before?"

"No," said Lovelace. "I'm not afraid of it, but maybe this drink would help."

"Wait awhile," said Shafter and pushed the whiskey away. The front door opened and a file of troopers came briskly in, headed by a sergeant. The sergeant bawled: "All out for the ferry. Make it sharp now, boys. Get away from that bar—cash in. I won't be tellin' you twice." The detail tramped out.

"We'll go out and circle the place to the back room," said Lovelace. The music stopped and Shafter and Lovelace moved with the crowd into the sparkling, damp air. Voices called through the blind fog and somewhere a woman started to laugh and kept on until she ran out of breath. He heard the patrol sergeant shouting in and out of the Point's various dens. Lights died here and there as Lovelace led him around the corner of the Stud Horse, past a group of waiting troopers. He heard one of them say:—

"That's that new sergeant of A Company."

"Can he fight?"

"He licked Donovan."

"He's my oyster, boys. Where'd that damned patrol go to?"

Lovelace led him to the rear of the building and opened a door into a little room crowded with A troopers. A lamp burned on the table and smoke filled the place. Donovan said:—

"You're a man to keep a date on the dot, Professor. Nine it is. The patrol's gone by."

"Hold it a minute," said Sergeant McDermott. "Hackett is patrol sergeant tonight and he knows about this. So he said, don't start a fight until he gets out of hearin'."

"You think of everything," said Donovan.

"There's a right way to fix things—and a wrong way," said McDermott. "Lovelace, how many L men did you see?"

"Eight or nine."

"The agreement was not more than ten to a side," said McDermott, "but you got to watch that outfit. It is not to be trusted."

Shafter counted noses. He said: "We've got twelve here, Mac."

"That's entirely different," said McDermott. "Just in case they got more."

Shafter grinned at the men around him, at Donovan's scarred professional fighting face, at the wholly unconcerned Bierss, at Lovelace who was worried and tried to hide it, at Tinney whom he felt to be treacherous, at the other troopers standing shoulder to shoulder around the room; it was the troop spirit that drew them here—the pride of it in their bones and the rank lust of living in their blood. They would be bruised and they would be hurt and some of them would carry scars afterwards, but still it was the faith of one man to another that brought them here.

There was a scratching and a murmuring out in the big room. McDermott said: "That's them," and opened the little room's inner door and stepped through with A's troopers behind him. McDermott looked across the room at the L troopers drawn into a kind of line; he said, politely formal, "Well, gentlemen, here we are. How many have you got?"

There was a sergeant to speak for L—a rawboned heavy man with pure-black mustaches roping down from either side of his mouth. "You can count, Mac."

"So I can, and I count thirteen. That's more than ten."

"Ain't it, though," retorted L's sergeant. "And I can count, too, and I count twelve. You tryin' to fool us again?"

"I said to the boys," said McDermott, "that you could never trust L. I was right, wasn't I?"

"Twelve and twelve then," said L's sergeant, and turned to point a finger at one of his men. "You, Gatch, stand aside and stay out of it."

McDermott took a look at the discarded L trooper and was derisive. "Him? Hell, leave him in the fun. He ain't goin' to be of any use to you anyhow."

The two troops had spread out and had gradually drifted nearer. A man came from the bar, speaking to them: "What you pick my place for? I get the worst of it all the time. Take your scrap over to the City of Paris for a change. You bust up any more poker tables for me and I'm goin' to turn you in to Custer."

"Yeah," said McDermott, "you do that. He'll pay the bill." But then he stopped his forward drifting and stabbed an arm at one of the troopers in front of him. "Conboy, what're you doin' here? This is strictly between A and L."

But L's sergeant said in a cool and crafty voice: "Nothin' was said about that."

Conboy was built short and broad and muscular. He had a bull's neck and a jet-black head of hair cropped close to his skull and when he looked out upon A Company's ranks he dropped his head and scanned them from beneath his heavy brows. He was a knuckle-scarred man, flat of lip and flat of nose, and he rubbed his shoes gently back and forth on the floor, his knees springing into a slight crouch. Donovan protested at once. "Nothin' was said about bringin' in outside bruisers, either. Is this an honest fight, or ain't it?"

"Now will you listen to who's speakin' those words?" jeered L's sergeant.

"All right," said Donovan. "Pair off as you want, but I'll take Conboy."

"I've licked you before, Donovan," said Conboy, now speaking for himself. "I want fresh meat this time."

"So you've got down to pickin' your meat easy," said Donovan with heavy sarcasm. "You should be proud of that, Conboy."

"I'll take one man," said Conboy with a kind of insolent weariness. "When I have done him up I'll back off. That leaves things even enough."

"Who's the man?" demanded McDermott.

"Him," said Conboy and pointed at Shafter. "I hear he thinks he's a fighter."

McDermott was outraged at the affair and said so. "Martin," he said to L's sergeant, "if that damned misfit outfit of yours is so afraid of itself that it has got to ring in professional talent to win a scrap, you can go to hell before you get any further consideration from us."

Donovan had drifted beside Shafter and now whispered. "The man is a bruiser. He fought all the big ones in England. I have fought him twice. He's better than me, Professor. He's better than you."

Conboy stood watching Shafter with an idle, lowering light in his pale-blue eyes, with his scarred head dropped after the fashion of a dangerous bull half ready to charge. He was barrel-chested and he had massive legs but his girth bulged out from his hips like pillow stuffings; he was past his prime and no longer kept himself hard, but the crafty skill of his long years was more than enough among amateurs. He was, Shafter guessed, beyond thirty-five.

Conboy said: "You ready?"

Shafter moved to the bar and peeled off his overcoat and blouse and shirt. He heard Conboy say in a vast, confident voice: "The rest of you lads hold off your fight till we have ours. I like a proper audience."

"A knockdown is a round?" asked Donovan. "You back off when he's on the floor?"

"So it is," said Conboy shortly.

"Then it is understood," said Donovan. "Everything proper. If you forget that, Conboy, I'll come up behind you with a chair."

Conboy had stripped to the waist, and now he squatted slightly, one foot forward and both enormous fists cocked stiffly before him. Shafter squared off before him, standing balanced with his arms down. Conboy stared at him from under his shaggy brows. "Get your guard up, you fool. I'll not play around with a green man. Come on, guinea, give me a fight—give me a fight."

The troopers had fashioned a circle to watch this; other troopers were returning to the Stud Horse, drawn by the rumor of trouble. Shafter looked at Conboy's feet, so solidly planted on the floor, anchored there by the man's vast bulk, and experimentally he slowly circled Conboy at a distance, watching Conboy's shoes make little shuffling turns; suddenly Shafter whipped back in the opposite direction and saw Conboy's feet stop and reverse. Conboy's footwork had been slow and Conboy knew it as well as Shafter, for his pale eyes heated up and he let out a huge roar and came rushing forward with his head down and his big hands reaching out in feinting punches. Shafter slid by him, hooked a hard jab into the man's belly, swung and caught Conboy on the side of the neck. Conboy, never off balance, whirled catlike and launched his rush; he missed with his right hand and reached full out with his left fist and caught Shafter on the shoulder, shaking Shafter backward. He followed up his chance, pursuing Shafter. Shafter wheeled aside, swinging behind Conboy and waiting there.

Conboy came around with an irritated scowl. "Come on—quit the fancy stuff and give me a fight!" He stood still, his flanks heaving softly to his breathing. He jiggled his fists up and down, feinting as he remained in his tracks and watching Shafter with his alert and crafty eyes. L Company's men were beginning to ride Shafter with their comment:—

"That's monseer, the dancer."

"Take a crack at him, Shafter. It won't hurt any worse to get killed now than later."

Shafter moved sidewise again, slowly turning a circle while Conboy irritably wound about. Shafter heard Donovan murmur: "Take your time Professor. Make him come to you. The big tub of guts is too heavy to move."

Conboy heard it and flung his head aside to shout at Donovan: "I moved fast enough for you, lad—"

Shafter slipped in, cracked him on the side of the face and laced a jab into his flank; he had learned something about the man at the first exchange of punches, and learned something now, for Conboy's ruffled temper gave him speed and he came around in a flash and smashed through Shafter's fending arm and hit him with a left-hand blow on the chest. It had a crushing effect, turning Shafter cold. All he saw for that moment was Conboy's red face and pale-blue eyes moving against him; he ducked and barely avoided a killing punch that went windy past his cheek; in self-defense he fell against Conboy, locked Conboy's arms and laid his weight against Conboy. Donovan yelled: "That's it—that's it!"

Conboy roared, "Is it now?" and threw his bullet round head forward, cracking Shafter hard on lip and nose. Shafter locked his fingers together behind Conboy's back and squeezed, but it was like squeezing into sponge rubber; he could not spring the man's ribs. He bore Conboy backward by his dead weight, he shifted his legs to protect his crotch against the up-driving of Conboy's knees and he brought his heel hard down on Conboy's instep. The heavy man had grown angry and his wind began to trouble him as he tried to fling Shafter away. They had wheeled around the circle, with the circle giving away, and now they came to the bar. Conboy used a sudden concentration of energy to swing and hurl Shafter against the bar. Shafter, who realized what the man wanted to do, let himself be carried around and then flung his own strength into the wrestling.

Conboy, overbalanced, struck the bar and was pinned to it. Shafter surged against him, driving the man's shoulders backward. He heard Conboy grunt and wheeze and he pushed Conboy far enough to draw one of the man's legs from the ground. He let go, smashed him under the neck with two hard side-swinging punches, saw Conboy's arms lift and then drove in with his knee full into Conboy's belly.

For a little while he had Conboy cornered and he grew reckless of his own defense. He battered Conboy's kidneys, he flung himself against the man again with all his weight and threw his forearm across Conboy's windpipe, springing the man's back on the edge of the bar. He matched Conboy's strength with his own and he balanced his weight against Conboy's. He heard L Company shouting at him, outraged at the turn of the affair and disliking this kind of fighting.

He heard something crash and then the truce snapped and the troopers rushed yelling at one another.

He saw Conboy's face grow crimson from strain and he felt the man's oxlike heart slug through his shirt. He let go the pressure and stepped back and drove a right-hand blow with all the power he had into Conboy's belly. He saw Conboy sag; but that was all he saw. Fired up and aggressive, he momentarily forgot that this man had spent a lifetime learning rough-and-tumble; suddenly out of nowhere Conboy's fist caught him on the head and the explosion of it lighted his brain brilliantly and he felt himself spin away and go backward. He never knew when he hit the floor.

When he awoke he had a thundering headache and a sick hollowness in his belly. There was a stillness in the saloon and out of the stillness a man said: "That patrol will be back here in a minute. Maybe we had better carry him."

He couldn't see who did the talking, but he said: "Damned if you will," and rolled and put the palms of his hands on the floor, pushing himself up. Then he heard Donovan's husky, gravelly voice close by. "Now that's the lad, Professor. A drink will fix it, and we've just got time for one."

He stood up with the help of Donovan's arm. Donovan's face was a shimmering object behind a fog; it moved gradually out of the fog and became clear. Looking around him he saw A Company's men, worse for the wear and tear of a hard brawl; but he saw L's troopers here too. The affair seemed to be over and no bad feelings left. He spotted Conboy at the bar, both elbows hooked to its edge. Conboy's face was still red and he looked tired. Shafter walked over to his blouse and overcoat and put them on, feeling the pull of his sore places; the ache of his head pounded steadily on.

McDermott slapped the bar with his palm. "Let's get that drink, boys. We can't hold off that patrol all night."

"Conboy," said Shafter, "what'd you hit me with?"

"Me hand, damn you," said Conboy, morosely. He swung himself around to the bar and leaned on it, a tired man and a disgruntled one. Donovan stood by Shafter, feeling good.

"Next time, Conboy, he'll lick you."

"Will he," said Conboy, sourly. "Will he indeed?"

"A month's pay he will," said Donovan.

Conboy gave Donovan a pale and dismal stare and downed his whiskey at a toss and looked dourly at the empty glass. "A man's a fool to be doin' this thing forever."

This crowd was tired, the ferment spilled out of it in one sudden climax of brawling; but it was cheerful. Troopers stood along the bar shoulder to shoulder and drank the cheap Stud Horse whiskey in content while the houseman bitterly complained.

"Who's payin' for those tables? Who's in charge here? By God, I'll go over to the fort tomorrow."

Conboy turned his sour glance to Shafter. "What's the 'Professor' for?"

"Just a jackleg title," said Shafter.

"You'll do," said Conboy grudgingly. "I had to work for that hundred dollars."

Donovan gave him a look. "What hundred dollars?"

There was a man beside Conboy, a trooper with a dandy's haircut and a weakly handsome face; and this one said softly to Conboy, "Shut up, Conboy."

McDermott had gone out of the saloon, and now came hurriedly back. "Back door—back door. Patrol's comin'."

The troopers made a run for the saloon's rear doorways and went scrambling into the darkness; out front the sergeant of the patrol made an unnecessary racket with his command. "Patrol, halt! Patrol at ease! Jackson, you go over to the City of Paris while I see if everything's clear in the Stud Horse!" His voice carried clearly through the misty, cold night; it was a fire-alarm warning to everybody before him, as he knew it would be. Donovan caught Shafter's arm. "Come on, Professor. No use causin' Hackett any trouble."

"Donovan," said Shafter. "Who was the slick one with Conboy?"

"Him? That's Lieutenant Garnett's striker. Purple's his name."

McDermott herded his band together, softly grumbling: "Follow me," and led the way down the bluff and across the sandy lowlands to the river. Lovelace trotted into the darkness and presently called: "Down here." Following his voice, the A Company detachment came upon two boats drawn upon the beach. "Six to a boat," said McDermott. "Pile in."

They shoved the boats into the water, troopers wading out and climbing aboard. These boats were average size and the weight of six troopers pulled them down until the oarlocks were a bare six inches above the water. Donovan had the oars in Shafter's boat and he swore placidly at the troopers crouched on the bottom. "How the hell can I brace my legs?" There was a steady wind out of the north—the cold all-day wind with its bite of winter; as soon as they cleared the beach small waves began to lick against them. McDermott said: "Don't get this damned thing broadside, Donovan, or we'll swamp."

"Say," said Corporal Bierss, "can anybody swim?"

Nobody answered him. The laden boat rose sluggishly with the swells but never quite made the summit; water broke at the bow and sprayed inboard. Somebody let out a yell. "Fine," said Bierss, "I'm glad one man can walk home if we sink."

"Listen," said somebody else in an uneasy voice, "let's go back."

"Shut up," said Bierss. "Other people want to enjoy the music."

"What music?"

"Ah," said Bierss, "the fiddles of heaven are playing."

Donovan had the nose slightly swung toward the west bank and therefore the waves, coming close upon each other in this narrow stretch of water took the boat on the quarter and gave it a twisting, heaving motion. The fog had closed densely in, shutting off the lights from the fort, the Point, and the stars. The second boat had disappeared and the sound of the troopers in it faded somewhere downstream. They were in a black gut that had no direction, with the wind beating down the river's shallow canyon and the boat wallowing. The Missouri came aboard in flat sheets and somebody stirred, and drew protest from McDermott.

"Lie still."

Bierss said in his idle, unexcitable voice: "If anybody gets sick on this packet, just remember which way the wind blows."

"We ought to be near shore. How wide is this damned creek?"

"It runs from bank to bank," drawled Bierss. "But my mother always liked to say that no river was as wide as it looked and no chore as hard as it seemed."

"Was she ever on the Missouri in the middle of the night with a bunch of drunks?"

Lovelace spoke up, distinguishable to Shafter by his more careful use of words. "Next time I think I could lick that fellow."

Four men spoke up practically in unison. "You licked him this time."

There was a silence, and then Lovelace said in a surprised, greatly elated voice: "Did I? Did I really lick him? You know, he wasn't a bad fellow."

"Why," said Bierss, "none of 'em are bad after you've had a fight with them."

Donovan had said nothing all this while, being full of labor at the oars and extremely careful in his management of the boat. Now suddenly either his vigilance wavered or the wind swung a curler from a broader angle, for the boat rose on its side, took the shock of the wave's wallop nearly broadside and went teetering into a trough. It dipped into the river like a bucket, whereupon one trooper lifted himself off the floor and further unbalanced the boat. There was a moment of real danger. Shafter felt the craft sink and felt it grow unmanageable. Water rolled back and forth along the bottom.

"Bierss and Mack," he said, "overboard and hang on." He was at the bow and swung and straddled it and let himself into the river, hanging to the bow's point. He heard Bierss say cheerfully: "Nature's own way of taking a bath." Shafter felt the boat lighten as it lost something like five hundred pounds of load. "Donovan," he called, "you can't row upstream with the three of us dragging. Just keep the nose angling toward the bank and let the current set you over." He went under as a wave broke across the bow—and he came up spitting. Wind made a sibilant rough sound on the river. Bierss was saying:—

". . . and so Reginald said to Mary, 'Will you walk hand and hand down life's pathway with me?' And so she did and her oldest son grew up to join the cavalry. Donovan, stop long enough for me to shake the water out of my boots."

"It ain't so damned funny," grumbled somebody.

There was a dull crystal glow above them, which would be the fort lights coming through the fog, and the waves had lost force. Donovan rowed steadily and a last curler broke over Shafter's head, the muddiness of it making a taste in his mouth. Now with calmer water, Donovan swung the nose of the craft and headed directly for shore, and presently Shafter felt bottom beneath his feet. He walked into shallower water, pulling the boat with him.

The troopers got out and hauled the boat to dry land while McDermott murmured, "Wait," and disappeared in the downstream darkness. Donovan also moved away and in a little while returned. "We're half a mile below Post Ten." Somewhat later McDermott came back with the troopers who had been in the other boat.

"This river," said Donovan thoughtfully, "ain't anything to fool with. I never did like water."

The party walked upstream into the cutting wind. Shafter felt coldness slice through him; water drained down his body and collected in his boots and his boots squealed as he stepped forward. After ten minutes of this forward groping McDermott whispered back: "Follow me," and tackled the bluff.

They moved Indian file to the bluff's edge and lay flat, waiting the sentry's passage. It was now past taps with the lights of barracks darkened, but a glow came on from Officers' Row and from the buildings scattered outside the post proper. A shape emerged from the misty blackness, paused and faced the river. McDermott waited a decent interval and then called softly forward:—

"For God's sakes, Killen, move on to the end of your post. We're cold."

The sentry growled: "Keep your mouth shut. You want me to violate the articles of war?" He walked into the darkness.

The file of troopers rose up, passed the stables and crept to the rear of the barrack. McDermott opened the door and led the way into the room's warm darkness; one by one the troopers groped to their bunks, the sound of water-logged boots betraying them. Shafter stripped naked, laid his clothes at the foot of the bunk and slid into his blankets.

The night was over, leaving him with his bruises and his headache; the left side of his face was numb from the last blow landed by Conboy. Otherwise he felt content, relieved of his cares and made sweet again by the swift burning-out of excess energy; all through the barrack he heard men whispering and the soft laughter of troopers as they remembered back—and this sound was a good sound and gave him peace.

Then he recalled Conboy's hundred-dollar chore and realized it was Garnett who had offered the money to have Conboy cut him into ribbons; he had been tired but now he lay long awake, his fresh hatred rising. He was still awake when Hines stepped from the orderly room with a lantern and played its light upon the row of bunks; he had stayed discreetly away until he was certain of the party's return and now, like an indulgent father, came to see if all were accounted for.

☆ 9 ☆

Word from the Past

One day, the restless Custer took his wife and brother Tom east for winter; he took with him also the driving energy which whipped the regiment's temper, so that without his presence the Seventh settled into a slower routine. Early winter rains slashed out of slate-colored skies lifting the Missouri a full five feet and driftwood wheeled down the river's mud-greasy surface while the quickening current began to undercut the crumbling bluffs. Standing near A Company's stable, Shafter watched huge sections of earth crash into the water and send small tidal waves onward. Two soldiers were caught in a squall while crossing from the Point and were never seen again. Three babies were born within the post and a sergeant's wife on Laundress Row committed suicide.

Continued reports of disaffection came from the various Indian agencies. Runners arrived with news that the Sioux, half starved for want of enough government-issued beef, were beginning to leave the reservations and return to their own lands westward. The Seventh, now under Reno, scouted steadily in that direction to turn stragglers back, but it was like spreading a net against the wind. The spirit of revolt and resistance was a growing thing throughout the Indian bands as Sitting Bull's couriers traveled from village to village. Near the end of November Calhoun and thirty men had a brush with a fleeing party of Sioux on the Heart River in which one trooper was injured; the Sioux disappeared in the darkness.

A hundred recruits arrived from Jefferson Barracks to fill the Seventh's thin ranks. Lieutenant Benny Hodgson, about to surrender his commission and return to civil life, decided to stay through the summer campaign which he felt to be coming, and was made battalion adjutant under Reno. Young Jim Sturgis, the colonel's son, newly minted from West Point, joined his father's regiment and was attached to M Company quartered at Rice. There was the rumor of a War Department scandal coming out of the East as well as half-verified news of army plans being laid by Grant and Sherman and Sheridan for a winter campaign to crush the Sioux. Custer, the post learned, was in New York, being feted and dined and enjoying the company of that great Shakespearean actor Lawrence Barrett. General Terry, the department commander at St. Paul, sent on urgent orders for the Seventh to overhaul its equipment and to whip its recruits into shape as rapidly as possible; whereby on the windy bitter mornings the troops went through their monotonous evolutions on the parade, marched outside the fort for rifle-range practice, and daily scouted westward. Freighters broke the first light snowfall with supplies for the quartermaster and commissary depots on the reservation. Miners began to stream back from the Black Hills, forced out by weather and by the fear of Sioux revenge in the spring. The Far West, Captain Grant Marsh commanding, came downriver and stopped briefly to report he had been fired on four times in four days along the upper stretches of the Missouri. On December 6 the telegraph flashed news from the East that couriers would be sent out to instruct the recalcitrant Sioux to come into the reservations by January 31, or be treated thereafter as hostiles. That same day the first hard blizzard swept out of the north and pounded Lincoln for thirty-six hours, marking the end of train service from the East until spring.

First Sergeant Hines opened the orderly room directly after morning sick call and waggled a finger at Shafter. When he reached the room, Shafter found Captain Moylan at the little desk with a letter in his hand. The captain said: "Hines, step out a moment," and waited until the old sergeant had gone.

"Kern," said Moylan, and nodded at the letter, "this came to headquarters three or four days ago. Cooke gave it to me to handle as I saw fit." He handed it to Shafter and he sat back to watch Shafter's face as the latter looked down on the single page with its scent so familiar, with its light quick handwriting:—

The Commanding Officer,
Seventh Cavalry,
Fort Lincoln, D.T.

As a particular favor to one who is vitally interested in knowing the whereabouts of Kern Shafter, is he a member of your regiment?

Very truly,
ALICE MACDOUGALL

The scent raced across the years and the sight of that handwriting made him vividly remember the smiling and the laughter and the love that once had been without bottom or boundary. Her personality was a fire glowing against the blackness of time; her voice was a light bell stroking its melody through long emptiness, rousing his memories so fully that the hurt of all that had been was a physical pain. He folded the page into smaller and smaller squares, tore it across, and dropped the pieces into the iron stove in the middle of the orderly room.

"No answer?" asked Moylan.

Shafter turned his head slowly from side to side. "None at all."

"I remember her very distinctly," said Moylan. "Last time was behind the lines at Fredericksburg." He sat idle, a heavy, sandy-haired, bluff-featured man with memories in turn sweet and acid. "You were the officer then, and I was the sergeant. Very odd to recall. You've never seen her since?"

"Once," said Shafter. "Once in Baltimore."

The captain said in a careful way: "I always wondered one thing. Did Garnett marry her?"

"No."

"God damn him," growled the captain, "he's got a lot to answer for on Judgment Day." He looked up. "She still remembers you. Is this the first time you've heard of her—since Baltimore?"

"No," said Shafter. "I have heard indirectly of her many times. She has spent a fortune tracing me."

"She has a fortune to spend," said Moylan.

"She always had everything she wanted," said Shafter.

"Until she met Garnett," amended Moylan. "Then she had nothing." He sat heavily in thought, and at last shook his head. "It didn't take her long to find out she guessed wrong, did it? She has apparently been sorry for ten years—and wishes to see you. That's a long time for a woman to regret a thing. Doesn't it have any effect on you?"

"No," said Shafter.

Moylan looked at Shafter with steady attention. "It is logical that you should hate Garnett. He'll not be easy with you around here. He'll use his weight on you where he can. He's already tried, has he not?"

"Yes," said Shafter. "But that can work both ways, Myles."

"Do nothing you'll regret."

"Regret?" said Shafter and gave the captain a metal-sharp glance. "If it were in my power to put a bullet through his heart, I'd have no regrets."

"That is not what I meant," said Moylan. "He ruined you professionally once. Do not open yourself to that again by any act."

Shafter said nothing and the captain knew the man well enough to realize his words made no effect on one who, ten years before, had been a wild and headlong kind of warrior. The intervening years had settled Shafter, had given him some wisdom and some tolerance; it had not changed his essential character at all. He was now what he had always been, the proof of it being his return to soldiering after long absence. That caused Moylan a question.

"What brought you back to the uniform, Kern?"

"I was never very happy out of it."

"The old songs, the old bugle calls, the old duties—"

"Not sentiment, Myles. I'm a little old for that, and a little too jaded to be romantic. Maybe I got tired of being my own man doing whatever I pleased, and therefore doing nothing."

"I know you better," said Moylan. "The answer is that soldiering was your lot, as it is to some men more than others. The dust and misery of it, and the content of it as well. The romance of soldiering, of course, is all nonsense in the hands of civilians who know no better. The real part of soldiering is a thing they never know—to come off a scout dirty and frozen to the bone—and to sit at night in comfort and to know you've done a day's good work, and that other men around you have done it, too." He stopped his talking, looked down at his broad hands, and said in a different voice: "We've got need of a sergeant to ride the mail. I told Cooke I had the man for it. You are the man."

"Yes, sir," said Shafter and smiled a little. "You want me out of the post this winter."

"I want no collision between you and Garnett," said Moylan. "Report to Cooke for further instructions. You're listed on A's roster as detached beginning today."

He sat back after Shafter had gone. Hines returned and set about the ritual of paper work. Moylan said: "I gave him the job."

"Does he know about bad weather?"

"Yes," said Moylan and drew a piece of paper before him. He dipped the pen and stroked the corners of his mustaches for a moment and then began:—

My dear General:

It would require the colonel's approval to carry this matter to the adjutant general's attention. Therefore, I write directly to you as an old friend, to bring to your attention the case of Kern Shafter, once an officer of the Fourteenth Ohio . . .

"Captain," said Hines, "is there a feelin' between Shafter and the Lieutenant Garnett?"

"Why?" asked the captain.

"It is information among the boys that Garnett paid Conboy a hundred dollars to bruise up the lad."

Moylan grumbled in his throat and sat heavy at the table, his silence giving

Hines assent. Hines said discreetly: "There are other things, regardin' the lieutenant's habits—"

Moylan swung about. He stared at Hines. "A woman?"

"A woman."

"I know about that," said Moylan. "But keep your mouth shut, Hines."

Shafter pulled on his heavy coat and Berlin mittens and moved into the white outer world. The wind, driving from the north, had banked all exposed walls of the post eave-high with snow, had laid a two-foot covering across the parade. The roofs of the buildings were puffed up like thatched cottages, the glittering white surface broken only by the dark smudge of chimney. The wind which at the height of the storm had blown at a sixty-mile rate had ceased entirely so that the post had a dampered stillness across which the voices of men carried with a lively sharpness. Shafter moved along the narrow shoulder-high lane carved out by the shovel details, and reported to the adjutant's office. Cooke gave him his instructions.

"You'll have a sleigh and two mules and a week's rations. You'll eat and be quartered along the route, but the rations will be for emergency if you get snowed in anywhere. The round trip to Fargo is approximately two weeks, depending on weather. You'll be wise to follow the railroad closely. You can't see the track but the telegraph poles will always guide you. Here is a list of ranches and shelters along the way. Better spend the morning picking your team and putting your storm pack together. Draw on the quartermaster for extra robes and blankets. Leave at reveille tomorrow. Get the pouches at the fort's post office and drop back here for special despatches. You'll also take the outgoing mail from Bismarck. That is a courtesy to the town. I have no more to add, except that you should watch your weather most closely. Sometimes you'll never have more than an hour's warning of a blizzard."

Shafter saluted and left the adjutant's office, going out to the big mule barn behind the post to pick a team. He spent an hour doing this, and the rest of the morning stowing the sleigh. Then, with nothing more on his mind and being his own master while on detached duty, he hitched his mules to the sleigh and left the fort for a trial run. In the middle of the afternoon he drew up before Josephine Russell's house and saw her come to the door.

"If you're staying awhile," she called, "drive your outfit into the barn."

He circled the house, left the team and sleigh tied in the barn's runway, and struggled back to the house. The snow was fresh and needed both settling and hardening in order to make decent footing for the mules; a cold night, he thought, ought to put it in shape. He slid out of his heavy coat in the room's warmth and stood with his back to the heater's isinglass windows, watching Josephine's clever hands work at her knitting needles. She sat near a window for the sake of the light, her face now lifting to him, now dropping to her work. She had on a dress the color of dark roses, with a large cameo brooch pinned at the neck; and she seemed pleased with his presence. There were certain things which always gave a woman a cozy, demure air; knitting, he decided, was one of those things.

"What's your errand today, Kern?"

"Just trying out a pair of mules, for the Fargo mail run."

She stopped her work to give him a serious appraisal. "Did you put in for that?"

"It was assigned to me, but I have no objections."

Her smile came quickly up through the soberness of her face, giving it warmth and charm. He watched her lips softly change. "No," she said, "you wouldn't object. When I first met you, Kern, I thought you were a very sophisticated character. In fact I thought perhaps you were of the faded gentleman type. When I heard you had joined the Seventh I thought, 'There goes a man with delusions of romantic adventure.' " She smiled again to remove whatever sting there might have been in her words. "But you have done very well for yourself. Is that little purple spot on your temple the place Conboy hit you?"

"Who tells you of these things, Josephine?"

"An army post is the biggest whispering gallery on earth."

"I got knocked out," he said and stretched his feet before him, loose in the chair and very comfortable. The girl went about her knitting, her head bent. She had turned sober again and he thought she held some displeasure of him behind her silence. After a little while she murmured:—

"What do the women look like in that place?"

He came to his own defense immediately. "Do you think my tastes are on that level?"

"Then what were you there for?" she asked, and looked at him with sharp criticism.

"It was a little family affair between A and L Companies," he said. "The boys asked me to join the party." He thought it over and added: "You could call it my initiation into the troop."

She held herself still, once more debating him in her mind. "The opinion of other men means a great deal to you, Kern."

"The opinion of my kind of men," he amended.

"Are they your kind?" she asked. "The ones you bunk with and march with? Are they really?"

"That's why I joined," he said. "To get back where I belong."

She shook her head, murmuring, "You're strange," and resumed her knitting. "You've had education and many pleasant things, but you go back to a raw and very rough kind of life. Doesn't it cause you any remorse to give up those nice things?"

He sat silent, turning it over in his own mind. Nothing had bothered him since joining, no regrets and no moments of indecision. He remembered now that he had felt at home when he stepped onto Fort Lincoln's parade; weight and care had fallen from him, and the feeling of emptiness within him had somehow been filled. Not one day since that time had he lacked peace of mind.

"You are thinking that I'm ducking out of civil life because it was too hard—letting the government do my thinking in return for eighteen dollars a month."

"It has occurred to me," she said.

"I had no obligations in civil life," he told her. "I had nothing—and I knew it. A man must feel he belongs to something. As long as he floats around space doing little chores that start and end with his hands and never reach his heart, he's no good to himself. Some things are real and some are only tinsel paper that people wrap themselves in, having nothing more important to do with their time. Dust is an honest thing, and so is sweat and the bruises you get from fighting."

"Do you suppose these other troopers think of that?" she said.

"Some do and some don't. Some are good and some are pretty bad. But the point is that when the trumpet blows boots and saddles, they'll all swing up together, and when action begins they'll run forward together. That is what men were made for, Josephine."

She held her eyes down to her work while he talked; she kept them there. Shafter sank low in the chair, the back of his hair ruffled against it and his body sprawled in lank and bony lines. He watched her fingers move with the knitting needles, making little half circles of gracefulness. Small shades of expression softly darkened and softly lightened her face and her lips made their elusive changes as her thinking varied. He got up to fill the stove and noticed that the woodbox was empty; he left the house and got an armload of wood and brought it back. The silence of the house was a pleasant silence; he tipped his head, watching the ceiling, listening to the ticking of a clock. Now and then an echo from Bismarck's main street reached out.

"How old are you, Kern?"

"Thirty-two."

Her knitting needles wove in and out beneath her absorbed eyes, her profile against the strong light of the window was full-lipped and serene.

"Have you ever been married?"

"No," he said.

"Engaged?"

"Yes."

"Are you now?"

"No," he said.

She laid down her knitting and let her hands lie idle in her lap while she gave him an exacting appraisal. She was thoroughly serious, wholly wrapped up by her momentary interest in him. "It was something painful, wasn't it?"

He nodded and let that serve for an answer. Her glance searched all the way through him, and presently she shook her head and took up her knitting again, speaking as much to herself as to him. "It has left its effect. It isn't that you are cynical about women. I've never caught that in your talk, but you distrust women. You look at them as though they had qualities which men should be on guard against."

"Women," he said in his idle, speculative way, "are the only real beauty in the world. What good is a lovely sunset if a man can't embrace it? There is a need in him that neither sky nor earth nor music can fill. Only a woman can fill it."

She murmured: "You say that as if you believed it but didn't want to believe it."

"A woman is a wind, wild and sweet. A woman is a song. I have never thought differently."

"Kern," she said, "your trouble was that you wanted too much. No woman can be all that."

"There are rare meetings like that—of a man carrying to a woman all that he feels and needs, and receiving from her all that he hoped for."

"You have been deeply disappointed," she said.

"A man's not entitled to disappointment," he said. "The fault is more apt to be in him than in the woman. Therefore, he draws back and forgets about it."

"You have not forgotten."

"I have not forgotten that I was a fool," he said, quite careful with his words. "I will not be a fool twice."

She kept her attention on her knitting, her mouth drawn together in almost severe lines. She made no attempt to break the silence; she seemed done with him. Presently, in a little gesture of impatience, she put the needlework aside and rose and went into the kitchen. He heard her call back:—

"When does A Company have its ball for the enlisted men?"

"Two weeks away, I believe."

"It will remind you of other days."

"I had no intention of attending," he said.

She came out in a little while with a cup of coffee for him, and one for herself. She took her chair again. "One stretch of road between here and Fargo you'll want to watch. There's no shelter of any kind for thirty miles if a blizzard should catch you. It is between Romain's ranch and a little section house called Fossil Siding. When do you leave—when will you be back?"

"Leave in the morning. Should return in ten or twelve days unless the weather stops me."

She put her coffee cup aside and rose and stood at the window with her back to him. Her shoulders were square but rounded softly at the points and her black hair lay rolled and heavy on her head. She touched the pane idly and turned to him, looking across the room with a restless light in her eyes. He sat still, meeting her glance and seeing the shadow and shape of odd things come and vanish. She wasn't smiling but the thought of a smile was a hint at the corners of her mouth, in the tilt of her head. She took his coffee cup and went into the kitchen. He heard her move and then stand still; and suddenly his mind was fully on her and the thought of her went through him and kicked up its reaction. He got up and reached for his coat.

"This is a lazy man's life."

She came into the living room. "Have supper here."

"There's the team on my hands. Otherwise I'd accept."

She watched him button up the big overcoat and grow bulky. His shoulders made a sweep and the uniform took much of the first-noticed softness from him, toughening him. She noticed the scars on his knuckles.

"So you had your fight and crossed the river on a dark, rough night—and almost swamped. Is that what you like?"

He grinned. "That's what I like," he said. "It was a good party."

"I haven't been to a dance since early fall," she murmured.

He looked at her a moment. "It's strictly an enlisted man's ball. No officers and officers' ladies."

"So then?"

"You're for gentlemen and officers, Josephine."

"Am I?" she asked him, coolly meeting his attention. "How do you know that?"

He saw in her at that moment a reckless spirit. She had wanted something and she had asked for it; her eyes held his glance, with the hint of a temper as aggressive as his own. He said: "I can't be put in the position of refusing a lady's wish. Will you go to the ball with me?"

"Of course," she said.

She was smiling slightly, knowing what she had done to him, knowing also the boldness of her asking. He moved to the door and turned there; she was alert, she was carefully exploring his face with her eyes for things she seemed to want to know. "You gave yourself away," she told him. "If you weren't a gentleman it wouldn't have been difficult to refuse me."

"Maybe," he said, "I really wanted to take you." But he shook his head at her. "It is not a good thing for you. It will cut you out from being invited to officers' dances. When you let yourself be seen with an enlisted man, you are crossing one of the toughest boundaries in the world."

She started to tell him something, thought better of it, and moved around him to open the door. Then she said: "You are a rough-and-tumble man, Sergeant. But I think I can hold my own with you."

He grinned as he lifted his cap, and then went into the snow, openly laughing, and presently curled around the house with the sleigh. She was on the front porch and waved at him as he went by. She stood a considerable while in the biting, still air, now wishing she had told Shafter that Garnett had invited her to officers' ball and that she had accepted. It was the reason she had deliberately forced an invitation to the enlisted men's ball from Shafter. She knew, as a matter of intuition, that he disliked the officer. This, then, was her way of balancing the situation, of taking the edge from any resentment he might feel toward her for going with Garnett.

She turned into the house and closed the door, and stood with her back to it. "Why should I bother to go to the trouble of saving his feelings? What do his feelings matter to me? I am simply another woman he means to keep at a proper distance."

She remembered all that he had said, and she knew much that he had not said—the streaks of hopelessness and resentment, the imagination that he could not entirely subdue, the hunger that no amount of self-discipline could kill. He had partly given himself away, she realized. "The woman," she thought, "left her marks all over him. She must have been brutal about it, to produce his present state of mind. Yet even now he is not sure he doesn't love her. That's behind it all."

She moved across the room, despising the woman, whoever she was; ashamed of the woman, and outraged at a story she could only guess at.

☆ 10 ☆

Mr. Garnett Tries His Luck

At reveille he was up; by eight o'clock he had put the fort and the river behind him. There was a hundred pounds of mail in the sleigh, a week's emergency rations and a roll of bedding, and extra grain for the mules. Bismarck dropped behind a steel-gray winter haze—its housetops and its little winding columns of smoke; ahead of him stretched a white smoothness broken only by the line of telegraph poles and, at great intervals, the low-lying smudge of a ranch house. That first day out he saw several of these ranches; and put up at one of them that night. The second day brought a duller sky and a greater emptiness. The mules went steadily on, hauling the sleigh at a brisk clip where the snow lay thoroughly hardened by alternate freezing and thawing. When they reached soft patches the team fell to a slow, exhausting struggle. He passed two houses on the second day; on the third, he ran almost his whole trip with nothing in sight but the telegraph poles. He crossed little creeks frozen to the bottom, he flushed small bands of antelopes and saw where they had scratched away the snow for forage. The fourth day he came upon a party of warriors cutting out of the north on a hunting trip; they saw him and advanced until they identified his uniform and then turned away, sending back their insolent cries. The fifth evening brought him to a stalled freight train waiting for a snowplow; he stayed that night in the train's caboose, stabling the mules in an abandoned sod hut. The following afternoon, passing close-grouped farms, he came into Fargo—which was only another version of Bismarck. By daybreak the following morning he was on his way back, bearing not only mail but several packages for Bismarck merchants and a little pouch of despatches from department headquarters at St. Paul.

He brought with him also a week's collection of newspapers and read them at night, in one ranch house or another. President Grant had taken the Indian matter into his hands and had ordered a winter campaign to follow the failure of the Indians to return peacefully to their reservations on the deadline of January 31. One headline said: CUSTER WILL LEAD WINTER EXPEDITION. CAN BOY GENERAL REPEAT BRILLIANT WASHITA STRATEGY? The *New York Tribune* had a long and tempered essay on the ills and evils of Indian affairs, deplored the instances of corruption and misdealing which had characterized so much of white relations with the savage, but sadly concluded that the march of white man's progress could not be stopped, therefore making rigorous treatment of the Indian the most humane in the long run. The *Boston Post* bitterly assailed the greed of the white man and the white man's consistent disregard of his obligations.

The history of relations between white man and red has been an unbroken story of rapacity, cruelty and of complete lack of feeling on the part of the white. Nothing has been constant with him except his sacred right to seize whatever land he wished from whatever Indian tribe he wished. We have no reason to be proud of our dealings with the weaker savage race. We have no right to call ourselves a civilized or cultured people with that record against us.

But the *St. Louis Globe* reflected the view of the western settler and trader and land-hungry emigrant.

There is no use entering into a discussion of the morals of the white man versus the red man. All the debate in Christendom cannot blink the fact that the white man is a surging tide of conquest, of settlement and progress, whereas the Indian is content to rove nomadically across the land as he has done for the tens of thousands of years, ignoring an earth which could provide him riches were he industrious enough to cultivate it. Primitive indolence and barbaric narrowness is his character, nor does he wish for anything we call civilization. Let us not shed tears over the ills done poor Lo. Poor Lo has been at the business of killing and raiding and stealing for many centuries before the white man came. It is his one great object in life, it is his profession and his pastime. Whereas a white boy is taught to believe that the purpose of a man is scientific and literary and social advancement, the one and only training an Indian boy ever receives is to go out and kill his enemy, thereby becoming great in his own tribe. Were the race of the Indian to die off tomorrow there would be no permanent handiwork behind him, no inventions, no scholarship except a few primitive daubs on this or that rock, no system of ethics at all, not one worthy thing to justify his tenantry upon the fairest of all continents. By contrast look upon the white man's record in a brief 250 years here. That should be answer enough to all the silly sentimentality current in the East. It is time now to end the endless marching and countermarching of skeleton cavalry columns commanded by officers who know nothing of savage warfare. It is time now to send in one large and determined expedition to crush savage resistance permanently and to confine the red man to the reservation, so that at last the white race may get on with its appointed destiny, which is to harness the continent and to build civilization's network across it.

The system of post traderships was under fire and Congressman Clymer had asked the House for authority to investigate the Indian Bureau and the War Department, suggesting scandal. Secretary of War Belknap was quoted as saying that yellow journalism made a mockery of an honest man's attempt at efficient administration. There was definitely, in all the papers, a growing preoccupation with the Indian question—and a growing scent of trouble brewing. There were also many items regarding Custer. He had given a talk at the Lotus Club. His spectacular presence was noted and admired at the theater.

Custer [said the *New York Herald*] has as much right as any man living to speak of Indians. His statement that one regiment of cavalry—with pardonable pride he mentions his own Seventh—could handle the Sioux in one campaign as effectively as ten years of treaty making and treaty breaking, must be seriously regarded. In any such campaign, who else has the skill, the matchless daring to equal his leadership? The Boy General of 1864 is now the mature Indian fighter, the darling of his troops, and in the full prime of his great powers.

There was the smell of bad weather in the air as Shafter moved westward over the empty, dull-glittering plain toward Lincoln.

They had been to see "Julius Caesar" played by their closest friend, Lawrence Barrett; and afterwards they had gone up to a mansion facing Central Park where, surrounded by money and power and considerable beauty, Custer had dominated the conversation both by his exuberance and by his reputation. Now, at two o'clock in the morning, the general and his wife returned to their hotel rooms.

The general was keyed up by the fullness of the evening, and at the mercy of his inexhaustible energy; he flung his hat and cape and dress coat the full length of the room and missed the chair at which he aimed. He let them lie and walked a circle of the sitting room while his wife went into the adjoining bedroom.

"Vacation's about gone, old girl," he called out. "We're coming to the end of our period in heaven."

"I'll regret going back," she said. "I've had such a nice time. And you've enjoyed yourself so much."

"No more shows, no more parties for another year. Maybe for two or three years. The army is a strange thing. A little glitter at retreat when the band plays and everybody's in full dress. A little of that followed by hours of drudgery and tedium. It is the tedium that eats out an officer's heart. Year after year of it."

She came out to him in her robe. "Autie, you shouldn't be restless. We've had such a good time. It's nice to have a famous husband. We're welcome in the homes of the rich, the powerful, the artistic, the intelligent. George Armstrong Custer rings the bell and the door opens. I thought of that tonight, watching you talk. I was very proud of you."

He looked at her, he smiled at her; he stood in a moment's rare repose, gentled by her softness, by her love. But it was only for a moment. He had supped at the table of the mighty, and the mighty had been deferent to him because he was General Custer; now he saw that ended as he turned back to his frontier post. He saw more than that. He saw the undramatic years stretch out ahead of him—a continuation of the long eleven years which had followed the Civil War. And as he thought of those years of patience and plodding and unspectacular duties performed, he had his fear. He was a child of adventure; his fame had come of moments of crisis and headlong action. Routine was death to him, but he saw nothing forward but routine. He had reached the pinnacle at twenty-five and all the subsequent years had been anticlimax, a wasting away of those precious hours which a man so meagerly possessed— those hours in which he had his chance at everlasting glory. At thirty-six he was less than he had been at twenty-five. In another ten years he would be forty-six, one more middle-aged Civil War officer whose greatness was only a fading memory with the people, whose place in the sun was taken by younger men seizing their moments of luck.

"Oh, Libby," he said, almost groaning, "I'm in a blind alley. There's no chance open, nothing to reach for. I see the stupid and the dull all around me, rising above me, fawning or tricking their way to power. My enemies are in command of the War Department, cheating me out of chances, giving other men places I ought to have, entrusting incompetent officers to places of responsibility to which I'm entitled. I'm handcuffed. If there was a break I might make, if there was an alley, an opening anywhere, I'd seize it."

"Autie," said Mrs. Custer, whose softness was strength, whose quietness was the only discipline he knew, "what more could you want?"

He sighed greatly and smiled at her. He went forward and kissed her, turned obedient and teasing. "You have a hell of a time with me, don't you, Libby?"

She said: "Civilization is not too good for you. I think we will be happier when we return to the command." But a cloud passed across her expressive face as she remembered that spring was not far away. Spring was her dread, spring was a black cloud that shut out her life's sun—for spring meant campaigning, it meant Autie marching away. Suddenly she turned back into the bedroom.

Custer seized the day's paper and lay out full length on the floor of the room to read it. He became engrossed in a front-page story concerning Congressman Clymer's proposed investigation of the War Department; and presently he sprang up, went to the writing table and sat down at it. Mrs. Custer heard his pen scratching violently through the quietness.

"To whom are you writing, Autie?"

"I'm offering my services as witness to Clymer. I think we shall get the bottom of some scandal, and I know enough of it to lend a hand."

She was silent a moment, then spoke again. "Do you think it wise?"

"Wise or not," he said, "I shall do it."

He finished his letter, addressed the envelope and sealed it; he leaned back in the chair, feeling a thrust of hope. It might lead somewhere; it might lead to an opportunity. It might give him an opportunity to smash at his enemies, to bring him before the people on an issue. It was, at least, an opening—and openings were rare things for a frontier officer. He studied this and grew slightly excited at the thought. He saw himself once more in the current, as he had been before; he saw himself out of the slack water at last. He had to have action to survive, since action was his only gift; and survival and triumph and public acclaim were to him the same sources of life they were to the other public men who fought tooth and claw for them. Fame was a jungle in which predatory beasts roamed; there were no rules in that jungle, only a bitterest kind of fighting. And at fighting he had considerable skill.

* * *

Garnett called for Josephine at eight, stood a moment in the Russell living room to give her his full admiring glance and murmured: "You must forgive me for using a very old phrase. I had no idea you were so—" he paused and seemed to search himself for the word, and went on in an impulsive way—"so damned beautiful."

She was round and mature within a black dress whose solid coloring was broken by little streaks of gold thread along her breasts and sleeves. Her hair, extremely black, lay high and shining on her head, exposing white neck and ears, and a pair of earrings moved slightly as her head turned. She watched him, smiling but not entirely taken in. "I hear you're a gallant man, Lieutenant."

He gave her a keen answering smile and stood sharp-eyed before her. The smile gradually faded. "I suppose so," he agreed. "I suppose the presence of women inclines me toward the kind of speech they want to hear. My feeling is that a woman living out here, with little enough in the way of comfort or luxury, has got something extremely fine in her soul. Even the washerwoman who follows her sergeant from one dismal hovel to another."

"Particularly that woman," corrected Josephine.

"Gallantry or not," he said and was wholly serious, "I mean what I say about you."

"It is at least pleasant to hear."

"And now to the ball," he said, suddenly returned to his high humor; and escorted her to the cutter. They made a rapid passage to the fort and came upon the commissary building, which served as the ballroom, its stores pushed aside and its bare walls and rafters decorated with colored paper shields, crossed arms and bunting. The regimental band sat on a platform at one end of the room. Major Reno, commanding in the absence of Custer, led the grand march with his wife; afterwards the crowd broke into sets for the quadrille.

The officers of the five companies stationed at Lincoln were present in full dress uniforms, gold epaulets, sash and regimental cord draped over the shoulder; and this color flashed and glittered against the dresses of the ladies, and there was a sharp exuberance in all of them, a health and a happiness and a childlike response to one night's freedom. The Benteens and DeRudios and Gibsons came up from Rice where H and M Companies were stationed—and remembrances were spoken for the five troops on far-away station—for Captain Keogh's I Company and Captain Ilsley's E Company at Fort Totten, and for B, G and K in distant Louisiana. The regiment was a clannish thing even though it had not been together as a complete unit for many years; in spite of its jealousies and cliques and animosities, the Seventh was tied together by its traditions, its decade of service.

There were other townspeople, besides Josephine, at the ball; and now and then she saw Charley Reynolds, reputed to be the best scout in the West, come shyly inside and watch the proceedings. He was a small man, very quiet and very soft of speech, dressed in a neat blue suit and black tie; somewhere he had a past which he never mentioned but his eyes were sad blue eyes above a round, smooth face and a semicircle mustache carefully kept. Other officers from the infantry companies stationed at the post were likewise in attendance.

They danced the sets, they danced the polka, the schottische and the waltz. Josephine went swinging away in the arms of this officer or that one; she stood in one little group or another, all of them gay and all charged with little bursts of gossip and laughter and bantering. They stood at the punch bowl—lemonade made with citric acid—they lightly ridiculed one another, out of familiar association, repeating the old, old jokes and the ancient recollections.

"I admire that dress," said Mrs. Smith to Josephine.

"I bought it this fall in the East. I suppose it's the last new one I'll have for three or four years."

"Why," said Mrs. Smith, "I'm wearing one six years old."

Mrs. Calhoun smiled regretfully. "I bought this in 1869. I've never been close enough to the East to get another. It has been altered and let out so often that it is nothing but a mass of thread and stitches. Miss Russell makes old women out of all of us."

Annie Yates and her husband joined the group. Captain Yates ran the back of his fingers across his yellow mustaches. "Myles, I hear your saddler got drunk and snowbound last night."

Moylan nodded. "We are thawing him out one section at a time."

"It shows," said Yates slyly, "what drunkenness will do for a company."

Moylan grinned. "Just have your first sergeant mention it to my first sergeant, if you want to know which outfit is the best at indoor fighting. For recommendations, ask L Company."

"What about that fracas?" asked Yates, turning to Garnett.

Garnett gave Moylan a quick glance and met the captain's cool attention. He flushed a little when he answered Yates. "I know nothing of it."

"Quite a brawl, I heard," said Yates indifferently and moved to his partner as the music began. Major Barrows bowed at Josephine and led her away, leaving his wife for Garnett's attention. Garnett put his arm about her slim waist, adjusted himself at the proper waltz distance and swung her out upon the floor.

Neither of them spoke for a considerable time, he staring over the top of her dark hair and she watching the couples about her with an expressionless disinterest. Now and then she caught sight of Josephine and followed the girl with a narrowed glance, her lips moving together by a pure reaction over which she had no control. Finally she said in her coolest voice: "Your taste is excellent, Edward."

Garnett said, equally cool, "Do you object?"

"Why should I?"

But he knew she was furious, and the knowledge pleased him. "I wish," he murmured, "I might hold you closer."

"Be careful," she murmured, "my husband is watching."

"Does he suspect?"

"It is never possible to know what he thinks or what he knows, Edward. But we must be very discreet."

"I shall have the cutter at the same place tomorrow afternoon."

"No," she murmured, "not so soon. I can't always be finding reasonable excuses to go to town."

He said nothing but when she looked up she noticed the shadow of sulkiness on his face; the tips of her fingers dug into his shoulder. "Don't," she whispered. "Don't, Edward."

"I can't help it," he said.

She grew coldly, politely angry with him. "You can help it well enough to bring a very pretty girl to the ball. Don't act out a part."

They danced the rest of it in complete silence, once around the huge hall. The music found them at the far end. He took her arm and walked her slowly back toward her husband. He looked straight ahead of him when he spoke. "Tomorrow afternoon, Margaret?"

They had almost rejoined the group when he heard her soft smothered answer: "All right." Then she turned from him to her husband who stood by with his usual taciturnity. She smiled at him. "Are you having a good time, Joseph?"

He looked down at her in the manner with which she was so familiar—some part of his mind and heart loving her, some part of him grimly hanging to his iron reserve. "I always enjoy myself when I see you having a good time."

She kept her eyes on him until he turned to speak to Calhoun; and then she ventured a surreptitious side glance at Josephine Russell, who stood beside Garnett. She hated the girl in the proud way of a beautiful woman recognizing loveliness in another woman; and knowing Garnett, she wondered what secrets might lie behind Josephine's calm. Benteen came up to claim her, his cheeks scarlet against the silver-white magnificence of his hair. Crusty and contentious as he was, he unbent to her. "My pleasure, Mrs. Barrows."

At two in the morning the ball ended and the various couples met in one house or another for coffee and bacon, and carefully treasured eggs long packed down in water glass. At three, Garnett returned Josephine to her house and at her invitation stepped inside. The elder Russell sat asleep in a rocker with a stout fire going; and woke and moved off to bed. Garnett stood in the middle of the room, holding his dress hat tucked under an arm, letting his glance openly admire the girl. She removed her coat and stood by the stove, as fresh and as awake now as she had been seven hours before; there was a tremendous amount of vitality in her, and a great deal of practical wisdom which now and then came out with its faint irony, and a capacity for emotion lying well down within her. He wondered if any man had stirred it.

"Thank you, Mr. Garnett, for the most delightful kind of an evening."

He made a little bow with his head, still watching her with his appreciative eyes. She turned to warm her hands at the stove and her attitude at the moment—the straightness of her body with its round, and full outlines—kicked a hard emotion through him. He was so interested in her that when she suddenly turned her head she caught him with this unguarded appreciation in his eyes; and her glance came back to him knowing what he thought. He was a handsome creature whose judgment was critical and therefore his interest was a flattering thing; she admitted that to herself. He was dangerous as well—his smile, his gallantry, and his words.

"Am I welcome in this house?" he asked.

"Yes," she said.

"I should like to pick you up for a ride in the cutter some morning."

She didn't answer it; she simply nodded. He drew a breath and walked toward her until she was within reach of him and he looked down at her and waited for a break in her eyes.

"Don't spoil a good impression, Mr. Garnett."

"You're still thinking I am particularly solicitous of ladies, aren't you?"

"I think," she said, "they are a challenge to your talents."

Sometimes she threw him off stride by her frankness; in moments like this, when he wished for tenderness and emotion, her words were cold water flung in his face. He flushed somewhat. "I find myself in a bad situation with you. I don't want you to suspect me. Women have played their light games of flirt with me. I have responded in kind. You seem to be aware of that."

"Let's not be too serious at three o'clock in the morning."

"I don't want to be misunderstood. I want you to know I'm dead serious toward you. This is no game with me, Josephine. When I leave here tonight I'll be troubled with myself all the way home."

"Now why, for mercy's sakes?" she demanded, really surprised.

He shrugged his shoulders. "As you stood there at the stove just now I grew completely disgusted with myself. I never thought any woman could humble me in that manner. Do you see what I mean?"

"Perhaps," she said, studying him with considerable penetration. She had a great deal of self-control, and much pride. She was, he thought, as strong a woman emotionally as he had seen; but in her lips, in her voice tones, in the slanted glances she sometimes gave him there was the hint of powerful convictions and will. He had the feeling that she could, if necessary, draw a revolver and shoot a man down and not go to pieces afterwards; it was that thing he chiefly discovered as he analyzed her, that courage and simplicity of action which was near to being primitive. The truth was, he knew less of her from observation than he knew of most women; her character had a way of eluding his inspection.

"Why should we be too involved in all this, Edward?"

He made a little bow to her and said "Good night," and turned to the door. As he opened it he swung back, and said with a complete confidence: "You must know me for what I am. I mean to have you. I mean to make you want me."

Trooper Lovelace ate his supper in a hurry, a fact noticed and commented on by Bierss. "What's the matter with your appetite, Lovelace?"

The young lad flushed under the attention of the roundabout troopers and got up from the table. "Nothing," he said. "Nothing at all."

"Love's bad for the appetite," said Bierss. But he went easy on Lovelace. Crude and obscene as his comment could be, he forbore using it now. All he added was, "You got Purple to beat, Lovelace. He's stickin' close to Suds Row."

"Who said anything about Suds Row?" retorted Lovelace and left the mess hall. He was relieved to get away from the crowd, for he lived in deadly fear that one of the troopers might say something concerning Mary which would compel him to fight. It wasn't the fighting which troubled him so much; it was her name being mentioned at all in the barrack. He wrapped his heavy coat around him and passed into the frigid night; and eagerness to see her again caused him to buck his way rapidly through the snow.

When he came before Mulrane's house he stopped, the shyness in him making it difficult for him to knock on the door and face the family. He stepped away and moved on toward the bluff, but he hadn't gone far when he saw a pair coming up the street, and heard Mary's voice carry forward in the brittle-cold air. The other figure was tall against her, whereby he knew it was Purple.

He went dead cold and his stomach turned over. He hated Purple violently, and he was shocked at Mary; but most of all he felt the humiliation of standing here as they came forward and saw him. They moved on until he saw Purple's grinning face—and heard Purple speak to him like a grown man making talk to a little boy: "You're out late, son."

"Is that so?" said Lovelace, and felt self-disdain for so feeble an answer. Mary's face was round and troubled in the darkness. Her voice was softly hurried.

"Frank," she said, "we're going in the house now. Come on."

"No," he said, "I was just walking by," and cut around them and went on. He heard Purple say something, and laugh; and the sound of it burned like an iron through him. He stopped at the edge of the bluff and swung around. They were before her house and a little later he heard Purple's boots go gritting through the snow. The house door opened, and closed. She had gone inside. Lovelace moved up the street, thinking of a dozen sharp and challenging things he might have said to Purple, in answer to the man's arrogant manner. He thought of them now; but now they were too late. He passed the Mulrane house with his head down, and heard Mary speak to him.

"Frank," she said, "wait a minute."

She had opened and closed the door, but she hadn't gone in. She stood in the shadows, waiting for him, and as he came up she lifted her head and smiled for him. "Come in now, Frank."

"No," he said.

"You're angry."

"No," he said. "I didn't mean to butt in."

"I didn't know you were coming," she said. "How was I to know?" Then she grew a little irritated. "Am I supposed to just sit around and wait for you and turn everybody away?"

"No," he said. "Not at all."

"Well, then," she said, "don't be foolish."

"A little cold for taking a walk, wasn't it?"

She tossed her head at him. "I've walked in colder weather, with you."

"And kissed him, too, I suppose."

She delayed her answer, watching him, troubled and uncertain with this scene. "I let him kiss me," she admitted slowly.

"Well," he said, stricken dull, "good night."

"Wait. A girl has to know things, doesn't she? She has to know whether she thinks more of one man than another. A girl isn't a bolt of cloth to be wrapped up and set on the shelf by the first man that comes along. She's got to know who's right. A man looks around to find the right one, doesn't he?"

"Well," said Lovelace, "maybe he's the right one, and maybe I'm not. When I kiss a girl I'm not fooling around."

"You shouldn't say that to me, Frank. I'll do what I please until I make up my mind."

He descended lower and lower into a sweltering gloom. He sank like a rock through layers of disillusion and renouncement and broken dreams. He said, "All right, Mary," and moved up the street with personal tragedy weighting his shoulders down.

Her voice came after him: "Aren't you going to invite me to your troop ball?"

"No," he said. "Good-by, Mary."

He moved through the guard gate and tramped along the row of barracks; he went all the distance to the north guard gate and turned back to company quarters. He stretched out on his bunk, face up; he was wholly crushed and there was no hope in him. He thought of deserting and going to Mexico. Then he said to himself: "No, I'll stay here until summer campaign. She'll see."

☆ 11 ☆

Memory of a Woman

Shafter reached Fort Lincoln thirteen days after his departure from it and dropped off his mail and despatches. He had brought back from Fargo a barrel of apples, something rarely had on the frontier. Half of the barrel he left in the barrack room; the other half he divided into three sacks, taking one to Mrs. Moylan and one to Lieutenant Smith's wife. Both ladies were genuinely appreciative. Mrs. Smith looked at them and took up one and laid it against her cheek. "When I was a child in New York, Sergeant, I used to do this to take the winter chill out of them. We had a big root cellar with bins on each side for apples and potatoes. Sometimes the snow got so deep between the house and the root cellar that we tunneled a passageway between." She looked beyond the sergeant, the vision of it very clear to her, drawing her back to her younger years. "Apples and nuts and home-cured raisins at night around the big fireplace. There were eight of us—eight children, and now they're scattered all over the earth." She gave him a bright short smile. "Your present took me back, Sergeant. Thank you."

He carried the mail on through for Fort Rice that same afternoon and returned to Lincoln next noon. This was Saturday, and the men of the troop had spent most of the day dressing up the quartermaster building for their ball that night. Receiving Moylan's permission to use the mail sleigh, Shafter presented himself at Josephine's house promptly at seven-thirty.

When she came to the door, he was astonished at the rough shock that went through him. Her presence did that to him, the smile breaking over her lips, the touch of her hand on his arm, the sudden view of loveliness she presented to him. He closed the door and stood against it, watching her move away and turn and face him. She said: "It is a little early. Take off your overcoat for a moment."

He was a tall sharp shape inside the coat's length and heaviness. It fitted snug against shoulders and chest and added to his height. He stood wholly attentive as he watched her, a black-haired man with long and broad bones and a face whipped by the wind; and the wind and darkness—and the sight of her— sharpened his eyes. She noticed it and made a slight turn and a slight gesture with her arms and stood before him for his inspection, the smile steady. "Will I do for your ball, Kern?"

He said: "I've not seen anyone like you."

"Come now," she said, "you've seen no woman at all for a week. That's no comparison."

"I can go farther back than that," he said, soberly deliberate.

She tipped her head, immensely curious as to his past, caring about it with a genuine emotion. Her smile changed and grew smaller. "How far back must you go to find a woman you'd want to stand beside me?"

"Once," he said, "a long time ago, there was one."

"She meant a great deal?" asked Josephine, very softly.

He nodded. "At the time it was one of those affairs which seemed—" and a self-amused and slightly harder tone came into his voice—"eternal. The kind you make everlasting vows on. When the earth is wonderful and everything is fair to behold and you could fight all the dragons on earth."

She had ceased to smile; the glow left her face and she stood still, listening. "Where is she now?"

"Somewhere, alive."

"Alive in you. I hear her walking around your heart."

"All you hear is echoes."

"How long since you've seen her?"

"Eight years."

"Echoes don't last that long. Only hope does."

"Or disillusion. I have no desire to hope."

She turned slowly away, moving toward the corner table in the room. She put her hands lightly on a book, and moved the book, and spoke over her shoulder. "It must have been an intense affair to leave so lasting an impression."

"A man and woman in love," he said, "is scarcely a mild thing, is it?"

"That depends on the woman and on the man."

"I'm speaking for myself."

"Yes, you have a great deal of depth. I have only recently discovered that in you."

"A man learns to cover himself and protect himself from further commitments which will break him apart. He goes sour and skeptical."

"You're not."

"You've not heard me express it."

She turned about. "Kern, I don't think I like to be the instrument which brings back those memories to you."

Humor moved into his eyes. He had an edge to his spirits, and appreciation of her was a clear print on his face. He had changed a great deal in the short time he had been in the army, she thought; he was a more aggressive man, a simpler and less involved man enjoying the physical sensations, the hearty pleasures, the old, sentimental loyalties. Still, she remembered his one grim remark concerning disillusion, and was troubled by it, though she failed to understand why she should let it disturb her. For a moment the fine, glowing feeling of his presence had left her; suddenly she shrugged her shoulders and smiled again.

"What a strange way to start an evening. Time to go, isn't it?"

He moved over the room to lift her coat from a chair. He held it for her and was for the moment close to her, so that when she turned to him and looked up she saw the image of her face in his eyes. His lids crept together as he watched her, as her presence hit him again with its sound jolt. She saw what was happening to him but she stood still, her lips slightly apart. She thought: "This is foolish," and felt the heavy undertow of feeling sweep against her, unsettle her resolution, and turn her reckless. She made one sharp move to break that moment, and wheeled away. He stood still and presently she swung back, her face almost severe in its darkness, but her eyes glowing against him. For a moment they watched each other, completely still; and then she lifted her chin, breaking the turbulence of feeling between them, and took his arm.

"Time to go," she repeated.

He brought her back at one in the morning and escorted her to the door. He lifted his hat and he said: "Thank you. Now you've tried the high and the low. Good night."

She said: "Come in for coffee."

"No," he said.

She had a way of lifting her head in a sudden motion when she was angry and when she was determined. She said: "Tie the mules and put the blankets over them. Then come in, Sergeant."

When he had taken care of the mules he came into the house and found Russell standing sleepily by the stove. Russell said: "My girl is staying out late. Three last week and one o'clock tonight."

"My record is better than the lieutenant's by two hours," said Shafter.

"That's right," said Russell and left the room. Josephine had dropped her coat on a chair and for a moment had watched Shafter's face; now she went into the kitchen. Shafter stood with his back to the stove, hearing her move about the other room. He got a cigar from his pocket and lighted it and he drew in the heavy smoke and relished it, at the same time thinking of the waltz tune swinging them around and around the hall. It was Sergeant Hines who had privately said to him, during a break in the dancing: "You're flyin' high, Shafter. She was at officers' ball last week with Garnett."

He listened to her footfalls and admitted that she drew his attention, and he recalled that he had thought of her during the thirteen days between Fargo and Bismarck. He pulled the cigar from his mouth and stood with his face tipped toward the floor, gravely aware of what was happening to him and stubbornly convinced that he had to prevent it from happening.

She came from the kitchen with coffee for both of them and a little tray with bread and honey and cheese. She put these things on a table and motioned to him. He brought up a chair and sat down opposite her. She sat back with her coffee, her eyes scanning him over the rim of the cup, quite thoughtful. "Who told you about my going with Garnett?"

"One of the boys."

"I should have told you two weeks ago that I planned to go with him."

"If I'd known it I wouldn't have taken you."

"Why?"

"A woman can't play both sides of the line. I'm on one side of it and Garnett's on the other. You're an officer's woman. In going with me you have shut yourself out of being invited to the officers' side again."

"Isn't that my affair more than yours?"

"No," he said.

She sipped at her coffee, never for a moment taking her eyes from him. He was seemingly at ease, but she knew he was violently angry and she hated to have him that way.

"It really isn't that," she told him. "It's Garnett, isn't it?"

"Let's forget it."

"Nothing would please me better," she coolly answered. "But you have no intention of forgetting it. So it had better be talked out before it gets worse."

He used his calm, stubborn voice on her. "How would it help?"

"I don't know," she said. "That's what I'm trying to discover. You were embarrassed by him in this house once. Is that the cause of your disliking him so greatly?"

"Josephine," he said, "I hope you had a pleasant evening," and rose. He smiled at her, but he had drawn away from her. She sat still, watching him pull into his coat, and she wanted to ask him if common jealousy lay at the roots of his change toward her but she could not bring herself to the direct question.

"It started out very well, Kern," she told him, "and ended badly. But I really forced myself on you, so I shall not complain." Abruptly she began to feel a slow outrage at the whole situation. "I have liked most of the changes I have seen in you. I do not like this one at all."

It broke through the reserve behind which he seemed to want to take shelter. "It is Garnett," he admitted. "But it goes a long way back. There's no use adding to that."

"If it is so far in the past, why bring it forward to influence your judgment of me? I have nothing to do with your past, or your quarrels."

"That's right," he said, very dry. "You're also trying to tell me I have no business in making an issue of your going with Garnett."

"Yes," she said. "I was trying to tell you that."

"You're right. And that leaves the matter pretty straight. As I said before, you're an officer's woman and I have no business here at all." He took up his dress hat and bowed slightly at her and turned to the door.

"Is that your way of saying good-by, Kern?"

He swung. She had shaken him out of his hardness and she had made him sad. She saw the sadness lie darkly around his eyes and his mouth. He nodded. "I don't believe in tangling up somebody's life—and I've spent a good many years trying to untangle my own."

She rose and spoke in an almost antagonistic tone. "Where is the tangling? Aren't you taking in too much territory to make anything out of a dinner, a few visits and a dance?"

"You misjudge yourself, Josephine," he said.

She had not convinced him, she had not changed him, and she was not holding him. Knowing it she hit him with deliberate unfairness. "Did you run from Garnett once before—as you're doing now?"

He let an enormous sigh out of his chest as he came back to her. She hated what she had done and she was ashamed of herself and stood still when he looked down with his gray, dismal expression. "You don't know me very well," he said and took her arms and pulled her forward. "It would have been better if you'd left me alone." He dropped his head and kissed her, holding her so strongly with his hands that she felt pain in her ribs. Then he stepped back. "That was foolish," he said.

"Was it?" she asked.

"You knew it was coming," he said, thoughtfully watching her.

"I usually know when a man wants to kiss me."

"That's not hard to read on a man. The difficult thing is to know what he means by the kiss."

"Last time you kissed me it was for the purpose of offending me and getting rid of me. What was your meaning this time?"

"We're fighting now," he said. "It isn't worth that."

"What would you fight for?"

"A crooked deal at cards," he said, "a spilled drink, a dirty name—a shove in the ribs."

His words deliberately crowded her out, deliberately kept him inside a man's world. She was hurt by the way he spoke, and she thought she knew why he had spoken. "You've had one fight over a woman and now you think there's no woman worth that trouble. You have taken most of the nonsense out of your life, haven't you, Kern? You are very safe with your little comforts."

She was greatly embittered and she wanted to punish him. Even so she listened carefully to him when he spoke, seeking to pull aside the screening of his words to fathom what terrible experience had left him so dull and without faith.

"A woman is beauty, Josephine, and all men worship beauty. Some men always see it from a safe distance and die happy with their illusion. Some men come upon a woman and touch her and possess her and never regret it. But there are men who have no such luck. When they come upon their shrine and touch the beauty they have worshiped from afar for so long—all that beauty fades and dies out." He paused a moment and then added the one and terrible comment: "It is hard for a man to come upon this shrine and see the finger marks of other worshipers before him."

"From you," she said, pitying him even as she hated him. "From you who have rolled in the dust and been beaten down in barroom brawls."

"Different," he said with his gray smile remaining. "A man's sins are honest. He wants his beauty to be the same way." He looked at her with the smile disappearing. "How did I come to speak of all this?"

"I drew you out. I don't like you, Kern."

"The first honest thing said tonight." Then he shook his head. "No, the kiss was also honest. But it is better to end a thing properly than to nourish miserable illusions."

She said: "You will never cease to nourish your illusions."

"Then," he said, "I'm a fool."

She threw his words back to him. "Yes, you're a fool. But for the opposite reason. For thinking you can live without illusions. You'll never have anything else half as real. Good night."

She listened to him cross the porch and drop into the snow. Later she heard him run the sleigh and team around the house, heading away for the post. He was still before her in the room, his shape, his height, his face with its swings of feeling. Until this night he had guarded himself well, and then had let the screen slip aside to expose the wreckage within—the old love that had run through him like a fire and had burned out to leave nothing but the charred skeleton of hope behind. "I was right," she thought, "I should never have permitted myself to be interested in him."

It surprised her that he had so profoundly shaken her, had aroused a momentary fury against him, and then a pity. He was a man emptied out by catastrophe and now living in a state of guarded suspense, fearing that some other catastrophe might shake him again. He had pulled away from all the fine prodigal emotions of living because of that. Yet she corrected herself, knowing she had wrongly estimated him. He had too much in him deliberately to starve out all his feelings and therefore he had retreated to the world of men.

It was a tragedy and she felt it. She stood still, wondering why it should go so hard with her, and presently she understood. She had allowed herself to put her first hopes in him, his smile, his strength, his imagination and tenderness—all those things which made a man sound and good; and now stood by and watched him throw those things contemptuously aside. It hurt her badly.

☆ 12 ☆

The Gods Cease to Smile

Shafter was in Fargo on Christmas Day. He had dinner at the railroad restaurant and moved to the saloon to play poker until the mood went out of him and he bucked his way through a hard-driving snowstorm to the hotel and lay long awake, listening to the wind whining thin and sharp along the wall of the building. Darkness pressed down upon Fargo so heavily that the town's lights, passing through window pane and doorway, were at once absorbed. On the blackened, weather-riddled street a gunfight erupted and briefly lasted. Somewhere in the hotel a music machine pricked out sentimental tunes steadily; he listened to those little tinny melodies and was carried back and carried down until he turned savage from the memories of his life.

The storm pounded the earth for three days. It screamed through the town and drove drifts against the windward side of buildings until men were able to walk out of second-story windows. It snapped telegraph lines eastward and stopped trains from St. Paul. It moved out of the northern emptiness like great wild sea waves, higher and higher, more and more violent, until the impact of this fury thundered against Fargo's walls and carried away all insecure things, and shook each building on its foundation. Fargo's citizens counted ranks and named those who had been caught away from home and knew that death rode abroad.

There was a rope stretched from the hotel to the restaurant and from the restaurant to the saloon; along this confined pathway the citizens blindly moved. Men who had come in from the outskirts of town at the beginning of the blizzard dared not attempt the half-mile journey to their homes. They slept in the hotel, ate in the restaurant and spent the rest of their hours in the saloon. A poker game, started on the first day, went intermittently on to the end; and when Shafter rose from the table on the morning of the fourth day and heard the strange, hollow stillness abroad, he had five hundred dollars in his pockets.

It was beyond New Year, however, before the mail from St. Paul came in; and the homeward journey across the drift-drowned land took him ten days. When he came into A Company's barracks, Hines said: "Where were you when it started?"

"Fargo."

"The boys were bettin' even money you were caught out."

That night Garnett dropped into Josephine's house for dinner and mentioned the arrival of the mail. Josephine said: "Did he have trouble getting through?"

"Shafter? I don't know." He observed the girl's lightened spirits and after the elder Russell had taken himself off to bed, Garnett commented on it. "You have a fancy for him don't you?"

"I'd worry about any man traveling in this weather," she said.

It was not a direct answer, Garnett realized, and he pushed his point. "That wasn't what I asked."

"Yes," she told him, "I like the sergeant."

He smiled his best smile. "I envy any living thing which has part of your heart or your interest."

"Edward, did you know him before he came here?"

He had been smiling at her, and he still smiled; but she noticed him change within, grow reticent, grow cautious. He struggled with his answer, not wishing to answer her, but she kept the pressure of her glance on him, making him say with great reluctance: "Yes, I knew him."

"Were you once friends?"

He said, "Good friends, once."

"Why did you quarrel?"

"Do you have to know that, Josephine?"

"I suppose I'm too curious," she said, and turned away from him to the far corner of the room. She sat down and picked up her knitting, at once absorbed in it. She changed the conversation by saying: "This is your first winter out here, isn't it? You must watch the weather from now until April. It can be very treacherous."

"I've heard that," he said. But he was troubled at the way the scene had gone, and dissatisfied at the showing he made with her. A woman's mind was a fertile thing. She would perhaps ask him no more about his past, but she would invent one answer after another to fill in the unsolved story—and by this process he might be injured in her eyes. He sat in the chair with a posed ease, the warmth of the room making his ivory cheeks ruddy; his hair tumbled forward on his head and gave him a negligent handsomeness. He tapped the chair with the index finger of his right hand—a broad, long hand with a heavy diamond ring showing out its glitter; he dropped into a somber study.

She looked up and saw him thus off guard and tried to fathom the realness of the man. There were times when he deliberately put himself on his best behavior toward her; she always knew these times and always discounted them. There were other moments when she felt he wanted her to see him for whatever he was, when he tried to be only human and natural, as though he had discovered in her a realism which cut through any pose he might adopt. He knew his own striking appearance and he took pains to be seen at his best, and yet, in his own way, he had much of the rough masculinity she had observed in Shafter. Always, in studying Garnett, she had Shafter in her mind; he was a constant reminder in her head so that now he was somewhere in the room, looking at her with his gray eyes and with his smile which covered his real feelings.

"Edward," she murmured, "don't chase your thoughts around."

"Well," he said, "I've never been noted for heavy thinking. I'm surprised at myself. The things I keep going back to, the things I keep stumbling over. Regrets—and all that."

"What regrets?"

"Things that would have been better undone."

"Women, I suppose."

"Looking at you, they're just shadows."

"That's a strange thing to say."

"It is strange for me to be here wishing I could say what I want to say."

"I never knew you to lack self-expression."

"I never have," he admitted. "That's it. I have told other women how beautiful I thought they were. I have even told a woman I was in love with her. I have said those things, not entirely meaning them. Now I want to say them because I mean them. I wish I had never used those words before."

"You're frank at least."

"It is my only chance, with you." He got up, walking toward her. He looked down. "Do you expect him tonight? He came back today. I suppose he'll come to see you."

"I don't think so," she said.

"You've been kind to me lately. Do you have any particular feeling toward him, Josephine?"

She answered him with an almost irritable impatience. "No."

"Do you trust me?"

She ceased her knitting and looked up, carefully choosing her answer. "Yes," she said, "I trust you."

It made a tremendous impression on him. He grew buoyant, he made a swift motion with his arms. "I'd like to wrap you in fur and drive you down the Avenue in the most elegant cab in New York. I'd like to dine you at Terry's and take you to the theater. I'd like to sit by and watch your lips grow red when you smile. You are the most beautiful woman in the world in evening clothes. There is body and strength to you. There's—"

"Edward," she said, "don't."

His intemperate feelings controlled him. "You see," he murmured, "that's how I feel. If you trust me, believe me also." He swung around and got his coat and shrugged himself into it. She laid aside her knitting to watch him and noticed how, unconsciously, he straightened himself before her to show himself to best advantage; it was a thing he couldn't help. "There's a place in New Orleans, in the Quarter. When I think of it I think of you. A restaurant down an alley, with a back courtyard and an old man who plays the violin while you eat—"

"Did you take a woman last time you were there?"

"Yes."

"Shame on you for wishing to take me there then."

"I know," he said. "I know. You see how it is? Well, let's go for a sleigh ride out to the Benson farm tomorrow."

"Don't you ever have duty at the post?"

"Winter's a dreary time for soldiering. Nothing to do. Old stories, old faces. We all get sick of one another, and therefore try to keep away from each other. Two o'clock?"

She murmured: "We had a drive two days ago. Let's wait another week, Edward."

"Then invite me to supper."

"I shall," she said. "But not this week."

He said quietly, "I understand."

She found herself irritated. "What do you understand, Edward?"

"You do expect Shafter. Good night, Josephine."

He was not a humble man and therefore it was remarkable to her that he left with so much quietness. She took up her knitting but held it still; she listened to the wall clock strike nine and restlessness destroyed her sense of comfort. She put the knitting aside and got her coat and hat and an old wool muffler and stepped into the night. Coldness held both wind and blackness in its frozen grip and the sliding of her feet on the snow brought up crackling echoes which went abnormally large before her. She turned into Bismarck's street and strolled along it, almost alone. The night marshal passed her and stopped to leave his warning. "Twenty-seven below, Josephine. Don't stay out in this too long." She went on until she reached the post office. It was closed, as she knew it would be, but she looked both ways on the street with hope in her heart, and then turned into her father's store.

The night clerk was serving a last customer before closing time. She moved idly around the counter and got herself a cracker and cut a piece of cheese and dipped a pickle from the big barrel; she sat on the counter's edge and swung one leg while she ate. Two squaws came in and made signs for tobacco. She made the transaction, speaking a few Sioux words to them, and watched them leave.

"Why don't you go home, Jo?" asked the clerk. "That pickle will spoil your sleep."

She wrapped the muffler around her neck and stepped back into the night's iron-hard cold and saw Shafter standing at the edge of the walk, facing her. He had come along in the sleigh and had gotten out of it.

She realized then that this was the hope that had brought her here; but now she was uncertain, and uncertainty made her turn half away, and stop and turn back. His glance had followed her and was intently on her. He lifted his hat.

"You're going home alone?"

"Yes," she said.

He made a motion toward the sleigh. He came forward and took her arm and gave her a hand into it. "Better wrap that muffler tighter. Part of your ear is exposed."

She said: "Did the storm catch you?"

"I was in Fargo," he said and sent the mules walking down the street. "Didn't get away until after New Year."

"I wondered if you were safe," she said.

"Two weeks in Fargo," he said, "is a dull experience."

"There must have been a poker game."

"That runs out, too."

They turned the corner and moved over the gap toward her house. He brought the sleigh before the door and held the mules in check. "Nice Christmas?"

"The Calhouns had a party at the fort. Somebody had sent in a plum pudding; and we had Tom-and-Jerries without the eggs. There were three eggs, but they all turned out bad. The band played Christmas carols and we went around singing until Major Reno ordered us back to shelter before we froze. Yes, it was a pleasant Christmas. Only one shooting in Bismarck."

"Christmas . . ." he started to say, and shook his head and let it go like that. He looked at her in the way she best knew him, smiling and easy—all this covering up the heat in him. She sat still a long moment, gripping her hands together beneath the robe. She thought: "I should ask him inside. I should break this wall between us." But her pride was harder than her wishes and presently she slipped from the sleigh. "Good night."

"Good night," he said and lifted the reins. He was ten feet on when she called to him. She said, "Happy New Year, Kern."

He swung in the seat, the glow from the snowbound earth shining faintly on him. "And many of them," he said and disappeared.

She waited until she no longer saw the outline of the sleigh and no longer heard the sibilant slicing of team and runners on the snow; then she turned inside, profoundly sad.

He was in Fargo in February when news came over the wire that the Indian Commissioner had surrendered control of all Sioux not on their reservations to the War Department. He was at Fort Lincoln a week later when Terry's order to be ready for a winter campaign came to the Seventh. Making his back-and-forth circuit during the following weeks, Shafter watched the story unfold. The Sioux and Cheyenne, frightened by the intentions of the War Department, fled from their reservations, going back through bitterest weather to their old grounds on the Powder, on the Rosebud, on the Tongue. The General of the Army, Sherman, had given Terry full freedom of action. Meanwhile Sherman had despatched a column under Crook north from Fetterman, the intent being that Crook and Terry, coming from different directions, should catch the Sioux in a nut cracker. Crook's column beat its way through terrible weather, launched a surprise attack on the village of Crazy Horse, on the upper sources of the Powder, and for a moment had victory within its grasp. But Crazy Horse, fighting in desperate recklessness, gathered his warriors and threw Crook's column into disorder and drove it back to Fetterman. Terry, meanwhile, found his plans wrecked by the steady succession of blizzards blowing over the land and delayed his campaign.

Early in March, the long simmering scandal which had sent its forewarning taint out of Washington for a year or more boiled over. A broker in New York came forward with evidence that Belknap, or Belknap's wife, had taken money as reward for aiding certain men to secure profitable post-traderships. Belknap resigned as Secretary of War on the eve of a Congressional investigation. At the same time Custer, whose leave had expired, took the train west to St. Paul with his wife and there reported to General Terry.

Terry gave him his orders. Custer was to go on to Lincoln at once, to put his regiment in readiness and to march at the first break of weather, to meet the

Sioux and to gather them in or to crush them. "I had hoped to be started long before this," said Terry, "in order to work in conjunction with Crook. As soon as practicable, Sherman will get Crook in motion again, headed north."

Custer took a special train from St. Paul. Halfway between Fargo and Lincoln the blizzard snowed him in and he cooled his impatient heels in a frigid coach until a detachment from Lincoln came out to his rescue. Once at the fort, his nervous, driving, impetuous will galvanized the seven troops of the regiment into feverish action; and at the same time, departmental orders went out from Washington, sending the three companies in Louisiana and the two at Fort Totten back to Lincoln. For the first time in many years the regiment was again to be whole. Custer flung himself into his job with all the terrific energy of a man who could not bear quietness.

He had scarcely returned to duty, however, when a telegram arrived from the Congressional investigating committee ordering his return to Washington in order to testify against Belknap. On the eve of a campaign, with all the glory that might accrue to the regiment and to him, his own indiscreet offer to Clymer had at last caught up with him. In this dilemma he wired his appeal to the committee:—

I AM ENGAGED UPON AN IMPORTANT EXPEDITION. . . . I EXPECT TO TAKE THE FIELD EARLY IN APRIL. . . . MY PRESENCE HERE IS DEEMED VERY NECESSARY. . . . WOULD IT NOT BE POSSIBLE TO ALLOW ME TO RETURN MY REPLIES BY MAIL?

The committee thought not, and so near the end of March Custer returned to Washington. Sergeant Hines spoke his mind confidentially to Shafter about this.

"If the general would keep his mouth shut maybe he wouldn't get in so much trouble."

Terry had based his plans on Custer since the latter was to his mind the best Indian campaigner under his command. Therefore the campaign lagged, waiting Custer's return from Washington. The days and the weeks dragged on while the committee slowly worked its way through the mass of testimony, prejudice, politics and recrimination. One by one the lost companies of the Seventh returned from their out-of-way assignments and the quarters at Lincoln, never meant for a full regiment, spilled over. The ice in the river went out one day with a grinding and a crashing like unto the cannonade of an artillery battle but the weather still was dangerous, now clear, now swinging down with its northern fury. Day after day the regiment drilled and made its preparations, and by means of the newspapers followed the testimony of their commander in Washington who, prodded by question upon question, at last produced this one startling thing:—

"Fraud among the sutlers could not have been carried on without the connivance of the Secretary of War. . . . You ask me of the morale and character of the army. The service has not been demoralized even though the head of it, the Secretary of War, has shown himself to be so unworthy."

Captain Benteen, consistent in his hatred of Custer, smiled a wintry smile when he read that. "The Goddamned fool," he said to his lieutenant, Francis Gibson. "Belknap was President Grant's friend. In saying Belknap was a scoundrel, Custer is telling the people publicly that he thinks the President is a scoundrel. Do you think Grant will stand that in silence? It is a matter of discipline. No little jackass lieutenant colonel in the United States Army can speak of the commander-in-chief that way. Right or wrong, an officer keeps his mouth shut. But Custer never had sense enough to know that. He has court-martialed many a man within his regiment for insubordination, and now exhibits the worst insubordination possible. Wait and see what Grant does to him."

Out in St. Paul, General Terry waited for Custer's release from Washington. All arrangements had been made, now that spring was close by. Crook was to start up from Fetterman again. General Gibbon, with all the troops he could scrape together from the isolated and remote posts of Montana Territory, was to march east, reach the Yellowstone, and follow it until he joined with the Seventh Cavalry which meanwhile would be marching west. Thus the three columns, flushing Sioux before them, would drive the red men into a pocket, there to trap them and induce them to return to the reservation, or to subdue them by pitched battle. The plan was made and Terry waited for the commander of the Fort Lincoln column to return from Washington.

The Congressional committee finished its initial hearings but held Custer in the capital for future use. Now, with the campaign hourly growing nearer, Custer saw himself in danger of being left behind—his regiment marching without him. He appealed to Sherman, who was the General of the Army. Sherman said: "You had better see the President. It is in his hands entirely."

"I have been there twice. He refuses to see me," said Custer.

"Better try again," said Sherman.

Custer went wearily back to the White House and handed in his card. He sat in the anteroom, a lank, flamboyant man slowly being humbled and made conscious of his own helplessness as the hours passed. Men went by him, in and out of the President's office. Old officer friends from the Civil War paused to say hello, but he thought there was constraint in their manner. The sun had ceased to shine upon him. At five o'clock in the evening, as gray day came to its end, the President's secretary came out with his message.

"The President," said the secretary, "will not see you."

Custer stood up, paling a little. He remained still, the dash and the rankling vigor for the moment crushed from him. Then he murmured, "Very well, sir," and left the room. That night, with his wife, he caught the train west. As he stepped from the train at Chicago to transfer for St. Paul an aide of General Sheridan's came to him, offered a polite salute and handed to him a copy of a telegram despatched from Sherman to Terry:—

GENERAL: I AM AT THIS MOMENT ADVISED THAT GENERAL CUSTER STARTED LAST NIGHT FOR ST. PAUL AND FORT ABRAHAM LINCOLN. HE WAS NOT JUSTIFIED IN LEAVING WITHOUT SEEING THE PRESIDENT OR MYSELF. PLEASE INTERCEPT HIM AT CHICAGO OR ST. PAUL AND ORDER HIM TO HALT AND WAIT FOR FURTHER ORDERS. MEANWHILE, LET THE EXPEDITION FROM FORT LINCOLN PROCEED WITHOUT HIM.

Custer gave his wife an odd, desperate glance—the wildness of feeling rushing to his bony face, into his piercing eyes. "Libby," he said, "they have stripped me of my command."

Discipline had reached out and struck him with its brutal hand; and the hand was Grant's, whose reputation Custer had so rashly impugned before the Congressional committee. Custer at once boarded the train for St. Paul with Libby. He was afraid—he who never had known fear before. He was humiliated and humbled and felt the sting of it so keenly that all the appreciation of life went from him. His vaulting amibition to challenge the President, with the public as an audience to the combat, fell completely out of him; his audacity wavered and his intense physical energy, with its accompanying self-assurance, faltered. He who had been the darling of America stood bereft of his power, brought short up, stripped and held still by the brooding presence in the White House. His entire career lay in the hollow of Grant's stubby palm.

Reason and persuasion were methods for which Custer held a secret contempt, because of his impetuous nature; but force was a thing he understood, and this blunt blow reduced him to the stature of a man begging for his life. As soon as he reached St. Paul he went directly to his immediate superior, Terry. Terry, he knew, had always liked him, and had faith in him as a fighter. Terry was now his last resort.

"I am entirely in your hands, General," said Custer. "Neither Sherman nor Sheridan will intercede for me. The President would not see me, although I repeatedly attempted to see him. When I found it was useless, I took the train west. Now I am condemned for not having visited the President before I left. What was I to do? They have me trapped in a cage and it pleases them to poke sticks at me. If it is the President's wish to humiliate me before the country, he is succeeding. I do not believe I deserve it."

Terry was a mild man, a man deeply humane, tolerant and sympathetic. There was a Christian mellowness in him, and a great capacity of forbearance. Even so, he delivered a gentle reprimand.

"You should have known better. You've been in the service long enough to know the impropriety of making public comment on your superiors."

At any other time Custer would have reiterated his fiery impatience with hypocrisy. Now he played a meek hand. "I have never been anything but a soldier, General. I do not understand politicians. They have used me."

"No man can be used unless he permits himself to be used. Or unless he is very stupid. Certainly you're not stupid."

Custer flushed, but held his peace. Terry thoughtfully considered the problem and was at loss for an answer. He had counted on Custer for the campaign. "I have definite instructions not to take you. Even if it were possible to take you, I now propose to go as commander of the eastern column."

"Put yourself in my place," said Custer. "If my regiment marches without me I shall be intolerably disgraced."

Terry thought about that, slowly and with great doubt. "I have learned not to question the orders of my superiors. That is a lesson I doubt if you've learned. But you must learn it. Impetuousness has been your lifelong creed. It is an admirable thing until it runs into something else, which is insubordination. An officer of your rank, commanding the lives of eight hundred men, must have respect for order and for caution. The lives of all these men are entirely at your disposition. I have complete faith in you as a fighter and I should feel much better with you in personal command of the Seventh, but I cannot deny that the President has cause enough to suspend you from duty."

"Is there no way you can put in a word for me?" said Custer.

Terry turned to his desk and took up his pen, very carefully composing a message; upon finishing, he passed it to Custer. It read:—

I have no desire to question the orders of the President. Whether Lieutenant Colonel Custer shall be permitted to accompany the column or not, I shall go in command of it. I do not know the reasons upon which the orders given rest; but if these reasons do not forbid it, Lieutenant Colonel Custer's services would be very valuable with his regiment.

Custer's relief came up strong and ruddy to his face; his spirits rushed from extreme depth to extreme height. He said: "I am forever under debt to you, General," and left the room.

There was now nothing to do but wait while the slow wheels ground; and days passed, intolerably long to Custer, and to his wife who had to bear his moods which were penitent and hopeful and downcast and bitter by turn. The message went to the division commander at St. Louis, General Sheridan, who added his endorsement.

On a previous occasion, in 1868, I asked executive clemency for Colonel Custer to enable him to accompany his regiment against the Indians and I sincerely hope that if granted this time it may have sufficient effect to prevent him from again attempting to throw discredit upon his profession and his brother officers.

It was then forwarded to General Sherman who despatched it to the White House, and there it rested in the hands of Grant—a man whose convictions were as immovable as polar ice, whose enemies were seldom forgiven, whose injuries were always remembered. Yet the President was a military man and the western campaign waited, and Terry had expressed an inclination for Custer's services. Somewhere during the same day upon which he received Terry's application, he weighed his personal feelings in relation to the wishes of Terry, an old soldier whose faithfulness was unquestioned; and so he despatched his answer to Sherman, who wired it to Terry:—

THE PRESIDENT SENDS ME WORD THAT IF YOU WANT GENERAL CUSTER ALONG, HE WITHDRAWS HIS OBJECTIONS. ADVISE CUSTER TO BE PRUDENT, NOT TO TAKE ANY NEWSPAPERMEN, WHO ALWAYS MAKE MISCHIEF, AND TO ABSTAIN FROM PERSONALITIES IN THE FUTURE.

Nothing but a sense of propriety restrained a wild whoop of triumph from Custer when Terry gave him the news. All his restlessness and vitality and abundant confidence came back at a single bound. He stood by to hear Terry's final instructions: "Return to Lincoln by the first train and pull your regiment together. I shall join you at the first opportunity. I wish to march as soon as I arrive."

Custer left Terry's office and repaired immediately to his hotel. In the lobby he met Captain Ludlow, who once had campaigned with him and now was passing through the city. His troubles were common knowledge among the army, and Ludlow expressed a friendly sorrow. "But," he said, "you look uncommonly cheerful for a disgraced man."

"I've been restored to duty," said Custer. "I am taking the next train west."

"Capital," said Ludlow. "When will Terry join you?"

"Directly."

"You'll be under an excellent officer. A little on the cautious side for a man of your temper, but an able one. I hope it won't cramp your freedom of action too much."

Custer gave him a smile and a rash, penetrating glance. "Oh, once we're in the field, I shall pull away from Terry."

Ludlow lifted his eyebrows and stifled a comment. Custer gave him a hearty slap on the back, departing. When he entrained for Lincoln, he was a man with a fixed idea. Behind him lay intolerable injustice and deep personal humiliation; but ahead of him lay redemption in the form of one more glorious opportunity. The Seventh was his regiment, as all the country knew; his name and the Seventh were inseparable. It would be the Seventh which seized the chance and pressed it—and restored his prestige. Who then could stand before him? In this game of power—played before the audience of the nation—he meant to produce a trump against Grant. He meant to seize his chance, by whatever means it had to be obtained. He looked ahead, and saw no great difficulty in gaining complete freedom of movement from Terry, once he was in the field.

☆ 13 ☆

The Past Comes Forward

Spring came slowly, fitfully to the plains; now with the pale sun dissolving the snow, now with half-warmed rains pelting down, now with nights of searing coldness. The Missouri boiled yellow and heavy between its crumbling banks and rose until it lapped at the foundation timbers of the Point. All across the flatlands the river eddied and cut its way, and great chunks of earth dropped into an already mud-engorged stream. The *Far West,* Captain Marsh commanding, nosed up from Yankton and tied at the fort to take on supplies which it would carry upstream for the troops, as far as the Powder and the Tongue, or even beyond if Terry so ordered. In memory of past ambuscades, Captain Marsh had the sides of the engine room double-planked and the pilot house shielded with thin iron plates against Sioux rifle fire.

Toward the middle of April, Shafter left Lincoln for what he believed would be the last mail trip. Snow still blanketed the ground and lay bank-full in the coulees; but here and there on the railroad's right-of-way it had begun to shrink back, permitting section crews to repair the unsettled grade and the warped track. Trains would be soon in operation.

Four miles from Fargo, he passed the Benson farm and stopped long enough to pick up their private mail. The earliest spring birds were returning, sweeping in graceful clouds upon the small knolls swept clear of snow; and high overhead at night he heard the honking of geese—the earliest vanguard of itinerant millions to follow. The weather was raw and windy, but in the wind was the rank smell of winter's breakup, of rotted earth about to come alive. By early morning he crossed swales coated with ice; by late afternoon similar swales farther east had turned into brimming lakes under the wan warmth of the day. Here and there, the receding snow line disgorged its tragedies, a buffalo fallen, a cow long dead but still intact from its winter's refrigeration. Far away on the horizon he saw the smoke of a work train.

He arrived at Yankton to find the despatches not yet arrived from St. Paul, and was delayed a week, waiting their arrival. The mail, the newspapers and the telegraph wires were teeming with news of freshened activity. Great things were stirring, great plans were making, and hopes ran high for a permanent settlement of the Indian problem; the campaign was drawing near. Crook had already started north from Fetterman to carry out his part of the plan, which was to box the Sioux on the south, to drive them north toward the Missouri or to prevent them from drifting away from the Missouri. Meanwhile, in Montana, General Gibbon had formed a column from troops stationed at Forts Shaw and Ellis and had gotten under way the middle of March, pushing through the bitterest of winter weather in order that he might fulfill the orders Terry had given him. Coming out of the west, Gibbon was to push east to the Yellowstone and follow it, scouting, making contact with the Sioux, and pressing them toward the Dakota column which would be advancing from Lincoln. Somewhere in the almost unknown region west of the Missouri and south of the Yellowstone, Terry's plan called for a junction of these three columns—his own, Crook's and Gibbons. Somewhere in that same area the Sioux moved like shadows upon the earth, keyed up by their great leaders and their medicine men.

The despatches from St. Paul arrived at last on a Saturday train. Shafter went to the post office, got the pouches for Fort Lincoln and Bismarck and returned to his hotel with them late in the afternoon. Afterwards he dropped by the stable to have a look at the mules, and went to the hotel for supper. Darkness came down again and a rough wind whirled through the town. He sat awhile in the saloon, half interested in a poker game, and finally gave it up and climbed to his room.

A week of inaction was a hard thing. He made a slow circle around the cold room, half of a mind to go back to the saloon; there was this restlessness in him which had lately grown greater, destroying his satisfaction. He thought, "Same thing as cabin fever. It's been a hell of a long winter. A little sunshine, a little sweat and a smell of dust will cure it." He stopped and stood by the window, listening to the wind with an experienced ear. It made a racket and it shook the hotel with its force; but the venom had gone out of it. Spring was on the way. In another sixty days the regiment would be in motion across the plains; the thought of it cheered him enormously. "Probably this is my last mail trip," he reflected. "Snowplows and work trains are halfway to Bismarck now. Should be a train in there next week."

Somebody knocked on his door and he said, "Come in," but for a moment he remained at the window, interested in a little scene on the street below. A dray, drawn by four horses, came around the corner, the horses breast high in the snow. They stalled there and the driver, seeing trouble ahead of him, now tried to back out and got his two teams snarled. Presently Shafter remembered the knock at his door and turned. A woman stood in the doorway and made a little gesture with her hand. She tried to smile and failed; and suddenly she closed the door and placed her back to it.

"Kern," she said. "Kern. Come to me."

It was like springing out of a sound sleep. The same physical shock went through him, the same quick and heavy pounding of his heart oppressed him. A queer thought came to him. "Why," he said, "she's ten years older." He saw that at once. Her shape was the same straight and lovely shape he had known so long ago; her face was the same expressive face, the lips warm and ready, the eyes watching him and willing to respond. She had always worn excellent clothes, and wore them now; the jade pendants at her ears reminded him somehow of the night he had found her with Garnett; perhaps they were the same ones. She wore the ring he had given her, the sight of which had a far-away effect on him, as though he turned back the pages of a book and saw himself as a man half familiar, half strange.

"Hello, Alice," he said.

"Come to me Kern."

He kept thinking that she was ten years older. There was nothing he could see on her to prove it; but the effect of those years was somewhere in her. They had made a change, the nature of which he could not tell. He lowered his eyes and remembered how many hundreds of times he had called her back to his mind and had created the image of her. The image was clear and distinct, engraved in his memory by the years of recollection. He lifted his glance quickly, to match the image with her presence before him; and there was an instant in which the image lay upon the reality and made a small blur. The two did not perfectly blend. Then the image died and the realness of her presence was with him. But he remembered that one moment and he thought: "Ten years have made a difference."

She had waited for him and he had not moved. She said: "I've spent a long time looking for you, Kern. Years of looking for you. I found you were at Lincoln. I was on my way to Lincoln. Then I saw you tonight on the street. After all that, can't you come the last ten feet?"

But she saw he had no intention of coming and, with a gesture of her shoulders, she walked toward him, her eyes holding his attention completely. There was a blackness and a care in her eyes; there was a terrible concentration of feeling in them, as though her life depended upon him. She touched him and looked up, and then she slid her arms around him and brought her body to him and give him a full and long kiss.

He made a gesture of placing his arms around her and a great embarrassment went through him at his lack of response. She felt it as well and presently stepped back, hopelessness and half-terror in her eyes. She murmured: "Would it do any good to go all the way back, Kern? To explain the kind of a girl I was, the foolishness in me, the strange things I seemed to want and then found out I didn't want? Would it help if I said I made a mistake, and knew it as soon as you were gone, and have lived ever since trying to find you and repair the mistake?"

"No," he said, "it wouldn't do any good."

"I can't believe the deepness of all we felt could die out entirely. I can't believe it would die at all. It was everything to us. How could it be nothing now?"

"Was it everything to you?"

"When it was too late, I knew it was. But you were always the steadfast one. I never expected to come to you and find there wasn't a trace of me left in your heart. I knew I had hurt you as badly as if I'd shot you. That's been on my mind ten years—to make it up. But I thought you'd remember me, and remember the best of what we had. That maybe you would carry a hope, as bitter as you were toward me, that someday it might be different. That we could go back."

He heard, in her words, all that he himself had secretly believed. He had nourished the wish, even as he had closed himself up, made himself over, and sought simplicity for his life. His disillusion, he realized, was a screen behind which he covered his hope. Now she was here—and he could revive the hope. Yet, with Alice MacDougall before him, he had no desire to revive it. Something had happened to him. Maybe it was the weariness of ten years. Maybe it was something else. He wanted to express all this to her, and found it impossible; and only shook his head.

She looked closely at him. She begged him in silence to change, to come to her; she begged him to lie to her and say the things, out of pity, that he didn't believe. The wish and the appeal was on her face; the willingness to come to him on any terms was there. He knew it and felt the shame of her position and was embarrassed again. "No," he said, "nothing can come back, for us."

She made a sharp turn from him and walked across the room to the door. She swung back. The capacity for crying was burned out of her, he guessed; her expression was dull and indifferent.

"Kern," she said, "it would help me if I knew one thing. Do you hate me so much?"

"No. I don't hate you at all."

"Then," she said, "I know you never loved me as deeply as you thought you did. I haven't really wrecked your life. I only wrecked my own."

He wished he could answer that. He wanted to tell her how the long years had been with him, how empty they had been, how far he had traveled to escape the memory of her, how long he had dreamed of her. But he saw that she was comforted by her belief that he had failed in depth of emotion. It restored her self-respect. She stood still, giving him a long and smileless glance; she was a woman taking away some final memento to mark the end of a part of her life. She murmured: "You've changed very little. You look well." She drew a breath, she said in a low and uneven voice: "Remember, Kern, I tried to come back." Then she opened the door and went away.

He walked over and closed the door. He stood with his face to it, trying to explain to himself why the memory of her had been so powerful in him and now meant nothing. He was free in a way he had not been free before; there was nothing left of her now but a sentimental recollection. He thought: "Something's happened and I have not been aware of it."

He left Fargo on a dull and lowering morning. Winter this year had been one of the most severe on record; it released its grip for a few hours, and renewed it again with its bleak, slicing winds. At Hatton's Ranch he woke to a bright morning. A bland warm wind blew from the south, and all that day the snow beneath him turned to slush and the mules carried a thin vapor of steam around their flanks from sudden sweating. That night, at Bell T Ranch, old George MacGoffin warned him.

"Too damned sudden and too damned fair. It's like a woman hatin' you all year and then beginnin' to smile. There's a knife in that smile."

"Never had the experience of a woman throwing a knife at me," said Shafter.

"My experience has been with Injun women," said MacGoffin. "I ain't had no chance at the other kind."

That morning he started with one day's run into Lincoln remaining, and therefore was on the road earlier than usual. The previous day's thaw had hardened by night into a tough crust which made bad footing for the mules. At noon Shafter stopped to boil his coffee and fry his bacon. Before resuming his journey he buckled on to each mule a set of smaller leather snowshoes designed to give better traction. Far ahead of him, barely visible in the steel-colored haze, lay Romain's ranch and, beyond that, the Benson ranch which was four miles short of Bismarck.

As he rode forward the haze thinned and gave him a better view of the horizons; at three o'clock he passed the Romain ranch and pointed toward Benson's house. Somewhere in the course of the next hour a feeling rolled through him and ruffled his flesh, a queer sensation that had no apparent origin. He sat still, alert to the feeling and now aware of a forming darkness distant in the north. The air was wholly motionless and the sound of mules and sleigh made more than the usual racket in an increasingly thin air. His feet and the exposed flesh of his face registered the increased bite of weather, by which he knew the temperature had swung sharply down in one of the prairie's freak twists. It was the weather change, then, that had made its reaction in him.

The Romain ranch was by then an hour behind him, the Benson house two hours ahead. He thought of the possibilities of shelter between those two points —the culverts into which a man might dig his way and find scant comfort, and one small section house. These were his secondary defenses against the storm now displaying itself northward in the shape of a ragged wall of cloud columns kicked high by wind.

He had played his game with these blizzards all during the winter; had seen them form and come on, sometimes slowly, sometimes with the speed of an express train. On occasion he had been given far-away warning; on other occasions he had been struck within a period of ten minutes. So now he studied the clouds with a searching attention over a quarter hour, sending the sleigh along at a fast clip. It would be a storm of some severity, he decided, but probably not as dangerous as those of midwinter had been and not possessing that dense drive of snow which completely blotted out the earth. By this time he had reached the halfway point between Romain's and Benson's. In one sudden flip of decision he made up his mind to continue to Benson's.

He had enough experience to possess great respect for those northern clouds bearing down upon him; therefore he checked his position in relation to the nearest culvert on the railroad and made a quick guess of the length of time it would take him to reach Benson's. He oriented himself carefully, knowing that when darkness closed in he would have to depend entirely on the feeling of the earth as it lifted and dropped beneath the sleigh. The telegraph poles ran die-straight westward, the yellow station house at Tie Siding marched up and fell behind. He got out his watch and marked the time he passed it. If the storm closed in he would then have one kind of a bearing when he turned about.

Nothing yet disturbed the cold still air around him; up north the height and breadth of the jagged clouds told of a tremendous wind rushing forward—and behind the clouds marched a spreading blackness in which fury lived. The sight of it made him revise his judgment, made him take out his compass and get a course on the Benson house. It lay directly along the telegraph poles, one point south of due west. As long as light lasted the telegraph poles would be sufficient, but when the storm's strange night fell, with its wild crying and its pressure against the team and its smother of snow, the poles would be indistinguishable ten feet distant.

At four o'clock, the Benson house was forty-five minutes before him and in clear view. At ten minutes after four there was no Benson house to be seen. Day drained out of the sky and through the stillness he heard the distant reverberation of wind, like the trembling echo of a waterfall, like the shuddering of volcanic action. He looked into the sleigh's bed to see if his mail and light cargo were secure; he snugged his collar around his neck and lifted his scarf to the bridge of his nose and suddenly put the team to a run. He had sensed a possibility of outracing the storm by a scant margin.

In another ten minutes he hauled the team down to a steady walk. He had lost his race even then and realized he had to conserve the mules for the emergency which would come when the blizzard struck. Blackness moved over the sky like an unrolling carpet and one first streak of wind puffed softly across the stillness. The mules had been plugging steadily along but now the touch of the wind disturbed them and they broke into a trot. Shafter let them keep the pace, meanwhile watching the gray wall, boiling from earth to heaven, move on with its stately terrible power; great lances of grayness puffed forward from its crests, like the spray blown from mile-wide, mile-high waves. Wind grew brisker about Shafter and as the churning blackness rushed upon him he heard the voice of the storm slowly lift at him with its mixture of tortured sounds. He looked at his watch, putting his head close to the dial. The time was then twenty-five minutes past four and the Benson house was another thirty minutes ahead. Looking up from the watch he thought he saw a flash of light reach forward from the house, but at once realized it was a single wafer of snow whipping by. He had scarcely stuffed the watch into his pocket when the full pressure of the blizzard, moving across the earth at fifty miles an hour, came upon him and round about him and seized him and shook him in the sleigh's seat and became a great yelling in his ears. A wall of hardened snow hit him and closed steadily down until he had only a vague sight of the mules.

He felt them give to the wind's pressure and pulled them back, northward, and felt them give again. He changed course slightly, passing a telegraph pole within arm's distance and calculating the location of the next pole; in this way, fighting the team's drift, he made his departure from one pole and his landfall on another, observing that he missed the poles by wider and wider margins as he went on. The pressure of the storm thus grew greater and his forward progress became a game of guessing how far northward it was necessary to swing. Meanwhile he took to counting the poles, realizing he could not read the watch in the pit-black darkness now surrounding him. He made his rapid estimate of distance. It was a rough four miles to Benson's and there were thirty poles to the mile; that would make 120 poles between this point and Benson's, the poles standing 176 feet apart.

He drew hard to the north. He counted the approximate distance before the next pole should show its thin blur near by, and saw nothing; he hauled hard to the north again, tension pulling at the muscles of his belly. He counted the seconds slowly in his head. He thought: "Maybe I'm swinging too much," and strain piled up in him. But the force of the wind had gotten always greater and he knew his own senses were tricking him and therefore kept drawing to the right until it appeared to him he was traveling due north.

He had by then gone a distance sufficient to include three poles and had seen nothing. There was only one way left him of checking his whereabouts. Pulling around through what seemed a forty-five-degree turn, he headed full into the teeth of the wind. The team fought him and fell off against the wind; he brought it back and used the ends of his reins to push it on. The sleigh rose with a roll of snow and tipped down and he felt the runners grit and bump along spotty covering over the railroad ties. He had struck the right-of-way.

He turned with it and followed it. A snowplow had recently cut a partial way through here, leaving shoulders to either side of the track; thus more or less guided, the mules could not swing off as freely, and now settled to a steady pulling. Meanwhile he counted the poles he could not see, judging the distance between. When he passed the thirtieth pole he started from the beginning again and in this manner covered the second mile.

The wind and the sheer weight of the coldness got through him. He felt it first in his legs as a stiffness and then as a pain; and then he felt it in his bones. He began to kick his feet against the sleigh's floor. "Twenty-three," he said, and kicked the floor, "twenty-four," and kicked again. He had the muffler drawn twice around his head, but the wind flung its rioting racket against his ears until the steady pulse of sound bothered him.

This was the first break in a man's armor, the first aperture through which the blizzard flung itself eventually to break down sense of direction, to destroy hope, to bring on the panic that made men disbelieve themselves and at last turn with the wind and let it carry them to destruction. It was the incessant sound which first drummed the balance out of a man's mind, and afterwards it was a knowledge of legs slowly freezing. He was in the center of blackness, feeling the blackness whirl around him so swiftly and so powerfully that he grew dizzy. For a moment he closed his eyes. When he opened them the team had stopped.

He brought the reins sharply down on the mules rumps. He said, "Thirty. Two more miles."

The mules started, went a few halfhearted feet, and again stopped. He lifted the ends of the reins, but suddenly remembered that there was a short low trestle over a coulee two miles east of Benson's house; the mules had come upon the trestle and were afraid of it. Pulling them around, he drove over a hump of snow and sighted a pole as it slid by, and now once more he aimed his course from pole to pole.

He was in the middle of the third mile when he realized the mules were playing out. The poles came up from the blackness more slowly and the team swung farther from the wind and was harder to rein back. At the twenty-sixth pole on the third mile the team faltered and came to a stop.

He lashed out with the end of his reins and got the sleigh going. He said "Twenty-seven," and waited what seemed a long while for the twenty-eighth pole. He picked it up and then sat back for the next one. Suddenly he thought: "I was pretty slow in reaching out to slap those mules." He had thought he had swung his arm instantly, but now that he got to studying it, he realized he had sat motionless for a good ten seconds. The bitter cold had begun to paralyze his mind and the knowledge of it flashed the sense of danger through him. He stamped his feet on the sleigh's floor and he yelled into the wind, "Now I'll stretch my right arm," and felt his muscles gradually respond. It was like sending a ball rolling down a bowling alley and waiting for it to strike—his will moving that reluctantly toward his muscles.

He reached the first pole of the fourth mile. The wind keeled him on the seat; the force of it shoved the sleigh sidewise and the screaming sound of the storm grew more and more shrill until his ears vibrated with the steadiness of the impact. He pulled the mules around with greater difficulty and knew that he could afford to waste little more energy in this kind of wrestling and turned the team north again, rising onto a shoulder of snow and dropping into the railroad cut. It took a great load off his mind thus to be traveling in a certain direction; at the same time he began again to count slowly, thereby estimating the passage of the telegraph poles, which he could not see. The thirtieth pole should, if his calculations had been right, bring him opposite Benson's house. If he missed Benson's, the road would carry him directly into Bismarck, but he knew he could not nurse the team the additional five miles.

He kept stamping his feet until he discovered he had lost all feeling in them; his right side, so steadily pounded by the wind, had grown stiff. He stopped the team as soon as he thus realized he was slowly freezing, and stepped from the sleigh. He held the reins and walked forward, no sensation of weight on his feet, and got to the head of the team and led it forward.

The physical exertion warmed him, but it tired him. He thought: "I'm not that soft," and knew at once how much the blizzard had sapped him. He put the reins over his shoulder, guiding the mules as well as pulling them on against their inclination to stop. He had passed the fiftieth pole when he began to watch the left forward distance for Benson's house lights. He thought he saw those lights and stared steadily until the mealy agitation of snow made a heaving up-and-down confusion in his brain. He closed his eyes and walked half a dozen paces, and opened them again. There were no lights.

When he had counted the twentieth pole he began to visualize the ten poles remaining. He made a picture of them in his mind and saw how far they stretched out and he thought: "I may have to let the team go and walk on." But he argued himself out of the impulse. He had a terrible feeling of futility and a growing conviction that he lacked the energy to cover the distance. Then he pushed the doubt out of his mind by arguing with himself about the mules again. "It's too good a team to abandon. The off mule is a little the smartest, and a little the meanest. Same as people are. The smarter they are the crueler they can be. Something there for me to think about when I reach Lincoln. Can't give up the mules. Or the mail . . ."

He walked straight into a signal post stuck up beside the right-of-way and struck it with his face. It should have hurt him badly, but the pain was something that traveled very slowly to his consciousness. The team had stopped behind him. He put his hand on the post and felt upward until he reached the square board on top of the post—and he stood still, the wind pushing him against the post and the scream of the wind pulling his thoughts apart. He put them patiently together again, trying to make a picture of the railroad as it moved toward Bismarck, trying to spot the signal board's location.

"Why, hell," he said, "this is the Benson whistle-stop sign. The house is two hundred feet straight south."

The discovery shot a jet of warmth through him. He crawled back along the side of the near mule and got into the sleigh and he squared the team into the south, with the wind full at his back. Then he said: "There's one more sign, a mile away from the Benson sign, but I can't have misjudged my distance that much." The whole thing now was a toss-up, for he was no longer certain, and he sat still, knowing that if he failed to strike the Benson house at the first try, the team would not face the weather and return to the track. Suddenly he brought the rein ends down on the mules. "Hya—hya," he yelled. "Get on Babe. Butcher!"

They had stood still too long and now were slow in starting. He slashed their rumps with the reins and got them into motion. He felt them strain upward on the ridge of snow and falter. He hit them again and yelled at the top of his voice. The sleigh tilted, came to the snow's summit and dropped down. The mules, driven by the wind, slogged slowly through the snow.

He was again counting time slowly, and guessing distance. He stared ahead of him for Benson's lights and he grumbled, "Come on—put that lamp in the window. Forty-two seconds, forty-three seconds . . ."

There was a flurry of snow in front of him, a flickering screen of it across his eyes; and then he realized it was a ray of house light which had made the snow visible. The mules had stopped again and when he watched the snow a moment he saw the light shining ahead. He was directly against the house's porch.

It never occured to him to step down and go to the house. Instead, he guided the team to the left and made a patient circle, driving the sleigh close by the walls. Darkness came solidly down again as soon as the house light faded, but he had the picture of Benson's yard wholly clear in his mind and went on with confidence. When the team stopped, Shafter got down and went ahead, touching the wall of Benson's barn. He scraped his hand along the wall until he found a door latch and rolled the door open and pulled team and sleigh into the barn's runway. He hauled the door almost shut and turned and put his back to it. He spoke to himself aloud, with a drunken man's labored distinctness:—

"Better stay here until I thaw out. Better not go into a warm house."

Exhaustion hit him on the head like a maul. He felt his feet slide forward a little so that he was braced against the wall. His belly was empty and his throat dry; and his body was a patchwork of feeling and stinging aches and numbness. He slapped his hands together and he said: "They're all right." He took off his Berlin gloves and slid his hands underneath the muffler which lay ice-cemented around his throat and ears. He pinched his ears. He pulled away the muffler and began a steady rubbing. Streaks of colored light swam across his pupils and he was distinctly unbalanced from the pounding of the storm, and for a little while the quietness in the barn bothered him. He felt the wind lean against the wall and strain it and he heard the shrilling of the eaves and the rattle of sleet against the roof. Sensation came to his ears.

He walked through the darkness toward the mules. He said: "Babe—Butch," and walked around and around the sleigh, stamping his feet as he traveled. He was greatly tired and wanted to sit down, but he kept himself moving. He said, "Babe," again and unhitched the team and groped in the dark for a quarter hour to remove the harness. He was as weak as a man recovering from a long fever, every motion of his hand, requiring a deliberate push of his will. He let the harness fall on the ground and he let the mules go and turned to the door. When he stepped outside, the storm nailed him to the wall so that he had to wheel sideways and go shoulder first into the wind; he guided himself by the faint light he saw and reached the house's back door. He hit it once with his hand, opened the door and passed into a dark room. There was a farther door open, through which a light burned with extraordinary brilliance. He went through the doorway and saw two blurred forms ahead of him. A woman's voice came sharply at him.

"Kern—where've you been?"

She came to him, reaching toward the scarf around his neck and when she pulled it away, the crusted ice rattling on the floor, she laid her hands on his ears. "Kern," she said, "you can't stay in a warm room."

"That's all right, I thawed out in the barn." He closed his eyes and pushed his fingers against the lids, and opened them to find Josephine watching him.

"I'll get you some coffee. Are you sure your feet are all right?"

"Coffee's fine," he said. He looked at the man standing near the stove in the corner of the room, but the pounding of the weather still affected his eyes and the heat of the room put a film on them. Josephine had gone back toward the kitchen. He looked around the room and saw an army cot made up like a divan and he went to it and sat down. He bent over and supported his head with his hands braced against his knees. This was uncomfortable and presently he lay back on the cot.

When Josephine returned he was sound asleep. She stood over him a moment, worrying about him. "He was coming from Fargo and got caught in it. He must have lost his team. Edward, help me take his boots and socks off. If his feet are frozen we'll have to wake him up."

Garnett said irritably: "It is a strange thing he should come to this house, with two hundred miles of space between Fargo and Bismarck."

She looked back at the lieutenant. "Under the circumstances, I'm very glad he's here. Help me with his boots."

Garnett said: "I'd do anything for you, Josephine, but I will not touch him."

"This is no time to be hating him. He may lose his feet."

"Let him crawl around on his hands and knees."

"Edward," she said, shocked, "no human being should carry that kind of thought in his head."

"You don't know," he murmured. "You can't possibly know how I feel about him, or how he feels about me. There is no use of hiding it. I'd be lying to you if I said I was sorry for him. I regret he survived the storm. For his part, he would stand over me and let me die and never lift a hand."

He stood back and watched her haul at Shafter's boots. She got them off and stripped away his heavy wool socks. She put her hands on Shafter's feet; she pinched the white skin around his ankles and watched a faint spot of color come to the flesh. Garnett's expression turned distasteful as he viewed this. A protest came out of him. "Don't dirty your beautiful hands on him."

"I wish I knew what was between you two. You've done something to him, haven't you, Edward?"

"I have done my best to ruin him," said Garnett coolly. "As he has done his best to ruin me."

"I think he has more generosity in him than you have, Edward."

Garnett's mouth formed a small, acid smile. "Wait and see." Then he remained still a long while, his hands laced behind him, darkly speculating. "Josephine," he said finally, "no matter what happens next, please remember I have never said an insincere thing to you."

"Why? What can happen?"

"Wait and see," said Garnett.

☆ 14 ☆

A Sinner Turned Holy

Shafter woke with one thought uppermost in his mind: "I've got to get up and find a place to sleep tonight." The room was dark, and the windows showed the blackness of the outer world. The storm had blown itself away, its abrupt end a surprise to him. He turned his head to see a light in the kitchen and a woman moving about. He lifted himself on the cot; his clothes were on but his shoes had been removed, and he had blankets over him. The weariness was gone. This little half hour's nap had freshened him and taken even the memory of the storm's beating from his head; he felt fine, and said to himself: "I'm almost as good now at thirty-two as I was at twenty." Almost as good, but not quite, for no man could expect to keep forever the bubble of energy of that younger age; and when a man got older he got wiser—and wisdom always had a little bit of fear in it. "When you're young," he thought, "you're too dumb to know all the things that could kill you."

He got up and moved into the kitchen to find Josephine at the stove. The little kitchen table was set and the smell of coffee and bacon was a stimulant to him. Josephine said: "How do you feel?" She smiled at him.

"Fine," he said, "fine. Half an hour's rest does a lot."

"Nearer ten hours," she said. "It is six o'clock in the morning."

He looked out of the window; he looked at his watch. "That's a strange one," he said, and went to the back porch. He cracked the ice from a water bucket and washed his face. Josephine opened the door briefly to hand him a towel, and he stood in the brittle stillness of the morning, savoring the softer, warmer smell that this day brought. Light made a dull crack in the east, but there was a silver haze hanging over the land—the kind of fog that would last indefinitely and shut out the sun. Snowdrifts lay in molded shapes against the walls of the house, banked halfway up the windows. The blizzard had punished him, and left his skin as tender as though it had been seared by fire, but even so he had already forgotten the misery of that four-mile ride. He was in good spirits, and hungry, and pleased with his survival as he turned back into the kitchen.

He sat down to breakfast. Josephine poured coffee for him and for herself and took a place opposite. She sat quietly by, her face rose-colored and pretty by the stove's heat; she sipped her coffee, now and then watching him but offering no comment.

"How do you come to be here?" he asked.

"We were out for a ride and saw the blizzard coming. We got here about two hours before you did. Where were you when it started?"

"Halfway between here and Romain's. What time did I get here?"

224

"It was half-past seven."

"Four miles in two hours and a half," he said. He shook his head. "I didn't think it took that long. No wonder I got cold."

"You were dead-beat," she said.

He ate his meal and sat back with his cigar. Josephine rose to pour him another cup of coffee, a serene and thoughtful expression composing her face. He noticed it now as he had so often before. "Where are the Bensons?" he asked.

"They were on the way to Bismarck when we passed them. So I suppose the storm held them in town."

Daylight slowly seeped through the windows, muddy and sullen. He got up from his place, now thinking about his mules. "Time to get on. It was a first-class blizzard. The last shot in the carbine, I guess, before spring comes. I doubt if we'll have another. My last trip, more than likely. The train will be running next week."

He heard somebody stepping along the front room, behind him, and he noticed the girl's face tighten. He thought nothing about it as he stood there; he felt like a man who had gone through a big drunk—bruised and sore but all sweet and cleaned out inside. Everything was fine and he had no bad memories or cares.

"Where did you get that cut on your head?"

He raised his hand to it and ran a finger along a welt which stretched from the bridge of his nose back to the line of his hair. He had to stop to think about it before he remembered. "I walked into the signal post out in front of the house. That's what saved my bacon. I knew I was on top of Benson's then. It steered me right in."

"You took chances, Kern."

"I thought I could beat out the storm. I guess I got a little careless." He turned around and faced the living-room doorway, and at that same moment he saw Garnett come across the front room and stop. Garnett looked at him, his eyes narrowed, his mouth pulled long and firm; there was a thin and bright attentiveness in his glance and he held himself on guard, as though he knew trouble had to come between them.

Shafter removed his cigar. Red color showed freshly along his neck and a rough expression tumbled over his face. He looked, the girl thought, like a man who suddenly had stumbled upon something dangerous and unpleasant, something for whom he had maintained a lifelong animosity. He held the cigar in his hand, reading Garnett, and being read by Garnett. Presently Shafter turned his head to the girl and she saw what he thought.

"This is the man you came riding with?"

"Yes," she said. "It is as I explained to you. The storm caught us."

"I know," said Shafter, very quietly. Then he asked her an odd question. "Has he had breakfast?"

"No. But why?"

He almost smiled as he pointed to the revolver and belt on Garnett's waist. "He eats breakfast with his gun."

"You know why it's there," said Garnett.

"Why is it?" Josephine asked.

"He's away from the fort," said Shafter, murmuring the words.

"There's nothing on this side of the river to be afraid of," she pointed out. "These Indians on the east bank are all right."

"That's right," said Shafter. "But I'm here."

"You see?" said Garnett to her. "He knows why I've got it."

She studied the two, worried and gradually growing impatient. "I think you are both fools."

"That's probably true," said Shafter.

"You've had your meal," said Garnett. "Go on, get out of here."

Shafter's face held its creased half-smile. He had his head slightly bent as he watched the lieutenant. He murmured: "Up to the same old tricks, Garnett?"

The girl caught the meaning of it and spoke quietly, ignoring the chance to grow furious at him. "I told you how it was. You were caught in the same blizzard, weren't you?"

"Don't explain anything to him," said Garnett sharply.

"That's right," agreed Shafter. "The lieutenant never explains. There isn't time enough—even if he lived to be an old man—for him to explain all he's got behind him."

"Sergeant," said Garnett coolly, "mind what I tell you or I'll have you court-martialed for disobeying me."

"Stand aside from the door," said Shafter. "I'm going in there to get my cap and I don't want to get the smell of a scoundrel on me."

"According to the record," said Garnett in a jeering tone, "who's the scoundrel? You're making a scene for the lady. If I had you in my company I'd break you."

"If I were in your company," said Shafter, "somebody would be broken in due time, no doubt. Stand aside, Beau."

The name, the girl noticed, pricked Garnett's coldness. His eyes heated and for a moment he balanced in the doorway, thinking of the answer he wanted to make. Then he stepped into the kitchen and cleared the doorway. Shafter went past him and crossed the room to the cot. He got his cap off the floor and he took his muffler from a wall hook where it had been hung by Josephine to dry during the night. He stood with his back to the kitchen while he wrapped the muffler around his neck. He started to put on his overcoat, but then he got a thought in his head which turned his face tough, and he folded the coat over his arm and went back to the kitchen.

Garnett had taken a seat at the end of the table. He sat on the edge of the chair, his body turned so that he might watch Shafter, who now came through the doorway and paused. Shafter looked at the girl. He said softly: "My advice to you is to get out of this house."

She was under strain, fearing what might happen. "Kern," she said, "don't say any more. You've said enough."

"That's right," he agreed. "I've talked enough." He dropped the coat and came against the back of Garnett's chair. Garnett started to rise, but Shafter's arms closed about him and pinned him to the chair; then he let go with one arm and used the butt of his palm to crack Garnett on the temple, and after that he reached down and knocked away Garnett's hand as it struggled to reach the gun. He caught the gun out of Garnett's holster and stepped back and threw it to the far corner of the kitchen. He was laughing quietly.

"Now, Beau."

Garnett sat still a long dragged-out moment, his head sagged down. The girl mistook his silence and sharply spoke: "Kern, you've injured him! Don't you know what he can have done to you—"

Garnett made a springing rush from the chair, avoiding Shafter's outreaching arm. He raced through the doorway, momentarily out of sight. Shafter wheeled and started after him, hearing Josephine's voice suddenly grow shrill:—

"Benson's rifle—on the wall!"

He rushed through the door in time to see Garnett rip the rifle from the wall and bring it up to him. The round, dark muzzle centered on Shafter and wavered a moment. He whirled and ducked as the roar of the gun filled the room with its dry crash and he felt the wind of the bullet against him and heard it tick through the far wall. He charged straight against Garnett as the latter took two backward steps. He knocked the gun aside and hit Garnett with the point of his shoulder and smashed him against the wall; he brought up one arm and rammed it across Garnett's windpipe, and seized the gun and got it free and flung it into a corner. He stepped back again, his head still slightly bent as he watched the man.

"Now's the time, Beau."

"Do you know what I'll have done to you?" cried Garnett.

"You're hiding behind somebody else again," said Shafter. "You're always trying to find somebody else to settle your scores. Like Conboy. Like other times I could bring back to you. But right now, it is just the two of us. Do you know what I'm going to do, Beau? I am going to destroy an illusion of manliness. I am going to cripple you past the point where any other woman will want you. When I think of the women—"

Josephine, now at the kitchen doorway, cried at Shafter: "Don't, Kern!"

Garnett stepped sidewise along the wall, toward a corner, as Shafter watched him. Suddenly Garnett reached a chair and seized it and flung it up over his head and came forward, his face slashed by the intensity of his thinking as he swung the chair and flung it down and forward. Shafter raised one arm and took the blow, and shunted the chair aside. He stepped on and drove a punch deep into Garnett's flank, into the soft flesh just above the hip. Garnett cried out a hurt breath and let the chair drop and wheeled and sprang at Shafter, both hands swinging. One of his fists struck Shafter on the cheek, sending Shafter back.

But he was still hunting for a weapon, and momentarily turned his head, thus exposing himself. Shafter jumped in and staggered the lieutenant with a blow against his belly. Garnett struck the wall and his mouth sprang open and in this defenseless moment he was at Shafter's mercy. Shafter hit him slantingly on the mouth, drawing blood. He watched Garnett's head drop and roll aside. He waited for his chance and when he saw it he hooked another side blow across Garnett's nose. He knew he had done the man damage, for he heard Garnett's yell rise.

Garnett came against him and took his punishment; he seized Shafter around the waist and held on and pushed Shafter toward the stove with a great burst of strength. He shoved Shafter against its hot sides and he stiffened his legs behind him and spent all his remaining energy in that one effort to hold Shafter there.

The smell of Shafter's scorched clothing began to stink in the room. Shafter felt the flare of pain on the backs of his legs. He got an arm around Garnett's head and gave it a twist that threw the man off balance. He slid suddenly aside and saw Garnett throw both hands against the hot top of the stove to keep himself upright. Garnett cried out and drew back with his hands half open before him. The pain of it made him forget Shafter who, now behind him, came up and sledged him on the side of the neck and drove him across the room. Garnett turned and shoved his arms defensively before him. Shafter hit him on the mouth and drove a punch into his belly and watched the man drop.

He stood over Garnett, breath drawing deep, and bitterly regretted he had not more premanently damaged those handsome features which had caused so much ruin. This was not like his fight with Conboy, in which the end of the struggle brought also an end to bad feeling; this was like no other fight in his life. He was dissatisfied, his thirst unquenched; he looked down and hated the man more violently than before, and knew he would never cease to hate him. He waited there with the hope that Garnett would rise up and try again. He said: "Now's the time, Beau. Get up. Just one more try. Maybe you can reach another chair. Maybe you can get one of the guns. You can try, Beau. If you shot me, you wouldn't be held for it. You know that. Get up and try it."

He stepped back another pace, giving Garnett a chance to make his turn, his jump, his lunge. He thought the man's silence was faked; he thought Garnett heard him, and waited. Blood rolled down Garnett's lips and he breathed in the shallow, fast and sucking way of an exhausted man; suddenly he gave a hard groan and rolled to his back and laid a hand over his broken nose. Shafter got a glance at the man's eyes and knew then the fight was over.

He stood still with the memory of a ten-year injustice burning through him, unquenched. He murmured: "God damn you, Garnett, you've always got a way of sliding out. You'll crawl out of this, like you crawled out before, and you'll carry your rotten business on. I ought to break your back."

Garnett swayed gently from side to side, on the floor. His legs rose and dropped as steady reflexes of pain pulsed through him. He groaned: "You've broken my nose."

"I hope it heals crooked," said Shafter. He had grown cooler and now he shrugged his shoulders and turned into the kitchen. Halfway to the rear door he wheeled rapidly, entered the living room again and picked up Benson's rifle. He ejected the shells and put them in his pocket and laid the gun on its rack; in the kitchen he retrieved Garnett's revolver and removed its loads and left the gun empty on the table.

Josephine had come into the kitchen. When he moved toward the back door she halted him with her voice.

"He'll have you courtmartialed. You have put yourself in his hands."

He had forgotten her for a little while. He stared at her, aware of her beauty as he always was. She was a fair woman, with hungry dreams seeking answer; and Garnett, whose profession was women, had at once known the vividness of her dreaming, her eagerness to believe and to respond to those things which seemed to come as answers to all longings. It was a cheap and easy and dirty profession, preying upon the near things of a woman's soul, betraying them and leaving the woman stripped of illusion.

"No," he said. "He won't. He can't bring charges against me without explaining the circumstances and involving you. He won't do that. Not that he'd have any scruples about giving you away, but he'd be exposing himself."

"Exposing himself to what?" she asked.

"To other women who now think they share his interest exclusively," said Shafter.

She stood stone-quiet, her face fixed in a cold distasteful expression. She murmured: "You make this a very unpleasant affair, don't you?"

"I know the man," said Shafter.

"Do you know me?" she said.

"You went out for an afternoon's ride," he said. "That was all."

Her answer tumbled swiftly back at him. "Where is the wrong, Kern? Dig down as deep as you want and find me an answer—the worst answer you can find."

"There's your answer," he said and pointed through the door toward the living room. Garnett had risen from the floor and now walked slowly forward and supported himself in the doorway. He looked upon these two with his battered face, his crushed lips and his bold nose now broken at the bridge; he looked at them with a dull indifference, and listened as though their words came through fog to him.

"What has he to do with me?" she demanded.

"Everything he touches—"

She cut in and finished the phrase for him. "Turns bad. That's what you think. You were hurt once, and you stopped growing. You have spent the last years of your life shrinking smaller, drawing away for fear of getting hurt again. You've done a good job of making a very unimportant man out of yourself, Kern. You might have been a big one. I've thought of that often and it has troubled me to see so much turn into so little. There's more fun and honesty in living than you know about. It has passed you by. You think Edward is evil? So are you. Evil in the way you let hate and suspicion feed upon your soul."

Shafter bowed his head slightly. "You may be right," he said, and left the room.

She stood still, hearing his feet crackle through the snow crust as he went toward the barn; she was very attentive to that, forgetting the presence of Garnett. The anger died out of her and her face lost its temper; her shoulders dropped.

"That's the girl," said Garnett. "You've hit him hard. I know how he looks when he's been beaten. I know the look on his face."

She had her back to Garnett. "Edward, as soon as Kern has driven away, get your team and cutter ready. We're going home."

He said: "Look at me."

She kept her position for a little while and when she did turn she was sorry to show him the feeling she knew he would see. He was a clever man with his eyes; he read what lay within people—that was his gift. He had, she realized, frequently read her mind or her wishes and had changed his mood to suit her, his manner to please her. In a way it was a versatility not quite honest, a skill that came of practice. She remembered then what Kern had said about him: "To other women who now think they share his interest exclusively."

"I'm sorry, Edward," she said.

He said: "You liked me yesterday. You don't like me now. Where was the change?"

She shook her head. "Never mind. Let's go."

"He made the change, didn't he? You believe what he said about me?"

"Let's not bother to go into it. A thing changes. People change."

"No," he said, "you believe him. And all those hard words you used on him meant nothing."

"Yes," she said, "I meant them."

He managed a thin smile. "You intended to hurt him, but you never intended to drive him off. You want him to come back. It is a very old way with a woman."

"You would know, wouldn't you?" she said quietly.

"It has been used on me more than once." He looked at her, withdrawing his smile. "I never have tried to cover up my weaknesses to you, Jo. I knew it was no good. If you had been just another woman with me, I would have used all the tricks in the book."

"You know the book very well."

"I don't deny it." He sighed and struggled with the pain pulsing through him. "When I saw you I knew I had come to something serious. You are the first woman with whom I have ever wanted to be honest. As soon as I realized that, I was afraid. I knew what was behind me. I knew you'd discover it sooner or later—as any woman will come to know about a man. That's why I told you to believe in me, whatever happened. I wanted you to know I meant to play the game right with you." He shrugged his shoulders, the weight of his thoughts fatally on him. "A sinner turned holy—and confronted with his sins."

"I believe you," she told him quietly.

"But now believing is not enough," he murmured. "There's too much behind me, and too little left in me."

"Yes," she said. "Let's go home."

He went back to the living room and got into his coat and left the house, soon bringing the cutter around. He helped her up and turned toward Bismarck through a lowering overcast which closed the horizons down. She looked for the shape of Shafter's sleigh in the distance and didn't see it.

"Edward," she said, "don't use your power as an officer over him now. Let all this die."

He gave a strange, almost irrational laugh which made her glance sharply at him. She said, "You're hurt, aren't you?"

"That's another thing about a woman. She goes through storm and then expects sunshine to erase the memory of storm. You misjudge me and you misjudge Shafter. Nothing will stop the way we feel. Nothing will stop me from getting at him."

"Edward," she said, "don't make yourself less than you are."

He shook his head and said nothing more until they reached the front of her house. She dropped out of the cutter and looked back at him a moment, sad for the way things had been, sorry that she had hurt him. He read that in her, too, with his eyes. He said:—

"I shan't see you again, I suppose."

"No."

He nodded. Then he said: "But you must understand something else about Shafter. I know him better than any other person. You believe he'll come back because—as you have already discovered—he's in love with you." He smiled in his bitter way. "But he won't come back. He never goes back to anything. Good-by, Jo."

☆ 15 ☆

Boots and Saddles

One night the regiment lay crowded within the walls of Fort Lincoln; at tattoo on the following evening it camped in tents on a level plain three miles south of the fort. Winter was done and waiting was done. Terry's orders had come through and the Seventh stretched its legs in the open once more and smelled the old good odor of canvas and grass and campfire. There would be a period of preparation before Terry arrived from St. Paul to lead the expedition on its way.

The regiment was whole again, all its twelve companies lined up side by side on the plain, each with its company street and line of tents leading off the main regimental street. Across the regimental street stood the tent of the commander, now occupied by Major Reno. Beside the tent of the commanding officer sat the other tents of the adjutant and staff. Adjoining the cavalry troops were two companies of the Seventeenth Infantry and one of the Sixth Infantry; here also were three Gatling guns in charge of two infantry officers and thirty-two men—an innovation looked upon by the cavalry with mixed emotions. Still farther on lay the wagon park with its one hundred fifty wagons to carry the quartermaster and commissary supplies, near which camped a hundred and seventy-five civilian teamsters in their own clannish group. With the regiment as well was a small party of Ree scouts, Charley Reynolds, and two interpreters —Fred Girard and the Negro Isaiah Dorman. The scout detachment had been placed under the command of Lieutenant Charles Varnum.

Here it lay under the early May sunshine, a sprawling unit on the plain, the white tops of its tents softly shining, the year's early dust rising from its steady activity, its day hourly marked by the throaty summons of the trumpets, with despatch riders whirling in from Lincoln and Bismarck and slow freight caravans arriving to round out the regiment's supplies; with scout details trotting out for their daily sweeps westward and returning jaded at night, one day coated with dust and the next day freckled with the mud of a seasonal shower. Throughout the hours the companies drilled, the sharp calls of officers and noncoms flatting through the bland late-spring air and the horses wheeling and crowding and moving with the precision of long training, and metal gear singing its minor metal tunes, and saddle leather squealing, and carbines slapping on their slings. Throughout the hours, too, details filed away to the foot of a small ridge for target practice.

This was the shake-down of a regiment whose units had been long separated. Men sweated off the fat of winter and refreshed their memories of duties grown vague by disuse. Equipment was overhauled, and replaced, guns tested and clothing mended or newly issued. Old men coached recruits and hazed them with the time-yellowed tricks of the service. New cavalry mounts were broken at the corrals and officers found bizarre flaws in old horses in order to secure younger stock for their commands. The pieces and parts of the regiment came together, stiffly from long lack of contact and then smoothly as they daily made union. At night campfires blazed on the earth, yellow dots against the velvet shadowing of the land, and men sang, or sat still, or argued, or wrote last letters homeward, or thought of home and never wrote; and they sorted out their possessions and extra equipment and mementoes long prized and sent them back to barracks to await their return when the campaign was done. All sabers were boxed and stored and dress uniforms put away. Threadbare trousers and battered campaign hats appeared, decorated by the frail blue and yellow flowers now coloring the prairie.

New faces appeared with the returned companies—Lieutenants Godfrey and Hare of K, Godfrey with a huge nose and a stringy mustache and long goatee; Captain McDougal, transferred from E to command B; Lieutenant McIntosh with the strain of Indian blood in him, and Lieutenant Wallace with the long neck and serious manner; Benny Hodgson, a youngster loved by the command for a sunny disposition; and Porter of I Company, and Captain Myles Keogh of I, a sharp-eyed, swarthy-skinned man with a pointed black imperial and indigo black mustache. It was Hines who described Keogh to Shafter. "There's three soldiers of fortune in this outfit. Nowlan and DeRudio and Keogh have served in Europe. Nowlan is a fine one and DeRudio is all right when he don't get excited and start talkin' Eyetalian at us. This Keogh, now, is the hardest of the lot, a martinet when he's sober and one that will throw the back of his hand at a trooper when he feels like it. We're goin' into this campaign in need of officers, Professor. We should have thirty-six or more and we've got but twenty-eight, and some of them are far from bein' the best in the world. For that matter, we could stand a few more men. Eight hundred to the regiment is not enough. It is Custer's idea that we can lick all the Sioux in the West. It is not mine."

"It looks like Reno in command instead of Custer," said Shafter.

Sergeant Hines gave him a look, shrugged his shoulders and turned away.

On May tenth the guardhouse trumpet cracked the afternoon with its sharp flourish for a general officer and Terry and his staff, and Custer, whirled out of the prairie and down the regimental street. It was as though an electrical shock passed through the command, stiffening it and exciting it. The presence of Terry meant the beginning of the campaign; and the presence of Custer meant that ease was over and long marches begun and sudden strains and unexpected shocks would come to the command. That night after retreat, the story of Custer was common knowledge in the camp, spoken of by officers in the presence of the sergeant major, and mentioned by him to the company sergeants, and in turn passed down the line. The regiment was a family with no secrets.

Hines said: "There Custer was in St. Paul, the President with a thumb on him and pushin' down for the things he'd said in Washington. And Sherman was out of patience with him, and Sheridan too. So he was a spanked boy watchin' his regiment go away and him not with it. Can you see the general pacin' up and down, cursin' the world because he wasn't out in front wavin' his big hat and sayin' 'Come on boys'?" Hines looked around him and grinned.

"So he writes this letter very humble to the President and Terry writes a nice letter to back him up, and Sherman likewise. Well, then, the President finally says back to Terry that if Terry thinks Custer will help on the campaign he'll let Custer go. But you know what Sherman wired Terry?" Hines's grin broadened into a laugh and he slapped the mess table with his hand. "Sherman wires Terry to tell Custer to be prudent, not to take any newspapermen along with him to write up his glorious deeds, and to quit makin' remarks about his superior officers in the future. So we got Custer back."

"Lickin' his wounds," said Sergeant McDermott. "He was spanked before the country and he knows it. The more he thinks of it, the worse it will hurt."

"That's a fact," said Hines.

"You know what he'll do to us now?"

"He'll take it out on us," said Hines. "Be ready to sweat."

"It is not the sweatin' I think of," said McDermott. "He will be devisin' ways to make the ones that spanked him look foolish. He will try to make a big man out of himself again, before the country. He will whip the Sioux, and then he'll be a hero once more. What I'm thinkin' is he'll ride this regiment into hell to do it."

"I guess he'll find hell enough out there to ride into," said Hines imperturbably. "There is no able-bodied Sioux left on the reservations. They're out west waitin' for us to come."

"A man in the Seventh," said McDermott glumly, "shouldn't be a family man."

"There's Terry to hold him down," said Hines.

"He'll do as he did before with Stanley. He'll listen to orders and march away and disobey 'em."

But Hines scratched his chin, long thinking. He shrugged his shoulders. "It may all be so. Still, I feel better with him around. I like to soldier under a man that is masterful at leadin'. Wherever we go, McDermott, he'll be at the front of us. We'll never have to look back to see if he's comin'."

"If he don't pull out and leave us to fight it alone," said McDermott. "Like he did Major Elliot at Washita."

"That," said Hines, "was a long time ago, and a thing full of argument. Let it be forgotten."

Shafter said: "You're an old horse smelling smoke, Hines."

"The truth," said Hines. "In spring my bones begin to ache with the memory of twenty-eight years of campaignin' and I sleep light and wake early and I think of a lot of lads I knew and a lot of fights we've had, and I want to be at it. I am a fool to think it, for the feelin' of bein' old has gotten at me lately. I guess this will be my last campaign."

It was as Hines knew, and as all the regiment suspected. The winter's ordeal had left Custer raw of nerve and pride; it had increased his terrific animal energy. His rough hand seized the regiment and shook it into redoubled activity. Officers' call was a repeated summons through the day and the drill period lengthened and men toiled late at special-duty chores. Inspections were repeated, company by company, with Custer's sharp eyes on everything. By day he was everywhere, whirling out of camp to the fort, the drill field or rifle range, or simply rushing headlong into the prairie to give himself a run; at retreat his nervous, staccato voice cracked across the plain; late after taps the guards saw his tent lights burning and his shadow pacing. There was no rest in him.

Crook, the grapevine rumors said, was well under way; and Gibbon was already as far as the Bighorn, having fought his way out of the West through the last winter storms. The May weather turned variable, one day warm and the next day sending down its riotous sheets of rain which turned the porous earth into spongy mud and set all the tents a-steaming. The *Far West* had already departed upriver with supplies, which would be left at a base designated by Custer. Terry had, meanwhile, made every effort to secure advance information of the Sioux whereabouts, and scouts drifted in fugitively with their information and drifted secretively out. The Rees, under Bloody Hand, arrived in camp on the fifteenth and pitched their tents. On the sixteenth general orders went out; the command would march the following morning. That night, on the eve of departure, the officers held a ball on the regimental street and all the ladies came out from Lincoln, and in the bland evening the music of the regimental band swung them around and around while the light of campfires glowed on colored dresses and faded fatigue uniforms.

Shafter stood back, watching the couples—the cheerfulness upon the men and the gaiety upon their women. This was the time, he thought, when a woman looked upon a man with a sharpened tenderness, when she noticed the things upon a man's face with a memorizing care, and stored in her mind the little things said, and matched his carefree air and held back from him the hard anxiety which lay like a lump in her heart. And this was the time when a man felt the goodness and the excitement of soldiering and yet had his own anxieties and tried to conceal them from the woman with a greater buoyancy. This was the time when they laughed and concealed harsher thoughts.

He moved back to his tent at tattoo and stretched out on his bunk. McDermott was writing a letter by candlelight, making hard work out of it. McDermott looked up at him, scowling. "If you're going to soldier, Shafter, don't get married."

"Where's your family?"

"Iowa—Cedar Rapids." McDermott leaned back. "I've got a boy who's three. Haven't seen him for eight months. I'll be glad when this enlistment's up." He returned to his letter and struggled with it and stopped again. "I suppose you've done your writing already."

"No," said Shafter.

"Better do it. I ain't been in the army ten years for nothing. I know when a campaign's just a march and I know when it's going to be a fight. This one's going to be a fight. I've seen it come all winter."

Shafter left the tent, moving down the company street into the darkness. The band music floated through the windless air, the swing and lift and melody of it carrying him back through his memories, evoking scenes half forgotten and feelings long buried. It shocked him to know suddenly how powerfully the music swayed him, embittering him for things that had been and now were not, making him sad out of reasons he could not understand, creating in him an acute loneliness.

"Here," he said to himself, "you're thirty-two and past sentiment. You've gotten rid of your dreams. That's what you wanted, wasn't it?"

He could not stop the outreaching of his thoughts, the strange swirl of his imagination. He remembered a lace fan lifted before a woman's face; and then the fan fell and he saw the sharp curve of her red mouth as she laughed at him, provocation in every soft curve of her cheeks, and the sound of her voice came over the great distance like a bell. The ball long since had turned silent, but the echo remained.

He remembered in sharp, stinging regret the kind of young man he had been; he recalled the wild flavor of his ambitions, the endless taste he had for life, the hopes and tempers and formless dreams which had buoyed him. Faith had been in that young Kern Shafter, and enthusiasm had made the world a fair place. He stopped walking; he put his hands behind his back and laced his fingers together, looking into the lush shadows of the night. Even now he caught the end of that hot vivid past, and suddenly said to himself: "When did I stop believing in things?" Somewhere along the line—and he knew when it was and how it was—he had flung himself upon the sharp point of disillusion, and it had opened him up and had drained out his faith; since that time he had walked as a bloodless man, turned stringy and colorless and heated only by a hatred.

But he saw that lace fan lift again over a woman's face and he heard her voice speaking to him, and then the fan dropped and the face was fair and smiling before him. It was another face—it was Josephine Russell's face and the smile was for him as long as it lasted. He watched it darken and die and he watched the glow of her eyes grow strange. He swung back on his heels; the music was still warm and beautiful in the night when he crawled into his blankets; and from the regimental street drifted the quick, stray phrases and laughter of the officers and their ladies.

Lieutenant Smith whirled his wife gallantly around, outward beyond the crowd. The music still played on but he broke away and took her arm and strolled across the slick prairie grass. "That makes me think of Saratoga," he said. "We had fun, old girl. Seems like a long time back. Just five years, though."

She said: "Do you know where I'd like to go again? Remember that little Connecticut town we passed through? All the houses painted white. The elms around them."

"We'll have our bills paid by fall," he said slowly. "Then I shall ask for leave." He stopped and turned her and looked down at her. "I regret all the things you've missed," he said, and kissed her.

She stepped back but she held both his arms. "This is the first time I've ever felt so afraid."

"It shouldn't be a long campaign. We are very well equipped, and we're going out in substantial numbers. This won't be another Fetterman affair. I think we'll have it done with by late August and be on the way home."

"I'm afraid," she whispered.

"Terry's a sound, safe man."

She shook her head, still clinging to him. It was a rare thing for her to be upset in this manner; both of them had a little ritual about these partings, which was to make them gay and very casual. But tonight she could not play the part, and his own feelings were strange in his chest. "I'm afraid," she said in a still lower, more breathless voice. "I've been that way all winter."

"You've stuck too long on the frontier."

"No," she said, "it isn't that." She pulled herself together and spoke with a pent-up feeling. "I wish the President had kept Custer away."

"Now—now," he said. "Anyhow, Custer will be under Terry's orders."

"If he sees a chance for a grand coup," she said, "he'll disobey his orders. I hate that man."

"Look here," he said gently, "we're in this regiment for another twenty years. You must not let your emotions shake you too much."

"Sometimes," she said, "I wish you were not in the army. I know it is your life and you want no other. But what have you gotten for all your faithfulness and service? You are beginning to turn gray. The hard usage of campaigning has done it to you. What do we have for it? A dozen silver spoons and a few cracked plates."

He was deeply disturbed and walked on without speaking. Presently she touched his arm and stopped. He saw a smile come uncertainly to her face. She murmured: "I won't send you off this way. Be good and take no unnecessary chances."

"I shall write you faithfully each night," he said. "We'll be in Connecticut this winter. Fresh apples, fresh vegetables. New clothes and old friends." He grinned at her and put his arms around her and kissed her once more; and so they stood in the darkness clinging to each other and reluctant to part while the long moments ran by.

In the four-o'clock darkness the drums of the infantry and the cavalry trumpets sounded the general and the glowing tops of the tent city collapsed as by the stroke of a single hand. Details moved on their crisscross errands, rolling and packing the canvas and stowing it away in supply wagons. Water details moved to the river and came back and orderlies rushed through the wan light of first daylight. Assembly blew and companies formed, each trooper's voice harking to roll call. Officers crisply shouted, swinging the companies into regimental line. The band was ahead and the colors swung by and Custer and his aids whirled up spectacularly. In the distance a bugler sounded "Forward" and at the same moment the band broke into tune. An ancient excitement rippled through Shafter, reviving the recollections of a hundred other marches in the past. After long waiting and long preparation, they were under way; over eight hundred troopers and infantrymen with scouts and guides and the long lumbering train of wagons rolling behind. The Seventh, in camp a collection of many men, now became a single-minded weapon, flexible, obedient and responsive. Ahead, Custer's huge campaign sombrero swung up in a wide gesture.

Shafter rode as right guide, the captain beside him, Moylan said: "We're parading through the fort. When we get beyond it we'll stop to let the wagon train catch up. There will be time for anybody so wishing to ride back and say so-long. Pass that word along, Hines." Then the captain looked at Shafter. "You got somebody to speak to?"

"No," said Shafter.

Moylan sat straight and blocky in the saddle—a man growing old in his uniform. He had an excellent soldier's face, square and calm and shrewd; he was a good commander, his strictness tempered with practical wisdom. He saw many things he pretended not to see; but he always saw what needed to be seen. Lieutenant Smith rode half down the line. The second lieutenant, Varnum, had been detached with Hare to command the Ree scouts. These rode ahead of the regiment.

Somewhere between midnight and reveille it had briefly rained, so that all the grass stems were beaded with moisture. Morning's sun came up to lighten a faint fog and a courier galloped back from the head of the column at a headlong pace. As the troopers approached the walls of Lincoln they filed past Ree women gathered wailing and weeping to watch their men go. Moylan looked thoughtful when he heard it. "That's odd," he said. At Laundress Row the sergeants' families were likewise gathered and likewise crying. McDermott, reminded of his own wife and children, began to curse. Young Lovelace looked down upon the women and presently he found Mary there; she too had tears in her eyes.

The band struck up the regimental tune, "Garryowen," and so passed through the gate and marched across the parade. Along Officers' Row the families had assembled, and townspeople had come over from Bismarck for the departure. The infantry companies left in charge of the post were drawn up in rank to salute the passing column; a handful of troopers, on sick list or detached duty, marched beside their companions a little distance to say good-by. Thus the regiment passed through the main guard gate to the north and swung westward toward the ridge west of the post.

As A Company filed through the gate, Shafter saw more townspeople gathered and, looking over toward the little building of the commissary sergeant, he saw Josephine.

She didn't notice him at the moment. Her glance was on the column and she seemed to be scanning it very closely, her glance running through the stretched-out file with a hurried intentness. Presently she discovered him and her eyes stayed on him as he rode forward; he observed her face grow tighter than before and he saw her lips move. He lifted his hat and when he rode on he felt the effect of her glance. It seemed to remain with him, to follow him.

Half a mile onward the regiment halted to wait for the supply wagons to come forward; and the ranks broke, the officers and married men riding back to perform their own private farewells. Shafter stood beside his horse, watching them go; he got out his pipe and filled it and drew smoke heavily into his lungs. He squatted down on the hard earth, hard in thought, hearing the cross fire of talk of other troopers around him.

Bierss said: "Your last chance, Bill, on that gal you been goin' with. She'll have another soldier when you come back."

"I can get another gal."

"Them Sioux women ain't tame," said Bierss.

Frank Lovelace walked rapidly down the hill with the rest of the back-tracking men. He passed groups of people at the north gate, he heard them talking and laughing—and he saw a woman put both her hands on a trooper's shoulder, look long at him, and begin to weep. He moved across the parade's long length toward the south side, blindly pulled toward Mary. He hadn't talked to her for many weeks—not since the night of the quarrel—and he knew that the tears he had seen on her face were for her father who was also marching away. Or maybe they were for Purple. Still, he kept going; he couldn't help it. When he had gotten halfway across the parade he saw her come toward him. She was running.

He said, "Ah, Mary, don't run!" He raced toward her. She was speaking to him but he couldn't hear what she was saying. He stopped just in time to avoid striking her; her arms went around him and he felt the hard pounding of her heart and her tears ran hot along his cheeks when he kissed her.

She pulled back to look at him, the terror in her eyes. "I didn't want you to go away like that, Frank!"

"I was coming to you," he said.

"It didn't mean anything," she said. "I'm sorry you were angry. If you'd only turned back instead of walking away."

"I wanted to come back," he said. "I guess I was a big fool."

The trumpet was blowing from the hill, summoning them back. The sound of it went hard through him; it made a pain in him. Her hands dug into his arms and she was trembling—and once more terror widened her eyes. "Frank—Frank—"

"I'll be back," he said.

"My father likes you. Frank—"

He kissed her again and turned, pulled by the music. Men were streaming over the parade and somebody called at him to come along. She clung to him, so that he had to lift her arms from him; and though he was very young, he did something that was as gallant as any mature man could ever do. He lifted her hand and kissed it, and he smiled and said again, "I'll be back," and trotted toward the north gate. After a few feet, he looked behind and noticed that she was walking after him. He called, "No. Mary." He shook his head and broke into a run. When he reached the north gate he again looked back and saw her standing in the center of the parade with her hand raised to him. The sight of her, so small and lonely on the parade ground's empty sweep, hit him in the heart.

Several officers had ridden down from the ridge to have a final moment with their families. Garnett came with them and went into bachelor's quarters to pick up a small notebook he had forgotten; when he came out of quarters he looked along Officers' Row and observed Mrs. Barrows standing before her house; her face turned toward him and he saw the care and the shadowing cast upon her features by her thinking. Then she looked away from him and he noticed the major coming across the parade toward her. Garnett climbed to his saddle and trotted briskly toward the north gate.

Lieutenant Smith had meanwhile dismounted before his wife, campaign hat in hand. He said: "I shall write you faithfully, by each courier. I really think we'll be back by August. Be a good girl, keep your hands busy and your mind out of mischief."

"What mischief is there to be found in an army post with all the healthy men gone?"

"Always one or two handsome beggars floating around."

"Pooh," she said, "I can't flirt with old men. That's all you're leaving me with."

They were light and foolish with each other. He said: "I shall come back with a mustache a foot long. One of the scratchy kind."

"I shall divorce you if you appear with mutton chops."

"It won't be divorce you'll be thinking of, when I show up."

"You're very egotistical."

The sound of the trumpet came again from the hill; and their smiling died. He took her to him and he said in a hard, grating voice: "I shall miss you like hell."

"Ah," she said, "be careful—oh, be careful!"

He held her as long as he dared and then wheeled and stepped up to his horse. He was again smiling, and looking down sharply at her until she brought a smile resolutely to her lips. "That's it," he said. "This winter, old girl, we're going to Connecticut. Good-by, my dear."

Shafter sat on the ground, looking down at the post, his thoughts wholly with Josephine. What stuck with him was the picture she made, her shoulders against the wall of the commissary sergeant's house, her eyes so carefully searching the column and at last stopping upon him. He said to himself: "She can have little interest in me," but her lips had said something to him across the distance. Very definitely she had spoken to him. Suddenly he realized he had to go back to her and discover if she had spoken to him, if she had anything to say to him. He rose and went into the saddle, dropping down the hill.

He came to the officers' club and skirted the post gardens. There were a lot of soldiers and people crowded around the gate and he didn't immediately see her and he thought she had perhaps returned to the ferry. Troopers had begun to come out of the fort, bound back to the column, and from his point of view he could see the long wagon train crawl around the west edge of the fort, now nearly caught up with the command; and from the main column came the sharp notes of the trumpet, summoning the stragglers. Threading the crowd, he saw her. She still stood by the house of the commissary sergeant and she had seen him and was watching him. He came before her and lifted his hat.

"Nice of you," he said, "to come here to watch us go."

"I suppose," she said, "you'll be away all summer."

"Never know. Nothing's certain."

She had nothing to add, and for his part he was caught in a silence which held him fast. Troopers streamed through the north gate. Captain Moylan passed, saying: "Time to go, Sergeant." Shafter watched her, with the clearest impression of her beauty and her strength. These were the things in her which most had appealed to him—these which gave her a capacity for laughter and teasing and gave her, too, a will which could be as hard as iron.

"Good luck," he said.

"You're the one to need that, Kern. I should be wishing you the luck."

"Wish it, then," he said.

"If you think it worth remembering," she said, soft and calm, "I do wish you luck."

He stirred on his saddle. There was a question in his mind, and a wish and an uncertainty he wanted to be rid of; and he remembered how sweet her lips were and the vibrations of her voice when she was stirred. He was on the edge of dismounting and he had made a move toward it when Garnett rode up from the guard gate and saw him there. Garnett's voice hit him like a stone.

"Get back to your outfit, Sergeant."

Shafter saw her throw a glance toward Garnett, who swung from his horse and now stood by her. She looked at Garnett with an odd expression, and turned her smiling glance again to Shafter, still and sweet. He bowed his head at her, wheeled the horse and trotted to A Company.

Custer rushed by, lithe and magnificent on his horse, the feeling of motion and activity exciting the general. All down the line the sergeants were bawling at their men. A single word rippled through the column.

"Forward!"

The Seventh moved with a kind of elastic stretching; and the white-topped wagon trains made a sinuous half-mile trail behind. The ground sloped upgrade toward the little ridge west of the fort and one by one the companies came to the summit, tipped over and had a last backward look at Lincoln, lying under the sun-brightened morning haze. Shafter swung in his saddle to catch that picture, and Hines said:—

"Long time before we see it again."

They moved down the ridge into a rolling, broken land—headed toward the Heart River, the Bad Lands, the Powder and the Tongue and the Yellowstone and the Rosebud—to all that crisscross of strange names and colorful and mysterious names—to the mysterious depth of a land almost unknown to them. In that direction somewhere lay the Sioux. The band had ceased to play and the column tilted over the ridge in thoughtful silence. With the general rode his adjutant, his orderly and Charley Reynolds. With him too rode Marc Kellogg, representing the *New York Tribune,* one of those newspapermen whom Sherman had warned Custer not to take along.

From her place at the side of the commissary sergeant's house, Josephine Russell watched the regiment move up to the summit of the ridge and fall away. At that moment the sun brightened the haze and she noticed that a shadow was thrown upward by the column. The shadow strengthened into a mirage, so that she clearly saw the regiment marching through the sky and slowly fading in the sky.

She thought for a moment it was an illusion of her own; but then she heard people around her speak of it, half in excitement, half in wonder. One man near by shook his head and turned his eyes from it. "That's a sign. I'm damned glad I'm not along."

She swung back to the ferry, walking with her head lowered; she got to her horse and stepped to the saddle. "It might have been better," she thought. "But Edward came between us again. I expected too much. Now there's nothing left to expect." She thought she heard the far-off sound of the regimental band playing "Garryowen," and listened until she was certain it was only her imagination.

☆ 16 ☆

Westward March

That afternoon, the column marched thirteen miles and camped in a grassy bottom beside the Heart River. Water and wood details went immediately away and men took up clubs to clear the area of rattlesnakes. The horses were placed on picket down the middle of each street and the guards were pacing their rounds by the time the cook fires began to stain the shadows. Another detail went out to slaughter the beef issue from the herd of cattle driven with the column. At headquarters tent, Terry and Custer sat in close conference while pay call blew and the regiment filed by the paymaster.

Shafter said: "You going to walk down to the corner saloon now, Hines?"

"It is Terry's doin'," said Hines. "If the boys had gotten their pay last night in the fort we'd have a column of drunks this mornin'. Now it will keep till we get home."

Reveille blew at four on the following morning and the general sounded at five. By six the column was under way, a mile-long line sinuously following the contours of the land, with flankers to left and right and advance points far ahead, with the Ree scouts fading into the distance and creeping back as quietly in the late day. Rains came down in tempestuous squalls and they crossed the Sweetbriar in a slashing hail storm and crawled through bottom-land with the wagons hub-deep and double-teamed. Despatch riders arrived from Lincoln with the latest mail and later rode back. On the twenty-first they crossed the Big Muddy and moved through sharp showers and slept wet at night and rose sullen. The little creeks they came upon were bank-full from the steady downfall; the quick-bred mosquitoes swarmed thickly around them, driving the livestock frantic. Alkali patches began to appear and on the left forward horizon the Bad Lands showed as fairyland spires and grotesque, vari-colored minarets; at night burning lignite beds sent up their dull red columns, like signals of warning. They crossed the crooked loops of Davis Creek ten times in one day's march, moved through huge cottonwood groves and put the Little Missouri behind them. That day Terry sent Custer forward on scout but found no sign of Indians.

It rained again and grew cold and snow fell three inches deep. Wet buffalo chips smoldered without burning and horses grew hungry for want of good grass. Scouts came out of the broken land from Major Moore's detachment— who had been sent forward to establish a supply base—to report he had reached Stanley's Stockade and that the *Far West* waited there with supplies. The same despatches brought news from Gibbon to the effect that his Montana column was in motion down the Yellowstone. Terry sent back orders for Gibbon to halt and wait, and for the *Far West* to deliver one boat-load of supplies to the mouth of the Powder.

They followed the Beaver into rising, broken country, the column weaving around and about gullies and low masses of rusty sandstone. They forded Cabin Creek and traversed a barren country glittering with mica. Beyond O'Fallon's Creek they crossed a divide into the basin of the Powder and from the heights, in a short interval of sunlight, they saw far away the rugged, contorted bluffs of the Yellowstone. Thoroughly weary, and wet again from the intermittent rain, they camped on the Powder, which was at this point two hundred feet wide and two feet deep.

It was June 8, with the patient and thorough Terry growing unaccountably restless. Next morning he took Moylan's and Keogh's troops and rode down the Powder to the Yellowstone where the *Far West* waited and where also Major Brisbin of Gibbon's column waited. Terry left the two cavalry troops and proceeded up the river on the *Far West* to the Tongue where he had a conference with Gibbon. Then he came back on the boat to the Powder and returned with his two escort troops to the camp of the Seventh. That night Hines, having talked with the sergeant major, passed on the news.

"The base of supply will be at mouth of the Powder. The *Far West* will move Major Moore and the supplies to there from Stanley's Stockade. Meanwhile Gibbon's been ordered to go back up the Yellowstone to the Rosebud and wait until we march to him. The country over that way is full of Indians. Gibbon's outfit has been fightin' 'em in small details all the way along."

Now it was a game of hide and seek, with all the responsibility of making contact falling upon Terry's shoulders. Before him lay a rough area of land about one hundred miles square, bounded on the north by the Yellowstone, on the south by the fore edge of the Bighorns, on the west by the Bighorn and on the east—where he stood poised with the Seventh—by the Powder. In that area lay the main bodies of the Sioux, their tracks plain to his scouts, their smaller bands weaving rapidly from place to place as bait to confuse him and draw him off scent. Now, patiently, he set about a thorough scouting job to establish the whereabouts of the enemy's weight. Crook, somewhere around the Bighorns, acted as a fence on the south and Gibbon, camped at the mouth of the Rosebud, would bar the Sioux from westward retreat.

"The trouble is," said McDermott, "we're too slow and we're too few to make a good fence. If Crazy Horse or Gall or Two Moons or Red Cloud want to break out of this country, they can circle and be a hundred miles away before we get turned around. Now here's Terry tryin' to find where to hit. Meanwhile the Sioux scouts know where we are. We can be seen forty miles away. We ain't goin' to strike the Sioux by surprise."

"That," said Hines, "is what Terry's got Custer for. We'll just march here and there across the country until Terry's got it figured where they are. Then one night we'll set out under Custer and we'll go fast. We'll make a big jump and catch 'em before they see us."

On the tenth of June, Terry despatched Reno with six companies of cavalry and one Gatling gun to explore the upper part of the Powder. "You will go as far as the junction of the Little Powder," he told Reno. "Then go due west to the headwaters of the Mizpah Creek, cross and continue to the Pumpkin, and go down the Pumpkin to the Tongue. Then proceed down the Tongue to the Yellowstone where you will meet me. You will throw out smaller parties as you march, exploring the intervening ground. I wish it thoroughly scouted, although I feel certain the hostiles are not in body this far east. I think we shall find them beyond the Tongue. Do not, however, go beyond the Tongue."

Thus he intended thoroughly to convince himself of the emptiness of this smaller area before pushing ahead to where he believed the action lay. Reno left early in the afternoon with his wing, A Company included, and struck directly up the Powder. Faithful to his orders, he turned west at the Little Powder, touched the headwaters of the Mizpah and moved on to Pumpkin Creek. He had his feelers out all the way in the form of the Ree scouts led by Bloody Hand; and each night they brought back the story of renewed trails sweeping up from the southeast and going on toward the northwest, on beyond the Tongue toward the Rosebud, toward the Bighorn. Bloody Hand, to indicate the size of that far-away gathering, reached down and cupped the clodded earth in his hands and let it spill out. "That many," he said.

Reno had long service as an officer and a creditable Civil War record; but now when he reached the Tongue he faced the problem of an independent commander operating beyond the reach of his superior officer. He had his strict orders not to go beyond the Tongue, but his scouts all were in accord as to the presence of Sioux over that way; and he judged his mission to be that of finding definite clues. Therefore, wrestling with the problem, he broke the bonds of his orders and crossed the Tongue to the Rosebud, feeling right and left constantly, and on the nineteenth he stopped near the Yellowstone and sent a despatch to Terry of his whereabouts and what he had discovered.

Terry meanwhile had been moving westward along the Yellowstone with the rest of the Seventh, keeping in contact with the Montana column and with Moore by courier; and now slowly, as news drifted in, he began to tie the ends of his expedition together. Gibbons he held at the Rosebud. At the Tongue he met Reno's returning party and the three men, Terry and Custer and Reno, held a conference. Terry listened to Reno's report and explanation of his going beyond his orders without comment, being a mild and reserved officer. All he said was: "It is as I believed. The Sioux are beyond. On the Rosebud and westward in the direction of the Bighorn. General—" indicating Custer—"you will move the Seventh on to the mouth of the Rosebud and join Gibbon. I shall take the *Far West* up there."

Custer and Reno left the general, Custer walking with a heavy irritable silence that Reno immediately noticed; and for his part he had his dislike of Custer and now revealed it with a sour, caustic question:—

"I seem to gather from your manner that you disapprove of my stretching my instructions."

"When Terry gave you those orders," said Custer, "he already knew there was a concentration west of the Tongue. Therefore your march in that direction was a waste of six days' time."

"I judged the orders on their intent," said Reno stiffly. "I think I have an average intelligence."

"I do not question it," snapped Custer and walked away. He was in a bad frame of mind, his nervous energy goading him to an impetuous action he could not embrace because of Terry's restraining hand.

On June 20, the *Far West* landed Terry at the mouth of the Rosebud where Gibbon and his column waited. That same afternoon the Seventh arrived and a general meeting was held aboard the boat—Terry, Custer, Gibbon and Gibbon's second in command, Brisbin. Terry laid his big campaign map on the table and made his estimate of the situation.

"The Sioux are southwest of us, somewhere between the Rosebud and the Bighorn. General Gibbon's column will ascend the Bighorn. It will swing when it reaches the Little Bighorn and follow that stream. You will leave in the morning, Custer, with your regiment, and go up the Rosebud. The intent of this maneuver is that the two columns will act as an anvil and sledge, with the Sioux between. We shall require a close consideration of the time. General Gibbon, at what time can you be at the mouth of the Little Bighorn?"

Gibbon took a long look at the map and made his calculations; at this stage of the game the element of time and distance grew vital and therefore he arrived at his estimation with a great deal of care. "I shall," he said, "be at the Little Bighorn on the morning of the twenty-sixth."

"That is for your information, Custer," said Terry. "Your marches should be based upon Gibbon's arrival at that creek at the agreed time. Now," he went on, still speaking to Custer, "as you proceed up the Rosebud, you will explore right and left. When you reach Tullock's Creek you will send a man down that creek to meet Gibbon's scouts and thereby transmit such information as you have acquired to him. This country will no doubt be full of hostiles. Therefore you need a good scout to make it."

"Let me give him Herendeen," said Gibbon. "I'll talk to Herendeen."

Custer nodded absent-mindedly.

"At the upper reaches of the Rosebud," Terry said, "you will scout toward the Little Bighorn. But I wish you to constantly feel toward your left. I do not wish to hamper you with unnecessary orders, but you should adjust your marches so as to give Gibbon time to come along. On the morning of the twenty-sixth, therefore, you should be in some position southeast of the Sioux while Gibbon is somewhere northwest of them, the two of you closing in on either side. Do not rush the thing. Do not permit yourself to engage before Gibbon is up for support. Now, how are your supplies and how do you feel about your men? Do you need something added to the Seventh? Gibbon could give you Brisbin's battalion of cavalry."

Custer sat in glum thought, staring at the floor. "No," he said, "I'll need nothing more than I have. The Seventh is wholly able to take care of what it meets. The addition of outside cavalry would only interfere with our freedom of movement."

Terry considered him a thoughtful moment, knowing his man; and Gibbon and Brisbin studied him. Irritableness worked in Custer; an uncharacteristic gloom showed on him, as though the winter's injuries and humiliations, never healed, now freshly hurt him.

"Gibbon," said Terry, "give Custer part of your Crow scouts. Give him Bouyer and Girard. They know this country better than Reynolds. They can assist Reynolds." He stroked his smooth chin and had a commander's natural grave wondering; for he had made his explorations, formed his judgments and had arranged his maneuvers. Now the job was in the hands of his field officers. He sat still, checking all these things seriously in his mind. "Crook should be somewhere near us, and it would be a relief to have him in support. But I have heard nothing from him and have no idea at all where he is. Nor can I wait longer, for fear the Sioux will slip through us. You have a slightly farther distance to go, Gibbon, therefore put your troops in motion today for the Bighorn. Custer will leave first thing in the morning. That is all. I shall go with Gibbon's column and—" turning to Custer—"if all goes well, I shall meet you on the twenty-sixth."

Custer rose, saying, "I'll pass on the orders," and left the tent. Gibbon, Terry and Brisbin all watched him depart, their glances following his long shape, as it moved with impatient treading toward his own headquarters tent.

Officers' call ran through the Seventh, summoning them to Custer who sat in his portable easy chair, a lank figure in buckskin, with a scarlet flowing kerchief and a head of hair grown ragged. The sun had scorched his face scarlet, making his eyes a deeper blue. He sat still before his officers, with none of the electric energy showing in his talk or his muscles. He seemed to their sharp eyes unusually depressed.

"Gibbon marches up the Bighorn while we march up the Powder. We shall leave in the morning, light marching order. The wagon train stays. Each troop is assigned twelve mules which are to carry hardtack, coffee and sugar for fifteen days, bacon for twelve days. Use your strongest mule in each troop for extra ammunition, two thousand rounds per troop. You'll have to load extra forage on the mules also. Each trooper will carry one hundred rounds of carbine ammunition and eighteen rounds of revolver. And twelve pounds of oats."

The twenty-eight officers stood gravely before him, stained with a month's hard marching, their buckskins caked with old mud, their blue trousers faded out, their mustaches unkempt. They were a hard crew to look upon in the falling twilight; and they were silent long after he had fallen silent, until at last he said in his always touchy voice:—

"Are there any suggestions, gentlemen?"

It was Moylan who spoke. "That's not enough mules, General. You'll break them down with the load you propose."

"Wagons are out of the question. Additional mules will slow us too greatly."

French of M Company had a word. "Once your mules start to lag you'll slow down anyhow."

Custer slapped the arms of his portable chair with a gesture of open temper; his voice carried its rasp of anger. "Well, gentlemen, carry what you please, but remember you are responsible for your companies. The present arrangement of wings is abolished. Each commander reports directly to me. The extra forage was only a suggestion, but bear in mind we will follow the trail for fifteen days unless we catch them before that time."

Captain McDougall said: "Are we to push on at will? I thought I understood you to say we were operating in conjunction with General Gibbon."

Custer was now moving back and forth along the ground, nervous and wholly out of patience with his officers. "We shall follow the Sioux, no matter how long it takes. We may not see the steamer again." He swung on his adjutant. "Cooke, make out the orders so troop commanders may have them tonight. Assign a sergeant and six privates from each company to take charge of the pack train. McDougall, your troop will guard the pack train. There is at present an unequal distribution of officers among the companies. I shall make temporary reassignments in order that each troop may be properly officered. That's all."

He meant it to be all, but the officers lingered, not wholly satisfied. McDougall said: "I don't think a few extra mules would be unwise, General."

Custer wheeled, his voice turned shrewish and sardonic: "Twelve mules to a company. Take what you wish on them. Take nothing if you are prepared to starve your troop. For that matter you'd better take salt along. You may have to live on horsemeat before we're finished with this." Having said it, he whirled into his tent.

The officers turned and moved backward toward their companies in small groups. Godfrey moved beside Edgerly and quietly spoke his mind. "I have never seen him like that before."

"You must remember," said Edgerly, "he is smarting under the rebuke he received from the President. He is a very proud man."

Godfrey shook his head. "The smell of powder is usually a tonic to him—and the smell of powder is thick around here tonight. He is singularly depressed. In fact he has depressed me."

Darkness came and mess fires bloomed along the Yellowstone's bluff. Details moved back to the supply train to break out the extra rations and ammunition to be loaded on mule-back on the morrow; and off to one corner of the camp, the Indian scouts were in full voice with their own strange ceremony—the echoes of it sharp and mournful in this wild empty corner of the earth. In his tent, Lieutenant Smith was at the moment writing this letter to his wife:—

My dear: We leave in the morning on what seems to be the final part of the campaign. It will soon be over and then I shall look forward to the return—to leave this fall. I know how you feel when I am away. I have often thought of the hardness of it on you and I wish often that I were a more demonstrative man so that I could tell you how the sight of you and the nearness of you sometimes affects me. We are a sober lot tonight. The general is in an edgy frame of mind and there's not the usual racket along the company street. But that is as it always is before action. Be cheerful. There is no great prospect of danger here . . .

Lieutenant Porter stepped into Lieutenant Van Reilly's tent and found Harrington there; and stood by while these two made mutual wills. "My effects to you," said Harrington, "if I die and you survive. If you die and I survive, I shall take your things to your wife."

"Agreed," said Van Reilly. "Now in case we're both killed, let's have Porter do that chore."

"Agreed," said Porter. "And either of you is to look after my possessions and return them to my wife in case of my death. Is there a drink of hard liquor in this tent?"

Van Reilly found a bottle and measured it by candlelight. "One drink for tonight. One for tomorrow night. After that we shall not need it, being uplifted by victory, I sincerely trust."

In his tent, Custer was at the moment composing his nightly letter to Libby; and all along the regiment men made their casual disposition of their effects, or wrote final thoughtful messages home, or lay back and were silent, or played poker by candlelight, or walked abroad in the camp darkness. On the *Far West* a game of poker had started with Grant Marsh, Keogh, Tom Custer, Calhoun and Garnett playing; and on the bluff of the river Shafter stood alone, watching the steamboat's lights make their yellowed, wrinkled lanes across the water. The river was a steady washing tone in the night, and wind came down from the north, and somewhere southward a low moon shed a partial glow through the fog. The Crows and the Ree were steadily chanting out their strangely barbaric tune of farewell and warning—that beating rhythm a pulse of premonition all through the camp. One by one the lights of the regiment died and tattoo sounded softly. Shafter watched the black shadows thicken in the Yellowstone's canyon, and he looked backward and saw his life as an empty thing and found no clear answer for his future. His life marched to this point, void of hope or ambition, without sweet memories or faith—and tomorrow held nothing that made him anxious to be traveling toward it.

So the regiment settled down to sleep on the eve of its march. On that same night and at that same hour, one hundred miles southward, Crook's command lay with double guards around it and licked the wounds of a sharp defeat inflicted by Crazy Horse four days earlier. For the second time in five months Crook grew cautious and doubtful and now sent despatches back to Laramie— to be wired to Sheridan at Chicago—that he would not advance without additional re-enforcements. Of all this Terry knew nothing as he sat awake on the *Far West* and reviewed his plans.

☆ 17 ☆

Custer Pulls Away

A damp mist hung heavily over the water and the canyon, through which the cursing of the mule packers came in muffled explosions. The peremptory notes of assembly laid a rough hand upon the troopers, and the companies formed one by one on the rolling bench above the river. Custer swung to his horse and crossed the camp at a full gallop to join Terry, Gibbon and Brisbin who tarried behind their own column in order to see the Seventh away. Custer rounded in beside the three, his horse fiddling briskly. Down the bench rose Reno's shout of command, which placed the regiment in forward motion. There was no music to lead them on this parade; the band had been left at the Powder River base.

They came past the reviewing group, Reno saluting as he went by, each company commander swinging his head to the right and rendering a like salute. They moved on, company by company, stained by weather and a month's hard marching—dark and toughened and competent men made surly by early morning. There was none of a dress parade's flash or fancy display about them this day. Their clothes were ragged and their whiskers long, and they carried with them the bulky impedimenta of a field campaign—bedding roll lashed behind saddle cantle; haversacks, lariat and picket pins, nose bags and extra pouch of oats, carbine and revolver, extra bandoliers of ammunition, trenching tools, canteen—all these things attached to various quarters of man or horse, all slapping and clattering and shifting to the motion of the mount.

Terry watched them pass with a thoughtful eye. For the troops he had nothing but commendation. "You have a good regiment, Custer. I do not know of a better one in the service."

Custer showed a flash of his old spirit. He smiled, the constriction of it half closing his eyes and brightening them into audacity. "My regiment, General, has been the best in the army for ten years."

Terry smiled. Gibbon said nothing. Brisbin, a member of the Third Cavalry and a truculent man, gave Custer a sharply irritated glance and returned his eyes to the Seventh. It had always been a flashy regiment, more troublesome and more picturesque than any other, with ten years of campaigning to its credit, with its roll of honorable dead, with its actions and skirmishes and engagements a worthy list on its record. Its companies, never at full strength, had been further pulled down by details left at the Powder River base so that its eight hundred had diminished to seven hundred. But it had a strong core of old-time noncommissioned men and its captains were largely good, some seasoned and faithful like Moylan, some wild-tempered like Keogh, some stubborn and cool as was the white-haired Benteen who never forgot a hatred or a liking.

The companies were under-officered and Custer had made some changes of assignment. Moylan still had A Company, B was McDougall, C had been given to Tom Custer while Weir kept D. Algernon Smith had been taken from A to command E Company. F was Yates and G was led by Donald McIntosh, the officer with Indian blood. Benteen had H and I was commanded by Keogh and Godfrey led K. Custer's brother-in-law, Calhoun, rode in front of L. French retained M. There was also some shuffling of other officers to insure for each troop better leadership.

"The heart of a regiment," said Terry, "is faith in itself. I have every confidence in the Seventh."

The column went by. Sun began to break through the fog and the day promised to be fair and warm. Terry, laboring under natural weight of spirit, saw the sun as an omen and slightly nodded to himself, and then fixed a sharp blue eye on the pack train of 160 mules now passing under the escort of six troopers from each company, followed by McDougall's company as guard. The mules were improperly loaded and made a ragged, recalcitrant column. The general scowled at the sight of it.

"That's a poor shift for a supply train," he said with some degree of sharpness. "You're going to have trouble with it."

Custer flushed in embarrassed irritation and bit his lips. He looked straight before him. "We'll get it shaken down before the day's over."

"Better have been gotten in shape before you started," stated Terry. "Everything depends on the timetable we have set. Let nothing disturb that, even if you have to cut your worst mules out and let them go."

The last file passed and the better part of a half-hour had gone by. Terry lifted a folded paper from his pocket and handed it to Custer. "This is the written statement of the instructions I gave you yesterday. I have left them purposely indefinite in certain things. I have too much faith in your judgment as a commander to impose fixed orders upon you."

Custer accepted the paper, gave it a careless glance and thrust it into his pocket. He was impatient to be away and his body communicated that feeling to the horse beneath him. It fiddled and danced in the spongy earth, carrying him around until he faced Terry.

Terry said: "I shall be with Gibbon and we shall be on the Little Bighorn the morning of the twenty-sixth. Be sure, when you reach the head of Tullock's Creek, to send Herendeen back along it to communicate with Gibbon. That will be a verification of your whereabouts. One last thing. I expect both columns to work in close conjunction. We cannot beat the Indians in detail, or surround them in detail. This movement depends entirely upon both columns striking at the same approximate time. Be sure to have your scouts always well ahead to establish contact with Gibbon at the first opportunity. I wish you luck."

Custer grasped Terry's hand and shook it with his swift impulsiveness, briefly accepted the hands of Gibbon and Brisbin, and whirled around. Just before he broke his horse into a gallop, Brisbin called after him:—

"Now Custer, don't be greedy. Wait for us."

Custer looked back, flushed and smiling. He flung up his hand, his horse springing up beneath him, and so making a figure of dash and gallantry in the day's growing sunlight. "I won't," he said. With that enigmatic answer he let his horse go, and rushed away toward the column's head.

A mile from the Yellowstone, Custer halted the command for a brief rest and divided the Indian scouts into two sections to cover each side of the Rosebud; after that he stood at the head of his horse and looked awhile into the haze slowly developing southward. Cooke was with him, waiting for anything the general might have to say, but Custer made no comment. Wrapped in an unusual kind of taciturnity, Custer presently mounted and swung up his hand for the forward march; and led the column over the Rosebud to the west bank.

From his saddle, Shafter watched the broken country unroll before him. The Rosebud lay at the bottom of a shallow canyon and the column, now without the impediment of wagons, took the most practicable course—sometimes following the edge of the water, sometimes traveling on a narrow benchland half up the side of the canyon, and sometimes rising to the top of the bluff. All this was a powder-gray, fine-grained land with grass and sage tufting it; all of it was a land scorched by summer's heat and scarified by severe winters. Now and then the command passed through willow growths. Otherwise there was no break in the rough rolling of the country.

A Company had a new officer. Smith had been put in command of E and Varnum was in charge of the scout detail; therefore Custer had assigned Garnett to A, and Garnett now rode at the foot of the troop. Shafter felt him as he would have felt a cold wind at the back of his neck; and all his thoughts of Garnett were cold and full of hate, shaking him out of his solemn, indifferent frame of mind.

Hines said: "Reminds me of the country around the Washita. It's gettin' hot. I never knew it to be any other way when the outfit went into a fight. Cold as hell or hot enough to give a man a stroke. Soldierin' is a funny life."

They bivouacked at noon, ate and lay idle in the warming drowse. The regiment now was definitely pointed into action, hourly penetrating deeper into the heart of Sioux country, and therefore men were more silent than usual, more withdrawn to their own thoughts—and more watchful. In the afternoon the regiment moved on, still following the Rosebud as it angled to the southwest; scouts returned with their news and sometimes this news came down the line, as overheard by some officer or enlisted man. Once Moylan spurred ahead, spoke to the adjutant and dropped back.

"Plenty of tracks ahead of us. The Sioux seem headed toward a general meeting on our forward right."

"Soldierin'," repeated Hines, "is a funny life. I knew I'd get sore bones out of this, but I wanted to come. Ten years from now I'll smoke a pipe and tell some youngster how Grandpaw fought the Sioux—and I'll lie like hell. It will seem wonderful to me, lookin' back at it. But right now my bones are sore."

"It ain't your bones," said Bierss.

Hines retorted: "My bottom's a damned sight tougher than yours, Cawpril. It has scrubbed leather a lot of years longer."

"You ain't had the fun I've had," said Bierss. "You never got run out of as many bedrooms. Ah, Sarge, you're a serious man. When you're dead you'll regret that."

"In heaven," said McDermott, "I wonder if a man could get chevrons put on his wings."

"If it takes as long to get a promotion in heaven as in this army," said Bierss, "you'll be fifty years a rookie."

"A good man's a good man, heaven or here," said McDermott virtuously. "Gabriel will have me runnin' a platoon inside of a week."

"All I want out of heaven," said Bierss, "is a bed and three meals and no work. And a woman who won't cry when I leave her."

"You'll be lookin' for a second-story window to jump through," said McDermott.

"No windows in heaven, you fool," put in Hines. "It is a city of glass. Everybody sees everybody. No dark corners and no walls."

"Good God," said Bierss, "can't a man have privacy anywhere?" He grinned at Shafter. "Professor, you've read books. What's heaven like?"

"A tunnel," said Shafter. "No light and no sound. You'll never know when you walk into it and you'll never reach the other end. In fact, Bierss, you'll never know you're there."

Bierss rummaged that conception through his mind for a quarter mile and made no headway. "I don't see that at all. It sounds like bein' buried underground forever."

"Who knows?" murmured Shafter.

"Professor," stated Bierss, "if that is what a book does for a man, then books are damned dangerous and I'm glad I never read one."

The column camped short of twilight, still on the Rosebud; and fires twinkled along the earth and guards threw a vigilant ring around camp. The Crow and the Rees slid mysteriously away and from afar presently came softly the repeated hoot of an owl, to be elsewhere echoed. An orderly summoned the officers to Custer's fire. He stood at the blaze with his officers ringed around it, and firelight played upon him somberly and brightly danced in their eyes. Cooke, the giant adjutant, stood near Custer, as did the mild and self-effacing Charley Reynolds.

"From now on," said Custer, "there will be no more bugle calls. Stable guards will waken the troops at 3 A.M. March will be resumed at five. I shall regulate the making and breaking of camp. Otherwise each commander is responsible for the actions of his company. You will observe proper interval between companies. Do not get ahead of the scouts and do not let the column stretch out. We must remain compact."

He spoke in a suppressed manner; he seemed jaded, he seemed half indifferent, half uncertain. None of the brusque and intolerant stridency so characteristic of him showed this night; and after his initial announcement he stared long in the fire and presently pulled himself out of a kind of reverie.

"Gentlemen, I have complete faith in this regiment and I have entire confidence in your loyalty and your entire support. I call on you particularly now to give me the best of your judgment and all of your talents."

He pushed his hands into his pockets and broke off, hard engaged in thought, his bony face tipped down, his thin long lips half hidden behind his mustache, his face in a shadowed, disillusioned repose. The ring of officers waited for him to continue, closely watching, carefully listening to this new tone, this somber reflection so unlike him. Silence weighted the circle. Benteen looked upon his commander with his ruddy, dogmatic face holding a steadfast reserve, an ingrained dislike; and Reno studied the man out of his dark-ringed eyes.

"We can," continued Custer, "expect to meet a thousand warriors or more. The trails are growing heavy, pointing ahead of us and west of us. It may be more than a thousand. It might be fifteen hundred. We came here to find Indians and we shall find them. We shall find them if I have to march this regiment all the way down to Nebraska or back to the Agencies. Let there be no misunderstanding as to our purpose. I have too much pride in the Seventh to go back empty-handed and I know you feel the same way. I ought to mention that General Terry offered me Brisbin's battalion of cavalry. I refused it. Frankly, I felt that there might be jealousy between the two groups and I wanted nothing to break the present knit spirit of our command." Then he paused and took on a moment's show of his old spirit. "Moreover, I am confident the Seventh can handle whatever it faces. If the hostiles can whip the Seventh, they can whip any re-enforcements we might have. That is all I have to say tonight, except you should be prepared for marches of between twenty-five and thirty miles a day."

The group slowly dissolved, walking in twos and threes back through the shadows toward the vague line of the troops lying like windrows along the earth. Godfrey and McIntosh and Wallace moved together toward the far end of camp, none of them speaking for a long spell. It was Wallace who broke the silence.

"You know, I think Custer is going to be killed."

"Why, what makes you believe that?" asked Godfrey.

"I have never seen him so disheartened before," said Wallace. "There is a shadow distinctly over him."

McIntosh made a troubled remark. "The general speaks of going as far as

Nebraska if he must. I had the impression that Terry had definitely restricted us to a fifteen-day sortie."

"You know the general," said Godfrey, whereupon the three broke off, each going his own direction. Godfrey's troop was well along the camp and presently he passed a fire, around which he saw the interpreter Mitch Bouyer and three Crows squatting. Godfrey stopped and likewise squatted. One of the Indians looked at him and then spoke in Crow to Bouyer, who turned to Godfrey.

"Half Yellow Face wants to know if you've ever fought Sioux before."

"Tell him I have," said Godfrey.

Bouyer passed it back to Half Yellow Face. The Indian asked another question which Bouyer relayed. "How many do you expect to find this time?"

"Oh, ten or fifteen hundred," said Godfrey. "What does he think?"

"He wants to know if you think you can whip that many?"

"I guess so."

Bouyer spoke for himself. "Well, I can tell you we're going to have a damned big fight and I ain't so sure. Neither are the Crows."

"How big a fight—how soon?" asked Godfrey.

"Soon," said Bouyer. "Don't expect the Sioux to retreat any more. They got their families with them. A big fight. All the fight you'll ever want."

The regiment was up at three and again in motion at five, with the troopers silent and stale. Within two miles they crossed the looping Rosebud three times and stopped once for watering. The day grew hot and the sun began to bite down for the first time during the long campaign and the porous earth changed from slick mud to dust by noon. The scouts, now working constantly ahead, reported back the mark of sign not over two days old. The long day wheeled on and the scanty foraging of the horses began to tell upon them; after thirty-three miles the regiment went into camp, ate and fell asleep. Once again at three it rose and at five was again marching.

Shafter said to Hines: "What's the date?"

Hines couldn't remember it and had to draw his roster book from his shirt pocket. "Twenty-fourth, but what's a day to you?"

"Birthday."

"Well," said Bierss, "tonight we'll bake a cake."

Captain Moylan, riding at his usual place beside Shafter, turned and said: "Good luck."

"Any kind of luck is all right."

The Crows sent back word of fresh sign and presently the column began to pass the round dead-grass spots where lodges had stood and the blackened char of old campfires. At noon the command halted for dinner—bacon and hardtack and coffee—and was hurried into the saddle by Custer. But after a brief forward march, he stopped the regiment at one o'clock. The Crows, vigilantly rummaging the distance, had sent back word of a camp freshly deserted at the forks of the Rosebud. Custer swung forward with two troops to investigate while the regiment rested. He was back in the middle of the afternoon and now began to throw his scouts in widening circles all around him. Seated cross-legged against the earth, Shafter knew that the trail had grown suddenly hot from the way the scouts ran in and out.

At five, Custer swung the command forward and now the trail passed into a valley whose short brown grass grew smooth and slick from a dry, stiff wind ruffling over it. The tracks of lodgepole travois scratched the ground everywhere and they came upon the skeleton frames of wickiups where a camp had been, and a sundance lodge. An officer left the column and moved to the lodge and rode back presently with a scalp lifted in his hand. Presently news came down the column:—

"White man's scalp hanging on that lodge. Cooke says it must have been one of Gibbon's troopers killed on the Yellowstone last month."

Custer seemed now to be pulled by the lively scent, for he moved the column steadily on through the last sunlight and into the blue-running dusk. The land tilted upward and the Rosebud made a shallow semicircle toward the southwest, fringed with willows. Beyond them, in the distance, lay a shallow knob.

Herendeen, who had been Gibbon's scout, now trotted up the line and reached Custer and spoke to him. "General, we're as close to the head of Tullock's Creek as we'll get. It's off there—" pointing to the right. "This is where I'm supposed to leave you and go down the creek to find Gibbon's scouts."

He waited for Custer's order on the subject and for whatever message Custer intended to convey to Gibbon. It was a night's ride down the creek, through the heart of Sioux-held ground and a risky prospect for a lone man. Gibbon had known this and had promised Herendeen extra pay for the venture. So now Herendeen waited for Custer's order to go, and rode silently beside the commander. Custer gave him a brief glance out of his deep-set eyes, out of his bony, thought-hardened face; and then Custer put his glance into the forward blue distance and rode on without speaking. He had no answer for Herendeen and, after a half mile of this kind of traveling, Herendeen saw he was to be given no order. Being a man with a frontier touchiness, he wheeled away and dropped back along the column until he had reached his place. Apparently the general had changed his mind about sending back a messenger; it was just as well to Herendeen, who had no intention of risking his skin unless Custer definitely requested it.

At seven o'clock the command halted in sundown's last yellow flare of light and made camp with a dry, hard wind rolling the desert's smoke-fine dust at them. An orderly trotted through camp in lieu of officers' call and presently all officers stood in circle around Custer and Custer's headquarter's pennant. Benteen, whose mind always had an acid realism, stared at the flag with his unfavorable thought, at the two stars of a major general stitched on the pennant's field. This was what Custer had once been, in the Civil War, but no longer was; therefore in Benteen's critical opinion the commander had no right to the use of the two stars. It was a display of vanity that he held against Custer, adding it to his list of Custer's many other faults.

They stood stiff and spraddle-legged and dusty in the forming twilight, watching Custer's hawkish face swing around upon them; and, since all of them were in his hands and all their futures were at his disposal, they watched him closely, analyzing his unpredictable temper. The sourness and the gloominess had given way, but his buoyancy had not returned. He stood eager and straining in the windy evening, anxiously bedeviled by the nearness of the Indians, with all the consequent possibilities of a spectacular sweep against them; he was gnawed by the thought that he might miss them and lose that chance. All this was evident in the staccato manner of his talk.

"We have come seventy-five miles from the mouth of the Rosebud. I have sent Varnum forward with the scouts. We're no more than thirty miles from the hostiles. I do not know yet which way they're running but I propose to find out."

Benteen's dry voice interrupted. "Are you sure they're running, General?"

Custer's voice had a special usage for Benteen; it was stiff and formal and brief: "If they were not running; we should have struck them before now."

"They know where we are," Benteen pointed out. "They know we're coming. It is my idea they may be picking their own spot to fight on."

"We'll see—we'll see," said Custer in his dismissing tone. "I propose to make a sudden jump at them. Troop commanders had better change your details on the pack train. May not get another chance. Look to your equipment. I suggest you water again tonight."

The pushing wind caught at the standard, whose end was plunged in the sandy earth, and suddenly knocked it over. Godfrey bent down and lifted it and jammed it into the ground again. It fell again, whereupon Godfrey patiently repeated the operation. All the officers watched this until Custer said: "Nothing more, gentlemen," and then they turned back to their various company streets, walking with a sprung-legged weariness. DeRudio said to Godfrey: "That was a bad sign."

Shafter lay back on his blankets, head pillowed on the McClellan saddle. Wind lifted the silt-fine sand from the ground and threw it against his face; the smell of dust was constant in his nostrils, and turned his throat dry. Night fell with its desert suddenness and the stars were very bright against the black bedding of the sky. Moylan had returned and spoke to Hines, who in turn spoke to Sergeant Easley. "Get six men and go relieve the troop's pack-train detail."

At nine o'clock, Lieutenant Varnum returned from his scout and reported to Custer who sat cross-legged in the darkness. Varnum crouched down to make his report.

"We went ten miles forward. Same kind of tracks as we've been crossing. We saw what looked like signal fires during the afternoon. They were off to the right."

Custer said: "The Crows tell me there's a high point on the divide between the Rosebud and the Little Bighorn where they used to go to steal Sioux horses. It is a lookout place called Crow Peak. It commands a view of the Little Bighorn valley. I want a responsible white man to go up there with the Crows tonight and have a look from there first thing in the morning and send word back to me. I'll be coming forward."

"I expect," said Varnum, "that means me."

"Take Reynolds and Bouyer with you, and whatever Indians you please."

Varnum had been in the saddle for many hours straight and was extremely weary. He got up and stamped his feet on the ground. "Daylight will be about four or a little after."

"Send back word as soon as practicable. What do your Crows say about the Sioux?"

"They guess a couple thousand. They counted the lodge marks at the last camp we passed."

Custer said: "These Rees are dead afraid of a Sioux. One Sioux is five to them. I doubt if the Crows have much more courage in that respect."

"I'd argue that, General. They're strong fighters."

"Send back word as soon as possible," repeated Custer and thus sent the dog-tired Varnum away. Cooke came up from the darkness and looked down from his great height. "Anything more, General?"

"No," said Custer. "Better roll in."

After Cooke had gone away, the general remained in his cross-legged attitude, solemnly thoughtful. The Rosebud, shallow and fickle, ran with a slight murmuring along the base of the low bluff before him. Behind him lay the regiment, soon asleep. He heard the sentries pacing, the occasional murmuring of their voices and the click of their guns. The wind had somewhat lessened but the scent of dust was strong, and the smell of horses and mules blew through the camp. He sat very still, his impulsive mind grasping the ends of his problem, and darting here and there, and jumping far ahead to the eventual scene which he knew he must make real—the scene of the Seventh smashing the Sioux in surprise attack. There was never any doubt in his mind as to the Seventh, never any doubt as to victory; the only thing which had ever worried him was his ability to catch up with the hostiles before they slipped from his grasp, before Terry's time limit expired, before Gibbon came up to join him.

He had a fighter's heart, this Custer, and a fighter's tremendous energy. He scorned the cautions which held other commanders back, he had a blind faith in the naked power of the sudden surprise rush and the naked power of a cavalry charge. On dash and surprise and swiftness he had made himself a general out of a boy lieutenant in four years and he could not change now. Nor wanted to change. Impatience and restlessness and a self-faith that never wavered were the stars that shone brightest before him, and moved him and made him.

So he sat, jealous of the chance before him and wanting neither Terry nor Gibbon to share it; and he thought of the ordeal through which he had passed during the winter—the humiliation put upon him by Grant, by Sherman, even by Sheridan, and all this he hated until the hatred squeezed out of him everything but the one dominating passion to strike and destroy the Sioux camp, and so recover his prestige. He had been a household name in his country, and still was; and once he whirled down upon the Sioux and scattered them to the winds not even the President would be able to stay the public applause or the public clamor for his advancement.

To himself he was a candid man. He knew what he wanted, and what he would do to get what he wanted—and never did he attempt to conceal it from himself. He had no hypocrisy in him, no political caution and none of that mellowness whereby a man might smooth himself a pathway through other men. The egotism which lies in the tissues of all men was thicker in him than in others; the hunger for applause which is a thirst in all men was a greater craving in him. The sense of drama which made quieter men silently wish they had the stature and the daring to play great parts was in George Armstrong Custer so vivid that it gave him the stature and the daring. He created the color which other men shrank from, even as they wanted it. He played his part straight as would a great actor and believed in himself and in his part until the two were one; in him was none of that critical self-reflection which caused others to draw short of appearing ridiculous. He was a simple man so hungry for greatness that he could ride roughshod over the personal feelings of other men and not be aware of it; he was so naïve in his judgments that even as he knew his enemies, he treated them in the manner of one who knows them to be entirely wrong and therefore to be treated charitably, indulged. He could be harsh and brutal for the sake of a soldierly ideal, but there was no gentle insight in him, no compassion, no deep sympathy. As inspiring a commander as he knew himself to be and as proud of his regiment as he was, he knew nothing of that man-to-man affection which tied a command together. One moment indulgent and the next instant full of fiery intolerance, he lacked any semblance of balance and was so blind to his own character that he needlessly broke army regulations out of a sense of complete virtue, and yet would instantly condemn and punish a subordinate officer for the slightest breach. All these things he was—an elemental complex of emotions and hungers and dreams never cooled, never disciplined, never refined by maturity; for he had never grown up.

He lay back, somewhere during the night, on his blankets and fell into that instant sleep for which he was famous. But the last thing on his mind had been a fear of losing the Sioux and the first thing to return to it when he woke near midnight was that same fear. He lay quiet for half an hour, thinking of it; and suddenly rose up and called to his orderly.

"Wake the company commanders and tell them to be ready to march at one o'clock."

☆ 18 ☆

The Ordeal Begins

The command struggled out of dead sleep and stumbled through the curdled blackness; and horses pitched a little and men cursed with bitter violence and sergeants' voices prodded the weary-drunk companies into formation. There was no talk as the Seventh moved forward. Horses sneezed and dust rose thick around the command; now and then an orderly ran down the column, and later ran back. They traveled with the Rosebud as it circled and slowly moved upgrade, and the land all around was a series of streaky black layers against which some heavier chunk of land thrust a deeper blackness. At three o'clock, this blackness began to move in muddy gray waves and at four light came, one dark tone moving into a tone less dark until a pearl dawn lay over the earth. A rippled order came back along the column, through the dense dry dust.

"Fall out for breakfast."

Shafter unsaddled and searched for the makings of a fire. Hines had dropped almost at once on his haunches and part of the command curled up and fell asleep again, wanting rest more than food. Shafter boiled his coffee and fried his bacon and put his hardtack in the bacon grease to soften it. He saw Captain Moylan standing near by and he beckoned him over and split his breakfast with his commander. Moylan squatted in the dust, his eyes bloodshot. The creek water had alkali in it, turning the coffee bad. Hines came over and sat down, groaning as he touched the ground. "This is soldierin' for you, Shafter. Don't stay in it as long as I'm stayin'. If I was thirty again—"

Shafter said: "I remember a night march from Chambers to Shaw Gap, during the war. It was worse, Hines."

"Much worse," said Moylan and grinned at Shafter. "There was a tougher commander along. He was in a hurry."

Hines looked at both of them and softly said: "So. Same outfit, hey?"

Garnett walked forward and stopped by the fire. He looked down at Moylan: "Any orders, Captain?"

"None that I know of," said Moylan. "Get off your feet, Garnett. It is a long day coming and nobody knows what's at the end of it."

Shafter looked up at Garnett and met the man's cool glance; he gave back the same arrogant stare and saw the flush of temper in Garnett's face. Presently the lieutenant moved away. Shafter heard Hines murmur: "There comes somebody," and turned his attention to the little hill ahead, down which a rider rode rapidly, rounding in before the head of the column. Shafter dropped back on his shoulder blades.

"Today's the day, Hines. Want to lay a bet?"

"What you bettin' on?"

"A fight," said Shafter. "I feel it in the middle of my belly."

Hines looked around him to the troopers scattered on the brown grass. "Some of those lads ain't heard the sound of bullets before."

Shafter lay idle, staring at the sky. One small cloud fluff sailed alone overhead and the sunlight had begun to brighten the blue arch. The day would be hot. "War," he murmured, "is a woman—beautiful when first kissed."

The mention of a woman brought the near-by Bierss upright from his prone position. "I'm a dumb one, Professor, but I get that."

"I don't," said Hines.

Bierss grinned at Shafter. "And you didn't get it out of no book."

Custer came down the camp, riding bareback. He stopped near Moylan. "Be ready to move at eight. Varnum sends word there is a concentration of hostiles to the west of the divide." He rode on. Shafter closed his eyes and fell instantly asleep. Presently he heard a trumpet blowing far away and somebody dug him urgently in the ribs and Bierss was saying: "Come on, rise and shine."

The regiment collected itself, slowly and with effort, and moved forward. From his place in the saddle, Shafter saw Custer and a small party riding on ahead. Dust began to steam up around the column again.

Custer galloped forward with Girard, one of the civilians lent him by Gibbon. Two miles on, he found Charley Reynolds waiting for him at the foot of Crow Peak. Reynolds led him up the slope toward a round knob from which the country fell away in its broken wrinkled outline. To the north, they could see the long cavalry file move forward in a smoky, serpentine line, gradually following the creek bed and sheltered from sight by the ridges to either side of the creek. Here, adjacent to Crow Peak, was the height of land which marked the head of the Rosebud's valley. To the west the land ran in small gullies and tangled ridges toward the Little Bighorn.

Varnum and Bouyer and Reynolds stood near the general; the Crows made a group of their own nearby. Custer lifted his glasses on the valley to the west and gave it a careful scrutiny, a prolonged attention. He lowered his glasses. "I see nothing," he said in a disappointed tone.

"Look beyond the valley to the top of the bluffs," urged Varnum. "The Sioux horse herd is there. A big one."

Custer tried again, and shook his head. "I see nothing."

"Look for worms wiggling along the ground," said Varnum.

Custer took one more try with his glasses. Varnum waited in silence worn down by his steady riding and feeling the weight of his responsibility. Custer shook his head as he lowered his glasses. "No, I make out nothing."

Varnum showed his disappointment. "The Crow are quite certain of a big camp over there. We saw smoke rising on that plateau an hour ago. Dust smoke from horses. The Crow are also quite sure we have been seen by Sioux scouts."

"No," said Custer arbitrarily, "we haven't been seen. We've been riding under the rim of the valley."

"The Crow are sure we have been," stated Varnum. "They think the Sioux are off there in great numbers, waiting for us."

Charley Reynolds, always an extremely quiet man, now put in his advice. "You're going to have a big fight, General. A hell of a big fight."

"What do you base that on, Charley?" asked Custer.

Charley thought about it in his mild, thoughtful manner. "On my medicine," he said. "I have lived in the West a long while. I know what's up when I get a feelin'. I have seen enough tracks to convince me and enough dust to be certain." He pointed west and said seriously: "There are more Indians over there, General than you ever saw in one place before."

One of the Crows gave a grunt and pointed to the northwest. Looking down from the knob, Custer and the rest of the party saw four Indians riding rapidly through a coulee toward the Rosebud. They had been somewhere near the crest of the divide, blended with the brown and gray soil; now they traveled away fast, their ponies breaking the dust.

"We've been spotted for certain," said Varnum.

"I doubt it," said Custer. "They couldn't see the regiment from there."

Charley Reynolds and Girard and Bouyer and Varnum gave the general a silent attention, forbearing to say more. Suddenly he turned off the knob, got to his horse and led the group downgrade. The head of the regiment had reached the foot of the ridge and now halted at his command. He said to his trumpeter orderly: "Officers' call," and sat on the ground, waiting for his officers to assemble. His buckskins were powdered with dust, his bright red kerchief silvered with it. Three days of hard sun had scorched his extremely fair skin. Beneath the flare of his great-brimmed hat, his bony features were soberly composed, his hawkish nose dipped and his eyes narrowly fixed upon the earth before him. He dug his fingers into the soil and lifted dust through them as he considered his problem with his restless will, his driving wishes. Presently he stood up to meet his officers.

They came forward on slow feet, all men worse for the wear, wanting sleep and suffering from a thirst the alkali water of the region could not slake. Dust and heat had gotten into all of them; even Major Reno's sallow cheeks were flushed; and Benteen's naturally florid complexion was scarlet. They stood jaded and lackluster around him.

"The camp," said Custer, "seems to be over that way," and motioned his arm westward. "The Crows are certain of it. I am not. The Crows likewise think we have been discovered. I am now inclined to agree. In any event, we move that way as soon as troops are in order. We will now break the command into three wings. Reno, you take M, A and G Companies. The scouts and guides will also be attached to you, and Doctors Porter and DeWolfe will follow your battalion. Hodgson will be your adjutant. Benteen, you will have your own company and also D and K. McDougall will remain as guard for the pack animals, and the arrangement of six men and a noncom from each troop to handle the animals will likewise remain as it is. Mathey will command that detail. I shall take C, E, F, I and L. Doctor Lord will go with me. You had better fill canteens and water the horses. We may not have time to do that later."

The officers went doggedly away, and presently watering details broke for the creek. A hot sun poured down from straight above and the air was thin and still. Custer stood alone by his horse, the old flame of haste burning in him, the old impatience nagging at him. He turned sharp to his adjutant who remained faithfully near by. "Cooke, ride through the command and take the report of the troop commanders when they're ready."

Shafter filled his canteen and brought his horse to water and watched it test the surface of the creek with its sensitive nose. It blew against the water, it smelled the water and expelled a breath and tried to skim the surface away, and lifted its head. The alkaline taste was too strong. Boots and saddles cracked the warming day, and at half-past twelve he was mounted again, moving forward.

The column rose with the divide, leaving the creek behind it, and now filed westward through the wings of a shallow pass. The horses were worn down and the command began to stretch out and a warning kept running back: "Close up —close up!" Moylan turned his head and beckoned at Garnett who rode near the foot of the troop. Garnett came up briskly to join Moylan. Shafter heard the captain speaking.

"I shall tell you this while we have time to speak of it. I do not give many commands, since my noncommissioned officers are all old hands at the business. But when I do sing out, I want quick answers. Half or better of the company has not been under fire. Therefore these men will shoot too fast and waste ammunition. You must constantly watch for this on the skirmish line. Keep the fire steady but hold down the hotheads. You must keep counseling these green men not to fire unless they have something to hit. You must also keep the company closed up. The Sioux always try to split a command into detail and chop up the pieces. Let nobody straggle or fall back on your wing. That is the main thing I want to tell you. Keep this company always together." He nodded, sending Garnett back.

Hines turned to McDermott and murmured: "You're top kick if I drop. Remember to get the duty roster out of my breast pocket."

There were three sergeants with the troop, Hines, McDermott and Shafter, the others having been detached for various duties; there were four corporals, and forty-one privates now riding two and two down the western slope of the broken hills. Ahead of them at a distance lay the half view of a valley stretching along the timber-fringed Little Bighorn, gray and dark olive and tawny in the hazy heat fog. Benteen suddenly swung out from the column's head and drew his three troops with him. Shafter heard Reno call out:—

"Where you going, Benteen?"

Benteen waved an arm at the rough hills to the south of him. "Goin' to scout that—and drive everything before me." He had, always, a dry voice and it was impossible to tell how much irony lay in it now. He shouted back and drew his own company after him, and Weir's and Godfrey's. These three rattled away.

A Company now was the head of the column; and suddenly Cooke dropped back from the general, who rode fifty yards ahead. Cooke reined around beside Reno. "The general," he said, "directs you take specific command of M, A and G."

"Is that all?" asked Reno.

"That is all he said," confirmed Cooke, and galloped forward.

The pitch of the hills steepened and the way wound between gray chunks of earth and clacked across a rocky underfooting. There was a little stream to the right of them dropping in liquid bubbling toward the Bighorn. Dust thickened and the horses grunted with the effort required to check their descent. Custer swung in his saddle and pointed at Reno, and then pointed across the creek; Reno at once crossed his column over. Now the two battalions marched side by side, Custer's to the one hand of the creek and Reno on the other. Meanwhile the pass widened as it descended and the ground before them showed the chopped tracks of fresh Indian travel. Moylan looked at those tracks with considerable thought.

The troopers moved through the dense dust, sweating and cursing, steeped in their own misery, gaunt from weariness and from thirst; but the pace quickened and a strange, lively feeling got into Shafter—the same warning of battle which had gone through him so many times before. The guides were ranging ahead, lifting up and down the little rolls of land which now and then shut out the valley before them.

Custer shouted at Reno and waved his hat in signal, whereupon Reno swung the column over the creek again, bringing the two battalions together. Suddenly they capped a ridge and saw a lone tepee standing in the valley before them.

Custer flung up his hand, halting the command, and the Ree scouts went forward in stooped, lithe positions, like scurrying dogs closing in on a scent. Girard swung to the right, climbing a small ridge which gave him a view of the land beyond. Meanwhile the Rees, growing bold, reached the lodge. One of them entered—and came out, crying at Bouyer. Bouyer said to Custer: "A dead Sioux inside."

Girard shouted down from his vantage point on the ridge. "Injuns, runnin' down the valley!"

The Rees had set fire to the tepee. Custer spurred up the ridge beside Girard and had his look into the valley and turned and rushed down the ridge, yelling at the Ree chief, Bloody Hand: "Tell your people to follow them!"

Bloody Hand spoke back at the Ree. They stood still, saying nothing and not moving, and presently Bloody Hand shook his head at Custer. Custer cried out: "Forward," and started down the creek with the two columns racking after him. The little ridge which had blocked their view now petered out into the plain of the valley and gave them view of the creek as it looped toward the brush and willows which marked the course of the Bighorn. Dust in the valley showed where the fleeing Indians had been. The two columns pitched forward, men rolling in their saddles and sergeants shouting back. Cooke and Captain Keogh rode over from Custer's column and fell beside Reno, all of them at a canter. Cooke said:—

"The Indians are across the Little Bighorn, about two miles ahead of us, now. The general directs that you follow them as fast as you can and charge them. He will support you with the other battalion."

The Indian trail crossed the creek. Reno's battalion went splashing over the water and pointed at the Little Bighorn in its grove of trees. The valley continued beyond those trees, not visible to the troopers. Looking back, Shafter saw the column under Custer veer away in another direction, and presently slide behind a knoll of ground. In that direction the valley rose to a line of high bluffs.

Reno struck the Bighorn at a place where the trees were thinnest and yelled back, "Don't let the horses stop to drink!" Moylan turned to Shafter and repeated the command. Shafter dropped out of his file and stood with his mount belly-deep in the water. Corporal Bierss' animal came to a dead halt and thrust its muzzle eagerly down. Bierss sawed at the reins and cursed it, and then Shafter spurred near and gave it a hard kick with his toe and sent it on. But the little delay had broken the compactness of the line and troopers were tangled midstream, their animals half crazed by thirst. Shafter and McDermott ranged among them, kicking them on. A horse stumbled and went down and water sprayed up, wonderfully cool. Moylan's great voice bawled from the far bank and McIntosh of D and French of M were laying words about them like ax handles.

The column crossed, fought through the willows and came upon the broadened valley before them. To the right, across the stream, a bluff lifted and grew taller as it moved away until, two or three miles south, it was a ridge crowned by round-topped peaks; on the left the valley was held in by a low, slow-rising slope. Ahead of them, at a distance, a wooded bend of the river closed out the farther view of the valley; a mass of dust rose beyond those trees. At this moment Cooke came splashing across the ford and shouted at Reno. "Scout reports there's a hell of a lot of Indians under that dust smoke—beyond those trees."

"All right—all right," said Reno. He sat on his horse while troopers straggled out of the river. The companies had lost formation and officers were calling and sergeants swore their men into formation. Horses plunged, turned frantic by the excitement, and one horse took the bit in its mouth and raced a hundred yards away before the company checked it down.

"Take your time," said Reno. "There's enough ahead for all of us. Form up— form up!" He shouted at Cooke who now had wheeled back into the water on his return trip to Custer. "Where's Custer?"

Cooke turned in his saddle, shook his head, and pointed vaguely; and disappeared. The three companies had formed and now were in columns of fours. Men sat with hard-handed grip on the reins, dusty and water-splashed, reddened by the hard scorching of the sun, half exhausted and hungry. Reno called: "McIntosh, you're reserve. Varnum, take your scouts out on the left flank." He rose in his saddle to give the forward command, but changed his mind and turned to look at the valley. There was no Indian to be seen on it yet, but the whole floor showed the scarring of their ponies—and the distant dust column rose heavily behind the trees. Suddenly he spoke aside to his orderly. "Ride back to Custer. Tell him the Indians are in force in front of us." Now he rose in his stirrups again and shouted:—

"Left into line—guide center—gallop!"

The column broke like a fan, fours slanting out and coming into a broad troop front. The two advance companies formed a spaced skirmish line sweeping at a gallop down the valley, A to the left and M to the right, Reno, Hodgson, Moylan and French riding forward, and Garnett and DeRudio behind. G Company made a second line in the rear. Over to the left, skirting the edge of the footslopes, Varnum commanded his Ree scouts; with him were Reynolds and the two half-breed Jacksons, Girard, Herendeen, and the Negro Dorman.

☆ 19 ☆

Charge and Retreat

It was a two-mile run down the length of that valley toward the trees which barred their farther view. Dust thickened steadily behind the trees, and puffs of dust rolled forward around them and something flashed in the core of the dust —like lances glittering. Reno, out in the lead, turned in the saddle as he galloped and looked back anxiously toward the crossing of the river, looked for the support Custer had promised. The plain was empty. At the same time DeRudio shouted: "That's Custer waving his hat on the bluff!" Shafter, throwing his glance to the high bluffs to the right, across the river, thought he saw a single horseman on that far crest move slowly out of sight.

They were nearly abreast the trees which formed a screen; they swung to pass the trees and so continue down the valley. On the left, Varnum was cursing above the racketing roll of sound, above the thud and jingle and the heaving and the crying of men. "Goddammit, come back—come back!" His Rees had been watching the dust in the foreground and they had sighted the onracing shape of Sioux; now they turned and fled. Bloody Hand, their leader, called and beckoned; but when he saw them run he flung up an arm and turned back to Varnum and the white scouts remaining. It left a gap in the left end of Reno's line. Suddenly Reno cried through the turmoil at McIntosh. His voice failed to carry but the gesture of his arm was enough. McIntosh spurred G Company forward into the line.

They skirted the timber and pushed by it. The dust storm was ahead of them, no more than two hundred yards away, and now the shadows within the dust leaped out of it and rushed on—Sioux warriors bending and swaying and crying. One wave of them wheeled and made for the left flank of Reno's line, meaning to turn it. Reno tossed up his arm and his mouth formed a phrase that was seen but scarcely heard: "Prepare to fight on foot!"

Horses went crazy in the sudden milling halt, in the sing of rifle fire, and for a moment the line was beyond control. One young trooper let out a screaming yell and plunged into the dust, his horse uncontrollable. Shafter watched him disappear, never again seeing him. Troopers dropped from their saddles, and in groups of threes flung their reins to a fourth trooper who wheeled and ran back with the mounts. The line became a crescent of kneeling men; the officers dropped behind to unmask the fire of their companies. Reno walked calmly to the rear of his command; he stood with his legs apart and his revolver drawn, taking careful aim and firing with deliberation.

The trees now were behind the command and the solid dust in front; and suddenly a wave of Sioux broke forward and curled around the left, where Varnum was posted with his guides. Firing rattled up from the troopers' thin ranks and Varnum's little group was in the thick of a swift, wicked melee. Sioux lead struck the earth hard by throwing up little streamers of dust, and men ducked and grunted at the sight of it. Hines knelt beside Shafter, sweat making straggling marks down the patched dust of his face; his complexion was purple but his lips were pulled apart as if he were grinning. "Professor," he said, "I wish I was thirty years younger."

The Sioux shots made a thin rain along the earth; their lead breathed hotly past. An arrow struck short and wavered snakelike on the dust. A man to the right of Shafter gave one soft grunt and settled forward on both knees. Hines turned his head in that direction. He called: "Cobb, you hit?" Hines had a grim stretch to his lips and he raised a hand to dash the sweat from his face; but the hand went halfway up, halted there and dropped. His head jerked from the impact of a bullet, his eyes rolled. He said, "Ah," and dropped dead.

Reno shouted, "Forward," and Moylan repeated it. Shafter reached to

Hines's breast pocket and pulled out the roster book. He looked around him and saw other figures lying still; he saw McDermott shake his head. Wallace trotted toward Moylan and Reno. "Pressure's getting very strong. We're going to have our left flank caved in. Can't we send back to Custer for support?"

The Sioux were wheeling crisscross through the dust, charging and firing and rushing away. They made a greater and greater pressure, against which Reno's line slowly moved until it could move no more; men settled to their knees for better fire. Over on the left, Shafter watched Sioux suddenly appear out of the wrinkled high ground and sweep behind the cavalry line. To the right, where the river lay, he saw the cloudy shapes of Indians darting through the willows. Reno saw it too and stood still to think of his position. Wallace had trotted toward Varnum's position; now he came back with Billy Jackson, one of the half-breed guides.

"You want to go back and find Custer?" asked Reno.

The dust had rolled over them and beyond them; there was no view of the valley in any direction. Billy Jackson saw all this and shook his head. "They've cut us off. No man could get through."

The horseholders, a hundred feet behind the line, were firing into the smoky haze, now being attacked from the side. Reno said to McIntosh: "Pull out your company and go guard the horses."

McIntosh and Wallace both signaled G Company out of the skirmish line. Firing began to strike at them from other angles, left and right. Young Lovelace cursed his gun and reached for a knife to dig a stuck shell from the chamber. Shafter stood up to look for McDermott, whereupon Bierss grinned at him. "Damn you and your black tunnel. It bothers me."

Shafter called at a youngster wildly firing: "Take your time—take your time! You're hitting nothing!" He saw Garnett standing a yard behind the line, as tall as if he were on parade. The lieutenant had his revolver half lifted and his eyes strained into the dust mist, waiting for a target. Whiskers darkened his sallow face; his mouth was trap-tight. Shafter moved back in time to see George Busby drop. Donovan raised a crimson face and called at Shafter. "We can't hold this place. Somebody better tell Reno that while there's time."

Reno knew it and Reno had made up his mind and had given his orders. Moylan was shouting those orders through the steady slam of gunfire. "Drop back to the timber!"

The line rose, ragged and broken, and slowly retreated, followed by the bold and confident Sioux who charged closer and closer to the cavalry guns. They were sweeping down in greater numbers on the left, and their lead came out of the river willows. Under this crosswhip of fire some of the green troopers began to break and run for the timber; the voices of the officers struck them and seized them and settled them to an orderly withdrawal. Pace by pace, the line gave way and presently got to the protecting edge of the brush and timber and stepped inside it.

As soon as they left the open ground they lost contact with each other; the battalion lost unity and runners began to crease through the brush, seeking the major for his orders. Reno had taken stand in a little clearing in the middle of the timber. He had his adjutant Hodgson with him, and his trumpeter; he listened to the firing slash its way through the loose brush and strike the tree trunks and ricochet on in whining tangents. He ducked as one of these sounds came close, and swore at himself. He said to his trumpeter: "Get the horseholders up here in this clearing."

A runner sifted through the undergrowth. "Captain French says the Sioux are massing on the other side of the Bighorn and mean to make a crossing and cut us off!"

"Tell French to swing his company against the river side," said Reno. Then he turned to Hodgson. "Go see where A and G have got themselves placed."

Shafter crouched at the edge of the timber and watched the Sioux shapes lace the thickening dust before him. They raced forward through it, firing at the timber; and wheeled and faded away; they were curling around the grove, drawing a tighter ring about the command. The woods reverberated with the steady echoes of the troopers' firing and he heard men crying questions through the thicket. The men of A Company were spaced so far apart in the brush that he saw only the nearest files. Donovan was on his left, coolly waiting, coolly firing. Bierss knelt at his right. Bierss was a heavy man and had dripped his sweat all the way up the Rosebud, but now Bierss had no moisture left in him and gave Shafter a glance of pure misery. "Pretty soon I got to crawl to the river for a drink, Professor." Shafter passed him his canteen.

The pressure increased against the grove. Shafter had the feeling that the troopers on his left flank had drifted toward the center of the area. There was no longer any resemblance of order. Cut off from their commands, the men grew afraid.

"Bierss," he said, "how much ammunition have you left?"

"Fifty rounds. Where the hell you suppose Custer is? He was goin' to support us."

Shafter got up and broke through the brush to his left. He found Lovelace and Ryan and Corporal Mudd; after a ten-yard gap he discovered O'Dale. He said: "You seen McDermott?"

"No," said O'Dale. "I ain't seen anybody. Where's the rest of the outfit? I'm all alone here."

A bullet touched a willow and went on with the sound of a hard-plucked banjo string. He pushed farther on to make contact with the lost fragments of his company; he parted the brush before him, at the same time hearing carbine fire strengthen behind him. That would be the Sioux crossing the river. He lifted his voice, calling: "McDermott!" Suddenly, knocking the thicket aside with the barrel of his carbine, he came face to face with a Sioux, all naked save for a breech clout. The Sioux took a backward pace and flung up his carbine. Shafter had that one instant in which to see black shock dilate the man's lids, to see a reaction stretch the red man's face broad. He fired and heard his bullet tear through the Sioux's chest, and for the briefest moment, he watched the Sioux fall and turn and die.

Deeper in the trees he heard Garnett shouting: "Moylan, where are you?" He turned back, not knowing the Sioux were filtering into the woods and that in a little while the battalion would be completely surrounded and completely trapped. He passed O'Dale and then struck off toward the heart of the timber and had gone fifty feet when he met Moylan.

"We can't stay here, Captain. We'll be out of ammunition in fifteen minutes."

"Reno's debating a retreat," said Moylan. "The Indians have crossed the river and broken our flank there."

"They're coming in on this side, too."

"I'll go tell Reno that. Pull the company back toward the center."

Shafter retraced his path to O'Dale. "Give way to the middle of the timber." He went along the line again repeating it, and reached Bierss. "Swing to your right and tell the lads to collect in the center clearing." Then he turned to the left once more, seeking to find the other flank of A Company, lost somewhere in the thicket. He passed the dead Indian and drove his shoulder through the small willows, listening to the steady crackle of gunfire. Dust came into the woods from the plain and presently he caught a smell that was something else than dust—the taint of leaves burning. Directly after that he heard the dry rustle of flames. The Sioux had fired the grove.

He found three A troopers together in an isolated spot and sent them back; now crouched and running, he moved twenty feet and came upon Doctor Porter, kneeling over Charley Reynolds. "Fall back, Doctor," said Shafter. "Toward the center."

"Give me a hand with Charley," said the doctor and turned to Reynolds. He put a hand on Reynolds' chest and shook his head. "No, never mind," he said and got up. The Negro Dorman lay dead ten feet away with a little ring of cartridges around him—and a trooper from M was near at hand, also dead. Shafter ran across a clearer patch of ground with the doctor behind him; when he reached the middle clearing he saw the remnants of the battalion gathering from the edges of the grove, and the horseholders standing ready. Reno waited by his horse, his feet apart and his face flushed and dark; he was an anxious, uncertain man with a terrible decision riding his shoulders.

He said: "Where's McIntosh—where's DeRudio?"

Shafter moved down A Company's half-assembled ranks. He said, "Bierss, have you seen McDermott?" Bierss shook his head, too tired to answer. Heat lay through the trees in smothering pressure and the flung-up dust grew heavy and the smell of smoke increased. Carbine fire rattled all through the timber and men straggled forward, so spent that they dragged the butts of their guns on the ground. Lead from the Sioux guns whipped the clearing. Moylan and Wallace and French waited—and grew tired of waiting. French said: "This position is becoming untenable, Reno."

The Ree leader, Bloody Hand, swung up to his pony and murmured, "Better go—better go."

Reno cast a strained eye around a command grown thinner from casualties and from strays still lost in the grove. The weight of his decision grew so great that it deadlocked his mind. But suddenly he said, "We'll charge back up the valley and cross the river to the bluffs." He swung to his saddle, close by the waiting Bloody Hand. Moylan and French were calling to their troops and men rushed toward the horseholders and the confusion grew into half panic.

McIntosh plunged breathless from the woods, his hat gone and his dark face pinched.

"Column of fours!" roared Moylan.

"My troop's not collected!" said McIntosh.

French shouted at him, "We can't wait, Tosh. You go first, Moylan. I'll follow. Bring up the rear, Tosh!"

Reno had swung his horse around; and at that instant a Sioux bullet made its sightless track across the clearing and punched its way through Bloody Hand's brain, showering blood on the near-by Reno. The major flung up a hand to his face, so badly shaken that be jumped from the saddle and said, "Wait!" The loose-formed column began to break apart under the pressure of bullets singing and sighing all around. The smell of smoke came to the horses and fright grew among them. Reno shook his head and clawed his way to the saddle. He yelled, "Forward!" and set his horse to a gallop.

The column, not yet untangled, followed in loose disorder—all the officers laboring to get the battalion in some sort of shape. They were in full motion when they came out of the timber into the valley, into the rolling clouds of dust raked up by the Sioux who had now swept around the grove and set up their sharp fire at the column's head. Horses slammed together under excitement and troopers, venting strange needs, began to yell full voice. Reno and Hogdson led the way, Reno swaying hatless in his saddle. Moylan galloped beside Shafter, now and then looking back at his troop. When the head of the column had gotten a hundred yards from the grove, Shafter glanced behind him and saw M Company directly following; but beyond M Company, G came in scattered, straggling bunches.

Wallace tore forward, overtaking Reno. He yelled: "For God's sakes men, don't run! Don't let them whip us!"

Reno turned his head and harked out a savage answer. "I am in command here, sir!"

Dust rolled heavier and heavier and suddenly the Sioux darted in, riding parallel to the column. They made dark, shining figures on their horses; they flung up their carbines, took bobbing aim, and fired. They made sudden dead-on runs at the column until their horses scraped against the running mounts of the troopers and presently the column, pouring forward at a full run, was engaged in a deadly, hand-to-hand wrestling.

Shafter jammed his carbine into its boot and now used his revolver point-blank. He saw his targets waver and he turned to watch an Indian fall and noticed Lovelace locked in a Sioux's tight grasp—the Sioux seeking to unhorse the lad. Shafter wheeled and blew a hole in the Sioux's flank and gave a sudden push to Lovelace, who was three quarters out of his saddle. But the Sioux were racing up in greater numbers, pressing in with a daring that came from sure knowledge of their victory; and the close fire struck home and troopers fell screaming and riderless horses bolted away. Shafter saw Lieutenant McIntosh running alone beside the column with two Indians boxing him. He swung over, but was too late. McIntosh flung up both hands and his head bobbed down. Shafter watched him disappear beneath the hoofs of the oncoming Indians. Far back he noticed a little isolated band of troopers drop out of sight as the Sioux cut across and blocked their escape.

It seemed an endless, hopeless run down the valley. The battalion was a skeleton, its identity half buried in the smothering, close-riding Sioux; the horses ran in the loose gate of near-exhaustion. Shafter galloped beside Bierss who rolled like a drunk in the saddle. Bierss' face had a stoniness on it, an unrecognizing blankness. Shafter cried: "Sit up, Bierss! Hang on!"

"Ah," murmured Bierss. "A long day—a long day."

Reno had swung the column toward the river, apparently meaning to cross. This maneuver brought them close by the bordering willows and thus they ran with the bright flash of the water beckoning them at the foot of a bank which ran sheerly up and down, too high to jump. Across the river stood the wrinkled hard slopes of bluffs whose rough-crowned tops promised safety.

One trooper wheeled from the column, came to the edge of the bank and made his desperate fifteen-foot leap. Horse and rider struck in a great spray and afterwards the horse struggled on alone, the rider never coming to the surface. Garnett, so far at the foot of A Company, now put spurs to his horse and drew forward until he rode abreast Reno, and he cried out, "Here's a ford," and rushed down a crack in the bluff.

The battalion followed that narrow cut to the edge of water. The leading horses, crazed by thirst, slackened and tore the reins free from the troopers' tight grasp. They stopped belly-deep in the stream and made a barricade which spread back and blocked the small pathway down the bluff; the men of the battalion, coming on in desperate haste, fanned out and took to the river from whatever point they found themselves. Carbine fire began to whip at the troopers in the water.

Shafter had crossed the river when he saw Donovan's horse drop, sending Donovan to the ground. Donovan got up and shouted as troopers fled by him toward the rising slopes of the bluff. Donovan lifted his pistol and took his stand, firing back across the river, blood-flushed but cool. Shafter ran beside him and kicked one foot out of his near stirrup. Donovan put his foot in the stirrup and lifted himself behind Shafter, whose horse now dropped to a slow and weary walk.

"There goes Benny Hodgson!" shouted Donovan.

Hodgson had fallen midstream, waist-deep. He got to his feet and staggered forward. A passing trooper paused long enough for the boy lieutenant to seize a stirrup and in this manner he was towed out of the river, turning around and around, dragging his limp feet. He was on the gravel shore when a second bullet dropped him. For a moment the trooper paused and was on the impulse of dismounting; then he saw Hodgson to be dead and rushed at the slope.

Halfway up that hard, bitter incline, Shafter saw Doctor DeWolfe die, struck by a bullet from the heights. Troopers dotted the trail, some racing far ahead, some still coming over the water; they slashed the last grain of energy out of their half-dead horses, they scrambled afoot; they stopped to fire, they plugged on, one weary yard at a time; they collapsed and sat in momentary agony, and got up and went on again. They fell and lay still.

Not far from the summit Shafter saw Garnett reel in his horse, make a futile grab to save himself, and fall shoulder first. He was crawling upgrade on his belly when Shafter passed him and he turned his head hopefully and looked up, about to ask for help; but when he saw Shafter he closed his mouth and groaned and resumed his painful inching progress.

Shafter reached the crest and found Reno with half a dozen troopers already arrived. Reno stood hatless, watching his broken battalion come up with a gray, dazed expression on his face. He kept saying: "Spread out and cover the others." Donovan dropped off and Shafter dismounted and fell to his stomach on the edge of the crest, bringing his carbine into play. For a moment he lay wholly still, his heart painfully pumping, his throat parched dry and his chest aflame. He felt himself half groggy and for a moment he had to squeeze down on the carbine to keep himself from fainting.

One by one troopers reached the crest and fell in their tracks. Moylan arrived and French came up, both going to Reno. "We had better arrange a defense here," said Moylan. "The Sioux will re-form and attack."

Far down, near the water's edge, Shafter saw the Sioux rush toward dark figures on the ground, bend and describe a swift motion, and rise and run on. Garnett lay flat on the ground, three hundred feet below, apparently dead; but presently Garnett raised his head slightly and looked up to the crest—and lowered his head again, turned still. Across the river, back in the valley out of which the battalion had made its way, the Sioux were swinging and racing toward the grove; they were streaming around the grove to the valley's lower end, beyond sight.

"They're not following up their attack," said Moylan.

"I'm damned glad of that," said French. "We're out of ammunition."

He heard someone yell, "Here comes Benteen," and he looked to his left, eastward along the bumpy spine of the bluffs. Benteen's three companies moved briskly forward and Benteen jumped from his saddle. He said: "Where's Custer?"

"I'll be damned if I know," said Reno. "He was to have supported me. We got down there and took one hell of a beating. Where's McDougall and the pack train?"

"Coming," said Benteen.

"Send somebody back to him. Tell him to cut out one ammunition mule and get it here as soon as possible."

The Sioux made a long, cloudy line on the plain, racing away, and Moylan murmured: "I don't understand that." Then, in the following half silence, all of them, heard one far-away volley westward.

"There's Custer," said Benteen. "In a fight."

Troopers continued to struggle up the slope, their eyes glazed by exertion; and now other troopers, partly rested, moved back down from the summit to rescue the wounded stragglers. Shafter heard the officers talking nearby, but he paid no attention. He had his eyes pinned to Garnett's motionless shape. He watched the man, and a steady hatred held him still. Bierss crawled beside him and groaned and lay full length. "Professor," he murmured, "it was bad."

"We're here," said Shafter.

"A lot of us ain't," said Bierss. "There's Hines and McDermott—"

"But we're here," said Shafter roughly. He laid aside his carbine and slid down the slope. A stray Sioux bullet struck near him and in the thin heated silence the crack of it sounded on and on. He got to Garnett and crouched. "You alive?"

Garnett slowly turned his head on the dust. He looked at Shafter's feet, murmuring, "You got any water?"

"No," said Shafter. He hooked Garnett around the shoulders with his arms and sat him upright. He braced the man against his legs and heaved again, pulling Garnett up. He balanced him a moment, doubting his own strength; then he crouched and in one sharp effort he got Garnett on his shoulder and went up the hill. His feet ground into the soft, rocky underfooting and slid back. A bullet struck short and ricocheted with a liquid whining; elsewhere a carbine flatted an answer. He said at the extreme end of his lungs, "You dog, I shouldn't be doing this." Fifty feet from the summit, Donovan came down and gave him a hand.

At five o'clock, a dust-red sun flamed low on the western horizon and from the west now and then came the pulse of gunfire, so faint that some men heard it and others were uncertain. It was the worried and impatient ones who heard it; it was the exhausted who neither heard it nor cared. The valley below was almost empty of Sioux but in the rocky crevices of the two higher points surrounding this peak Indians lay and intermittently fired. Benteen, salty and cool under disaster, moved briskly around the rim of the peak, posting the companies while the jaded Reno moved aimlessly from point to point, unafraid but dazed by what he had undergone and what he feared he must yet endure. The walking wounded toiled painfully up the stiff slope; details were bringing up those critically injured, while Doctor Porter moved among them, making such shifts as he could.

McDougall's B Company had arrived with the pack train and extra ammunition. Captain Weir, one of Custer's nearest friends, stood arguing with Reno, half pleading, half in ill-covered anger. "We should be moving out to support Custer. He is very definitely engaged at the lower end of the valley."

"So were we very definitely engaged," said Reno, irritably. "My orders were to attack and that I would be supported. I attacked. I was not supported. I had no orders at all to support Custer. It is only by God's miracle we survived to reach this hill."

"He may be in extreme trouble," said Weir.

"He may be," said Reno. "And so are we. Take a look around you, Weir. Does this look like a battalion presently fit for service?"

"Definite orders or not," said Weir stubbornly, "you have your judgment to exercise. I should think judgment would indicate supporting the wing now in need of help. My God, there are a thousand or two thousand Sioux down there fighting him."

"I'm better aware of it than you are," said Reno, dryly. "I have just come out of all that. My judgment is first to protect my own battalion. We shall be attacked again."

Weir went stamping angrily away and Shafter saw him move over to his lieutenant, Edgerly. The two remained in considerable conversation, after which Weir mounted his horse and came back toward Reno. He dismounted and said something to Reno, and then got on his horse and moved out to the north alone. Within five minutes Edgerly pulled D Company into formation and followed Weir. In that direction the faint volleying sounded again.

Benteen came up to Reno. "Where's Weir going?"

"Damned if I know."

"You're in charge here, aren't you?" said Benteen acidly. "I'd suggest you pull him back."

"No," said Reno, temporarily resolute. "We'll move out and see if we can support Custer, wherever he is."

The troops drearily assembled. Blankets were opened and the wounded placed upon them, four men to a blanket. In the harsh, swimming sunlight of late afternoon the battalion started west along the rough summit of the bluffs. A mile onward they got to a high peak and saw the lower end of the valley, all hazy with the churning of Sioux horses, and on a lower peak they discovered Sioux madly circling into sight and riding down out of sight again. Beyond that lower peak was a hidden extension of the valley; and from it came one last volley, followed only by the popping of an occasional gun.

Weir was ahead and now Weir stopped, his troopers dismounting. The crooked ravines before Weir suddenly disgorged Sioux and within five minutes he was in a bitter fight, gradually retreating until he came upon the main command. "Now, dammit," cried Reno to Weir, "you see what it's like!"

Indians erupted over the lower peak and slashed forward; they struck up from the long slopes to the north; they clambered forward on the rocky outcrop of the sheer bluff to the south. The battalion, thus abruptly faced with fire from three sides, slowly jockeyed itself into position. D took the force of the attack while the remnants of A and G painfully moved backward with the wounded. Presently M replaced D and then Godfrey dismounted K and made a screen for the rest of the command; thus beyond six o'clock Reno's battalion, exhausted by a steady twenty-four-hour march and half destroyed by an afternoon's fighting, reached its original peak and flung itself into defensive position. Benteen paced back and forth, maneuvering the companies in a rough circle to defend the knob; there was a shallow depression in the middle area of the knob and here he posted the pack horses and made a breastworks of the packs, behind which he placed the wounded.

"Wallace," he said, "put G here," and indicated the place with his arm.

Wallace said wearily: "There are just three men left in G."

"Very well. Place those three here."

The sun was low and the light had changed. Now at this hour, the Sioux poured back, clambering up the bluff, sidling along the ravines and rock barriers, boiling across the river. From the two adjoining higher peaks the Sioux fire began to break, plunging down upon the exposed circle. That leaden rain splashed up the dust and furrowed the sandy earth, biting into men and animals and packs.

"God damn that sun," panted Bierss. "Why don't it set?"

Shafter lay flat, watching the distant rocks, waiting for a fair shot. Donovan died silently beside him; a crazed horse rocketed around the circle and stepped on his outstretched legs and charged down the slope, and tripped itself on its dropped reins and went end over end in a small avalanche of shale all the way to the river. There was no letup while daylight lasted; that pelting storm played cruelly and fatally upon them all as they crouched and dismally took punishment. The command was a half-unconscious body, quivering to each added lash but unable to strike back. At eight o'clock the sun fell and the shadows came mercifully to end the gunfire; in the twilight and in the onset of peace, Shafter stirred out of his position like a man drugged and heard a trooper crying among the wounded.

☆ 20 ☆

Farewell to Glory

Now men who had been wounded and who had said nothing of it began to move toward the center of the area where Doctor Porter steadily worked and voices began to lift, shaken by agony. "Who's got some water?" The officers stirred around, taking check of their companies. Moylan said to Shafter: "We have got to dig in tonight. They'll be at us when daylight comes. We've got to throw up breastworks. Where's Garnett?"

"Over there," said Shafter.

"Alive?"

"I don't know," said Shafter.

He got his bacon and hardtack out of his haversack and sat down to his first meal since the night before; but he had no water and his mouth was too dry to dissolve the hardtack and therefore he chewed on the raw bacon for its moisture, and presently grew thirstier. The groaning of the wounded got steadily worse and one of these men had a question that never left his tongue: "Where's Custer? Why don't he come?"

Somebody, anonymous in the darkness, flung back an answer: "He's pulled out and left us, like he did Major Elliot at Washita."

Moylan spoke up, coolly. "Let that go, boy."

Pickets were sent down-slope and presently stragglers, trapped in the grove or the river's willows during the valley fight, began to creep in. Shafter listened to their hard breathing and the sudden grunt that came out of them when they sat down. He moved along A Company's line. "Start digging. Dig yourself a hole. Make yourself a shelter."

"What with, Sarge?" asked O'Dale.

"A knife or a spoon if you've got nothing else." He came to Bierss and found the corporal sound asleep. He stood a little while, hating to break that exhausted slumber; he nudged Bierss with his foot and then he had to reach down and shake the corporal. "Bierss—dig yourself in."

"The blacker the tunnel the better," murmured Bierss. "What you meant was just to rest and forget, wasn't it, Professor? Sounds better now than it did before."

The call for water from the wounded was a thing that rubbed Shafter's nerves raw; it was worse than anything that had gone before. Some of A Company's men were over there in Doctor Porter's compound; he thought he heard Lovelace and stepped over and found the boy. Lovelace had a hole in his leg above the knee, and he was trying to endure it without complaining, but his voice shook when he spoke. "Jesus, I hope this thing don't get so bad they have to cut it off. You got a drink, Sarge?"

Shafter unhooked Lovelace's canteen; he collected a dozen canteens and searched for Moylan in the shadows. "I'm going down to the river."

"The valley is crawling with Sioux," said Moylan. "Hear all those owls hooting?"

"I can hoot as well," said Shafter. "Remember when we crawled through the rebel lines?"

"The rebels weren't as smart as these Sioux."

"Where do you think Custer is, Myles?"

Moylan thought about it a long while and let his voice fall to a murmur. "Maybe he broke through and went on to meet Terry, but I don't think so. I think he's dead. I think they're all dead."

"So he waved his big hat and went out to meet his beloved."

"I don't mind that so much," said Moylan. "But he took more than two hundred men with him. Terry's all we've got to hope for now, and he'd better come soon. There's three thousand Sioux in that damned valley and they'll all be at us first thing morning comes."

Shafter dropped down the slope, softly calling to the pickets. He tried to make a quiet trip of it, but the loose shale crumbled beneath his boots and rolled away. Half-descended, he stopped and listened into the night; at the lower end of the valley he saw Sioux campfires burning and he heard strange rhythms and strange echoes drift forward. He crouched in the muddy darkness for ten minutes and then proceeded with greater caution until he got to the softer ground at the bottom of the bluff; and went directly to the water's edge. He flattened on his belly and drank sparingly and drew back to feel that cold wetness spring through him like an acid injected into his veins; it was the sharpest possible sensation through every part of his body. He put his arms into the water when he drank again; he ducked his head under and drew back once more, licking his tongue against his dripping mouth.

He filled the canteens and crouched still. There was a sibilance in the willows, and a slight steamy echo from the river as it flowed past, these sounds sharpening his feeling of danger. He swung his head to orient one sound or another and he watched the shadows pulse around him. He thought: "This is the last drink for God knows how long," and regretted leaving the river; and drank again, until he felt slightly sick. Gathering up the canteens he turned back to the bluff.

The canteens weighted him down and they made a small racket which betrayed his position. A third of the distance up the bluff he sat down, suddenly so weak that he doubted if he could carry the load. Somewhere now he definitely heard a body gritting along the nearby surface of the bluff, and in a little while a voice said: "They're up this ravine. Come on." He sat still and let the party go on ahead of him. He wanted to call to them for help, but the night was too still to take the risk.

He grew less cautious, once they were ahead of him, and now tackled the slope again, each foot of advance using up his wind; his leg muscles ached and he seemed to have a hole in him through which his strength poured like sand. Presently he sat down, feeling the dogged beating of his heart. "When I was twenty, this would have been easy." It was harder to rise and the steepness of the slope dragged at him and pulled him back. Dried out as he was, he began to sweat. He thought: "If I stop again I'll throw away some of the canteens, so I had better keep going." Beyond the halfway point he had ceased to think of the Sioux creeping around him and he no longer troubled to walk quietly. He created a racket in the night, plugging one foot before him, making strange sounds with his mouth, shoving himself on. A picket's voice came at him:—

"Who's that?"

"Give me a push," said Shafter.

"You got water?"

"Not for you," said Shafter.

"To hell with you then," said the picket.

Shafter churned the rubble under him; the whole weight of the bluff bore against him and pushed him. His lungs had a spongy, bubbling ferment in them and his pulse slugged at his temples, his neck, his wrists. He was a man on the edge of collapse, indecently listening to his own weakness. When he came to the summit he stumbled and fell, flinging the canteens into the darkness. The liquid sound of them brought men at him on the run; he heard them searching the ground for the canteens. He rolled over, suddenly furious. He got up and struck a bent shadow. He panted, "Leave those alone!"

Bierss called at him from a short distance. "You want help there, Sarge?"

He got his canteens together and walked over to Doctor Porter's stockade, where the wounded lay. Doctor Porter crouched beside a man, a stub end of a candle lighting his work. "A little water," said Shafter.

Porter paused a moment and gave the canteens the sharpest kind of stare; his own thirst tortured him and he showed the struggle on his face. Then he called quietly into the darkness. "Toomey, come here and dole out this water. None for you, Toomey, and none for any who is able-bodied."

Shafter kept his own canteen. He saw Lovelace near by and he bent and propped up the boy and gave him a small drink and watched inexpressible relief slash sharp lines on Lovelace's face. He stood up, oppressed by the sound of misery around him, and by the smell of misery. Men lay under the feeble circle of the candlelight, they were shadows beyond the candlelight. He heard them calling: "Toomey—for God's sakes bring me a drink!" Porter suddenly leaned back from his patient and gave the man a long look. "Nothing more for you until we can get you in a better place."

"You don't have to tell me that way, Porter."

Shafter looked around, recognizing Garnett's voice. He stood undecided in his tracks, hearing Porter answer. "I haven't told you anything, Garnett," he said, and moved on to the next man. Shafter bent, seeing Garnett's pale face grow rough with the knowledge of his own dying. Garnett's eyes were wide and his pupils were big; he stared up at Shafter.

"Light's bad," he whispered. "That's you, Kern?"

Shafter unscrewed his canteen top. "Take a drink."

"You're wasting it. I'll be dead in a little while."

"A man's got a right to die with a drink in him," said Shafter. He stared down, not even now able to feel sympathy. His hatred was as rank as it ever had been; this was a man he despised, a man whose memory he would always carry like the scar of a wound treacherously inflicted. It even rankled him that Garnett should refuse water in order that the living might have it; none of that charity or goodness had ever been in Garnett.

Garnett sighed. "Give me the drink, then," he said.

Shafter slid the flat of his hand behind Garnett's head and lifted it; he listened to the greedy sucking sound of Garnett's lips on the canteen. He pulled the canteen away. "That's enough to die on."

Garnett moved his head, side to side. He murmured: "I think the bullet smashed my spine. I can feel nothing from the hips down."

"This time," said Shafter, "you couldn't duck."

Garnett said: "I was never afraid of anything and you damned well know it." Garnett stared at him with a kind of malicious satisfaction. "You're waiting for me to cry for mercy—or pity. You're alive and I'm dying, and you're pleased as hell and you think I'm going to go out on my hands and knees, crawling and afraid. You're wasting your time. I'm not sorry for a thing I've ever done."

"It is a good thing to know you'll never ruin another woman."

A shadow came upon Garnett's face. He lay still and thought about that. "Why," he said finally, "it was a game with me. The only game that ever interested me. A man and a woman. A man in pursuit of a woman. But you've got the wrong view of that, too, Kern. I am a kind of a specialist in women and I guess I ought to know what lies in them as well as anybody. Now that I look back I doubt if I ever ruined any woman. I doubt if I ever made a woman do something she hadn't made up her mind to do. Do you understand that, Kern?"

"No," said Shafter.

Garnett had a dying man's patience and now slowly brought his thoughts to bear upon the thing he wanted to say. "A man is supposed to be the hunter and the woman the hunted. Who started that idea? A man did. A man always figures himself the one who does the chasing and the winning. I have looked into the eyes of many a woman and I have said to myself: 'I can make her want me.' But that was really a delusion. It is women who really make the conquests. They get what they want, Kern, but the blame goes to the men. That's the way a woman holds a man—laying the blame on him. She surrenders but she captures. I was smart enough to know that. I played the game just as women wanted it played. But I never let myself get captured."

"You believe that?" said Shafter. "Would you do it all over?"

"I'd do every bit of it over," said Garnett.

"You're better dead," said Shafter.

"You're thinking of Alice," murmured Garnett. "A dead man doesn't have to be a gentleman, Kern, so I'll tell you something about her. She was my kind, not yours. You think I took her away from you. I had damned little to do with it. She was after me and I played the game. She knew you and I were friends. She broke up that friendship without the least scruple. But after she got me, she didn't want me. She was looking for fresh meat. She was a beautiful woman, Kern, and she had no trouble at all in making me want her. I had my illusions about her, as you did. I thought the whole world was in her eyes, as you did. Then afterwards I discovered the coldness behind her beauty. She cured me of my illusions. I have never respected another woman. Is that candle going out? It's getting dark."

"No," said Kern. "It is still burning."

"Then I'm the one going out," murmured Garnett softly. "What a hell of a mess today's been. Where's Custer?"

"Nobody knows."

"I wish you luck for tomorrow," said Garnett.

Shafter had no answer for that. He watched Garnett with an impersonal attention; he watched the man's face lose its sharpness one line at a time, its definiteness one degree upon another, until presently Garnett was a spirit quietly withdrawing, half free but not wholly free of his body. Nothing, he thought, stopped Garnett from immediately ceasing to breathe except the mortal fear of the last long jump into space and blackness. Garnett held on, dreading the step.

"In pain?" asked Shafter.

"No."

"The easy way," said Shafter, "is to just shut your eyes and die."

"Kern," said Garnett, "do me one favor. See that I'm buried deep enough to keep the coyotes from digging me up." Then the faint malicious tone came back. "If you are alive to do it."

"Anybody you want a letter written to?"

"Don't be hypocritical, Kern. How could you compose a letter of soldierly regret concerning me?"

"I could say you were dead, nothing more. Have you got anybody who might care enough to hear it?"

"You always were a fellow who hated to change," murmured Garnett. "You would burn your bridge rather than go back over it." He was silent for so long that Shafter thought he had died; then his head moved on the ground. He looked up into the night, at the far stars winking. "The earth is my pillow, the earth is my mistress. The earth is a woman and, like all women, stronger than any man can be. Men are the vessels God made to carry illusions. Women are the realists; they are the strength of the race. They love, they hate, they bear.

They pray and they sin. But they are stronger than love or sin. If I had it to do over again—" He ceased to speak, coming upon his final convictions and knowing them and struggling with them. "I should not do the same things. That's what you're waiting to hear, Kern—the cry of a man afraid."

"I am disappointed in you," said Shafter.

"The last woman was the one I wanted and could not have because of what I had been before I met her. That is something you didn't know about me. I was more of a man of honor in her presence than you supposed."

"Josephine?" said Shafter.

"Josephine," whispered Garnett and died.

Doctor Porter moved past, dropping his question. "How's Garnett?"

"Finished."

"Fortunate," said Porter and knelt down with his candle beside another man. Shafter got up and moved on his stiff, dead legs toward the northern edge of the defense circle. He passed Moylan, standing solitary in the dark. He said, "Here's a drink, Myles," and handed over the canteen. The captain accepted the canteen. He shook it and judged its contents and for a long moment he struggled with his thirst, and handed it back unopened. "Spread it thin among the boys," he said.

"Garnett's dead," said Shafter.

"Poor soul," said Moylan. "Feel sorry for him?"

"No."

"You had better catch a wink. Tomorrow's a bad thing to think of."

Shafter found Bierss lying on his back. Bierss had scooped himself a hollow spot the size of his body and had tossed the dirt up as a breastwork and now he slept in the depression with the dirt for a pillow. Shafter settled down, feeling the dullness of his body throughout. He thought: "I've got to dig my own shelter," and dreaded the chore. He was sore of muscle and dried out and his lungs burned from exertion and dust; he was tired in a way he had never been tired—made stupid and indifferent by it. His mind moved slowly and his will had little effect, but exhaustion had put a kind of poison in him which would not let him sleep. He lay still, feeling the heat die out of the earth and the air. Some of the wounded mercifully slept but for others the agony went on and their groaning made him grit his teeth and turn on the ground; over there in the improvised hospital men were going through a hell that would leave its scratches on them forever. This was the glory of battle—this was the end of the band playing and the bright pennants flying and all the dreams of gallantry and personal triumph; a man dreamed of glory and it came to this. A lithe figure in a buckskin suit and a flowing red tie stood up in his stirrups and flung his great hat impetuously over his head and the regiment went into battle line, the voices of men shouting out their power and their excitement, and afterwards the smoke and heat and dust folded over them and death struck and long later in the aftermath's stillness men lay physically and spiritually smashed and thought only of water and rest and peace.

Yet Garnett was right. Men were vessels to carry the dreams of the race—the bright visions of gallantry and courage and daring which made the life stream

fresh and quick, the steadfast visions of honor and loyalty, and the great flame
of faith.

The good and the bad died for those visions, never wholly realizing why they
fought; the good and the bad lived to enjoy the peace which came of nights like
these, never fully understanding how their peace was secured for them.

The name of this little battle in a remote western valley would fade as time
went on until few people knew of it or the reason for it. But even if they forgot
it, it would still be a part of that red thread which ran continuously through the
fabric of the country. Battles of the past had stained the thread, and this battle
now would add its scarlet color, and other battles yet to come. Some of these
battles were just and some were unjust, some were necessary struggles of survival, some need never have been fought; but there was never any way of
knowing.

A man was faithful and he fought, and had his hopes of betterment; and
somewhere else a man stopped his plow and looked upon the long furrows with
his mind fertile with ambition; a river packet steamed down the Ohio with its
cargo of two hundred people asleep while the pilot smoked his stogy in the
wheelhouse and watched the dark river bend; a jockey at Saratoga sat on his
horse at the barrier and wickedly waited for his break; a man in some New York
tenement room sat before his table and wrote his pamphlet inciting the oppressed to rise against the barons of coal and steel; a boy and a girl walked
through moonlight under the hickory trees of Indiana and knew nothing except
each other's presence; a married woman stood in a room and looked across it,
beyond the crowd and beyond her husband to her lover, and met his glance and
knew what it meant. The just and the unjust, the faithful and the crooked, the
pure and the sinful—all were one, breathing a common air and pacing a common earth, the most pure with his temptations and the most dissolute with his
moments of grandeur. All were one, walking forward through the sunlight and
the dark, each with his end but each a part of the life stream which came out of
time and went on into time.

This was his country and this was his part and his place. He thought of Hines
dead and Bierss alive; one an upright man and one a lewd scoundrel. But each
had taken his place in the ranks of men and each had been faithful, one with his
duties discharged and one yet to suffer before his grace was achieved. Tonight
the camp lay at fitful rest and each of the living nourished his memories, his
wishes and his hatreds but all were waiting together for tomorrow—and again
would stand together. Their lot was a common one; the commonness of it made
all of them good.

He thought: "I've got nothing but a spoon and a knife to work with." He rose
to a sitting position and found his haversack and got out his knife and began to
dig the sandy-powdered soil. He worked mechanically, his muscles reluctantly
answering his will. This was the bitter end of a day now twenty hours old and
pieces of that day worked through his mind as strange and vivid pictures tele-
scoped together. He remembered many mixed sounds, and the shock of cold
water at the first ford went sharp through him; he recalled the way Cooke had
turned at the ford and had gone away, his Dundreary whiskers flowing to the
breeze of his gallop; he remembered the terrified face of young Adkins, whose

horse had bolted straight into the dust and toward the Sioux. He thought: "I shouted at him to fall off the saddle, but he didn't hear." He scooped the loose earth into a mound and recollected Bloody Hand's sudden shudder in the saddle and the violent blood splashing against Reno's face. He could not recall when he had last seen McDermott. He tried to recollect McDermott on the firing line; he tried to follow McDermott from that point. "Dead and scalped," he concluded.

Reno came tramping around the circle and stopped near Moylan. Shafter heard the major speak with an exhausted incoherence. "How in God's name can a man possibly sleep?"

"Who's asleep?"

"Benteen," said the major. "Sound asleep."

At midnight or beyond, Shafter had a shallow depression scooped out. He thought, "There'll be hell around here at daylight. They've got positions higher up and they'll scorch us." But he had done all he could and now settled in his depression, uncomfortably lying on his cartridge belt; he made some attempt to adjust himself, and fell asleep.

☆ 21 ☆

Bugles in the Afternoon

He woke with a sudden upfling of his body from the ground, startled by the sound of a single shot. Day trembled through morning's twilight and the peaks to either side of this one now came into view; below him a mist moved thinly over the Little Bighorn. Benteen strode past, sharp of voice and full of vigor. "Keep under cover, boys. The music's starting again."

A second shot arrived, slitting the dust behind Shafter, the echoes of it rolling on and on through morning's stilled air. Bierss grunted to himself and pointed westward to the adjacent peak, whose heights commanded this knob on which they lay. "Comin' from there, but I don't see a damned thing."

Moylan came forward and sat down by Shafter. He said: "You take the left wing of the company, I'll take the right."

"Myles," said Shafter, "don't expose yourself."

"I am too old to duck," said Moylan. He crossed his legs tailor fashion and stared a long while at the hill from which the fire now came more strongly. Lead arrived, breaking up dust and forming a thin haze on the knoll. "Boys," called Moylan, "watch those rocks and wait till you see something to shoot at. We have got all day." Far below, fresh waves of Sioux came up the valley and flung themselves at the river willows and made the water crossing; they dismounted and began to work their way forward on the slope, climbing in crisscross fashion and dropping behind the rough furrows of earth, the frequent slabs of rock. The sun rose, the first touch of it reminding Shafter of his thirst and his hunger. This day would be hot.

"Give me your carbine," said Moylan and took it from Shafter and braced his elbows on his knees and snugged the gun to his cheek. He waited a long while, holding the muzzle dead on one spot; the gun roared and the recoil slightly swayed him. His mouth creased. He returned the carbine to Shafter, nodding.

Bierss said: "For God's sakes, Cap'n, get down."

"Kern," said Moylan, "I wrote a letter a month ago to General Summers. You remember him?"

"Yes."

"He's close to Sherman. I told him to open a case that had been shut too long."

Shafter said, "You ought to let dead things alone. They'll never touch it."

"I did Summers a good turn once when he was a young captain. He owes me a turn and I told him I wanted it. A word from him to Sherman will be enough. A word from Sherman will do all of it. That would be a good thing."

"Once," said Shafter, "it would have mattered. Now, I don't care."

"Yes," said the captain, "you do. Otherwise what brought you back to the uniform?"

"I could think of nothing else to do."

"So you did the thing which was in your mind, my boy. You came back. You'll be soldiering until you're mustered out an old man, or until you're buried on the battlefield."

Shafter turned in his hole and smiled at the captain. "A bunk to sleep in, a payday for a little whiskey and a little poker—that's enough, Myles."

"We shall see," said the captain and moved away, strolling as though he were on Lincoln's parade ground with no care in his mind.

Company A held the east segment of the circle, facing the higher peak, from which Sioux fire now strengthened. H and K lay overlooking the ford to the south and M guarded the west, taking the fire from the peak which stood as a high point in that direction. To the north, where the ridge ran gradually downward into flat land, B and D and the pitiful remnant of G had been placed. It was from this direction Reno and Benteen expected attack.

The sun came full up. At nine o'clock the firing had grown to an outright engagement and the Sioux had apparently begun an encircling movement. A constant, down-plunging leaden rain came from the two peaks to north and south. Along the lower rocks, between the south rim and the ford, the brown Sioux bodies made a spotty, shifting pattern against the gray earth. Reno came over to look down that way and spoke his judgment.

"They wish to draw our attention. The main attack is shaping to the north."

Over there the land fell gently, slashed by frequent gullies into which the Sioux filtered in quick sallies; a great party moved around the base of the southern peak, made a wide sweep and rushed forward into the gullies. Benteen, vigilant and calm, came up to Reno.

"If they get any nearer, they'll swamp us with a sudden charge. We've got to attack."

"You'll lose every man you take out there," said Reno.

"We have got to drive at them," repeated Benteen.

Reno said irritably: "If you can get a party together you have my assent to it."

The firing never let up. Horses began to drop in the center of the area and the smell of powder lay acrid in the air. Bierss snugged himself into his shallow pit, fired and loaded and fired again until the barrel of his Springfield was too hot to grasp. Moylan sat behind his section of the company, loading guns and passing them to his troopers with his calm counsel. "Take your time. Wait until you see the sweat on their bellies."

Shafter had gone to the left of the troop line; he stood here watching the earth around him show dimpled jets of dust. Behind him Benteen's voice made a strong, steady call and troopers were gathering themselves for a rush. The Indian line, now drawing about the knoll from all sides, brought a heavier gunfire to bear. It grew into fury, echoes all blended into one rolling, crackling racket. Shafter watched A Company's thin line wilt on the ground; he watched men die and he saw them flinch and roll helplessly aside and turn wild glances upon him. Bierss moved a little in his hole, as if settling for a better aim; the corporal's gun steadied on the nearby peak and the corporal's body lifted and fell to his breathing. Shafter turned his head for a brief while to watch Reno trot toward the other side of the area. "Benteen," said Reno, "I'll take this." Swinging his glance back again, Shafter noticed Bierss' gun tipped idle over the dust parapet. Bierss had flattened himself full length and seemed to be taking a short rest.

"Bierss," said Shafter, "look alive."

Trooper O'Dale looked about and shook his head. Shafter stepped forward until he saw that Bierss had a bullet through his brain.

Reno's voice came back through the hark and the snarl of gunfire. "Forward!" Shafter swung and ran after him as the major jumped forward with his revolver, leading his troopers downgrade toward the nearest gully. Shafter came abreast of the line and ran with it. He remembered the way Bierss had relished his worldly pleasures, but he remembered, too, how Bierss had marched and endured and fought and had grinned through all his misery.

The skirmish line rushed on toward the gully, firing as it ran. Reno had no hat and his lank hair jiggled down over his forehead; he kept discharging his revolver at the gully and he kept shouting: "Forward—jump 'em!" Men whimpered a little and paused and sat slowly down and were left behind. Twenty yards from the gully, Shafter watched Sioux spring out of it and run backward toward the next lower gully. The slope of the plain boiled with dust and his heart began to slug in his ribs again from the run. Reno had stopped and turned. "That does it," he said, his eyes round and black-ringed. "Back to the top." The line swung, trotting upgrade, pushed now by the danger to the rear. Bullets whipped by and scraped up flinty showers of earth. Shafter breathed from the bottom of his lungs, he heard men from the higher parapet call him forward. He reached the top and half turned to look behind him, and at that moment he was struck hard in the body and he dropped to his hands and knees and was puzzled at his fall. He started to rise again, and saw Lieutenant Edgerly striding toward him. He reached out for Edgerly's hand, but his own arm grew too heavy and fell back. For the smallest interval of time there was a roar in his head like the breaking of surf; after that all sound ceased.

The sortie had driven the Sioux back from the near coulee and the firing slackened and men began to reach out for the wounded. A pair of D troopers carried Shafter to the pack barricade before Porter, who worked on his knees, his sleeves rolled up and his long hands blood-stained. He gave Shafter a single, hard look and said to the troopers, "Take his shirt off," and returned to his immediate job.

Moylan came up a little later and found Porter working on Shafter. Moylan said: "Where's he hit?"

"Near the kidney," said the doctor and leaned back to dash the sweat from his nose.

"What's that on his face?"

"He hit a rock when he fell."

"Porter," said Moylan, "how much does a man have to suffer to earn salvation?"

Porter shook his head and returned to his labors. He rolled back Shafter's eyelids and peered down and sat a moment, making up his mind; and got up and turned to the next man.

At noon, half a dozen desperate troopers ran the gantlet to the river and came back with water. The sun moved on, blistering the earth with its heat, and the wounded began to stir under it and cry out when they could no longer be still. At two o'clock, the Sioux fire grew brisk and for half an hour the command fought doggedly; in the following lull the officers held a conference.

"Custer must have gone on to Terry," said Weir.

"Terry," said Godfrey, "was due at the mouth of the Little Bighorn this morning. He should be here."

Moylan shook his head. "If he's anywhere around this valley he's in one hell of a fight, same as we are."

Captain French made a short roundabout gesture with his hand. "Time can't be held much longer. We're being cut to ribbons. We have got to move to one of those two higher points tonight."

"We have got to get water tonight," added McDougall.

Reno said dourly: "We have got to have help, or we won't last tonight."

"By God, sir," said Benteen brusquely, "we'll last."

He had fallen asleep and now he was awake, and he had slept so hard that his body was numb below the hips. He looked at the sun crawling half down the sky; it had been straight overhead when he last saw it. "How could I have slept for three hours?" he wondered. He rocked his head from side to side and recognized the barricade of packs and discovered men lying in a row beyond him, some still and some groaning. Then he knew he had been hit and he tried to move his legs and had no luck. Pain began to move through him; it trickled like water and seemed to have no source.

Toomey, Doctor Porter's orderly, was nearby. He said: "What's the matter with me, Toomey?"

"You got a hole in your guts," said Toomey.

Shock sickened him and a bitter fright yelled through him; but that was only temporary. The wave of vitality passed, and left him dull. He thought: "I must be dying."

The pain began to take on the rhythm of his pulse, slow and steady, and in a little while he was a mass of flame. "Four days ago," he thought, "we were at the mouth of the Rosebud and Custer led us. Twenty-four hours ago we were coming over the pass. Then we sighted the lone tepee." It was far back; it might have been a month ago. He remembered how the troop had looked when it marched away from the Yellowstone and he visualized the men he knew to be dead, and then he visualized the troop without these men. "My God," he said, "we're not enough to mount a guard."

He watched the sun slide west and he heard the firing come in fitful volleys. A bullet occasionally struck the barricade of packs with a sharp thump, and now and then a bullet bounced from the earth and screamed through the thin hot air like a suddenly burst piano wire. Moylan came over and looked down. "How are you, Kern?"

"All right."

"Terry ought to be up to relieve us pretty soon."

"I hope he's got a better hill than we have."

"The Indians have quit massing against us," said Moylan. He watched Shafter a moment in an extraordinarily sharp way—the way of a man who looks upon death; and then Moylan went away.

There were fewer and fewer exchanges of firing. The men at the parapets began to rise, dusty and parched, and to move around with the looseness of physical exhaustion. The smell of the wounded hung in the air, faintly sweet, faintly foul; the dead man next to him had begun to swell in the belly. Details formed and moved the horses downgrade toward the river, and he heard Reno talking to Benteen.

"They've gone back toward the foot of the valley."

"They wouldn't be leaving us unless they were threatened elsewhere," said Benteen. "That will be Terry or Custer."

A detail returned with water for the wounded. Moylan came over to give Shafter a drink, and sprinkled some of it on Shafter's face. There was smoke in the air.

"Sioux burning the grass in the valley," said Moylan. Godfrey called to him and he went back toward the south rim of the peak.

"Look there," said Godfrey.

The Sioux had broken camp at the lower end of the valley and now were passing up the same area across which Reno's troop had charged. The column was as wide as the valley itself and it stretched on and on, braves and squaws and travois and horse herd. All the officers and men lined the brow of the hill to watch it pass and swing south into the broken land.

"A mile wide and three miles long," said Benteen, estimating the column. "Fully three thousand warriors in that party. That's what we ran into."

The sun had begun to set, its long rays flashing on Indian lance and gun; the murmur of that vast band—the sound of voices and the rattle of gear—came up the slope like the faint babble of geese in the distant sky. Benteen said suddenly: "There are white men in that outfit."

"White men's clothes," said Godfrey; and then all of them heard the notes of a cavalry trumpet—a pure blast without orderly meaning—come from the column.

"Clothes and trumpet," said Moylan. "There's your answer. Stripped from dead troopers."

"I wish," said Weir in a groaning voice, "Custer would come."

Moylan and the other officers only looked at him.

Night came down, the stars bright and immense in the sky. Moylan brought Shafter a cup of coffee and said: "You want some bacon, Kern?"

"No," said Shafter, "I'm not hungry, but I could drink a gallon of water."

He turned on his side, but a great bomb of pain exploded in his belly and sent out its waves of agony. He stretched his arms and dug his fingers into the ground and slowly sweated and felt sick. A wind came up and cooled him slightly; and thus partly relieved, he fell asleep. When he awoke the wind still blew but he was increasingly hot and he called softly for Toomey and got another drink; and lay listening to the little sounds in the camp, to the pacing of the sentries and the snoring of exhausted men and the suppressed sighing and gritted suspirations of the wounded around him. He saw light break through the east and when day came he was a thousand years old, with strange thoughts in his head; and he had made his exploration into the sub-world which the living and healthy never see, and heat burned throughout him; then he fell asleep a second time.

When he awoke again the sun had started up and he saw a column of riders come over the hill's crest, General Terry in the lead. Terry got down and reached out and shook Reno's hand and Benteen's hand. There were tears in Terry's eyes.

"General," said Reno, "where is Custer?"

"Custer," said Terry, and nodded to the west, "is three miles down there, dead."

"Where's his battalion?"

"Dead," said Terry. His voice broke and he bent his head, wrestling with his self-control. "All of them, every man and every beast. A terrible blunder—a terrible, tragic, unnecessary blunder."

The group of officers stood around him in stunned silence; their own ordeal had taken much capacity of feeling out of them, yet this was a shock that all felt, this complete extinction of five companies, all their officers and all their men who had ridden away the previous afternoon. Reno lifted a hand and surreptitiously wiped moisture from his eyes. Weir, who had loved Custer, flung up a hand and turned aside. Terry looked around him and saw the remnant of Reno's command and the brutal evidence of its ordeal.

"What are your casualties?"

"I have got thirty dead and forty wounded. There are others missing." Reno passed a hand over his face, at the end of his physical resources. "I do not entirely know."

Terry stood still, looking into space, a sad and weary and troubled man whose campaign, so carefully planned, so thoughtfully and painfully arranged, had turned into greatest disaster. This regiment which had marched up the Rosebud in high hope, its colors flying and its commander dreaming of gallantry, now lay as a broken thing on the dry hot earth, more than 250 of its men dead and another sixty wounded. The regiment had come upon the Sioux at the high flood of their power, upon the greatest concentration of strength ever seen upon the plains. Uncaptured and undefeated, that Sioux power now slowly moved away while Terry with his battered command could not follow.

He knew, as he stood so gravely here upon the scene of defeat, how that defeat had come about. His trap, designed to snap shut, had been prematurely set off by the impetuous disregard of General Custer of his orders; wanting glory and blindly believing in himself and his regiment, Custer had not waited; the power of waiting was not in him. More than that the expected help of Crook had not come. With a command greater than Terry's, Crook dallied on the upper Powder, cautiously sealing himself in with double-strength pickets, made afraid by his defeat and calling for help. Of this Terry then knew nothing; it only mattered that the campaign had failed.

He turned to his adjutant and said slowly: "Send a man back to the *Far West* and tell Marsh to push the boat upstream as far as he dares. We shall be bringing on the wounded, who must be taken to Lincoln. Remind him to have plenty of wood aboard and to arrange the lower deck as a hospital. We must have details out at once to bury the dead. Waste no time. We have got to pull out."

From his place behind the packs, Shafter saw the command's sudden activity with a disinterested eye. Fever thinned his blood and lifted him so that sometimes he seemed weightless above the ground. The talk of men moved around him and left no impression. He saw Moylan bend down and he heard Moylan speak, and nodded in return. He saw the dead carried away and never quite understood why. Later he was lifted into a blanket litter slung from poles, two mules fore and aft on the poles; with this motion cradling and easing him he slept and woke and saw the sky bright, and slept again, later to wake and find the sky black. He heard Lovelace's voice somewhere near him and Lovelace was saying: "I'll be back. I'll be back." Three days later he was on the *Far West* and only vaguely was aware of it; there was a different smell and a different motion—and the sight of the sky disappeared. From time to time he heard a whistle blowing and always he heard the murmur of men—their sighing and their suppressed words. Some of the words came from him.

On the third of July, the *Far West* blew its whistle for the landing at Fort Lincoln and, with its jack staff black-draped and its flag at half-mast, touched shore. A runner went out immediately with the news and in the middle of the night officers reluctantly walked toward Officers' Row to notify the wives of the dead. The wounded were carried to the post infirmary. In Bismarck, a telegrapher sat at his key to flash the news east, and at midnight exactly someone rapped on the door of the Russell house. Josephine had heard the boat's whistle. Now, moved by the intimations of fear, she rose and dressed and hurried to the post.

☆ 22 ☆

"It Was Written in the Book"

THERE WAS SPACE around and above and below him; he swept through it, back and forth, as though in a giant swing. At times he rose directly upward and fell down and down yet never touched earth. Occasionally, great storms swept this space and he was whirled end over end with the screaming tumult of the storm filling his ears; then calmness would come and he floated without motion or sound or feeling. There were moments when he drifted near consciousness and heard voices, and recognized his own voice among them, and felt the touch of the bed and sometimes the cold pressure of a hand on his face. Sensations of fire and suffocation made him turn and protest; and after that he lost these sensations and floated into complete blackness and knew nothing. When he returned to near-consciousness he always knew he had been away, and his mind always tried to distinguish the real from the unreal but never quite succeeded.

On those occasions when he came out of blackness and approached the border of awareness he seemed always to ask himself: "How long has it been?" and his mind strained to answer the problem. Now it was but a moment he had been away, now it was a hundred years. Time was something that would not stay fixed; it had nothing definite about it, nothing real. It was a distance between two points—but the points were forever moving, so that the distance was never the same. He walked back and forth between those points time after time with his watch in his hand. It always took him fifty-seven minutes, no matter how near each other the points were, no matter how far apart they were. Then he changed his way of calculation. He dug deep holes and buried posts and laid rocks against them so they could not move, so they would always be exactly in the same places. Now he walked back and forth between them and found he could make the trip sometimes in one minute, sometimes in six hours. But there was no difference between the minute and the six hours. His mind strained onward toward truth, reaching out and out and almost grasping a thought but never quite touching it. It excited him and he put all his will into it. He said: "There is no such thing as time," and felt a great wave of peace roll cool and wonderful through him. He would never have to worry about time any more.

He stood again by one of the posts he had planted deep in the ground and he looked around him. Where was north? Where was down and where was up?

Distance marched away, but it had no ending. It began where he stood, but the place on which he stood was nothing; it did not exist—and space marched out from nowhere through nowhere, to nowhere. There were no boundaries. When he walked away from the post he walked into emptiness, and emptiness was all around him and it made no difference which way he traveled, for there was no such thing as direction.

Then he returned to the post and he said, "But this is somewhere—this is solid. I am here. This is here." He reached out and touched the post to feel its solidness, and discovered the post was an illusion, for his hand passed through the squareness and the definiteness of it and there was no squareness, no definiteness, no post. It did not exist. It was only something he had wanted to be there. It was only a wish, a dream. Suddenly he swept his hand back to his chest, to feel his own solidness, and his hand passed through his chest, and he looked down at his hand, and it was not there. He was not there. He was a shadow in shadows. He was less than that—he was emptiness floating in emptiness. "No," he said, "that can't be true. I think and I feel—and I see." But what did he see and what was it he felt? He sought for his answer, patiently and stubbornly. He was alone, a bodiless thing in a space that had no beginning, no form and no end. He was a voice that had not sound, he was a wish, a dream, a spark of being. His mind worked at it, pushing at the thought and pressing it narrower and narrower. He was a spirit. Where came that spirit and what gave it power and what was its form, its meaning or its purpose? He was still now; he was motionless in the motionless void around him; but somewhere in the void was a presence waiting for his answer. "What am I?" he asked. Then he said: "I am something."

He awoke as he had wakened thousands of other times; consciousness arrived softly and he opened his eyes and saw the walls around him, the stove in the room, the iron frame at the foot of his bed, the gray blanket folded there, and the orderly looking down at him. Josephine sat beside the bed.

"Hello, Kern," she said.

"What time is it?"

The orderly gave him an odd glance and pulled out his watch. "Nine in the morning."

"What morning?"

"Saturday morning. July 6."

"This Fort Lincoln?"

"Yes."

Shafter lay with his head turned, watching these two, Josephine and the orderly. They were solid figures silhouetted against the daylight streaming through the hospital windows, their voices made full sounds, and Josephine's lips were red and real and there was a strange moist shining in her eyes. He said, "Bend forward," and put out his hand. It had weight and the weight was hard for him to manage, but he touched her cheek, and felt its smoothness and its reality. He murmured, "A very odd thing," and then, as though this one gesture had worn him out, he fell asleep.

* * *

He came awake again somewhere during the night and felt the hollow, exhausted peace within his body. His lips were rough when he touched them with his tongue and a great lassitude made it impossible for him to move. But he was thinking of the strange things which had been in his mind and now he tried to bring them back, grasp their meaning and their dark importance. They would not come; it were as if, close to the margin of death, a gate had drawn aside to permit him a glimpse of another world. But he had cheated death and the gate had slammed shut and some power was even now at work, erasing within him the half-revealed secrets which did not belong to him as long as he was in this world. "A man could not endure living," he thought, "if he saw both sides of the fence." He slept into the middle of the following day and woke and was fed. Josephine came in for a short time and sat at his bed. She watched him, darkly and without a smile; it was the way he knew her best, her pride making her strong, her will giving her force.

"Garnett's dead," he said.

"I know." Then she added, "Why do you think of that before you think of other things?"

"He spoke your name." He thought of that a moment, and added: "Of all the women he knew, you were the one he remembered."

"Did he ask you to tell me anything?"

"No."

"Why are you speaking of him now?"

"A woman should know when a man dies with her memory in him."

"And the memory of other women."

"No," said Shafter, "he wasn't thinking of the others."

"Do you want me to thank you for telling me all this?"

"I am only doing a chore."

She watched him and he held his eyes on her, wondering what emotions lay behind her self-control. He wanted some sign from her, but she gave him none. She had closed up on him entirely so that he no longer saw in her eyes or on her lips, nor heard in the cadence of her voice, the telltale warmness of her heart. He felt irritated at it, at her, and at himself.

She said: "Better sleep," and went away.

A little later he saw Mary Mulrane pass him. He watched her stop at a far bed and bend over; he raised himself a little and thought he recognized Lovelace in the bed. When Mary returned he stopped her. He said: "How's Frank?"

She was happy, he saw; and she had been crying. "He's all right," she said. "The doctor says he's all right. If I knew about my father—"

"Your father," said Shafter, "was stationed at the Powder River base. He's safe."

She looked at him and was tempted to speak of something; and struggled with it, and spoke. "What happened to Jack Purple?"

"He died with his troop." He looked at her and felt free to give her some advice. "Mary," he said, "don't waste a tear on him. Your boy is better."

"Oh," she said, "I know that. I always knew that. I am just sorry—I'm sorry for all of them."

Major Barrows and his wife called that afternoon. They talked a little while, the major inquiring about his officer companions, those living and those dead. Mrs. Barrows sat by, scarcely speaking, but attentive, and presently the major murmured, "Stay a moment, Margaret. I want to speak to Doctor Jordan." He gave his wife a sharp glance and strolled down the room.

Mrs. Barrows said: "It was terrible for all of you, wasn't it?"

"It was a hard fight," he said.

She pressed her lips together and sat in silence, looking at him in a rather desperate way. She turned her head to notice that her husband was at the far end of the room and now she swung her glance back to Shafter, suddenly grown strained and harassed. "Sergeant," she murmured, "how did Edward Garnett die?"

He knew then how it was with her. He said to himself: "So he got her, too." She loved the man and was tortured now. He thought of what he was to say very carefully, and said it: "We were halfway up the hill when he was hit. He got to the top and lasted until that night. But he wasn't in much pain. He knew he was dying and it didn't matter to him."

She absorbed his words. She sat still, waiting for him to continue, her eyes begging him to add something she seemed in an actual agony to hear. Presently she drew a long sigh and spoke in a tone scarcely above a whisper. "Were you with him when he died?"

"Yes."

"Did he speak of me at all?"

This was what she wanted to hear, so urgently that she had stripped herself of her honor before him. It meant life or death to her.

"Yes," he said, "he called your name when he died."

Feeling rushed across her face and filled her eyes. She drew a ragged breath and her hands came together and whitened with pressure. She started to speak to him but found no voice. She bowed her head, struggling with her composure, and in a little while the major returned from the far end of the room. Shafter noticed the way his eyes surreptitiously touched his wife. Then the major said quietly: "We mustn't wear him out, Margaret."

She stood up, very cool again. She said: "God be with you, Sergeant," and for the first time she smiled.

Major Barrows had started away, but now came back and looked down at Shafter. "Sergeant," he said, "how could it have happened? How could it have been possible?"

Shafter murmured: "I've been thinking of it. General Terry split his forces into two sections, to approach from different sides of the Sioux. That turned out to be a mistake. Then Custer split his regiment into three pieces—and that was a mistake. He was to have waited for Gibbon to come up. He was to have sent a scout through to check with Gibbon. He didn't send the scout through, and he didn't wait. Both mistakes. We had counted on Crook, but Crook never came. Add all those things together."

Barrows said: "If Terry had held his command together, if Custer had waited—"

"We still would have been beaten, I think. There were too many Sioux."

"A tragedy of errors," sighed Barrows and shook his head.

Shafter looked at the major. He looked at the major's wife. What he said was for both of them. "Men do the best they can. That's all they can do. This thing was written in the book. The hand that writes in the book is one over which we have no control."

"It is as good an answer as any," said Barrows and led his wife away.

The wind blew rough and dry across the parade as the major and his wife stepped from the hospital. The major took her arm and looked at her with a consideration that was odd in him. "Turn your face from it, Margaret."

"I'm not that fragile."

"This land is hard on precious things," he said.

She gave him a startled glance. "Why, Joseph, I haven't heard you say that for so long—"

"I know," he murmured. "I know."

Shafter lay in a still and wonderful ease while his mind turned the case of Mrs. Barrows patiently over and over. She had been a woman racked with terrible emotions, with feelings so urgent that she had bared herself to him; and then in one phrase he had restored within her some faith, some flame, some spiritual loveliness more necessary to her than her loyalty to her husband. Maybe she had been lonely most of her days, the grace and romance of life slowly shriveling until Garnett had come along to see her need and to prey upon it. Perhaps she had feared or suspected it was a cheap thing with him, nothing more than a conquest in return for all her passionate giving, and so she had come to him, to Shafter, for one word which would restore her faith. Well, he had given her the thing she wanted to hear. He had supplied Garnett's memory with a dignity the man himself did not possess.

But he thought of other women Garnett had captured by his charm and it occurred to him that all of these women had seen in Garnett something which he was not. How had they seen it then? He puzzled over it until he remembered Mrs. Barrows' eyes. It was a dream they sought to make real. These women all had hungered for the music, the color and the vivid richness of living; it was a cry in them, to be important, to fill the empty tissues of existence with those full and beautiful experiences for which the human spirit was created. They had come to Garnett, crowded of heart and body, and had made their surrender in hopes of a like return. That was their fulfillment—to love and to be loved.

He remembered the stillness on Josephine's face, the stillness upon her lips; and he slept.

The hospital orderly brought him a letter the next morning. "Came last week," said the orderly. "War Department."

It was from the adjutant general. It said:—

By order of the General of the Armies, please be informed that your record has been reviewed and certain findings set aside. This is your authority to request re-instatement, as first lieutenant of cavalry, United States Army. If you wish to act upon this authority, make application through the adjutant, Seventh Cavalry, submit to physical examination and return papers to this office for approval.

Moylan, he thought, had done that. When Josephine came that afternoon he showed the letter to her and watched her eyes move back and forth over the writing. She had an intent, interested expression on her face, and her lips stirred and she looked at him with a lively expression playing behind her reserve.

"Are you going to accept it?"

"Yes."

"Many things have happened to you, Kern. Some of them have been harsh. Or were you a wild young man?"

"It was a woman with whom I was in love," he said. "Garnett was my best friend in those days."

"He took her from you, Kern?"

"Or she went to him. Who knows about those things? In any event, the world fell down. She had come down behind the lines to see me. This was in the Shenandoah Valley, in a little town. When I got away to go to the town to meet her I found Garnett with her. The hotel room," he added irrelevantly, "had rosebud wallpaper. I drew my sword on him and we fought all the way downstairs and out through the door. I slashed him and he fell. He was senior to me as an officer and naturally preferred charges. Neither of us could explain the cause of the quarrel and therefore it stood as insubordination on my part. I was dismissed from the army, enlisted under another name and served the rest of the war as a private."

She listened to him with an absorbed attention. She said swiftly: "You saw her again. You told me that once. When you saw her, Kern, did you have any great feeling about her? Did you hate her greatly, or still want her greatly?"

"I saw her in Fargo, on my last mail trip. It was all gone—everything. You can't restore faith. I was very young and love is a terrible thing when you're young."

"But not when you're a mature man, Kern?"

He shrugged his shoulders.

She said: "I can understand why you hated Garnett. You still do, don't you?"

"No," he said. "It would be difficult for me to hate any man, living or dead, who rode down that valley with me."

"But he changed your life for you."

"Maybe I did my own changing. I lay no blame on anybody for what I am."

She spoke out of a dark, cold distance. "He always walked between you and other people. Whenever he did that, you were never the same. He destroyed your faith. You have never had it since. Not in anything or anybody."

"Could I have a drink of water?"

She poured out of a jug into a glass. She started to hand it to him, then bent and slipped an arm under his head and lifted him and held it. Her hand was warm and firm on his back, her eyes intently searched him, her lips stern. He dropped back, hearing sharpness in her voice.

"You're so thin, Kern."

"I'll be standing retreat one month from now," he said. "In this regiment."

"At least," she said, as though to herself, "you have faith left in one thing, in your kind of men. That's all. For all other things, you are an empty man. Garnett and that woman killed so much in you. They left you a bare, bleached skeleton."

"Why, Josephine," he said. "He's dead and she's two thousand miles away."

"Are they?" she said and rose. She looked down at him in a way he well remembered, hating him bitterly for his lack of trust in her, injured by his unspoken judgment. It was the same look she had given him when he had faced her in the kitchen of the Benson house. "I don't think so, Kern. Whatever he touched he ruined for you. You don't forget and you don't change your mind." The anger in her was real. Her feeling in the matter was a growing storm. "Perhaps," she said, "he destroyed many things for me, too."

Mrs. Custer came to see him, and Algernon Smith's wife. They sat by him, forlorn women now, each made aimless by a Sioux bullet. Mrs. Smith took his hand and silently held it, asking for comfort rather than giving it. He listened to the pacing of the sentry on the baked earth and he heard the echoes strike hollow through the emptied garrison. He had his recollections of Hines and McDermott and of Bierss. There was a woman over at the Point of whom Bierss had often spoken; she was a woman to whom any soldier could go, but she had been fond of Bierss. He thought: "I'll go over there and tell her about Bierss." He slept soundly the night through and woke and was restless throughout the morning and spent a long afternoon. He ate supper and watched the lights go out and irritably composed himself for the night.

When Josephine came the next afternoon she gave him a keen look. "You're better," she said. "You're cranky. Now I shan't have to come as often."

"When did you first come?"

"The night the boat brought you down. It was twelve o'clock at night. Who shaved you this morning?"

"The orderly."

"He left a mustache on you. Don't grow a mustache, Kern."

He had his head on the edge of the pillow, uncomfortably turned to look at her. She watched him a moment, and bent forward to lift his head and replace the pillow. She drew back her arm, but held her position, looking straight down upon his face; feeling roughened the smoothness of her lips.

"I can't reach up," he said.

"Do you want to?"

"Yes."

"Do you always want your own way? Do you always expect people to come back after you've knocked them down?"

"When you hate a man," he said, "your eyes turn dead black."

"It isn't hate," she whispered. "But I've got too much to give you to even let myself start—if I can't be sure you have something for me."

"Remember the last time I kissed you?"

"Yes."

"Was it a very mild thing, Josephine?"

Her lips were near and all her fragrance came to him; he saw her lips move and become heavy, he watched her eyes darken. She made a little gesture and put herself on the edge of the bed and lowered her face to him, and her warmth and her weight came impulsive and fully meant against him. She drew her mouth away, whispering into his ear. "Will you keep me close, will you never tire, will you never be less than you are now?" She waited for no answer, knowing him well; and came to him again. It was like a tall fire springing up through the black sky, touching heaven; and by its light the land around lay full and mysterious and wonderful.

THE SEARCHERS

by

Alan LeMay

To my grandfather, Oliver LeMay, who died on the prairie;
and to my grandmother, Karen Jensen LeMay,
to whom he left three sons under seven.

"These people had a kind of courage that may be the finest gift of man: the courage of those who simply keep on, and on, doing the next thing, far beyond all reasonable endurance, seldom thinking of themselves as martyred, and never thinking of themselves as brave."

Like so many of the very best writers of the West, including three of the four in this volume, ALAN LEMAY came to his fictional material by choice, not by birth. He was born in 1899, in Indianapolis, Indiana, attended Stetson University in Florida in 1916, then joined the U.S. Army as an infantryman in 1918. After military service, he earned a degree at the University of Chicago and, while still in college, sold a short story to *Adventure,* one of the very best of the pulp magazines—which continued to publish his work for many years. After college, LeMay worked as a journalist before writing fiction became his career.

A frequent contributor to the magazine markets in the mid 1920s, LeMay sold his work not only to *Adventure* but to many others, including *Western Story Magazine, Dime Western, Thrilling Ranch Stories* and *Star Western.* By 1929, with a couple of novels, *Painted Ponies* among them, under his belt, he broke into *Collier's,* where his fiction was then published regularly. Writing for the pulps in addition to the slicks in order to supplement his erratic income as a California ranchowner, he adopted pseudonyms, including Whiskers Beck and the anagrammatic Alan M. Emley. LeMay was published in hardcover by Harper, Doubleday, and Farrar and Rinehart.

Unlike many of his peers LeMay enjoyed (if that is the word) a full career in Hollywood as a screenwriter, film producer, and director. Many of his novels were adapted to the screen, including *Useless Cowboy* (with Gary Cooper) and *Thunder in the Dust,* which became *The Sundowners* (for which he wrote the screenplay, produced, and directed). Just as *The Searchers* ranks among the best western novels ever written, the film, directed by John Ford and starring John Wayne, is a recognized classic of its genre. The intensity and vigor of LeMay's prose is transmuted into visual images of equal power and suspense.

LeMay was married twice, his first marriage ending in divorce in 1938, and had four children. He died in 1964, in Pacific Palisades, California.

1

Supper was over by sundown, and Henry Edwards walked out from the house for a last look around. He carried his light shotgun, in hopes the rest of the family would think he meant to pick up a sage hen or two—a highly unlikely prospect anywhere near the house. He had left his gun belt on its peg beside the door, but he had sneaked the heavy six-gun itself into his waistband inside his shirt. Martha was washing dishes in the wooden sink close by, and both their daughters—Lucy, a grown-up seventeen, and Debbie, just coming ten—were drying and putting away. He didn't want to get them all stirred up; not until he could figure out for himself what had brought on his sharpened dread of the coming night.

"Take your pistol, Henry," Martha said clearly. Her hands were busy, but her eyes were on the holster where it hung empty in plain sight, and she was laughing at him. That was the wonderful thing about Martha. At thirty-eight she looked older than she was in some ways, especially her hands. But in other ways she was a lot younger. Her sense of humor did that. She could laugh hard at things other people thought only a little bit funny, or not funny at all; so that often Henry could see the pretty sparkle of the girl he had married twenty years back.

He grunted and went out. Their two sons were on the back gallery as he came out of the kitchen. Hunter Edwards, named after Martha's family, was nineteen, and as tall as his old man. He sat on the floor, his head lolled back against the adobe, and his mind so far away that his mouth hung open. Only his eyes moved as he turned them to the shotgun. He said dutifully, "Help you, Pa?"

"Nope."

Ben, fourteen, was whittling out a butter paddle. He jumped up, brushing shavings off his blue jeans. His father made a Plains-Indian sign—a fist pulled downward from in front of his shoulder, meaning "sit-stay." Ben went back to his whittling.

"Don't you forget to sweep them shavings up," Henry said.

"I won't, Pa."

They watched their father walk off, his long, slow-looking steps quiet in his flat-heeled boots, until he circled the corrals and was out of sight.

"What's he up to?" Ben asked. "There ain't any game out there. Not short of the half mile."

Hunter hesitated. He knew the answer but, like his father, he didn't want to say anything yet. "I don't know," he said at last, letting his voice sound puzzled. Within the kitchen he heard a match strike. With so much clear light left out-side, it was hard to believe how shadowy the kitchen was getting, within its thick walls. But he knew his mother was lighting a lamp. He called softly, "Ma . . . Not right now."

His mother came to the door and looked at him oddly, the blown-out match smoking in her hand. He met her eyes for a moment, but looked away again without explaining. Martha Edwards went back into the kitchen, moving thoughtfully; and no light came on. Hunter saw that his father was in sight again, very far away for the short time he had been gone. He was walking toward the top of a gentle hill northwest of the ranch buildings. Hunter watched him steadily as long as he was in sight. Henry never did go clear to the top. Instead he climbed just high enough to see over, then circled the contour to look all ways, so that he showed himself against the sky no more than he had to. He was at it a long time.

Ben was staring at Hunter. "Hey. I want to know what—"

"Shut up, will you?"

Ben looked astonished, and obeyed.

From just behind the crest of the little hill, Henry Edwards could see about a dozen miles, most ways. The evening light was uncommonly clear, better to see by than the full glare of the sun. But the faint roll of the prairie was deceptive. A whole squadron of cavalry could probably hide itself at a thousand yards, in a place that looked as flat as a parade ground. So he was looking for little things— a layer of floating dust in the branches of the mesquite, a wild cow or an antelope disturbed. He didn't see anything that meant much. Not for a long time.

He looked back at his house. He had other things, the stuff he worked with —barn, corrals, stacks of wild hay, a shacky bunkhouse for sleeping extra hands. But it was the house he was proud of. Its adobe walls were three and four feet thick, so strong that the first room they had built had for a long time been called the Edwards Fort. They had added on to it since, and made it even more secure. The shake roof looked burnable, but it wasn't, for the shakes were laid upon two feet of sod. The outside doors were massive, and the windows had heavy battle shutters swung inside.

And the house had luxuries. Wooden floors. Galleries—some called them porches, now—both front and back. Eight windows with glass. He had made his family fairly comfortable here, at long last, working patiently with his hands through the years when there was no money, and no market for cows, and nothing to do about it but work and wait.

He could hardly believe there had been eighteen years of that kind of hang-ing on. But they had come out here that long ago—the same year Hunter had been born—drawn by these miles and miles of good grass, free to anyone who dared expose himself to the Kiowas and Comanches. It hadn't looked so dan-gerous when they first came, for the Texas Rangers had just pushed the Wild Tribes back out of the way. But right after that the Rangers were virtually disbanded, on the thrifty theory that the Federal Government was about to take over the defense. The Federal troops did not come. Henry and Martha held on and prayed. One year more, they told each other again and again . . . just another month . . . only until spring. . . . So the risky years slid by, while no military help appeared. Their nearest neighbors, the Pauleys, were murdered off by a Comanche raid, without survivors except a little boy less than two years old; and they heard of many, many more.

Six years of that. Then, in 1857, Texas gave up waiting, and the Rangers bloomed again. A tough line of forts sprang up—McKavitt, Phantom Hill, Bell's Stockade. The little strongholds were far strung out, all the way from the Salt Fork to the Rio Grande, but they gave reassurance nonetheless. The dark years of danger were over; they had lasted out, won through to years of peace and plenty in which to grow old—or so they thought for a little while. Then the War Between the States drained the fighting men away, and the Kiowas and Comanches rose up singing once more, to take their harvest.

Whole counties were scoured out and set back to wilderness in those war years. But the Edwardses stayed, and the Mathisons, and a few more far-spread, dug-in families, holding the back door of Texas, driving great herds of longhorns to Matagorda for the supply of the Confederate troops. And they waited again, holding on just one year more, then another, and one more yet.

Henry would have given up. He saw no hope that he would ever get a foothold out here again, once he drew out, but he would gladly have sacrificed their hopes of a cattle empire to take Martha and their children to a safer place. It was Martha who would not quit, and she had a will that could jump and blaze like a grass fire. How do you take a woman back to the poverty of the cotton rows against her will? They stayed.

The war's end brought the turn of fortune in which they had placed their faith. Hiring cowboys on promise, borrowing to provision them, Henry got a few hundred head into the very first drive to end-of-track at Abilene. Now, with the war four years past, two more drives had paid off. And this year he and Aaron Mathison, pooling together, had sent north more than three thousand head. But where were the troops that peace should have released to their defense? Bolder, wilder, stronger every year, the Comanches and their Kiowa allies punished the range. Counties that had survived the war were barren now; the Comanches had struck the outskirts of San Antonio itself.

Once they could have quit and found safety in a milder land. They couldn't quit now, with fortune beyond belief coming into their hands. They were as good as rich—and living in the deadliest danger that had overhung them yet. Looking back over the years, Henry did not know how they had survived so long; their strong house and everlasting watchfulness could not explain it. It must have taken miracles of luck, Henry knew, and some mysterious quirks of Indian medicine as well, to preserve them here. If he could have seen, in any moment of the years they had lived here, the endless hazards that lay ahead, he would have quit that same minute and got Martha out of there if he had had to tie her.

But you get used to unresting vigilance, and a perpetual danger becomes part of the everyday things around you. After a long time you probably wouldn't know how to digest right, any more, if it altogether went away. All that was behind could not explain, exactly, the way Henry felt tonight. He didn't believe in hunches, either, or any kind of spirit warnings. He was sure he had heard, or seen, or maybe even smelled some sign so small he couldn't remember it. Sometimes a man's senses picked up dim warnings he didn't even recognize. Like sometimes he had known an Indian was around, without knowing what told him, until a little later the breeze would bring the smell of the Indian a little stronger—a kind of old-buffalo-robe smell—which of course had been the warning before he knew he smelled anything. Or sometimes he knew horses were coming before he could hear their hoofs; he supposed this came by a tremor of the ground so weak you didn't know you felt it, but only knew what it meant.

He became aware that he was biting his mustache. It was a thin blond mustache, trailing downward at the corners of his mouth, so that it gave his face a dour look it didn't have underneath. But it wasn't a chewed mustache, because he didn't chew it. Patiently he studied the long sweep of the prairie, looking steadily at each quadrant for many minutes. He was sorry now that he had let Amos go last night to help the Mathisons chase cow thieves; Amos was Henry's brother and a rock of strength. It should have been enough that he let Martin Pauley go along. Mart was the little boy they had found in the brush, after the Pauley massacre, and raised as their own. He was eighteen now, and given up to be the best shot in the family. The Mathisons hadn't been satisfied anyway. Thought he should send Hunter, too, or else come himself. You can't ever please everybody.

A quarter mile off a bedded-down meadow lark sprang into the air, circled uncertainly, then drifted away. Henry became motionless, except for his eyes, which moved continually, casting the plain. Five hundred yards to the right of the spot where the meadow lark had jumped, a covey of quail went up.

Henry turned and ran for the house.

2

Martin Pauley had found this day a strange one almost from the start. Twelve riders had gathered to trail some cow thieves who had bit into the Mathisons'; and the queer thing about it was that five out of the twelve soon disagreed with all the others as to what they were following.

Aaron Mathison, who owned the run-off cattle, was a bearded, calm-eyed man of Quaker extraction. He had not been able to hold onto the part of his father's faith which forswore the bearing of arms, but he still prayed, and read the Bible every day. Everything about the Mathison place was either scrubbed, or raked, or whitewashed, but the house was cramped and sparsely furnished compared to the Edwards'. All the money Aaron could scrape went into the quality of his livestock. Lately he had got his Lazy Lightning brand on ten head of blood bulls brought on from Kansas City. These had been held, by the chase-'em-back method, with a small herd on the Salt Crick Flats. This was the herd that was gone.

They picked up the churned trail of the stolen herd shortly after dawn, and followed it briskly, paced by the light-riding Mathison boys on their good horses. Martin Pauley lagged back, dogging it in the early hours. He had a special grouch of his own because he had looked forward to a visit with Laurie Mathison before they set out. Laurie was eighteen, like himself—straight and well boned, he thought, in terms he might have used to judge a filly. Lately he had caught her unwary gray eyes following him, now and then, when he was around the Mathisons'. But not this morning.

Laurie had been flying around, passing out coffee and quick-grab breakfast, with two of the Harper boys and Charlie MacCorry helping her on three sides —all of them clowning, and cutting up, and showing off, till there was no way to get near. Martin Pauley was a quiet boy, dark as an Indian except for his light eyes; he never did feel he cut much of a figure among the blond and easy-laughing people with whom he was raised. So he had hung back, and never did get to talk to Laurie. She ran out to his stirrup, and said, "Hi," hardly looking at him as she handed him a hunk of hot meat wrapped in bread—no coffee—and was gone again. And that was the size of it.

For a while Martin kept trying to think of something cute he might have said. Didn't think of a thing. So he got bored with himself, and took a wide unneedful swing out on the flank. He was casting the prairie restlessly, looking for nothing in particular, when presently he found something that puzzled him and made him uneasy.

Mystified, he crossed the trail and swung wide on the other flank to take a look at the ground over there; and here he found Amos, doing the same thing. Amos Edwards was forty, two years older than his brother Henry, a big burly figure on a strong but speedless horse. He was some different from the rest of the Edwards family. His heavy head of hair was darker, and probably would have been red-brown, except that it was unbrushed, without any shine to it. And he was liable to be pulled back into his shell between rare bursts of temper. Just now he was riding lumpily, hands in his pockets, reins swinging free from the horn, while he guided his horse by unnoticeable flankings with the calves of his legs and two-ounce shifts of weight. Martin cleared his throat a few times, hoping Amos would speak, but he did not.

"Uncle Amos," Martin said, "you notice something almighty fishy about this trail?"

"Like what?"

"Well, at the jump-off I counted tracks of twelve, fifteen ponies working this herd. Now I can't find no more than four, five. First I supposed the rest had pushed on ahead, and their trails got tromp out by cows—"

"That's shrewd," Amos snubbed him. "I never would have thunk of it."

"—only, just now I find me a fit-up where two more ponies forked off—and they sure didn't push on ahead. They turned back."

"Why?"

"Why? Gosh, Uncle Amos—how the hell should I know? That's what itches me."

"Do me one thing," Amos said. "Drop this 'Uncle' foolishness."

"Sir?"

"You don't have to call me 'Sir,' neither. Nor 'Grampaw,' neither. Nor 'Methuselah,' neither. I can whup you to a frazzle."

Martin was blanked. "What should I call you?"

"Name's Amos."

"All right. Amos. You want I should mosey round and see what the rest of 'em think?"

"They'll tell you the same." He was pulled back in his shell, fixing to bide his time.

It was straight-up noon, and they had paused to water at a puddle in a coulee, before Amos made his opinion known. "Aaron," he said in tones most could hear, "I'd be relieved to know if all these boys realize what we're following here. Because it ain't cow thieves. Not the species we had in mind."

"How's this, now?"

"What we got here is a split-off from an Indian war party, running wild loose on a raid." He paused a moment, then finished quietly. "Maybe you knowed that already. In case you didn't, you know it now. Because I just told you."

Aaron Mathison rubbed his fingers through his beard and appeared to consider; and some of the others put in while he did that. Old Mose Harper pointed out that none of the thieves had ridden side by side, not once on the trail, as the tracks showed plain. Indians and dudes rode single file—Indians to hide their numbers, and dudes because the horses felt like it—but white men rode abreast in order to gab all the time. So the thieves were either Indians or else not speaking. One t'other. This contribution drew partly hidden smiles from Mose Harper's sons.

Young Charlie MacCorry, a good rough-stock rider whom Martin resented because of his lively attentions to Laurie Mathison, spoke of noticing that the thieves all rode small unshod horses, a whole lot like buffalo ponies. And Lije Powers got in his two cents. Lije was an old-time buffalo hunter, who now lived by wandering from ranch to ranch, "stopping by." He said now that he had "knowed it from the fust," and allowed that what they were up against was a "passel of Caddoes."

Those were all who took any stock in the theory.

Aaron Mathison reasoned in even tones that they had no real reason to think any different than when they had started. The northeasterly trend of the trail said plainly that the thieves were delivering the herd to some beef contractor for one of the Indian Agencies—maybe old Fort Towson. Nothing else made any sense. The thieves had very little start; steady riding should force a stand before sundown tomorrow. They had only to push on, and all questions would soon be answered.

"I hollered for a back track at the start," Amos argued. "Where's the main war party these here forked off from? If they're up ahead, that's one thing. But if they're back where our families be—"

Aaron bowed his head for several moments, as if in prayer; but when his head came up he was looking at Amos Edwards with narrowed eyes. He spoke gently, slipping into Quakerish phrasings; and Martin Pauley, who had heard those same soft tones before, knew the argument was done. "Thee can turn back," Aaron said. "If thee fears what lies ahead or what lies behind, I need thee no more."

He turned his horse and rode on. Two or three hesitated, but ended by following him.

Amos was riding with his hands in his pockets again, letting his animal keep up as it chose; and Martin saw that Amos had fallen into one of his deadlocks. This was a thing that happened to Amos repeatedly, and it seemed to have a close relationship with the shape of his life. He had served two years with the Rangers, and four under Hood, and had twice been up the Chisholm Trail. Earlier he had done other things—bossed a bull train, packed the mail, captained a stage station—and he had done all of them well. Nobody exactly understood why he always drifted back, sooner or later, to work for his younger brother, with never any understanding as to pay.

What he wanted now was to pull out of the pursuit and go back. If he did turn, it could hardly be set down to cowardice. But it would mark him as unreliable and self-interested to an unforgivable degree in the eyes of the other cowmen. A thing like that could reflect on his whole family, and tend to turn the range against them. So Amos sat like a sack of wheat, in motion only because he happened to be sitting on a horse, and the horse was following the others.

His dilemma ended unexpectedly.

Brad Mathison, oldest of Aaron's boys, was ranging far ahead. They saw him disappear over the saddle of a ridge at more than two miles. Immediately he reappeared, stopped against the sky, and held his rifle over his head with both hands. It was the signal for "found." Then he dropped from sight beyond the ridge again.

Far behind him, the others put the squeeze to their horses, and lifted into a hard run. They stormed over the saddle of the ridge, and were looking down into a broad basin. Some scattered bunches of red specks down there were cattle grazing loose on their own. Aaron Mathison, with his cowman's eyes, recognized each speck that could be seen at all as an individual animal of his own. Here was the stolen herd, unaccountably dropped and left.

Brad was only about a mile out on the flats, but running his horse full stretch now toward the hills beyond the plain.

"Call in that damn fool," Amos said. He fired his pistol into the air, so that Brad looked back.

Aaron spun his horse in close circles to call in his son. Brad turned reluctantly, as if disposed to argue with his father, but came trotting back. Now Aaron spotted something fifty yards to one side, and rode to it for a closer look. He stepped down, and the others closed in around him. One of the young blood bulls lay there, spine severed by the whack of an axe. The liver had been ripped out, but no other meat taken. When they had seen this much, most of the riders sat and looked at each other. They barely glanced at the moccasin prints, faint in the dustfilm upon the baked ground. Amos, though, not only dismounted, but went to his knees; and Martin Pauley stooped beside him, not to look wise, but trying to find out what Amos was looking for. Amos jabbed the carcass with his thumb. "Only nine, ten hours old," he said. Then, to Lije Powers, "Can you tell what moccasins them be?"

Lije scratched his thin beard. "Injuns," he said owlishly. He meant it for a joke, but nobody laughed. They followed Mathison as he loped out to meet his son.

"I rode past five more beef kills," Brad said when they came together. He spoke soberly, his eyes alert upon his father's face. "All these down here are heifers. And all killed with the lance. Appears like the lance wounds drive deep forward from just under the short ribs, clean through to the heart. I never saw that before."

"I have," Lije Powers said. He wanted to square himself for his misfire joke. "Them's Comanche buffler hunters done that. Ain't no others left can handle a lance no more."

Some of the others, particularly the older men, were looking gray and bleak. The last five minutes had taken them ten years back into the past, when every night of the world was an uncertain thing. The years of watchfulness and struggle had brought them some sense of confidence and security toward the last; but now all that was struck away as if they had their whole lives to do over again. But instead of taking ten years off their ages it put ten years on.

"This here's a murder raid," Amos said, sending his words at Aaron like rocks. "It shapes up to scald out either your place or Henry's. Do you know that now?"

Aaron's beard was sunk on his chest. He said slowly, "I see no other likelihood."

"They drove your cattle to pull us out," Amos hammered it home. "We've give 'em free run for the last sixteen hours!"

"I question if they'll hit before moonrise. Not them Commanch." Lije spoke with the strange detachment of one who has seen too much for too long.

"Moonrise! Ain't a horse here can make it by midnight!"

Brad Mathison said through his teeth, "I'll come almighty close!" He wheeled his pony and put it into a lope.

Aaron bellowed, "Hold in that horse!" and Brad pulled down to a slamming trot.

Most of the others were turning to follow Brad, talking blasphemies to their horses and themselves. Charlie MacCorry had the presence of mind to yell, "Which place first? We'll be strung out twenty mile!"

"Mathison's is this side!" Mose Harper shouted. Then to Amos over his shoulder, "If we don't fight there, we'll come straight on!"

Martin Pauley was scared sick over what they might find back home, and Laurie was in his mind too, so that the people he cared about were in two places. He was crazy to get started, as if haste could get him to both places at once. But he made himself imitate Amos, who unhurriedly pulled off saddle

and bridle. They fed grain again, judging carefully how much their animals would do best on, and throwing the rest away. The time taken to rest and feed would get them home quicker in the end.

By the time they crossed the saddleback the rest of the riders were far spaced, according to the judgment of each as to how his horse might best be spent. Amos branched off from the way the others took. Miles were important, now, and they could save a few by passing well west of Mathison's. Amos had already made up his mind that he must kill his horse in this ride; for they had more than eighty miles to go before they would know what had happened— perhaps was happening now—to the people they had left at home.

3

Henry Edwards stood watching the black prairie through a loophole in a batten shutter. The quartering moon would rise late; he wanted to see it coming, for he believed now that all the trouble they could handle would be on them with the moon's first light. The dark kitchen in which the family waited was closed tight except for the loopholes. The powder smoke was going to get pretty thick in here if they had to fight. Yet the house was becoming cold. Any gleam of light would so hurt their chances that they had even drawn the coals from the firebox of the stove and drowned them in a tub.

The house itself was about as secure as a house could be made. The loopholed shutters, strap-hinged on the inside, were heavy enough to stop a 30–30, if not a buffalo slug, and the doors were even better. Nine or ten rifles could hold the place forever against anything but artillery. As few as seven would have their hands full against a strong war party, but should hold.

There lay the trouble and the fear. Henry did not have seven. He had himself, and his two sons, and Martha. Hunter was a deadly shot, and Ben, though only fourteen, would put in a pretty fair job. But Martha couldn't shoot any too well. Most likely she would hold fire until the last scratch, in hopes the enemy would go away. And Lucy . . . Lucy might do for a lookout someplace, but her dread of guns was so great she would be useless even to load. Henry had made her strap on a pistol, but he doubted if she could ever fire it, even to take her own life in event of capture.

And then there was Deborah. The boys had been good shots at eight; but Debbie, though pushing ten, seemed so little to Henry that he hadn't let her touch a weapon yet. You don't see your own children grow unless there's a new one to remind you how tiny they come. In Henry's eyes, Debbie hadn't changed in size since she was brand new, with feet no bigger than a fingertip with toes.

Four rifles, then, or call it three and a half, to hold two doors and eight shuttered windows, all of which could be busted in.

Out in the work-team corral a brood mare gave a long whinny, then another after a moment's pause. Everyone in the kitchen held his breath, waiting for the mare's call to be answered. No answer came, and after a while, when she whinnied again, Henry drew a slow breath. The mare had told him a whole basket of things he didn't want to know. Strange ponies were out there, probably with stud horses among them; the mare's nose had told her, and the insistence of her reaction left no room for doubt. They were Indian ridden, because loose ponies would have answered, and horses ridden by friends would have been let to answer. The Indians were Comanches, for the Comanches were skillful at keeping their ponies quiet. They wove egg-size knots into their rawhide hackamores, so placed that the pony's nostrils could be pinched if he so much as pricked an ear. This was best done from the ground, so Henry judged that the Comanches had dismounted, leaving their ponies with horse holders. They were fixing to close on foot—the most dangerous way there was.

One thing more. They were coming from more than one side, because none would have approached downwind, where the mare could catch their scent, unless they were all around. A big party, then, or it would not have split up. No more hope, either, that the Comanches meant only to break fence on the far side of the corrals to run the stock off. This was a full-scale thing, with all the chips down, tonight.

Lucy's voice came softly out of the dark. "Debbie?" Then more loudly, with a note of panic, "Debbie! Where are you?" Everyone's voice sounded eery coming out of the unseen.

"Here I am." They heard the cover put back on the cookie crock at the far end of the room.

"You get back on your pallet, here! And stay put now, will you?"

Long ago, hide-hunting at the age of eighteen, Henry and two others had fought off more than twenty Kiowas from the shelter of nothing more than a buffalo wallow. They had fought with desperation enough, believing they were done for; but he couldn't remember any such sinking of the heart as he felt now behind these fort-strong walls. Little girls in the house—that's what cut a man's strings, and made a coward of him, every bit as bad as if the Comanches held them hostage already. His words were steady, though, even casual, as he made his irrevocable decision.

"Martha. Put on Debbie's coat."

A moment of silence; then Martha's single word, breathy and uncertain: "Now?"

"Right now. Moon's fixing to light us up directly." Henry went into a front bedroom, and quietly opened a shutter. The sash was already up to cut down the hazard of splintering glass. He studied the night, then went and found Martha and Debbie in the dark. The child was wearing moccasins, and hugged a piece of buffalo robe.

"We're going to play the sleep-out game," he told Debbie. "The one where you hide out with Grandma. Like you know? Very quiet, like a mouse?" He was sending the little girl to her grandmother's grave.

"I know." Debbie was a shy child, but curiously unafraid of the open prairie or the dark. She had never known her grandmother, or seen death, but she had been raised to think the grave on the hill a friendly thing. Sometimes she left little picnic offerings up there for Grandma.

"You keep down low," Henry said, "and you go quietly, quietly along the ditch. Then up the hill to Grandma, and roll up in your robe, all snug and cozy."

"I remember how." They had practiced this before, and even used it once, under a threat that blew over.

Henry couldn't tell from the child's whisper whether she was frightened or not. He supposed she must be, what with the tension that was on all of them. He picked her up in his arms and carried her to the window he had opened. Though he couldn't see her, it was the same as if he could. She had a little triangular kitty-cat face, with very big green eyes, which you could see would be slanting someday, if her face ever caught up to them. As he kissed her, he found tears on her cheek, and she hugged him around the neck so hard he feared he would have to pull her arms away. But she let go, and he lifted her through the window.

"Quiet, now—stoop low—" he whispered in her ear. And he set her on the ground outside.

4

Amos pulled up at the top of a long rise ten miles from home; and here Martin Pauley, with very little horse left under him, presently caught up. On the south horizon a spot of fire was beginning to show. The glow bloomed and brightened; their big stacks of wild hay had caught and were going up in light. The east rim still showed nothing. The raiders had made their choice and left Mathison's alone.

For a moment or two Martin Pauley and Amos Edwards sat in silence. Then Amos drew his knife and cut off the quirt, called a romal, that was braided into his long reins. He hauled up his animal's heavy head; the quirt whistled and snapped hard, and the horse labored into a heavy, rocking run.

Martin stepped down, shaking so hard all over that he almost went to his knees. He reset his saddle, and as he mounted again his beat-out pony staggered, almost pulled over by the rider's weight. Amos was out of sight. Mart got his pony into an uncertain gallop, guiding the placement of its awkwardly slung hoofs by the light of the high moon. It was blowing in a wind-broke roar, and when a patch of foam caught Martin in the teeth he tasted blood in it. Yet the horse came nearer to getting home than Martin could have hoped. Half a mile from the house the animal stumbled in a shallow wash and came down heavily. Twice the long head swung up in an effort to rise, but flailed down again. Martin drew his six-gun and put a bullet in the pony's head, then dragged his carbine from the saddle boot and went on, running hard.

The hay fires and the wooden barn had died down to bright beds of coals, but the house still stood. Its shingles glowed in a dozen smoldering patches where torches had been thrown onto the roof, but the sod beneath them had held. For a moment a great impossible hope possessed Martin, intense as a physical pain. Then, while he was still far out, he saw a light come on in the kitchen as a lamp was lighted inside. Even at the distance he could see that the light came through a broken door, hanging skew-jawed on a single hinge.

Martin slowed to a walk, and went toward the house unwillingly. Little flames still wandered across the embers of the hay stacks and the barn, sending up sparks which hung idly on the quiet air; and the house itself showed against the night in a dull red glow. On the back gallery lay a dead pony, tail to the broken door. Probably it had been backed against the door to break the bar. By the steps Amos' horse was down, knees folded under. The heavy head was nodded lower and lower, the muzzle dipping the dust; it would never get up.

Martin stepped over the legs of the dead Comanche pony and went into the kitchen, walking as though he had never learned to walk, but had to pull each separate string. Near the door a body lay covered by a sheet. Martin drew back the limp muslin, and was looking into Martha's face. Her lips were parted a little, and her open eyes, looking straight up, appeared perfectly clear, as if she were alive. Her light hair was shaken loose, the lamplight picking out the silver in it. Martha had such a lot of hair that it was hardly noticeable, at first, that she had been scalped.

Most of the batten shutters had been smashed in. Hunter Edwards lay in a heap near the splintered hall door, his empty hands still clawed as if grasping the duck gun that was gone. Ben had fallen in a tangled knot by the far window, his gangly legs sprawled. He looked immature and undersized as he lay there, like a skinny small boy.

Martin found the body of Henry Edwards draped on its back across the broad sill of a bedroom window. The Comanche knives had done eery work upon this body. Like Martha, Henry and both boys had been scalped. Martin gently straightened the bodies of Henry, and Hunter, and Ben, then found sheets to put over them, as Amos had done for Martha. Martin's hands were shaking, but he was dry-eyed as Amos came back into the house.

When Martin had got a good look at his foster uncle, he was afraid of him. Amos' face was wooden, but such a dreadful light shone from behind the eyes that Martin thought Amos had gone mad. Amos carried something slim and limp in his arms, clutched against his chest. As Amos passed the lamp, Martin saw that the thing Amos carried had a hand, and that it was Martha's hand. He had not drawn down the sheet that covered Martha far enough to see that the body lacked an arm. The Comanches did things like that. Probably they had tossed the arm from one to another, capering and whooping, until they lost it in the dark.

"No sign of Lucy. Or Deborah," Amos said. "So far as I could find in the lack of light." The words were low and came unevenly, but they did not sound insane.

Martin said, "We used to practice sending Debbie up the hill to Grandma's grave—"

"I been up. They sent her there. I found her bit of buffalo robe. But Debbie's not up there. Not now."

"You suppose Lucy—" Martin let the question trail off, but they had worked so much together that Amos was able to answer.

"Can't tell yet if Lucy went up with Debbie to the grave. Not till daylight comes on."

Amos had got out another sheet and was tearing it into strips. Martin knew Amos was making bandages to fix up their people as decently as he could. His hands moved methodically, going through the motions of doing the next thing he ought to do, little as it mattered. But at the same time Amos was thinking about something else. "I want you to walk to the Mathisons'. Get them to hook their buckboard, and bring their women on. . . . Martha should have clean clothes put on."

Probably Amos would have stripped and bathed the body of his brother's wife, and dressed it properly, if there had been no one else to do it. But not if a walk of fifteen miles would get it done a more proper way. Martin turned toward the door without question.

"Wait. Pull off them boots and get your moccasins on. You got a long way to go." Martin obeyed that, too. "Where's them pegs you whittled out? I figure to make coffins out of the shelves."

"Behind the woodbox. Back of the range." Martin started off into the night.

Martin Pauley was eight miles on the way to Mathisons' when the first riders met him. All ten who had ridden the day before were on their way over, riding fresh Mathison horses and leading spares. A buckboard, some distance back, was bringing Mrs. Mathison and Laurie, who must no longer be left alone with a war party on the loose.

The fore riders had been pressing hard, hoping against hope that someone was left alive over there. When they had got the word from Martin, they pulled up and waited with him for the buckboard. Nobody pestered at him for details. Laurie made a place for him beside her on the buckboard seat, and they rode in silence, the team at a good trot.

After a mile or two Laurie whimpered, "Oh, Martie . . . Oh, Martie . . ." She turned toward him, rested her forehead against the shoulder of his brush jacket, and there cried quietly for a little while. Martin sat slack and still, nothing left in him to move him either toward her or away from her. Pretty soon she straightened up, and rode beside him in silence, not touching him any more.

5

Dawn was near when they got to the house. Amos had been hard at work. He had laid out his brother Henry and the two boys in one bedroom, and put their best clothes on them. He had put Martha in another room, and Mrs. Mathison and Laurie took over there. All the men went to work, silently, without having to be told what to do. These were lonely, self-sufficient people, who saw each other only a few times a year, yet they worked together well, each finding for himself the next thing that needed to be done. Some got to work with saw, boxplane, auger, and pegs, to finish the coffins Amos had started, while others made coffee, set up a heavy breakfast, and packed rations for the pursuit. They picked up and sorted out the litter of stuff the Indians had thrown about as they looted, put everything where it had belonged, as nearly as they could guess, scrubbed and sanded away the stains, just as if the life of this house were going to go on.

Two things they found in the litter had a special meaning for Martin Pauley. One was a sheet of paper upon which Debbie had tried to make a calendar a few weeks before. Something about it troubled him, and he couldn't make out what it was. He remembered wishing they had a calendar, and very dimly he recalled Debbie bringing this effort to him. But his mind had been upon something else. He believed he had said, "That's nice," and, "I see," without really seeing what the little girl was showing him. Debbie's calendar had not been hung up; he couldn't remember seeing it again until now. And now he saw why. She had made a mistake, right up at the top, so the whole thing had come out wrong. He turned vaguely to Laurie Mathison, where she was washing her hands at the sink.

"I . . ." he said. "It seems like . . ."

She glanced at the penciled calendar. "I remember that. I was over here that day. But it's all right. I explained to her."

"Explained what? What's all right?"

"She made a mistake up here, so it all—"

"Yes, I see that, but—"

"Well, when she saw she had spoiled it, she ran to you. . . ." Her gray eyes looked straight into his. "You and I had a fight that day. Maybe it was that. But —you were always Debbie's hero, Martie. She was—she's still just a baby, you know. She kept saying—" Laurie compressed her lips.

"She kept saying what?"

"Martie, I made her see that—"

He took Laurie by the arms hard. "Tell me."

316

"All right. I'll tell you. She kept saying, 'He didn't care at all.' "

Martin let his hands drop. "I wasn't listening," he said. "I made her cry, and I never knew."

He let her take the unlucky sheet of paper out of his hand, and he never saw it again. But the lost day when he should have taken Debbie in his arms, and made everything all right, was going to be with him a long time, a peg upon which he hung his grief.

The other thing he found was a miniature of Debbie. Miniatures had been painted of Martha and Lucy, too, once when Henry took the three of them to Fort Worth, but Martin never knew what became of those. Debbie's miniature, gold-framed in a little plush box, was the best of the three. The little triangular face and the green eyes were very true, and suggested the elfin look that went with Debbie's small size. He put the box in his pocket.

6

They laid their people deep under the prairie sod beside Grandma. Aaron Mathison read from the Bible and said a prayer, while Martin, Amos, and the six others chosen for the pursuit stood a little way back from the open graves, holding their saddled horses.

It wasn't a long service. Daylight had told them that Lucy must have been carried bodily from the house, for they found no place where she had set foot to the ground. Debbie, the sign showed, had been picked up onto a running horse after a pitifully short chase upon the prairie. There was hope, then, that they still lived, and that one of them, or even both, might be recovered alive. Most of Aaron's amazing vitality seemed to have drained out of him, but he shared the cracking strain that would be upon them all so long as the least hope lasted. He made the ritual as simple and as brief as he decently could. "Man that is born of woman. . . ."

Those waiting to ride feared that Aaron would get carried away in the final prayer, but he did not. Martin's mind was already far ahead on the trail, so that he heard only the last few words of the prayer, yet they stirred his hair. "Now may the light of Thy countenance be turned away from the stubborn and the blind. Let darkness fall upon them that will not see, that all Thy glory may light the way of those who seek . . . and all Thy wisdom lead the horses of the brave. . . . Amen."

It seemed to Martin Pauley that old Aaron, by the humility of his prayer, had invited eternal damnation upon himself, if only the search for Lucy and Debbie might succeed. His offer of retribution to his God was the only word that had

been spoken in accusation or in blame, for the error of judgment that had led the fighting men away.

Amos must have had his foot in the stirrup before the end of the prayer, for he swung into the saddle with the last "Amen," and led off without a word. With Martin and Amos went Brad Mathison, Ed Newby, Charlie MacCorry, Mose Harper and his son Zack, and Lije Powers, who thought his old-time prairie wisdom had now come into its own, whether anybody else thought so or not. Those left behind would put layers of boulders in the graves against digging varmints, and set up the wooden crosses Martin Pauley had sectioned out of the house timbers in the last hours of the dark.

At the last moment Laurie Mathison ran to Martin where he sat already mounted. She stepped up lightly upon the toe of his stirruped boot, and kissed him hard and quickly on the mouth. A boldness like that would have drawn a blast of wrath at another time, but her parents seemed unable to see. Aaron still stood with bowed head beside the open graves; and Mrs. Mathison's eyes were staring straight ahead into a dreadful loneliness. The Edwardses, Mathisons, and Pauleys had come out here together. The three families had sustained each other while the Pauleys lived, and after their massacre the two remaining families had looked to each other in all things. Now only the Mathisons were left. Mrs. Mathison's usually mild and kindly face was bleak, stony with an insupportable fear. Martin Pauley would not have recognized her, even if he had been in a mood to notice anything at all.

He looked startled as Laurie kissed him, but only for a second. He seemed already to have forgotten her, for the time being, as he turned his horse.

7

Out in the middle of a vast, flat plain, a day's ride from anything, lay a little bad-smelling marsh without a name. It covered about ten acres and had cat-tails growing in it. Tules, the Mexicans called the cat-tails; but at that time certain Texans were still fighting shy of Mexican ways. Nowhere around was there a river, or a butte, or any landmark at all, except that nameless marsh. So that was how the "Fight at the Cat-tails" got its foolish-sounding name.

Seven men were still with the pursuit as they approached the Cat-tail fight at sundown of their fifth day. Lije Powers had dropped out on the occasion of his thirty-ninth or fortieth argument over interpretation of sign. He had found a headdress, a rather beautiful thing of polished heifer horns on a browband of black and white beads. They were happy to see it, for it told them that some Indian who still rode was wounded and in bad shape, or he would never have left it behind. But Lije chose to make an issue of his opinion that the headdress was Kiowa, and not Comanche—which made no difference at all, for the two tribes were allied. When they got tired of hearing Lije talk about it, they told him so, and Lije branched off in a huff to visit some Mexican hacienda he knew about somewhere to the south.

They had found many other signs of the punishment the Comanches had taken before the destruction of the Edwards family was complete. More important than other dropped belongings—a beaded pouch, a polished ironwood lance with withered scalps on it—were the shallow stone-piled Indian graves. On each lay the carcass of a horse of the Edwards' brand, killed in the belief that its spirit would carry the Comanche ghost. They had found seven of these burials. Four in one place, hidden behind a hill, were probably the graves of Indians killed outright at the ranch; three more, strung out at intervals of half a day, told of wounded who had died in the retreat. In war, no Indian band slacked its pace for the dying. Squaws were known to have given birth on the backs of traveling ponies, with no one to wait for them or give help. The cowmen could not hope that the wounded warriors would slow the flight of the murderers in the slightest.

Amos kept the beaded pouch and the heifer-born headdress in his saddle-bags; they might help identify the Comanche killers someday. And for several days he carried the ironwood lance stripped of its trophies. He was using it to probe the depth of the Indian graves, to see if any were shallow enough so that he could open them without falling too far back. Probably he hoped to find something that would give some dead warrior a name, so that someday they might be led to the living by the unwilling dead. Or so Martin supposed at first.

But he could not help seeing that Amos was changing. Or perhaps he was seeing revealed, a little at a time, a change that had come over Amos suddenly upon the night of the disaster. At the start Amos had led them at a horse-killing pace, a full twenty hours of their first twenty-four. That was because of Lucy, of course. Often Comanches cared for and raised captive white children, marrying the girls when they were grown, and taking the boys into their families as brothers. But grown white women were raped unceasingly by every captor in turn until either they died or were "thrown away" to die by the satiated. So the pursuers spent themselves and their horseflesh unsparingly in that first run; yet found no sign, as their ponies failed, that they had gained ground upon the fast-traveling Comanches. After that Amos set the pace cagily at a walk until the horses recovered from that first all-out effort, later at a trot, hour after hour, saving the horses at the expense of the men. Amos rode relaxed now, wasting no motions and no steps. He had the look of a man resigned to follow this trail down the years, as long as he should live.

And then Amos found the body of an Indian not buried in the ground, but protected by stones in a crevice of a sandstone ledge. He got at this one—and took nothing but the scalp. Martin had no idea what Amos believed about life and death; but the Comanches believed that the spirit of a scalped warrior had to wander forever between the winds, denied entrance to the spirit land beyond the sunset. Amos did not keep the scalp, but threw it away on the prairie for the wolves to find.

Another who was showing change was Brad Mathison. He was always the one ranging farthest ahead, the first to start out each morning, the most reluctant to call it a day as the sun went down. His well-grained horses—they had brought four spares and two pack mules—showed it less than Brad himself, who was turning hollow-eyed and losing weight. During the past year Brad had taken to coming over to the Edwardses to set up with Lucy—but only about once every month or two. Martin didn't believe there had been any overpowering attachment there. But now that Lucy was lost, Brad was becoming more involved with every day that diminished hope.

By the third day some of them must have believed Lucy to be dead; but Brad could not let himself think that. "She's alive," he told Martin Pauley. Martin had said nothing either way. "She's got to be alive, Mart." And on the fourth day, dropping back to ride beside Mart, "I'll make it up to her," he promised himself. "No matter what's happened to her, no matter what she's gone through. I'll make her forget." He pushed his horse forward again, far into the lead, disregarding Amos' cussing.

So it was Brad, again, who first sighted the Comanches. Far out in front he brought his horse to the edge of a rimrock cliff; then dropped from the saddle and led his horse back from the edge. And now once more he held his rifle over his head with both hands, signaling "found."

The others came up on the run. Mart took their horses as they dismounted well back from the edge, but Mose Harper took the leads from Mart's hands. "I'm an old man," Mose said. "Whatever's beyond, I've seen it afore—most likely many times. You go on up."

The cliff was a three-hundred-foot limestone wall, dropping off sheer, as if it might be the shoreline of a vanished sea. The trail of the many Comanche ponies went down this precariously by way of a talus break. Twenty miles off, out in the middle of the flats, lay a patch of haze, shimmering redly in the horizontal light of the sunset. Some of them now remembered the cat-tail marsh that stagnated there, serving as a waterhole. A black line, wavering in the ground heat, showed in front of the marsh haze. That was all there was to see.

"Horses," Brad said. "That's horses, there at the water!"

"It's where they ought to be," Mart said. A faint reserve, as of disbelief in his luck, made the words come slowly.

"Could be buffler," Zack Harper said. He was a shag-headed young man, the oldest son of Mose Harper. "Wouldn't look no different."

"If there was buffalo there, you'd see the Comanche runnin' 'em," Amos stepped on the idea.

"If it's horses, it's sure a power of 'em."

"We've been trailin' a power of 'em."

They were silent awhile, studying the distant pen scratch upon the world that must be a band of livestock. The light was failing now as the sunset faded.

"We better feed out," Brad said finally. He was one of the youngest there, and the veteran plainsmen were usually cranky about hearing advice from the young; but lately they seemed to listen to him anyway. "It'll be dark in an hour and a half. No reason we can't jump them long before daylight, with any kind of start."

Ed Newby said, "You right sure you want to jump all them?"

Charlie MacCorry turned to look Ed over. "Just what in hell you think we come here for?"

"They'll be took unawares," Amos said. "They're always took unawares. Ain't an Indian in the world knows how to keep sentries out once the night goes cold."

"It ain't that," Ed answered. "We can whup them all right. I guess. Only thing . . . Comanches are mighty likely to kill any prisoners they've got, if they're jumped hard enough. They've done it again and again."

Mart Pauley chewed a grass blade and watched Amos. Finally Mart said, "There's another way. . . ."

Amos nodded. "Like Mart says. There's another way." Mart Pauley was bewildered to see that Amos looked happy. "I'm talking about their horses. Might be we could set the Comanch' afoot."

Silence again. Nobody wanted to say much now without considering a long while before he spoke.

"Might be we can stampede them ponies, and run off all the whole bunch," Amos went on. "I don't believe it would make 'em murder anybody—that's still alive."

"This thing ain't going to be too easy," Ed Newby said.

"No," Amos agreed. "It ain't easy. And it ain't safe. If we did get it done, the Comanch' should be ready to deal. But I don't say they'll deal. In all my life, I ain't learned but one thing about an Indian: Whatever you know you'd do in his place—he ain't going to do that. Maybe we'd still have to hunt them Comanches down, by bunches, by twos, by ones."

Something like a bitter relish in Amos' tone turned Mart cold. Amos no longer believed they would recover Lucy alive—and wasn't thinking of Debbie at all.

"Of course," Charlie MacCorry said, his eyes on a grass blade he was picking to shreds, "you know, could be every last one of them bucks has his best pony on short lead. Right beside him where he lies."

"That's right," Amos said. "That might very well be. And you know what happens then?"

"We lose our hair. And no good done to nobody."

"That's right."

Brad Mathison said, "In God's name, will you try it, Mr. Edwards?"

"All right."

Immediately Brad pulled back to feed his horses, and the others followed more slowly. Mart Pauley still lay on the edge of the rimrock after the others had pulled back. He was thinking of the change in Amos. No deadlock now, no hesitation in facing the worst answer there could be. No hope, either, visible in Amos' mind that they would ever find their beloved people alive. Only that creepy relish he had heard when Amos spoke of killing Comanches.

And thinking of Amos' face as it was tonight, he remembered it as it was that worst night of the world, when Amos came out of the dark, into the shambles of the Edwards' kitchen, carrying Martha's arm clutched against his chest. The mutilation could not be seen when Martha lay in the box they had made for

her. Her face looked young, and serene, and her crossed hands were at rest, one only slightly paler than the other. They were worn hands, betraying Martha's age as her face did not, with little random scars on them. Martha was always hurting her hands. Mart thought, "She wore them out, she hurt them, working for us."

As he thought that, the key to Amos' life suddenly became plain. All his uncertainties, his deadlocks with himself, his labors without pay, his perpetual gravitation back to his brother's ranch—they all fell into line. As he saw what had shaped and twisted Amos' life, Mart felt shaken up; he had lived with Amos most of his life without ever suspecting the truth. But neither had Henry suspected it—and Martha least of all.

Amos was—had always been—in love with his brother's wife.

8

Amos held them where they were for an hour after dark. They pulled saddles and packs, fed out the last of their grain, and rubbed down the horses with wads of dry grass. Nobody cooked. The men chewed on cold meat and lumps of hard frying-pan bread left from breakfast. All of them studied the shape of the hills a hundred miles beyond, taking a line on the Comanche camp. That fly speck, so far out upon the plain, would be easy to miss in the dark. When the marsh could no longer be seen they used the hill contours to take sights upon the stars they knew, as each appeared. By the time the hills, too, were swallowed by the night, each had star bearings by which he could find his way.

Mose Harper mapped his course by solemnly cutting notches in the rim of the hat. His son Zack grinned as he watched his father do that, but no one else thought it comical that Mose was growing old. All men grew old unless violence overtook them first; the plains offered no third way out of the predicament a man found himself in, simply by the fact of his existence on the face of the earth.

Amos was still in no hurry as he led off, sliding down the talus break by which the Comanches had descended to the plain. Once down on the flats, Amos held to an easy walk. He wanted to strike the Comanche horse herd before daylight, but when he had attacked he wanted dawn to come soon, so they could tell how they had come out, and make a finish. There must be no long muddle in the dark. Given half a chance to figure out what had happened, the war party would break up into singles and ambushes, becoming almost impossible to root out of the short grass.

When the moon rose, very meager, very late, it showed them each other as

black shapes, and they could make out their loose pack and saddle stock following along, grabbing jawfuls of the sparse feed. Not much more. A tiny dolloping
whisk of pure movement, without color or form, was a kangaroo rat. A silently
vanishing streak was a kit fox. About midnight the coyotes began their clamor,
surprisingly near, but not in the key that bothered Mart; and a little later the
hoarser, deeper howling of a loafer wolf sounded for a while a great way off.
Brad Mathison drifted his pony alongside Mart's.

"That thing sound all right to you?"

Mart was uncertain. One note had sounded a little queer to him at one point,
but it did not come again. He said he guessed it sounded like a wolf.

"Seems kind of far from timber for a loafer wolf. This time of year, anyway,"
Brad worried. "Known 'em to be out here, though," he answered his own complaint. He let his horse drop back, so that he could keep count of the loose
stock.

After the loafer wolf shut up, a dwarf owl, such as lives down prairie dog
holes, began to give out with a whickering noise about a middle distance off.
Half a furlong farther on another took it up, after they had left the first one
silent behind, and later another as they came abreast. This went on for half an
hour, and it had a spooky feel to it because the owls always sounded one at a
time, and always nearby. When Mart couldn't stand it any more he rode up
beside Amos.

"What you think?" he asked, as an owl sounded again.

Amos shrugged. He was riding with his hands in his pockets again, as Mart
had often seen him ride before, but there was no feel of deadlock or uncertainty about him now. He was leading out very straight, sure of his direction,
sure of his pace.

"Hard to say," he answered.

"You mean you don't know if that's a real owl?"

"It's a real something. A noise don't make itself."

"I know, but that there is an easy noise to make. You could make it, or—"

"Well, I ain't."

"—or I could make it. Might be anything."

"Tell you something. Every critter you ever hear out here can sometimes
sound like an awful poor mimic of itself. Don't always hardly pay to listen to
them things too much."

"Only thing," Mart stuck to it, "these here all sound like just one owl, follering along. Gosh, Amos. I question if them things ever travel ten rods from
home in their life."

"Yeah. I know. . . . Tell you what I'll do. I'll make 'em stop, being's they
bother you." Amos pushed his lips out and sounded an owl cry—not the cry of
just any owl, but an exact repeat of the one they had just heard.

No more owls whickered that night.

As Mart let his pony drop back, it came almost to a stop, and he realized that
he was checking it, unconsciously holding back from what was ahead. He wasn't
afraid of the fighting—at least, he didn't think he was afraid of it. He wanted
more than anything in the world to come to grips with the Comanches; of that
he felt perfectly certain. What he feared was that he might prove to be a

coward. He tried to tell himself that he had no earthly reason to doubt himself, but it didn't work. Maybe he had no earthly reason, but he had a couple of unearthly ones, and he knew it. There were some strange quirks inside of him that he couldn't understand at all.

One of them evidenced itself in the form of an eery nightmare that he had had over and over during his childhood. It was a dream of utter darkness, at first, though after a while the darkness seemed to redden with a dim, ugly glow, something like the redness you see through your lids when you look at the sun with closed eyes. But the main thing was the sound—a high, snarling, wailing yammer of a great many voices, repeatedly receding, then rising and swelling again; as if the sound came nearer in search of him, then went past, only to come back. The sound filled him with a hideous, unexplained terror, though he never knew what made it. It seemed the outcry of some weird semihuman horde—perhaps of ghoulish and inimical dead who sought to consume him. This went on and on, while he tried to scream, but could not; until he woke shivering miserably, but wet with sweat. He hadn't had this nightmare in a long time, but sometimes an unnatural fear touched him when the coyotes sang in a certain way far off on the sand hills.

Another loony weakness had to do with a smell. This particularly worried him tonight, for the smell that could bring an unreasoning panic into him was the faintly musky, old-leather-and-fur smell of Indians. The queer thing about this was that he felt no fear of the Indians themselves. He had seen a lot of them, and talked with them in the fragments of sign language he knew; he had even made swaps with some of them—mostly Caddoes, the far-wandering peddlers of the plains. But if he came upon a place where Indians had camped, or caught a faint scent of one down the wind, the same kind of panic could take hold of him as he felt in the dream. If he failed to connect this with the massacre he had survived, it was perhaps because he had no memory of the massacre. He had been carried asleep into the brush, where he had presently wakened lost and alone in the dark; and that was all he knew about it firsthand. Long after, when he had learned to talk, the disaster had been explained to him, but only in a general way. The Edwardses had never been willing to talk about it much.

And there was one more thing that could cut his strings; it had taken him unawares only two or three times in his life, yet worried him most of all, because it seemed totally meaningless. He judged this third thing to be a pure insanity, and wouldn't let himself think about it at all, times it wasn't forced on him without warning.

So now he rode uneasily, dreading the possibility that he might go to pieces in the clutch, and disgrace himself, in spite of all he could do. He began preaching to himself, inaudibly repeating over and over admonishments that unconsciously imitated Biblical forms. "I will go among them. I will prowl among them in the night. I will lay hands upon them; I will destroy them. Though I be cut in a hundred pieces, I will stand against them. . . ." It didn't seem to do any good.

He believed dawn could be no more than an hour off when Brad came up to whisper to him again. "I think we gone past."

Mart searched the east, fearing to see a graying in the sky too soon. But the night was still very dark, in spite of the dying moon. He could feel a faint warm breath of air upon his left cheek. "Wind's shifted to the south," he answered. "What little there is. I think Amos changed his line. Wants to come at 'em up wind."

"I know. I see that. But I think—"

Amos had stopped, and was holding up his hand. The six others closed up on him, stopped their horses and sat silent in their saddles. Mart couldn't hear anything except the loose animals behind, tearing at the grass. Amos rode on, and they traveled another fifteen minutes before he stopped again.

This time, when the shuffle of their ponies' feet had died, a faint sound lay upon the night, hard to be sure of, and even harder to believe. What they were hearing was the trilling of frogs. Now, how did they get way out here? They had to be the little green fellows that can live anywhere the ground is a little damp, but even so—either they had to shower down in the rare rains, like the old folks said, or else this marsh had been here always, while the dry world built up around.

Amos spoke softly. "Spread out some. Keep in line, and guide on me. I'll circle close in as I dare."

They spread out until they could just barely see each other, and rode at the walk, abreast of Amos as he moved on. The frog song came closer, so close that Mart feared they would trample on Indians before Amos turned. And now again, listening hard and straining their eyes, they rode for a long time. The north star was on their right hand for a while. Then it was behind them a long time. Then on their left, then ahead. At last it was on their right again, and Amos stopped. They were back where they started. A faint gray was showing in the east; their timing would have been perfect, if only what they were after had been here. Mose Harper pushed his horse in close. "I rode through the ashes of a farm," he said to Amos. "Did you know that? I thought you was hugging in awful close."

"Hush, now," Amos said. "I'm listening for something."

Mose dropped his tone. "Point is, them ashes showed no spark. Amos, them devils been gone from here all night."

"Catch up the loose stock," Amos said. "Bring 'em in on short lead."

"Waste of time," Mose Harper argued. "The boys are tard, and the Comanches is long gone."

"Get that loose stuff in," Amos ordered again, snapping it this time. "I want hobbles on 'em all—and soon!"

Mart was buckling a hobble on a pack mule when Brad dropped on one knee beside him to fasten the other cuff. "Look out yonder," Brad whispered. "When you get a chance."

Mart stood up, following Brad's eyes. A faint grayness had come evenly over the prairie, as if rising from the ground, but nothing showed a shadow yet. Mart cupped his hands over his eyes for a moment, then looked again, trying to look beside, instead of straight at, an unevenness on the flat land that he could not identify. But now he could not see it at all.

He said, "For a minute I thought—but I guess not."

"I swear something showed itself. Then took down again."

"A wolf, maybe?"

"I don't know. Something funny about this, Mart. The Comanch' ain't been traveling by night nor laying up by day. Not since the first hundred miles."

Now followed an odd aimless period, while they waited, and the light imperceptibly increased. "They're out there," Amos said at last. "They're going to jump us. There's no doubt of it now." Nobody denied it, or made any comment. Mart braced himself, checking his rifle again and again. "I got to hold fast," he kept telling himself. "I got to do my share of the work. No matter what." His ears were beginning to ring. The others stood about in loose meaningless positions, not huddled, not restless, but motionless, and very watchful. When they spoke they held their voices low.

Then Amos' rifle split the silence down the middle, so that behind lay the quiet night, and ahead rose their hour of violence. They saw what Amos had shot at. A single file of ten Comanches on wiry buffalo ponies had come into view at a thousand yards, materializing out of the seemingly flat earth. They came on at a light trot, ignoring Amos' shot. Zack Harper and Brad Mathison fired, but weren't good enough either at the range.

"Throw them horses down!" Amos shouted. "Git your backs to the marsh and tie down!" He snubbed his pony's muzzle back close to the horn, picked up the off fetlock, and threw the horse heavily. He caught one kicking hind foot, then the other, and pig-tied them across the fore cannons. Some of the others were doing the same thing, but Brad was in a fight with his hotblood animal. It reared eleven feet tall, striking with fore hoofs, trying to break away. "Kill that horse!" Amos yelled. Obediently Brad drew his six-gun, put a bullet into the animal's head under the ear, and stepped from under as it came down.

Ed Newby still stood, his rifle resting ready to fire across the saddle of his standing horse. Mart lost his head enough to yell, "Can't you throw him? Shall I shoot him, Ed?"

"Leave be! Let the Comanch' put him down."

Mart went to the aid of Charlie MacCorry, who had tied his own horse down all right and was wrestling with a mule. They never did get all of the animals down, but Mart felt a whole lot better with something for his hands to do. Three more of the Comanche single-file columns were in sight now, widely spread, trotting well in hand. They had a ghostly look at first, of the same color as the prairie, in the gray light. Then detail picked out, and Mart saw the bows, lances bearing scalps like pennons, an occasional war shield carried for the medicine in its painted symbols as much as for the bullet-deflecting function of its iron-tough hide. Almost half the Comanches had rifles. Some trader, standing on his right to make a living, must have taken a handsome profit putting those in Comanche hands.

Amos' rifle banged again. One of the lead ponies swerved and ran wild as the rider rolled off into the grass. Immediately, without any other discernible signal, the Comanches leaned low on their ponies and came on at a hard run. Two or three more of the cowmen fired, but without effect.

At three hundred yards the four Comanche columns cut hard left, coming into a single loose line that streamed across the front of the defense. The cowmen were as ready as they were going to be; they had got themselves into a ragged semi-circle behind their tied-down horses, their backs to the water. Two or three sat casually on their down horses, estimating the enemy.

"May as well hold up," Mose Harper said. His tone was as pressureless as a crackerbox comment. "They'll swing plenty close, before they're done."

"I count thirty-seven," Ed Newby said. He was still on his feet behind his standing horse.

Amos said, "I got me a scalp out there, when I git time to take it."

"Providin'," Mose Harper tried to sound jocular, "they don't leave your carcass here in the dirt."

"I come here to leave Indian carcasses in the dirt. I ain't made no change of plan."

They could see the Comanche war paint now as the warriors rode in plain sight across their front. Faces and naked bodies were striped and splotched in combinations of white, red, and yellow; but whatever the pattern, it was always pointed up with heavy accents of black, the Comanche color for war, for battle, and for death. Each warrior always painted up the same, but it was little use memorizing the paint patterns, because you never saw an Indian in war paint except when you couldn't lay hands on him. No use remembering the medicine shields, either, for these, treated as sacred, were never out of their deerskin cases until the moment of battle. Besides paint the Comanches wore breech clouts and moccasins; a few had horn or bear-claw headdresses. But these were young warriors, without the great eagle-feather war bonnets that were the pride of old war chiefs, who had tallied scores of coups. The ponies had their tails tied up, and were ridden bareback, guided by a single jaw rein.

Zack Harper said, "Ain't that big one Buffalo Hump?"

"No-that-ain't-Buffer-Hump," his father squelched him. "Don't talk so damn much."

The Comanche leader turned again and circled in. He brought his warriors past the defenders within fifty yards, ponies loosely spaced, racing full out. Suddenly, from every Comanche throat burst the screaming war cry; and Mart was paralyzed by the impact of that sound, stunned and sickened as by a blow in the belly with a rock. The war cries rose in a high unearthly yammering, wailing and snarling, piercing to his backbone to cut off every nerve he had. It was not exactly the eery sound of his terror-dream, but it was the spirit of that sound, the essence of its meaning. The muscles of his shoulders clenched as if turned to stone, and his hands so vised upon his rifle that it rattled, useless, against the saddle upon which it rested. And at the same time every other muscle in his body went limp and helpless.

Amos spoke into his ear, his low tone heavy with authority but unexcited. "Leave your shoulders go loose. Make your shoulders slack, and your hands will take care of theirselves. Now help me git a couple!"

That worked. All the rifles were sounding now from behind the tied-down horses. Mart breathed again, picked a target, and took aim. One Comanche after another was dropping from sight behind his pony as he came opposite the waiting rifles; they went down in order, like ducks in a shooting gallery, shamming a slaughter that wasn't happening. Each Comanche hung by one heel and a loop of mane on the far side of his pony and fired under the neck, offering only one arm and part of a painted face for target. A pony somersaulted, its rider springing clear unhurt, as Mart fired.

The circling Comanches kept up a continuous firing, each warrior reloading as he swung away, then coming past to fire again. This was the famous Comanche wheel, moving closer with every turn, chewing into the defense like a racing grindstone, yet never committing its force beyond possibility of a quick withdrawal. Bullets buzzed over, whispering "Cousin," or howled in ricochet from dust-spouts short of the defenders. A lot of whistling noises were arrows going over. Zack Harper's horse screamed, then went into a heavy continuous groaning.

Another Indian pony tumbled end over end; that was Amos' shot. The rider took cover behind his dead pony before he could be killed. Here and there another pony jerked, faltered, then ran on. A single bullet has to be closely placed to bring a horse down clean.

Amos said loud through his teeth, "The horses, you fools! Get them horses!" Another Comanche pony slid on its knees and stayed down, but its rider got behind it without hurt.

Ed Newby was firing carefully and unhurriedly across his standing horse. The buzzbees made the horse switch its tail, but it stood. Ed said, "You got to get the shoulder. No good to gut-shot'em. You fellers ain't leading enough." He fired again, and a Comanche dropped from behind his running horse with his brains blown out. It wasn't the shot Ed was trying to make, but he said, "See how easy?"

Fifty yards out in front of him Mart Pauley saw a rifle snake across the quarters of a fallen pony. A horn headdress rose cautiously, and the rifle swung to look Mart square in the eye. He took a snap shot, aiming between the horns, which disappeared, and the enemy rifle slid unfired into the short grass.

After that there was a letup, while the Comanches broke circle and drew off. Out in front of the cowmen lay three downed ponies, two dead Comanches, and two live ones, safe and dangerous behind their fallen horses. Amos was swearing softly and steadily to himself. Charlie MacCorry said he thought he goosed one of them up a little bit, maybe, but didn't believe he convinced him.

"Good God almighty," Brad Mathison broke out, "there's got to be some way to do this!"

Mose Harper scratched his beard and said he thought they done just fine that trip. "Oncet when I was a little shaver, with my pa's bull wagons, a couple hundred of 'em circled us all day long. We never did get 'em whittled down very much. They just fin'y went away. . . . You glued to the ground, Zack? Take care that horse!"

Zack got up and took a look at his wounded horse, but didn't seem to know what to do. He stood staring at it, until his father walked across and shot it.

Mart said to Amos. "Tell me one thing. Was they hollering like that the time they killed my folks?"

Amos seemed to have to think that over. "I wasn't there," he said at last. "I suppose so. Hard to get used to, ain't it?"

"I don't know," Mart said shakily, "if I'll ever be able to get used to it."

Amos looked at him oddly for some moments. "Don't you let it stop you," he said.

"It won't stop me."

They came on again, and this time they swept past at no more than ten yards. A number of the wounded Comanche ponies lagged back to the tail of the line, their riders saving them for the final spurt, but they were still in action. The Comanches made this run in close bunches; the attack became a smother of confusion. Both lead and arrows poured fast into the cowmen's position.

Zack whimpered, "My God—there's a million of 'em!" and ducked down behind his dead horse.

"Git your damn head up!" Mose yelled at his son. "Fire into 'em!" Zack raised up and went to fighting again.

Sometime during this run Ed Newby's horse fell, pinning Ed under it, but they had no time to go to him while this burst of the attack continued. An unhorsed Comanche came screaming at Amos with clubbed rifle, and so found his finish. Another stopped at least five bullets as a compadre tried to rescue him in a flying pickup. There should have been another; a third pony was down out in front of them, but nobody knew where the rider had got to. This time as they finished the run the Comanches pulled off again to talk it over.

All choices lay with the Comanches for the time being. The cowmen got their backs into the job of getting nine hundred pounds of horse off Ed Newby. Mose Harper said, "How come you let him catch you, Ed?"

Ed Newby answered through set teeth. "They got my leg—just as he come down—"

Ed's leg was not only bullet-broken, but had doubled under him, and got smashed again by the killed horse. Amos put the shaft of an arrow between Ed's teeth, and the arrowwood splintered as two men put their weight into pulling the leg straight.

A party of a dozen Comanches, mounted on the fastest of the Indian ponies, split off from the main bunch and circled out for still another sweep.

"Hold your fire," Amos ordered. "You hear me? Take cover—but let 'em be!"

Zack Harper, who had fought none too well, chose this moment to harden. "Hold hell! I aim to get me another!"

"You fire and I'll kill you," Amos promised him; and Zack put his rifle down.

Most took to the ground as the Comanches swept past once more, but Amos stood up, watching from under his heavy brows, like a staring ox. The Indians did not attack. They picked up their dismounted and their dead; then they were gone.

"Get them horses up!" Amos loosed the pigging string and got his own horse to its feet.

"They'll scatter now," Mose Harper said.

"Not till they come up with their horse herd, they won't!"

"Somebody's got to stay with Ed," Mose reminded them. "I suppose I'm the one to do that—old crip that I be. But some of them Comanch' might circle back. You'll have to leave Zack with me."

"That's all right."

"And I need one fast man on a good horse to get me help. I can't move him. Not with what we got here."

"We all ought to be back," Amos objected, "in a couple of days."

"Fellers follering Comanches don't necessarily ever come back. I got to have either Brad Mathison or Charlie MacCorry."

"You get Mathison, then," Charlie said. "I'm going on."

Brad whirled on Charlie in an unexpected blast of temper. "There's a quick way to decide it," he said, and stood braced, his open hand ready above his holster.

Charlie MacCorry looked Brad in the eye as he spat at Brad's boots and missed. But after that he turned away.

So three rode on, following a plume of dust already distant upon the prairie. "We'll have the answer soon," Amos promised. "Soon. We don't dast let 'em lose us now."

Mart Pauley was silent. He didn't want to ask him what three riders could do when they caught up with the Comanches. He was afraid Amos didn't know.

9

They kept the feather of dust in sight all day, but in the morning, after a night camp without water, they failed to pick it up. The trail of the Comanche war party still led westward, broad and plain, marked at intervals with the carcasses of buffalo ponies wounded at the Cat-tails. They pushed on, getting all they could out of their horses.

This day, the second after the Fight at the Cat-tails, became the strangest day of the pursuit before it was done, because of something unexplained that happened during a period while they were separated.

A line of low hills, many hours away beyond the plain, began to shove up from the horizon as they rode. After a while they knew the Comanches they followed were already into that broken country where pursuit would be slower and more treacherous than before.

"Sometimes it seems to me," Amos said, "them Comanches fly with their elbows, carrying the pony along between their knees. You can nurse a horse along till he falls and dies, and you walk on carrying your saddle. Then a Comanche comes along, and gets that horse up, and rides it twenty miles more. Then eats it."

"Don't we have any chance at all?"

"Yes. . . . We got a chance." Amos went through the motions of spitting, with no moisture in his mouth to spit. "And I'll tell you what it be. An Indian will chase a thing until he thinks he's chased it enough. Then he quits. So the same when he runs. After while he figures we must have quit, and he starts to loaf. Seemingly he never learns there's such a thing as a critter that might just keep coming on."

As he looked at Amos, sitting his saddle like a great lump of rock—yet a lump that was somehow of one piece with the horse—Mart Pauley was willing to believe that to have Amos following you could be a deadly thing with no end to it, ever, until he was dead.

"If only they stay bunched," Amos finished, and it was a prayer; "if only they don't split and scatter . . . we'll come up to 'em. We're bound to come up."

Late in the morning they came to a shallow sink, where a number of posthole wells had been freshly dug among the dry reeds. Here the trail of the main horse herd freshened, and they found the bones of an eaten horse, polished shiny in a night by the wolves. And there was the Indian smell, giving Mart a senseless dread to fight off during their first minutes in this place.

"Here's where the rest of 'em was all day yesterday," Amos said when he had wet his mouth; "the horse guards, and the stole horses, and maybe some crips Henry shot up. And our people—if they're still alive."

Brad Mathison was prone at a pothole, dipping water into himself with his tin cup, but he dropped the cup to come up with a snap. As he spoke, Mart Pauley heard the same soft tones Brad's father used when he neared an end of words. "I've heard thee say that times enough," Brad said.

"What?" Amos asked, astonished.

"Maybe she's dead," Brad said, his bloodshot blue eyes burning steadily into Amos' face. "Maybe they're both dead. But if I hear it from thee again, thee has chosen me—so help me God!"

Amos stared at Brad mildly, and when he spoke again it was to Mart Pauley. "They've took an awful big lead. Them we fought at the Cat-tails must have got here early last night."

"And the whole bunch pulled out the same hour," Mart finished it.

It meant they were nine or ten hours back—and every one of the Comanches was now riding a rested animal. Only one answer to that—such as it was: They had to rest their own horses, whether they could spare time for it or not. They spent an hour dipping water into their hats; the ponies could not reach the little water in the bottom of the posthole wells. When one hole after another had been dipped dry they could only wait for the slow seepage to bring in another cupful, while the horses stood by. After that they took yet another hour to let the horses crop the scant bunch grass, helping them by piling grass they cut with their knives. A great amount of this work gained only the slightest advantage, but none of them begrudged it.

Then, some hours beyond the posthole wells, they came to a vast sheet of rock, as flat and naked as it had been laid down when the world was made. Here the trail ended, for unshod hoofs left no mark on the barren stone. Amos remembered this reef in the plain. He believed it to be about four miles across by maybe eight or nine miles long, as nearly as he could recall. All they could do was split up and circle the whole ledge to find where the trail came off the rock.

Mart Pauley, whose horse seemed the worst beat out, was sent straight across. On the far side he was to wait, grazing within sight of the ledge, until one of the others came around to him; then both were to ride to meet the third.

Thus they separated. It was while they were apart, each rider alone with his tiring horse, that some strange thing happened to Amos, so that he became a mystery in himself throughout their last twenty-four hours together.

Brad Mathison was first to get around the rock sheet to where Mart Pauley was grazing his horse. Mart had been there many hours, yet they rode south a long way before they sighted Amos, waiting for them far out on the plain.

"Hasn't made much distance, has he?" Brad commented.

"Maybe the rock slick stretches a far piece down this way."

"Don't look like it to me."

Mart didn't say anything more. He could see for himself that the reef ended in a couple of miles.

Amos pointed to a far-off landmark as they came up. "The trail cuts around that hump," he said, and led the way. The trail was where Amos had said it would be, a great welter of horse prints already blurred by the wind. But no other horse had been along here since the Comanches passed long before.

"Kind of thought to see your tracks here," Brad said.

"Didn't come this far."

Then where the hell had he been all this time? If it had been Lije Powers, Mart would have known he had sneaked himself a nap. "You lost a bed blanket," Mart noticed.

"Slipped out of the strings somewhere. I sure ain't going back for it now." Amos was speaking too carefully. He put Mart in mind of a man half stopped in a fist fight, making out he was unhurt so his opponent wouldn't know, and finish him.

"You feel all right?" he asked Amos.

"Sure. I feel fine." Amos forced a smile, and this was a mistake, for he didn't look to be smiling. He looked as if he had been kicked in the face. Mart tried to think of an excuse to lay a hand on him, to see if he had a fever; but before he could think of anything Amos took off his hat and wiped sweat off his forehead with his sleeve. That settled that. A man doesn't sweat with the fever on him.

"You look like you et something," Mart said.

"Don't know what it could have been. Oh, I did come on three-four rattle-snakes." Seemingly the thought made Amos hungry. He got out a leaf of jerky, and tore strips from it with his teeth.

"You sure you feel—"

Amos blew up, and yelled at him. "I'm all right, I tell you!" He quirted his horse, and loped out ahead.

They off-saddled in the shelter of the hump. A northering wind came up when the sun was gone; its bite reminded them that they had been riding deep into the fall of the year. They huddled against their saddles, and chewed corn meal. Brad walked across and stood over Amos. He spoke reasonably.

"Looks like you ought to tell us, Mr. Edwards." He waited, but Amos didn't answer him. "Something happened while you was gone from us today. Was you laid for? We didn't hear no guns, but . . . Be you hiding an arrow hole from us by any chance?"

"No," Amos said. "There wasn't nothing like that."

Brad went back to his saddle and sat down. Mart laid his bedroll flat, hanging on by the upwind edge, and rolled himself up in it, coming out so that his head was on the saddle.

"A man has to learn to forgive himself," Amos said, his voice unnaturally gentle. He seemed to be talking to Brad Mathison. "Or he can't stand to live. It so happens we be Texans. We took a reachin' holt, way far out, past where any man has right or reason to hold on. Or if we didn't, our folks did, so we can't leave off, without giving up that they were fools, wasting their lives, and wasted in the way they died."

The chill striking up through Mart's blankets made him homesick for the Edwards' kitchen, like it was on winter nights, all warm and light, and full of good smells, like baking bread. And their people—Mart had taken them for granted, largely; just a family, people living alone together, such as you never thought about, especially, unless you got mad at them. He had never known they were dear to him until the whole thing was busted up forever. He wished Amos would shut up.

"This is a rough country," Amos was saying. "It's a country knows how to scour a human man right off the face of itself. A Texan is nothing but a human man way out on a limb. This year, and next year, and maybe for a hundred more. But I don't think it'll be forever. Someday this country will be a fine good place to be. Maybe it needs our bones in the ground before that time can come."

Mart was thinking of Laurie now. He saw her in a bright warm kitchen like the Edwards', and he thought how wonderful it would be living in the same house with Laurie, in the same bed. But he was on the empty prairie without any fire—and he had bedded himself on a sharp rock, he noticed now.

"We've come on a year when things go hard," Amos talked on. "We get this tough combing over because we're Texans. But the feeling we get that we fail, and judge wrong, and go down in guilt and shame—that's because we be human men. So try to remember one thing. It wasn't your fault, no matter how it looks. You got let in for this just by being born. Maybe there never is any way out of it once you're born a human man, except straight across the coals of hell."

Mart rolled out to move his bed. He didn't really need that rock in his ribs all night. Brad Mathison got up, moved out of Amos' line of sight, and beckoned Mart with his head. Mart put his saddle on his bed, so it wouldn't blow away, and walked out a ways with Brad on the dark prairie.

"Mart," Brad said when they were out of hearing, "the old coot is just as crazy as a bedbug fell in the rum."

"Sure sounds so. What in all hell you think happened?"

"God knows. Maybe nothing at all. Might be he just plainly cracked. He was wandering around without rhyme or principle when we come on him today."

"I know."

"This puts it up to you and me," Brad said. "You see that, don't you? We may be closer the end than you think."

"What you want to do?"

"My horse is standing up best. Tomorrow I'll start before light, and scout on out far as I can reach. You come on as you can."

"My horse got a rest today," Mart began.

"Keep saving him. You'll have to take forward when mine gives down."

"All right." Mart judged that tomorrow was going to be a hard day to live far behind on a failing pony. Like Brad, he had a feeling they were a whole lot closer to the Comanches than they had any real reason to believe.

They turned in again. Though they couldn't know it, until they heard about it a long time after, that was the night Ed Newby came out of his delirium, raised himself for a long look at his smashed leg, then put a bullet in his brain.

 10

By daylight Brad Mathison was an hour gone. Mart hadn't known how Amos would take it, but there was no fuss at all. They rode on in silence, crossing chains of low hills, with dry valleys between; they were beginning to find a little timber, willow and cottonwood mostly along the dusty streambeds. They were badly in need of water again; they would have to dig for it soon. All day long the big tracks of Brad Mathison's horse led on, on top of the many-horse trample left by the Comanche herd; but he was stirring no dust, and they could only guess how far he must be ahead.

Toward sundown Amos must have begun to worry about him, for he sent Mart on a long swing to the north, where a line of sand hills offered high ground, to see what he could see. He failed to make out any sign of Brad; but, while he was in the hills alone, the third weird thing that could unstring him set itself in front of him again. He had a right to be nerve-raw at this point, perhaps; the vast emptiness of the plains had taken on a haunted, evilly enchanted feel since the massacre. And of course they were on strange ground now, where all things seemed faintly odd and wrong, because unfamiliar. . . .

He had dismounted near the top of a broken swell, led his horse around it to get a distant view without showing himself against the sky. He walked around a ragged shoulder—and suddenly froze at sight of what stood on the crest beyond. It was nothing but a juniper stump; not for an instant did he mistake it for anything else. But it was in the form of similar stumps he had seen two or three times before in his life, and always with the same unexplainable effect. The twisted remains of the juniper, blackened and sand-scoured, had vaguely the shape of a man, or the withered corpse of a man; one arm seemed upraised in a writhing gesture of agony, or perhaps of warning. But nothing about it explained the awful sinking of the heart, the terrible sense of inevitable doom, that overpowered him each of the times he encountered this shape.

An Indian would have turned back, giving up whatever he was about; for he would have known the thing for a medicine tree with a powerful spirit in it, either telling him of a doom or placing a doom upon him. And Mart himself more or less believed that the thing was some kind of a sign. An evil prophecy is always fulfilled, if you put no time limit upon it; fulfilled quite readily, too, if you are a child counting little misfortunes as disasters. So Mart had the impression that this mysteriously upsetting kind of an encounter had always been followed by some dreadful, unforeseeable thing.

He regarded himself as entirely mature now, and was convinced that to be filled with cowardice by the sight of a dead tree was a silly and unworthy thing. He supposed he ought to go and uproot that desolate twist of wood, or whittle it down, and so master the thing forever. But even to move toward it was somehow impossible to him, to a degree that such a move was not even thinkable. He returned to Amos feeling shaken and sickish, unstrung as much by doubt of his own soundness as by the sense of evil prophecy itself.

The sun was setting when they saw Brad again. He came pouring off a long hill at four miles, raising a reckless dust. "I saw her!" he yelled, and hauled up sliding. "I saw Lucy!"

"How far?"

"They're camped by a running crick—they got fires going —look, you can see the smoke!" A thin haze lay flat in the quiet air above the next line of hills.

"Ought to be the Warrior River," Amos said. "Water in it, huh?"

"Didn't you hear what I said?" Brad shouted. "I tell you I saw Lucy—I saw her walking through the camp—"

Amos' tone was bleak. "How far off was you?"

"Not over seventy rod. I bellied up a ridge this side the river, and they was right below me!"

"Did you see Debbie?" Mart got in.

"No, but—they got a bunch of baggage; she might be asleep amongst that. I counted fifty-one Comanch'—What you unsaddling for?"

"Good a place as any," Amos said. "Can't risk no more dust like you just now kicked up. Come dark we'll work south, and water a few miles below. We can take our time."

"Time?"

"They're making it easy for us. Must think they turned us back at the Cat-tails, and don't have to split up. All we got to do is foller to their village—"

"Village? You gone out of your mind?"

"Let 'em get back to their old chiefs and their squaws. The old chiefs have gone cagy; a village of families can't run like a war party can. For all they know—"

"Look—look—" Brad hunted desperately for words that would fetch Amos back to reality. "Lucy's there! I saw her—can't you hear? We got to get her out of there!"

"Brad," Amos said, "I want to know what you saw in that camp you thought was Lucy."

"I keep telling you I saw her walk—"

"I heard you!" Amos' voice rose and crackled this time. "*What* did you see walk? Could you see her yellow hair?"

"She had a shawl on her head. But—"

"She ain't there, Brad."

"God damn it, I tell you, I'd know her out of a million—"

"You saw a buck in a woman's dress," Amos said. "They're game to put anything on 'em. You know that."

Brad's sun-punished blue eyes blazed up as they had at the pothole water, and his tone went soft again. "Thee lie," he said. "I've told thee afore—"

"But there's something I ain't told you," Amos said. "I found Lucy yesterday. I buried her in my own saddle blanket. With my own hands, by the rock. I thought best to keep it from you long's I could."

The blood drained from Brad's face, and at first he could not speak. Then he stammered, "Did they—was she—"

"Shut up!" Amos yelled at him. "Never ask me what more I seen!"

Brad stood as if knocked out for half a minute more; then he turned to his horse, stiffly, as if he didn't trust his legs too well, and he tightened his cinch.

Amos said, "Get hold of yourself! Grab him, Mart!" Brad stepped into the saddle, and the gravel jumped from the hoofs of his horse. He leveled out down the Comanche trail again, running his horse as if he would never need it again.

"Go after him! You can handle him better than me."

Mart Pauley had pulled his saddle, vaulted bareback onto the sweaty withers, and in ten jumps opened up all the speed his beat-out horse had left. He gained no ground on Brad, though he used up what horse he had in trying to. He was chasing the better horse—and the better rider, too, Mart supposed. They weighed about the same, and both had been on horses before they could walk. Some small magic that could not be taught or learned, but had been born into Brad's muscles, was what made the difference. Mart was three furlongs back as Brad sifted into the low hills.

Up the slopes Mart followed, around a knob, and onto the down slope, spurring his wheezing horse at every jump. From here he could see the last little ridge, below and beyond as Brad had described it, with the smoke of Comanche campfires plain above it. Mart's horse went to its knees as he jumped it into a steep ravine, but he was able to drag it up.

Near the mouth of the ravine he found Brad's horse tied to a pin-oak scrub; he passed it, and rode on into the open, full stretch. Far up the last ridge he saw Brad climbing strongly. He looked back over his shoulder, watching Mart without slowing his pace. Mart charged through a dry tributary of the Warrior and up the ridge, his horse laboring gamely as it fought the slope. Brad stopped just short of the crest, and Mart saw him tilt his canteen skyward; he drained it unhurriedly, and threw it away. He was already on his belly at the crest as Mart dropped from his horse and scrambled on all fours to his side.

"God damn it, Brad, what you doing?"

"Get the hell out of here. You ain't wanted."

Down below, at perhaps four hundred yards, half a hundred Comanches idled about their business. They had some piled mule packs, a lot of small fires in shallow fire holes, and parts of at least a dozen buffalo down there. The big horse herd grazed unguarded beyond. Most of the bucks were throwing chunks of meat into the fires, to be snatched out and bolted as soon as the meat blackened on the outside. No sign of pickets. The Comanches relied for safety upon their horsemanship and the great empty distances of the prairies. They didn't seem to know what a picket was.

Mart couldn't see any sign of Debbie. And now he heard Brad chamber a cartridge.

"You'll get Debbie killed, you son-of-a-bitch!"

"Get out of here, I said!" Brad had his cheek on the stock; he was aiming into the Comanche camp. He took a deep breath, let it all out, and lay inert, waiting for his head to steady for the squeeze. Mart grabbed the rifle, and wrenched it out of line.

They fought for possession, rolling and sliding down the slope. Brad rammed a knee into Mart's belly, twisted the rifle from his hands, and broke free. Mart came to his feet before Brad, and dived to pin him down. Brad braced himself on one hand, and with the other swung the rifle by the grip of the stock. Blood jumped from the side of Mart's head as the barrel struck. He fell backward, end over end; then went limp, rolled slackly down the hill, and lay still where he came to rest.

Brad swore softly as he settled himself into firing position again. Then he changed his mind and trotted northward, just behind the crest of the ridge.

Mart came to slowly, without memory or any idea of where he was. Sight did not return to him at once. His hands groped, and found the rocky ground on which he lay; and next he recognized a persistent rattle of gunfire and the high snarling of Comanche war cries, seemingly some distance away. His hands went to his head, and he felt clotting blood. He reckoned he had got shot in the head, and was blind, and panic took him. He struggled up, floundered a few yards without any sense of balance, and fell into a dry wash. The fall knocked the wind out of him, and when he had got his breath back his mind had cleared enough so that he lay still.

Some part of his sight was coming back by the time he heard a soft footstep upon sand. He could see a shadowy shape above him, swimming in a general blur. He played possum, staring straight up with unwinking eyes, waiting to lose his scalp.

"Can you hear me, Mart?" Amos said.

He knew Amos dropped to his knees beside him. "I got a bullet in my brain," Mart said. "I'm blind."

Amos struck a match and passed it before one eye and then the other. Mart blinked and rolled his head to the side. "You're all right," Amos said. "Hit your head, that's all. Lie still till I get back!" He left, running.

Amos was gone a long time. The riflery and the war cries stopped, and the prairie became deathly still. For a while Mart believed he could sense a tremor in the ground that might mean the movement of many horses; then this faded, and the night chill began to work upward out of the ground. But Mart was able to see the winking of the first stars when he heard Amos coming back.

"You look all right to me," Amos said.

"Where's Brad?"

Amos was slow in answering. "Brad fit him a one-man war," he said at last. "He skirmished 'em from the woods down yonder. Now, why from there? Was he trying to lead them off you?"

"I don't know."

"What'd you do? Get throwed?"

"I guess."

"Comanches took him for a Ranger company, seemingly. They're long gone. Only they took time to finish him first."

"Was he scalped?"

"Now, what do you think?"

After he had found Mart, Amos had backed off behind a hill and built a signal fire. He slung creosote bush on it, raised a good smoke, and took his time sending puff messages with his saddle blanket.

"Messages to who?"

"Nobody, damn it. No message, either, rightly—just a lot of different-size hunks of smoke. Comanches couldn't read it, because it didn't say nothing. So they upped stakes and rode. It's all saved our hair, once they was stirred up."

Mart said, "We better go bury Brad."

"I done that already." Then Amos added one sad, sinister thing. "All of him I could find."

Mart's horse had run off with the Comanche ponies, but they still had Brad's horse and Amos'. And the Comanches had left them plenty of buffalo meat. Amos dug a fire pit, narrow but as deep as he could reach, in the manner of the Wichitas. From the bottom of this, his cooking fire could reflect only upon its own smoke, and he didn't put on stuff that made any. When Mart had filled up on buffalo meat he turned wrong side out, but an hour later he tried again, and this time it stuck.

"Feel like you'll be able to ride come daylight?"

"Sure I'll ride."

"I don't believe we got far to go," Amos said. "The Comanch' been acting like they're close to home. We'll come up to their village soon. Maybe tomorrow."

Mart felt much better now. "Tomorrow," he repeated.

11

Tomorrow came and went, and showed them they were wrong. Now at last the Comanche war party split up, and little groups carrying two or three horses to the man ranged off in ten directions. Amos and Mart picked one trail at random and followed it with all tenacity as it turned and doubled, leading them in far futile ways. They lost it on rock ledges, in running water, and in blown sand, but always found it again, and kept on.

Another month passed before all trails became one, and the paired scratches of many travois showed they were on the track of the main village at last. They followed it northeast, gaining ground fast as the trail grew fresh.

"Tomorrow," Amos said once more. "All hell can't keep them ahead of us tomorrow."

That night it snowed.

By morning the prairie was a vast white blank; and every day for a week more snow fell. They made some wide, reaching casts and guesses, but the plains were empty. One day they pushed their fading horses in a two-hour climb, toiling through drifts to the top of a towering butte. At its craggy lip they set their gaunted horses in silence, while their eyes swept the plain for a long time. The sky was dark that day, but near the ground the air was clear; they could see about as far as a man could ride through that clogging snow in a week. Neither found anything to say, for they knew they were done. Mart had not wept since the night of the massacre. Then he had suffered a blinding shock, and an inconsolable, aching grief so great he had never expected to cry again. But now as he faced the emptiness of a world that was supposed to have Debbie in it, yet was blank to its farthest horizons, his throat began to knot and hurt. He faced away to hide from Amos the tears he could no longer hold back; and soon after that he started his horse slowly back down that long, long slope, lest Amos hear the convulsive jerking of his breath and the snuffling of tears that ran down inside his nose.

They made an early, snowbound camp, with no call to hurry any more or stretch the short days. "This don't change anything," Amos said doggedly. "Not in the long run. If she's alive, she's safe by now, and they've kept her to raise. They do that time and again with a little child small enough to be raised their own way. So . . . we'll find them in the end; I promise you that. By the Almighty God, I promise you that! We'll catch up to 'em, just as sure as the turning of the earth!"

But now they had to start all over again in another way.

What Mart had noticed was that Amos always spoke of catching up to "them"

339

—never of finding "her." And the cold, banked fires behind Amos' eyes were manifestly the lights of hatred, not of concern for a lost little girl. He wondered uneasily if there might not be a peculiar danger in this. He believed now that Amos, in certain moods, would ride past the child, and let her be lost to them if he saw a chance to kill Comanches.

They were freezing miserably in the lightweight clothes in which they had started out. Their horses were ribby shells, and they were out of flour, grease, block matches, coffee, and salt. Even their ammunition was running dangerously low. They were always having to shoot something to eat—a scrawny antelope, a jackrabbit all bones and fur; nothing they shot seemed to last all day. And it took two cartridges to light a fire—one to yield a pinch of powder to be mixed with tinder, a second to fire into the tinder, lighting it by gun flash. They needed to go home and start again, but they could not; there was much they could do, and must do, before they took time to go back.

President Grant had given the Society of Friends full charge of the Indian Agencies for the Wild Tribes, which in the Southwest Plains included Indians speaking more than twenty languages. Important in strength or activity were the Cheyennes, Arapahoes, and Wichitas; the Osages, a splinter of the Sioux; and, especially, that most murderous and irreconcilable alliance of all, the Comanches and Kiowas. The gentle and unrequiring administration of the Quakers very quickly attracted considerable numbers of these to the Agencies as winter closed. Besides government handouts, this got them a snow-weather amnesty from the trouble stirred up by their summer raids. Traders, Indian Agents, and army officers ransomed captive white children from winter peace-lovers like these every year. Failing this kind of good fortune, the situation still offered the best of opportunities to watch, to listen, and to learn.

Mart and Amos swung south to Fort Concho, where they re-outfitted and traded for fresh horses, taking a bad beating because of the poor shape their own were in. Amos seemed to have adequate money with him. Mart had never known how much money was kept, variously hidden, around the Edwards' place, but during the last two or three years it had probably been a lot; and naturally Amos wouldn't have left any of it in the empty house. The two riders headed up the north fork of the Butterfield Trail, laid out to provide at least one way to El Paso, but abandoned even before the war. Fort Phanton Hill, Fort Griffin, and Fort Belknap—set up to watch the Tonkawas—were in ruins, but still garrisoned by worried little detachments. At these places, and wherever they went, they told their story, pessimistically convinced that information was best come by in unlikely ways, being seldom found where you would reasonably expect it. Amos was posting a reward of a thousand dollars for any clue that would lead to the recovery of Debbie alive. Mart supposed it could be paid out of the family cattle, or something, if the great day ever came when it would be owed.

Laboriously, sweatily, night after night, Mart worked on a letter to the Mathison family, to tell them of the death of Brad and the manner in which he died. For a while he tried to tell the facts in a way that wouldn't make his own part in it look too futile. But he believed that he had failed, perhaps unforgivably, at the Warrior River, and that if he had been any good, Brad would still be alive.

So in the end he gave up trying to fix any part of it up, and just told it the way it happened. He finally got the letter "posted" at Fort Richardson—which meant he left it there for some random rider to carry, if any should happen to be going the right way.

At Fort Richardson they struck north and west, clean out of the State of Texas. Deep in Indian Territory they made Camp Wichita, which they were surprised to find renamed Fort Sill—still a bunch of shacks but already heavily garrisoned. They stayed two weeks; then pushed northward again, far beyond Sill to the Anadarko Agency and Old Fort Cobb. By a thousand questions, by walking boldly through the far-strung-out camps of a thousand savages, by piecing together faint implications and guesses, they were trying to find out from what band of Comanches the raiders must have come. But nobody seemed to know much about Comanches—not even how many there were, or how divided. The military at Fort Sill seemed to think there were eight thousand Comanches; the Quaker Agents believed there to be no more than six thousand; some of the old traders believed there to be at least twelve thousand. And so with the bands: there were seven Comanche bands, there were sixteen, there were eleven. When they counted up the names of all the bands and villages they had heard of, the total came to more than thirty.

But none of this proved anything. The Comanches had a custom that forbade speaking the name of a dead person; if a chief died who had given himself the name of his band, the whole outfit had to have a new name. So sometimes a single village had a new name every year, while all the old names still lived on in the speech of Comanches and others who had not got the word. They found reason to think that the River Pony Comanches were the same as the Parkanowm, or Waterhole People; and the Widyew, Kitsa-Kahna, Titcha-kenna, and Yapa-eena were probably all names for the Rooteaters, or Yampareka. For a time they heard the Way-ah-nay (Hill Falls Down) Band talked about as if it were comparable to the Pennetecka (Honey-eaters), which some said included six thousand Comanches by itself. And later they discovered that the Way-ah-nay Band was nothing but six or seven families living under a cut-bank.

The Comanches themselves seemed unable, or perhaps unwilling, to explain themselves any more exactly. Various groups had different names for the same village or band. They never used the name "Comanche" among themselves. That name was like the word "squaw"—a sound some early white man thought he heard an Indian make once back in Massachusetts; the only Indians who understood it were those who spoke English. Comanches called themselves "Nemmenna," which meant "The People." Many tribes, such as the Navajo and Cheyenne, had names meaning the same thing. So the Comanches considered themselves to be the total population by simple definition. Nothing else existed but various kinds of enemies which The People had to get rid of. They were working on it now.

Mart and Amos did learn a few things from the Comanches, mostly in the way of tricks for survival. They saved themselves from frozen feet by copying the Comanche snow boots, which were knee length and made of buffalo hide with the fur turned inside. And now they always carried small doeskin pouches of tinder, made of punkwood scrapings and fat drippings—or lint and kerosene, which worked even better, when they had it. This stuff could be lighted by boring into dry-rotted wood with a spinning stick. But what they did not learn of, and did not recognize until long after, was the mortal danger that had hung over them as they walked through those Comanche camps—such danger as turned their bellies cold, later, when they knew enough to understand it.

Christmas came and went unnoticed, for they spent it in the saddle; they were into another year. Mart was haunted by no more crooked stumps in this period, and the terror-dream did not return. The pain of grief was no longer ever-present; he was beginning to accept that the people to whom he had been nearest were not in the world any more, except, perhaps, for the lost little child who was their reason for being out here. But they were baffled and all but discouraged, as well as ragged and winter-gaunted, by the time they headed their horses toward home, nearly three hundred miles away.

Night was coming on as they raised the lights of the Mathison ranch two hours away. The sunset died, and a dark haze walled the horizon, making the snow-covered land lighter than the sky. The far-seen lights of the ranch house held their warmest promise in this hour, while you could still see the endless emptiness of the prairie in the dusk. Martin Pauley judged that men on horse-back, of all creatures on the face of the world, led the loneliest and most frost-blighted lives. He would have traded places with the lowest sodbuster that breathed, if only he could have had four walls, a stove, and people around him.

But as they drew near, Mart began to worry. The Mathisons should have got his letter two months ago, with any luck. But maybe they hadn't got it at all, and didn't even know that Brad was dead. Or if they did know, they might very likely be holding Brad's death against him. Mart turned shy and fearful, and began to dread going in there. The two of them were a sorry sight at best. They had been forced to trade worn-out horses four times, and had taken a worse beating every swap, so now they rode ponies resembling broke-down dogs. Amos didn't look so bad, Mart thought; gaunted though he was, he still had heft and dignity to him. Thick-bearded to the eyes, his hair grown to a great shaggy mane, he looked a little like some wilderness prophet of the Lord. But Mart's beard had come out only a thin and unsightly straggle. When he had shaved with his skinning knife he was left with such a peaked, sore-looking face that all he needed was a running nose to match. His neck was wind-galled to a turkey red, and his hands were so scaly with chap that they looked like vulture's feet. They had no soap in many weeks.

"We're lucky if they don't shoot on sight," he said. "We ain't fitten to set foot in any decent place."

Amos must have agreed, for he gave a long hail from a furlong out, and rode in shouting their names.

The Mathison house was of logs and built in two parts in the manner of the southern frontier. One roof connected what was really two small houses with a wind-swept passage, called a dog-trot, running between. The building on the left of the dog-trot was the kitchen. The family slept in the other, and Mart didn't know what was in there; he had never been in it.

Brad Mathison's two brothers—Abner, who was sixteen, and Tobe, fifteen—ran out from the kitchen to take their horses. As Abner held up his lantern to make sure of them, Mart got a shock. Ab had the same blue eyes as Brad, and the same fair scrubbed-looking skin, to which no dirt ever seemed to stick; so that for a moment Mart thought he saw Brad walking up to him through the dark. The boys didn't ask about their brother, but they didn't mention Mart's letter, either. Go on in, they said, the heck with your saddles, Pa's holding the door.

Nothing in the kitchen had changed. Mart remembered each thing in this room, as if nothing had been moved while he was gone. His eyes ran around the place anyway, afraid to look at the people. A row of shined-up copper pots and pans hung over the wood range, which could feed a lot of cowhands when it needed to; it was about the biggest in the country. Everything else they had here was homemade, planed or whittled, and pegged together. But the house was plastered inside, the whole thing so clean and bright he stood blinking in the light of the kerosene lamps, and feeling dirty. Actually he smelled mainly of juniper smoke, leather, and prairie wind, but he didn't know that. He felt as though he ought to be outside, and stand downwind.

Then Aaron Mathison had Mart by the hand. He looked older than Mart remembered him, and his sight seemed failing as his mild eyes searched Mart's face. "Thank thee for the letter thee wrote," Mathison said.

Mrs. Mathison came and put her arms around him, and for a moment held onto him as if he were her son. She hadn't done that since he was able to walk under a table without cracking his head, and to give him a hug she had to kneel on the floor. He vaguely remembered how beautiful and kind she had seemed to him then. But every year since she had gradually become dumpier, and quieter, and less thought about, until she had no more shape or color than a sack of wheat. She still had an uncommonly sweet smile, though, what times it broke through; and tonight as she smiled at Mart there was such wistfulness in it that he almost kissed her cheek. Only he had not been around people enough to feel as easy as that.

And Laurie . . . she was the one he looked for first, and was most aware of, and most afraid to look at. And she was the only one who did not come toward him at all. She stood at the wood range, pretending to get ready to warm something for them; she flashed Mart one quick smile, but stayed where she was.

"I have a letter for you," Aaron said to Amos. "It was brought on and left here by Joab Wilkes, of the Rangers, as he rode by."

"A what?"

"I have been told the news in this letter," Aaron said gravely. "It is good news, as I hope and believe." Amos followed as Aaron retired to the other end of the kitchen, where he fumbled in a cupboard.

Laurie was still at the stove, her back to the room, but her hands were idle. It occurred to Martin that she didn't know what to say, or do, any more than he did. He moved toward her with no clear object in view. And now Laurie turned at last, ran to him, and gave him a peck of a kiss on the corner of his mouth. "Why, Mart, I believe you're growing again."

"And him on an empty stomach," her mother said. "I wonder he doesn't belt you!"

After that everything was all right.

12

They had fresh pork and the first candied yams Mart had seen since a year ago Thanksgiving. Tobe asked Amos how many Comanch' he had converted in the Fight at the Cat-tails.

"Don't know." Amos was at once stolid and uncomfortable as he answered. "Shot at two-three dozen. But the other varmints carried 'em away. Worse scared than hurt, most like."

Tobe said, "I bet you got plenty scalps in your saddle bags!"

"Not one!"

"He just stomp' 'em in the dirt," Mart explained, and was surprised to see Amos' eyes widen in a flash of anger.

"Come morning," Amos said to Mart, wrenching clear of the subject, "I want you borry the buckboard, and run it over to my place. The boys will show you which team. Round up such clothes of mine, or yours, as got overlooked."

That "my place" didn't sound just right to Mart. It had always been "Henry's place" or "my brother's place" every time Amos had ever spoken of it before.

"Load up any food stores that wasn't stole or spoilt. Especially any unbust presarves. And any tools you see. Fetch 'em here. And if any my horses have come in, feed grain on the tail gate, so's they foller you back." There was that "my" again. "My horses" this time. Amos had owned exactly one horse, and it was dead.

"What about—" Mart had started to ask what he must do about Debbie's horses. Debbie, not Amos, was heir to the Edwards' livestock if she lived. "Nothing," he finished.

When they had eaten, Aaron Mathison and Amos got their heads together again in the far end of the room. Their long conference partly involved tally books, but Mart couldn't hear what was said. Laurie took her sewing basket to a kind of settle that flanked the wood range, and told Mart by a movement of her eyes that she meant him to sit beside her.

"If you're going over—over home," she said in a near whisper, "maybe I ought to tell you about—something. There's something over there. . . . I don't know if you'll understand." She floundered and lost her way.

He said flatly, "You talking about that story, the place is haunted?"

She stared at him.

He told her about the rider they had come on one night, packing up toward the Nations on business unknown. This man had spoken of heading into what he called the "old Edwards place," thinking to bed down for the night in the deserted house. Only, as he came near he saw lights moving around inside. Not like the place was lived in and lighted up. More like a single candle, carried around from room to room. The fellow got the hell out of there, Mart finished, and excuse him, he hadn't meant to say hell.

"What did Amos say?"

"He went in one of his black fits."

"Martie," Laurie said, "you might as well know what he saw. You'll find the burnt-out candle anyway."

"What candle?"

"Well . . . you see . . . it was coming on Christmas Eve. And I had the strongest feeling you were coming home. You know how hard you can know something that isn't so?"

"I sure do," Mart said.

"So . . . I rode over there, and laid a fire in the stove, and dusted up. And I —you're going to laugh at me, Martie."

"No, I ain't."

"Well, I—I made a couple of great gawky bush-holly wreaths, and cluttered up the back windows with them. And I left a cake on the table. A kind of a cake —it got pretty well crumbed riding over. But I reckoned you could see it was meant for a cake. You might as well fetch home the plate."

"I'll remember."

"And I set a candle in a window. It was a whopper—I bet it burned three-four days. That's what your owl-hoot friend saw. I see no doubt of it."

"Oh," said Mart. It was all he could think of to say.

"Later I felt foolish; tried to get over there, and cover my tracks. But Pa locked up my saddle. He didn't like me out so long worrying Ma."

"Well, I should hope!"

"You'd better burn those silly wreaths. Before Amos sees 'em, and goes in a 'black fit.' "

"It wasn't silly," Mart said.

"Just you burn 'em. And don't forget the plate. Ma thinks Tobe busted it and ate the cake."

"It beats me," Mart said honestly. "How come anybody ever to take such trouble. I never see such a thing."

"I guess I was just playing house. Pretty childish. I see that now. But—I just love that old house. I can't bear to think of it all dark and lonely over there."

It came to him that she wanted the old house to be their house to make bright and alive again. This was the best day he had ever had in his life, he supposed, what with the promising way it was ending. So now, of course, it had to be spoiled.

Two rooms opened off the end of the kitchen opposite the dog-trot, the larger being a big wintry storeroom. The other, in the corner nearest the stove, was a cubbyhole with an arrow-slit window and a buffalo rug. This was called the grandmother room, because it was meant for somebody old, or sick, who needed to be kept warm. Nowadays it had a couple of rawhide-strung bunks for putting up visitors without heating the bunkhouse where the seasonal hands were housed.

When the family had retired across the dog-trot, Amos and Mart dragged out a wooden tub for a couple of long-postponed baths. They washed what meager change of clothes they had, and hung the stuff on a line back of the stove to dry overnight. Their baggy long-handled underwear and footless socks seemed indecent, hung out in a room where Laurie lived, but they couldn't help it.

"What kind of letter you get?" Mart asked. The average saddle tramp never got a letter in his life.

Amos shook out a pair of wet drawers, with big holes worn on the insides of the thigh, and hung them where they dripped into the woodbin. "Personal kind," he grunted, finally.

"Serves me right, too. Don't know why I never learn."

"Huh?"

"Nothing."

"I been fixing to tell you," Amos began.

"That ain't needful."

"What ain't?"

"I know that letter ain't none of my business. Because nothing is. I just set on other people's horses. To see they foller along."

"I wasn't studying on no letter. Will you leave a man speak? I say I made a deal with old Mathison."

Mart was silent and waited.

"I got to be pushing on," Amos said, picking his words. Passing out information seemed to hurt Amos worse every day he lived. "I won't be around. So Mathison is going to run my cattle with his own. Being's I can't see to it myself."

"What's he get, the increase?"

"Why?"

"No reason. Seemed the natural thing to ask, that's all. I don't give a God damn what you do with your stock."

"Mathison come out all right," Amos said.

"When do we start?"

"You ain't coming."

Mart thought that over. "It seems to me," he began. His voice sounded thin and distant to himself. He started over too loudly. "It seems to me—"

"What you hollering for?"

"—we started out to look for Debbie," Mart finished.

"I'm still looking for her."

"That's good. Because so am I."

"I just told you—by God, will you listen?" It was Amos' voice raised this time. "I'm leaving you here!"

"No, you ain't."

"What?" Amos stared in disbelief.

"You ain't telling me where I stay!"

"You got to live, ain't you? Mathison's going to leave you stay on. Help out with the work what you can, and you'll know where your grub's coming from."

"I been shooting our grub," Mart said stubbornly. "If I can shoot for two, I can shoot for one."

"That still takes ca-tridges. And a horse."

Mart felt his guts drop from under his heart. All his life he had been virtually surrounded by horses; to ride one, you only had to catch it. Only times he had ever thought whether he owned one or not was when some fine fast animal, like one of Brad's, had made him wish it was his. But Amos was right. Nothing in the world is so helpless as a prairie man afoot.

"I set out looking for Debbie," he said. "I aim to keep on."

"Why?"

Mart was bewildered. "Because she's my—she's—" He had started to say that Debbie was his own little sister. But in the moment he hesitated, Amos cut him down.

"Debbie's my brother's young'n," Amos said. "She's my flesh and blood—not yours. Better you leave these things to the people concerned with 'em, boy. Debbie's no kin to you at all."

"I—I always felt like she was my kin."

"Well, she ain't."

"Our—I mean, her—her folks took me in off the ground. I'd be dead but for them. They even—"

"That don't make 'em any kin."

"All right. I ain't got no kin. Never said I had. I'm going to keep on looking, that's all."

"How?"

Mart didn't answer that. He couldn't answer it. He had his saddle and his gun, because Henry had given him those; but the loads in the gun were Amos', he supposed. Mart realized now that a man can be free as a wolf, yet unable to do what he wants at all.

They went on to bed in silence. Amos spoke out of the dark. "You don't give a man a chance to tell you nothing," he complained. "I want you to know something, Mart—"

"Yeah—you want me to know I got no kin. You told me already. Now shut your God damned head!"

One thing about being in the saddle all day, and every day, you don't get a chance to worry as much as other men do once you lie down at night. You fret, and you fret, and you try to think your way through—for about a minute and a half. Then you go to sleep.

13

Mart woke up in the blackness before the winter dawn. He pulled on his pants, and started up the fire in the wood range before he finished dressing. As he took down his ragged laundry from behind the stove, he was of a mind to leave Amos' stuff hanging there, but he couldn't quite bring himself to it. He made a bundle of Amos' things, and tossed it into their room. By the time he had wolfed a chunk of bread and some leavings of cold meat, Tobe and Abner were up.

"I got to fetch that stuff Amos wants," he said, "from over—over at his house. You want to show me what team?"

"Better wait while we hot up some breakfast, hadn't you?"

"I et already."

They didn't question it. "Take them little fat bays, there, in the nigh corral—the one with the shelter shed."

"I want you take notice of what a pretty match they be," said Tobe with shining pride. "We call 'em Sis and Bud. And pull? They'll outlug teams twice their heft."

"Sis is about the only filly we ever did bust around here," Abner said. "But they balanced so nice, we just couldn't pass her by. Oh, she might cow-kick a little—"

"A little? She hung Ab on the top bar so clean he just lay there flappin'."

"Feller doesn't mind a bust in the pants from Sis, once he knows her."

"I won't leave nothing happen to 'em," Mart promised.

He took the team shelled corn, and brushed them down while they fed. He limbered the frosty straps of the harness with his gloved hands, and managed to be hooked and out of there before Amos was up.

Even from a distance the Edwards place looked strangely barren. Hard to think why, at first, until you remembered that the house now stood alone, without its barn, sheds, and haystacks. The snow hid the black char and the ash of the burned stuff, as if it never had been. Up on the hill, where Martha, and Henry, and the boys were, the snow had covered even the crosses he had carved.

Up close, as Mart neared the back gallery, the effect of desolation was even worse. You wouldn't think much could happen to a sturdy house like that in just a few months, but it already looked as if it had been unlived in for a hundred years. Snow was drifted on the porch, and slanted deep against the door itself, unbroken by any tracks. In the dust-glazed windows Laurie's wreaths were ghostly against empty black.

When he had forced the door free of the iced sill, he found a still cold inside, more chilling in its way than the searing wind of the prairie. A thin high music that went on forever in the empty house was the keening of the wind in the chimneys. Almost everything he remembered was repaired and in place, but a gray film of dust lay evenly, in spite of Laurie's Christmas dusting. Her cake plate was crumbless, centering a pattern of innumerable pocket-mouse tracks in the dust upon the table.

He remembered something about that homemade table. Underneath it, an inch or so below the top, a random structural member made a little hidden shelf. Once when he and Laurie had been five or six, the Mathisons had come over for a taffy pull. He showed Laurie the secret shelf under the table, and they stored away some little square-cut pieces of taffy there. Afterward, one piece of taffy seemed to be stuck down; he wore out his fingers for months trying to break it loose. Years later he found out that the stubbornly stuck taffy was really the ironhead of a lag screw that you couldn't see where it was, but only feel with your fingers.

He found some winter clothes he sure could use, including some heavy socks Martha and Lucy had knitted for him. Nothing that had belonged to Martha and the girls was in the closets. He supposed some shut trunks standing around held whatever of their stuff the Comanches had left. He went to a little chest that had been Debbie's, with some idea of taking something of hers with him, as if for company; but he stopped himself before he opened the chest. I got these hands she used to hang onto, he told himself. I don't need nothing more. Except to find her.

He was in no hurry to get back. He wanted to miss supper at the Mathisons for fear he would lash out at Amos in front of the others; so, taking his time about everything he did, he managed to fool away most of the day.

A red glow from the embers in the stove was the only light in the Mathison house as he put away the good little team, but a lamp went up in the kitchen before he went in. Laurie was waiting up, and she was put out with him.

"Who gave you the right to lag out till all hours, scaring the range stock?"

"Amos and me always night on the prairie," he reminded her. "It's where we live."

"Not when I'm waiting up for you." She was wrapped twice around in a trade-blanket robe cinched up with a leather belt. Only the little high collar of her flannel nightgown showed, and a bit of blue-veined instep between her moccasins and the hem. Actually she had no more clothes than he had ever seen her wear in her life; there was no reason for the rig to seem as intimate as it somehow did.

He mumbled, "Didn't go to make work," and went to throw his rag-pickings in the grandmother room.

Amos was not in his bunk; his saddle and everything he had was gone.

"Amos rode on," Laurie said unnecessarily.

"Didn't he leave no word for me?"

"Any word," she corrected him. She shook down the grate and dropped fresh wood in the firebox. "He just said, tell you he had to get on." She pushed him gently backward against a bench, so that he sat down. "I mended your stuff," she said. "Such as could be saved."

He thought of the saddle-worn holes in the thighs of his other drawers. "Goddle mighty," he whispered.

"Don't know what your purpose is," she said, "getting so red in the face. I have brothers, haven't I?"

"I know, but—"

"I'm a woman, Martie." He had supposed that was the very point. "We wash and mend your dirty old stuff for you all our lives. When you're little, we even wash you. How a man can make out to get bashful in front of a woman, I'll never know."

He couldn't make any sense out of it. "You talk like a feller might just as leave run around stark nekkid."

"Wouldn't bother me. I wouldn't try it in front of Pa, was I you, so long as you're staying on." She went to the stove to fix his supper.

"I'm not staying, Laurie. I got to catch up with Amos."

She turned to see if he meant it. "Pa was counting on you. He's running your cattle now, you know, along with his own—"

"Amos' cattle."

"He let both winter riders go, thinking you and Amos would be back. Of course, riders aren't too hard to come by. Charlie MacCorry put in for a job."

"MacCorry's a good fast hand," was all he said.

"I don't know what you think you can do about finding Debbie that Amos can't do." She turned to face him solemnly, her eyes very dark in the uneven light. "He'll find her now, Mart. Please believe me. I know."

He waited, but she went back to the skillet without explanation. So now he took a chance and told her the truth. "That's what scares me, Laurie."

"If you're thinking of the property," she said, "the land, the cattle—"

"It isn't that," he told her. "No, no. It isn't that."

"I know Debbie's the heir. And Amos has never had anything in his life. But if you think he'd let harm come to one hair of that child's head on account of all that, then I know you're a fool."

He shook his head. "It's his black fits," he said; and wondered how he could make a mortal danger sound so idiotic.

"What?"

"Laurie, I swear to you, I've seen all the fires of hell come up in his eyes, when he so much as thinks about getting a Comanche in his rifle sights. You haven't seen him like I've seen him. I've known him to take his knife . . ." He let that drop. He didn't want to tell Laurie some of the things he had seen Amos do. "Lord knows I hate Comanches. I hate 'em like I never knew a man could hate nothin'. But you slam into a bunch of 'em, and kill some—you know what happens to any little white captives they got hold of, then? They get their brains knocked out. It's happened over and over again."

He felt she didn't take any stock in what he was saying. He tried again, speaking earnestly to her back. "Amos is a man can go crazy wild. It might come on him when it was the worst thing could be. What I counted on, I hoped I'd be there to stop him, if such thing come."

She said faintly, "You'd have to kill him."

He let that go without answer. "Let's have it now. Where's he gone, where you're so sure he'll find her?"

She became perfectly still for a moment. When she moved again, one hand stirred the skillet, while the other brought a torn-open letter out of the breast of her robe, and held it out to him. He recognized the letter that had been left with Aaron Mathison for Amos. His eyes were on her face, questioning, as he took it.

"We hoped you'd want to stay on," she said. All the liveliness was gone from her voice. "But I guess I knew. Seems to be only one thing in the world you care about any more. So I stole it for you."

He spread out the single sheet of ruled tablet paper the torn envelope contained. It carried a brief scrawl in soft pencil, well smeared.

Laurie said, "Do you believe in second sight? No, of course you don't. There's something I dread about this, Martie."

The message was from a trader Mart knew about, over on the Salt Fork of the Brazos. He called himself Jerem (for Jeremiah) Futterman—an improbable name at best, and not his own. He wasn't supposed to trade with Indians there any more, but he did, covering up by claiming that his real place of business was far to the west in the Arroyo Blanco, outside of Texas. The note said:

I bought a small size dress off a
Injun. If this here is a peece of
yr chiles dress bring reward, I know
where they gone.

Pinned to the bottom of the sheet with a horseshoe nail was a two-inch square of calico. The dirt that grayed it was worn evenly into the cloth, as if it had been unwashed for a long time. The little flowers on it didn't stand out much now, but they were there. Laurie was leaning over his shoulder as he held the sample to the light. A strand of her hair was tickling his neck, and her breath was on his cheek, but he didn't even know.

"Is it hers?"

He nodded.

"Poor little dirty dress . . ."

He couldn't look at her. "I've got to get hold of a horse. I just got to get me a horse."

"Is that all that's stopping you?"

"It isn't stopping me. I'll catch up to him. I got to."

"You've got horses, Martie."

"I—what?"

"You've got Brad's horses. Pa said so. He means it, Martie. Amos told us what happened at the Warrior. A lot of things you left out."

Mart couldn't speak for a minute, and when he could he didn't know what to say. The skillet started to smoke, and Laurie went to set it to the back of the range.

"Most of Brad's ponies are turned out. But the Fort Worth stud is up. He's coming twelve, but he'll outgame anything there is. And the good light gelding —the fast one, with the blaze."

"Why, that's Sweet-face," he said. He remembered Laurie naming that colt herself, when she was thirteen years old. "Laurie, that's your own good horse."

"Let's not get choosey, Bub. Those two are the ones Amos wanted to trade for and take. But Pa held them back for you."

"I'll turn Sweet-face loose to come home," he promised, "this side Fiddler's Crick. I ought to cross soon after daylight."

"Soon after—By starting when?"

"Now," he told her.

He was already in the saddle when she ran out through the snow, and lifted her face to be kissed. She ran back into the house abruptly, and the door closed behind her. He jabbed the Fort Worth stud, hard, with one spur. Very promptly he was bucked back to his senses, and all but thrown. The stallion conveyed a hard, unyielding shock like no horse Mart had ever ridden, as if he were made all of rocks and iron bands. Ten seconds of squealing contention cleared Mart's head, though he thought his teeth might be loosened a little; and he was on his way.

━━⟩⟩ 14 ⟨⟨━━

When Laurie had closed the door, she stood with her forehead against it a little while, listening to the violent hammer of hoofs sometimes muffled by the snow, sometimes ringing upon the frozen ground, as the Fort Worth stud tried to put Mart down. When the stud had straightened out, she heard Mart circle back to pick up Sweet-face's lead and that of the waspish black mule he had packed. Then he was gone, but she still stood against the door, listening to the receding hoofs. They made a crunch in the snow, rather than a beat, but she was able to hear it for a long time. Finally even that sound stopped, and she could hear only the ticking of the clock and the winter's-night pop of a timber twisting in the frost.

She blew out the lamp, crossed the cold dog-trot, and crept softly to her bed. She shivered for a few moments in the chill of the flour-sack-muslin sheets, but she slept between two deep featherbeds, and they warmed quite soon. For several years they had kept a big gaggle of geese, especially for making featherbeds. They had to let the geese range free, and the coyotes had got the last of them now; but the beds would last a lifetime almost.

As soon as she was warm again, Laurie began to cry. This was not like her. The Mathison men had no patience with blubbering women, and gave them no

sympathy at all, so Mathison females learned early to do without nervous out-
lets of this kind. But once she had given way to tears at all, she cried harder and
harder. Perhaps she had stored up every kind of cry there is for a long time.
She had her own little room, now, with a single rifle-slit window, too narrow for
harm to come through; but the matched-fencing partition was too flimsy to be
much of a barrier to sound. She pressed her face deep into the feathers, and
did her best to let no sound escape. It wasn't good enough. By rights, everybody should have been deep asleep long ago, but her mother heard her anyway,
and came in to sit on the side of her bed.

Laurie managed to snuffle, "Get under the covers, Ma. You'll catch you a
chill."

Mrs. Mathison got partly into the bed, but remained sitting up. Her work-
stiffened fingers were awkward as she tentatively stroked her daughter's hair.
"Now, Laurie. . . . Now, Laurie. . . ."

Laurie buried her face deeper in the featherbed. "I'm going to be an old
maid!" she announced rebelliously, her words half smothered.

"Why, Laurie!"

"There just aren't any boys—men—in this part of the world. I think this
everlasting wind blows 'em away. Scours the whole country plumb clean."

"Come roundup there's generally enough underfoot, seems to me. At least
since the peace. Place swarms with 'em. Worse'n ants in a tub of leftover
dishes."

"Oh!" Laurie whimpered in bitter exasperation. "Those hoot-owlers!" Her
mind wasn't running very straight. She meant owl-hooters, of course—a term
applied to hunted men, who liked to travel by night. It was true that the hands
who wandered out here to pick up seasonal saddle work were very often
wanted. If a Ranger so much as stopped by a chuck wagon, so many hands
would disappear that the cattlemen had angrily requested the Rangers to stay
away from roundups altogether. But they weren't professional badmen—not
bandits or killers; just youngsters, mostly, who had got into some trouble they
couldn't bring themselves to face out. Many of the cattlemen preferred this
kind, for they drifted on of their own accord, saving you the uncomfortable job
of firing good loyal riders who really wanted to stick and work. And they were
no hazard to home girls. They didn't even come into the house to eat, once
enough of them had gathered to justify hiring a wagon cook. Most of them had
joked with Laurie, and made a fuss over her, so long as she was little; but they
had stopped this about the time she turned fifteen. Nowadays they steered
clear, perhaps figuring they were already in trouble enough. Typically they
passed her, eyes down, with a mumbled, "Howdy, Mam," and a sheepish tug at
a ducked hat brim. Soon they were off with the wagon, and were paid off and
on their way the day they got back.

Actually, Laurie had almost always picked out some one of them to idolize,
and imagine she was in love with, from a good safe distance. After he rode on,
all unsuspecting, she would sometimes remember him, and spin daydreams
about him, for months and months. But she was in no mood to remember all
that now.

Mrs. Mathison sighed. She could not, in honesty, say much for the temporary hands as eligible prospects. "There's plenty others. Like—like Zack Harper. Such a nice, clean boy—"

"That nump!"

"And there's Charlie MacCorry—"

"*Him.*" A contemptuous rejection.

Her mother didn't press it. Charlie MacCorry hung around a great deal more than Mrs. Mathison wished he would, and she didn't want him encouraged. Charlie was full of high spirits and confidence, and might be considered flashily handsome, at least from a little distance off. Up close his good looks seemed somehow exaggerated, almost as in a caricature. What Mrs. Mathison saw in him, or thought she saw, was nothing but stupidity made noisy by conceit. Mentioning him at all had been a scrape at the bottom of the barrel.

She recognized the upset Laurie was going through as an inevitable thing, that every girl had to go through, somewhere between adolescence and marriage. Mrs. Mathison was of limited imagination, but her observation was sound, and her memory clear, so she could remember having gone through this phase herself. A great restlessness went with it, like the disquiet of a young wild goose at the flight season; as if something said to her, "Now, now or never again! Now, or life will pass you by. . . ." No one who knew Mrs. Mathison now could have guessed that at sixteen she had run away with a tinhorn gambler, having met him, in secret, only twice in her life. She could remember the resulting embarrassments with painful clarity, but not the emotions that had made her do it. She thought of the episode with shame, as an unexplainable insanity, from which she was saved only when her father overtook them and snatched her back.

She had probably felt about the same way when she ran off a second time— this time more successfully, with Aaron Mathison. Her father, a conservative storekeeper and a pillar of the Baptist Church, had regarded the Quakers in the Mathison background as benighted and misled, more to be pitied than anything else. But the young shaggy-headed Aaron he considered a dangerously irresponsible wild man, deserving not a whit more confidence than the staved-off gambler—who at least had the sense to run from danger, not at it. He never spoke to his daughter again. Mrs. Mathison forever after regarded this second escapade as a sound and necessary move, regarding which her parents were peculiarly blind and wrong-headed. Aaron Mathison in truth was a man like a great rooted tree, to which she was as tightly affixed as a lichen; no way of life without him was conceivable to her.

She said now with compassion, "Dear heart, dear little girl—Martin will come back. He's bound to come back." She didn't know whether they would ever see Martin Pauley again or not, but she feared the outrageous things—the runaways, the cheap marriages—which she herself had proved young girls to be capable of at this stage. She wanted to give Laurie some comforting hope, to help her bridge over the dangerous time.

"I don't care what he does," Laurie said miserably. "It isn't that at all."

"I never dreamed," her mother said, thoughtfully, ignoring the manifest untruth. "Why, you two always acted like—more like two tomboys than anything. How long has . . . When did you start thinking of Mart in this way?"

Laurie didn't know that herself. Actually, so far as she was conscious of it, it had been about an hour. Mart had been practically her best friend, outside the family, throughout her childhood. But their friendship had indeed been much the same as that of two boys. Latterly, she recalled with revulsion, she had idiotically thought Charlie MacCorry more fun, and much more interesting. But she had looked forward with a warm, innocent pleasure to having Mart live with them right in the same house. Now that he was suddenly gone—irrecoverably, she felt now—he left an unexpectedly ruinous gap in her world that nothing left to her seemed able to fill. She couldn't explain all that to her mother. Wouldn't know how to begin.

When she didn't answer, her mother patted her shoulder. "It will all seem different in a little while," she said in the futile cliché of parents. "These things have a way of passing off. I know you don't feel that way now; but they do. Time, the great healer . . ." she finished vaguely. She kissed the back of Laurie's head, and went away.

◄── 15 ──►

After days of thinking up blistering things to say, Mart judged he was ready for Amos. He figured Amos would come at him before they were through. Amos was a respected rough-and-tumble scrapper away from home. "I run out of words," Mart had heard him explain many a tangle. "Wasn't nothing left to do but hit him." Let him try.

But when he caught up, far up the Salt Fork, it was all wasted, for Amos wouldn't quarrel with him. "I done my best to free your mind," Amos said. "Mathison was fixing to step you right into Brad's boots. Come to think of it, that's a pair you got on. And Laurie—she wanted you."

"Question never come up," Mart said shortly.

Amos shrugged. "Couldn't say much more than I done."

"No, you sure couldn't. Not without landing flat on your butt!" Mart had always thought of Amos as a huge man, perhaps because he had been about knee high to Amos when he knew him first. But now, as Amos for a moment looked him steadily in the eye, Mart noticed for the first time that their eyes were on the same level. Mrs. Mathison had been right about Mart having taken a final spurt of growth.

"I guess I must have left Jerem's letter lying around."

"Yeah. You left it lying around." Mart had meant to ball up the letter and throw it in Amos' face, but found he couldn't now. He just handed it over.

"This here's another thing I tried to leave you out of," Amos said. "Martha put herself out for fifteen years bringing you up. I'll feel low in my mind if I get you done away with now."

"Ain't studying on getting done away with."

" 'Bring the reward,' he says here. From what I know of Jerem, he ain't the man to trust getting paid when he's earned it. More liable to try to make sure."

"Now, he ought to know you ain't carrying the thousand around with you!"

"Ain't I?"

So he was. Amos did have the money with him. Now there's a damn fool thing, Mart considered. Aloud he said, "If he's got robbery in mind, I suppose he won't tell the truth anyway."

"I think he will. So he'll have a claim later in case we slip through his claws."

"You talk like we're fixing to steal bait from a snap trap!"

Amos shrugged. "I'll admit one thing. In a case like this, two guns got about ten times the chance of one."

Mart was flattered. He couldn't work himself up to picking a fight with Amos after that. Things dropped back to what they had been before they went home at all. The snow melted off, and they traveled in mud. Then the weather went cold again, and the wet earth froze to iron. More snow was threatening as they came to Jerem Futterman's stockade, where Lost Mule Creek ran into the Salt Fork. The creek had not always been called the Lost Mule. Once it had been known as Murder River. They didn't know why, nor how the name got changed, but maybe it was a good thing to remember now.

Jerem Futterman was lightly built, but well knit, and moved with a look of handiness. Had he been a cow-horse you might have bought him, if you liked them mean, and later shot him, if you didn't like them treacherous. He faced them across a plank-and-barrel counter in the murk of his low-beamed log trading room, seeming to feel easier with a barrier between himself and strangers. Once he had had another name. Some thought he called himself Futterman because few were likely to suspect a man of fitting such a handle to himself, if it wasn't his right one.

"Knew you'd be along," he said. "Have a drink."

"Have one yourself." Amos refused the jug, but rang a four-bit piece on the planks.

Futterman hesitated, but ended by taking a swig and pocketing the half dollar. This was watched by four squaws hunkered down against the wall and a flat-faced breed who snoozed in a corner. Mart had spotted four or five other people around the place on their way in, mostly knock-about packers and bull-team men, who made up a sort of transient garrison.

The jug lowered, and they went into the conventional exchange of insults that passed for good humor out here. "Wasn't sure I'd know you standing up," Futterman said. "Last I saw, you were flat on your back on the floor of a saloon at Painted Post."

"You don't change much. See you ain't washed or had that shirt off," Amos said; and decided that was enough politeness. "Let's see the dress!"

A moment of total stillness filled the room before Futterman spoke. "You got the money?"

"I ain't paying the money for the dress. I pay when the child is found—alive, you hear me?"

The trader had a trick of dropping his lids and holding motionless with cocked head, as if listening. The silence drew out to the cracking point; then Futterman left the room without explanation. Mart and Amos exchanged a glance. What might happen next was anybody's guess; the place had an evil, trappy feel. But Futterman came back in a few moments, carrying a rolled-up bit of cloth.

It was Debbie's dress, all right. Amos went over it, inch by inch, and Mart knew he was looking for blood stains. It was singular how often people west of the Cross Timbers found themselves searching for things they dreaded to find. The dress was made with tiny stitches that Amos must be remembering as the work of Martha's fingers. But now the pocket was half torn away, and the square hole where the sample had been knifed out of the front seemed an Indian kind of mutilation, as if the little dress were dead.

"Talk," Amos said.

"A man's got a right to expect some kind of payment."

"You're wasting time!"

"I paid twenty dollars for this here. You lead a man to put out, and put out, but when it comes to—"

Amos threw down a gold piece, and Mart saw Futterman regret that he hadn't asked more.

"I had a lot of other expense, you realize, before—"

"Bull shit," Amos said. "Where'd you get this?"

One more long moment passed while Jerem Futterman gave that odd appearance of listening. This man is careful, Mart thought; he schemes, and he holds back the aces—but he's got worms in his craw where the sand should be.

"A young buck fetched it in. Filched it, naturally. He said it belonged off a young'n—"

"Is she alive?"

"He claimed so. Said she was catched by Chief Scar the tail end of last summer."

"Take care, Jerem! I never heard of no Chief Scar!"

"Me neither." Futterman shrugged. "He's supposed to be a war chief with the Nawyecky Comanches."

"War chief," Amos repeated with disgust. Among the Comanches any warrior with a good string of coups was called a war chief.

"You want me to shut up, say so," Futterman said testily. "Don't be standing there giving me the lie every minute!"

"Keep talking," Amos said, relaxing a little.

"Scar was heading north. He was supposed to cross the Red, and winter-in at Fort Sill. According to this buck. Maybe he lied."

"And maybe you lie," Amos said.

"In that case, you won't find her, will you? And I won't get the thousand."

"You sure as hell won't," Amos agreed. He stuffed Debbie's dress into the pocket of his sheepskin.

"Stay the night, if you want. You can have your pick of them squaws."

The squaws sat stolidly with lowered eyes. Mart saw that a couple of them, with the light color of mixed blood, were as pretty as any he had seen. Amos ignored the offer, however. He bought a skimpy mule load of corn for another twenty dollars, with only a token argument over the outrageous price.

"I expect you back when you find her," Futterman reminded him, "to pay the money into this here hand." He showed the dirty hand he meant.

"I'll be back if I find her," Amos said. "And if I don't."

Little daylight was left as they struck northward along Lost Mule Creek. The overcast broke, and a full moon rose, huge and red at first, dwindling and paling as it climbed. And within two hours they knew that the lonely prairie was not half lonely enough, from the standpoint of any safety in this night. Mart's stud horse told them first. He began to prick his ears and show interest in something unseen and unheard, off on their flank beyond the Lost Mule. When he set himself to whinny they knew there were horses over there. Mart picked him up sharply, taking up short on the curb, so the uproar the stud was planning on never come out. But the horse fussed and fretted from then on.

Though the stud could be stopped from hollering, their pack mule could not. A little farther on he upped his tail, lifted his head, and whipsawed the night with a bray fit to rouse the world.

"That fool leatherhead is waking up people in Kansas," Mart said. "You want I should tie down his tail? I heard they can't yell at all, failin' they get their tail up."

Amos had never seen it tried, but he figured he could throw off on that one by percentage alone. "That's what I like about you," he said. "Man can tell you any fur-fetched thing comes in his head, and you'll cleave to it for solemn fact from then on."

"Well, then—why don't we split his pack, and stick a prickle pear under his tail, and fog him loose?"

"He'd foller anyway."

"We can tie him. Shoot him even. This here's the same as traveling with a brass band."

Amos looked at him with disbelief. "Give up a fifteen-dollar mule for the likes of Jerem? I guess you don't know me very well. Leave the brute sing."

The thing was that nothing answered the mule from beyond the creek. The stud might have scented a band of mustangs, but mustangs will answer a mule same as a horse. Their animals were trying to call to ridden horses, probably Spanish curbed.

"I see no least reason," Mart said, "why they can't gallop ahead and dry-gulch us any time they want to try."

"How do you know they haven't tried?"

"Because we ain't been fired on. They could pick any time or place they want."

"I ain't led you any kind of place they want. Why you think I swung so far out back there a few miles? That's our big advantage—they got to use a place I pick."

They rode on and on, while the moon shrunk to a pale dime, and crossed the zenith. The mule lost interest, but the stud still fretted, and tried to trumpet. The unseen, unheard stalkers who dogged them were still there.

"This can't run on forever," Mart said.

"Can't it?"

"We got to lose 'em or outrun 'em. Or—"

"What for? So's they can come on us some far place, when we least expect?"

"I can't see 'em giving up," Mart argued. "If this kind of haunting has to go on for days and weeks—"

"I mean to end it tonight," Amos said.

They off-saddled at last in the rough ground from which the Lost Mule rose. Amos picked a dry gully, and they built a big tenderfoot fire on a patch of dry sand. Mart did what Amos told him up to here.

"I figure I got a right to know what you aim to do," he said at last.

"Well, we might make up a couple of dummies out o'—"

Mart rebelled. "If I heard one story about a feller stuffed grass in his blanket and crawled off in the buck brush, I heard a million! Come morning, the blanket is always stuck full of arrows. Dozens of 'em. Never just one arrow, like a thrifty Indian would make do. Now, you know how hard arrows is to make!"

"Ain't studyin' on Indians."

"No, I guess not. I guess it must be crazy people."

"In poker, in war," Amos said, "what you want is a simple, stupid plan. Reason you hear about the old flim-flams so much is they always work. Never try no deep, tricky plan. The other feller can't foller it; it throws him back on his common sense—which is the last thing you want."

"But this here is childish!"

Amos declared that what you plan out never helps much any; more liable to work against you than anything else. What the other fellow had in mind was the thing you wanted to figure on. It was the way you used *his* plan that decided which of you got added to the list of the late lamented. But he said no more of dummies. "You hungry? I believe they'll stand off and wait for us to settle down. We got time to eat, if you want to cook."

"I don't care if I never eat. Not with what's out there in the dark."

Only precaution they took was to withdraw from the ember-lighted gully, and take cover under a low-hung spruce on the bank. About the first place a killer would look, Mart thought, once he found their camp. Mart rolled up in his blankets, leaving Amos sitting against the stem of the spruce, his rifle in his hands.

"You see, Martie," Amos went back to it, "a man is very liable to see what he's come expecting to see. Almost always, he'll picture it all out in his mind beforehand. So you need give him but very little help, and he'll swindle hisself. Like one time in the Rangers, Cap Harker offered five hundred dollars reward for a feller—"

"Now who ever give the Rangers five hundred dollars? Not the Texas legislature, I guarandamtee."

"—for taking a feller alive, name of Morton C. Pettigrew. Cap got the description printed up on a handbill. Middling size; average weight; hair-colored hair; eye-colored eyes—"

"Now wait a minute!"

"Shut up. Temperment sociable and stand-offish; quiet, peaceable, and always making trouble."

"Never see such a damn man."

"Well, you know, that thing got us more than forty wanted men? Near every settlement in Texas slung some stranger in the calabozo and nailed up the door. We gathered in every size and shape, without paying a cent. A little short redhead Irishman, and a walking skeleton a head taller'n me, and a Chinaman, and any number of renegade Mex. Near every one of 'em worth hanging for something, too, except the Chinaman; we had to leave him go. Cap Harker was strutting up and down Texas, singing 'Bringing home the sheaves,' and speaking of running for governor. But it finished him."

"How?"

"Marshal down at Castlerock grobe a feller said he *was* Morton C. Pettigrew. We sent a man all the way back to Rhode Island, trying to break his story. But it was his right name, sure enough. Finally we had to make up the reward out of our own pants."

Mart asked nervously, "You think they'll try guns, or knives?"

"What? Who? Oh. My guess would be knives. But you let them make the choice. We'll handle whichever, when it comes. Go'n to sleep. I got hold of everything."

All they really knew was that it would come. No doubt of that now. The stud was trumpeting again, and stammering with his feet. Mart was not happy with the probability of the knives. Most Americans would rather be blown to bits than face up to the stab and slice of whetted steel—nobody seems to know just why. Mart was no different. Sleep, the man says. Fine chance, knowing your next act must be to kill a man, or get a blade in the gizzard. And he knew Amos was a whole lot more strung-up than he was willing to let on. Amos hadn't talked so much in a month of Sundays.

Mart settled himself as comfortably as he could for the sleepless wait that was ahead; and was asleep in the next half minute.

The blast of a rifle wakened him to the most confusing ten minutes of his life. The sound had not been the bang that makes your ears ring when a shot is fired beside you, but the explosive howl, like a snarl, that you hear when it is fired toward you from a little distance off. He was rolling to shift his probably spotted position when the second shot sounded. Somebody coughed as the bullet hit, made a brief strangling noise, and was quiet. Amos was not under the spruce; Mart's first thought was that he had heard him killed.

Down in the gully the embers of their fire still glowed. Nothing was going on down there at all; the action had been behind the spruce on the uphill side. He wormed on his belly to the place where he had heard the man hit. Two bodies were there, instead of one, the nearer within twenty feet of the spot where he had slept. Neither dead man was Amos. And now Mart could hear the hoofdrum of a running horse.

From a little ridge a hundred feet away a rifle now spoke twice. The second flash marked for him the spot where a man stood straight up, firing deliberately down their back trail. Mart leveled his rifle, but in the moment he took to make

sure of his sights in the bad light, the figure disappeared. The sound of the running horse faded out, and the night was quiet.

Mart took cover and waited; he waited a long time before he heard a soft footfall near him. As his rifle swung, Amos' voice said, "Hold it, Mart. Shootin's over."

"What in all hell is happening here?"

"Futterman held back. He sent these two creeping in. They was an easy shot from where I was. Futterman, though—it took an awful lucky hunk of lead to catch up with that one. He was leaving like a scalded goat."

"What the devil was you doing out there?"

"Walked out to see if he had my forty dollars on him." It wasn't the explanation Mart was after, and Amos knew it. "Got the gold pieces all right. Still in his pants. I don't know what become of my four bits."

"But how come—how did you make out to nail 'em?"

What can you say to a man so sure of himself, so belittling of chance, that he uses you for bait? Mart could have told him something. There had been a moment when he had held Amos clean in his sights, without knowing him. One more pulsebeat of pressure on the hair-set trigger, and Amos would have got his head blown off for his smartness. But he let it go.

"We got through it, anyway," Amos said.

"I ain't so sure we're through it. A thing like this can make trouble for a long, long time."

Amos did not answer that.

As they rode on, a heavy cloud bank came over the face of the lowering moon. Within the hour, snow began to fall, coming down in flakes so big they must have hissed in the last embers of the fire they had left behind. Sunrise would find only three low white mounds back there, scarcely recognizable for what they were under the blanketing snow.

16

Winter was breaking up into slush and sleet, with the usual freezing setbacks, as they reached Fort Sill again. The Indians would begin to scatter as soon as the first pony grass turned green, but for the present there were many more here than had come in with the early snows. Apparently the Wild Tribes who had taken the Quaker Peace Policy humorously at first were fast learning to take advantage of it. Three hundred lodges of Wichitas in their grass beehive houses, four hundred of Comanches in hide tepees, and more Kiowas than both together, were strung out for miles up Cache Creek and down the Medicine Bluff, well past the mouth of Wolf Creek.

Nothing had been seen of the Queherenna, or Antelope Comanches, under Bull Bear, Black Horse, and Wolf-Lying-Down, or the Kotsetaka (Buffalo-followers) under Shaking Hand, all of whom stayed in or close to the Staked Plains. The famous war chief Tabananica, whose name was variously translated as Sound-of-Morning, Hears-the-Sunrise, and Talks-with-Dawn-Spirits, was not seen, but he was heard from: He sent word to the fort urging the soldiers to come out and fight. Still, those in charge were not heard to complain that they hadn't accumulated Indians enough. A far-sighted chief named Kicking Bird was holding the Kiowas fairly well in check, and the Wichitas were quiet, as if suspicious of their luck; but the Comanches gleefully repaid the kindness of the Friends with arrogance, insult, and disorderly mischief.

Mart and Amos were unlikely to forget Agent Hiram Appleby. This Quaker, a graying man in his fifties, looked like a small-town storekeeper, and talked like one, with never a "thee" nor "thou"; a quiet, unimpressive man, with mild short-sighted eyes, stains on his crumpled black suit, and the patience of the eternal rocks. He had watched the Comanches kill his milch cows, and barbecue them in his dooryard. They had stolen all his red flannel underwear off the line, and paraded it before him as the outer uniform of an improvised society of young bucks. And none of this changed his attitude toward them by the width of a whistle.

Once they watched a Comanche buck put a knife point to Appleby's throat in a demand for free ammunition, and spit in the Agent's face when it didn't work. Appleby simply stood there, mild, fusty looking, and immovable, showing no sign of affront. Amos stared in disbelief, and his gun whipped out.

"If you harm this Indian," Appleby said, "you will be seized and tried for murder, just as soon as the proper authorities can be reached." Amos put away his gun. The Comanche spat in an open coffee bin, and walked out. "Have to make a cover for that," Appleby said.

They would never understand this man, but they could not disbelieve him, either. He did all he could, questioning hundreds of Indians in more than one tribal tongue, to find out what Mart and Amos wanted to know. They were around the Agency through what was left of the winter, while Comanches, Kiowas, and Kiowa Apaches came and went. When at last Appleby told them that he thought Chief Scar had been on the Washita, but had slipped away, they did not doubt him.

"Used to be twelve main bands of Comanches, in place of only nine, like now," Appleby said, with the customary divergence from everything they had been told before. "Scar seems to run with the Wolf Brothers; a Comanche peace chief, name of Bluebonnet, heads them up."

They knew by now what a peace chief was. Among Comanches, some old man in each family group was boss of his descendants and relatives, and was a peace chief because he decided things like when to move and where to camp— anything that did not concern war. When a number of families traveled together, their peace chiefs made up the council—which meant they talked things over, sometimes. There was always one of the lot that the others came to

look up to, and follow more or less—kind of tacitly, never by formal election—
and this one was *the* peace chief. A war chief was just any warrior of any age
who could plan a raid and get others to follow him. Comanche government was
weak, loose, and informal; their ideas of acceptable behavior were enforced
almost entirely by popular opinion among their kind.

"Putting two and two together, and getting five," Appleby told them, "I get
the idea Bluebonnet kind of tags along with different bunches of Nawyeckies.
Sometimes one bunch of 'em, sometimes another. Too bad. Ain't any kind of
Comanche moves around so shifty as the Nawyecky. One of the names the
other Comanches has for 'em means 'Them As Never Gets Where They're
Going.' Don't you believe it. What it is, they like to lie about where they're
going, and start that way, then double back, and fork off. As a habit; no reason
needed. I wouldn't look for 'em in Indian Territory, was I you; nor anyplace else
they should rightfully be. I'd look in Texas. I kind of get the notion, more from
what ain't said than what they tell me, they wintered in the Pease River breaks.
So no use to look there—they'll move out, with the thaw. I believe I'd look up
around the different headwaters of the Brazos, if I was doing it."

"You're talking about a hundred-mile spread, cutting crosswise—you know
that, don't you? Comes to tracing out all them branches, nobody's going to do
that in any one year!"

"I know. Kind of unencouraging, ain't it? But what's a man to say? Why don't
you take a quick look at twenty-thirty miles of the Upper Salt? I know you just
been there, or nigh to it, but that was months ago. Poke around in Canyon
Blanco a little. Then cut across and try the Double Mountain Fork. And Yellow
House Crick after, so long as you're up there. If you don't come on some kind
of Nawyeckies, some place around, I'll put in with you!"

He was talking about the most remote, troublesome country in the length of
Texas, from the standpoint of trying to find an Indian.

Amos bought two more mules and a small stock of trade goods, which Appleby helped them to select. They took a couple of bolts of cotton cloth, one
bright red and one bright blue, a lot of fancy buttons, spools of ribbon, and junk
like that. No knives, because the quality of cheap ones is too easily detected,
and no axe heads because of the weight. Appleby encouraged them to take half
a gross of surplus stock-show ribbons that somebody had got stuck with, and
shipped out to him. These were flamboyant sateen rosettes, as big as your hand,
with flowing blue, red, or white ribbons. The gold lettering on the ribbons
mostly identified winners in various classes of hogs. They were pretty sure the
Indians would prize these highly, and wear them on their war bonnets. No
notions of comedy or fraud occurred either to Appleby or the greenhorn traders
in connection with the hog prizes. A newcomer might think it funny to see a
grim-faced war chief wearing a First Award ribbon, Lard-Type Boar, at the
temple of his headdress. But those who lived out there very early got used to
the stubbornness of Indian follies, and accepted them as commonplace. They
gave the savage credit for knowing what he wanted, and let it go at that.

And they took a great quantity of sheet-iron arrowheads, the most sure-fire
merchandise ever taken onto the plains. These were made in New England,

and cost the traders seven cents a dozen. As few as six of them would some-times fetch a buffalo robe worth two and a half to four dollars.

So now they set out through the rains and muck of spring, practicing their sign language, and learning their business as they went along. They were travel-ing now in a guise of peace; yet they trotted the long prairies for many weeks without seeing an Indian of any kind. Sometimes they found Indian signs—warm ashes in a shallow, bowl-like Comanche firepit, the fresh tracks of an unshod pony—but no trail that they could follow out. Searching the empty plains, it was easy to understand why you could never find a village when you came armed and in numbers to destroy it. Space itself was the Comanche's fortress. He seemed to live out his life immune to discovery, invisible beyond the rim of the world; as if he could disappear at will into the Spirit Land he described as lying beyond the sunset.

Then their luck changed, and for a while they found Comanches around every bend of every creek. Mart learned, without ever quite believing, the dif-ference between Comanches on raid and Comanches among their own lodges. Given the security of great space, these wildest of horsemen became amiable and merry, quick with their hospitality. Generosity was the key to prestige in their communal life, just as merciless ferocity was their standard in the field. They made the change from one extreme to the other effortlessly, so that war-riors returning with the loot of a ravaged frontier settlement immediately be-came the poorest men in their village through giving everything away.

Their trading went almost too well for their purposes. Comanche detach-ments that had wintered in the mountains, on the borders of Piute and Sho-shone country, were rich in furs, particularly fox and otter, far more valuable now than beaver plews since the passing of the beaver hat. A general swap, big enough to clean out a village, took several days, the first of which was spent in long silences and casual conversations pretending disinterest in trade. But by the second day the Comanche minds had been made up; and though Mart and Amos raised their prices past the ridiculous, their mules were soon so loaded that they had to cache their loot precariously to keep an excuse for continuing their search.

Once the first day's silences were over, the Indians loved to talk. Caught short of facts they made up stories to suit—that was the main trouble when you wanted information from them. The searchers heard that Debbie was with Woman's Heart, of the Kiowas; with Red Hog, with Wolves-talk-to-him, with Lost Pony in the Palo Duro Canyon. They heard, in a face-blackened ritual of mourning, that she had died a full year before. Later they heard that she had been dead one month. Many Indians spoke of knowing Scar. Though they never knew just where he was, he was most often said to ride with Bluebonnet —a name sometimes translated as "the Flower." Mart and Amos both felt cer-tain that they were closing in.

That was the summer a sub-chief of the Nocona Comanches, named Double Bird, tried to sell them a gaggle of squaws. They didn't know what he was driving at, to begin with. He signed that he had something to show them, and walked them out of his squalid ten-lodge village to the banks of the Rabbit Ear. Suddenly they were looking down at a covey of eight or nine mother-naked

Indian girls, bathing in a shallow pool. The girls yipped and sat down in the water as the strangers appeared. Double Bird spoke; slowly the girls stood up again, and went on washing themselves in a self-conscious silence, lathering their short-cropped hair with bear grass.

Double Bird explained in sign language that he found himself long on women, but short of most everything else—especially gunpowder. How did they like these? Fat ones. Thin ones. Take and try. Amos told the chief that they didn't have his price with them, but Double Bird saw no obstacle in that. Try now. You like, go get gunpowder, lead; he would like a few dozen breech-loading rifles. Squaw wait.

Some of the young squaws were slim and pretty, and one or two were light-skinned, betraying white blood. Amos looked at Mart, and saw that he was staring with glassy eyes.

"Wake up," Amos said, jabbing him with a thumb like the butt of a lance. "You going to pick some, or not?"

"I know one thing," Mart said, "I got to give up. Either give up and go back, or give up and stay out."

"That's just the trouble. Pretty soon it's too late. Longer you're out, the more you want to go back—only you don't know how. Until you don't fit any place any more. You'll end up a squaw man—you can mark my word. You see why I tried to leave you home?"

During this time Mart had one recurrence of the terror-dream. He had supposed he would never have it any more, now that he had a pretty fair idea of how it had been caused. But the dream was as strong as ever, and in no way changed. The deathly dream voices in the reddish dark were as weird and unearthly as ever, only vaguely like the yammering war cries he had heard at the Cat-tails. Amos shook him out of it, on the theory he must be choking on something, since he made no sound. But he slept no more that night.

Nevertheless, he was steadying, and changing. His grief for his lost people had forked, and now came to him in two ways, neither one as dreadful as the agony of loss he had felt at first. One way was in the form of a lot of little guilt-memories of unkindnesses that he now could never redress. Times when he had talked back to Martha, hadn't had time to read to Debbie, failed to thank Henry for fixing him up a saddle—sometimes these things came back in cruelly sharp detail.

The other way in which his grief returned was in spells of homesickness. Usually these came on him when things were uncomfortable, or went wrong; while they lasted, nothing ahead seemed to offer any hope. He had no home to which he could ever go back. No such thing was in existence any more on this earth. This homesickness, though, was gradually being replaced by a loneliness for Laurie, who could give him worries of another kind, but who at least was alive and real, however far away.

A more immediate frustration was that he could not seem to catch up with Amos in learning Comanche. He believed this to be of the utmost importance. Sign language was adequate, of course, for talking with Indians, but they wanted to understand the remarks not meant for their ears. Maybe Mart was trying too hard. Few Comanche syllables had anything like the sound of anything in English. But Amos substituted any crude approximate, whereas Mart was trying to get it right and could not.

Then Mart accidentally bought a squaw.

He had set out to buy a fox cape she was wearing, but ran into difficulty. His stubbornness took hold, and he dickered with her whole family for hours. At one point, Amos came and stood watching him curiously, until the stare got on Mart's nerves. "What the devil you gawkin' at? Y'see somepin' green?"

"Kind of branching out, ain't you?"

"Caught holt of a good hunk o' fur—that's all!"

Amos shrugged. "Guess that's one thing to call it." He went away.

Mart fingered the fox skins again. They still looked like prime winter stuff to him. He closed the deal abruptly by paying far too much, impatient to get it over with. And next he was unable to get possession. Amos had already diamond-hitched the mule packs, and it was time to go. But the squaw would only clutch the cape around her, chattering at him. When finally she signed that she would be back at once, and ran off among the lodges, Mart noticed that an uncomfortable number of Comanches were pressed close around him, looking at him very strangely. Bewildered and furious, he gave up, and pushed through them to his horse.

By the time he was set to ride, the young squaw had unexpectedly reappeared, exactly as she had promised. She was mounted bareback on an old crowbait that evidently belonged to her, and she carried her squaw bag, packed to bulging, before her on the withers. Behind her massed a whole phalanx of her people, their weapons in their hands. Mart sign-talked at the scowling bucks, "Big happy present from me to you," in rude gestures dangerously close to insult; and he led out, wanting only to be away from there.

The Comanche girl and her old plug fell in behind. He ignored her for a mile, but presently was forced to face it: She thought she was going with them. Brusquely he signed to her to turn her pony. She wheeled it obediently in one complete revolution, and fell in behind them again. He signaled more elaborately, unmistakably this time, telling her she must go back. She sat and stared at him.

Amos spoke sharply. "What the hell you doing?"

"Sending her home, naturally! Can't leave her tag along with—"

"What for God's sake you buy her for, if you didn't want her?"

"*Buy her?*"

"Mean to tell me—" Amos pulled up short and glared at him with disbelief—"You got the guts to set there and say you didn't even know it?"

"Course I didn't know it! You think I—" He didn't finish it. Comprehension of his ridiculous situation overwhelmed him, and he forgot what he had had in mind.

Amos blew up. "You God damned chunkhead!" he yelled. "When in the name of the sweet Christ you going to learn to watch what you're doing?"

"Well, she's got to go back," Mart said sullenly.

"She sure as hell is not going back! Them bastards would snatch our hair off before sundown, you flout 'em like that!"

"Oh, bloody murder," Mart moaned. "I just as lief give up and—"

"Shut up! Fetch your God damned wife and come along! What we need is distance!"

Wife. This here can't be happening, Mart thought. Man with luck like mine could never last. Not even this far. Should been killed long ago. And maybe I was—that's just what's happened. This horse ain't carrying a thing but a haunted saddle. . . .

He paid no more attention to her, but when they camped by starlight she was there, watering and picketing their animals, building their fire, fetching water. They wouldn't let her cook that night, but she watched them attentively as they fried beans and antelope steak, then made coffee in the same frying pan. Mart saw she was memorizing their motions, so that she would someday be able to please them. He furtively looked her over. She was quite young, a stocky little woman, inches less than five feet tall. Her face was broad and flat, set woodenly, for the time being, in a vaguely pleasant expression. Like most Comanche women, her skin was yellowish, of a lighter color than that of the males, and her hair was cropped short, in accordance with Comanche custom. Her long, entirely unlearnable name, when Amos questioned her about it, sounded like T'sala-ta-komal-ta-nama. "Wants you to call her Mama," Amos interpreted it, and guffawed as Mart answered obscenely. Now that he was over his mad, Amos was having more fun out of this than anything Mart could remember. She tried to tell them in sign language what her name meant without much success. Apparently she was called something like "Wild-Geese-Fly-Over-in-the-Night-Going-Honk," or, maybe, "Ducks-Talk-All-Night-in-the-Sky." In the time that she was with them Mart never once pronounced her name so that she recognized it; he usually began remarks to her with "Look—" which she came to accept as her new name. Amos, of course, insisted on calling her Mrs. Pauley.

Time came to turn in, in spite of Mart's efforts to push it off as long as he could. Amos rolled into his blankets, but showed no sign of dozing; he lay there as bright-eyed as a sparrow, awaiting Mart's next embarrassment with relish. Mart ignored the little Comanche woman as he finally spread out his blankets, hoping that she would let well enough alone if he would. No such a thing. Her movements were shy, deferential, yet completely matter-of-fact, as she laid her own blankets on top of his. He had braced himself against this, and made up his mind what he must do, lest he arm Amos with a hilarious story about him, such as he would never live down. He did not want this Comanche woman in the least, and dreaded the night with her; but he was determined to sleep with her if it killed him.

He pulled his boots, and slowly, gingerly, doubled the blankets over him. The Comanche girl showed neither eagerness nor hesitation, but only an acceptance of the inevitable, as she crept under the blankets, and snuggled in beside him. She was very clean—a good deal cleaner than he was, for the matter of that. The Comanche women bathed a lot when they had any water—they would break ice to get into the river. And often steeped themselves in sage smoke, particularly following menstruation, when this kind of cleansing was a required ritual. She seemed very small, and a little scared, and he felt sorry for her. For a moment he thought the night was going to be all right. Then, faint, but living, and unmistakable, the smell of Indian. . . . It was not an offensive odor; it had to do, rather, with the smoke of their fires, with the fur and wild-tanned leather they wore, and with the buffalo, without which they did not know how to live. He had supposed he had got used to the smoky air of lodges, and outgrown the senseless fear that had haunted his childhood. But now he struck away the blankets and came to his feet.

"Need water," he said in Comanche. She got up at once, and brought him some. A choking sound came from where Amos lay; Mart had a glimpse of Amos' compressed mouth and reddening face before Amos covered his head, burying the laughter he could not repress. Anger snatched Mart, so violent that he stood shaking for a moment, unable to turn away. When he could, he walked off into the dark in his sock feet; he was afraid he would kill Amos if he stood there listening to that smothered laughter.

He had figured out an excuse to give her by the time he came back. He explained in signs that his power-medicine was mixed up with a taboo, such that he must sleep alone for a period of time that he left indefinite. She accepted this tale readily; it was the kind of thing that would seem logical, and reasonable, to her. He thought she looked mildly relieved.

At their noon stop on the third day, Amos believed they had come far enough to be safe. "You can get rid of her, now, if you want."

"How?"

"You can knock her on the head, can't you? Though, now I think of it, I never seen you show much stomick for anything as practical as that."

Mart looked at him a moment. He decided to assume Amos was fooling, and let it pass without answer. Amos doubled a lead rope, weighted it with a couple of big knots, and tested it with a whistling snap. "Show you another way," he said; and started toward the Comanche girl.

Suddenly Mart was standing in front of him. "Put that thing down before I take it away from you!"

Amos stared. "What the hell's got into you now?"

"It's my fault she's here—not hers. She's done all she possibly could to try to be nice, and make herself helpful, and wanted. I never seen no critter try harder to do right. You want to rough something—I'm in reach, ain't I?"

Amos angered. "I ought to wrap this here around your gullet!"

"Go ahead. But when you pick yourself up, you better be running!"

Amos walked away.

The Comanche girl was with them eleven days, waiting on them, doing their work, watching them to foresee their needs. At the end of the eleventh day, in the twilight, the girl went after water, and did not come back. They found their bucket grounded in the shallows of the creek, and traced out the sign to discover what they were up against. A single Indian had crossed to her through the water; his buffalo pony had stood in the damp sand while the girl mounted behind the rider. The Indian had been the girl's lover most likely. They were glad to have him take her, but it made their scalps crawl to consider that he must have followed them, without their at all suspecting it, for all that time.

Though he was relieved to be rid of her, Mart found that he missed her, and was annoyed with himself for missing her, for many weeks. After a while he could not remember what had made him leap up, the night she had crept into the blankets with him; he regretted it, and thought of himself as a fool. They never saw her again. Years later Mart thought he heard of her, but he could not be sure. A Comanche woman who died a captive had told the soldiers her name was "Look." Mart felt a strange twinge, as of remorse without reason for remorse, as he remembered how a sad-eyed little Comanche woman had once got that name.

He had realized she had been trying to teach him Comanche, though without letting him notice it any more than she could help. When she talked to him in sign language she pronounced the words that went with the signs, but softly, so that he could ignore the spoken speech, if he wished. She responded to his questions with a spark of hidden eagerness, and with the least encouragement told hour-long stories of wars and heroes, miracles and sorceries, in this way. He wouldn't have supposed he could learn anything in so short a time after beating his skull against the stubborn language for so long. But actually it was a turning point; the weird compounds of Comanche speech began to break apart for him at last. When next he sat among Comanches he became aware that he was able to follow almost everything they said. Amos presently began to turn to him for translations; and before the end of that summer, he was interpreter for them both.

Understanding the Comanches better, Mart began to pick up news, or at least rumors filtered through Indian minds, of what was happening upon the frontier. Most of the Comanches didn't care whether the white men understood their tales of misdeeds or not. The Wild Tribes had as yet been given little reason to think in terms of reprisals. Returning raiders boasted openly of the bloodiest things they had done.

There were enough to tell. Tabananica, having again challenged the cavalry without obtaining satisfaction, crept upon Fort Sill in the night, and got off with twenty head of horses and mules out of the Agency corral. White Horse, of the Kiowas, not to be outdone, took more than seventy head from the temporary stake-and-rider corral at the Fort itself. Kicking Bird, bidding to regain prestige lost in days of peace, went into Texas with a hundred warriors, fought a cavalry troop, and whipped it, himself killing the first trooper with his short lance. Wolf-Lying-Down walked into Sill in all insolence, and sold the Quaker agent a little red-haired boy for a hundred dollars. Fast Bear's young men got similar prices for six children, and the mothers of some of them, taken in a murderous Texas raid. The captives could testify to the wholesale murder of their men, yet saw the killers pick up their money and ride free. The Peace Policy was taking effect with a vengeance—though not quite in the way intended.

Often and often, as that summer grew old, the searchers believed they were close to Debbie; but Bluebonnet somehow still eluded them, and War Chief Scar seemed a fading ghost. They saw reason to hope, though, in another way. The Comanches held the Peace Policy in contempt, but now leaned on it boldly, since it had proved able to bear their weight. Surely, surely all of them would come in this time, when winter clamped down, to enjoy sanctuary and government rations in the shadow of Fort Sill. For the first time in history, perhaps, the far-scattered bands would be gathered in a single area—and fixed there, too, long enough for you to sort through them all.

So this year they made no plans to go home. As the great buffalo herds turned back from their summer pastures in the lands of the Sioux and the Blackfeet, drifting down-country before the sharpening northers, the two pointed their horses toward Fort Sill. Soon they fell into the trail of a small village—twenty-five or thirty lodges—obviously going to the same place that they were. They followed the double pole scratches of the many travois lazily, for though they were many weeks away from Fort Sill, they were in no great hurry to get there. It took time for the Indians to accumulate around the Agency, and the kind they were looking for came late. Some would not appear until they felt the pinch of the Starving Moons—if they came at all.

Almost at once the fire pits they rode over, and the short, squarish shape of dim moccasin tracks, told them they were following Comanches. A little later, coming to a place where the tracks showed better detail, they were able to narrow that down. Most Comanches wore trailing heel fringes that left faint, long marks in the dust. But one bunch of the Kotsetakas—the so-called Upriver branch—sewed weasel tails to the heels of their moccasins, leaving broader and even fainter marks. That was what they had here, and it interested them, for they had seen no such village in the fourteen months that they had searched.

But still they didn't realize what they were following, until they came upon a lone-hunting Osage, a long way from the range where he belonged. This Indian had an evil face, and seemingly no fear at all. He rode up to them boldly, and as he demanded tobacco they could see him estimating the readiness of their weapons, no doubt wondering whether he could do the two of them in before they could shoot him. Evidently he decided this to be impractical. In place of tobacco he settled for a handful of salt, and a red stock-prize ribbon placing him second in the class for Aged Sows. He repaid them with a cogent and hard-hitting piece of information, conveyed in crisp sign language, since he spoke no Comanche.

The village they were following, he said, was two sleeps ahead. Twenty-four lodges; six hundred horses and mules; forty-six battle-rated warriors. Tribe, Kotsetaka Comanche, of the Upriver Band (which they knew, so that the Osage's statements were given a color of truth); Peace Chief, Bluebonnet; War Chiefs, Gold Concho, Scar; also Stone Wold, Pacing Bear; others.

Amos' signs were steady, casual, as he asked if the village had white captives. The Osage said there were four. One woman, two little girls. One little boy. And two Mexican boys, he added as an afterthought. As for himself, he volunteered, he was entirely alone, and rode in peace. He walked the White Man's Way, and had never robbed anybody in his life.

He rode off abruptly after that, without ceremony; and the two riders went into council. The temptation was to ride hard, stopping for nothing, until they overtook the village. But that was not the sensible way. They would be far better off with troops close at hand, however tied-down they might be. And the gentle Quakers were the logical ones to intercede for the child's release, for they could handle it with less risk of a flare-up that might result in hurt to the child herself. No harm in closing the interval, though. They could just as well pick up a day and a half, and follow the Indians a few hours back to cut down chance of losing them in a mix with other Indians, or even a total change of plans. Anyway, they had to put distance between themselves and that Osage, whose last remarks had convinced both of them that he was a scout from a war party, and would ambush them if they let him.

They made a pretense of going into camp, but set off again in the first star-light, and rode all night. At sunrise they rested four hours for the benefit of their livestock, then made a wide cast, picked up the trail of the village again, and went on. The weather was looking very ugly. Brutal winds screamed across the prairie, and at midday a blue-black wall was beginning to rise, obscuring the northern sky.

Suddenly the broad trail they were following turned south at a right angle, as if broken square in two by the increasing weight of the wind.

"Are they onto us?" Mart asked; then repeated it in a yell, for the wind so snatched his words away that he couldn't hear them himself.

"I don't think that's it," Amos shouted back. "What they got to fear from us?"

"Well, something turned 'em awful short!"

"They know something! That's for damn sure!"

Mart considered the possibility that the Osages had thrown in with the Chey-ennes and Arapahoes, and gone to war in great force. Forty-six warriors could only put their village on the run, and try to get it out of the path of that kind of a combination. He wanted to ask Amos what he thought about this, but speech was becoming so difficult that he let it go. And he was already beginning to suspect something else. This time the apprehension with which he watched developments was a reasoned one, with no childhood ghosts about it. The sky and the wind were starting to tell them that a deadly danger might be coming down on them, of a kind they had no means to withstand.

By mid-afternoon they knew. Swinging low to look closely at the trail they followed, they saw that it was now the trail of a village moving at a smart lope, almost a dead run. The sky above them had blackened, and was filled with a deep-toned wailing. The power of the wind made the prairie seem more vast, so that they were turned to crawling specks on the face of a shelterless world. Amos leaned close to shout in Mart's ear. "They seen it coming! They've run for the Wichita breaks—that's what they done!"

"We'll never make it by dark! We got to hole up shorter than that!"

Amos tied his hat down hard over his ears with his wool muffler. Mart's muffler snapped itself and struggled to get away, like a fear-crazed thing, as he tried to do the same. He saw Amos twisting in the saddle to look all ways, his eyes squeezed tight against the sear of the wind. He looked like a man hunting desperately for a way of escape, but actually he was looking for their pack mules. Horses drift before a storm, but mules head into it, and keep their hair. For some time their pack animals had shown a tendency to swivel into the wind, then come on again, trying to stay with the ridden horses. They were far back now, small dark marks in the unnatural dusk. Amos mouthed unheard curses. He turned his horse, whipping hard, and forced it back the way they had come.

Mart tried to follow, but the Fort Worth stud reared and fought, all but going over on him. He spurred deep, and as the stud came down, reined high and short with all his strength. "Red, you son-of-a-bitch—" Both man and horse might very easily die out here if the stallion began having his way. The great neck had no more bend to it than a log. And now the stud got his head down, and went into his hard, skull-jarring buck.

Far back, Amos passed the first mule he came to, and the second. When he turned downwind, it was their commissary mule, the one with their grub in his packs, that he dragged along by a death-grip on its cheek strap. The Fort Worth stud was standing immovable in his sullage as Amos got back. Both Mart and the stud horse were blowing hard, and looked beat out. Mart's nose had started to bleed, and a bright trickle had frozen on his upper lip.

"We got to run for it!" Amos yelled at him. "For God's sake, get a rope on this!"

With his tail to the wind, the stud went back to work, grudgingly answering the rein. Mart got a lead rope on the mule, to the halter first, then back to a standing loop around the neck, and through the halter again. Once the lead rope was snubbed to the stud's saddle horn the mule came along, sometimes sitting down, sometimes at a sort of bounding trot, but with them just the same.

It was not yet four o'clock, but night was already closing; or rather a blackness deeper than any natural night seemed to be lowering from above, pressing downward implacably to blot out the prairie. For a time a band of yellow sky showed upon the southern horizon, but this narrowed, then disappeared, pushed below the edge of the world by the darkness. Amos pointed to a dark scratch near the horizon, hardly more visible than a bit of thread laid flat. You couldn't tell just what it was, or how far away; in that treacherous and failing light you couldn't be sure whether you were seeing half a mile or fifteen. The dark mark on the land had better be willows, footed in the gulch of a creek—or at least in a dry run-off gully. If it was nothing but a patch of buckbrush, their chances were going to be very poor. They angled toward it, putting their horses into a high lope.

Now came the first of the snow, a thin lacing of ice needles, heard and felt before they could be seen. The ice particles were traveling horizontally, parallel to the ground, with an enormous velocity. They made a sharp whispering against leather, drove deep into cloth, and filled the air with hissing. This thin bombardment swiftly increased, coming in puffs and clouds, then in a rushing stream. And at the same time the wind increased; they would not have supposed a harder blow to be possible, but it was. It tore at them, snatching their breaths from their mouths, and its gusts buffeted their backs as solidly as thrown sacks of grain. The galloping horses sat back against the power of the wind as into breechings, yet were made to yaw and stumble as they ran. The long hair of their tails whipped their flanks, and wisps of it were snatched away.

In the last moments before they were blinded by the snow and the dark, Mart got a brief glimpse of Amos' face. It was a bloodless gray-green, and didn't look like Amos' face. Some element of force and strength had gone out of it. Most of the time Amos' face had a wooden look, seemingly without expression, but this was an illusion. Actually the muscles were habitually set in a grim confidence, an almost built-in certainty, that now was gone. They pushed their horses closer together, leaning them toward each other so that they continually bumped knees. It was the only way they could stay together, sightless and deafened in the howling chaos.

They rode for a long time, beaten downwind like driven leaves. They gave no thought to direction; the storm itself was taking care of that. It was only when the winded horses began to falter that Mart believed they had gone past whatever they had seen. His saddle was slipping back, dragged toward the stud's kidneys by the resistance of the mule. He fumbled at the latigo tie, to draw up the cinch, but found his hands so stiff with cold he was afraid to loosen it, lest he slip his grip, and lose mule, saddle, horse, and himself, all in one dump. This thing will end soon, he was thinking. This rig isn't liable to stay together long. Nor the horses last, if it does. Nor us either, if it comes to that. . . . His windpipe was raw; crackles of ice were forming up his nose. And his feet were becoming numb. They had thrown away their worn-out buffalo boots last spring, and had made no more, because of their expectations of wintering snugly at Fort Sill.

No sense to spook it, he told himself, as breathing came hard. Nothing more a man can do. We'll fall into something directly. Or else we won't. What the horses can't do for us won't get done. . . .

Fall into it was what they did. They came full stride, without warning, upon a drop of unknown depth. Seemingly they struck it at a slant, for Amos went over first. His horse dropped a shoulder as the ground fell from under, then was gone. Even in the roar of the storm, Mart heard the crack of the pony's broken neck. He pulled hard, and in the same split second tried first to sheer off, and next to turn the stud's head to the drop—neither with the least effect, for the rim crumbled, and they plunged.

Not that the drop was much. The gully was no more than twelve-feet deep, a scarcely noticeable step down, had either horse or man been able to see. The stud horse twisted like a cat, got his legs under him, and went hard to his knees. The mule came piling down on top of the whole thing, with an impact of enormous weight, and a great thrashing of legs, then floundered clear. And how that was done without important damage Mart never knew.

He got their two remaining animals under control, and groped for Amos. They hung onto each other, blind in the darkness and the snow, leading the stud and the mule up the gully in search of better shelter. Within a few yards they blundered upon a good-sized willow, newly downed by the wind; and from that moment they knew they were going to come through. They knew it, but they had a hard time remembering it, in the weary time before they got out of there. They were pinned in that gully more than sixty hours.

In some ways the first night was the worst. The air was dense with the dry snow, but the wind, rushing with hurricane force down a thousand miles of prairie, would not let the snow settle, or drift, even in the crevice where they had taken refuge. No fire was possible. The wind so cycloned between the walls of the gulch that the wood they lighted in the shelter of their coats immediately vanished in a shatter of white sparks. Mart chopped a tub-sized cave into the frozen earth at the side, but the fire couldn't last there, either. Their canteens were frozen solid, and neither dry cornmeal nor their iron-hard jerky would go down without water. They improvised parkas and foot wrappings out of the few furs they had happened to stuff into the commissary pack, and stamped their feet all night long.

Sometime during that night the Fort Worth stud broke loose, and went with the storm. In the howling of the blizzard they didn't even hear him go.

During the next day the snow began rolling in billows across the prairie, and their gully filled. They were better off by then. They had got foot wrappings on their mule, lest his hoofs freeze off as he stood, and had fed him on gatherings of willow twigs. With pack sheet and braced branches they improved their bivouac under the downed willow, so that as the snow covered them they had a place in which a fire would burn at last. They melted snow and stewed horse meat, and took turns staying awake to keep each other from sleeping too long. The interminable periods in which they lay buried alive were broken by sorties after wood, or willow twigs, or to rub the legs of the mule.

But the third night was in some ways the worst of all. They had made snow-shoes of willow hoops and frozen horsehide, tied with thongs warmed at the fire; but Mart no longer believed they would ever use them. He had been beaten against the frozen ground by that murderous uproar for too long; he could not hear the imperceptible change in the roar of the churning sky as the blizzard began to die. This nightmare had gone on forever, and he accepted that it would always go on, until death brought the only possible peace.

He lay stiffened and inert in their pocket under the snow, moving sluggishly once an hour, by habit, to prevent Amos from sleeping himself to death. He was trying to imagine what it would be like to be dead. They were so near it, in this refuge so like a grave, he no longer felt that death could make any unwelcome difference. Their bodies would never be found, of course, nor properly laid away. Come thaw, the crows would pick their bones clean. Presently the freshets would carry their skeletons tumbling down the gulch, breaking them up, strewing them piecemeal until they hung in the driftwood, a thighbone here, a rib there, a skull full of gravel half buried in the drying streambed.

People who knew them would probably figure out they had died in the blizzard, though no one would know just where. Mart Pauley? Lost last year in the blizzard . . . Mart Pauley's been dead four years . . . ten years . . . forty years. No—not even his name would be in existence in anybody's mind, anywhere, as long as that.

Amos brought him out of that in a weird way. Mart was in a doze that was dangerously near a coma, when he became aware that Amos was singing—if you could call it that. More of a groaning, in long-held, hoarse tones, from deep in the galled throat. Mart lifted his head and listened, wondering, with a desolation near indifference, if Amos had gone crazy, or into a delirium. As he came wider awake he recognized Comanche words. The eery sound was a chant.

> The sun will pour life on the earth forever . . .
>   (I rode my horse till it died.)
> The earth will send up new grass forever . . .
>   (I thrust with my lance while I bled.)
> The stars will walk in the sky forever . . .
>   (Leave my pony's bones on my grave.)

It was a Comanche death song. The members of some warrior society—the Snow Wolf Brotherhood?—were supposed to sing it as they died.

"God damn it, you stop that!" Mart shouted, and beat at Amos with numbed hands.

Amos was not in delirium. He sat up grumpily, and began testing his creaky joints. He grunted, "No ear for music, huh?"

Suddenly Mart realized that the world beyond their prison was silent. He floundered out through the great depth of snow. The sky was gray, but the surface of the snow itself almost blinded him with its glare. And from horizon to horizon, nothing on the white earth moved. The mule stood in a sort of well it had tromped for itself, six feet deep in the snow. It had chewed the bark off every piece of wood in reach, but its hoofs were all right. Mart dragged Amos out, and they took a look at each other.

Their lips were blackened and cracked, and their eyes bloodshot. Amos' beard had frost in it now that was going to stay there as long as he lived. But they were able-bodied, and they were free, and had a mule between them.

All they had to do now was to get through a hundred and ten miles of snow to Fort Sill; and they could figure they had put the blizzard behind them.

17

They took so many weeks to make Fort Sill that they were sure Bluebonnet's village would be there ahead of them; but it was not. They were in weakened, beat-down shape, and they knew it. They slept much, and ate all the time. When they went among the Indians they moved slowly, in short hauls, with long rests between. Hard for them to believe that only a year and a half had passed in their search for Debbie. Many thought they had already made a long, hard, incredibly faithful search. But in terms of what they had got done, it wasn't anything, yet.

Living things on the prairie had been punished very hard. The buffalo came through well, even the youngest calves; only the oldest buffalo were winter killed. Things that lived down holes, like badgers, prairie dogs, and foxes, should have been safe. Actually, animals of this habit were noticeably scarcer for the next few years, so perhaps many froze deep in the ground as they slept. The range cattle were hit very hard, and those of improved breeding stood it the worst. Where fences had come into use, whole herds piled up, and died where they stood. Hundreds had their feet frozen off, and were seen walking around on the stumps for weeks before the last of them were dead.

After the blizzard, a period of melt and freeze put an iron crust on the deep snow. A lot of the cattle that had survived the storm itself now starved, unable to paw down to the feed with their cloven hoofs. Horses did considerably better, for their hoofs could smash the crust. But even these were fewer for a long time, so many were strewn bones upon the prairie before spring.

Yet all this devastation had come unseasonably early. After the first of the year the winter turned mild, as if it had shot its wad. Once travel was practicable, more Indians streamed into the sanctuary of Fort Sill than ever before. Their deceptively rugged tepees, cunningly placed, and anchored by crossed stakes driven five feet into the ground, had stood without a single reported loss; and the villages seemed to have plenty of pemmican to feed them until spring. Perhaps they had been awed by the power of the warring wind spirits, so that they felt their own medicine to be at a low ebb.

They were anything but awed, however, by the soldiers, whom the Peace Policy tied down in helplessness, or by the Society of Friends, whose gentle pacifism the Wild Tribes held in contempt, even while they sheltered behind it. Appears-in-the-Sky, Medicine Chief of the Kiowas, who claimed a spirit owl as his familiar, in January moved out a short distance through the snow to murder four Negro teamsters. Two cowboys were killed at Sill's beef corral, barely half a mile from the fort, and a night wrangler was murdered and scalped closer than that. Half a dozen Queherenna, or Antelope Comanches—the military were calling them Quohadas—stole seventy mules out of Fort Sill's new stone corral, and complacently camped twenty miles away, just as safe as upon their mothers' backboards.

Both Kiowas and Comanches were convinced now of the integrity of the Quakers. They pushed into the Quakers' houses, yanked buttons off the Agent's clothes; helped themselves to anything that caught the eye, then stoned the windows as they left. Those Quakers with families were ordered to safety, but few obeyed. Resolute in their faith, they stood implacably between their Indian charges and the troops. It was going to be a hard, rough, chancy year down below in Texas.

Meanwhile Mart and Amos searched and waited, and still Bluebonnet did not come in. As spring came on they bought new horses and mules, replenished their packs and once more went looking for Indians who forever marched and shuffled themselves in the far lost wastes of their range.

18

Most of that second trading summer was like the first. Being able to understand what the Indians said among themselves had proved of very little use, so far as their search was concerned. They did hear more, though, of what was happening back home, upon the frontier their wanderings had put so far behind. Mart, particularly, listened sharply for some clue as to whether the Mathisons still held, but heard nothing he could pin down.

In Texas the outlying settlers were going through the most dreadful year in memory. At least fourteen people were dead, and nine children captive, before the middle of May. Only a stubbornness amounting to desperation could explain why any of the pioneers held on. Bloody narratives were to be heard in every Comanche camp the searchers found. A party of surveyors were killed upon the Red River, and their bodies left to spoil in a drying pool. The corpses of three men, a woman and a child were reduced to char in a burning ranch house, cheating the raiders of the scalps. Oliver Loving's foreman was killed beside his own corral. By early summer, Wolf-Lying-Down had stolen horses within sight of San Antonio; and Kiowas under Big Bow, crossing into Mexico near Laredo, had killed seventeen vaqueros, and got back across Texas with a hundred and fifty horses and a number of Mexican children.

General Sherman, who habitually took Texan complaints with a grain of salt, finally had a look for himself. He appeared in Texas along about the middle of the summer, with an escort of only fifteen troopers—and at once nearly added himself to a massacre. Near Cox Mountain a raiding party of a hundred and fifty Comanches and Kiowas destroyed a wagon train, killing seven, some by torture. Unfortunately, for it would have been the highlight of his trip, General Sherman missed riding into this event by about an hour and a half. Proceeding to Fort Sill, Sherman supervised the arrest of Satanta, Satank, and Big Tree, showing a cool personal courage, hardly distinguishable from indifference, in the face of immediate mortal danger. He presented the three war chiefs in handcuffs to the State of Texas; and after went away again.

All this, the two riders recognized, was building up to such a deadly, all-annihilating showdown as would be their finish, if they couldn't get their job done first. But for the present they found the Comanches in high and celebrative mood, unable to imagine the whirlwind that was to come. The warriors were arrogant, boastful, full of the high-and-mighty. Yet, luckily, they remained patronizingly tolerant, for the time, of the white men who dared come among them in their own far fastnesses.

During this time the terror-dream of the red night and the unearthly voices came to Mart only once, and he saw no copy of the unexplained death tree at all. Yet the attitudes of the Indians toward such things were beginning to influence him, so that he more than half believed they carried a valid prophecy. The Comanches were supposed to be the most literal-minded of all tribes. There are Indians who live in a poetic world, half of the spirit, but the Comanches were a tough-minded, practical people, who laughed at the religious ceremonies of other tribes as crazy-Indian foolishness. They had no official medicine men, no pantheon of named gods, no ordered theology. Yet they lived very close to the objects of the earth around them, and sensed in rocks, and winds, and rivers, spirits as living as their own. They saw themselves as of one piece with a world in which nothing was without a spirit.

In this atmosphere, almost every Comanche had a special spirit medicine that had come to him in a dream, usually the gift of some wild animal, such as an otter, a buffalo, or a wolf—never a dog or horse. By the time a Comanche was old, he was either a medicine man, believed to know specific magics against certain ills or disasters, or a black-magic sorcerer, feared because he could maim or kill from far away.

You could never learn to understand an Indian's way of thinking, or guess what he was about to think next. If you saw an Indian looking at the sky, you might know why you would be looking at the sky in his place—and be sure the Indian had some different reason. Yet sometimes they ran into a Comanche, usually an old one, who knew something there was no possible way for him to know.

"You speak Nemenna very well," an old Nocona said to Mart once. (The names of the bands were turning themselves over again; in a single year the name "Nawyecky" had fallen into almost total disuse.) Mart supposed the old man had heard of him, for he had not opened his mouth. He pretended not to understand, hoping to discredit a rumor of that kind. But the old Comanche went on, smiling at Mart's effort to dissimulate. "Sometimes you come upon a spirit in the form of a dead tree," he said. "It is blackened; it looks like a withered corpse, struggling to free itself from the earth."

Mart stared, startled into acknowledgment that he understood the old man's speech. At this the Comanche grinned derisively, but went on in grave tones. "You do not fear death very much, I think. Last year, maybe; not this year any more. But you will do well to fear the evil tree. Death is a kind and happy thing beside the nameless things beyond the tree."

He sat back. "I tell you this as a friend," he finished. "Not because I expect any kind of gift. I wish you well, and nothing more. I want no gift at all." Which of course meant that he did.

By middle fall the mood of the Comanches had begun to change. Raids were lacing into Texas at an unprecedented pace; Colorado was heavily scourged, and Kansas hurt to the very borders of Nebraska. Almost every village they came to was waiting in brooding quiet for a great war party to return, if it were not whooping up a scalp dance to celebrate a victory, or a glory dance for sending a party out. But now both Texas and the United States Army were fighting back. The Texas Rangers were in the saddle again, losing men in every skirmish, but making the Indians pay three and four lives for one. The Fort Sill garrison was still immobilized, but Fort Richardson, down on the West Fork of the Trinity, was beyond the authority of the Friends. From Richardson rode Colonel Mackenzie with a regiment and a half of yellowlegs; his forced marches drove deep into the land of the Quohadas. Shaking Hand's Kotsetakas got out of his way, and the great Bull Bear of the Antelopes, with such war chiefs under him as Black Horse, Wolf Tail, Little Crow, and the brilliant young Quanah, threatened briefly in force but drew back.

Old chiefs were losing favorite sons, and you could see black death behind their eyes when they looked at white men. Warrior societies who scalp-danced for victory after victory counted their strength, and found that in the harvest season of their greatest success they were becoming few. The searchers learned to scout a village carefully, to see if it were in mourning for a raiding party decimated or destroyed, before they took a chance on going in. Over and over, white captives were murdered by torture in revenge for losses sustained upon the savage raids. Mart and Amos rode harder, longer, turning hollow-eyed and gaunted. Their time was running out, and very fast; already they might be too late.

Yet their goal, while it still eluded them, seemed always just ahead. They never had come to any point where either one of them could have brought himself to turn back, from the first day their quest had begun.

Then, as the snow came again, they struck the trail they had hunted for so long. It was that of twenty-two lodges led by Bluebonnet himself, and he had a captive white girl in his village, beyond any reasonable doubt. The horse-trampled parallel lines left by the many travois led south and eastward, crossing the high ground between the Beaver and the Canadian; they followed it fast and easily.

"Tomorrow," Amos said once more as they rode. The captive girl had been described to them as smallish, with yellow hair and light eyes. As they went into camp at twilight he said it again, and now for the last time: "Tomorrow. . . ."

19

Mart Pauley woke abruptly, with no notion of what had roused him. Amos breathed regularly beside him. Each slept rolled in his own blankets, but they shared the wagon sheet into which they folded themselves, heads and all, for shelter from the weather. The cold air stiffened the slight moisture in Mart's nostrils as he stuck his head out. Only the lightest of winds whispered across the surface of the snow. The embers of their fire pulsed faintly in the moving air, and by these he judged the time to be after midnight.

At first he heard nothing; but as he held his breath a trick of the wind brought again the sound that must have come to him in his sleep, so faint, so far off, it might have been a whispering of frost in his own ears.

He closed his grip slowly on Amos' arm until he waked. "Whazzamatter?"

"I swear I heard fighting," Mart said, "a long way off."

"Leave the best man win." Amos settled himself to go back to sleep.

"I mean big fighting—an Indian fight. . . . There! . . . Ain't that a bugle way off down the river?"

A few small flakes of snow touched their faces, but the night turned sound-less again as soon as Amos sat up. "I don't hear nothing."

Neither did Mart any more. "It's snowing again."

"That's all right. We'll come up with Bluebonnet. Snow can never hide him from us now! It'll only pin him down for us!"

Mart lay awake for a while, listening hard; but no more sound found its way through the increasing snowfall.

Long before daylight he stewed up a frying-pan breakfast of shredded buffalo jerky, and fed the horses. "Today," Amos said, as they settled, joint-stiff, into their icy saddles. It was the first time they had ever said that after all the many, many times they had said "Tomorrow." Yet the word came gruffly, without exultation. The day was cold, and the snow still fell, as they pushed on through darkness toward a dull dawn.

By mid-morning they reached the Canadian, and forded its unfrozen shal-lows. They turned downstream, and at noon found Bluebonnet's village—or the place it had seen its last of earth.

They came to the dead horses first. In a great bend of the river, scattered over a mile of open ground, lay nearly a hundred head of buffalo ponies, their lips drawing back from their long teeth as they froze. The snow had stopped, but not before it had sifted over the horses, and the blood, and the fresh tracks that must have been made in the first hours of the dawn. No study of sign was needed, however; what had happened here was plain. The cavalry had learned long ago that it couldn't hold Comanche ponies.

Beyond the shoulder of a ridge they came upon the site of the village itself. A smudge, and a heavy stench of burning buffalo hair, still rose from the wreck-age of twenty-two lodges. A few more dead horses were scattered here, some of them the heavier carcasses of cavalry mounts. But here, too, the snow had covered the blood, and the story of the fight, and all the strewn trash that clutters a field of battle. There were no bodies. The soldiers had withdrawn early enough so that the Comanche survivors had been able to return for their dead, and be gone, before the snow stopped.

Mart and Amos rode slowly across the scene of massacre. Nothing meaning-ful to their purpose was left in the burnt-out remains of the lodges. They could make out that the cavalry had ridden off down the Canadian, and that was about all.

"We don't know yet," Mart said.

"No," Amos agreed. He spoke without expression, allowing himself neither discouragement nor hope. "But we know where the answer is to be found."

It was not too far away. They came upon the bivouacked cavalry a scant eight miles below.

20

Daylight still held as Mart and Amos approached the cavalry camp, but it was getting dark by the time they were all the way in. The troopers on duty were red-eyed, but with a harsh edge on their manners, after the night they had spent. An outlying vedette passed them into a dismounted sentry, who called the corporal of the guard, who delivered them to the sergeant of the guard, who questioned them with more length than point before digging up a second lieutenant who was Officer of the Day. The lieutenant also questioned them, though more briefly. He left them standing outside a supply tent for some time, while he explained them to a Major Kinsman, Adjutant.

The major stuck a shaggy head out between the tent flaps, looked them over with the blank stare of fatigue, and spat tobacco juice into the snow.

"My name," Amos began again, patiently, "is—"

"Huntin' captives, huh?" The shaggy head was followed into the open by a huge frame in a tightly buttoned uniform. "Let's see if we got any you know." Major Kinsman led the way, not to another tent, but to the wagon park. They followed him as he climbed into the wagonbed of a covered ambulance.

Under a wagon sheet, which the adjutant drew back, several bodies lay straight and neatly aligned, ice-rigid in the cold. In the thickening dark inside the ambulance, Mart could see little more than that they were there, and that one or two seemed to be children.

"Have a light here in a minute," Major Kinsman said. "Orderly's filling a lantern."

Mart Pauley could hear Amos' heavy breathing, but not his own; he did not seem able to breathe in here at all. A dreadful conviction came over him, increasing as they waited, that they had come to the end of their search. It seemed a long time before a lighted lantern was thrust inside.

The bodies were those of two women and two little boys. The older of the women was in rags, but the younger and smaller one wore clean clothes that had certainly belonged to her, and shoes that were scuffed but not much worn. She appeared to have been about twenty, and was quite beautiful in a carved-snow sort of way. The little boys were perhaps three and seven.

"Both women shot in the back of the head," Major Kinsman said, objectively. "Flash-burn range. Light charge of powder, as you see. The little boys got their skulls cracked. We think this woman here is one taken from a Santa Fe stagecoach not many days back. . . . Know any of them?"

"Never saw them before," Amos said.

Major Kinsman looked at Mart for a separate reply, and Mart shook his head.

They went back to the supply tent, and the adjutant took them inside. The commanding officer was there, sorting through a great mass of loot with the aid of two sergeants and a company clerk. The adjutant identified his superior as Colonel Russell M. Hannon. They had heard of him, but never seen him before; he hadn't been out here very long. Just now he looked tired, but in high spirits.

"Too bad there wasn't more of 'em," Colonel Hannon said. "That's the only disappointing thing. We were following the river, not their trail. Wichita scouts brought word there must be a million of 'em. What with the snow, and the night march, an immediate attack was the only course permissible."

He said his troops had killed thirty-eight hostiles, with the loss of two men. Comanches, at that. A ratio of nineteen to one, as compared to Colonel Custer's ratio of fourteen to one against Black Kettle at the Battle of the Washita. "Not a bad little victory. Not bad at all."

Mart saw Amos stir, and worried for a moment. But Amos held his tongue.

"Four hundred ninety-two ponies," said Hannon. "Had to shoot 'em, of course. Wild as antelope—no way to hold onto them. Four captives recovered. Unfortunately, the hostiles murdered them, as we developed the village. Now, if some of this junk will only show *what* Comanches we defeated, we'll be in fair shape to write a report. Those Wichita scouts know nothing whatever about anything; most ignorant savages on earth. However—"

"What you had there," said Amos wearily, "was Chief Bluebonnet, with what's left of the Wolf Brothers, along with a few Nawyecky. Or maybe you call 'em Noconas."

"Get this down," the colonel told the clerk.

It was going to take a long time to find out just who had fought and died at the riverbend—and who had got away into the night and the snow, and so still lived, somewhere upon the winter plain. Even allowing for the great number of dead and dying the Comanches had carried away uncounted, somewhere between a third and a half of Bluebonnet's people must have escaped.

They were glad to help sort through the wagonload of stuff hastily snatched up in the gloom of the dawn before the lodges were set on fire. Some of the pouches, quivers, and squill breastplates were decorated with symbols Mart or Amos could connect with Indian names; they found insignia belonging to Stone Wolf, Curly Horn, Pacing Bear, and Hears-the-Wind-Talk. The patterns they didn't know they tried to memorize, in hopes of seeing them again someday.

Especially valued by Colonel Harmon, as exonerating his attack in the dark, was certain stuff that had to be the loot from raided homesteads: a worn sewing basket, an embroidered pillow cover, a home-carved wooden spoon. Hard to see what the Comanches would want with a store-bought paper lamp shade, a wooden seat for a chamber pot, or an album of pressed flowers. But if someone recognized these poor lost things someday, they would become evidence connecting the massacred Comanches with particular crimes. One incriminating bit was a mail pouch known to have been carried by a murdered express rider. The contents were only half rifled; some Comanche had been taking his time about opening all the letters—no man would ever know what for.

But the thing Mart found that hit him hard, and started his search all over again, was in a little heap of jewelry—Indian stuff mostly: Carved amulets, Mexican and Navajo silver work, sometimes set with turquoise; but with a sprinkling of pathetic imitation things, such as frontiersmen could afford to buy for their women. Only thing of interest, at first sight, seemed to be a severed finger wearing a ring which would not pull off. Mart cynically supposed that any stuff of cash value had stayed with the troopers who collected it.

Then Mart found Debbie's locket.

It was the cheapest kind of a gilt-washed metal heart on a broken chain. Mart himself had given it to Debbie on the Christmas when she was three. It wasn't even a real locket, for it didn't open, and had embarrassed him by making a green spot on her throat every time she wore it. But Debbie had hung on to it. On the back it said "Debbie from M," painfully scratched with the point of his knife.

Both officers showed vigorous disinterest as Mart pressed for the circumstances in which the locket had been found. These were professionals, and recognized the question as of the sort leading to full-dress investigations, and other chancy outcomes, if allowed to develop. But Amos came to Mart's support, and presently they found the answer simply by walking down the mess line with the locket in hand.

The locket had been taken from the body of a very old squaw found in the river along with an ancient buck. No, damn it, the colonel explained, of course they had not meant to kill women and children, and watch your damn tongue. All you could see was a bunch of shapeless figures firing on you—nothing to do but cut them down, and save questions for later. But one of the sergeants remembered how these two bodies had come there. The squaw, recognizable in hindsight as the fatter one, had tried to escape through the river on a pony, and got sabered down. The old man had rushed in trying to save the squaw, and got sabered in turn. Nothing was in hand to tell who these people were.

Colonel Hannon saw to it that the locket was properly tagged and returned to the collection as evidence of a solved child stealing. Restitution would be made to the heirs, upon proper application to the Department, with proof of loss.

"She was there," Mart said to Amos. "She was there in that camp. She's gone with them that got away."

Amos did not comment. They had to follow and find the survivors—perhaps close at hand, if they were lucky; otherwise by tracing them to whatever far places they might scatter. This time neither one of them said "Tomorrow."

21

They had been winter-driven that first time they went home, all but out of horseflesh, and everything else besides. But after the "Battle" of Deadhorse Bend they went home only because all leads very soon staled and petered out in the part of the country where they were. Otherwise, they probably would have stayed out and kept on. They had lived on the wild land so long that they needed nothing, not even money, that they did not know how to scratch out of it. It never occurred to them that their search was stretching out into a great extraordinary feat of endurance; an epic of hope without faith, of fortitude without reward, of stubbornness past all limits of reason. They simply kept on, doing the next thing, because they always had one more place to go, following out one more forlorn-hope try.

And they had one more idea now. It had been spelled out for them in the loot Colonel Hannon's troopers had picked up in the wreckage of Bluebonnet's destroyed village. Clear and plain, once you thought of it, though it had taken them weeks of thinking back over the whole thing before they recognized it. Amos, at least, believed that this time they could not fail. They would find Debbie now—if only she still lived.

Their new plan would carry them far into the southwest, into country hundreds of miles from any they had ever worked before. And so long as they had to go south, home was not too far out of the way. Home? What was that? Well, it was the place they used to live; where the Mathisons still lived—so far as they knew—and kept an eye on the cattle that now belonged to Debbie. Mart would always think of that stretch of country as home, though nothing of his own was there, nor anybody waiting for him.

As they rode, a sad, dark thing began to force itself upon their attention. When they came to the country where the farthest-west fringe of ranches had been, the ranches were no longer there. Often only a ghostly chimney stood, solitary upon the endless prairie, where once had been a warm and friendly place with people living in it. Then they would remember the time they had stopped by, and things they had eaten there, and the little jokes the people had made. If you hunted around in the brush that ran wild over all, you could usually find the graves. The remembered people were still there, under the barren ground.

More often you had to remember landmarks to locate where a place had been at all. Generally your horse stumbled over an old footing or something before you saw the flat place where the little house had been. Sometimes you found graves here, too, but more usually the people had simply pulled their house down and hauled the lumber away, retreating from a place the Peace Policy had let become too deadly, coming on top of the war. You got the impression that Texas had seen its high tide, becoming little again as its frontier thinned away. Sundown seemed to have come for the high hopes of the Lone Star Republic to which Union had brought only war, weakening blood losses, and the perhaps inevitable neglect of a defeated people.

On the morning of the last day, with Mathison's layout only twenty-odd miles away, they came upon one more crumbling chimney, lonely beside a little stream. Mart's eyes rested upon it contemplatively across the brush at five hundred yards without recognizing it. He was thinking what a dreadful thing it would be if they came to the Mathisons, and found no more than this left of the place, or the people. Then he saw Amos looking at him strangely, and he knew what he was looking at. Surprising that he had not known it, even though he had not been here in a long time. The chimney marked the site of the old Pauley homestead; the place where he had been born. Here the people who had brought him into the world had loved him, and cared for him; here they had built their hopes, and here they had died. How swiftly fade the dead from people's minds, if he could look at this place and not even know it! He turned his horse and rode toward it, Amos following without question.

He had no memory of his own of how this homestead had looked, and no faintest images of his people's faces. He had been taken over this ground, and had all explained to him when he was about eight years old, but no one had ever been willing to talk to him about it, else. And now, except for the chimney, he couldn't locate where anything had been at all. The snow had gone off, but the ground was frozen hard, so that their heels rang metallically upon it as they dismounted to walk around. The little stream ran all year, and it had a fast ripple in it that never froze, where it passed this place; so that the water seemed to talk forever to the dead. This creek was called the Beanblossom; Mart knew that much. And that was about all.

Amos saw his bewilderment. "Your old m— your father wagoned the Santa Fe Trail a couple of times," he said, "before he settled down. Them Santa Fe traders, if any amongst 'em died, they buried 'em ahead in the trail; so every dang ox in the train tromped over the graves. Didn't want the Indians to catch on they were doing poorly. Or maybe dig 'em up. So your father was against markers on graves. Out here, anyways. Knowing that, and after some argument, we never set none up."

Mart had supposed he knew where the graves were anyway. They had been plainly visible when he had been shown, but now neither mound nor depression showed where they were. The brush had advanced, and under the brush the wind and the rain of the years had filled and packed and planed and sanded the sterile earth until no trace showed anywhere of anything having crumbled to dust beneath.

Amos picked a twig and chewed it as he waded into the brush, taking cross-sightings here and there, trying to remember. "Right here," he said finally. "This is where your mother lies." He scraped a line with the toe of his boot, the frozen ground barely taking the mark. "Here's the foot of the grave." He stepped aside, and walked around an undefined space, and made another mark. "And here's the head, here."

A great gawky bunch of chaparral grew in the middle of what must be the side line of the grave. Mart stood staring at the bit of earth, in no way distinguishable from any other part of the prairie surface. He was trying to remember, or to imagine, the woman whose dust was there. Amos seemed to understand that, too.

"Your mother was a beautiful girl," he said. Mart felt ashamed as he shoved out of his mind the thought that whatever she looked like, Amos would have said that same thing of the dead. "Real thin," Amos said, mouthing his twig, "but real pretty just the same. Brown eyes, almost what you'd call black. But her hair. Red-brown, and a lot of it. With a shine in it, like a gold kind of red, when the light struck through it right. I never seen no prettier hair."

He was silent a few moments, as if to let Mart think for a decent interval about the mother he did not remember. Then Amos got restless, and measured off a long step to the side. "And this here's Ethan—your father," he said. "You favor him, right smart. He had a black-Welsh streak; marked his whole side of the family. It's from him you got your black look and them mighty-near crockery eyes. He was just as dark, with the same light eyes."

Amos turned a little, and chewed the twig, but didn't bother to pace off the locations of the others. "Alongside lies my brother—mine and Henry's brother. The William you've heard tell of so many, many times. I don't know why, but in the family, we never once did call him Bill. . . . William was the best of us. The best by far. Good looking as Henry, and strong as me. And the brains of the family—there they lie, right there. He could been governor, or anything. Except he was less than your age—just eighteen. . . ." Mart didn't let himself question the description, even in his mind. You could assume that the first killed in a family of boys was the one who would have been great. It was what they told you always.

"Beyond, the three more—next to William lies Cash Dennison, a young rider, helping out Ethan; then them two bullwhackers that lived out the wagon-train killing, and made it to here. One's name was Caruthers, from a letter in his pocket; I forget the other. Some blamed them for the whole thing—thought the Comanches come down on this place a-chasing them two. But I never thought that. Seems more like the Comanch' was coming here; and it was the wagon train they fell on by accident on their way."

"You got any notion—does anybody know—did they get many of the Comanches? Here, the night of this thing?"

Amos shook his head. "A summer storm come up. A regular cloudburst—you don't see the like twice in twenty year. It washed out the varmints' trail. And naturally they carried off their dead—such as there was. Nobody knows how many. Maybe none."

Waste, thought Mart. Useless, senseless, heartbreaking waste. All these good, fine, happy lives just thrown away. . . .

Once more Amos seemed to answer his thought. "Mart, I don't know as I ever said this to anybody. But it's been a long time; and I'll tell you now what I think. My family's gone now, too—unless and until we find our one last little girl. But we lived free of harm, and the Mathisons too, for full eighteen years before they struck our bunch again. You want to know what I think why? I think your people here bought that time for us. They paid for it with their lives."

"Wha-at?" No matter what losses his people had inflicted on the raiders, Comanches would never be stopped by that. They would come back to even the score, and thus the tragic border war went on forever. But that wasn't what Amos meant.

"I think this was a revenge raid," Amos said. "It was right here the Rangers come through, trailing old Iron Shirt's band. They cut that bunch down from the strongest there was to something trifling, and killed Iron Shirt himself. So the trail the Rangers followed that time had a black history for Comanches. They come down it just once in revenge for their dead—and Ethan's little place was the farthest out on this trail. And it was a whole Indian generation before they come again. That's why I say—your people bought them years the rest of us lived in peace. . . ."

Mart said. "It's been a long time. Do you think my father would mind now if I come and put markers on them graves? Would that be a foolishness after all this while?"

Amos chewed, eating his twig. "I don't believe he'd mind. Not now. Even could he know. I think it would be a right nice thing to do. I'll help you soon's we have a mite of time." He turned toward the horses, but Mart wanted to know one thing more that no one had ever told him.

"I don't suppose—" he said—"well, maybe you might know. Could you show me where I was when Pa found me in the brush?"

"Your Pa? When?"

"I mean Henry. He always stood in place of my own. I heard tell he found me, and picked me up. . . ."

Amos looked all around, and walked into the brush, chewing slowly, and taking sights again. "Here," he said at last. "I'm sure now. Right—exactly— here." The frost in the earth crackled as he ground a heel into the spot he meant. "Of course, then, the brush was cleared back. To almost this far from the house." He stood around a moment to see if Mart wanted to ask anything more, then walked off out of the brush toward the horses.

This place, this very spot he stood on, Mart thought, was where he once awoke alone in such terror as locked his throat, seemingly; they had told him he made no sound. Queer to stand here, in this very spot where he had so nearly perished before he even got started; queer, because he felt nothing. It was the same as when he had stood looking at the graves, knowing that what was there should have meant so much, yet had no meaning for him at all. He couldn't see anything from here that looked familiar, or reminded him of anything.

Of course, that night of the massacre, he hadn't been standing up better than six feet tall in his boots. He had been down in the roots of the scrub, not much bigger than his own foot was now. On an impulse, Mart lay down in the tangle, pressing his cheek against the ground, to bring his eyes close to the roots.

A bitter chill crept along the whole length of his body. The frozen ground seemed to drain the heat from his blood, and the blood from his heart itself. Perhaps it was that, and knowing where he was, that accounted for what happened next. Or maybe scars, almost as old as he was, were still in existence down at the bottom of his mind, long buried under everything that had happened in between. The sky seemed to darken, while a ringing, buzzing sound came into his ears, and when the sky was completely black it began to redden with a bloody glow. His stomach dropped from under his heart, and a horrible fear filled him—the fear of a small helpless child, abandoned and alone in the night. He tried to spring up and out of that, and he could not move; he lay there rigid, seemingly frozen to the ground. Behind the ringing in his ears began to rise the unearthly yammer of the terror-dream—not heard, not even remembered, but coming to him like an awareness of something happening in some unknown dimension not of the living world.

He fought it grimly, and slowly got hold of himself; his eyes cleared, and the unearthly voices died, until he heard only the hammering of his heart. He saw, close to his eyes, the stems of the chaparral; and he was able to move again, stiffly, with his muscles shaking. He turned his head, getting a look at the actual world around him again. Then, through a rift in the brush that showed the creek bank, he saw the death tree.

Its base was almost on a level with his eyes, at perhaps a hundred feet; and for one brief moment it seemed to swell and tower, writhing its corpse-withered arms. His eyes stayed fixed upon it as he slowly got up and walked toward it without volition, as if it were the only thing possible to do. The thing shrunk as he approached it, no longer towering over him twice his size as it had seemed to do wherever he had seen it before. Finally he stood within arm's length; and now it was only a piece of weather-silvered wood in a tormented shape, a foot and a half shorter than himself.

An elongated knot at the top no longer looked like a distorted head, but only a symbol representing the hideous thing he had imagined there. He lashed out and struck it, hard, with the heel of his right hand. The long-rotted roots broke beneath the surface of the soil; and a twisted old stump tottered, splashed in the creek, and went spinning away.

Mart shuddered, shaking himself back together; and he spoke aloud. "I'll be a son-of-a-bitch," he said; and rejoined Amos. If he still looked shaken up, Amos pretended not to notice as they mounted up.

22

Martin Pauley was taken by another fit of shyness as they approached the Mathison ranch. He was a plainsman now, a good hunter, and a first-class Indian scout. But the saddle in which he lived had polished nothing about him but the seat of his leather pants.

"I tried to leave you back," Amos reminded him. "A couple of burr-matted, sore-backed critters we be. You got a lingo on you like a Caddo whiskey runner. You know that, don't you?"

Mart said he knew it.

"Our people never did have much shine," Amos said. "Salt of the earth, mind you; no better anywhere. But no book learning, like is born right into them Mathisons. To us, grammar is nothing but grampaw's wife."

Mart remembered the times Laurie had corrected his speech, and knew he didn't fit with civilized people. Not even as well as before, when he was merely a failure at it. But someway he was finally herded into the Mathison kitchen.

Laurie ran to him and took both his hands. "Where on earth have you been?"

"We been north," he answered her literally. "Looking around among the Kiowas."

"Why up there?"

"Well . . ." he answered lamely, "she might have been up there."

She said wonderingly, "Martie, do you realize how long you've been on this search? This is the third winter you've been out."

He hadn't thought of the time in terms of years. It had piled up in little pieces—always just one more place to go that would take just a few weeks more. He made a labored calculation, and decided Laurie was twenty-one. That explained why she seemed so lighted up; probably looked the best she ever would in her life. She was at an age when most girls light up, if they're going to; Mexicans and Indians earlier. A look at their mothers, or their older sisters, reminded you of what you knew for certain: All that bright glow would soon go out again. But you couldn't ever make yourself believe it.

Laurie made him follow her around, dealing out facts and figures about Kiowas, while she helped her mother get dinner. He didn't believe she cared a hoot about Kiowas, but he was glad for the chance to have a look at her.

There was this Indian called Scar, he explained to her. Seemed he actually had one on his face. They kept hearing that Scar had taken a little white girl captive. He showed her how the Indians described the scar, tracing a finger in a sweeping curve from hairline to jaw. A well-marked man. Only they couldn't find him. They couldn't even find any reliable person—no trader, soldier, or black hat—who had ever seen an Indian with such a scar. Then Mart had happened to think that the sign describing the scar was a whole lot like the Plains-Indian sign for sheep. The Kiowas had a warrior society called the Sheep, and he got to wondering if all those rumors were hitting around the fact that the Kiowa Sheep Society had Debbie. So they went to see. . . .

"A pure waste of time, and nobody to blame but me. It was me thought of it."

"It was I," she corrected him.

"You?" he fumbled it; then caught it on the bounce. "No, I meant—the blame was on I."

"There's going to be a barn party," she told him. "Mose Harper built a barn."

"At his age?"

"The State of Texas paid for it, mainly; they're going to put a Ranger stopover in part of it, and store their feed there next year—or the year after, when they get around to it. But the party is right away. I bet you knew!"

"No, I didn't."

"Bet you did. Only reason you came home."

He thought it over, and guessed he would give her some real comical answer later; soon as he thought of one.

After supper Aaron Mathison and Amos Edwards got out the herd books and ledgers, as upon their visit before. Aaron's head bent low, eyes close to the pages, so that Mart noticed again the old man's failing sight, much worse than it had been the last time.

And now Mart made his next mistake, rounding out his tally for the day. He set up camp, all uninvited, on the settle flanking the stove where he had sat with Laurie before; and here, while Laurie finished picking up the supper things, he waited hopefully for her to come and sit beside him. He had a notion that all the time he had been gone would melt away, once they sat there again.

But she didn't come and sit there. Had to get her beauty sleep, she said. Great long drive tomorrow; probably no sleep at all tomorrow night, what with the long drive home.

"Harper's is seven miles," Mart said. "Scarcely a real good spit."

"Don't be coarse." She said good night, respectfully to Amos and briskly to Mart, and went off across the dog-trot into that unknown world in the other section of the house, which he had never entered.

Mart wandered to the other end of the room, intending to join Amos and Aaron Mathison. But "G'night" Amos said to him. And Mathison gravely stood up to shake hands.

"It comes to me," Mart said, "I've been a long time away."

"And if we stayed for the damn barn burning," Amos said, "we'd be a long time off the road." Amos believed he knew where he was going now. All that great jackstraw pile of Indian nonsense was straightening itself in his mind. He could add up the hundreds of lies and half truths they had ridden so far to gather, and make them come out to a certain answer at last.

"You be stubborn men," Aaron Mathison said, "both of you."

Mart tried to share Amos' fire of conviction, but he could not. "Man has to live some place," he said, and slung on his coat, for they were to sleep in the bunkhouse this time. The coat was a long-skirted bearskin, slit high for the saddle; it was big enough to keep his horse warm, and smelled like a hog. "The prairie's all I know any more, I guess." He went out through the cold dark to his bed.

23

Mart was up long before daylight. Some internal clockwork always broke him out early nowadays. In summer the first dawn might be coming on, but in the short days he woke in the dark at exactly half-past four. He started a fire in the bunkhouse stove, and set coffee on. Then he went out to the breaking corral into which they had thrown the horses and mules Amos had picked for the next leg of their perpetual trip.

He grained them all, then went back to the bunkhouse. He set the coffee off the fire, and studied Amos for signs of arisal. He saw none, so he went out to the corral again. They carried three mules now, on account of the trading, and a spare saddle horse, in case one should pull up lame when they were in a hurry. Mart picked himself a stocky buckskin, with zebra stripes on his cannons and one down his back. He snubbed down, saddled, and bucked out this horse with his bearskin coat on; all horses took outrage at this coat, and had to be broke to it fresh every day for a while, until they got used to it.

He laid aside the bearskin to top off the great heavy stock horse he supposed Amos would ride. Its pitch was straight, and easy to sit, but had such a shock to it that his nose bled a little. Finally he got the pack saddles on the mules, and left them standing hump-backed in a sull. By this time the gray bitter dawn was on the prairie, but the white vapor from the lungs of the animals was the only sign of life around the place as yet.

Amos was sitting up on the edge of his bunk in his long-handled underwear, peering at the world through bleary lids and scratching himself.

"Well," Mart said, "we're saddled."

"Huh?"

"I say I uncorked the ponies, and slung the mule forks on."

"What did you do that for?"

"Because it's morning, I suppose—why the hell did you think? I don't see no smoke from the kitchen. You want I should stir up a snack?"

"We're held up," Amos said. "We got to go to that roof-raising."

"Thought you said we had to flog on. Jesus, will you make up your mind?"

"I just done so. By God, will you clean out your ears?"

"Oh, hell," Mart said, and went out to unsaddle.

24

The barn party was just a rough-and-ready gathering of frontier cattle people, such as Mart knew perfectly well. He knew exactly how these people spent every hour of their lives, and he could do everything they knew how to do better than most of them. What bothered him was to see such a raft of them in one place. They filled the big new barn when they all got there. Where had these dozens of scrubbed-looking girls come from, in all shapes and sizes? All this swarming of strangers gave Mart an uncomfortable feeling that the country had filled up solid while he was gone, leaving no room for him here.

Mart had got stuck with the job of bringing along the pack mules, for Amos wanted to get started directly from Harper's without going back. In consequence, Mart hadn't seen any of the Mathison family after they got dressed up until they appeared at the party. Aaron Mathison was patriarchal in high collar and black suit, across his vest the massive gold chain indispensable to men of substance; and Mrs. Mathison was a proper counterpart in a high-necked black dress that rustled when she so much as turned her eyes. They joined a row of other old-timers, a sort of windbreak of respectability along the wall, suggestive of mysteriously inherited book learning and deals with distant banks.

But it was Laurie who took him by shock, and for whom he was unprepared. She had made her own dress, of no prouder material than starched gingham, but it was full-skirted and tight at the waist, and left her shoulders bare, what time she wasn't shawled up against the cold. He would have been better off if he could have seen this rig at the house, and had time to get used to it. He had never seen her bare shoulders before, nor given thought to how white they must naturally be; and now he had trouble keeping his eyes off them. A wicked gleam showed in her eyes as she caught him staring.

"Honestly, Mart—you act as though you came from so far back in the hills the sun must *never* shine!"

"Listen here," he said, judging it was time to take her down a peg. "When I first rode with you, you was about so high, and round as a punkin. And you wore all-overs made of flour sack. I know because I seen a yearling calf stack you wrong end up in a doodle of wild hay, and you said 'Steamboat Mills' right across the bottom."

She giggled. "How do you know I still don't?" she asked him. But her eyes were searching the crowd for somebody else.

He drew off, to remuster according to plan; and when next he tried to go near her, she was surrounded. The whole place was curdled up with lashings of objectionable young jaybirds he had never seen before in his life, and Laurie

392

had rings in the noses of them all. Some of them wore borrowed-looking store clothes, generally either too long in the sleeves or fixing to split out someplace. But more had come in their saddle outfits, like Mart, with clean handkerchiefs on their necks and their shirts washed out by way of celebration. He took them to be common saddle pounders, mostly. But he imagined a knowingness behind their eyes, as if they were all onto something he did not suspect. Maybe they knew what they were doing here—which was more than he could say for himself. Tobe and Abner knew everybody and mixed everywhere, leaving Mart on his own. Brad had been his best friend, but these younger brothers seemed of a different generation altogether; he had nothing in common with them any more.

Some of the boys kept sliding out the back way to the horse lines, and Mart knew jugs were cached out there. He had taken very few drinks in his life, but this seemed a good time for one. He started to follow a group who spoke owlishly of "seeing to the blankets on the team," but Amos cut him off at the door.

"Huh uh. Not this time." Amos had not had a drop, which was odd in the time and place. Mart knew he could punish a jug until its friends cried out in pain, once he started.

"What's the matter now?"

"I got special reasons."

"Something going to bust?"

"Don't know yet. I'm waiting for something."

That was all he would say. Mart went off and holed up in a corner with old Mose Harper, who asked him questions about "present day" Indians, and listened respectfully to his answers—or the first few words of them, anyway. Mose got the bit in his teeth in less than half a minute, and went into the way things used to be, in full detail. Mart let his eyes wander past Mose to follow Laurie, flushed and whirling merrily, all over the place. The country-dance figures kept people changing partners, and Laurie always had a few quick words for each new one, making him laugh, usually, before they were separated again. Mart wondered what on earth she ever found to say.

"In my day," Mose was telling Mart, "when them Tonkawas killed an enemy, they just ate the heart and liver. Either raw or fussy prepared—didn't make no difference. What they wanted was his medicine. Only they never ate a white man's vitals; feared our medicine wouldn't mix with theirs, seemingly, though they respected our weepons. . . ."

Mart more than half expected that Laurie would come around and try to pull him into a dance, and he was determined he wasn't going to let her do it. He was making up speeches to fend her off with, while he pretended to listen to Mose.

"Nowadays," Mose explained, "they've took to eating the whole corpse, as a food. 'Tain't a ceremony, any more, so much as a saving of meat. But they still won't eat a white man. 'Tain't traditional."

Laurie never did come looking for Mart. She made a face at him once, as she happened to whirl close by, and that was all. Holding back became tiresome pretty fast, with no one to insist on anything different. He got into the dance, picking whatever girls caught his eye, regardless of whom they thought they belonged to. He was perversely half hoping for the fight you can sometimes get into that way, but none started.

He had been afraid of the dancing itself, but actually there wasn't anything to it. These people didn't party often enough to learn any very complicated dances. Just simple reels, and stuff like that. Sashay forward, sashay back, swing your lady, drop her slack. You swing mine, and I'll swing yours, and back to your own, and everybody swing. At these family parties, out here on civilization's brittle edge, they didn't even swing their girls by the waist—a dissolute practice to be seen mainly in saloons. Man grabbed his lady by the arms, and they kind of skittered around each other, any way they could. He got hold of Laurie only about once every two hours, but there were plenty of others. The fiddles and the banjos whanged out a rhythm that shook the barn, and the time flew by, romping and stomping.

Through all this Amos stood by, withdrawn into the background and into himself. Sometimes men he had known came to shake hands with him, greeting him with a heartiness Amos did not return. They were full of the questions to be expected of them, but the answers they got were as short as they could civilly be, and conveyed nothing. No conversation was allowed to develop. Amos remained apart, neither alone nor with anybody. Small use speculating on what he might be waiting for. Mart presently forgot him.

It was long after midnight, though nobody but the nodding old folks along the wall seemed to have noticed it, when the Rangers came in. There were three of them, and they made their arrival inconspicuous. They wore no uniforms—the Rangers had none—and their badges were in their pockets. Nobody was turned nervous, and nobody made a fuss over them, either. Rangers were a good thing, and there ought to be more of them. Sometimes you needed a company of them badly. Didn't need any just now. So long as no robbery or bloody murder was in immediate view, Rangers ranked as people. And that was it.

That, and one thing more: Everyone knew at once that they were there. Within less than a minute, people who had never seen any of these three before knew that Rangers had come in, and which men they were. Mart Pauley heard of them from a girl he swung but once, and had them pointed out to him by the next girl to whom he was handed on. "Who? *Him?*" The youngest of the three Rangers was Charlie MacCorry.

"He enlisted last year sometime."

As they finished the set, Mart was trying to make up his mind if he should go shake hands with Charlie MacCorry, or leave him be. He never had liked him much. Too much flash, too much swagger, too much to say. But now he saw something else. Amos and one of the older Rangers had walked toward each other on sight. They had drawn off, and were talking secretly and intently, apart from anyone else. Whatever Amos had waited for was here. Mart went over to them.

"This here is Sol Clinton," Amos told Mart. "Lieutenant in the Rangers. I side-rode him once. But that was long ago. I don't know if he remembers."

Sol Clinton looked Mart over without to-do, or any move to shake hands.

This Ranger appeared to be in his forties, but he was so heavily weathered that he perhaps looked older than he was. He had a drooping sandy mustache and deep grin lines that seemed to have been carved there, for he certainly wasn't smiling.

"I'm that found boy the Edwards family raised," Mart explained, "name of—"

"Know all about you," Sol Clinton said. His stare lay on Mart with a sort of tired candor. "You look something like a breed," he decided.

"And you," Mart answered, "look something like you don't know what you're talking about."

"Stop that," Amos snapped.

"He's full of snakehead," Mart stood his ground. "I can smell it on him."

"Why, sure," the Ranger conceded mildly. "I've had a snort or two. This is a dance, isn't it? Man can't haul off and dance in cold blood."

"Mind your manners anyway," Amos advised Mart.

"That's all right," Sol said. "You know a trader calls himself Jerem Futterman up the Salt Fork of the Brazos?"

Mart looked at Amos, and Amos answered him. "He knows him, and he knows he's dead."

"Might let him answer for himself, Amos."

"Sol was speaking of us riding to Austin with him," Amos went on stolidly, "to talk it over."

Mart said sharply, "We got no time for—"

"I explained him that," Amos said. "Will you get this through your damn head? This is an invite to a neck-tie party! Now stop butting in."

"Not quite that bad," Clinton said. "Not yet. We hope. No great hurry, either, right this minute. Best of our witnesses broke loose on us; got to catch him again before we put anything together. Most likely, all we'll want of you fellers is to pad out a good long report. Show zeal, you know." He dropped into a weary drawl. "Show we're unrestin'. Get our pay raised—like hell."

"I guarantee Mart Pauley will come back to answer," Amos said, "same as me."

"I guess the same bond will stretch to cover you both," Sol Clinton said. "I'll scratch down a few lines for you to sign."

"It's a wonderful thing to be a former Ranger," Amos said. "It's the way everybody trusts you—that's what gets to a man."

"Especially if you're also a man of property," Clinton agreed in that same mild way. "Amos put up a thousand head of cattle," he explained to Mart, "that says you and him will come on into Austin, soon as you finish this next one trip."

"Aaron Mathison told me about this," Amos said. "I couldn't believe he had it right. I got to believe it now."

"They know about this, then. They knew it all the time. . . ."

"I stayed on to make sure. There's nothing more to wait on now. Go and tell the Mathisons we're leaving."

"Stay on awhile," Sol Clinton suggested. "Have a good time if you want."

Martin Pauley said, "No, thanks," as he turned away.

He went looking for Laurie first. She wasn't dancing, or anywhere in the barn. He went out to the barbecue pit, where some people were still poking around what was left of a steer, but she wasn't there. He wandered down the horse line, where the saddle stock was tied along the length of a hundred-foot rope. He knew some of the women had gone over to Mose Harper's house; a passel of young children had been bedded down over there, for one thing. He had about decided to go butt in there when he found her.

A couple stood in the shadows of a feed shelter. The man was Charlie Mac-Corry; and the girl in his arms was Laurie Mathison, as Mart somehow knew without needing to look.

Martin Pauley just stood there staring at them, his head down a little bit, like some witless cow-critter half knocked in the head. He stood there as long as they did. Charlie MacCorry finally let the girl go, slowly, and turned.

"Just what the hell do *you* want?"

A weakness came into Mart's belly muscles, and then a knotting up; and he began to laugh, foolishly, sagging against the feed rack. He never did know what he was laughing at.

Charlie blew up. "Now you look here!" He grabbed Mart by the front of the jacket, straightened him up, and slapped his face fit to break his neck. Mart lashed out by reflex, and Charlie MacCorry was flat on his back in the same tenth of a second.

He was up on the bounce, and they went at it. They were at it for some time.

They had no prize ring out in that country; fights were many but unrehearsed. These men were leathery and hard to hurt, but their knuckle brawls were fought by instinct, without the skill they showed with other weapons. Mart Pauley never ducked, blocked, nor gave ground; he came straight in, very fast at first, later more slowly, plodding and following. He swung workmanlike, slugging blows, one hand and then the other, putting his back into it. Charlie MacCorry fought standing straight up, circling and sidestepping, watching his chances. He threw long-armed, lacing blows, mostly to the face. Gradually, over a period of time, he beat Mart's head off.

They never knew when Laurie left them. A close circle of men packed in around them, shouting advice, roaring when either one was staggered. Amos Edwards was there, and both of MacCorry's fellow Rangers. These three stood watching critically but impassively in the inner circle, the only silent members of the crowd. Neither fighter noticed them, or heard the yelling. Somewhere along the way Mart took a slam on the side of the face with his mouth open, and the inside of his cheek opened on his own teeth. Daylight later showed frozen splotches of bright red over a surprising area, as if a shoat had been slaughtered. Mart kept on moving in, one eye puffed shut and the other closing; and suddenly this thing was over.

The blow that ended it was no different than a hundred others, except in its luck. Mart had no idea which hand had landed, let alone how he did it. Charlie MacCorry went down without notice, as if all strings were cut at once. He fell forward on his face, and every muscle was slack as they turned him over. For a couple of moments Mart stood looking down at him with a stupid surprise, wondering what had happened.

He turned away, and found himself facing Sol Clinton. He spit blood, and said, "You next?"

The Ranger stared at him. "Who? Me? What for?" He stood aside.

A dawn as cheerless as a drunkard's awakening was making a line of gray on the eastern horizon. Mart walked to their mules after passing them once and having to turn back. Any number of hands helped him, and took over from him, as he went about feeding their animals, so he took time to take the handkerchief from his neck, and stuff it into his cheek. The sweat with which it was soaked stung the big cut inside his cheek, but his mouth stopped filling up.

Charlie MacCorry came to him. "You all right?" His nose showed a bright blaze where it had hit the frozen ground as he fell.

"I'm ready to go on with it if you are."

"Well—all right—if you say. Just tell me one thing. What was you laughing at?"

"Charlie, I'll be damned if I know."

Watching him narrowly, Charlie said, "You don't?"

"Don't rightly recall what we was fighting about, when it comes to that."

"Thought maybe you figured I cross-branded your girl."

"I got no girl. Never had."

Charlie moved closer, but his hands were in his pockets. He looked at the ground, and at the cold streak of light in the east, before he looked at Mart. "I'd be a fool not to take your word," he decided. Charlie stuck out his hand, then drew it back, for it was swollen to double size around broken bones. He offered his left hand instead. "God damn, you got a hard head."

"Need one, slow as I move." He gave Charlie's left hand the least possible shake, and pulled back.

"You don't move slow," Charlie said. "See you in Austin." He walked away.

Amos came along. "Stock's ready."

"Good." Mart tightened his cinch, and they rode. Neither had anything to say. As the sun came up, Amos began to sing to himself. It was an old song from the Mexican War, though scarcely recognizable as Amos sang it. A good many cowboys had replaced forgotten words and turns of tune with whatever came into their heads before the song got to Amos.

> Green grow the rushes, oh,
> Green grow the rushes, oh,
> Only thing I ever want to know
> Is where is the girl I left behind. . . .

Well, it had been sung a good many thousand times before by men who hadn't left anything behind, because they had nothing to leave.

25

They angled southwest at a good swinging pace, their animals fresh and well grained. At Fort Phantom Hill they found the garrison greatly strengthened and full of aggressive confidence for a change. This was surprising enough, but at Fort Concho they saw troop after troop of newly mustered cavalry; and were told that Fort Richardson was swarming with a concentration of much greater strength. Southwest Texas was going to have a real striking force at last. They had prayed for this for a long time, and they welcomed it no less because of a sardonic bitterness in it for those to whom help had come too late.

Beyond the Colorado they turned toward the setting sun, through a country with nothing man-made to be seen in it. So well were they moving that they outrode the winter in a couple of weeks. For once, instead of heading into the teeth of the worst weather they could find, they were riding to meet the spring. By the time they rounded the southern end of the Staked Plains the sun blazed hot by day, while yet the dry-country cold bit very hard at night. The surface of the land was strewn with flints and black lava float; it grew little besides creosote bush, chaparral, and bear grass, and the many, many kinds of cactus. Waterholes were far apart, and you had better know where they were, once you left the wagon tracks behind.

Beyond Horsehead Crossing they rode northwest and across the Pecos, skirting the far flank of the Staked Plains—called Los Llanos Estacados over here. They were reaching for New Mexico Territory, some hundred and fifty miles above, as a horse jogs; a vulture could make it shorter, if he would stop his uncomplimentary circling over the two riders, and line out. Their time for this distance was much worse than a week, for half of which they pushed into a wind so thick with dust that they wore their neckerchiefs up to their eyes.

When finally they crossed the Territory line, they didn't even know it, being unable to tell Delaware Creek from any other dry wash unfed by snows. Dead reckoning persuaded them they must be in New Mexico, but they wouldn't have known it. Where were the señoritas and cantinas, the guitars and tequila, Amos had talked about? He may have confused this lately Mexican country he had never seen with the Old Mexico he knew beyond the lower Rio Grande. Without meaning to, probably, he had made the Southwest sound like a never-never country of song and illicit love, with a streak of wicked bloody murder interestingly hidden just under a surface of ease and mañana. The territory didn't look like that. Nor like anything else, either, at the point where they entered it. There wasn't anything there at all.

But now the wind rested, and the air cleared. The country recovered its characteristic black and white of hard sun and sharp shadows. Mart dug Debbie's miniature out of his saddle bags to see how it had come through the dust. He carried the little velvet box wrapped in doeskin now, and he hadn't opened it for a long time. The soft leather had protected it well; the little portrait looked brighter and fresher in the white desert light than he had ever seen it. The small kitty-cat face looked out of the frame with a life of its own, bright-eyed, eager, happy with the young new world. He felt a twinge he had almost forgotten—she seemed so dear, so precious, and so lost. From this point on he began to pull free from the backward drag of his bad days back home. No, not back home; he had no home. His hopes once more led out down the trail.

For now they were in the land of the Comancheros, toward which they had been pointed by the loot of Deadhorse Bend. Here Bluebonnet must have traded for the silverwork and turquoise in the spoils; here surely he would now seek refuge from the evil that had come upon him in the north.

That name, Comanchero, was a hated one among Texans. Actually the Comancheros were nothing but some people who traded with Comanches, much as Mart and Amos themselves had often done. If you were an American, and traded with Comanches from the United States side, basing upon the forts of West Texas and Indian Territory, you were a trader. But if you were a Mexican, basing in Mexico, and made trading contact with Comanches on the southwest flank of the Staked Plains, you were not called a trader, but a Comanchero.

During the years of armed disagreement with Mexico, the Comancheros had given Texans plenty of reasons for complaint. When thousands of head of Texas horses, mules, and cattle disappeared into the Staked Plains every year, it was the Comancheros who took all that livestock off Indian hands, and spirited it into deep Mexico. And when great numbers of breech-loading carbines appeared in the hands of Comanche raiders, it was the Comancheros who put them there.

Of course, Amos had once traded some split-blocks of sulphur matches and a bottle of Epsom salts (for making water boil magically by passing your hand over it) for some ornaments of pure Mexican gold no Indian ever got by trading. But that was different.

Mart had always heard the Comancheros described as a vicious, slinking, cowardly breed, living like varmints in unbelievable filth. These were the people who now seemed to hold their last great hope of finding Debbie. The great war chiefs of the Staked Plains Comanches, like Bull Bear, Wild Horse, Black Duck, Shaking Hand, and the young Quanah, never came near the Agencies at all. Well armed, always on the fight, they struck deep and vanished. Amos was certain now that these irreconcilables did business only with the Comancheros —and that the Flower had to be with them.

Somewhere there must be Comancheros who knew every one of them well. Somewhere must be one who knew where Debbie was. Or maybe there isn't, Mart sometimes thought. But they're the best bet we got left. We'll find her now. Or never at all.

First they had to find the Comancheros. Find Comancheros? Hell, first you had to find a human being. That wasn't easy in this country they didn't know. Over and over they followed trails which should have forked together, and led

some place, but only petered out like the dry rivers into blown sand. There had
to be people here someplace, though, and eventually they began to find some.
Some small bunches of Apaches, seen at a great distance, were the first, but
these shied off. Then finally they found a village.

This was a cluster of two-dozen, mud-and-wattle huts called jacals, around a
mud hole and the ruins of a mission, and its name was Esperanza. Here lived
some merry, friendly, singing people in possession of almost nothing. They had
some little corn patches, and a few sheep, and understood sign language. How
did they keep the Apaches out of the sheep? A spreading of the hands. It was
not possible. But the Apaches never took all the sheep. Always left some for
seed, so there would be something to steal another year. So all was well, thanks
to the goodness of God. Here were some guitars at last, and someone singing
someplace at any hour of day or night. Also some warm pulque, which could
bring on a sweaty lassitude followed by a headache. No señoritas in evidence,
though. Just a lot of fat squawlike women, with big grins and no shoes.

Once they had found one village, the others were much more easily discover-
able—never exactly where they were said to be, nor at anything like the distance which was always described either as "Not far" or "Whoo!" But land-
marked, so you found them eventually. They made their way to little places
called Derecho, Una Vaca, Gallo, San Pascual, San Marco, Plata Negra, and San
Philipe. Some of these centered on fortified ranchos, some on churches, others
just on waterholes. The two riders learned the provincial Spanish more easily
than they had expected; the vocabulary used out here was not very large. And
they became fond of these sun-sleepy people who were always singing, always
making jokes. They had voluble good manners and an open-handed hospitality.
They didn't seem to wash very much, but actually it didn't seem necessary in
this dry air. The villages and the people had a sort of friendly, sun-baked smell.

They looked much happier, Mart thought, than Americans ever seem to be.
A man built a one-room jacal, or maybe an adobe, if mud was in good supply
when he was married. Though he bred a double-dozen children, he never built
onto that one room again. As each day warmed up, the master of the house was
to be found squatting against the outer wall. All day long he moved around it,
following the shade when the day was hot, the sun when the day was cool; and
thus painlessly passed his life, untroubled. Mart could envy them, but he
couldn't learn from them. Why is it a man can never seem to buckle down and
train himself to indolence and stupidity when he can see what sanctuary they
offer from toil and pain?

But they found no Comancheros. They had expected a spring burst of fur
trading, but spring ran into summer without any sign of anything like that going
on. They were in the wrong place for it, obviously. And the real Comanchero
rendezvous would be made in the fall at the end of the summer-raiding season.
They worked hard to make sure of their Comancheros by the end of the summer—and they didn't learn a thing. The paisanos could retreat into a know-
nothing shell that neither cunning nor bribery could break down. A stranger
could see their eyes become placidly impenetrable, black and surface-lighted
like obsidian; and when he saw that he might as well quit.

Then, at Potrero, they ran into Lije Powers. They remembered him as an old fool; and now he seemed immeasurably older and more foolish than he had been before. But he set them on the right track.

Lije greeted them with whoops and exaggerated grimaces of delight, in the manner of old men who have led rough and lonely lives. He pumped their hands, and stretched eyes and jaws wide in great meaningless guffaws. When that was over, though, they saw that there wasn't so very much of the old man left. His eyes were sunken, his cheeks had fallen in; and his worn clothes hung on a rack of bones.

"You look like holy hell," Amos told him.

"I ain't been too well," Lije admitted. "I been looking for you fellers. I got to talk to you."

"You heard we came out here?"

"Why, sure. Everybody I seen in the last six months knows all about you. Come on in the shade."

Lije took them to a two-by-four cantina without even a sign on it where whiskey was to be had, for a new thing and a wonder.

"I been looking for Debbie Edwards," he told them.

"So have we. We never have quit since we seen you last."

"Me neither," Lije said. He had turned abstemious, sipping his whiskey slowly, as if with care. When it came time to refill the glasses, his was always still more than half full, and he wouldn't toss it off, as others did, but just let the glass be filled up. He didn't seem much interested in hearing what they had tried, or where they had been, or even if they had ever found any clues. Just wanted to tell at great length, with all the detail he could get them to stand for, the entire history of his own long search. He droned on and on, while Mart grew restless, then drunk, then sober again. But Amos seemed to want to listen.

"Guess you heard about the reward I put up," Amos said.

"I don't want the money, Amos," Lije said.

"Just been doing this out of the goodness of your heart, huh?"

"No . . . I'll tell you what I want. I want a job. Not a good job, nor one with too much riding. Bull cook, or like that, without no pay, neither, to speak of. Just a bunk, and a little grub, and a chai' by a stove. A place. But one where I don't never get throwed out. Time comes for me to haul off and die up, I want to be let die in that bunk. Not be throwed out for lack of the space I take up, or because a man on the die don't do much work."

There you had it—the end a prairie man could look forward to. Reaching out to accomplish some one great impossible thing at the last—as your only hope of securing just a place to lie down and die. Mart expected to hear Amos say that Lije was welcome to the bunk in any case.

"All right, Lije," Amos said. But he added, "If you find her."

Lije looked pleased; he hadn't expected anything more, nor been sure of this much. "So now lately, I been talking to these here Comancheros," he said.

"*Talking* to 'em?" Amos butted in.

"What's wrong with that? Ain't you been?"

"I ain't even seen one!"

Lije looked at him with disbelief, then with wonder; and finally with pity.

"Son, son. In all this time you been in the Territory, I don't believe you've seen one other dang thing else!"

Not that these peons knew much about what they were doing, he admitted. They hired on as trail drivers, or packers, or bullwhackers, when the work was shoved at them. Probably wouldn't want to name their bosses, either, to a stranger who didn't seem to know any of them. You had to find los ricos—the men who ran the long drives down into Old Mexico, too deep for anything ever to be recovered. He named about a dozen of these, and Amos made him go back over some of the names to be sure he would remember them all.

"Old Jaime Rosas—he's the one I'd talk to, was I you." (He pronounced it "Hymie Rosies.") "I swear he knows where Bluebonnet is. And the girl."

"You think she's alive?"

"I figure *he* thinks so. I figure he's seen her. I all but had it out of him. Then I was stopped."

"How stopped? Who stopped you?"

"You did. . . . Jaime got word you was in the territory. He wouldn't deal no more with me. I figure he believed he could do better for himself letting you come to him. Direct."

Find Jaime Rosas. It was all they had to do, and it shouldn't be too hard with the Comanchero willing to deal. He was around this border someplace for a part of every year. Most years, anyway. Find him, and this search is licked. Out of the rattle-brained old fraud of a broke-down buffalo hunter had come the only straight, direct lead they had ever had.

Amos gave Lije forty dollars, and Lije rode off in a different direction than Amos took. Said he wanted to check on some Caddoes he heard was running whiskey in. He always had seemed to have Caddoes on the brain. And Amos and Mart went looking for Jaime Rosas.

26

They did find old Jaime Rosas; or perhaps he had to find them in the end. It was the heartbreaking distances that held them back from coming up with him for so long. You were never in the wrong place without being about a week and a half away from the right one. That country seemed to have some kind of weird spell upon it, so that you could travel in one spot all day long, and never gain a mile. You might start out in the morning with a notched butte far off on your left; and when you camped at nightfall the same notched butte would be right there, in the same place. Maybe it was a good thing that a man and his plodding horse could not see that country from the sky, as the vultures saw it. If a man could have seen the vastness in which he was a speck, the heart would have gone out of him; and if his horse could have seen it, the animal would have died.

Now that they knew the names of the boss Comancheros, the people were more willing to help them, relaying news of the movements of Jaime Rosas. If they had no news they made up some, and this could prove a costly thing. If a peon wanted to please you he would give you a tale of some kind—never hesitating to send you ninety miles out of your way, rather than disappoint you by telling you he didn't know.

While they were hunting for Jaime Rosas, Martin Pauley's nights became haunted for a while by a peculiar form of dream. The source of the dream was obvious. One blazing day in Los Gatos, where they were held up through the heat of the siesta hours, Mart had wandered into a church, because it looked cool and pleasantly dark within the deep adobe walls. Little candles grouped in several places stood out in bright pinpoints, some of them red where they had burned down in their ruby glasses. Mart sat down, and as his eyes adjusted he began to see the images, life-size and dark-complected mostly, of saints and martyrs, all around him in the gloom. Painted in natural colors, with polished stones for eyes, they looked a lot like people, here in the dark. Except that they were unnaturally still. Not even the candle flames wavered in the quiet air. Mart sat there, fascinated, for a long time.

About a week after that, Mart dreamed of Debbie. In all this time he had never seen her in a dream before; perhaps because he rarely dreamed at all. But this dream was very real and clear. He seemed to be standing in the dark church. The images around him again, like living people, but holding unnaturally still. He could feel their presence strongly, but they seemed neither friendly nor hostile—just there. Directly in front of him a candlelighted shrine began to brighten, and there was Debbie, in the middle of a soft white light. She was littler than when she was lost, littler than in the miniature even, and with a different look and pose than the miniature had—more of a side-face position. She didn't look out at him, or move, any more than the images did, but she was alive—he knew she was alive; she fairly glowed with life, as if made of the light itself.

He stood holding his breath, waiting for her to turn and see him. He could feel the moment when she would turn to him coming nearer, and nearer, until the strain was unbearable, and woke him up just too soon.

The same dream returned to him on other nights, sometimes close together, sometimes many days apart, perhaps a dozen times. The whole thing was always as real and clear as it had been the first time; and he always woke up just before Debbie turned. Then, for no reason, he quit having that dream, and he couldn't make it come back.

Rumors found their way to them from Texas, most of them fourth- or fifth-hand tales of things that had happened months before. Yet there was enough substance to what they heard to tell that the smoldering frontier was blazing up into open war. A chief usually called Big Red Food, but whose name Mart translated as Raw Meat, charged a company of infantry close to Fort Sill, broke clean through it, and rode away. Wolf Tail drummed up a great gathering of warriors from many bands, dragging Quanah into it. For three days they pressed home an attack upon a party of buffalo hunters at Adobe Walls, charge after charge, but were beaten off with heavy loss. Every war chief they had ever known seemed to be up; but now Washington at last had had enough. The Friends were out of the Agencies, and the military was in the saddle. A finish fight seemed cocked and primed. . . .

But they had had no news for weeks, the night they found Jaime Rosas.

They had come after dark into Puerto del Sol, a village with more people in it than most. It had no hacienda and no church, but it did have a two-acre corral with high adobe walls, loopholed, so that the corral could be fought as a fort. Several unnecessarily large adobe stores, with almost nothing for sale in them, looked a lot like warehouses. A Comanchero base, sure enough, Mart thought.

The place had two cantinas, each with more volunteer guitar singers than it needed, cadging for drinks. Amos picked the smaller and better of the two, and as they went in, Mart saw that in Puerto del Sol the cantinas actually did have señoritas, for a rarity. They had been overanticipated for a long time, due to Amos' original confusion of this country with a part of Old Mexico that was the whole length of Texas away. The territory dance girls had been disappointing, what few times they had seen any—just stolid-faced little women like squaws, either too fat or with a half-grown look. These of Puerto del Sol didn't look much better, at first.

Amos fell in at once with a smart-looking vaquero with leather lace on his hat. A haciendado, or the son of one—if he wasn't one of the boss Comancheros. Mart bought a short glass of tequila and a tall glass of tepid water clouded with New Mexico Territory, and took them to a table in a corner. Amos didn't seem to like Mart standing by when he was angling for information. Sooner or later he was likely to include Mart in the conversation by some remark such as: "What the devil you haunting me for?" Or: "What in all hell you want now?" Since the dreams of Debbie had stopped, Mart was beginning to have a hard time remembering why he was still riding with Amos. Most days it was a matter of habit. He kept on because he had no plans of his own, nor any idea of where to head for if he split off.

The vaquero with the expensive hat went away, and came back with a shabby old man. Amos sat with these two, buying them drinks, but he seemed to have lost interest. All three seemed bored with the whole thing. They sat gazing idly about, with the placid vacuity common to the country, seeming to be trying to forget each other, as much as anything. Mart saw Amos make a Spanish joke he had worked out, something about the many flies drinking his liquor up, and the other two laughed politely. Amos wasn't finding out anything, Mart judged.

Mart's attention went back to the girls. There were five or six of them in here, but not the same ones all the time. They flirted with the vaqueros, and danced for them, and with them; and now and then a girl disappeared with one, whereupon another wandered in to take her place. They drank wine, but smelled mostly of vanilla-bean perfume and musk. These girls carried a sudden danger with them, as if death must be a he-goat, and liked to follow them around. Mart himself had seen one case of knife-in-the-belly, and had heard of a good many more. A girl let her eyes wander once too often, and the knives jumped with no warning at all. In the next two seconds there was liable to be a man on the dirt floor, and a surprised new face in hell. The girl screamed, and yammered, and had to be dragged away in a hollering tizzy; but was back the next night, with her eyes wandering just as much. Mart wondered if a girl got famous, and had songs made about her, if people pointed her out and said, "Five men are dead for that little one."

So he was watching for it, and able to handle it, when it almost happened to him. The tequila had an unpleasant taste, hard to get used to, as if somebody had washed his sox in it, but it hid a flame. As it warmed his brain, everything looked a lot prettier; and a new girl who came in looked different from all the others he had seen out here—or anywhere, maybe.

This girl was pert and trim, and her skirts flared in a whirl of color when she turned. Her Spanish-heeled shoes must have been a gift brought a long way, perhaps from Mexico City. The shoes set her apart from the others, who wore moccasins, at best, when they weren't barefoot altogether. She had a nose-shaped nose, instead of a flat one, and carried her head with defiance. Or anyhow, that was the way Mart saw her now, and always remembered her.

A lot of eyes looked this one up and down with appreciation, as if her dress were no more barrier to appraisal than harness on a filly. Martin Pauley dropped his eyes to his hands. He had a tall glass in one hand and a short glass in the other, and he studied this situation stupidly for a few moments before he swallowed a slug of warmish chalky water, and tossed off the rest of his tequila. He had drunk slowly, but a good many. And now the tequila looked up, fastened eyes upon the girl, and held without self-consciousness, wherever she went. There is a great independence, and a confident immunity to risk, in all drinks made out of cactus.

An old saying said itself in his mind. "Indian takes drink; drink takes drink; drink takes Indian; all chase squaw." It had a plausible, thoughtful sound, but no practical meaning. Presently the girl noticed him, and looked at him steadily for some moments, trying to make up her mind about him in the bad light. Nothing came of this immediately; a peonish fellow, dressed like a vaquero, but not a good one, took hold of her and made her dance with him. Mart sucked his teeth and thought nothing of it. He had no plans.

The girl had, though, and steered her partner toward Mart's table. She fixed her eyes on Mart, swung close, and kicked him in the shin. One way to do it, Mart thought. And here it comes. He drained a last drop from his tequila glass, and let his right hand come to rest on his leg under the table. Sure enough. The vaquero turned and looked him over across the table. His shirt was open to the waist, showing the brown chest to be smooth and hairless.

"Your eye is of a nasty color," the vaquero said poetically in Chihuahua Spanish. "Of a sameness to the belly of a carp."

Mart leaned forward with a smile, eyebrows up, as if in response to a greeting he had not quite caught. "And you?" he returned courteously, also in Spanish. "We have a drink, no?"

"No," said the vaquero, looking puzzled.

"We have a drink, yes," the girl changed his mind. "You know why? The gun of this man is in his right hand under the table. He blows your bowels out the door in one moment. This is necessary."

She extended an imperious palm, and Mart slid a silver dollar across the table to her. The vaquero was looking thoughtful as she led him away. Mart never knew what manner of drink she got into the fellow, but she was back almost at once. The vaquero was already to be seen snoring on the mud floor. A compadre dragged him out by the feet, and laid him tenderly in the road.

She said her name was Estrellita, which he did not believe; it had a picked-out sound to him. She sat beside him and sang at him with a guitar. The tequila was thinking in Spanish now, so that the words of the sad, sad song made sense without having to be translated in his head.

> I see a stranger passing,
>   His heart is dark with sorrows,
> Another such as I am,
>   Behind him his tomorrows . . .

This song was a great epic tragedy in about a hundred stanzas, each ending on a suspended note, to keep the listener on the hook. But she hadn't got through more than half a dozen when she stopped and leaned forward to peer into his eyes. Perhaps she saw signs of his bursting into tears, for she got him up and danced with him. A whole battery of guitars had begun wailing out a *baile* as soon as she stopped singing, and the tequila was just as ready to romp and stomp as to bawl into the empty glasses. As she came close to him, her musk-heavy perfume wrapped around him, strong enough to lift him off his feet with one hand. The tequila thought it was wonderful. No grabbing of arms in dancing with this one— you swung the girl by taking hold of the girl. The round neckline of her dress was quite modest, almost up to her throat, and her sleeves were tied at her elbows. But what he found out was that this was a very thin dress.

"I think it is time to go home now," she said.

"I have no home," he said blankly.

"My house is your house," she told him.

He remembered to speak to Amos about it. The young well-dressed vaquero was gone, and Amos sat head to head with the shabby old man, talking softly and earnestly. "All right if I take a walk?" Mart interrupted them.

"Where you going to be?" Amos asked the girl in Spanish.   She described a turn or two and counted doors on her fingers. Amos went back to his powwow, and Mart guessed he was dismissed. "Wait a minute," Amos called him back. He gave Mart a handful of silver dollars without looking up. Good thing he did. Running out of *dinero* is another first-class way to get in trouble around a cantina señorita.

Her *casa* turned out to be the scrubbiest horse stall of a jacal he had seen yet. She lighted a candle, and the place looked a little better inside, mostly because of a striped serape on the dirt floor and a couple tied on the walls to cover holes where the mud had fallen out of the woven twigs. The candle stood in a little shrine sheltering a pottery Virgin of Tiburon, and this reminded Mart of something, but he couldn't remember what. He blinked as he watched Es-

trellita cross herself and kneel briefly in obeisance. Then she came to him and presented her back to be unbuttoned.

All through this whole thing, Mart showed the dexterity and finesse of a hog in a sand boil, and even the tequila knew it. It was very young tequila at best, as its raw bite had attested, and it couldn't help him much after a point. One moment he was afraid to touch her, and in the next, when he did take her in his arms, he almost broke her in two. The girl was first astonished, then angry; but finally her sense of humor returned, and she felt sorry for him. She turned patient, soothing and gentling him; and when at last he slept he was in such a state of relaxation that even his toe nails must have been limp.

So now, of course, he had to get up again.

Amos came striding down the narrow *calle*, banging his heels on the hard dirt. One of his spurs had a loose wheel; it had always been that way. It never whispered when he rode, but afoot this spur made some different complaint at every step. Thug, ding, thug, clank, thug, bingle, went Amos as he walked; and the familiar sound woke Mart from a hundred feet away.

"Get your clothes on," Amos said, as soon as the door was open. "We're on our way."

Except for a slight queerness of balance as he first stood up, Mart felt fine. There is no cleaner liquor than tequila when it is made right, however awful it may taste. "Right now? In the middle of the night?"

"Look at the sky."

Mart saw that the east was turning light. "I suppose that old man seen Jaime Rosas some far-fetched place. Maybe last year, or the year before."

"That old man is Jaime Rosas."

Mart stared at Amos' silhouette, then stamped into his boots.

"He says Bluebonnet has a young white girl," Amos told him. "One with yaller hair and green eyes."

"Where at?"

"Rosas is taking us to him. We'll be there before night."

They had been in New Mexico more than two years and a half.

 27

They sat in a circle in the shade of a tepee eighteen feet across, three white men and seven war chiefs around a charred spot that would have been a council fire if a fire had been tolerable that day. The scraped buffalo hide of the tepee had been rolled up for a couple of feet, and the hot wind crept under, sometimes raising miniature dust devils on the hard dirt floor.

Bluebonnet, the elusive ghost they had followed for so long, sat opposite the entrance flap. Mart had long since stopped trying to believe there was any Comanche named Bluebonnet, or the Flower, or whatever his damned name meant in words. He judged Bluebonnet to be a myth, the work of an all-Indian conspiracy. Every savage in creation had probably heard of the two searchers by this time, and stood ready to join in the sport of sending them hither and yon in chase of a chief who did not exist. Yet there he was; and on the outside of the tepee, large as a shield, the oft-described, never-seen symbol of the Flower was drawn in faded antelope blood.

An oddly shimmering light, a reflection from the sun-blasted surface of the earth outside, played over the old chief's face. It was the broad, flat face common to one type of Comanche, round and yellow as a moon. Age was crinkling its surface in fine-lined patterns, into which the opaque eyes were set flush, without hollows.

The other six war chiefs weren't needed here. Bluebonnet had them as a courtesy—and to reassure his village that he wasn't making foolish trades behind the backs of his people. It wasn't much of a village. It numbered only fourteen lodges, able to turn out perhaps thirty or forty warriors by counting all boys over twelve. But it was what he had. His pride and his special notion of his honor were still very great, far though he was on his road to oblivion.

Jaime Rosas had four vaqueros with him, but he hadn't brought them into council. They were tall Indian-looking men, good prairie Comancheros, but he owed them no courtesies. The vaqueros had pitched a shade-fly of their own a little way off. Three of them slept most of the time, but one was always awake, day or night, whatever the time might be. Whenever several were awake at once they were to be heard laughing a good deal, or else singing a sad long song that might last a couple of hours; then all but one would go back to sleep again.

What was going on in the tepee was in the nature of a horse trade. The evening of their arrival had been devoted to a meager feast without dancing, the atmosphere considerably dampened by the fact that Rosas had brought no rum. The council began the next morning. It was a slow thing, with long stillnesses between irrelevant remarks conveyed in sign language. One thing about it, no one was likely to go off half cocked in a session like that. From time to time the pipe, furnished by Bluebonnet, was filled with a pinch of tobacco, furnished by Rosas, and passed from hand to hand, as a sort of punctuation.

They were in that tepee three days, the councils running from forenoon to sundown. Even a cowboy's back can get busted, sitting cross-legged as long as that. Jaime Rosas did all the talking done on the white men's side. This old man's face was weathered much darker than Bluebonnet's; his dirty gray mustache looked whiter than it was against that skin. His eyes had brown veins in the whites and red-rimmed lids. All day long he chewed slowly on a grass stem with teeth worn to brown stubs; by night he would have a foot-long stem eaten down to an inch or two. He could sit quiet as long as Bluebonnet could, and maybe a little longer; and when he unlimbered his sign language it ran as smoothly as Bluebonnet's, though this chief prided himself on the grace of his sign talk. The unpunctuated flow of compound signs made the conversation all but impossible to follow.

Rosas' hands might say, "Horse-dig-hole-slow-buffalo-chase-catch-no-enemy-run-chase-catch-no-sad." Mart read that to mean, "The horse is worthless—too slow for hunting or for war; it's too bad."

And Bluebonnet's answer, in signs of smooth speed and great delicacy: "Stiff-neck-beat-enemy-far-run-still-neck-horse-ride-leave-tepee-warriors-pile-up." They had him there, Mart admitted to himself. He believed Bluebonnet had said, "When a chief has run his enemies out of the country, he wants a horse he can ride with pride, like to a council." But he didn't know. Here came the pipe again.

"I'll never get no place in this dang country," he said to Amos. "It's a good thing we'll soon be heading home."

"Shut up." It was the first remark Amos had made that day.

Toward sundown of the first day Bluebonnet admitted he had a young white girl, blonde and blue-eyed, in his lodge.

"May not be the one," Amos said in Spanish.

"Who knows?" Rosas answered. "Man is the hands of God."

Around noon of the second day, Rosas presented Bluebonnet with the horse they had talked about most of the first day. It was a show-off palomino, with a stud-horse neck and ripples in its silver mane and tail. About what the old dons would have called a palfrey once. Mart wouldn't have wanted it. But the saddle on it, sheltered under a tied-down canvas until the moment of presentation, was heavily crusted with silver, and probably worth two hundred dollars. Rosas gave the old chief horse and rig upon condition that no present would be accepted in return. Bluebonnet turned wary for a while after that, as if the gift might have done more harm than good; but his eyes showed a gleam toward the end of the day, for what they talked about all afternoon was rifles.

Sundown was near on the third day when they came to the end at last. The abruptness of the finish caught Mart off guard. Rosas and Bluebonnet had been going through an interminable discussion of percussion caps, as near as Mart could make out. He had given up trying to follow it, and had let his eyes lose focus in the glow of the leveling sun upon the dust. He took a brief puff as the pipe passed him again, and was aware that one of the warriors got up and went out.

Amos said, "He's sent for her, Mart."

The desert air seemed to press inward upon the tepee with an unbelievable weight. His head swam, and he could not recognize a single familiar symbol among the next posturings of Bluebonnet's hands.

"He says she's well and strong," Amos told him.

Mart returned his eyes to Bluebonnet's hands. His head cleared, and he saw plainly the next thing the hands said. He turned to Amos in appeal, unwilling to believe he had properly understood.

"The girl is his wife," Amos interpreted.

"It doesn't matter." His mouth was so dry that the thick words were not understandable at all. Mart cleared his throat, and tried to spit, but could not. "It doesn't matter," he said again.

The warrior who had left the lodge now returned. As he entered, he spoke a Comanche phrase over his shoulder, and a young woman appeared. Her form was not that of a little girl; it hardly could have been after the lost years. This was a woman, thin, and not very tall, but grown. Her face and the color of her hair were hidden by a shawl that must once have been red, but now was dulled by the perpetually blowing dust.

His eyes dropped. She wore heel-fringed moccasins, a prerogative of warriors, permitted to squaws only as a high honor. But her feet were narrow and high-arched, unlike the short, splayed feet of Comanches. The ankles were tanned, and speckles of the everlasting dust clung to them, too, as if they were sprinkled with cinnamon; yet he could see the blue veins under the thin skin. She followed the warrior into the lodge with a step as light and tense as that of a stalking wolf. He realized with a sinking of the heart that the girl was afraid— not of the Flower, or his warriors, but of her own people.

Bluebonnet said in the Comanche tongue, "Come stand beside me."

The young woman obeyed. Beside Bluebonnet she turned reluctantly toward the council circle, still clutching the shawl that hid her face so that nothing was visible but the whitened knuckles of one hand. On one side of Mart, Amos sat, an immovable lump. On his other side, Rosas had thrown down his grass stem. His eyes were slitted, but his glance flickered back and forth between the girl and Amos' face, while he moved no other muscle. Over and over, white girls captured as children and raised by the Comanches have been ashamed to look white men in the face.

"Show them your head," Bluebonnet said in Comanche, Mart thought; though perhaps he had said "hair" instead of "head."

The white girl's head bowed lower, and she uncovered the top of it, to let them see the color of her hair. It was cropped short in the manner of the Comanches, among whom only the men wore long hair, but it was blonde. Not a bright blonde; a mousy shade. But blonde.

"Show your face," came Bluebonnet's Comanche words, and the girl let the shawl fall, though her face remained averted. The old chief spoke sharply at last. "Hold up your head! Obey!"

The girl's head raised. For a full minute the silence held while Mart stared, praying, trying to persuade himself of—what? The tanned but once white face was broad and flat, the forehead low, the nose shapeless, the mouth pinched yet loose. The eyes were green, all right, but small and set close together; they darted like an animal's, craving escape. Mart's mind moved again. Stare an hour, he told himself. Stare a year. You'll never get any different answer. Nor find room for any possible mistake.

This girl was not Debbie.

Mart got up, and blundered out into the reddening horizontal rays of the sunset. Behind him he heard Amos say harshly, "You speak English?" The girl did not answer. Mart never asked Amos what else was said. He walked away from the tepee of the Flower, out of the village, a long way out onto the thin-grassed flats. Finally he just stood, alone in the twilight.

28

Once more they went around the Staked Plains, passing to the south; but this time as they turned north they were headed home. They traveled by listless stages, feeling nothing much ahead to reach for now. Home, for them, was more of a direction than a place. It was like a surveyor's marker that is on the map but not on the ground: You're south of it, and you ride toward it, and after a while you're north of it, but you're never exactly there, because there isn't any such thing, except in the mind. They were nothing more than beaten men, straggling back down the long, long way they had traveled to their final defeat.

Fort Concho was deserted as they came to it, except for a token guard. But for once the emptiness had a difference. This was one garrison that had not been withdrawn by the fatheaded wishfulness that had disarmed more American troops than any other enemy. Three regiments under the colonel were on the march, riding northwest into the heart of the Comanche country. And these were part of a broad campaign, planned with thoroughness, and activated by a total resolution. For General Sheridan was in the saddle again, this time with a latitude of action that would let him put an end to rewarded murder once and for all.

North of Mackenzie's column, Colonel Buell was advancing; Colonel Nelson A. Miles was marching south from Fort Supply; Major William Price was coming into it from Fort Union beyond the Staked Plains. And at Fort Sill, Colonel Davidson, with perhaps the strongest force of all, to judge by the rumors they heard, hung poised until the other columns should be advantageously advanced. Under Sheridan there would be no more of the old chase, charge, scatter'em and go home. These troops would dog and follow, fighting if the Indians stood, but always coming on again. Once a column fastened upon a Comanche band, that band would be followed without turnoff, regardless of what more tempting quarry crossed between. And this would go on until no hostile could find a way to stay out and live.

When they had learned the scope of what was happening, Mart knew without need of words what Amos, with all his heart, would want to do now. It was the same thing he himself wanted, more than women, more than love, more than food or drink. They made a close study of their horses—a study about as needful as a close count of the fingers on their hands. Each horse had served as his rider's very muscles, day in and day out, for months. The two men were trying to persuade themselves that their horses were wiry, and wise in tricks for saving their strength, instead of just gaunted and low of head. But it couldn't be done, and not a horse was left at Fort Concho worth saddling.

411

Finally the two rode out and sat looking at the trail, stale and all but effaced, that the cavalry had made as it rode away. Up that trail hundreds of men were riding to what seemed a final kill—yet riding virtually blind for lack of just such scouts as Mart and Amos had become. But the column had so great a start it might as well have been on another world. Amos was first to shrug and turn away. Mart still sat a little while more, staring up that vacant trail; but at last drew a deep breath, let it all out again, and followed Amos.

They plodded north and east through a desolate land, for this year the country looked the worst they had ever seen it. The summer had been wickedly hot and totally dry; and on top of the drought great swarms of grasshoppers had come to chop what feed there was into blowing dust. The few bands of cattle they saw were all bones, and wild as deer. Only the aged cattle showed brands, for no one had worked the border ranges in a long time. Yet, if above all you wanted the cavalry to succeed, you had to look at the drought-ravaged range with a grim satisfaction. The cavalry carried horse corn, something no Indian would ever do, and the drought had given the grain-fed mounts an advantage that not even Comanche horsemanship could overcome this one year.

Toward noon of a colorless November day they raised the Edwards layout—"the old Edwards place," people called it now, if they knew what it was at all. And now came an experience worth forgetting altogether, except for the way it blew up on them later on. A thread of smoke rose straight up in the dead air from the central chimney of the house. They saw it from a great way off, and Mart looked at Amos, but they did not change the pace of their horses. Riding nearer, they saw a scratched-up half acre in front of the house, where Martha had meant to have a lawn and a garden someday. Here a bony rack of a mule was working on some runty corn stalks. It lifted its head and stood motionless, a rag of fodder hanging from its jaws, as it watched them steadily all the way in.

They saw other things to resent. Most of the corral poles were gone for firewood, along with a good many boards from the floors of the galleries. The whole homestead had the trashy look of a place where nothing is ever taken care of.

"Got a sodbuster in here," Amos said as they came up.

"Or a Mex," Mart suggested.

"Sodbuster," Amos repeated.

"I guess I'll ride on," Mart said. "I got no craving to see how the house looks now."

"If you hear shots," Amos said, "tell the Mathisons I ain't coming."

"Looking for trouble?"

"Fixing to make some."

That settled that. They tied their ponies to the gallery posts. The latch string whipped out of sight into its little hole in the door as Amos crossed the gallery. He kicked the door twice, once to test it, and once to drive it in. The bar brackets never had been repaired very well since the dreadful night when they were broken.

By the woodbox, as if he wanted to take cover behind the stove, a gaunt turkey-necked man was trying to load a shotgun with rattling hands. Automatically Mart and Amos moved apart, and their six-guns came out. "Put that thing down," Amos said.

"You got no right bustin' in on—"

Amos fired, and splinters jumped at the squatter's feet. The shotgun clattered on the floor, and they had time to take a look at what else was in the room. Five dirty children stood goggle-eyed as far back as they could get, and a malarial woman was frying jack rabbit; the strong grease smelled as if fur had got into it. A dress that had been Martha's dress hung loose on the woman's frame, and some of the children's clothes were Debbie's. He might have been sorry for all these saucer eyes except for that.

"You're in my house," Amos said.

"Wasn't nobody using it. We ain't hurting your—"

"Shut up!" Amos said. There was quiet, and Mart noticed the dirt, and some big holes in the chimney, the walls, the window reveals, where adobe bricks had been prized out.

"Been looking for something, I see," Amos said. "Let's see if you found it. Hold 'em steady, Mart." Amos picked up a mattock, and went into a bedroom, where he could be heard chunking a hole in the adobe with heavy strokes. He came back with an adobe-dusted tin box, and let them watch him pour gold pieces from it into a side pocket; Mart guessed there must be about four hundred dollars.

"I'll be back in a week," Amos said. "I want this place scrubbed out, and the walls patched and whitewashed. Fix them gallery floors out there, and start hauling poles for them corrals. Make all as it was, and might be I'll leave you stay till spring."

"I got no time for—"

"Then you better be long gone when I come!"

They walked out of there and rode on.

29

Nothing ever changed much at the Mathisons. The old, well-made things never wore out; if they broke they were mended stronger than they were before. Pump handles wore down to a high polish, door sills showed deeper hollows. But nothing was allowed to gather the slow grime of age. Only when you had been gone a couple of years could you see that the place was growing old. Then it looked smaller than you remembered it, and kind of rounded at the corners everywhere. Mart rode toward it this time with a feeling that the whole place belonged to the past that he was done with, like the long search that had seemed to have no end, but had finally run out anyway.

They didn't mean to be here long. Amos meant to ride on to Austin at once, to clear up the killings at Lost Mule Creek; and if he got held up, Mart meant to go there alone, and get it over. He didn't know what he was going to do after that, but it sure would be someplace else. He believed that he was approaching the Mathisons for the last time. Maybe when he looked over his shoulder at this place, knowing he would never see it again, then he would feel something about it, but he felt nothing now. None of it was a part of him any more.

The people had aged like the house, except a little faster and a little plainer to be seen. Mart saw at first glance that Aaron was almost totally blind. Tobe and Abner were grown men. And Mrs. Mathison was a little old lady, who came out of the kitchen into the cold to take him by both hands. "My, my, Martie! It's been so long! You've been gone five—no, it's more. Why, it's coming on six years! Did you know that?" No; he hadn't known that. Not to count it all up together that way. Seemingly she didn't remember they had been home twice in the meantime.

But the surprise was that Laurie was still here. He had assumed she would have gone off and married Charlie MacCorry long ago, and she had quit haunting him once he swallowed that. She didn't come out of the house as he unsaddled, but as he came into the kitchen she crossed to him, drying her hands. Why did she always have to be at either the stove or the sink? Well, because it was always coming time to eat again, actually. They were close onto suppertime right now.

She didn't kiss him, or take hold of him in any way. "Did you—have you ever—" Resignation showed in her eyes, but they were widened by an awareness of tragedy, as if she knew the answer before she spoke. And his face confirmed it for her. "Not anything? No least trace of her at all?"

He drew a deep breath, wondering what part of their long try needed to be told. "Nothing," he said, finally, and judged that covered it all.

"You've been out so long," she said slowly, marveling. "I suppose you talk Comanche like an Indian. Do they call you Indian names?"

"I sure wouldn't dast interpret the most of the names they call us," he answered automatically. But he added, "Amos is known to 'em as 'Bull Shoulders.'"

"And you?"

"Oh—I'm just the 'Other.'"

"I suppose you'll be going right out again, Other?"

"No. I think now she was dead from the first week we rode."

"I'm sorry, Martie," She turned away, and for a few minutes went through slow motions, changing the setting of the table, moving things that didn't need to be moved. Something besides what she was doing was going through her mind, so plainly you could almost hear it tick. Abruptly, she left her work and got her coat, spinning it over her shoulders like a cape.

Her mother said, "Supper's almost on. Won't be but a few minutes."

"All right, Ma." Laurie gave Mart one expressionless glance, and he followed her, putting his sheepskin on, as she went out the door to the dog-trot.

"Where's Charlie?" he asked, flat-footed, once they were outside.

"He's still in the Rangers. He's stationed over at Harper's, now; he's done well enough so he could politic that. But we don't see him too much. Seems like Rangers live on the hard run nowadays." She met his eyes directly, without shyness, but without lighting up much, either.

A small wind was stirring now, shifting the high overcast. At the horizon a line of blood-bright sunset light broke through, turning the whole prairie red. They walked in silence, well apart, until they had crossed a rise and were out of sight of the house. Laurie said, "I suppose you'll be going on to Austin soon."

"We've got to. Amos put up a thousand head—Of course, the Rangers can't collect until a judge or somebody declares Debbie dead. But they'll do that now. We got to go there, and straighten it out."

"Are you coming back, Martie?"

The direct question took him off guard. He had thought some of working his way up toward Montana, if the Rangers didn't lock him up, or anything. They were having big Indian trouble up there, and Mart believed himself well qualified to scout against the Sioux. But it didn't make much sense to head north into the teeth of winter, and spring was far away. So he said something he hadn't meant to say. "Do you want me to come back, Laurie?"

"I won't be here."

He thought he understood that. "I figured you'd be married long before now."

"It might have happened. Once. But Pa never could stand Charlie. Pa's had so much trouble come down on him—he always blamed himself for what happened to your folks. Did you know that? I didn't want to bring on one thing more, and break his heart. Not then. If I had it to do over—I don't know. But I don't want to stay here now. I know that. I'm going to get out of Texas, Mart."

He looked stupid, and said, "Oh?"

"This is a dreadful country. I've come to hate these prairies, every inch of 'em—and I bet they stretch a million miles. Nothing to look forward to—or back at, either—I want to go to Memphis. Or Vicksburg, or New Orleans."

"You got kinfolk back there?"

"No. I don't know anybody."

"Now, you know you can't do that! You never been in a settlement bigger'n Fort Worth in your life. Any gol dang awful thing is liable to happen to you in a place like them!"

"I'm twenty-four years old," she said bitterly. "Time something happened."

He searched for something to say, and came up with the most stilted remark he had ever heard. "I wouldn't want anything untoward to happen to you, Laurie," he said.

"Wouldn't you?"

"I've been long gone. But I was doing what I had to do, Laurie. You know that."

"For five long years," she reminded him.

He wanted to let her know it wasn't true that he hadn't cared what happened to her. But he couldn't explain the way hope had led him on, dancing down the prairie like a fox fire, always just ahead. It didn't seem real any more. So finally he just put an arm around her waist as they walked, pulling her closer to his side.

The result astonished him. Laurie stopped short, and for a moment stood rigid; then she turned toward him, and came into his arms. "Martie, Martie, Martie," she whispered, her mouth against his. She had on a lot of winter clothes, but the girl was there inside them, solider than Estrellita, but slim and warm. And now somebody began hammering on a triangle back at the house, calling them in.

"Oh, damn," he said, "damn, damn—"

She put her fingers on his lips to make him listen. "Start coughing soon's we go in the house. Make out you're coming down with a lung chill."

"Me? What for?"

"The boys put your stuff in the bunkhouse. But I'll work it out so you're moved to the grandmother room. Just you, by yourself. Late tonight, when they're all settled in, I'll come to you there."

Jingle-jangle-bang went the triangle again.

30

That night Lije Powers came back.

They were still at the supper table as they heard his horse; and the men glanced at each other, for the plodding hoofs seemed to wander instead of coming straight on up to the door. And next they heard his curiously weak hail. Abner and Tobe Mathison went out. Lije swayed in the saddle, then lost balance and buckled as he tried to dismount, so that Tobe had to catch him in his arms.

"Drunker than a spinner wolf," Tobe announced.

"Drunk, hell," Abner disagreed. "The man's got a bullet in him!"

"No, I ain't," Lije said, and went into a coughing fit that made a fool of Mart's effort to fake a bad chest. Tobe and Abner were both wrong; Lije was as ill a man as had ever got where he was going on a horse. At the door he tottered against the jamb, and clung to it feebly, preventing them from closing it against the rising wind, until the coughing fit passed off.

"I found her," Lije said, still blocking the door. "I found Deb'rie Edwards." He slid down the side of the door and collapsed.

They carried him into the grandmother room and put him to bed. "He's out of his head," Aaron Mathison said, pulling off Lije Powers' boots.

"I got a bad cold," Lije wheezed at them. He was glassy-eyed, and his skin burned their fingers. "But I'm no more out of my mind than you. I talked to her. She spoke her name. I seen her as close as from here to you. . . ."

"Where?" Amos demanded.

"She's with a chief named Yellow Buckle. Amos—you mind the Seven Fingers?"

Amos looked blank. The names meant nothing to him.

Aaron Mathison said, "Will you leave the man be? He's in delirium!"

"Be still!" Mart snapped at Aaron.

"I got a cold," Lije repeated, and his voice turned pleading. "Ain't anybody ever heard of the Seven Fingers?"

"Seems like there's a bunch of cricks," Mart said, groping for a memory, "west of the Wichita Mountains. . . . No, farther—beyond the Little Rainies. I think they run into the North Fork of the Red. Lije, ain't Seven Fingers the Kiowa name for them little rivers?"

"That's it! That's it!" Lije cried out eagerly. "Do this get me my rocking chai', Amos?"

"Sure, Lije. Now take it easy."

They piled blankets on him, and wrapped a hot stove lid to put at his feet, then spooned a little soup into him. It was what Mrs. Mathison called her "apron-string soup," because it had noodles in it. But Lije kept on talking, as if he feared he might lose hold and never be able to tell them once he let down.

"Yellow Buckle's squaws was feeding us. One comes behind me and she puts this calabash in my lap. Full of stewed gut tripe. . . . She bends down, and makes out like she picks a stick out of it with her fingers. And she whispers in my ear. 'I'm Deb'rie,' she says. 'I'm Deb'rie Edwards.' "

"Couldn't you get a look at her?"

"I snuck a quick look over my shoulder. Her head was covered. But I seen these here green eyes. Greener'n a wild grape peeled out . . ."

"Was that all?" Amos asked as the old man trailed off.

"I didn't see her no more. And I didn't dast say nothing, or ask."

"Who's Yellow Buckle with?" The answer was so long in coming that Mart started to repeat, but the sick man had heard him.

"I seen . . . Fox Moon . . . and Bull Eagle . . . Singin' Dog . . . Hunts-His-Horse—I think it was him. Some more'll come back to me. Do it get me my chai' by the stove?"

"You're never going to want for anything," Amos said.

Lije Powers rolled to the edge of the bunk in a spasm of coughing, and the blood he brought up dribbled on the floor.

"Lije," Mart raised his voice, "do you know if—"

"Leave be now," Aaron Mathison commanded them. "Get out of this room, and leave be! Or I put you out!"

"Just one more thing," Mart persisted. "Is Yellow Buckle ever called any other name?"

Aaron took a step toward him, but the thin voice spoke once more. "I think—" Lije said, "I think—some call him Cut-face."

"Get out!" Aaron roared, and moved upon them. This time they obeyed.

Mrs. Mathison stayed with the very ill old man, while Laurie fetched and carried for her.

"It upsets a man," Aaron said, all quietness again, when the door had closed upon the grandmother room. "But I find no word in it to believe."

Mart spoke up sharply. "I think he's telling the truth!"

"There's a whole lot wrong with it, Mart," Amos said. "Like: 'I'm Deb'rie,' she says. Nobody in our family ever called her 'Deb'rie' in her life. She never heard the word."

"Lije says 'Debrie' for the same reason he says 'prairuh,'" Mart disputed him. "He'd talk the same if he was telling what you said, or me."

"And them Indians. Fox Moon is a Kotsetaka, and so is Singing Dog. But Bull Eagle is a Quohada, and never run with no Kotsetakas. I question if he ever seen one!"

"Can't a sick old man get one name wrong without you knock apart everything he done?"

"We was all through them Kotsetakas—"

"And maybe passed her within twenty feet!"

"All right. But how come we never heard of any Yellow Buckle?"

"We sure as hell heard of Scar!"

"Sure," Amos said wearily. "Lije was the same places we been, Martie. And heard the same things. That's all."

"But he saw her," Mart insisted, circling back to where they had begun.

"Old Lije has been a liar all his life," Amos said with finality. "You know that well as me."

Mart fell silent.

"You see, Martin," Aaron Mathison said gently, "yon lies a foolish old man. When you've said that, you've said all; and there's the end on it."

"Except for one thing," Amos said, and his low voice sounded very tired. They looked at him, and waited, while for several moments he seemed lost in thought. "We've made some far casts, looking for a chief called Scar. We never found him. And Aaron, I believe like you: We never will. But suppose there's just one chance in a million that Lije is right, and I am wrong? That one slim shadow of a doubt would give me no rest forever; not even in my grave." He turned his head, and rested heavy eyes on Mart. "Better go make up the packs. Then catch the horses up. We got a long way more to go."

Mart ran for the bunkhouse.

31

In the bunkhouse Mart lighted a lamp. They had cracked their bedrolls open to get out clean shirts, and some of their stuff had got spread around. He started throwing their things together. Then he heard a scamper of light boots, and a whisk of wind made the lamp flutter as the door was thrown open. Laurie appeared against the dark, and she showed a tension that promised trouble.

"Shut the door," he told her.

She pressed it shut and stood against it. "I want the truth," she said. "If you start off again, after all this time—Oh, Mart, what's it supposed to mean?"

"It means, I see a chance she's there."

"Well, you're not going!"

"Who isn't?"

"I've dallied around this god-forsaken wind-scour for nearly six long years— waiting for you to see fit to come back! You're not going gallivanting off again now!"

It was the wrong tone to take with him. He no more than glanced at her. "I sure don't know who can stop me."

"You're a wanted man," she reminded him. "And Charlie MacCorry is less than half an hour away. If it takes all the Rangers in Texas to put handcuffs on you—they'll come when he hollers!"

He had no time to fool with this kind of an ambuscade, but he took time. He was clawing for a way to make her see what he was up against, why he had no choice. Uncertainly he dug out the doeskin packet in which he carried Debbie's miniature. The once-white leather was stained to the color of burlap, and its stiffened folds cracked as he unwrapped it; he had not dug it out for a long time. Laurie came to look as he opened the little plush case and held it to the light. Debbie's portrait was very dim. The dust had worked into it finally, and the colors had faded to shades of brown stain. No effect of life, or pertness, looked out from it any more. The little kitty-cat face had receded from him, losing itself behind the years.

Laurie hardened. "That's no picture of her," she said.

He looked up, appalled by the bitterness of her tone.

"It might have been once," she conceded. "But now it's nothing but a chromo of a small child. Can't you count up time at all?"

"She was coming ten," Mart said. "This was made before."

"She was eleven," Laurie said with certainty. "We've got the Edwards' family Bible, and I looked it up. Eleven—and it's been more than five years! She's sixteen and coming seventeen right now."

He had known that Debbie was growing up during all the long time they had hunted for her; but he had never been able to realize it, or picture it. No matter what counting on his fingers told him, he had always been hunting for a little child. But he had no reason to doubt Laurie. He could easily have lost a year in the reckoning some way, so that she had been a year older than he had supposed all the time.

"Deborah Edwards is a woman grown," Laurie said. "If she's alive at all."

He said, "If she's alive, I've got to fetch her home."

"Fetch what home? She won't come with you if you find her. They never do."

Her face was dead white; he stared at it with disbelief. He still thought it to be a good face, finely made, with beautiful eyes. But now the face was hard as quartz, and the eyes were lighted with the same fires of war he had seen in Amos' eyes the times he had stomped Comanche scalps into the dirt.

"She's had time to be with half the Comanche bucks in creation by now." Laurie's voice was cold, but not so brutal as her words. "Sold time and again to the highest bidder—and you know it! She's got savage brats of her own, most like. What are you going to do with them—fetch them home, too? Well, you won't. Because she won't let you. She'll kill herself before she'll even look you in the face. If you knew anything at all about a woman, you'd know that much!"

"Why, Laurie—" he faltered. "Why, Laurie—"

"You're not bringing anything back," she said, and her contempt whipped him across the face. "It's too late by many years. If they've got anything left to sell you, it's nothing but a—a rag of a female—the leavings of Comanche bucks—"

He turned on her with such a blaze in his eyes that she moved back half a step. But she stood her ground then, and faced up to him; and after a while he looked away. He had hold of himself before he answered her. "I'll have to see what Amos wants to do."

"You know what he wants to do. He wants to lead the yellowlegs down on 'em, and punish 'em off the face of creation. He's never wanted anything else, no matter how he's held back or pretended. Amos has leaned way backwards for love of his brother's dead wife—and not from regard for anything else on this earth or beyond it!"

He knew that was true. "That's why I've stayed with him. I told you that a long time ago."

"Amos has had enough of all this. I knew it the minute he stepped in the house. He's very patiently gone through all the motions Martha could have asked of him—and way over and beyond. But he's done."

"I know that, too," he said.

She heard the fight go out of his voice, and she changed, softening, but without taking hope. "I wanted you, Mart. I tried to give you everything I've got to give. It's not my fault it wasn't any good."

She had shaken him up, so that he felt sick. He couldn't lay hands on the purposes by which he had lived for so long, or any purpose instead. His eyes ran along the walls, looking for escape from the blind end that had trapped him.

A calendar was there on the wall. It had a strange look, because it picked up

beyond the lost years his life had skipped. But as he looked at it he remembered another calendar that hadn't looked just right. It was a calendar a little child had made for him with a mistake in it, so that her work was wasted; only he hadn't noticed that then. And he heard the little girl's voice, saying again the words that he had never really heard her say, but only had been told, and imagined: "He didn't care. . . . He didn't care at all. . . ."

"Do you know," Laurie said, "what Amos will do if he finds Deborah Edwards? It will be a right thing, a good thing—and I tell you Martha would want it now. He'll put a bullet in her brain."

He said, "Only if I'm dead."

"You think you can outride the yellowlegs—and Amos, too," she read his mind again. "I suppose you can. And get to Yellow Buckle with a warning. But you can't outride the Rangers! You've been on their list anyway for a long time! Charlie MacCorry is only seven miles away. And I'm going to fetch him—now!"

"You so much as reach down a saddle," he told her, "and I'll be on my way in the same half minute. You think there's a man alive can give me a fourteen-mile start? Get back in that house!"

She stared at him a moment more, then slammed her way out. When she was gone Mart put Debbie's miniature in his pocket, then retied his packs to be ready for a fast departure in case Laurie carried out her threat; and he left the lamp burning in the bunkhouse as he went back to the kitchen.

Laurie did not ride for Charlie MacCorry. As it turned out, she didn't need to. MacCorry arrived at the Mathisons in the next fifteen minutes, stirred up by the squatter to whom Amos had laid down the law in the Edwards house.

32

If you'd come in and faced it out, like you said," Charlie MacCorry told them, "I don't believe there'd ever been any case against you at all."

Four years in the Rangers had done Charlie good. He seemed to know his limitations better now, and accepted them, instead of noisily spreading himself over all creation. Within those limits, which he no longer tried to overreach, he was very sure of himself, and quietly so, which was a new thing for Charlie.

"I said I'd come in when I could. I was on my way to Austin now. Until I run into Lije as I stopped over."

"He spoke of that," Aaron Mathison confirmed.

Resentment kept thickening Amos' neck. He shouldn't have been asked to put up with this in front of the whole Mathison family. Mrs. Mathison came and went, staying with Lije Powers mostly. But there had been no way to get rid of

Tobe and Abner, who kept their mouths shut in the background, but were there, as was Laurie, making herself as inconspicuous as she could.

"And you had my bond of a thousand head of cattle, in token I'd come back," Amos said. "Or did you pick them up?"

"We couldn't, very well, because you didn't own them. Not until the courts declared Deborah Edwards dead, which hasn't been done. I don't think Captain Clinton ever meant to pick them up. He was satisfied with your word. Then."

"Captain, huh?" Amos took note of the promotion. "What are you—a colonel?"

"Sergeant," MacCorry said without annoyance. "You've been close to three years. Had to come and find you on a tip. Your reputation hasn't improved any in that time, Mr. Edwards."

"What's the matter with my reputation?" Amos was angering again.

"I'll answer that if you want. So you can see what us fellers is up against. Mark you, I don't say it's true." No rancor could be heard in MacCorry's tone. He sat relaxed, elbows on the table, and looked Amos in the eye. "They say it's funny you leave a good ranch, well stocked, to be worked by other men, while you sky-hoot the country from the Nations to Mexico on no reasonable business so far as known. They say you're almighty free with the scalping knife, and that's a thing brings costly trouble on Texas. They say you're a squaw man, who'd sooner booger around with the Wild Tribes than work your own stock; and an owlhoot that will murder to rob."

"You dare set there and say—"

"I do not. I tell you what's said. But all that builds up pressure on us. Half the Indian trouble we get nowadays is stirred up by quick-trigger thieves and squaw men poking around where they don't belong. And your name—names— are a couple that come up when the citizens holler to know why we don't do nothing. I tell you all this in hopes you'll see why I got to do my job. After all, this is a murder case."

"There ain't any such murder case," Amos said flatly.

"I hope you're right. But that's not my business. All I know, you stand charged with the robbery and murder of Walker Finch, alias Jerem Futterman. And two other deceased—"

"What's supposed to become of Yellow Buckle, while—"

"That's up to Captain Clinton. Maybe he wants to throw the Rangers at Yellow Buckle, with you for guide. You'll have to talk to him."

Watching Amos, Mart saw his mind lock, slowly turning him into the inert lump Mart remembered from long ago. He couldn't believe it at first, it was so long since he had seen Amos look like that.

"I'll ride there with you, Amos," Aaron Mathison said. "Sol Clinton will listen to me. We'll clear this thing once and for all."

Amos' eyes were on his empty hands, and he seemed incapable of speech.

"I'm not going in," Mart said to Charlie MacCorry.

"What?" The young Ranger looked startled.

"I don't know what Amos is of a mind to do," Mart said. "I'm going to Yellow Buckle."

"That there's maybe the worst thing I could hear you say!"

"All I want to do is get her out of there," Mart said, "before you hit him, or the cavalry hits. Once you jump him, it'll be too late."

"Allowing she's alive," Charlie MacCorry said, "which I don't—you haven't got a chance in a million to buy her, or steal her, either!"

"I've seen a white girl I could buy from an Indian."

"This one can talk. Letting her go would be like suicide for half a tribe!"

"I got to try, Charlie. You see that."

"I see no such thing. Damn it, Mart, will you get it through your head— you're under arrest!"

"What if I walk out that door?"

Charlie glanced past Aaron at Laurie Mathison before he answered. "Now, you ought to know the answer to that."

Laurie said distinctly, "He means he'll put a bullet in your back."

Charlie MacCorry thought about that a moment. "If he's particular about getting his bullets in front," he said to her, "he can walk out backwards, can't he?"

A heavy silence held for some moments before Amos spoke, "It's up to Sol Clinton, Mart."

"That's what I told you," Charlie said.

Amos asked, "You want to get started?"

"We'll wait for daylight. Seeing there's two of you. And allowing for the attitude you take." He spoke to Aaron. "I'll take 'em out to the bunkhouse; they can get some sleep if they want. I'll set up with 'em. And don't get a gleam in your eye," he finished to Mart. "I was in the bunkhouse before I come in here —and I put your guns where they won't be fell over. Now stand up, and walk ahead of me slow."

The lamp was still burning in the bunkhouse, but the fire in the stove was cold. Charlie watched them, quietly wary but without tension, while he lighted a lantern for a second light, and set it on the floor well out of the way. He wasn't going to be left in the dark with a fight on his hands by one of them throwing his hat at the lamp. Amos sat heavily on his bunk; he looked tired and old.

"Pull your boots if you want," Charlie MacCorry said. "I ain't going to stamp on your feet, or nothing. I only come for you by myself because we been neighbors from a long way back. I want this as friendly as you'll let it be." He found a chair with the back broken off, moved it nearer the stove with his foot, and sat down facing the bunks.

"Mind if I build the fire up?" Mart asked.

"Good idea."

Mart pawed in the woodbox, stirring the split wood so that a piece he could get a grip on came to the top.

Charlie spoke sharply to Amos. "What you doing with that stick?"

From the corner of his eye, Mart saw that Amos was working an arm under the mattress on his bunk. "Thought I heard a mouse," Amos said.

Charlie stood up suddenly, so that the broken chair overturned. His gun came out, but it was not cocked or pointed. "Move slow," he said to Amos, "and

bring that hand out empty." For that one moment, while Amos drew his hand slowly from under the tick, Charlie MacCorry was turned three-quarters away from Mart, his attention undivided upon Amos.

Mart's piece of cordwood swung, and caught MacCorry hard behind the ear. He rattled to the floor bonily, and lay limp. Amos was kneeling beside him instantly, empty-handed; he hadn't had anything under the mattress. He rolled Charlie over, got his gun from under him, and had a look at his eyes.

"You like to tore his noggin' off," he said. "Lucky he ain't dead."

"Guess I got excited."

"Fetch something to make a gag. And my light *reata*."

 33

They didn't know where the Seven Fingers were as well as they thought they did. West of the Rainy Mountains lay any number of watersheds, according to how far west you went. No creek had exactly seven tributaries. Mart had hoped to get hold of an Indian or two as they drew near. With luck they would have found a guide to take them within sight of Yellow Buckle's Camp. But Sheridan's long-awaited campaign had cleared the prairies; the country beyond the North Fork of the Red was deserted. They judged, though, that the Seven Fingers had to be one of two systems of creeks.

Leaving the North Fork they tried the Little Horsethief first. It had nine tributaries, but who could tell how many a Kiowa medicine man would count? This whole thing drained only seventy or eighty square miles; a few long swings, cutting for sign, disposed of it in two days.

They crossed the Walking Wolf Ridge to the Elkhorn. This was their other bet—a system of creeks draining an area perhaps thirty miles square. On the maps it looks like a tree. You could say it has thirty or forty run-ins if you followed all the branches out to their ends; or you could say it has eight, or four, or two. You could say it has seven.

The country had the right feel as they came into it; they believed this to be the place Lije had meant. But now both time and country were running out, and very fast. The murder charge against them might be a silly one, and liable to be laughed out of court. But they had resisted arrest by violence, in the course of which Mart had assaulted an officer with a deadly weapon, intending great bodily harm. Actually all he had done was to swing on that damn fool Charlie MacCorry, but such things take time to cool off, and they didn't have it. No question now whether they wanted to quit this long search; the search was quitting them. One way or the other, it would end here, and this time forever.

Sometimes they had sighted a distant dust far back on their trail, losing them when they changed direction, picking them up again when they straightened out. They hadn't seen it now for four days, but they didn't fool themselves. Their destination was known, within limits, and they would be come for. Not that they had any thought of escape; they would turn on their accusers when their work was done—if they got it done. But they must work fast now with what horseflesh they had left.

The Elkhorn Country is a land of low ridges between its many dust-and-flood-water streams. You can't see far, and what is worse, it is known as a medicine country full of dust drifts and sudden hazes. You can ride toward what looks like the smoke of many fires, and follow it as it recedes across the ridges, and finally lose it without finding any fire at all. Under war conditions this was a very slow-going job of riding indeed. Each swale had to be scouted from its high borders before you dared cut for sign; while you yourself could be scouted very easily, at any time or all the time, if the Indians you sought were at all wary of your approach.

Yet this whole complex was within three days military march from Fort Sill itself, at the pace the yellowlegs would ride now. No commander alive was likely to search his own doorstep with painful care, endlessly cordoning close to home, while the other columns were striking hundreds of miles into the fastnesses of the Staked Plains. Yellow Buckle had shown an unexampled craftiness in picking this hole-up in which to lie low, while the military storm blew over. Here he was almost certain to be by-passed in the first hours of the campaign, and thereafter could sit out the war unmolested, until the exhaustion of both sides brought peace. When the yellowlegs eventually went home, as they always did, his warriors and his ponies would be fresh and strong, ready for such a year of raids and victories as would make him legendary. By shrewdly setting aside the Comanche reliance upon speed and space, he had opened himself a way to become the all-time greatest war chief of the Comanches.

Would it have worked, except for a wobbly old man, whose dimming eyes saw no more glorious vision than that of a chair by a hot stove?

"We need a week there," Mart said.

"We're lucky if we've got two days."

They didn't like it. Like most prairie men, they had great belief in their abilities, but a total faith in their bad luck.

Then one day at daylight they got their break. It came as the result of a mistake, though of a kind no plainsman would own to; it could happen to anybody, and most it had happened to were dead. They had camped after dark, a long way past the place where they had built their cooking fire. Before that, though, they had studied the little valley very carefully in the last light, making sure they would bed down in the security of emptiness and space. They slept only after all reasonable precautions had been taken, with the skill of long-practiced men.

But as they broke out in the darkness before dawn, they rode at once upon the warm ashes of a fire where a single Indian had camped. They had been within less than a furlong of him all night.

He must have been a very tired Indian. Though they caught no glimpse of him, they knew they almost stepped on him, for they accidentally cut him off from his hobbled horse. They chased and roped the Indian pony, catching him very easily in so short a distance that Mart's back was full of prickles in expectation of an arrow in it. None came, however. They retired to a bald swell commanding the situation, and lay flat to wait for better light.

Slowly the sun came up, cleared the horizon haze, and leveled clean sunlight across the uneven land.

"You think he's took out on us?"

"I hope not," Amos answered. "We need the bugger. We need him bad."

An hour passed. "I figured he'd stalk us," Mart said. "He must be stalking us. Some long way round. I can't see him leaving without any try for the horses."

"We got to wait him out."

"Might be he figures to foller and try us tonight."

"We got to wait him out anyway," Amos said.

Still another hour, and the sun was high.

"I think it's the odds," Mart believed now. "We're two to one. Till he gets one clean shot. Then it's even."

Amos said with sarcasm, "One of us can go away."

"Yes," Mart said. He got his boots from the aparejos, and changed them for the worn moccasins in which he had been scouting for many days.

"What's that for?" Amos demanded.

"So's he'll hear me."

"Hear you doing what? Kicking yourself in the head?"

"Look where I say." Mart flattened to the ground beside Amos again. "Straight ahead, down by the crick, you see a little willer."

"He ain't under that. Boughs don't touch down."

"No, and he ain't up it neither—I can see through the leaves. Left of the willer, you see a hundred-foot strip of saw grass about knee high. Left of that, a great long slew of buckbrush against the water. About belt deep. No way out of there without yielding a shot. I figure we got him pinned in there."

"No way to comb him out if that's where he is," Amos said; but he studied the buckbrush a long time.

Mart got up, and took the canteens from the saddles.

"He'll put an arrow through you so fast it'll fall free on the far side, you go down to that crick!"

"Not without raising up, he won't."

"That's a seventy-five yard shot from here—maybe more. I ain't using you for bait on no such—"

"You never drew back from it before!" Mart went jauntily down the slope to the creek, swinging the canteens. Behind him he could hear Amos rumbling curses to himself for a while; then the morning was quiet except for the sound of his own boots.

He walked directly, unhurrying, to the point where the firm ground under the buckbrush mushed off into the shallow water at the saw-grass roots. He sloshed through ten yards of this muck, skirting the brush; and now his hackles crawled at the back of his neck, for he smelled Indian—a faint sunburnt smell of woodfires, of sage smoke, of long-used buffalo robes.

He came to the water, and stopped. Still standing straight up he floated the two canteens, letting them fill themselves at the end of their long slings. This was the time, as he stood motionless here, pretending to look at the water. He dared not look at the buckbrush, lest his own purpose be spoiled. But he let his head turn a little bit downstream, so that he could hold the buckbrush in the corner of his eye. He was certain nothing moved.

Amos' bullet yowled so close to him it seemed Amos must have fired at his back, and a spout of water jumped in the river straight beyond. Mart threw himself backward, turning as he fell, so that he came down on his belly in the muck. He didn't know how his six-gun came cocked into his hand, but it was there.

"Stay down!" Amos bellowed. "Hold still, damn it! I don't think I got him!" Mart could hear him running down the slope, chambering a fresh cartridge with a metallic clank. He flattened, trying to suck himself into the mud, and for a few moments lay quiet, all things out of his hands.

Amos came splashing into the saw grass so close by that Mart thought he was coming directly to where Mart lay.

"Yes, I did," Amos said. "Come looky this here!"

"Watch out for him!" Mart yelled. "Your bullet went in the crick!"

"I creased him across the back. Prettiest shot you ever see in your life!"

Mart got up then. Amos was standing less than six yards away, looking down into the grass. Two steps toward him and Mart could see part of the dark, naked body, prone in the saw grass. He stopped, and moved backward a little; he had no desire to see anything more. Amos reached for the Indian's knife, and spun it into the creek.

"Get his bow," Mart said.

"Bow, hell! This here's a Spencer he's got here." Amos picked it up. "He threw down on you from fifteen feet!"

"I never even heard the safety click—"

"That's what saved you. It's still on."

Amos threw the rifle after the knife, far out into the water.

"Is he in shape to talk?"

"He'll talk, all right. Now get your horse, quick!"

"What?"

"There's two Rangers coming up the crick. I got one quick sight of 'em at a mile—down by the far bend. Get on down there, and hold 'em off!"

"You mean fight?"

"No-no-no! Talk to 'em—say anything that comes in your head—"

"What if they try to arrest me?"

"Let' em! Only keep 'em off me while I question this Comanch'!"

Mart ran for his horse.

34

No Rangers were in sight a mile down the creek when Mart got there. None at two miles, either. By this time he knew what had happened. He had been sent on a fool's errand because Amos wanted to work on the Indian alone. He turned back, letting his horse loiter; and Amos met him at the half mile, coming downstream at a brisk trot. He looked grim, and very ugly, but satisfied with his results.

"He talked," Mart assumed.

"Yeah. We know how to get to Yellow Buckle now. He's got the girl Lije Powers saw, all right."

"Far?"

"We'll be there against night. And it's a good thing. There's a party of more than forty Rangers, with sixty-seventy Tonkawas along with 'em, on 'the hill by the Beaver'—that'll be old Camp Radziminski—and two companies of yellow-legs, by God, more'n a hundred of 'em, camped right alongside!"

"That's no way possible! Your Indian lied."

"He didn't lie." Amos seemed entirely certain. Mart saw now that a drop of fresh blood had trickled down the outside of Amos' scalping-knife sheath.

"Where is he now?"

"In the crick. I weighted him down good with rocks."

"I don't understand this," Mart said. He had learned to guess the general nature of the truth behind some kinds of Indian lies, but he couldn't see through this story. "I never heard of Rangers and cavalry working together before. Not in Indian territory, anyway. My guess is Sill sent out a patrol to chase the Rangers back."

Amos shrugged. "Maybe so. But the Rangers will make a deal now—they'll have to. Give the soldiers Yellow Buckle on a plate in return for not getting run back to Texas."

"Bound to," Mart said glumly, "I suppose."

"Them yellowlegs come within an ace of leaving a big fat pocket of Comanch' in their rear. Why, Yellow Buckle could have moved right into Fort Sill soon as Davidson marches! They'll blow sky high once they see what they nearly done. They can hit that village in two days—tomorrow, if the Rangers set the pace. And no more Yellow Buckle! We got to get over there."

They reset their saddles, and pressed on at a good long trot, loping one mile in three.

"There's something I got to say," Mart told Amos as they rode. "I want to ask one thing. If we find the village—"

"We'll find it. And it'll still be there. That one Comanche was the only scout they had out between them and Fort Sill."

"I want to ask one thing—"

"Finding Yellow Buckle isn't the hard part. Not now." Amos seemed to sense a reason for putting Mart off from what he wanted to say. "Digging the girl out of that village is going to be the hard thing in what little time we got."

"I know. Amos, will you do me one favor? When we find the village—Now, don't go off half cocked. I want to walk in there alone."

"You want—what?"

"I want to go in and talk to Yellow Buckle by myself."

Amos did not speak for so long that Mart thought he was not going to answer him at all. "I had it in mind," he said at last, "the other way round. Leave you stay back, so set you can get clear, if worst goes wrong. Whilst I walk in and test what their temper be."

Mart shook his head. "I'm asking you. This one time—will you do it my way?"

Another silence before Amos asked, "Why?"

Mart had foreseen this moment, and worked it over in his mind a hundred times without thinking of any story that had a chance to work. "I got to tell you the truth. I see no other way."

"You mean," Amos said sardonically, "you'd come up with a lie now if you had one to suit."

"That's right. But I got no lie for this. It's because I'm scared of something. Suppose this. Suppose some one Comanche stood in front of you. And you knew for certain in your own mind—he was the one killed Martha?"

Mart watched Amos' face gray, then darken. "Well?" Amos said.

"You'd kill him. And right there'd be the end of Debbie, and all hunting for Debbie. I know that as well as you."

Amos said thickly, "Forget all this. And you best lay clear like I tell you, too —if you don't want Yellow Buckle to get away clean! Because I'm going in."

"I got to be with you, then. In hopes I can stop you when that minute comes."

"You know what that would take?"

"Yes; I do know. I've known for a long time."

Amos turned in the saddle to look at him. "I believe you'd do it," he decided. "I believe you'd kill me in the bat of an eye if it come to that."

Mart said nothing. They rode in silence for a furlong more.

"Oh, by the way," Amos said. "I got something for you here. I believe you better have it now. If so happens you feel I got to be gunned down, you might's well have some practical reason. One everybody's liable to understand."

He rummaged in various pockets, and finally found a bit of paper, grease-marked and worn at the folds. He opened it to see if it was the right one; and the wind whipped at it as he handed it to Mart. The writing upon it was in ink.

Now know all men: I, Amos Edwards, being of sound mind, and without any known blood kin, do will that upon my death my just debts do first be paid. Whereafter, all else I own, be it in property, money, livestock, or rights to range, shall go to my foster nephew Martin Pauley, in rightful token of the help he has been to me, in these the last days of my life.

AMOS EDWARDS

Beside the signature was a squiggle representing a seal, and the signatures of the witnesses, Aaron Mathison and Laura E. Mathison. He didn't know what the "E" stood for; he had never even known Laurie had a middle name. But he knew Amos had fixed him. This act of kindness, with living witnesses to it, could be Mart's damnation if he had to turn on Amos. He held out the paper to Amos for him to take back.

"Keep hold of it," Amos said. "Come in handy if the Comanches go through my pockets before you."

"It don't change anything," Mart said bleakly. "I'll do what I have to do."

"I know."

They rode four hours more. At mid-afternoon Amos held up his hand, and they stopped. The rolling ground hid whatever was ahead but now they heard the far-off barking of dogs.

35

Yellow Buckle's village was strung out for a considerable distance along a shallow river as yet unnamed by white men, but called by Indians the Wild Dog. The village was a lot bigger than the Texans had expected. Counting at a glance, as cattle are counted, Mart believed he saw sixty-two lodges. Probably it would be able to turn out somewhere between a hundred fifty and two hundred warriors, counting old men and youths.

They were seen at a great distance, and the usual scurrying about resulted all down the length of the village. Soon a party of warriors began to build up just outside. They rode bareback, with single-rope war bridles on the jaws of their ponies, and their weapons were in their hands. A few headdresses and medicine shields showed among them, but none had tied up the tails of their ponies, as they did when a fight was expected. This group milled about, but not excitedly, until twenty or so had assembled, then flowed into a fairly well-dressed line, and advanced at a walk to meet the white men. Meanwhile three or four scouts on fast ponies swung wide, and streaked in the direction from which Mart and Amos had come to make sure that the two riders were alone.

"Seem kind of easy spooked," Mart said, "don't they?"

"I wouldn't say so. Times have changed. They're getting fought back at now. Seems to me they act right cocky, and sure."

The mounted line halted fifty yards in front of them. A warrior in a buffalo-horn headdress drew out two lengths, and questioned them in sign language: "Where have you come from? What do you want? What do you bring?" The conventional things.

And Amos gave conventional answers. "I come very far, from beyond the Staked Plains. I want to make talk. I have a message for Yellow Buckle. I have gifts."

A Comanche raced his pony back into the village, and the spokesman faked other questions, meaninglessly, while he waited for instructions. By the time his runner was back from the village, the scouts had signaled from far out that the strangers appeared to be alone, and all was well up to here. The two riders were escorted into the village through a clamoring horde of cur dogs, all with small heads and the souls of gadflies; and halted before a tepee with the black smoke flaps of a chief's lodge.

Presently a stocky, middle-aged Comanche came out, wrapped himself in a blanket, and stood looking them over. He was weaponless, but had put on no headdress or decoration of any kind. This was a bad sign, and the slouchy way he stood was another. Amos' gestures were brusque as he asked if this man called himself Yellow Buckle and the chief gave the least possible acknowledgment.

Visitors were supposed to stay in the saddle until invited to dismount, but Yellow Buckle did not give the sign. He's making this too plain, Mart thought. He wants us out of here, and in a hurry, but he ought to cover up better than this. Mart felt Amos anger. The tension increased until it seemed to ring as Amos dismounted without invitation, walked within two paces of the chief, and looked him up and down.

Yellow Buckle looked undersized with Amos looming over him. He had the short bandy legs that made most Comanches unimpressive on the ground, however effective they might be when once they put hands to their horses. He remained expressionless, and met Amos' eyes steadily. Mart stepped down and stood a little in back of Amos, and to the side. Getting a closer look at this chief, Mart felt his scalp stir. A thin line, like a crease, ran from the corner of the Comanche's left eye to the line of the jaw, where no natural wrinkle would be. They were standing before the mythical, the long-hunted, the forever elusive Chief Scar!

The Indian freed one arm, and made an abrupt sign that asked what they wanted. Amos' short answer was all but contemptuous. "I do not stand talking in the wind," his hands said.

For a moment more the Comanche chief stood like a post. Amos had taken a serious gamble in that he had left himself no alternatives. If Yellow Buckle—Scar—told him to get out, Amos would have no way to stay, and no excuse for coming back. After that he could only ride to meet the Rangers, and guide them to the battle that would destroy Scar and most of the people with him. It's what he wants, Mart thought. I have to stay if Amos rides out of here. I have to make what try I can, never mind what Amos does.

But now Scar smiled faintly, with a gleam in his eye that Mart neither understood nor liked, but which might have contained derision. He motioned Amos to follow him, and went into the tepee.

"See they keep their hands off the mule packs," Amos said, tossing Mart his reins.

Mart let the split reins fall. "Guard these," he said in Comanche to the warrior who had been spokesman. The Comanche looked blank but Mart turned his back on him, and followed Amos. The door flap dropped in his face; he struck it aside with annoyance, and went inside.

A flicker of fire in the middle of the lodge, plus a seepage of daylight from the smoke flap at the peak, left the lodge shadowy. The close air carried a sting of wood smoke, scented with wild-game stew, buffalo hides, and the faintly musky robe smell of Indians. Two chunky squaws and three younger females had been stirred into a flurry by Amos' entrance, but they were settling down as Mart came in. Mart gave the smallest of these, a half-grown girl, a brief flick of attention, without looking directly at her but even out of the corner of his eye he could see that her shingled thatch was black, and as coarse as a pony's tail.

Women were supposed to keep out of the councils of warriors, unless called to wait on the men. But the two squaws now squatted on their piled robes on the honor side of the lodge, where Scar's grown sons should have been, and the three younger ones huddled deep in the shadows opposite. Mart realized that they must have jumped up to get out of there, and that Scar had told them to stay. This was pretty close to insult, the more so since Scar did not invite the white men to sit down.

Scar himself stood opposite the door beyond the fire. He shifted his blanket, wrapping it skirtlike around his waist; and his open buckskin shirt exposed a gold brooch in the form of a bow of ribbon, hung around his neck on a chain. In all likelihood his present name, assumed midway of his career, commemorated some exploit with which this brooch was associated.

Amos waited stolidly, and finally Scar was forced to address them. He knew them now, he told them in smooth-running sign language. "You," he said, indicating Amos, "are called Bull Shoulders. And this boy," he dismissed Mart, "is The Other."

Amos' hands lied fluently in answer. He had heard of a white man called Bull Shoulders, but the Chickasaws said Bull Shoulders was dead. He himself was called Plenty Mules. His friends, the Quohadas, so named him. He was a subchief among the Comanchero traders beyond the Staked Plains. His boss was called the Rich One. Real name—"Jaime Rosas," Amos used his voice for the first time.

"You are Plenty Mules," Yellow Buckle's hands conceded, while his smile expressed a contrary opinion. "A Comanchero. This—" he indicated Mart—"is still The Other. His eyes are made of mussel shells, and he sees in the dark."

"This—" Amos contradicted him again—"is my son. His Indian name is No-Speak."

Mart supposed this last was meant to convey an order.

The Rich One, Amos went on in sign language, had many-heap rifles. (It was that sign itself, descriptive of piles and piles, that gave Indians the word "heap" for any big quantity, when they picked up white men's words.) He wanted horses, mules, horned stock, for his rifles. He had heard of Yellow Buckle. He had been told—here Amos descended to flattery—that Yellow Buckle was a great horse thief, a great cow thief—a fine sneak thief of every kind. Yellow Buckle's friend had said that.

"What friend?" Scar's hands demanded.

"The Flower," Amos signed.

"The Flower," Scar said, "has a white wife."

No change of pace or mood showed in the movement of Scar's hands, drawing classically accurate pictographs in the air, as he said that. But Mart's hair stirred and all but crackled; the smoky air in the lodge had suddenly become charged, like a thunderhead. Out of the corner of his eye Mart watched the squaws to see if Scar's remark meant anything to them in their own lives, here. But the eyes of the Comanche women were on the ground; he could not see their down-turned faces, and they had not seen the sign.

White wife. Amos made the throw-away sign. The Rich One did not trade for squaws. If the Yellow Buckle wanted rifles, he must bring horses. Many-heaps horses. No small deals. Or maybe—and this was sarcasm—Yellow Buckle did not need rifles. Plenty Mules could go find somebody else. . . . Amos was giving a very poor imitation of a man trying to make a trade with an Indian. But perhaps it was a good imitation of a man who had been sent with this offer, but who would prefer to make his deal elsewhere to his own purposes.

Scar seemed puzzled; he did not at once reply. Behind the Comanche, Mart could see the details of trophies and accoutrements, now that his eyes were accustomed to the gloom. Scar's medicine shield was there. Mart wondered if it bore, under its masking cover, a design he had seen at the Fight at the Cat-tails long ago. Above the shield hung Scar's short lance, slung horizontally from the lodgepoles. Almost a dozen scalps were displayed upon it, and less than half of them looked like the scalps of Indians. The third scalp from the tip of the lance had long wavy hair of a deep red-bronze. It was a white woman's scalp, and the woman it had belonged to must have been beautiful. The squaws had kept this scalp brushed and oiled, so that it caught red glints from the wavering fire. But Scar's lance bore none of the pale fine hair that had been Martha's, nor the bright gold that had been Lucy's hair.

Scar turned his back on them while he took two slow, thoughtful steps toward the back of the lodge and in that moment, while Scar was turned away from them, Mart felt eyes upon his face, as definitely as if a finger touched his cheek. His glance flicked to the younger squaws on the women's side of the lodge.

He saw her then. One of the young squaws wore a black head cloth, covering all of her hair and tied under her chin; it was a commonplace thing for a squaw to wear, but it had sufficed to make her look black-headed like the others in the uncertain light. Now this one had looked up, and her eyes were on his face in an unwavering stare, as a cat stares; and the eyes were green and slanted, lighter than the deeply tanned face. They were the most startling eyes he had ever seen in his life, strangely cold, impersonal yet inimical, and as hard as glass. But this girl was Debbie.

The green eyes dropped as Scar turned toward the strangers again and Mart's own eyes were straight ahead when the Comanche chief looked toward them.

Where were the rifles? Scar's question came at last.

Beyond the Staked Plains, Amos answered him. Trading must be there.

Another wait, while Mart listened to the ringing in his ears.

Too far, Scar said. Let the Rich One bring his rifles here.

Amos filled his lungs, stood tall, and laughed in Scar's face. Mart saw the Comanche's eyes narrow but after a moment he seated himself cross-legged on his buffalo robes under the dangling scalps and the shield. "Sit down," he said in Comanche, combining the words with the sign.

Amos ignored the invitation. "I speak no more now," he said, using his voice for the second time. His Comanche phrasings were slow and awkward but easily understood. "Below this village I saw a spring. I camp there, close by the Wild Dog River. Tomorrow, if you wish to talk, find me there. I sleep one night wait one day. Then I go."

"You spoke of gifts," Yellow Buckle reminded him.

"They will be there." He turned and, without concession to courtesy, he said in English, "Come on, No-Speak." And Mart followed him out.

36

Pringles ran up and down Mart's back as they rode out of that village with the cur dogs bawling and blaspheming again all around them, just beyond kick-range of their horses' feet. But until they were out of there they had to move unhurriedly, as if at peace and expecting peace. Even their eyes held straight ahead, lest so much as an exchange of glances be misread as a trigger for trouble.

Amos spoke first, well past the last of the lodges. "Did you see her? . . . Yeah," he answered himself. "I see you did." His reaction to the sudden climax of their search seemed to be the opposite of what Mart had expected. Amos seemed steadied, and turned cool.

"She's alive," Mart said. It seemed about the only thing his mind was able to think. "Can you realize it? Can you believe it? We found her, Amos!"

"Better start figuring how to stay alive yourself. Or finding her won't do anybody much good."

That was what was taking all the glory, all the exultation, out of their victory. They had walked into a hundred camps where they could have handled this situation, dangerous though it must always be. White captives had been bought and sold before time and again. Any Indian on earth but Scar would have concealed the girl, and played for time, until they found a way to deal.

"How in God's name," Mart asked him, "can this thing be? How could he let us walk into the lodge where she was? And keep her there before our eyes?"

"He meant for us to see her, that's all!"

"This is a strange Comanche," Mart said.

"This whole hunt has been a strange thing. And now we know why. Mart, did you see—there's scarce a Comanch' in that whole village we haven't seen before."

"I know."

"We've even stood in that same one lodge before. Do you know where?"

"When we talked to Singing Dog on the Little Boggy."

"That's right. We talked to Singing Dog in Scar's own lodge—while Scar took the girl and hid out. That's how they've kept us on a wild-goose chase five years long. They've covered up, and decoyed for him, every time we come near."

"We've caught up to him now!"

"Because he let us. Scar's learned something few Indians ever know: He's learned there's such a thing as a critter that never quits follering or gives up. So he's had enough. If we stood in the same lodge with her, and didn't know her, well and good. But if we were going to find her, he wanted to see us do it."

"So he saw—I suppose."

"I think so. He has to kill us, Mart."

"Bluebonnet didn't think he had to kill us."

"He never owned to having a white girl until Jaime Rosas made him a safe deal. And down there below the Llanos we was two men alone. Up here, we got Rangers, we got yellowlegs, to pull down on Scar. We rode square into the pocket where he was figuring to set until Davidson marched, and all soldiers was long gone. Scar don't dast let us ride loose with the word."

"Why'd he let us walk out of there at all?"

"I don't know," Amos said honestly. "Something tied his hands. If we knew what it was we could stretch it. But we don't know." Amos bent low over the horn to look back at the village under his arm. "They're holding fast so far. Might even let us make a pass at settling down at the spring. . . ."

But neither believed the Comanches would wait for night. Scar was a smart Indian, and a bitter one. The reason his squaws were on the honor side of the lodge where his sons should be was that Scar's sons were dead, killed in war raids upon the likes of Mart and Amos. He would take no chances of a slip-up in the dark.

"We'll make no two mistakes," Amos said, and his tone was thoughtful. "They got some fast horses there. You saw them scouts whip up when they took a look at our back trail. Them's racing ponies. And they got nigh two hours of daylight left."

They reached the spring without sign of pursuit, and dismounted. Here they had a good three-furlong start, and would be able to see horses start from the village when the Comanches made their move. They would not, of course, be able to see warriors who ran crouching on foot, snaking on their bellies across open ground. But the Comanches hated action afoot. More probably they would try to close for the kill under pretense of bringing fresh meat, perhaps with squaws along as a blind. Or the Comanches might simply make a horse race of it. The fast war ponies would close their three-eighths-mile lead very easily, with even half an hour of daylight left. Some Indians were going to be killed but there could hardly be but one end.

They set to work on the one thin ruse they could think of. Mart kicked a fire together first—about the least token of a fire that would pass for one at all—and set it alight. Then they stripped saddles and packs. They would have to abandon these, in order to look as though they were not going any place. Bridles were left on the horses, and halters on the mules.

"We'll lead out," Amos said, "like hunting for the best grass. Try to get as much more lead as we can without stirring 'em up. First minute any leave the village, we'll ease over a ridge, mount bareback—stampede the mules. Split up, of course—ride two ways—"

"We'll put up a better fight if we stay together," Mart objected.

"Yeah. We'd kill more Indians that way. There's no doubt of it. But a whole lot more than that will be killed if one of us stays alive until dark—and makes Camp Radziminski."

"Wait a minute," Mart said. "If we lead the yellowlegs on 'em—or even the Rangers, with the Tonkawas they got—there'll be a massacre, Amos! This village will be gutted out."

"Yes," Amos said.

"They'll kill her—you know that! You saw it at Deadhorse Bend!"

"If I didn't think so," Amos said, "I'd have killed her myself."

There was the substance of their victory after all this long time: One bitter taste of death, and then nothing more, forever.

"I won't do this," Mart said.

"What?"

"She's alive. That means everything to me. Better she's alive and living with Indians than her brains bashed out."

A blaze of hatred lighted Amos' eyes, while his face was still a mask of disbelief. "I can't believe my own ears," he said.

"I say there'll be no massacre while she's in that village! Not while I can stop it, or put it off!"

Amos got control of his voice. "What do you want to do?"

"First we got to live out the night. That I know and agree to. Beyond that, I don't know. Maybe we got to come at Scar some far way round. But we stay together. Because I'm not running to the troops, Amos. And neither are you."

Amos' voice was half choked by the congestion of blood in his neck. "You think the likes of you could stop me?"

Mart pulled out the bit of paper upon which the will was written, in which Amos left Mart all he had. He tore it slowly into shreds, and laid them on the fire. "Yes," he said, "I'll stop you."

Amos was silent for a long time. He stood with his shoulders slack, and his big hands hanging loose by his thighs, and he stared into space. When finally he spoke his voice was tired. "All right. We'll stay together through the night. After that, we'll see. I can't promise no more."

"That's better. Now let's get at it!"

"I'm going to tell you something," Amos said. "I wasn't going to speak of it. But if we fight, you got to murder all of 'em you can. So I'll tell you now. Did you notice them scalps strung on Scar's lance?"

"I was in there, wasn't I?"

"They ain't there," Mart said. "Not Martha's. Not Lucy's. Not even Brad's. Let's—"

"Did you see the third scalp from the point of the lance?"

"I saw it."

"Long, wavy. A red shine to it—"

"I saw it, I told you! You're wasting—"

"You didn't remember it. But I remember." Amos' voice was harsh, and his eyes bored into Mart's eyes, as if to drive the words into his brain. "That was your mother's scalp!"

No reason for Mart to doubt him. His mother's scalp was somewhere in a Comanche lodge, if a living Indian still possessed it. Certainly it was not in her grave. Amos let him stand there a moment, while his unremembered people became real to him—his mother, with the pretty hair, his father, from whom he got his light eyes, his young sisters, Ethel and Becky, who were just names. He knew what kind of thing their massacre had been, because he had seen the Edwards place, and the people who had raised him, after the same thing happened there.

"Let's lead off," Amos said.

But before they had gone a rod, the unexpected stopped them. A figure slipped out the willows by the creek, and a voice spoke. Debbie was there—alone, so far as they could see she had materialized as an Indian does, without telltale sound of approach.

She moved a few halting steps out of the willow scrub, but stopped as Mart came toward her. He walked carefully, watchful for movement in the thicket behind her. Behind him he heard the metallic crash as Amos chambered a cartridge. Amos had sprung onto a hummock, exposing himself recklessly while his eyes swept the terrain.

Mart was at four paces when Debbie spoke, urgently, in Comanche. "Don't come too close. Don't touch me! I have warriors with me."

He had remembered the voice of a child, but what he was hearing was the soft-husky voice of a grown woman. Her Comanche was fluent, indistinguishable from that of the Indians, yet he thought he had never heard that harsh and ugly tongue sound uglier. He stopped six feet from her; one more inch, he felt, and she would have bolted. "Where are they, then?" he demanded. "Let 'em stand up and be counted, if they're not afraid!"

Mystification came into her face; she stared at him with blank eyes. Suddenly he realized that he had spoken in a rush of English—and she no longer understood. The lost years had left an invisible mutilation as definite as if fingers were missing from her hand. "How many warriors?" he asked in gruff Comanche; and everything they said to each other was in Comanche after that.

"Four men are with me."

His eyes jumped then, and swept wide; and though he saw nothing at all, he knew she might be telling the truth. If she had not come alone, he had to find out what was happening here, and quick. Their lives might easily depend upon their next guess. "What are you doing here?" he asked harshly.

"My—" He heard a wary hesitancy, a testing of words before they were spoken. "My—father—told me come."

"Your *what?*"

"Yellow Buckle is my father."

While he stared at her, sure he must have misunderstood the Comanche words, Amos put in. "Keep at her! Scar sent her all right. We got to know why!"

Watching her, Mart was sure Debbie had understood none of Amos' Texan English. She tried to hurry her stumbling tale. "My father—he believes you. But some others—they know. They tell him—you were my people once."

"What did *you* tell him?"

"I tell him I don't know. I must come here. Make sure. I tell him I must come."

"You told him nothing like that," he contradicted her in Comanche. "He smash your mouth, you say 'must' to him!"

She shook her head. "No. No. You don't know my father."

"We know him. We call him Scar."

"My father—Scar—" she accepted his name for the chief—"He believes you. He says you are Comancheros. Like you say. But soon—" she faltered—"soon he knows."

"He knows now," he contradicted her again. "You are lying to me!"

Her eyes dropped, and her hands hid themselves in her ragged wash-leather sleeves. "He says you are Comancheros," she repeated. "He believes you. He told me. He—"

He had an exasperated impulse to grab her and shake her; but he saw her body tense. If he made a move toward her she would be gone in the same instant. "*Debbie*, listen to me! I'm *Mart!* Don't you remember me?" He spoke just the names in English, and it was obvious that these two words were familiar to her.

"I remember you," she said gravely, slowly, across the gulf between them. "I remember. From always."

"Then stop lying to me! You got Comanches with you—so you say. What do you want here if you're not alone?"

"I come to tell you, go away! Go tonight. As soon as dark. They can stop you. They can kill you. But this one night—I make him let you go."

"Make him?" He was so furious he stammered. "*You* make him? No squaw alive can move Scar a hand span—you least of all!"

"I can," she said evenly, meeting his eyes. "I am—bought. I am bought for—to be—for marriage. My—man—he pays sixty ponies. Nobody ever paid so much. I'm worth sixty ponies."

"We'll overcall that," he said. "Sixty ponies! We'll pay a hundred for you—a hundred and a half—"

She shook her head.

"My man—his family—"

"You own five times that many ponies yourself—you know that? We can bring them—many as he wants—and enough cattle to feed the whole tribe from here to—"

"My man would fight. His people would fight. They are very many. Scar would lose—lose everything."

Comanche thoughts, Comanche words—a white woman's voice and form . . . the meeting toward which he had worked for years had turned into a nightmare. Her face was Debbie's face, delicately made, and now in the first bloom of maturity; but all expression was locked away from it. She held it wooden, facing him impassively, as an Indian faces a stranger. Behind the surface of this long-loved face was a Comanche squaw.

He spoke savagely, trying to break through to the Debbie of long ago. "Sixty ponies," he said with contempt. "What good is that? One sleep with Indians— you're a mare—a sow—they take what they want of you. Nothing you can do would turn Scar!"

"I can kill myself," she said.

In the moment of silence, Amos spoke again. "String it out. No move from the village yet. Every minute helps."

Mart looked into the hard green eyes that should have been lovely and dear to him; and he believed her. She was capable of killing herself, and would do it if she said she would. And Scar must know that. Was this the mysterious thing that had tied Scar's hands when he let them walk away? An accident to a sold but undelivered squaw could cost Scar more than sixty ponies. It could cost him his chiefship, and perhaps his life.

"That is why you can go now," she said, "and be safe. I have told him—my father—"

His temper flared up. "Stop calling that brute your father!"

"You must get away from here," she said again, monotonously, almost dropping into a ritual Comanche singsong. "You must go away quick. Soon he will know. You will be killed—"

"You bet I'm getting out of here," he said, breaking into English. "And I got no notion of getting killed, neither! Amos! Grab holt that black mule! She's got to ride that!"

He heard leather creak as Amos swung up a saddle. No chance of deception now, from here on; they had to take her and run.

Debbie said, "What—?"

He returned to Comanche. "You're going with us now! You hear me?"

"No," Debbie said. "Not now. Not ever."

"I don't know what they have done to you. But it makes no difference!" He wouldn't have wasted time fumbling Comanche words if he had seen half a chance of taking her by main force. "You must come with me. I take you to—"

"They have done nothing to me. They take care of me. These are my people."

"Debbie, Debbie—these—these Nemenna murdered our family!"

"You lie." A flash of heat-lightning in her eyes let him see an underlying hatred, unexpected and dreadful.

"These are the ones! They killed your mother, cut her arm off—killed your own real father, slit his belly open—killed Hunter, killed Ben—"

"Wichitas killed them! Wichitas and white men! To steal cows—"

"*What?*"

"These people saved me. They drove off the whites and the Wichitas. I ran in the brush. Scar picked me up on his pony. They have told me it all many times!" He was blanked again, helpless against lies drilled into her over the years.

Amos had both saddles cinched up. "Watch your chance," he said. "You know now what we got to do."

Debbie's eyes went to Amos in quick suspicion, but Mart was still trying. "Lucy was with you. You know what happened to her!"

"Lucy—went mad. They—we—gave her a pony—"

"Pony! They—they—" He could not think of the word for rape. "They cut her up! Amos—Bull Shoulders—he found her, buried her—"

"You lie," she answered, her tone monotonous again, without heat. "All white men lie. Always."

"Listen! Listen to me! I saw my own mother's scalp on Scar's lance—there in the lodge where you live!"

"Lies," she said, and looked at him sullenly, untouched. "You Long Knives— you are the evil ones. You came in the night, and started killing us. There by the river."

At first he didn't know what she was talking about; then he remembered Deadhorse Bend and Debbie's locket that had seemed to tell them she had been there. He wondered if she had seen the old woman cut down, who wore her locket, and the old man sabered, as he tried to save his squaw.

"I saw it all," she said, as if answering his thought.

Mart changed his tone. "I found your locket," he said gently. "Do you remember your little locket? Do you remember who gave it to you? So long ago. . . ."

Her eyes faltered for the first time; and for a moment he saw in this alien woman the little girl of the miniature, the child of the shrine in the dream.

"At first—I prayed to you," she said.

"You what?"

"At first—I cried. Every night. For a long time. I cried to you—come and get me. Take me home. You didn't come." Her voice was dead, all feeling washed out of it.

"I've come now," he said.

She shook her head. "These are my people. You—you are Long Knives. We hate you—fight you—always, till we die."

Amos said sharply, "They're mounting up now, up there. We got to go." He came over to them in long, quick strides, and spoke in Comanche, but loudly, as some people speak to foreigners. "You know Yellow Buckle thing?" he demanded, backing his words with signs. "Buckle, Scar wear?"

"The medicine buckle," she said clearly.

"Get your hands on it. Turn it over. Can you still read? On the back it says white man's words 'Ethan to Judith.' Scratched in the gold. Because Scar tore it off Mart's mother when he killed and scalped her!"

"Lies," Debbie repeated in Comanche.

"Look and see for yourself!"

Amos had been trying to work around Debbie, to cut her off from the willows and the river, but she was watching him, moving enough to keep clear. "I go back now," she said. "To my father's lodge. I can do nothing here." Her movements brought her no closer to Mart, but suddenly his nostrils caught the distinct, unmistakable Indian odor, alive, immediate, near. For an instant the unreasoning fear that this smell had brought him, all through his early years, came back with a sickening chill of revulsion. He looked at the girl with horror.

Amos brought him out of it. "Keep your rifle on her, Mart! If she breaks, stun her with the butt!" He swayed forward, then lunged to grab her.

She wasn't there. She cried out a brief phrase in Comanche as she dodged him, then was into the brush, running like a fox. "Git down!" Amos yelled, and fired his rifle from belt level, though not at her; while simultaneously another rifle fired through the space in which Debbie had stood. Its bullet whipped past Mart's ear as he flung himself to the ground. The Comanche who had fired on him sprang up, face to the sky, surprisingly close to them, then fell back into the thin grass in which he had hidden.

Dirt jumped in Mart's face, and a ricochet yowled over. He swiveled on his belt buckle, and snap-fired at a wisp of gunsmoke sixty yards away in the brush. He saw a rifle fall and slide clear of the cover. Amos was standing straight up, trading shots with a third sniper. "Got him," he said, and instantly spun half around, his right leg knocked from under him. A Comanche sprang from an invisible depression less than thirty yards away, and rushed with drawn knife. Mart fired, and the Indian's legs pumped grotesquely as he fell, sliding him on his face another two yards before he was still. All guns were silent then; and Mart went to Amos.

"Go on, God damn it!" Blood pumped in spurts from a wound just above Amos' knee. "Ride, you fool! They're coming down on us!"

The deep thrumming of numberless hoofs upon the prairie turf came to them plainly from a quarter mile away. Mart sliced off a pack strap, and twisted it into a tourniquet. Amos cuffed him heavily alongside the head, pleading desperately. "For God's sake, Mart, will you ride? Go on! Go on!"

The Comanches weren't yelling yet, perhaps wouldn't until they struck. Of all the Wild Tribes, the Comanches were the last to start whooping, the first to come to close grips. Mart took precious seconds more to make an excuse for a bandage. "Get up here!" he grunted, stubborn to the bitter last; and he lifted Amos.

One of the mules was down, back broken by a bullet never meant for it. It made continual groaning, whistling noises as it clawed out with its fore hoofs, trying to drag up its dead hindquarters. The other mules had stampeded, but the horses still stood, snorting and sidestepping, tied to the ground by their long reins. Mart got Amos across his shoulders, and heaved him bodily into the saddle. "Get your foot in the stirrup! Gimme that!" He took Amos' rifle, and slung it into the brush. "See can you tie yourself on with the saddle strings as we ride!"

He grabbed his own pony, and made a flying mount as both animals bolted. Sweat ran down Amos' face; the bullet shock was wearing off, but he rode straight up, his wounded leg dangling free. Mart leaned low on the neck, and his spurs raked deep. Both horses stretched their bellies low to the ground, and dug out for their lives, as the first bullets from the pursuit buzzed over. The slow dusk was closing now. If they could have had another half hour, night would have covered them before they were overtaken.

They didn't have it. But now the Comanches did another unpredictable, Indian kind of a thing. With their quarry in full view, certain to be flanked and forced to a stand within the mile, the Comanches stopped. Repeated signals passed forward, calling the leaders in; the long straggle of running ponies lost momentum, and sucked back upon itself. The Comanches bunched up, and sat their bareback ponies in a close mass—seemingly in argument.

Things like that had happened before that Mart knew about, though never twice quite the same. Sometimes the horse Indians would fight a brilliant battle, using the fast-breaking cavalry tactics at which they were the best on earth —and seem to be winning; then unexpectedly turn and run. If you asked them later why they ran, they would say they ran because they had fought enough. Pursued, they might turn abruptly and fight again as tenaciously as before—and explain they fought then because they had run enough. . . .

This time they came on again after another twenty-five minutes; or, at least, a picked party of them did. Looking back as he topped a ridge, Mart saw what looked like a string of perhaps ten warriors, barely visible in the last of the light, coming on fast at three miles. He turned at a right angle, covered by the ridge, and loped in the new direction for two miles more. The dusk had blackened to almost solid dark when he dismounted to see what he could do for Amos.

"Never try to guess an Indian," Amos said thickly, and slumped unconscious. He hung to the side of the horse by the saddle strings he had tied into his belt, until Mart cut him down.

Camp Radziminski was twenty miles away.

37

Martin Pauley sprawled on a pile of sacked grain in Ranger Captain Sol Clinton's tent, and waited. With Amos safe under medical care, of sorts, Mart saw a good chance to get some sleep; but the fits and starts of a wakeful doze seemed to be the best he could make of it. The Ranger was still wrangling with Brevet-Colonel Chester C. Greenhill over what they were about to do, if anything at all. He had been over there for two hours, and it ought to be almost enough. When he got back, Mart would hear whether or not five years' search could succeed, and yet be altogether wasted.

Camp Radziminski was a flattish sag in the hills looking down upon Otter Creek—a place, not an installation. It had been a cavalry outpost, briefly, long ago; and an outfit of Rangers had wintered here once after that. In the deep grass you could still fall over the crumbling footings of mud-and-wattle walls and the precise rows of stones that had bordered military pathways; but the stockaded defenses were long gone.

Mart had been forced to transport Amos on a travois. This contraption was nothing but two long poles dragged from the saddle. The attached horse had shown confusion and some tendency to kick Amos' head off, but it hadn't happened. Mart found Radziminski before noon to his own considerable surprise. And the dead Comanche scout was proved to have told the truth with considerable exactness under Amos' peculiarly effective methods of questioning.

Here were the "more than forty" Rangers, their wagon-sheet beds scattered haphazardly over the best of the flat ground, with a single tent to serve every form of administration and supply. Here, too, were the two short-handed companies of cavalry—about a hundred and twenty men—with a wagon train, an officer's tent, a noncom's tent, a supply tent, and a complement of pup tents sheltering two men each. This part of the encampment was inconveniently placed, the Rangers having been here first; but the lines of tents ran perfectly straight anyway, defying the broken terrain.

And here, scattered up and down the slopes at random, were the brush wickiups of the "sixty or seventy" Tonkawas, almost the last of their breed. These were tall, clean, good-looking Indians, but said to be cannibals, and trusted by few; now come to fight beside the Rangers in a last doomed, expiring effort to win the good will of the white men who had conquered them.

As Mart had suspected, the Army and the Rangers were not working together at all. Colonel Greenhill had not, actually, come out to intercept the Rangers. Hadn't known they were there. But, having run smack into them, he conceived his next duty to be that of sending them back where they belonged. He had been trying to get this done without too much untowardness for several days; and all concerned were now fit to be tied.

In consequence, Mart found Captain Sol Clinton in no mood to discuss the murder charge hanging over Mart and Amos, by reason of the killings at Lost Mule Creek. From this standpoint, Clinton told Mart, he had been frankly hopeful of never seeing either one of them again. Seeing's they saw fit to thrust themselves upon him, he supposed he would have to do something technical about them later. But now he had other fish to fry—and by God, they seemed to have brought him the skillet! Come along here, and if you can't walk any faster than that you can run, can't you?

He took Mart to Colonel Greenhill who spent an hour questioning him in what seemed a lot like an effort to break his story; and sent him to wait in Clinton's tent after. Sol Clinton had spoken with restraint while Mart was with them, but as Mart walked away he heard the opening guns of Sol's argument roar like a blue norther, shaking the tent walls. "I'm sick and tired of war parties murdering the be-Jesus out of Texas families, then skedaddling to hide behind you yellowlegs! What are you fellers running, a damn Wild Indian sanctuary up here? The chief purpose of this here Union is to protect Texas—that's how *we* understood it! Yonder's a passel of murderers, complete with Texican scalps and white girl captive! I say it's up to you to protect us from them varmints by stepping the hell to one side while I—"

They had been at it for a long time, and they were still at it, though with reduced carrying power. Mart dozed a little, but was broad awake instantly as Sergeant Charlie MacCorry came in. Charlie seemed to have worked up to the position of right-hand man, or something, for he had stood around while Captain Clinton first talked to Mart, and he had been in Colonel Greenhill's tent during Mart's session there as well. His attitude toward Mart had seemed non-committal—neither friendly nor stand-offish but quiet, rather, and abstracted. It seemed to Mart an odd and overkindly attitude for a Ranger sergeant to take toward a former prisoner who had slugged him down and got away. And now Charlie seemed to have something he wanted to say to Mart, without knowing how to bring it up. He warmed up by offering his views on the military situation.

"Trouble with the Army," Charlie had it figured, "there's always some damn fool don't get the word. A fort sends some colonel chasing all over creation after a bunch of hostiles; and he finds 'em, and jumps 'em, and makes *that* bunch a thing of the past; and what does he find out then? Them hostiles was already coming into a different fort under full-agreed truce. Picked 'em off right on the doorstep, by God. Done away with them peaceful Indians all unawares. Well! Now what you got? Investigations—boards—court-martials—and wham! Back goes the colonel so many files he's virtually in short pants. Happens every time."

He paced the tent a few moments, two steps one way, two steps back, watching Mart covertly, as if expecting him to speak.

"Yeah," Mart said at last.

Charlie seemed freed to say what he had on his mind. "Mart . . . I got a piece of news."

"Oh?"

"Me and Laurie—we got married. Just before I left."

Mart let his eyes drop while he thought it over. There had been a time, and it had gone on for years, when Laurie was always in his mind. She was the only girl he had ever known very well except those in the family. Or perhaps he had never known her, or any girl, at all. He reached for memories that would bring back her meaning to him. Laurie in a pretty dress, with her shoulders bare. Laurie joking about her floursack all-overs that had once read "Steamboat Mills" across her little bottom. Laurie in his arms, promising to come to him in the night . . .

All that should have mattered to him, but he couldn't seem to feel it. The whole thing seemed empty, and dried out, without any real substance for him any more. As if it never could have come to anything, no matter what.

"Did you hear me?" Charlie asked. "I say, I married Laurie."

"Yeah. Good for you. Got yourself a great girl."

"No hard feelings?"

"No."

They shook hands, briefly, as they always did; and Charlie changed the subject briskly. "You sure fooled me, scouting up this attack on Scar. I'd have swore that was the last thing you wanted. Unless you got Debbie out of there first. Being's they're so liable to brain their captives when they're jumped. You think they won't now?"

"Might not," Mart said dully. He stirred restlessly. "What's happened to them king-pins over there? They both died, or something?"

Charlie looked at him thoughtfully, unwilling to be diverted. "Is she—Have they—" He didn't know how to put it, so that Mart would not be riled. "What I'm driving at—has she been with the bucks?"

Mart said, "Charlie, I don't know. I don't think so. It's more like—like they've done something to her mind."

"You mean she's crazy?"

"No—that isn't it, rightly. Only—she takes their part now. She believes them, not us. Like as if they took out her brain, and put in an Indian brain instead. So that she's an Indian now inside."

Charlie believed he saw it now. "Doesn't want to leave 'em, huh?"

"Almost seems like she's an Indian herself now. Inside."

"I see." Charlie was satisfied. If she wanted to stay, she'd been with the bucks all right. Had Comanche brats of her own most likely.

"I see something now," Mart said, "I never used to understand. I see now why the Comanches murder our women when they raid—brain our babies even —what ones they don't pick to steal. It's so we won't breed. They want us off the earth. I understand that, because that's what I want for them. I want them dead. All of them. I want them cleaned off the face of the world."

Charlie shut up. Mart sounded touched in the head, and maybe dangerous. He wouldn't have slapped Mart's face again for thirty-seven dollars.

Sol Clinton came in, now, at last. He looked angry, yet satisfied and triumphant all at once. "I had to put us under his command," the Ranger captain said. "I don't even know if I legally can—but it's done. Won't matter, once we're out ahead. We're going to tie into 'em, boys!"

"The Tonks, too?"

"Tonkawas and all. Mart, you're on pay as civilian guide. Can you find 'em again in the dark? Can you, hell—you've got to! I want to hit before sunrise— leave Greenhill come up as he can. You going to get us there?"

"That I am," Mart said; and smiled for the first time that day.

38

Scouting ahead, Mart Pauley found Scar's village still where he had seen it last. Its swarming cur dogs yammered a great part of every night, and their noise placed the village for him now. The Comanches claimed they could always tell what the dogs were barking at—wolves, Indians, white men, or spooks—and though Mart only partly believed this he reconnoitered the place from a great way out, taking no chances. He galloped back, and met Captain Sol Clinton's fast-traveling Rangers less than an hour before dawn.

"We're coming in," he said to Captain Clinton, turning his horse alongside. "I should judge we're within—" He hesitated. He had started to say they were within three to five miles, but he had been to very few measured horse races, and had only a vague idea of a mile. "Within twenty minutes trot and ten minutes walk," he put it. "There you top a low hogback, looking across flat ground; and the village is in sight beyond."

"In sight from how far?"

There it was again. Mart thought the hogback was about a mile from the village, but what's a mile? "Close enough to see trees, too far to see branches," he described it.

That was good enough. "Just about what we want," Sol accepted it. Everything else had been where Mart had said it would be throughout the long night's ride. The captain halted his forty-two Rangers, passing the word back quietly along the loose column of twos.

His men dismounted without further command, loosened cinches, and relieved themselves without military precision. They looked unhurried, but wasted no motions. These men supplied their own clothes, saddles, and weapons, and very often their own horses; what you had here was a bunch of individuals, each a tough and weathered fighting man in his own right, but also in his own manner.

Behind them the sixty-odd Tonkawas pulled up at an orderly interval, a body of riders even more quiet than the Rangers. They stepped down and looked to their saddles, which included every form of museum piece from discarded McClellans to Indian-craft rigs with elkhorn trees. Each dug a little hole in which to urinate, and covered it over when he was done.

A word from Clinton sent a young Ranger racing forward to halt the point, riding a furlong or so ahead in the dark. They were in their last hour before action, but the Ranger captain made no inspection. He had inspected these men to their roots when he signed them on, and straightened them out from

446

time to time after, as needed; they knew their business if they were ever going to.

Clinton sharpened a twig, picked his teeth with it, and looked smug. He had made a good march, and he knew it, and judged that the yellowlegs would be along in about a week. He cast an eye about him for the two cavalry troopers who had ridden with them as runner-links with Colonel Greenhill. They didn't seem to be in earshot. Captain Clinton spoke to Lieutenant Bart Lester, a shadowy figure in the last of the night. "Looks like we might get this thing cleaned up by breakfast," he said, "against something different goes wrong." Before Colonel Greenhill comes up, he meant. "Of course, when's breakfast is largely up to Scar. You can't—Who's this?"

Charlie MacCorry had come galloping up from the rear, where he had been riding tail. Now he pulled up, leaning low to peer at individuals, looking for Captain Clinton.

"Here, Charlie," Sol spoke.

"Hey, they're on top of us!"

"Who is?"

"The yellowlegs! They're not more than seven minutes behind!"

The toothpick broke between Sol Clinton's teeth, and he spit it out explosively as he jumped for his horse. "Damn you, Charlie, if you've let—"

"Heck, Sol, we didn't hear a thing until the halt. It's only just this minute we—"

"Bart!" Clinton snapped. "Take 'em on forward, and quick! Lope 'em out a little—but a lope, you hear me, not a run! I'll be up in a couple of minutes!" He went into his loose-cinched saddle with a vault, like a Comanche. He was cussing smokily, and tightening the cinch with one hand as he started hell-for-leather to the rear. The word had run fast down the column, without any shouting, and some of the Rangers were already stepping into their saddles. Charlie ducked his head between his shoulders. "Knew I'd never git far in the Rangers." Mart followed as Charlie spurred after Clinton who was riding to the Tonkawas.

"We can run for it," Charlie offered hopefully as Sol pulled up. "I believe if we hold the Tonks at a slow gait behind us—"

"Oh, shut up," Clinton said. He had to send the Tonkawas on, so that his own men would be between the Tonkawas and the cavalry when they went into action. The Cavalry couldn't be expected to tell one Indian from another, Clinton supposed, in the heat of action. The Tonks would race forward, anyway, pretty soon. No power on earth could hold those fools once the enemy was sighted.

"Hey, Spots!" Clinton called. "Where are you?"

Spotted Hog, the war chief commanding the Tonkawas, sprang onto his pony to ride the twenty yards to Clinton. "Yes, sir," he said in English of a strong Texan accent.

"Tell you what you do," Clinton said. "We're pretty close now; I'm sending you on in. I want—"

Spotted Hog whistled softly, a complicated phrase, and they heard it repeated and answered some distance to the rear.

"Wait a minute, will you? Damn it, Spots, I'm telling you what I want—and nothing no different!"

"Sure, Captain—I'm listening."

"The village is still there, right where it was supposed to be. So—"

"I know," Spotted Hog said.

"—so swing wide, and find out which side the crick they're holding their horses. Soon as you know—"

"The west side," the Tonkawa said. "The ponies are on the west side. Across from the village."

"Who told you to put your own scouts out? Damnation, if you've waked up that village—Well, never mind. You go hit that horse herd. The hell with scalps —run off that herd, and you can have the horses."

"We'll run 'em!"

"All right—get ahead with it."

"Yes, sir!" Spotted Hog jumped his pony off into the dark where a brisk stir of preparation could be heard among the Tonkawas.

"I got to send Greenhill some damn word," Clinton began; and one of the cavalry troopers was beside him instantly.

"You want me, sir?"

"God forbid!" Clinton exploded. "Git forward where you belong!" The trooper scampered, and Clinton turned to MacCorry. "Charlie . . . No. No. What we need's a civilian—and we got one. Here, Mart! You go tell Greenhill where he's at."

"What when he asks where you are?"

"I'm up ahead. That's all. I'm up ahead. And make this stupid, will you? If he gives you orders for me, don't try to get loose without hearing 'em; he'll only send somebody else. But you can lose your way, can't you? You're the one found it!"

"Yes, sir," Mart said with mental reservations.

"Go on and meet him. Come on, Charlie." They were gone from there, and in a hurry.

Galloping to the rear, past the Tonkawas, Mart saw that they were throwing aside their saddles, and all gear but their weapons, and tying up the tails of their ponies. No war paint had been seen on them until now, but as they stripped their shirts their torsos proved to be prepainted with big circles and stripes of raw colors. Great, many-couped war bonnets were flowering like turkey tails among them. Each set off, bareback, as soon as he was ready, moving up at the lope; there would be no semblance of formation. The Tonkawas rode well, and would fight well. Only they would fight from the backs of their horses, while the Comanches would be all over their ponies, fighting from under the necks, under the bellies—and still would run their horses the harder.

Once clear of the Tonkawas, Mart could hear the cavalry plainly. The noise they made came to him as a steady metallic whispering, made up of innumerable clinks, rattles, and squeaks of leather, perhaps five minutes away. Darkness still held as he reached them, and described the position of the enemy to Colonel Greenhill. The hundred and twenty cavalry-men wheeled twos into line.

"Has Clinton halted?" Greenhill asked.

"Yes, sir." Well . . . he had.

Some restrained shouting went on in the dark. The cavalry prepared to dismount, bringing even numbers forward one horse length; dismounted; reset saddles; and dressed the line. Colonel Greenhill observed that he remembered this country now; he had been over every foot of it, and would have recognized it to begin with, had he been booned with any decent kind of description. He would be glad to bet a barrel of forty-rod that he could fix the co-ordinates of that village within a dozen miles. If he had had so much as a single artillery piece, he would have shown them how to scatter that village before Scar knew they were in the country.

Mart was glad he didn't have one, scattering the Comanches being the last thing wanted. In his belief, the pony herd was the key. A Comanche afoot was a beaten critter; but let him get to a horse and he was a long gone Comanche— and a deadly threat besides. He felt no call, however, to expound these views to a brevet-colonel.

"Tell Captain Clinton I'll be up directly," Greenhill ordered him; and went briskly about his inspection.

Mart started on, but made a U-turn, and loped to the rear, behind the cavalry lines. At the far end of the dismounted formation stood four narrow-bowed covered wagons, their drivers at attention by the bridles of the nigh leaders. Second wagon was the ambulance; a single trooper, at attention by a front wheel, was the present sanitary detail. Martin Pauley rode to the tail gate, stepped over it from the saddle, and struck a shielded match. Amos lay heavily blanketed, his body looking to be of great length but little substance, upon a narrow litter. By his heavy breathing he seemed asleep, but his eyes opened to the light of the match.

"Mart? Where are we?"

"Pretty close on Scar's village. I was to it. Within dogbark, anyway. Sol sent the Tonks to make a try at their horses, and took the Rangers on up. He wants to hit before Greenhill finds what he's up to. How you feel?"

Amos stared straight upward, his eyes bleak and unforgiving upon the unseen night above the canvas; but the question brought a glint of irony into them, so that Mart was ashamed of having asked it.

"My stuff's rolled up down there by my feet," Amos said. "Get me my gun from it."

If he had been supposed to have it, the sanitary detail would have given it to him, but it was a long time since they had gone by what other people supposed for them. Mart brought Amos his six-gun, and his cartridge belt, and checked the loading. Amos lifted a shaking hand, and hid the gun under his blankets. Outside they heard the "Prepare to mount!"

"I got to get on up there." Mart groped for Amos' hand. He felt a tremor in its grip, but considerable strength.

"Get my share of 'em," Amos whispered.

"You want scalps, Amos?"

"Yeah. . . . No. Just stomp 'em—like I always done—"

Men and horses were beginning to show, black and solid against a general grayness. You could see them now without stooping to outline them against the stars, as Mart stepped from the wagon bed into the saddle. The cavalry had wheeled into column of twos and was in motion at the walk. Mart cleared the head of the column, and lifted his horse into a run.

39

Sol Clinton's forty-two Rangers were dismounted behind the last ridge below Scar's village as Mart came up. They had plenty of light now—more than they had wanted or intended. Captain Clinton lay on the crest of the ridge, studying the view without visible delight. Mart went up there, but Clinton turned on him before he got a look beyond.

"God damn you, Pauley, I—"

"Greenhill says, tell you he's coming," Mart got in hastily. "And that's all he says."

But Clinton was thinking about something else. "Take a look at this thing here!"

Mart crawled up beside Clinton, and got a shock. The fresh light of approaching sunrise showed Scar's village in clear detail, a scant mile from where they lay. Half the lodges were down, and between them swarmed great numbers of horses and people, the whole thing busy as a hoof-busted ant hill. This village was packing to march.

A hundred yards in front of the village a few dozen mounted warriors had interposed themselves. They sat about in idle groups, blanket-wrapped upon their standing ponies. They looked a little like the Comanche idea of vedettes, but more were riding out from the village as Mart and Sol Clinton watched. What they had here was the start of a battle build-up. Clinton seemed unsurprised by Scar's readiness. You could expect to find a war chief paying attention to his business once in a while, and you had to allow for it. But—"What the hell's the matter with you people? Can't you count? That band will mount close to three hundred bucks!"

"I told you he might want this fight. So he's got himself reinforced, that's all."

A rise of dust beyond the village and west of the Wild Dog showed where the Comanche horse herd had been put in motion. All animals not in use as travois horses or battle ponies—the main wealth of the village—were being driven upstream and away. But the movement was orderly. Where were the Tonkawas? They might be waiting upstream, to take the horses away from the small-boy herders; they might have gone home. One thing they certainly were not doing was what they had been told. Captain Clinton had no comment to waste on that, either.

He pulled back down the hill, moving slowly, to give himself time to think. Lieutenant Bart Lester came forward, dogged by the two uniformed orderlies. "Flog on back, boy," Clinton told one of them. "Tell Colonel Greenhill I am now demonstrating in front of the village to develop the enemy strength, and expedite his commitment. . . . Guess that ought to hold him. Mount 'em up, Bart."

The Rangers mounted and drifted into line casually, but once they were formed the line was a good one. These men might shun precision of movement for themselves, but they habitually exacted it from their horses, whether the horses agreed to it or not. Mart placed himself near the middle of the line and watched Clinton stoically. He knew the Ranger would be justified in ordering a retreat.

Clinton stepped aboard his horse, looked up and down the line of Rangers, and addressed them conversationally. "Well, us boys was lucky again," he said. "For once we got enough Comanches to go around. Might run as high as a dozen apiece, if we don't lose too many. I trust you boys will be glad to hear this is a fight, not a surprise. They're forming in front of the village, at about a mile. I should judge we won't have to go all the way; they'll come to meet us. What I'd like to do is bust through their middle, and on into the village; give Greenhill a chance to hit 'em behind, as they turn after us. This is liable to be prevented. In which case we'll handle the situation after we see what it is."

Some of the youngsters—and most of the Rangers were young—must have been fretting over the time Clinton was taking. The Cavalry would be up pretty quick, and Colonel Greenhill would take over; probably order a retirement according to plan, they supposed, without a dead Comanche to show. Clinton knew what he was doing, however. In broad daylight, lacking surprise, and with unexpected odds against him, he wanted the cavalry as close as it could get without telling him what to do. And he did not believe Greenhill would consider retreat for a second.

"In case you wonder what become of them antic Tonks," Clinton said, "I don't know. And don't pay them Comanches no mind, neither—just keep your eye on me. I'm the hard case you're up against around here—not them childish savages. If you don't hear me first time I holler, you better by God read my mind—I don't aim to raise no two hollers on any one subject in hand."

He pretended to look them over, but actually he was listening. The line stood steady and perfectly straight. Fidgety horses moved no muscle, and tired old nags gathered themselves to spring like lions upon demand, before a worse thing happened. And now they heard the first faint, far-off rustle of the bell-metal scabbards as the cavalry came on.

"I guess this sloppy-looking row of hay-doodles is what you fellers call a line," Sol criticized them. "Guide center! On Joe, here. Joe, you just follow me." Deliberately he got out a plug of tobacco, bit off a chew, and rolled it into his cheek. It was the first tobacco Mart had ever seen him use. "Leave us go amongst them," the captain said.

He wheeled his horse, and moved up the slope at a walk. The first direct rays of the sun were striking across the rolling ground as they breasted the crest, bringing Scar's village into full view a mile away. A curious sound of breathing could be heard briefly along the line of Rangers as they got their first look at what they were going against. A good two hundred mounted Comanches were now strung out in front of the village, where only the vedettes had stood before; and more were coming from the village in a stream. The war ponies milled a bit, and an increased stir built up in the village beyond, in reaction to the Ranger advance.

Clinton turned in his saddle. "Hey, you—orderly!"

"Yes, sir!"

"Ride back and tell Colonel Greenhill: Captain Clinton, of the Texas Rangers, presents his respects—"

"Yes, sir!" The rattled trooper whirled his horse.

"Come back here! Where the hell you going? Tell him the Comanches are in battle line east of the crick, facing south—and don't say you seen a million of 'em! Tell him I say there's a couple hundred. If he wants to know what I'm doing, I'm keeping an eye on 'em. All right, go find him."

They were at a thousand yards, and the stream of Comanches from the village had dwindled to a straggle. It was about time; their number was going to break three hundred easily. A line was forming in a practiced manner, without confusion, and it was going to be a straight one. It looked about a mile long, but it wasn't; it wouldn't be much longer than a quarter of a mile if the Comanches rode knee to knee. Still, Mart expected a quarter mile of Comanches to be enough for forty-two men.

Clinton waved an arm, and stepped up the pace to a sharp trot. He was riding directly toward the village itself, which would bring them against the Comanche center. A single stocky warrior, wearing a horn headdress, loped slowly across the front of the Comanche line. Mart recognized Scar first by his short lance, stripped of its trophy scalps for combat. Incredibly, in the face of advancing Rangers, Scar was having himself an inspection! At the end of the line he turned, and loped back toward the center, unhurrying. When he reached the center he would bring the Comanche line to meet them, and all this spooky orderliness would be over.

Captain Clinton let his horse break into a hand-lope, and the forty behind him followed suit in the same stride. Their speed was little increased, but the line moved in an easier rhythm. Scar's line still stood quiet, unfretting. The beef-up from the village had stopped at last; Scar's force stood at more than three hundred and fifty Comanches.

They were within the half mile. They could see the tall fanfeathered bonnets of the war chiefs, now, and the clubbed tails of the battle ponies. The warriors were in full paint; individual patterns could not yet be made out, but the bright stripes and splotches on the naked bodies gave the Comanche line an oddly broken color.

Now Scar turned in front of his center; the line moved, advancing evenly at a walk. Some of the veteran Indian fighters among the Rangers must have felt a chill down their backs as they saw that. This Indian was too cool, held his people in too hard a grip; his battle would lack the helter-skelter horserace quality that gave a smaller and better disciplined force its best opportunities. And he wasn't using a Comanche plan of attack at all. The famous Comanche grinding-wheel attack made use of horsemanship and mobility, and preserved the option to disengage intact. The head-on smash for which Scar was forming was all but unknown among Comanches. Scar would never have elected close grips to a finish if he had not been sure of what he had. And he had reason. Coolly led, this many hostiles could mass five deep in front of Clinton, yet still wrap round his flanks, roll him up, enfold him. The Rangers watched Sol, but he gave no order, and the easy rating of his horse did not change.

They were at the quarter mile. A great swarm of squaws, children, and old people had come out from the village. They stood motionless, on foot, a long, dense line of them—spectators, waiting to see the Rangers eaten alive. Scar's line still walked, unflustered, and Clinton still came on, loping easily. Surely he must have been expecting some break, some turn in his favor; perhaps he had supposed the cavalry would show itself by this time, but it had not. What he would have done without any break, whether he would have galloped steadily into that engulfing destruction, was something they were never going to know. For now the break came.

Out of the ground across the river the Tonkawas appeared, as if rising out of the earth. Nothing over there, not a ridge, not an arroyo, looked as though it would hide a mounted man, let alone seventy; yet, by some medicine of wits and skill, they appeared with no warning at all. The tall Tonkawas came in no semblance of a line; they rode singly, and in loose bunches, a rabble. But they moved fast, and as if they knew what they were doing, as they poured over the low swell that had somehow hidden them on the flank of the Comanches. A sudden gabble ran along Scar's line, and his right bunched upon itself in a confused effort to regroup.

And now the Tonkawas did another unpredictable thing that no Comanche could have expected because he never would have done it. On the open slope to the river the Tonkawas pulled up sliding, and dropped from their horses. They turned the animals broadside, rested their firearms across the withers, and opened fire. In enfilade, at four hundred yards, the effect was murderous. Ragged gaps opened in the Comanche right where riderless ponies bolted. Some of the bonneted war chiefs—Hungry Horse, Stiff Leg, Standing Elk, Many Trees —were among the first to go down, as crack shots picked off the marked leaders. A few great buffalo guns slammed, and these killed horses. Scar shouted unheard as his whole right, a third of his force, broke ranks to charge splashing through the river.

The Tonkawas disintegrated at once. Some faded upstream after the horse herd, but scattered shots and war cries could be heard among the lodges as others filtered into the village itself. More gaps opened in Scar's line as small groups turned back to defend the village and the horses.

"I'll be a son-of-a-bitch," Clinton said.

He gave the long yell, and they charged; and Scar, rallying his hundreds, rode hard to meet them. The converging lines were at a hundred feet when Clinton fired. Forty carbines crashed behind him, ripping the Comanche center. The

Rangers shifted their carbines to their rein hands, drew their pistols. Immediately the horses cannoned together.

It was Mart's first mounted close action, and what he saw of it was all hell coming at him, personally. A war pony went down under his horse at the first bone-cracking shock; his horse tripped, but got over the fallen pony with a floundering leap, and Comanches were all around him. Both lines disappeared in a yelling mix, into which Comanches seemed to lace endlessly from all directions. They rode low on the sides of their ponies, stabbing upward with their lances, and once within reach they never missed. If a man side-slipped in the saddle to avoid being gutted, a deep groin thrust lifted him, and dropped him to be trampled. Only chance was to pistol your enemy before his lance could reach you. The gun reached farther than the lance, and hit with a shock that was final; but every shot was a snapshot, and nobody missed twice. You had five bullets, and only five—the hammer being carried on an empty cylinder—to get you through it all.

A horse screamed, close by, through the war whoops and the gun blasting. Beside Mart a Ranger's horse gave a great whistling cough as it stumbled, and another as its knees buckled, then broke its neck as it overended. The shoulder of a riderless pony smashed Mart's knee. Struggling to hold up his staggered horse, he pistol-whipped a lance at his throat; the splintered shaft gashed his neck, but he fired into a painted face. A whipping stirrup somehow caught him on the temple. An unearthly, inhuman sound was cidered out of a Ranger as his knocked-down horse rolled over him, crushing his chest with the saddle horn.

The Comanches became a mass, a horde, seeming to cover the prairie like a buffalo run. Then abruptly he was clear of it, popped out of it like a seed. The battle had broken up into running fights, and he saw that most of the Rangers were ahead of him into the village. One last Comanche overtook him. Mart turned without knowing what warned him, and fired so late that the lance fell across his back, where it balanced weirdly, teetering, before it fell off.

He looked back, letting his horse run free as he reloaded; and now he saw the stroke that finished the battle, and won his respect for the cavalry forever. Greenhill was coming in at the quarter mile, charging like all hell-fire, in so tight a line the horses might have been lashed together. Scar massed his Comanches, and he outnumbered his enemies still; he struck hard, and with all he had. Into the packed war ponies the cavalry smashed head on, in as hard a blow as cavalry ever struck, perhaps. A score of the light war ponies went down under the impact of the solid line, and the rest reeled, floundered backward, and broke. Into the unbalanced wreckage the cavalry plowed close-locked, sabering and trampling.

Most of the village had emptied, but at the far end a great number of Comanche people—squaws, children, and old folks, mostly—ran like wind-driven leaves in a bobbing scatter. The Rangers were riding through to join the Tonkawas in the running fight that could be heard far up the Wild Dog; but they made it their business to stamp out resistance as they went. The dreadful thing was that the fleeing people were armed, and fought as they ran, as dangerous as a torrent of rattlesnakes. Here and there lay the body of an old man, a squaw, or a half-grown boy, who had died rather than let an enemy pass unmolested; and sometimes there was a fallen Ranger. Mart had to go through these people; he had to hunt through them all, and keep on hunting through them, until he found Debbie, or they got him.

A squaw as broad as a horse's rump, with a doll-size papoose on her back, whirled on him at his stirrup. Her trade gun blasted so close that the powder burned his hand, yet somehow she missed him. And now he saw Amos.

He couldn't believe it, at first, and went through a moment of fright in which he thought his own mind had come apart. Amos looked like a dead man riding, his face ash-bloodless, but with a fever-craze burning in his eyes. It seemed a physical impossibility that he should have stayed on a horse to get here, even if some bribed soldier had lifted him into the saddle.

Actually, witnesses swore later, there had been no bribed soldier. Amos had pistol-whipped one guard, and had taken a horse at gunpoint from another . . .

He must have seen Mart, but he swept past with eyes ahead, picking his targets coolly, marking his path with Comanche dead. Mart called his name, but got no response. Mart's blown horse was beginning to wobble, so that Amos pulled away, gaining yards at every jump; and though Mart tried to overtake him, he could not.

Then, ahead of Amos, Mart believed he saw Debbie again. A young squaw, slim and shawl-headed, ran like a deer, dodging among the horses. She might have got away, but she checked, and retraced two steps, to snatch up a dead man's pistol; and in that moment Amos saw her. The whole set of his laboring body changed, and he pointed like a bird dog as he charged his horse upon her. The lithe figure twisted from under the hoofs, and ran between the lodges. Amos whirled his horse at the top of its stride, turning it as it did not know how to turn; it lost footing, almost went down, but he dragged it up by the same strength with which he rode. Its long bounds closed upon the slim runner, and Amos leaned low, his pistol reaching.

Mart yelled, "Amos—no!" He fired wild at Amos' back, missing from a distance at which he never missed. Then, unexpectedly, Amos raised his pistol without firing, and shifted it to his rein hand. He reached down to grab the girl as if to lift her onto his saddle.

The girl turned upon the rider, and Mart saw the broad brown face of a young Comanche woman, who could never possibly have been Debbie. Her teeth showed as she fired upward at Amos, the muzzle of her pistol almost against his jacket. He fell heavily; his body crumpled as it hit, and rolled over once, as shot game rolls, before it lay still.

40

Only a handful of squaws, mostly with small children on their backs, had been taken prisoner. Mart talked to them, in their own tongue and in sign language, until the night grew old, without learning much that seemed of any value. Those who would talk at all admitted having known Debbie Edwards; they called her by a Comanche name meaning "Dry-Grass-Hair." But they said she had run away, or at least disappeared, three nights before—during the night following Mart and Amos' escape.

They supposed, or claimed to suppose, that she had run to the soldiers' camp on the Otter. Or maybe she had tried to follow Bull Shoulders and the Other, for she had gone the same way he himself had taken. Trackers had followed her for some distance in that direction, they said, before losing trace. They didn't know why she had gone. She had taken no pony nor anything else with her. If she hadn't found somebody to help her, they assumed she was dead; they didn't believe she would last long, alone and afoot, upon the prairie. Evidently they didn't think much of Dry-Grass-Hair in the role of an Indian.

"They're lying," Sol Clinton thought. "They've murdered her, is about the size of it."

"I don't think so," Mart said.

"Why?"

"I don't know. Maybe I just can't face up to it. Maybe I've forgot how after all this time."

"Well, then," Clinton humored him, "she must be between here and Camp Radziminski. On the way back we'll throw out a cordon. . . ."

Mart saw no hope in that, either, though he didn't say so, for he had nothing to suggest instead. He slept two hours, and when he awoke in the darkness before dawn he knew what he had to do. He got out of camp unnoticed, and rode northwest in a direction roughly opposite to that in which Camp Radziminski lay.

He had no real reason for doubting Clinton's conclusion that Debbie was dead. Of course, if it was true she was worth sixty horses, Scar might have sent her off to be hidden; but this did not jibe with Scar's bid for victory or destruction in open battle. The squaws' story didn't mean anything, either, even if they had tried to tell the truth, for they couldn't know what it was. The bucks never told them anything. His only excuse, actually, for assuming that Debbie had in truth run away, and perhaps still lived, was that only this assumption left him any course of action.

If she had run away it was on the spur of the moment, without plan, since

456

she had taken nothing with her that would enable her to survive. This suggested that she had found herself under pressure of some sudden and deadly threat—as if she had been accused, for instance, of treachery in connection with his own escape. In such a case she might indeed have started after Mart and Amos, as the squaws claimed. But he had a feeling she wouldn't have gone far that way without recoiling; he didn't believe she would have wanted to come to him. Therefore, she must have wanted only to get away from Comanches; and, knowing them, she would perhaps choose a way, a direction, in which Comanches would be unlikely to follow. . . .

He recalled that the Comanches believed that the mutilated, whether in mind or body, never entered the land beyond the sunset, but wandered forever in an emptiness "between the winds." They seemed to place this emptiness to the northwest, in a general way; as if long-forgotten disasters or defeats in some ancient time had made this direction which Debbie, thinking like an Indian, might choose if she was trying to leave the world of the living behind her. He had it all figured out—or thought he did.

This way took him into a land of high barrens, without much game, grass, or water. About a million square miles of broken, empty country lay ahead of him, without trails, and he headed into the heart of the worst of it. "I went where no Comanche would go," he explained it a long time after. He thought by that time that he had really worked it out in this way, but he had not. All he actually had to go on was one more vagueness put together out of information unnoticed or forgotten, such as sometimes adds itself up to a hunch.

He drifted northwest almost aimlessly, letting his weariness, and sometimes his horse, follow lines of least resistance—which was what a fugitive, traveling blindly and afoot, would almost inevitably have done. After a few miles the country itself began to make the decisions. The terrain could be counted on to herd and funnel the fugitive as she tired.

Toward the end of the first day, he saw vultures circling, no more than specks in the sky over a range of hills many hours ahead. He picked up the pace of his pony, pushing as hard as he dared, while he watched them circling lower, their numbers increasing. They were still far off as night closed down, but in the first daylight he saw them again, and rode toward them. There were more of them now, and their circles were lower; but he was certain they were a little way farther on than they had been when first seen. What they were watching still moved, then, however slowly; or at least was still alive, for they had not yet landed. He loped his stumbling pony, willing to kill it now, and go on afoot, if only he could come to the end before daylight failed him.

Early in the afternoon he found her moccasin tracks, wavering pitifully across a sand patch for a little way, and he put the horse full out, its lungs laboring. The vultures were settling low, and though they were of little danger to a living thing, he could wait no longer for his answer.

And so he found her. She lay in a place of rocks and dust; the wind had swept her tracks away, and sifted the dust over her, making her nearly invisible. He overrode, passing within a few yards, and would have lost her forever without the vultures. He had always hated those carrion birds of gruesome prophecy, but he never hated them again. It was Mart who picked—or blundered into—

the right quarter of the compass; but it was the vultures that found her with their hundred-mile eyes, and unwillingly guided him to her by their far-seen circles in the sky.

She was asleep, rather than unconscious, but the sleep was one of total exhaustion. He knew she would never have wakened from it of herself. Even so, there was a moment in which her eyes stared, and saw him with terror; she made a feeble effort to get up, as to escape him, but could not. She dropped into lethargy after that, unresisting as he worked over her. He gave her water first, slowly, in dribbles that ran down her chin from her parched lips. She went into a prolonged chill, during which he wrapped her in all his blankets, chafed her feet, and built a fire near them. Finally he stewed up shredded jerky, scraped the fibers to make a pulp, and fed it to her by slow spoonfuls. It was not true she smelled like a Comanche, any more than Mart, who had lived the same kind of life that she had.

When she was able to talk to him, the story of her runaway came out very slowly and in pieces, at first; then less haltingly, as she found he understood her better than she had expected. He kept questioning her as gently as he could, feeling he had to know what dreadful thing had frightened her, or what they had done to her. It no longer seemed unnatural to talk to her in Comanche.

They hadn't done anything to her. It wasn't that. It was the medicine buckle —the ornament, like a gold ribbon tied in a bow, that Scar always wore, and that had given him his change of name. She had believed Amos lied about its having belonged to Mart Pauley's mother. But the words that he had said were written on the back stayed in her mind. Ethan to Judith . . . The words were there or they weren't. If they were there, then Amos' whole story was true, and Scar had taken the medicine buckle from Mart's mother as she died under his knife.

That night she couldn't sleep; and when she had lain awake a long time she knew that somehow she was going to have to see the medicine buckle's back. Scar had been in council most of the night, but he slept at last. Mart had to imagine for himself, from her halting phrases, most of what had happened then. The slanting green eyes in the dark-tanned face were not cat's eyes as she told him, nor Indian's eyes, but the eyes of a small girl.

She had crawled out from between the squaws, where she always slept. With two twigs she picked a live coal out of the embers of the fire. Carrying this, she crept to the deep pile of buffalo robes that was Scar's bed. The chief lay sprawled on his back. His chest was bare, and the medicine buckle gleamed upon it in the light of the single ember. Horribly afraid, she got trembling fingers upon the bit of gold, and turned it over.

How had she been able to do that? It was a question he came back to more than once without entirely understanding her answer. She said that Mart himself had made her do it; he had forced her by his medicine. That was the part he didn't get. Long ago, in another world, he had been her dearest brother; he must have known that once. The truth was somewhere in that, if he could have got hold of it. Perhaps he should have known by this time that what the Indians call medicine is three-fourths the compelling ghosts of early associations, long forgotten. . . .

She had to lean close over the Comanche, so close that his breath was upon her face, before she could see the writing on the back of the medicine buckle. And then—she couldn't read it. Once, for a while, she had tried to teach Comanche children the white man's writing; but that was long ago, and now she herself had forgotten. But Amos had told her what the words were; so that presently the words seemed to fit the scratches on the gold: "Ethan to Judith . . ." Actually, the Rangers were able to tell Mart later, Amos had lied. The inscription said, "Made in England."

Then, as she drew back, she saw Scar's terrible eyes, wide open and upon her face, only inches away. For an instant she was unable to move. Then the coal dropped upon Scar's naked chest, and he sprang up with a snarl, grabbing for her.

After that she ran; in the direction Mart and Amos had gone, at first, as the squaws had said—but this was chance. She didn't know where she was going. Then, when they almost caught her, she had doubled back, like any hunted creature. Not in any chosen direction, but blindly, running away from everything, seeking space and emptiness. No thought of the limbo "between the winds" had occurred to her.

"But you caught me. I don't know how. I was better off with them. There, where I was. If only I never looked—behind the buckle—"

Sometime, and perhaps better soon than late, he would have to tell her what had happened to Scar's village after she left it. But not now.

"Now I have no place," Debbie said. "No place to go, ever. I want to die now."

"I'm taking you back. Can't you understand that?"

"Back? Back where?"

"Home, Debbie—to our own people!"

"I have no people. They are dead. I have no place—"

"There's the ranch. It belongs to you now. Don't you want to—"

"It is empty. Nobody is there."

"I'll be there, Debbie."

She lifted her head to stare at him—wildly, he thought. He was frightened by what he took to be a light of madness in her eyes, before she lowered them. He said, "You used to like the ranch. Don't you remember it?"

She was perfectly still.

He said desperately, "Have you forgotten? Don't you remember anything about when you were a little girl, at all?"

Tears squeezed from her shut eyes, and she began to shiver again, hard, in the racking shake they called the ague. He had no doubt she was taking one of the dangerous fevers; perhaps pneumonia, or if the chill was from weakness alone, he feared that the most. The open prairie had ways to bite down hard and sure on any warm-blooded thing when its strength failed. Panic touched him as he realized he could lose her yet.

He knew only one more way to bring warmth to her, and that was to give her his own. He lay close beside her, and wrapped the blankets around them both, covering their heads, so that even his breath would warm her. Held tight against him she seemed terribly thin, as if worked to the very bone; he wondered despairingly if there was enough of her left ever to be warmed again. But the chill moderated as his body heat reached her; her breathing steadied, and finally became regular.

He thought she was asleep, until she spoke, a whisper against his chest. "I remember," she said in a strangely mixed tongue of Indian-English. "I remember it all. But you the most. I remember how hard I loved you." She held onto him with what strength she had left; but she seemed all right, he thought, as she went to sleep.

WARHORSE

by

John Cunningham

JOHN CUNNINGHAM, though born in a small western Montana town, spent his early years in New York City, moved to and from New Jersey, California, and Virginia, and decided in college to become a writer because, "It was the only thing I was good at."

Being a writer, of course, afforded Mr. Cunningham the opportunity to pursue a mix of other careers: store-keeping on a Montana dude ranch for "rich juvenile delinquents," clearing firebreaks for a California chicken farmer for 50¢ a day, picking grapes, cultivating vineyards, and, on the high-tech side, installing a primitive electronic bookkeeping system in a San Francisco bank, reporting for the *New York Journal of Commerce*, and learning how to "make something out of nothing" for J. Walter Thompson. 1941 found Cunningham in Panama tracing Army shipments (most of which had been sunk by submarines), and he spent the next three years in the army, much of it in the South Pacific, the Philippines, and Japan.

After his army stint, he wrote stories for pulp magazines, choosing to write about the West because as he says, "I like the western scene, horses, and guns." His first story for *Collier's*, "Tin Star," later became the basis for the landmark movie *High Noon*. He went on to write for the *Saturday Evening Post, Cosmopolitan*, and *Redbook* among others. When the short-story market disappeared, Mr. Cunningham tried his hand at novels, of which *Warhorse* is his best known.

Of the western, Mr. Cunningham says, "While the western field is limited in many ways, it will last forever. The western (still) has a lot of unrealized dramatic potential to work on."

PART ONE

1

The Plains 80 Miles South of Ogalalla, Nebraska, at Frenchman's Creek July 8, 1882

The brim of Tucker's hat cut out the sky, a black shield against the immense, pale-blue desolation up above. He sat his horse on the best rise he could find, one knee hooked around the apple. The dry west wind passed his face gently, taking the sweat out of him without pain, cracking his lips and drying out his nose and mouth.

Northward, the pale-gold plains curved, and he could see the remote dust of Long's herd, already twenty miles north of him, a long day's push.

Southward the immense plain died far away into haze. The three thousand head of cattle which he drove, in trust, flowed in a long line down the fold between the low rises, moving fast toward the smell of water. He had been pushing them for a week, making twenty miles a day on this flat country, and the drag strung out half a mile. Those that got sore feet, he let drop behind for somebody else to pick up and bring in; and if he knocked a few pounds off the beef, it didn't matter—they were going on the northern range, not to Chicago. He was four days late now.

Everywhere the plain lay like a great golden ocean, just barely moving up and down, like the breast of a sleeper. It was not flat, there was no real roll, but it moved with a vast motion, obedient to the enormous surges of the wind.

"You got enough men," Tucker said to another rider, sitting before him, a little down the long slope toward the creek. There were five riders behind the fellow with the black mustache. "How come you need so much company, if you're so goddam legal?"

The mustache had a paper in his hands, the long legal kind with a blue back.

"I want you to read it," the mustache said. "I don't want to make any trouble. You just read it."

"What did you say your name was again?" Tucker asked politely.

"Spence," the mustache said. There was a wide, good-looking mouth under the mustache. It grinned, showing a good many wide, good-looking teeth, all natural in color. "Will Spence."

"And who did you say you were working for? This feller that won the suit?"

"Tommy Dickson. San Antonio."

467

"You don't mean Tommy Dickson the gambler, do you? The Little House feller?"

"That's right," Spence said, smiling patiently. It was a nice smile, guaranteed to work every time, just like an Edison light. You barged in, slammed the door, pulled the string, and there everything was, bright as day.

"Sure, that's where I seen you," Tucker said. "You were dealing faro at Dickson's old house on Yturri Street. Across from the Bull's Head. And now you want all my cows."

Spence nodded and smiled. "Just read the paper, Tucker." He held it out.

Tucker laughed. "Man, don't you know? I can't read. Now my cattle are coming down to the creek, and I got to be moving down there, just to be on hand. So you'll never mind if I move along, won't you?"

Tucker raised his left hand, lifting the reins, and his horse moved forward.

"Just a minute," Spence said. There was no smile, and his tone was just a little sharp and a little cool.

Tucker stopped his horse and said, "That sounds kind of like an order."

Spence said, "This is a court order from the Twenty-Second District Court and it's signed by Judge George H. Noonan."

"I know George Noonan. Him and I used to hunt ducks in the mud puddles over by the San Pedro Acequia. Noonan wouldn't take old Buford's cows. Now don't bother me no more with your damn legal papers, General Spence. George Noonan must be out of his mind—if what you say is true. Good-by."

Tucker turned his horse downhill again. Two of Spence's riders moved out and crossed his path and stopped, blocking him. Tucker pulled up short.

"You better sit and listen," Spence said. "I'll boil it down. The paper empowers me to seize any and all personal property of Buford Allen to satisfy a judgment of $630,000 rendered against him in a civil suit brought by Thomas Dickson in the Twenty-Second District Court, which includes Bexar County."

"Well, I'll be damned."

"I have a signed authority here making me Dickson's agent."

"Well, bless my old soul. Do tell."

Tucker sat still. Down the long slope, down the valley toward the creek, his three thousand head were coming, flowing like some kind of thick, brownish liquid. The soft rumble of hoofs was remote, but he caught the familiar smell. Black, red, buckskin, brindle, every color in cowdom, they streamed down, walking fast, nodding, bellowing, red-eyed, tired and mean.

Tucker's riders were looking up at him. They all sat quiet, letting the cattle go by, except the point riders.

"I never heard of no such of a thing," Tucker said, looking steadily at his men.

First one of the swing pair started up the long rise. Then the others saw him go, and they followed. Tucker sat a little easier in his saddle. The hoofs of the horses made a roll like a drum, and left a trail of dust growing out behind like a fuse smoke running along the ground.

Spence's boys heard the drumming, and the two blocking Tucker moved back, getting out from between. They all wore their customary arms, a Colt apiece and saddle guns, Winchesters or Ballards or Sharps. They sat in a line, now, facing the riders coming up the slope. The two riders down on the herd point were watching, but they didn't leave their posts.

Tucker said, "It's only eighty miles to Ogalalla. Mr. Allen will be there to meet us. Why don't you go on up there and argue with him?"

"I aim to sell these cattle as soon as we hit Ogalalla," Spence said.

Tucker laughed.

Spence's face lost its easy, pleasant look.

Tucker's four riders came up. Their horses fidgeted around, and the men looked from Spence to Tucker, quick and edgy, plainly primed, like a bunch of deer terriers smelling blood on a sack.

"Now, look here," Spence said, easing himself suddenly, "there's no call for hard feelings. Can any of you boys read?" he asked Tucker's riders. "He won't believe what I say about this paper."

One of them laughed.

"None of my boys can read," Tucker said. "They're all too dumb. Like me."

Spence bit nothing once, his jaw muscles twitching.

"Boys," Tucker said calmly to his men, "you better go on back down there and get that herd across. You tell Pete just bull 'em through, the water's fine; I tried it already. No sand, only about a twenty-foot swim. Don't lose no time, now."

His men glanced once at Spence's party, and turned and loped off back down the hill.

"You heard that court order," Spence said. His beautiful smile was gone. The string was broken.

"I heard something," Tucker said. He pulled a sack of bull out of his shirt pocket and began to shake a cigarette together.

"That was a court order," Spence said. He leaned forward in his saddle and his voice rose in proportion. "Don't you know what that means?"

"The Twenty-Second District Court takes in Bexar County, and Gomal and Atacosa, too, as far as that goes. But it don't take in the ass-end of Nebraska, which is where we are now. Ain't you slightly out of your jurisdiction?"

"That order is legal and I can attach Buford Allen's personal property anywhere I can find it."

"You mean, anywhere you're big enough. You got any carpetbagger blood in you, Mr. Spence? You are the most Republican-acting Texan I ever saw in my life."

Spence turned pink.

Tucker folded his cigarette together—it was too dry to roll—and hung it on his lip.

"Where's the next herd?" Spence asked. "Buford Allen started five herds. I've got attachments on all of them."

Tucker sighed.

"He started them out a day apart last spring," Spence said. "They ought still to be a day apart. Long told me that much."

"Long is a damn son of a bitch, and I'm going to tell him so in Ogalalla." Tucker fished a match out of his pocket.

"Are you going to force me to take this herd away from you?" Spence asked.

Tucker wiped the match on his pants and held the flare to his cigarette. He puffed and the blue smoke vanished, sucked out of his mouth by the wind. "The old man always did have his neck out," Tucker said. "But I never figured his friends would bankrupt him. But then," he said, inhaling slowly, "this Dickson who's bringing suit ain't a Texan, is he? I believe," he said, calmly recollecting, "the son of a bitch is an Englishman. Ain't he?"

He looked directly at Spence, mildly inquiring. He sucked on the cigarette. It had gone out. So he sucked on the paper.

Down below, the point men were in the water, bullying the old lead ox into the creek, keeping him head on. The others followed, with the swing men shoving the body of the herd up behind the point, crowding them bawling into the water.

They got halfway in and bawled and stalled and stood there protesting as their kindred shoved them deeper, trying to drown them. Then the ones in front gave up and struck out desperately for the far shore, swimming with their eyes bugged and nostrils wide as though the devil had hold of their tails. They only had twenty feet to swim before they stumbled on the bottom again and lunged on out through the shallows. On the far bank they spread up and down the creek, drinking.

Spence's face was set and heavy. "I'm taking this herd over right now," he said. "Don't make any trouble, Tucker. Don't try any shooting. I don't want those cattle scattered from here to Denver. I want you to ride down there and tell your men they are to take my orders from now on."

Tucker fished out another match. He let his hand down calmly to swipe it along the back of his pants, but instead, he dropped the match and pulled his Colt, cocking it as it came up. The rest of them sat there and looked at it.

"I don't want any shooting either," Tucker said, "but if there's going to be any, I'll start it." He smiled at Spence. "Son, you have bit the wrong wolf. I wouldn't give up these cows to the devil himself, much less a half-ass faro dealer and a spare-time pimp out of Yturri Street. You can fight me if you want, but you'll never get these cows. Because my boys will never let you get 'em gathered. Every time you get 'em bunched, we bust 'em hell, west, and crossways."

Spence looked at the solid old Colt, and then up at Tucker's quiet eyes, and then at the cattle, once more stringing out away from the creek on the north side.

"There's a sheriff in Ogalalla," Spence said. "He'll recognize this." He folded his paper. He turned to his men. "Joe, you and Taffy ride on down the trail and keep an eye on Allen's other outfits. They got a B A Bar trail brand like these. Don't let them turn off to Denver or some place. You other two stay and follow this outfit into Ogalalla."

Spence turned and smiled at Tucker, with his same old charm. "I'll be seeing you."

The whole bunch rode off.

Tucker sighed. His dead cigarette came apart in the wind and the tobacco dribbled out. He tore the paper off his lip and picked up his reins.

Down below, as he loped up along the herd, he smiled and called to his boys, "Twenty miles today, twenty miles! Keep 'em moving, boys, keep 'em moving!"

They grinned back through the dust.

"Eighty miles more, boys, eighty miles more!" he called to the swing, and they grinned back, licking their lips.

"Is it true?" one of the point men asked as Tucker came up and shambled down to a walk. "Is the old man broke?"

"He's been broke a thousand times," Tucker said.

"Let's leave that bastard," his top man said. "That fellow with the mustache. Let's point 'em to Cheyenne and sell 'em there."

"Ogalalla," Tucker said, rolling himself another cigarette. "I got my orders in San Antonio, and if Buford wants to change 'em, he can send a rider. Ogalalla it is, and screw the Englishman. If they want to fight, we'll give it to them there."

Cheyenne, Wyoming
July 8, 1882

Old man Buford Allen stood on the porch of the Elk Horn Hotel, combing his silky beard with one finger, scheming how to stall the tall gentleman at his right elbow. Mike Allen watched his father, and then Morton, and then went and leaned his elbows on the fancy railing and waited, looking down into Carey Avenue. The old man had to raise $300,000 by July 15, or lose an option on a ranch. That was all. Why did the old man care so hard? There were a thousand other ranches. But he had his fangs in this one, and he wouldn't let go, for some reason. Mike shrugged.

"Now, it ain't me," Morton said. "It's mostly my partners that's getting impatient for delivery, Mr. Allen."

The old man chuckled comfortably and single-fingered his beard. "The cows'll be along, they'll be right along. Tucker—my foreman—knows his business. Just a flood somewhere—held them up."

"Well, now," Morton said, "that wouldn't be my business, would it? The cause, and all that. My only concern is delivery. They're eight days overdue. I've had my men in camp north of town a week, sir, waiting."

"No need to worry, sir," Buford said, carefully maintaining his expression of calm cheer, of pleasant benignity. "Chicago's still going up. The longer you hold, the longer you wait, the more you'll gain. Take my advice, sir, don't hold these cows for fattening—ship 'em now. Send your men back to work and ship my beef out of Ogalalla, when they come. Let somebody else overstock the range. My advice is, clean up now."

He breathed deeply, with enough vigor to keep it out of the sigh class, carefully denoting *joie de vivre.* "Beautiful weather, beautiful weather," he said, smelling the wind. There was plenty on it besides the prairie grass and wild flowers. Nothing fazed the old boy, Mike thought, listening. He could draw a breath like that in the middle of the K.C. stockyards and sigh, "Beautiful, beautiful," and you'd believe it.

Across the street an old Blackfoot brave in a seamrotten cutaway threw up in the gutter. Down at the corner of 17th Avenue men were stringing wire for the new electric lights.

"My difficulty," Morton said smoothly, his voice as soft as she-duck's down, "is simple. Our contract—" He paused.

"I appreciate, I appreciate," Buford said with quiet good humor. "But I'll wager they're making twenty miles a day, Mr. Morton. By God, sir, I *am* sorry. If you want to fix a penalty, I'll take your figure, sir. I'll give you a draft for whatever you think is fair." The old man smiled, and the Wyoming wind lifted a bit of his white beard and let it fall again. It was a beautiful beard, soft and clean as soap and comb could make it.

Mike sat down and listened absently. Windy old Buford, him and his drafts. The only draft Buford could draw was out of a stein on hotel credit. But Buford was depending on Morton's gentlemanly instincts with all that talk about paying off, and it worked.

Morton's lean face turned ruddy. "Well, now, well, now, that's mighty square of you, but—"

"Of course," Buford said, "some day she'll keep on going up—but she hit $9.32 last May, and I'll bet a dollar that was the peak. I know well enough you could buy cattle any time—I'll let you go."

Morton turned his lean face slowly toward Buford, and his hard mouth curved in a hard smile. "I can't buy cattle in the open market at $55 a head, and you know it. There's nothing down at Ogalalla coming in much less than $60, and you know it. The only thing is, if she slips in Chicago, why, I might get cut down to a fifteen-percent profit before I can unload. You see . . ."

Mike Allen let the voices mumble away. The honey and treacle of his father's old Southern chuckle and the quiet, lipless misering of skinny-butt Morton, trying to hedge a penny this way and that, were just the same old two sides of the same old racket. The honey dripped on, promising delivery, promising this, that, promising good weather, promising higher prices, anything to stall Morton. Morton was cash, quick.

Cash in a hurry, Mike thought. $300,000 to collect in a week, before the old man lost his option. The old man had Morton on the ropes now, spinning daydreams.

But why? What was it about that crummy little ranch up in Montana that Buford wanted? He'd killed himself all spring, starting those five herds on the trail, to make that option—and Montana was full of ranches. But it was Montrose's he wanted.

What was it about Montrose and that ranch that made the old man so secretive? And every time the old man talked about the General, he got mean. The whole thing smelled of revenge—but on the face of it, it was just a simple business deal.

In a minute Buford would buy Morton a deep drink in the hotel bar, and Morton would wander back out to his cow camps north of town, lost in a fog of avarice, and spend the night in a mist of cow-pie smoke, dreaming about ten dollars he had dropped once in a game of Boston, and how he was going to get it back at last.

As far back as Mike could remember, there had been the dripping honey of his old man's voice, the fog and smoke of daydreams, and the glitter of the future. After a few years it made you sick to your stomach.

But the funny thing was, the old man was sincere. He actually believed it all himself—sometimes. Back of all the hot air there was a shrewd mind. There had to be, because old Buford was usually in the money. A man couldn't be a fool and make as much money as Buford. Of course, the fool in Buford that lost the money was easy to see. It was the other person behind the beard, the planner, that Mike in twenty-four years had not yet met.

Mike looked at Morton unobtrusively. A middle-sized wheel in the Cheyenne Club, tall, thin, a little stooped like a lot of tall, thin cowmen. Morton looked mighty dignified astride a horse, with about four hands trotting behind him, like one of the petty feudal barons Mike had read about in St. Mary's in San Antonio. And all he was, was just another back-country Northerner, up to his butt in debt like all of them, and getting deeper.

"By God, sir, but business is dry!" Buford cried out. *Here comes the drinks,* Mike thought. The idea was to get Morton all wound up tight, and then feed him a few fast ones. That would keep him in the right frame of mind—that is, looped—until he dried out tomorrow. Maybe by then the herd would be in. Maybe all of them would be in. They might all come at once. "Now come on in here and wet your whistle, Mr. Morton." "Wet your whistle" was a phrase old Buford would have gagged on privately, but he used it on Morton because of the homey, palsy touch it gave to his malarkey. It might make Morton feel like a boy again. God knew what would happen then.

"I tell you, sir, they have the best damn toddies in this hotel—"

Mike watched them go. He watched his father's big hand hovering at Morton's black-suited elbow, not touching. The old man had too much tact to touch the other. Mike saw him through—tact sticking out like hairs on a caterpillar, sensitive to every little intonation, every little nuance of expression. Buford could feel the touchiness in Morton from eight feet away—the independence, the pride, the stiffness. You might as well pat a coiled-up rattler.

Buford was wheeling Morton into the lounge with his voice alone. He had Morton trained like a cutting horse, after ten days of stalling. No hands, no reins, just a gentle word or two now and then and Morton would climb into the laundry chute and go down smiling.

A kind of pride rose up in Mike's belly, and then, from some other pole in his nature, the soft hurt of shame came up and matched it. He looked away, out over the rail, into Carey Avenue.

A granger's butcher-knife wagon groaned by, and then a three-span Anheuser-Busch outfit. Then came a little surrey, and in it he saw a girl.

A voice said behind him, "Good morning, Mr. Allen." Mike looked at the girl. The surrey pulled up at the hotel porch steps.

"Good morning, Mr. Allen," the voice said again. It was Holt, the manager. It would be about the bill.

"Wait a minute," Mike said in a soft voice, keeping his attention on the girl. She sat below him, and as he looked, Cheyenne seemed to rise from the earth and float away somewhere, and Mike was alone in silence, looking at her as though he'd never seen a woman before.

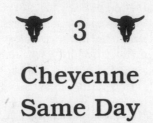

▼ 3 ▼

Cheyenne
Same Day

Sitting on the Elk Horn porch, Mike watched the girl in the surrey.

A thin-legged man with flat-heeled boots, unspurred, got out of the back, tail-on, so that all Mike could see was the black boots, the gray trousers, and the small-waisted black coat, almost military in cut. There was a colored man driving the single bay mare.

The girl sat there, looking like some kind of prisoner.

"I'm sure it won't take more than a few minutes of your time," the voice said, now at his shoulder. It was just another brand of treacle. "About the bill."

Mike closed his mind to the voice. The girl sat quite still, while the man in the gray pants came up the steps, head down. He was stiff, gray, and thin-shanked, but he moved smartly and neatly as he climbed the steps and went into the lobby.

"I beg your pardon," the voice said, a little louder, but with the same cool cheeriness.

"All right," Mike said, looking down at the girl. He knew what was the matter —the girl was hiding from Cheyenne. A man's town, full of men. There were six dozen of them on the hotel porch.

It was not her beauty that touched him, nor her sadness, though she had both. Her mouth was red and wide. Wide, red mouths were supposed to betoken a certain looseness or passion of character, and so most of the good girls in San Antonio spent hours before their plate mirrors practicing primness with properly pinched, though prettily curved, little lips that in later years would look about as beautiful and virtuous as a row of goose gizzards.

It was as though she had been wounded, and did not care, as she sat there in perfect simplicity, thinking of nothing, or perhaps of a wart on the back of the Negro's neck, or maybe remembering a flower at home.

"About the bill," the patient, crisp-apple voice said with a generous hospitality. Mr. Holt's hospitality never wore thin, but the sheriff came knocking nevertheless.

Her hair was dark, and evidently fine, for it made a kind of confusion of shadow rather than a prim cap. On her head there was some kind of scarf, or very light shawl, trying to hold all that gay, dark hair in some order.

The cheek was pale, and its long plane was slightly hollow, although plumpness was all the thing. What Mike wanted to do was reach out and touch the cheek with his finger, to make some gesture, the most delicate, the least offensive, to comfort and protect.

The girl lifted her head slightly and said something, probably to the Negro driver. The driver lifted the two new, light-tan lines and slapped them on the bay mare's rump, and the bay mare took off like a mechanical toy, trotting into the traffic with an action like a cancan girl operating in a Platte River bog.

Mike drew a breath and held it, and half rose from his chair. He watched her go, and one of his hands moved forward. He held the breath until the surrey turned the corner into 17th Avenue.

He turned around. "What about the bill?" he asked the man behind him, trying to suppress a certain sharpness.

A couple of faces turned their way.

Mr. Holt smiled and said softly, "Why not come into my office? It's a little more private."

Mike followed Holt inside. It was a big lobby with an enormous elk head hanging over the dining-room door, directly opposite the main entrance. The lobby was paneled with oak, freighted all the way from Ohio, and the oak columns holding up the ceiling were handsomely carved, by a German firm in Milwaukee, with a highly appropriate motif of oak leaves and acorns. Together with the molded plaster ceiling in cream and gold leaf and the purple-and-gold edgings in stained glass around the main windows, the whole place gave an effect of opulent confusion.

Everywhere there was the soft rumble of men's voices, and to the right, through a carved-oak archway, Mike saw the long, shining mahogany bar fading into the distance toward the billiard tables.

Mr. Holt's office door was made, like the mail-rack at the main desk, of polished cherry.

Mike sat down in a leather chair. "How much is the bill?"

Mr. Holt's smile warmed at his directness. He sat down too, behind his large oaken desk.

"Thirteen hundred and ninety-four dollars."

"It's a good thing it isn't an oyster month," Mike said. "He loves bluepoints and champagne. All his friends do too. How did he manage to run up such a bill without oysters?" Mike looked at the ten-foot ceiling, where plaster cherubs in bas-relief wound ribbons around Donatello fruit baskets.

"I was under the impression your father had considerable resources."

"He has the resources, too, only they're not cash. Not yet. We have five herds on the trail. That's about fifteen thousand head of cattle."

Mr. Holt raised his eyebrows. All of a sudden he seemed to relax. The blood seemed to run a little more freely in the veins on his nose.

Mike watched him.

Mr. Holt thought of something, and seemed to tighten up again.

"Don't worry," Mike said. "I can show you the contracts, if you like. All of them Cheyenne Club. Strictly cash, Mr. Holt. The first herd's overdue now. They may come tomorrow. They may come tonight. Tell me, what's the bar bill? It's only twenty dollars a day for those little rooms we've got, and we've only been here three weeks. That's only four hundred dollars."

Mr. Holt flicked a page over in his mind. "Five hundred and forty-four dollars. A very popular man, your father."

"I hope so."

"You may recall a number of dinners," Mr. Holt said. "Small affairs—modest, really—but still, about $150 a plate. And he never drinks New York wine."

"He's an ex-Confederate officer."

Somebody knocked on the door. One of the sub-clerks sidled in. "Pardon the interruption, Mr. Holt. A telegram. I saw Mr. Allen come in here—"

Mike took it. He pulled a dollar out of his pocket and gave it to the clerk. Mr. Holt's eyes narrowed on the dollar and the clerk backed out fast. The cherry door closed noiselessly, like the sealing of a tomb.

Mike opened the telegram. It read:

Ogalalla July 7 1882

Mr. Buford Allen   Elkhorn Hotel   Cheyenne
Longs herd is in hes making remarks about you ran out of Texas to beat your creditors advise you come down here and protect your name

Streeter

Mike folded the telegram and put it in the breast pocket of his coat. "Good news," he said. "According to this, a friend of ours just got into Ogalalla. His herd left Texas just a day before our first one. That means our first should be about a day south of Ogalalla. That means we should make delivery tomorrow, maybe."

Mr. Holt looked with not much cheer at the corner of the telegram sticking out of Mike's pocket. "I suppose you'll be going down to Ogalalla, then."

"It's only 160 miles east, Mr. Holt."

"Ah, yes." Mr. Holt looked glum. His two rather tired twinkling eyes watched his cigar go up in smoke.

"I regret our baggage isn't worth more," Mike said. "I'd be glad to leave it till we get back."

"Why don't you assign me one of your contracts as collateral?"

Mike's eyes smiled, but from a distance. "At $55 a head, 3,000 cattle are worth about $165,000. I guess you're joking."

Mr. Holt looked out the plate-glass window. The border of purple-and-yellow glass, leaded around the edges, cast a faintly gruesome gleam across one hand, lying inert on the desk.

He drew a deep breath. "No hard feelings. But I ought to enter a claim at the justice court this very day."

"Fine. You'll get a judgment, and when we can, we'll pay it. The trouble is, you'll crack our credit in half. Cheyenne Club cattlemen don't like to deal with bankrupts. The mere rumor is enough to ruin my old man." Mike looked at Holt for a moment. "You don't seem to understand how we do business. In Texas, and anywhere on the trail, we take each other's word. We have to. Things move too fast. They always have, and there never have been any courts. If a man breaks his word, Mr. Holt, he's through. For good."

Mr. Holt smiled. "I learned the hotel business in New York. I'll never get used to Wyoming. The way you people trust each other."

"The thing is, back in New York you could sue my old man and it wouldn't mean much. Out here, it would ruin him, because it would mean he had broken his word." Mike sat forward just a little. "That's why a man will kill somebody for calling him a liar, Mr. Holt. Because if he lets it stick, he's ruined. You understand now what I mean when I give you my word I'll pay you my father's bill, if he doesn't?"

Holt looked at the black pupils of Mike's eyes, in the dark-brown irises. It was like looking in an open window. "All right," Holt smiled without a twinkle. He looked like an aging bouncer after a hard night in a new saloon. He stuck out a hand, and Mike shook it.

"Just a minute," Mr. Holt said as Mike turned toward the cherry door. Holt stooped and pulled open a drawer in his roll-top desk. He turned back and held out a small, flat cigar box. "My compliments to your father," he said, his twinkle coming back. "A charming gentleman."

Mike took the box, saying nothing, and, disturbing the cherry door as little as possible, edged out.

He walked slowly over to the big plate-glass window and looked down into Carey Avenue, past the hairy ears and big hats, past the ornate railing. She was gone, really gone, Mike thought. He might have dreamed her. Maybe she had never been there at all.

He turned and walked toward the stairs. In any case, there was another woman in Texas, who had been very real for eight long years.

He forgot the face in the surrey, deliberately.

San Antonio, Texas
The Little House
July 8, 1882—4:30 P.M.

The doors of the Little House were open, but hardly anybody was there yet. The dealers loafed in the bar, practicing with various decks of cards of their own brand, and Maybelle, the cashier, who ordinarily sat like a large, buxom bird in her golden cage, smiling sweetly at the suckers, now sat in the ladies' bar with two other ladies, her handsome, pinchable knees spraddled far apart under her luminous yellow silk skirt, her shoes off under the table, and her full upper lip hiding coyly under a handsome white mustache of lager foam.

The other two ladies had large, dark, sad eyes. They looked upon the world of the Little House like lonely children, lost in dreams.

Their names were Eurydice and Amanda. However, they were called Bouncy and Fotts by their friends.

"Listen, Maybelle, for God's sake, can't you lend me anything at all?" This from the Poor Boy, also at the round table. "I only owe Dickson a thousand, and I can't raise it anywhere at all." It was hardly more than a loud whisper. He was so sick.

"Poor boy," Maybelle said. "Why don't you get out of town?"

"What's the use? He'd find me, wouldn't he?"

Maybelle looked with large blue eyes at the poor boy. He was a sweet lad named Hugh, no more than eighteen. His last name, which few people knew, was Buss. He had come down from St. Louis, where his father ran a small leather-skiving plant, to buy cattle hides and he was afraid to go home with neither the hides nor the $1700 he had come with.

"When you got to have it, Hughie?" Maybelle asked. There was a quality about her blue eyes which grew on people. They hardly ever changed. Men died in pools of blood, men lost thousands, men shot off guns at other men, men wept at the dice tables—the blue eyes never changed.

"In half an hour," Hughie said. He looked about a little wildly.

Maybelle shook her head slowly. "Poor boy." She thought, *He should never, never have left his mother.*

Fotts said nothing. Bouncy said nothing. They looked at Hugh with large, dark, sad eyes.

"Not even five dollars?" Maybelle said. "If you gave him five dollars he'd feel better. Tommy would never get mean if he knew you really tried to pay off."

Hughie shook his head slowly. "I lost my last five bucks in the Revolving Light, an hour ago. I've heard—uh—things about Mr. Dickson and—well, welshers. Only I'm not a welsher, Maybelle. I'm truly trying. I'm honestly trying. But is it true? Is it true, the things they say?"

"Of course not, Hughie," Maybelle said. "Those are just lies. Poor boy. Tommy wouldn't hurt a fly." There was a fly in the small puddle of beer on the table. Maybelle put a finger gently on the fly's back and pressed.

"Dear, dear," she said, giggling and wiping her finger delicately on the seat of her pants where it wouldn't show in the cage. "Dear me."

"Dear me what?" somebody said.

They all turned toward the entrance of the ladies' parlor.

"Why, Tommy, darling," Maybelle said, blowing him a kiss with her clean forefinger. "Sweetheart, come in and make us happy. We're all so bored."

Bouncy and Fotts lifted their upper lips slightly. Their teeth showed dully in the dim light, and their eyes shrank timidly.

"Hello, girls," Tommy said, sauntering in swinging his cane. "Not including you, of course, Hughie. What's my boy doing in the ladies' parlor?" He sat down on one of the bent-wire chairs. "Paul!" he shouted through the arched doorway. "Beer! Degen's!"

He sat, smiling, neat as a pin, in light-gray clothes, with a light-gray bowler on his head. There was a diamond in his tie, and another on his hand. He was as clean and cool as the north star, and indeed the whole place reflected Tommy Dickson's coolness, with its gray walls and oyster trim, its white shutters letting in cool, dim light, and the carpeting muffling all hard sounds.

Paul scuttled in. Tommy looked at the girls, and then at Hughie. His long, thin face, so clean and finely boned, was full of pleasant friendliness. "What a lovely party," he said, picking up his beer and smelling it. He put it down again. He spoke with a faint English accent.

"Nice to see you girls out," he said to Fotts. Fotts shrank and smiled at the same time.

"It's their afternoon off," Maybelle said. "Ain't it, girls?"

"Of course it is," Tommy said pleasantly. "My girls know the rules. Don't say 'ain't,' Maybelle. And please don't be sharp. There is a certain innate sharpness in you that sometimes escapes. Like Joanne, it alarms me."

"What's innate?" Maybelle said, swallowing beer. "Anything like naked?"

"Inside one," Tommy said. "Abiding, inherent."

"Like bowels," Bouncy said. She burbled interiorly three or four times, and blushed.

"Please," Tommy said. "Try to be delicate, girls. Delicacy pays. Respect, docility, humble willingness to please. That's your cue. Think of the young ones as your sons. Establish a personal relationship."

"Mr. Dickson," Hughie said, trying to look like somebody's son. There was a peculiar mixture of rank fear and utter adoration in his young face.

"Yes, Hughie?" Dickson said in a kindly voice.

"I tried like everything," Hughie said. "I tried all over town. The bank—"

"You lost your last five in the Revolving Light this afternoon," Dickson said. "You might at least have lost it in here. And I wouldn't go to Colonel Berry for money. Bankers never, never lend money to gamblers who lose. And it doesn't pay, Hughie, it really doesn't pay, to talk about our affairs with people like Colonel Berry. I wish you hadn't."

Hughie looked down, red. "Well, I'm sorry. But honest, Mr. Dickson, I'll get a job. I'll pay you back. Honest. A thousand dollars isn't much; I'll pay it back in a year. Honest."

Dickson looked at him down his long, thin nose. The bridge of Dickson's nose was unusually high, and the aloof, cool pleasantness of Dickson's gray eyes, together with the arch of that nose, had refreshed many a girl's illusions. He was obviously a gentleman, very refined; *he* never sweated.

"You see, Hughie," he said, "it isn't the money. It's the principle of the thing."

He waited. Hughie looked awed.

"You see, Hughie, so many people would take advantage of me, if I were simply to let you go. I wouldn't miss a thousand dollars, Hughie. A man named Buford Allen, for instance, owes me $300,000. I can't afford to have people think they can get away without paying me off on time. As Colonel Berry says, time is of the essence in the matter of negotiable instruments."

"Then what shall I do, sir?" Hughie asked in a kind of desperate, bedraggled squeak.

"We'll find a way," Dickson said, "to make everything right." He tapped the floor with his cane. "Come along, Hughie. Let's go for a walk. I have a couple of matters to attend to, and then we'll go home and think things over—at my house. You've never met my mother, have you? You'll like her."

Two tears came to Hughie's eyes. He stood up, fumbling for his hat on the wall, and knocked it to the floor.

"Well, ta-ta, girls," Tommy said, smiling cheerily and swinging his polished straight cane. "Enjoy yourself, Amanda—Eurydice. What charming names. So classic." They looked up with wooden faces and wooden smiles.

"Ta-ta, Maybelle," Tommy Dickson said.

Maybelle was looking at the fly, squashed in the beer. Her face was remote.

"Maybelle, dear," Tommy said, "you look a perfect bag when you sulk. Brighten up, my girl. Freshen up. That's the girl." He tapped twice on the floor with his cane, sharply, and Maybelle looked up, startled. She looked at his stiff, lean face, and quickly smiled.

"Sure, Tommy. You bet," she said in a quiet little voice. "You said it, Tommy."

She stood up timidly.

Tommy turned, whirling his cane once, and sauntered out the white archway. "Come along, Hughie."

Hughie followed, eyes hopeful and vacant.

"Maybelle," Bouncy said in a whisper, looking all around.

Maybelle looked up slowly.

"Is it true, what Dickson does?"

"I don't know," Maybelle said heavily. "I don't know nothing about his business affairs."

"You sleep with him," Fotts said simply.

"I don't know nothing about it!" Maybelle suddenly yelled, standing up. "Goddamit, so I sleep with him, you think I can read his goddam mind? Don't ask me no questions, you damn dumb tramps! How do I know what he does?" She stood there, her lips shaking.

There was complete silence in the bar, through the arch. After a moment, glasses began to clink again.

"I'm sorry, girls," Maybelle whispered. "I didn't mean what I said. He's such a son of a bitch, is all." She was crying, her lower lip shoving the upper one up toward her nose, squeezing the foam mustache out to the sides. Tears slid into the foam, and she licked it off, weeping.

"That's all right," Fotts said. "We're tramps," she sighed resignedly. She stood up. "Come along, Eurydice." She started sedately for the side door.

"You'll come back next Thursday, won't you, girls?" Maybelle asked, going after them. "I don't know what I'd do without your little visits."

Fotts turned. She said, soberly, close to Maybelle, "Listen, kid, you better get a hold of yourself. You got to keep your head in this business. You remember

Joanne, don't you, that used to come with us? The last time Dickson came around at the hotel collecting, she asked him for her money and he wouldn't give it to her—six months' earnings. She cussed him awful. So he sent her over to the other house across the creek. With all them stinking Mexicans and all them rough bush-beaters from the Brazos. She can't do a thing. If she tries to run, he'll have her throwed in the can for streetwalking, and then he'll bail her out and put her back in the house." Fotts's lips tightened.

"It's bad enough at the hotel, with all them fat German bastards. You watch your tongue, kid, or you'll be right in there with us."

Maybelle's eyes opened up wide. "He couldn't," she whispered. "He couldn't."

"Like hell he couldn't," Fotts said, her eyes as solid as a rock. "He can do anything he darn pleases; he'll find a way. I made four thousand dollars last year. The last time I asked him for it, to go home, he said I should leave it in the bank a while longer. I ain't got a dime, Maybelle. If I had, I'd go back to Tennessee. What can I do? If I was pretty enough to get him in bed once, I'd stab the son of a bitch in the heart." Her eyes gleamed secretly. "So watch yourself, Maybelle." Fotts smiled stiffly, and went out.

Maybelle blinked and stood staring vacantly after their dark, sedate, most sober figures, as they turned back toward the western edge of Irish Flats.

Tommy Dickson and Hughie walked up Yturri past the Bull's Head, east on Commerce Street to the main Plaza, on up Soledad past the 101 to Houston where the mule cars danged along back toward the Alamo Plaza. Everybody knew Tommy Dickson—he walked along nodding and smiling with cool civility.

They turned west on Houston Street, four doors, and went into the little bank. The teller took Tommy's name back, and Tommy waited, talking pleasantly with a bookkeeper.

Colonel Berry sat at his desk in the back, behind his partition, pondering over a few delinquent notes.

"In a minute," he said to the clerk in a low voice. "Give me two minutes." The clerk went out.

He had a love of paper, commercial paper, any kind of paper—Federal engraving paper, bond paper, it all felt good, like some delicate kind of hide. It almost hurt him when the interest payments ran off the bottom of a note and he had to have the teller pin on a new sheet.

He fingered the notes in his hand, slipping them gently between forefinger and thumb. Then his pet fox bit him again. There was nothing sentimental about an ulcer, and suddenly, as the pain started once more, the paper disgusted him. He picked up the glass of bicarbonate of soda at his elbow, drank, and belched. When he put down the glass, his eyes looked a little brighter, and the lines in his face not quite so deep. The fox was satisfied, for a while.

When the teller knocked again, he said, "All right," and stretched his thin, weak legs.

He did not get up when Dickson sauntered in. He smiled, and made no other move. The notes were in his hand like a full house.

"Good afternoon," Dickson said, waving his cane. He saw a chair, spread his coat tails, and sat down, lean and elegant. "I believe you know my young friend, Hugh Buss," he said, waving a hand in Hughie's direction. Hughie stood by the door, his hat in his hand, a strained, sick smile on his face.

"I do," the Colonel said. "Won't you sit down, Mr. Buss," he said wearily.

Mr. Buss sat down, his knees trembling.

"Mr. Buss and I thought we would drop by," Mr. Dickson said elegantly, "to tell you we have found a way out of his difficulties. His visit to you this morning was a bit impulsive."

The Colonel smiled. "Wonderful," he said. He was tired. The soda would last about half an hour. Then the fox would wake up again.

"Also, I thought you might have something for me," Mr. Dickson said. "A few more notes of Allen's somebody might have been holding. Surely everybody knows by now he won't come back."

"They should," the Colonel said pleasantly. "I have certainly made my opinion of him public enough. At least to knock his credit down to where we want it. Personally, I am beginning to wonder if he really did default on your suit."

"What do you mean?" Dickson said coldly.

"I mean, are you sure the deputy who served that summons up in Cheyenne really did see old Allen? Are you sure old Allen really did refuse to answer the summons to your suit? Judge Noonan is inclined to accept statements in evidence at their face value. Frankly, I am not."

Dickson sat forward slowly. "Are you implying that I bribed the deputy not to serve the summons and to swear that he did serve it? So that I could win the judgment by default? If you are—"

The Colonel laughed gently. "Now, now, Tom, don't get excited. All I am saying is that Allen may be quite slick, and yet not wholly dishonest. He may have a genuine intent to repay—in spite of all the hearsay and the, uh, rumors you and I have put about."

"And his default."

"If it was a default. Whatever one can say, Buford is a Texan. It was most unlike him to fail to pick up a challenge. I know him, after all. In any case, I believe his notes are worth more than fifty cents on the dollar."

"Indeed," Dickson said, sitting back and folding his hands on the top of his cane. "Why the buildup?"

The Colonel picked one of the notes out of his full house. He smiled. "Do you want it? A note for four thousand dollars made by Buford to Keppelbauer —the grocer. Six bits on the dollar."

"Speak English, Colonel."

"Seventy-five cents."

"Fifty cents is all I ever paid you."

"The market has changed. Six bits."

"Well, then," Dickson said, standing up, "keep it yourself and collect your own damn money." He turned toward the door. "Come along, Hughie."

"Now wait, now wait," the Colonel said. "Don't rush off, Tom."

Dickson stopped with his hand on the knob. "We had a strict agreement. I'd buy Allen's notes from you at fifty cents on the dollar, if you could pick them up at thirty-five, just to keep my name out of it until I had them all. Damn it, if you want to haggle like a Liverpool huckster, I'll knock you down to fifteen cents. I know how."

Colonel Berry looked a little bitterly at the notes. "Keppelbauer. Ernst Keppelbauer. Wholesale groceries. He sold Allen all his supplies for his trail crews."

Dickson raised his eyebrows and looked down at the paper. "Four thousand. So you paid him—$1400 for this. That's $1400 cash Keppelbauer's got I didn't know about."

"Is Ernst another of your clients?" the Colonel asked.

"Don't concern yourself with gambling debts, Colonel," Dickson said. "They aren't worth discussing." He picked up the note. "You want cash for this? Or you want me to credit your account at the Little House?"

"Cash," the Colonel said, reddening slightly. "Very well," Dickson said, and pulled a wallet out of his beautiful gray coat. "You are a greedy man, Colonel. Here is $2000." He laid the money on the desk. "Now, anybody else?"

"Why are you hounding old Allen?" The Colonel asked.

"My dear sir, he has almost a million dollars worth of cattle on the trail. I would hound anybody with a million dollars, if I thought I could get it—especially when he owes me $300,000 in gambling debts which I can't collect legally. It's very simple: he had legal debts amounting to half a million or so. If I could knock his credit down, I could buy them for half their face value, get a judgment, and collect the full value. That gives me my $300,000, roughly." He looked at the Colonel, smiling. "If you want to know how he managed to run up such a bill with me—all I can say is, I don't know. Buford is a lucky old bastard. He's a fool and a plunger, but he's very lucky. And then, too," he said, tucking the notes into his wallet, "I liked him, once. And then, too, he makes money fast—and I want it."

Dickson turned toward the door again. "Come along, Hughie. Good day to you, Colonel. Let me suggest more champagne, and less baking soda." He opened the door.

"Just a minute," the Colonel said in a different voice, leaning forward. He seemed almost a little shy.

Dickson took one look at him and said to Hughie, "Wait outside, dear boy." With Hughie gone, he shut the door.

"Where is Joanne?" the Colonel asked in a low voice.

Dickson looked blank.

"Joanne," the Colonel said. "You know the one I mean. The little blonde."

"Oh. Joanne. She left town."

The Colonel looked at him sharply. "I don't believe you. I told her last week I would talk to you about setting her up for myself, renting her a little house of her own. Why would she leave town? I was offering her a great deal."

"A very independent girl," Dickson said, somewhat absently. "Hot-tempered. All I know is, she is not at the hotel—she left. I don't know where she is. She simply said she was leaving San Antonio. What's the matter with Bouncy and Fotts and the others?"

"Oh, Bouncy and Fotts, Bouncy and Fotts."

"There are some new ones coming up from New Orleans next week."

A look of careful fear came into the Colonel's eyes and he reached for the soda.

"Farewell, *amigo*," Dickson said, putting on his hat. The Colonel didn't answer. Dickson opened the door and went out.

"The son of a bitch," the Colonel whispered. He sat there staring at his notes, lying on the table. He suddenly took a swipe at the papers and got up. He went to a picture on the wall, which showed about thirty officers in Federal uniform, in front of an old army building. They were all young. The uniforms were of ancient style.

He turned away, his face sick. "Joanne," he said. "Joanne."

He banged a bell with his fist, and one of the tellers ran in.

"Get me a man," the Colonel said, "a Mexican, an intelligent one. All I want him to do is follow somebody and see what he does. Any old brush-hunter will do, any old scout. Bring him quick. And bring me a quart of bourbon. The hell with this medical stuff."

The teller hurried out.

The Colonel's lean, sick face sharpened as he thought. It was evident that Dickson was a liar, for Bouncy had said Joanne had not left town, even though she was too scared to tell the truth in full.

He sat and waited, rattling his dry, papery fingers on the shadowy desk.

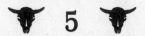 5

Cheyenne
The Old Man's Bedroom
Same Day

Mike walked up the main staircase of the Elk Horn, carefully sinking his feet into the pile with the feeling that he ought to be stealing something. It was like creeping through a twelfth-century forest, hunting a unicorn. He thought again of Sister Margaret Mary, for some reason—remembering her rather weak, whining voice, the insistent, sickly bee in black and white, boring at the ear through those long, deep, sultry afternoons by the little green river in San Antonio.

Of all those sisters, mostly so bright and cheery, she alone had been sickly and whiney. And yet, looking back, she was the only one, except the Mother Superior, whom he could remember.

Down the upper hallway he could see the old man's door standing open, reflecting light from its warm, cream surface into the dark hall. Bantering laughter. Buford was at it again, teasing some ancient chambermaid.

Mike stopped in the dark hall and listened to the bumbling laughter of his father, and the sniveling titters of the woman. Why did he do it? Maybe there was some kind of a devil in Buford, making him act, always act, in front of people. Mike listened to the bumbling, kindly voice. It was a lie.

He could understand Sister Margaret Mary better than he could understand his own father—she was a simple woman, very good, and what if she was cock-eyed about the San Antonio River? If Mike had told her of the bodies they hauled out of that limpid stream, of the blood that ran down the banks, of the vomit, of the stranglings and the drowning of drunks as well as the unending fornications, she would have said, "Well, that is just sin, isn't it? What do you expect?" And she would have gone on talking about the beauties of the river.

He went toward the door. The chambermaid backed out, giggling.

"And how old is the little darling?" Buford was asking. "As young as you? Ah, you'll see, she'll be a beauty too, one of these days."

The woman saw Mike's feet. She took one look at his black, silver eyes, and scuttled away down the hall.

"And how old is the next?" Buford was saying. Mike stood in the door and watched him, combing his beard in front of the bureau, the French cuffs of his beautiful, full-cut shirt turned back up over his hairy forearms. "Three? Four? Sure, I'll bet she's a beauty, too."

"She's eighty-nine if she's a day," Mike said quietly. "The little one will grow up to look like a horse's butt, just like her grandmother."

"Son," Buford said, "don't be bitter. I think what you need is a good woman, like your mother.".

"That reminds me," Mike said, sitting down on the bed. "I want to make a slight touch on you for $100,000."

"What?"

"I'll get to that later. Right now, here's a nice little box of cigars the manager sent you, with his compliments. It seems you are his dream-guest. Or will be, when I pay your bill."

"Son, now, son, you know these things always get taken care of. I talked to Holt once. I thought I had him taken care of."

"Taken care of. What does that mean? Driven crazy? Anyway, he's loony enough to send you some cigars, so smoke one. You can open the box yourself."

Mike lay back on the bed with his hands under his head. "A piece of news. General Montrose is in town. I heard from that slick-headed clerk on the desk."

Buford stopped combing his beard. "Interesting," he said, and thought for a long moment, his black eyes remote and shrewd. "Of course he's down here on account of money. Nobody ever does anything except for money."

"You mean, you don't."

"I mean, take long journeys, my boy. If they're poor, they go a long way for money; or if they're rich, they go a long way just to throw it away. Montrose ain't rich. Ergo, as my teachers used to say, ergo, he's either come down here to sell cattle or borrow money from a friend. If he's selling cattle, it means he really wants to move back East, and he might extend my option. If he's borrow-ing money, it means he's going to stick in the game, and he won't extend my option."

"Ergo—" Mike said, looking at the ceiling.

"Ergo," Buford said, looking rapidly around the marble bureau top for something. "I wish he would damn well stay put. I thought I had him taken care of."

"I don't think you've got anything taken care of, Pop. Today is the eighth of July. You've got to take up that option not later than the fifteenth. You've got to collect on all five herds in the next seven days, and not one has even come in sight."

Buford found his nail file. "Damn it, son, you talk like a man with a summons. If you can't be cheerful, kindly get the goddam hell out. I operate on faith." He delicately removed a grain of sand from beneath his left little fingernail.

"Don't think I won't, as soon as I get some of that cow money. Furthermore, how do you pay off?"

"If you mean Montrose, money paid in hand, or on deposit, up in Warhorse, Montana. They've got a stinking little hick bank I was going to wire it to. Run by one of those backwoods Rothschilds." Buford chuckled. "They're so crafty they catch themselves in their own mouse traps."

"You're cutting too fine on that option. You ought to have Montrose to dinner and kiss his butt for a while. Get a week's extension, anyway."

Buford threw down the nail file. "How can I do this with you nagging me? I don't want to see him. I don't want to talk to the stinking bastard. I saw enough of him in 1864."

Mike got up. "Then why do you want his ranch? Why do you go through all this just to get his ranch? There's thousands of others up there."

"That's a private matter, son." Buford picked up the nail file again.

"Like that locked suitcase?"

"I told you what was in that suitcase. Just dirty laundry."

"Then why do you keep it locked? Have you got some special kind of pedigreed flea you don't want to get crossed with these Northern fleas?"

Buford closed his eyes and sighed wearily. "For the God's sake, son, keep the peace. Some things are private. Do I pry into your affairs?"

Mike kept his mouth shut. The idea of the old man's prying into his affairs, or even showing any interest, was the last thing he would have thought of.

"Damn it," Buford said, digging away, "I suppose I better see him. It would be hell to lose that option by a day, if those damn cows were late. He's such a cold-blooded son of a bitch he wouldn't trust me for part of the money." Under his mustache, his lips twitched. "I could beg him on my knees." He sighed. "I better do it before I have to." He pulled down his white sleeves.

"It's a beautiful place, Mike, that ranch of Montrose's. You ought to see it." The old man smiled. "There's a good big log house, and good big barns, just between the summer and winter range. It's in between two spurs of the Warhorse Mountains up there, and a good creek goes down the valley."

Mike watched him dreaming, his big, rather sad eyes remotely smiling. "You're a Texan. Why would you be going to Montana? You were born in San Antonio."

Buford picked up his emerald cuff links. He folded back his left cuff. "I ain't nothing," he said, the eyes shrunk, wrinkled, and mean. "In the end, a man is just a sack of bones, and all you can hope for is maybe ten years of peace. That's all." He ran the emeralds through the fine broadcloth with big, clever fingers, without looking, unconsciously. "All you got in the end is what you love. That's all is left."

The sun from the window struck one of the emeralds as he moved, and the green light flashed brilliantly across the painted tin ceiling.

"Just tell me one thing, Pop," Mike asked. "Do you want me to bury that suitcase with you?"

Buford frowned. "You find General Montrose and invite him here for cock-tails."

"I haven't got your charm. Maybe you'd better invite him."

"You can kiss his butt as well as I. Damn it, convey my compliments. I'll get the son of a bitch drunk and make him write me a new option." Buford grinned and his white beard bristled out. "I'll show him who won the war. August first will give me time to breathe." He shrugged into his coat and picked up his silver comb again.

"I will on one condition," Mike said.

"Imagine that." Buford let the comb fall through his beard.

"Out of this haul you're going to make, I want a hundred thousand dollars so I can go home and marry Nancy Berry."

Buford held the comb in mid-stroke. "Quit dreaming," he said in a voice totally devoid of treacle. "Every cent of this cow money goes into Montrose's ranch. Miss Nancy Berry can marry you for yourself."

Mike pulled out the telegram and looked at it. "Every cent? What about Terman and the others in San Antonio? The ones you owe for the herds. And haven't you any gambling debts any more? What about the Little House? What about that bastard Dickson you were so thick with?"

"For God's sake, don't pin me down! All I meant was, there ain't no money for Nancy Berry." He rapped the comb lightly on the marble top of the bureau. "Why the hell should there be? Her old man damn near owns a bankful of it."

"You're a disgusting, profane old man."

Buford laughed. "Speak up son, I can't hear you."

"I said, you're a lovable old codger."

Buford stopped laughing and looked at himself in the mirror.

"I don't think Nancy Berry will marry me for myself," Mike said. "I mean, only myself. There's plenty of people just as good-looking as I am, in San Antonio, and there's a pack of them out at the Fort that's got uniforms besides."

Buford ran his fingers down through his beard. "All that gold braid must scratch like hell in bed."

"You're a disgusting, evil-minded old codger."

"What you all ought to do is go down to the bathhouse on the Island and let Nancy Berry take her pick by weight. Like cows. What are you trying to do? Buy Nancy Berry?"

"Nancy is just like most other girls. She wants to be taken care of. She's got an eye out for the future, and if she didn't she'd be a damn fool."

"How noble you are—in a cheap way. To your whole philosophy I may say one thing—it stinks." The old man lifted his chin and smoothed his neck hairs.

"Damn it, will you listen to what I say?"

"Don't shout so loud. This is a respectable hotel." Buford picked up the comb again and began parting his beard in the middle.

"All I'm trying to say is I need some of the cow money. I don't give a damn what you do with the rest, or if you pay Terman or not. Let 'em hang you, for all I care. Well, I don't mean that. But I need some of the money. What the hell can I do without money? All I know is riding and shooting. A fat lot you can learn in San Antonio."

"Then why didn't you go to the University of Virginia, like I said? They'd have taught you to drink like a gentleman, if nothing else. God knows I never learned."

Mike sat and kept his mouth shut. Buford was cutting his beard out to the sides in long sweeps. It never tangled, never caught in the comb. It looked, in this light, like white silk, just slightly touched with blue. Sometimes it looked a little yellow, like ivory.

"Don't you remember why I didn't go?" Mike asked.

"All I remember is your balky disposition. And your desire for a matched set of Remington revolvers. That was in 1875, I believe. Two years after the panic, and all you could think of for your birthday was a matched set of Remington revolvers. Cattle were worthless that year. We drove them north for the exercise."

"I hate to recall anyone of your dignity to reality. In 1875 you bought the steamboat. You had given up cattle. Remember the steamboat?"

Buford stopped sweeping his beard to the sides.

"You didn't have any money, you said. You bought the steamboat and lost your operating capital to that fellow from St. Louis who was supposed to bilk the passengers at monte. Remember that? He was supposed to split the percentage with you. But he didn't split what he took off you on the way down at Baton Rouge. Remember that? What I want now is a hundred thousand dollars to start my own damn cow business. With that, I can talk Nancy Berry into marrying me, and be a respectable young man in San Antonio society."

The unhappy look in Buford's eyes suddenly became rocklike, and then a kind of mask of bemused benignity descended over his face.

"How about it?" Mike asked.

"Son," Buford said.

"Don't say it," Mike interrupted. "Start out some other way. Every time you call me 'son' in that tone of voice, I come out screwed."

Buford jerked his neck up. "Goddamn it, don't cut me off like that."

Mike looked into the mirror, into the two hard, black, fierce eyes.

"All right," Mike said softly to the eyes. "I won't cut you off. Just give me my due and I'll clear out."

"Your due," Buford said, the eyes impenetrably black as cannon bores. "You've lived well with me. You've had plenty of money working with me. You've had your due."

"Like with the steamboat," Mike said.

Buford winced and his eyes dodged. His large fingers delicately tapped the marble bureau top. "What will all this get you?"

Mike slid to the edge of the bed and sat up straight. "I want a clean start of my own. You've got fifteen thousand head of cattle coming. You'll gross damn near nine hundred thousand dollars."

Suddenly the starch went out of Buford's back. He melted. His eyes went down. He opened a white palm toward Mike, and let it fall.

"You're right, son. I know you're right. Forgive me for not thinking about you more." He looked at Mike.

"I owe you plenty, Mike. I get mixed up. I know it. I get mixed up in these big schemes. Mike, don't you know why I keep trying to make a real killing? So I can quit. What I want is to give you a start, and to make a secure home for your mother and me. That's all. I forget sometimes, son, but it ain't because you aren't in my mind—it's just because I get so wrapped up in trying to do what I'm trying to do. Like this summer. Mike, listen—if there's money enough when we're all balanced off, I'll give it to you."

He saw the question of doubt in his son's eyes, and said, "Mike, I can't promise much hope. I can't lie to you now. I've strung you along in the past, but I can't now, because things are coming to a showdown with me. You know that, don't you?"

"No," Mike said quietly. "I didn't know that."

"Well, it's true." Buford was talking quietly, the lines in his face just normal for once, not blanded out with his second-rate poker face, nor engraved by phony drama. He looked at the Belgian carpet. "This is my last big chance, son. There's too many people in San Antonio got their hooks out for me. Too many people know me. I've fooled away too much of my credit. That damn gambling."

He looked away, beyond the wall, with a bitter half-smile. "After a while they wise up. You can't fool them forever."

He came back to his son, the black eyes familiar, intent, and frank. "Not that I ever tried to cheat anybody, Mike. You know that. It all came of getting too many obligations, trying to beat the son-of-a-bitching game."

Mike said, "That's what you're still trying to do. This summer."

Buford nodded. "Yes, I know. But this time I *can* beat it. This time it's breaking right."

Mike sighed. "You want me to play along with you? Suppose you lose it all again?"

Buford shook his head doggedly. "I can't lose. I haven't touched a card since March."

"Dad, that's a bunch of crap. You can lose. I don't know how. But you can lose it all. It isn't only cards. It's everything you do—it's all just one big damn game of monte."

Buford shook his head, his white beard wagging. "No. I can't lose this time."

Mike saw through him all at once. The old man wouldn't face it. He was shutting his eyes to something, and instinctively Mike knew that somewhere in the old man's figuring there was a wrong turn.

Mike said, "You owe about five hundred and twenty-five thousand for those herds. That's due the shippers."

Buford nodded. "That's right. That will leave me just about four hundred thousand. I can buy Montrose's ranch for three hundred thousand—if I can make the goddam option, that is." He turned suddenly away.

"That leaves me a hundred thousand as working capital. In other words, if you take any, I'm broke. How the hell can I work Montrose's ranch without capital? The damn banks eat you alive.

"Except once." He smiled suddenly. "Just once, I took a bank. Me and my troop, in 1862, on a raid up in Ohio. We hit them before they could run with the money, and we cleaned them out, every damn Yankee cent they had, even the nickels and dimes. I wish you had been with me in the war, boy. We would have been good, Mike.

"Nobody argued about money in the army, Mike. The hell with money. I had the best damned time I ever had in my life in the army, Mike, fighting. And I never chopped a man. I never put a stone to my saber in the whole four years. I never had to." He grinned. "I just whapped the bastards on the head or on the arm, and broke them. But they went home whole—mostly." He looked gloomily at the floor. "I never tried to kill none of those Yankee bastards. They were just a poor, ignorant lot of factory hands that didn't know what they were doing."

He looked up, his black eyes quiet. "It's money is the curse of the world, son. I keep trying to get it. A man's got to have it. How else can a man live? Why ain't there some country near by where we could ride down and take the son-of-a-bitching stuff away from them with a pistol? Like Mexico. Only it's against the law. By God, the law makes a man live like a mule in a field.

"All I do, all I've done for twenty years is scheme after money, the dirtiest, lowest, meanest stuff in the world. And scrabbling for it is the dirtiest, lowest, meanest thing a man can do. A man ought to live by his sword. Why ain't there some army where a man could fight forever? A man ought to live by his sword, and not scheme. A man ought to fight, he should live by his guns, and not be reduced to a goddam peddler, scratching and scritching in the dirt."

He suddenly turned away and stood with his hands on the marble slab with his head bowed. "This modern world is no place for a man, son. It's a goddam store-keeping world, son, and it's a son of a bitch. Don't you ever think it ain't. The one thing I want to do before I leave is to give it the goddamdest screwing it ever got."

He went over and sat wearily on the bed. "So there you are," he said. "I'll be lucky if I get out of this with my skin—much less Nancy Berry."

Mike looked at his father, sitting humped over on the bed. Where his coat stretched tight under the arms, there were small rolls of fat. There he sat, aging, dejected, and as Mike looked at the pulled seam, at the worn evidence of the old man's jovial indulgences, at the modest fat which would be rotted away not too long hence, at the bones which would be helpless, which would lie mute, he understood a little of his mother's long patience.

Buford pulled out a handkerchief and wiped his face. He cleared his throat and spat on the floor. "Well, damn it," he said, "go along and see Montrose."

"I'm sorry to have to bring this up now," Mike said soberly, pulling the telegram out of his pocket. "I just want to tell you, now, that I'll stick with you. We'll get hold of your ranch some way."

He threw the telegram on the bed.

San Antonio
Dickson's House—Same Day

After they left Colonel Berry's bank, Dickson and Hughie walked on down Houston Street and crossed the river. They turned north on St. Mary's Street and on up away from the crowds of cowmen, hunters, and soldiers from the Fort which boiled in and out of the places on the Plaza around the Cathedral.

The evening set in, cool and quiet in the tree shadows, with the noise becoming more and more remote south toward the plazas. They could almost hear the river, half a block away, running parallel to them on the west. Dickson slowed, and turned in at a walk. His house was simple and dignified, set back from the street and partly screened by trees.

Dickson swung the door open into a dark hall, and Hughie looked all around. It was dusk outside, gentle and luminous, and there was the smell of night jasmine already coming in through the doorway. Before him, down a long hall, parquet shone in the dull light from a distant French door, and beyond that, trees, toward the river.

A tall Negro came down the hall, carrying a three-branched silver candelabrum, the three orange-yellow flames, flowing backward, smoking. He was very tall and thin, his dark face old and sad, and he wore a plain black suit with a white shirt and a black string tie, like a country preacher.

"Get the boat ready, Harris," Dickson said. "I want Mr. Buss to meet my mother, and then perhaps we'll go for a little row on the river. Where is she?"

The Negro bowed his head slightly, as in prayer, and whispered, "The terrace." He bowed a little more and said, a little louder, "Mr. Keppelbauer is here, sir. In the front parlor." He was a West Indies man, and he had a clear, Anglicized accent.

Dickson smiled in the dusk. "Take him some sherry. Have you got anything cold for Mr. Buss? Hughie, you go with Harris here, and have a bite to eat. I am positive you had no lunch. Did you, now?" He smiled and gave Hughie a pat on the shoulder.

Hughie felt like crying. It was like being at home again. He followed Harris down the long, cool hall through the dusk.

Dickson opened the white door to the front parlor, gently clicking the shining brass latch. He went in. A man was sitting in shadow by the big bay window, an empty glass in his hand.

"Ah," Dickson said, shutting the door. "I see Harris has already brought the sherry." He looked out at the hibiscus growing beside the window, almost, now, without color. "Well, Keppelbauer, what good news have you got for me?"

The other stood up, "None, I am afraid," he said, smiling weakly.

"No money at all?" Dickson asked, surprised. He filled Keppelbauer's glass again. Keppelbauer was a staunchly paunched young man with full chin whiskers, placid of eye.

"I have to have something to run the business, Mr. Dickson."

Dickson eyed him through the dusk. "Surely, in a business the size of yours, there must be some profit. I could take a percentage."

Keppelbauer shrugged. "Bad debts. For instance, Buford Allen owed me $4,000."

"Why don't you sue?"

"What can I collect?"

"His hide," Dickson said, quietly and coldly. "Maybe I could take his hide on your account."

"Or mine?" Keppelbauer tried to smile. He set down his empty glass on a little table, with great care.

"I give you until August first. That is over three weeks. You owe me only $4,000. By the way, I heard you were in the Bull last night."

Keppelbauer drew up his chest and took a deep breath. "Is nothing my business?" The dim gray light hid most of his face, all but a dimple in his cheek, which came and went as his mouth worked.

Dickson pulled the note he had bought from Berry out of his pocket and held it in front of the other's nose. "You could have discounted this with me instead of with Berry. I would have given you better than thirty-five cents on the dollar; you could have reduced your debt. Instead, you had to have cash, to throw away in somebody else's house. I give you until the thirty-first of July, exactly at midnight. I advise you to sell your business."

Keppelbauer's fist opened and spread. "I can't sell my business. I don't dare try. If my connections knew the state it's in, they wouldn't give me credit. Nobody knows it but you. I have borrowed all I can, out of town."

Dickson turned toward the door. "Help yourself to the sherry, Mr. Keppelbauer. Perhaps you can let yourself out—Harris will be busy, I'm afraid. Remember, July thirty-first, midnight."

"Sherry," Keppelbauer said bitterly. "What do I want with your sherry?"

"My dear fellow, suit yourself. I merely offer you ordinary hospitality."

"And tomorrow you will take my hide, as you say."

"Tomorrow is tomorrow, my dear man. Everything in its proper place, in proper proportion. As you say, tomorrow I may take your hide. Tonight you may drink my sherry." He closed the door gently as he went out.

Moving quietly, Dickson went on down the long hall toward the French door at the end. He passed Hughie, eating in a small dining room.

He went out through the French door at the end, onto a terrace of flagstone. At the edge of the terrace a long, smooth lawn began, running down between rows of palm and oleander to a frame of trees at the river edge.

The last light of dusk floated like mist in the air, turning lavender. He could smell the night jasmine from the front, gentle at this distance, and there were two large tubs of heliotrope near the door behind him.

"And how is everything?" a voice said gently from the shadows near the heliotrope.

She was old, full of wrinkles, her sharp black eyes hidden in dark pouches, but she was smiling.

"Well enough, Mother," Dickson said.

He walked slowly back and forth on the terrace, scraping his cane here and there on the flagging. "I had to bring another one home."

"Oh," she said. "Well, if it's necessary, that's all there is to it. There's nothing else to do. It's simply one of the more disgusting aspects of this whole business." She sucked her lower lip. "But no aristocrat ever minded one commoner more or less."

"Aristocrats," he said heavily. "Aristocrats among the bananas. It's all a dream. Why did we ever start it?"

"Everything's a dream, my dear Tommy. If you line up ten corpses, stark-naked, how are you to tell which one is a king and which one is a baker? The only difference between one man and another is life and death—which one is left standing after the fight, which one is dead. You know that."

He stood in silence, looking down the long vista to the river, against the moon, and she sat watching her only child.

She had been a personal maid to the wife of an extremely wealthy landowner in the south of England, at the time of her first and only pregnancy. First and only not because of an otherwise speckless career, but simply because it was the only time she had been pregnant by a millionaire, and the thing had possibilities, so she let it run along for once. She and her son had been very happy for fifteen years, living on the old man's estate at Lamont. Unfortunately, he had died and the legitimate heirs (a wretched clutter of Manchester people involved somehow with yarn) had thrown the poor mother and son out without a penny. If only the old man's passions had been remotely approached by his foresight, all would have been well. But the impulsiveness which gave Thomas his life would hardly have been consistent with the prudence necessary to support it, in anyone. Nevertheless, they had had fifteen very happy years under that great roof, before the old man died. Twice she had been thrown out of that house— once by the mistress, when Thomas was born (the mistress had thought that her personal maid was pregnant by the butler, or perhaps even one of the footmen, until she saw how her husband carried on over the baby). The poor old woman had never been able to bear the old man even a daughter, and this was the whole spring of her hatred, that a mere personal maid should succeed in gestating a male heir—quite as though fertility had something to do with rank. The old mistress had even, after exhausting the resources of the Church of England, taken to local witchcraft, but to no avail. It was the recollection of money spent on witches (they were quite expensive) that enraged the old lady as much as anything else, and if England had not turned so disgustingly liberal in the last century, she would have thrown her maid not so much to the dogs as directly into the kennel. However, Liverpool was almost enough.

Much to everybody's joy, the old lady had died; and the old man, relieved of her morality and vituperation, had brought his little mistress and his beloved son back from the gutters of Liverpool (the old woman had intercepted all the money he had sent them) and they had lived in great happiness and simplicity, until Thomas was seventeen. What to do with a seventeen-year-old bastard? Simple enough—make him legitimate. But the old man had never got around to that.

Therefore, after the second eviction, it had been necessary for Thomas's mother to seduce her first and last true husband—a rather simple civil servant named Dickson. Then something terrible had happened—Dickson had been shipped to Jamaica, where his simplicity could do no harm; and Jamaica had been a nightmare to the mother and the son, a hell wherein England was inverted. There was nothing that she would not have done to escape that place. If she had ever been afraid of hell, she lost the fear with the thought that if the fires of that place of vengeance leaped exceeding high, at least it followed that the relative humidity was exceeding low, and that alone would make it better than Jamaica.

"We've been working only twelve years," she said. "That's not long. I am seventy. When you are seventy, you will be a peer. You have done wonders, Tommy dear. Simply wonders. How many other men have made three million dollars in twelve years?"

"Three million dollars and an English warrant."

"Never mind the warrant. With sufficient money you can turn all that into a signal service to the crown. After all, how would you ever have got a start, if you hadn't killed a man? And what better place could there have been to kill a man than in Jamaica? Nobody cares what happens in Jamaica, except Jamaicans."

The moon lighted her kindly, beaming old face. "Do you remember, when you were a tiny boy, how I used to carry you down into the Liverpool market? How many cabbages I have begged—or not quite begged."

She sucked her lip quietly, thinking.

"Your Aunt Cassie wrote that Lamont is up for sale again. Too remote for modern people. Nobody ever keeps it long."

"That's good," he said. "Let it sit a while. A house like that ought to be deserted. Everything is so damned improved in England nowadays—they even clip the box in some places. Can you imagine? Do you remember the box along the front terrace? Like clouds, and yet at the same time, like marble, so ponderous, and yet with such delicate texture."

"It's come down, too. Sixty thousand pounds was the last. No interest shown, either. How soon can we go back to England, Tommy?"

"Four million is the goal."

"Need it be quite so much?"

"One must have a goal. One must stick to it. Anyway, in another year, Lamont will be cheaper. People aren't interested in the old estates."

Somewhere a night bird called. He smiled. "You know how I remember it best? In the fall, with the trees all bare, and only the ivy green. Then it was sad, and all our country settled down, locking up tight against the winter—the streams, the ground, the trees. And do you remember how the horse's hoofs used to sound on that ground? By God! That was a world. We'd be so stiff with cold we could barely creak out of the saddles, and our feet would almost break, touching the ground—and we would come bustling in from the horses to the fire, and toddies all would be there. I can smell it, I can smell it now, horse sweat, toddies, fire." He sat silent, his cane in his hand. His mother said nothing.

"You will be like a queen there, Mother. As you should be. England, England, once again."

In the dark she smiled.

A candle gleamed beyond the door. It opened, and Harris came out, holding a silver candlestick. "The boat is ready, sir. Mr. Buss has finished."

Dickson stood up. "Then tell him to come along. And bring the blanket, Harris."

"A miserable business," the old lady said. "The fools. The worst of it is, the danger."

"No danger," Dickson said. "Nobody's dead without a corpse. The story will be that Hughie Buss just ran away from his debts, and evidently he was afraid to face his father—if the old man ever traces him from St. Louis." He sighed. "Anyway, it can't be helped. If I let one of them welsh and get away with it, they all will. I can't collect in court."

He walked restlessly about in the dark. The new moon gave only the faintest light. "Buford Allen is one I keep thinking about. He's due to collect close to a million. I'll squeeze him till he drips."

"They remind me of flies," the old lady said dreamily, "buzzing around a candle. They are so bestially stupid, the whole situation is so inappropriate, I am always heartily delighted when they burn to death. The fools. People with no brains really should leave cards alone."

The candle reappeared. Harris and Hughie came out, and Harris blew out the candle and set it down on the flags.

"Mother's not here this evening, Hughie," Dickson said in the dark as Hughie blinked at the moon. "Come along, we'll go for a row. It's almost like England here, Hughie. Such a gentle little river. Ever been to England? Come along, Harris, bring that blanket and the shovel."

"Shovel?" Hughie asked. "Are we going to dig something?"

"Mud bars," Dickson said. "Always need a shovel on mud bars."

"Oh," Hughie said, and stumbled off the terrace after Dickson.

Dickson was slashing at the oleanders under the palms with his cane.

"You know," Hughie said in a faint voice, "all of a sudden, I don't think I want to go. I think I'd better go home."

"How's that?" Dickson asked, amused. "It's lovely on the river at night. You'll see. We'll row down past Bowen's Island by the Old Mill crossing, and maybe have a beer at Wolframs. Ever been to Wolfram's Garden? It's a jolly place. Full of jolly Germans."

"But it's so dark," Hughie said, standing alone in the middle of the lawn with Harris silent behind him.

"Dark? Oh, that's rubbish. It isn't dark at Wolfram's. Come along, my boy. We'll talk over a job."

Hughie's head lifted at the idea of a job. He started walking again.

The boat was tied to a small floating pier at the foot of the lawn. The river slid by, almost invisible, making a slight murmur against the bank. Across, willows drooped into the black water, silver in the moon.

Behind them, Colonel Berry's Mexican brushhunter came waddling silently out of the oleander hedge and stood helplessly watching them float away down the stream. He started to follow them down the bank, but the garden shrubbery was too thick. They floated on, out of sight. He found a boat locked to a float at the foot of one of the gardens, and spent fifteen minutes getting it loose.

Harris sculled quietly in the stern. Hugh sat on the middle thwart, and Dickson faced him from the forward seat. They drifted in silence down the river, to a stretch under the willows. All around them lay the town, and they could hear the voices of people out in the cool evening. Ahead of them, the Travis Street bridge loomed up.

Under the bridge, Harris shipped his oar and took hold of a rock in the bridge pier, stopping the boat. A carriage rumbled across, overhead. A group of Mexicans went across, singing.

"What are we doing?" Hughie asked nervously. "What are we waiting for?"

"An interlude of silence," Dickson said, laying his cane across his knees.

"Please," Hughie said, looking at Dickson's pale, thin face. "I want to go on shore."

Dickson twisted the handle of his cane and pulled out a long blade. It shone dully in the light reflected into the gloom of the bridge from the water outside. Somewhere up the river, people were singing an old song.

"Why, what's that?" Hughie asked, amazed.

Dickson put the point of the blade on Hughie's coat over his heart, and shoved, lunging forward.

Hughie looked at him for one second with amazed eyes, and fell forward, dead.

Dickson pulled out the blade, cut it through the river water three times, and then carefully wiped it with his handkerchief. He threw the handkerchief away into the river. Harris threw the blanket over the body.

"A disgusting business," Dickson said. "A miserable business. It's much less fussy than shooting, but it's so beastly personal. You miserable little creature," he said to Hughie's body, "why do you force me into situations like this? Why don't you pay up as you ought? You miserable little fools. Row on down the river, Harris, down below Berg's Mill. You can bury him there, with the others."

7

Cheyenne—Same Night

In the hotel bedroom, Buford picked up the telegram Mike had thrown on the bed.

Long . . . Making remarks about you ran out of Texas to beat your creditors, Buford read. *Advise you come down here and protect your name.*

Buford got to his feet and stood still in the middle of the room, his shoulders slightly raised as though he were afraid of a blow from behind.

"The bastard," Buford whispered.

"Were you?" Mike asked mildly. "Running out?"

"Don't think I haven't dreamed of it," Buford said. "What could Long have heard?"

"He must have heard something on the trail up."

Buford stood there, shoulders up, hands half raised. "Who? Nobody could have passed Long. He drives too fast. Dodge—of course, Dodge. Somebody went up to Dodge on the cars and started the story and Long heard it when he hit Dodge. What son of a bitch left for Dodge after us?"

"Well, for God's sake, how would I know?" Mike said.

"Where's my gun? I'll teach that bastard to play around with my name," Buford said. "What's the world coming to? I'll have to kill the son of a bitch, that's all. I'll have to go down and kill him." He sat down on the bed.

"Why, I haven't killed a man in twenty years, Mike," the old man cried. "Why, the son of a bitch is going to make me kill him in my old age. Damn him, I'll have to stop his mouth, I'll have to make him publicly retract, and if he don't, I'll have to shoot his goddam head off. Do you realize—Do you realize—" His voice died and he sat staring at the carpet.

"What difference does it make what somebody said?" Mike asked quietly. "It's an insult. You can make him take it back. There's no need to get so excited about it."

"They'll be afraid to take my cattle," Buford said dully. "Morton and the rest."

"Why?"

"They'll think maybe there's a lien."

"Don't be silly. There can't be a lien without a judgment. Nobody's suing you. It's just slander, and all Morton cares is if he gets a proper bill of sale. Come on, let's go down to Ogalalla and settle this. If you don't kill him, I will. What will Colonel Berry think?"

Buford stood there hunched. "Get me my hat, son," he said wearily. He was still staring at nothing.

Mike found the old man's big buff hat and handed it to him. Buford took it and stood there, smiling faintly.

"What's the matter with you?" Mike asked sharply.

"I can't kill Long. The trouble is, he's half right."

"Why? You've got the money coming to pay off your shippers. He'll have to eat every damn word of it."

"There's a couple of things you don't know, Mike."

Mike looked at him for a moment, and then sat down on the bed. "All right. Let's have the truth, for once."

"I've got two private herds on the way north, son. Six thousand. I as good as stole them."

Mike asked, "What do you mean, stole them? When you sell them, you can pay off, and have the profit."

Buford said, "I ain't going to sell them. They're my seed herd, Mike. My one chance. I won't sell 'em, Mike." His eyes lost the dull look and settled down stubborn. "You can call me a liar or anything else you want. That herd goes with the ranch. Six thousand head for seed, son."

"Whose are they?"

"Mine."

"I mean, who trusted you to sell them?"

"They're mine, damn it. I got the bill of sale right here." Buford slapped himself on the breast pocket. "I got it, it's legal, they're mine."

"In a pig's eye they're yours. Who trusted you?"

"Well, Terman. I'll pay him back out of earnings. I'll pay him back double."

"Did he agree to that plan?"

"Hell, no, he didn't. But that's what it is." Buford turned away, putting his hat on, and roamed around like some old bear. "Where's that bottle?"

"Just a minute," Mike said. "That's stealing."

Buford whirled around. "So it's stealing. By God, I had to get out of Texas with something besides my lousy skin. Something to put on Montrose's ranch."

"Something you don't own to put on a ranch you don't own, either. By God, how do you do it? Stealing a man's cows to stock your ranch. By God, I bet you'd rob Montrose if he let you do it!"

"Sonny," Buford said, his eyes shining, "you said one hell of a mouthful. I only wish he was as big a fool as Terman; I'd get his goddam ranch for nothing."

They stood there glaring at each other, and Buford began to laugh, a hearty, warm chuckle. "Man, what a life. Let's have a drink. To a good ranch for your mother."

"Don't drag Mother into it!" Mike said. "She had nothing to do with your stealing your lousy cows."

"Well, by God, she'll have the ranch, and she'll eat the cows. We'll get there, all right."

"Over Terman's dead body," Mike said. "I hope you drown in your damn drink. I tell you one thing, Dad, you can ruin yourself if you want to, but not me. My credit's good and I want it to stay good." He took one step toward the old man, and Buford stopped smiling. "We're going down the trail and sell your damn six thousand as soon as we've delivered on our contracts up here. We'll sell them in Dodge, and we'll pay off Terman. You can buy seed cattle in Montana, anywhere, for cash."

"No," Buford said. "I ain't going back to Texas at all. The ones that get paid, get paid by draft."

"Where are those cattle?"

"I won't tell." The old man's eyes smiled. "They're the last thing I own in the world, and they're moving up the trail right now, headed for home. My last home."

"Who's driving those cows?"

"I won't tell." Buford's black eyes twinkled. He suddenly reminded Mike of a mischievous baby.

Mike erupted. "Six thousand head of cattle heading for a ranch that you got on an option that's about to run out. And you call it a home for Mother. Couldn't you spread it any thinner? Where do you want to spend your last years? In a cell? Dad, don't you know when to quit?"

The old man grinned, his beard bristling. "No. Mike, I'm washed up in Texas. I'll never get back down there. But I can start afresh in Montana. And I'm going to. They can hound me to hell, they can seize every damn cow of mine they can find, and they can seize my horses and my damn boots, but they won't get my seed herd, son. It's lost, right this minute. I lost it on purpose, in the Indian Country, and I told Colby—" He stopped.

"So it's Colby driving them."

"All right, it's Colby. But you'll never find them, and nobody else, because Colby's loyal to me, and I'll see the whole six thousand in hell before I give a one up."

He took a step toward Mike, and Mike backed away.

"And you know why?" The white beard jutted out and the black eyes lit up. " 'Cause they're my one chance, to set up as a man in a new country, with your mother in a decent house of her own. And as for Terman, why, screw Terman. I'd rob the goddam United States Treasury for less excuse than this." He laughed. "Where is that bottle?"

He found it in the bathroom and Mike listened to the gurgle. The old man came back with two glasses.

Mike said, "What you're doing is ruining me. You know that. If you run out on Terman, it's my name too. Why, Dad, you could sell those cattle in Dodge and clear a hundred thousand. You could settle down in San Antonio out of debt and live decent in your own town, instead of getting lost in Montana or some other place."

Buford held out one of the glasses. "Are you with me or against me?"

Mike said nothing.

"You can drink with me, and help me bull this thing through, as I will—or I'll do it alone. I'll go to Ogalalla alone, and I'll shoot that son of a bitch Long alone, too."

"Go ahead," Mike said. "I'm through."

Buford said, "You'd better come with me, boy. Like you said, if I'm ruined, you're ruined. You'd better take a long chance and play it out with me."

Mike looked at the glass Buford still held out.

"Go away," he said, "I want to think."

"All right," Buford said, and set down the glasses. "I'm going to the station to find out about trains."

Mike looked at him. The beard was warm, white, almost cream in the light from the window. "Why don't you want to go back to San Antonio? There's something behind all this that you're not telling."

"Some things are private, son."

"You were born there, like me. We both love it. What's the reason for Montana? What's the truth?" He waited.

Buford stood there without expression, his face as impassive as the plaster cherubs in Holt's office.

"You're always getting people to go on faith, you're always selling them a line. Why don't you let me in on the whole damn truth, for once?"

The sun struck a wide band across Buford's eyes. "Sometimes you get into something so deep," he said gently, "the only way out has got to be a little crooked. It wouldn't do any good if you knew the whole truth. Trust me, son. I will straighten it out. I swear it, I give you my word of honor. I will straighten everything out, or get killed trying." He smiled. "It's better for us to stick together. Ain't it?"

He opened the door and went out.

Mike sat alone. The odor of whiskey faded. A fly buzzed in the bathroom. He thought of Nancy Berry, far off by the little green river. Mike had the sensation of things falling away, dropping out of control. He sat with his head in his hands, trying to think.

The trouble was, a man couldn't join the crowd against his father. A man was stuck with what God gave him; you had to go along. And then, there was something about Buford, some unnameable quality, that made you love him, after you had got through hating him.

Sons of cheats had to go to other towns, it was always the way. So if the old man went down, he went down too, as far as San Antonio and Nancy were concerned. On the other hand, if, somehow, he could get the old man clear, and safely tucked away on his dream ranch in Montana, then he would have a clear field with Nancy Berry, and his mother could do as she liked.

The only hitch was this seed herd of the old man's, unpaid for, unallowed for, practically stolen. How had Buford got so desperate? What in the name of God could be driving him so hard? The only thing to do was to sell it, lever the bill of sale out of the old man some way.

Mike stood up, got himself a quick drink out of the bottle, and went down stairs. Buford was in the bar, buying toddies for a few compadres.

The headwaiter saw Mike and came over, smiling beautifully.

"I want a dinner," Mike said, "in one of the private rooms. There will be three. See if you can remember the kind of thing Mr. Allen usually eats, and have that."

"Ah, yes, Mr. Buford Allen I know well."

"That's a major delusion with many of us," Mike said and walked toward the front door, past the bar.

8

Cheyenne
Kuykendahl's–5:00 P.M.

The Negro woman holding the wide oaken door—maid, cook, whatever she was —looked at Mike with a dull, remote hostility.

"Is the General at home?" he asked, standing quietly under her mahogany examination. He handed her his card.

She shut the door in his face.

He looked down at himself. Was there something wrong with his blue lounge suit, or his button shoes? Then he understood. It was his accent. She must be from New Jersey, like the Montroses. He looked up at Kuykendahl's roof. The house was a monstrous English peasant's cottage: long, low, and ranchy-looking, the latest thing in architectural forgery, with a fake thatch roof.

The five-foot oak door swung open again. The old nanny looked at him, and then, with a barely suppressed expression of nausea, got out of his way. She shunted him into a small sitting room and shut the door on him.

He sat in the gloom and waited.

A door opened. He could see the dark figure, in a long gown that whispered, leaning over a table lamp.

A match flared, and he saw her face. It was the same girl he had seen in front of the hotel, and he remembered the old man coming up the steps. That, of course, had been the general.

The girl held the match to the round wick of the lamp and put back the mantle. Her figure had the same quality as her face—the same grave curves, gentleness, and grace. He watched her, entranced, smiling to himself.

She turned and, after a moment, saw him. She said, raising one hand a little, "Oh!"

He stood up slowly and she stood there. "My apologies," he said, trying to look like Lord Nelson. "I was waiting for your father."

"You were?" she asked. "My gracious. How long had you been sitting here in the dark?"

"Three days," he said.

She laughed. It was a nice, plain, warm laugh.

Nancy Berry had a kind of throaty voice, rich and somehow very attractive. Nancy Berry could say things softly, in that unsoft voice, and make them mean twice what anybody else would mean.

"I'll bet you twenty dollars your old nanny never even told the General I was here. She just brought me in here to starve."

"Oh, Herbia." She looked at him. "Who are you?"

501

"Michael Allen." He drew a deep breath. "My father and your father are—not very good friends."

"You want to buy our ranch."

"Yes."

"Well, kindly do so. I am sick of Montana."

Somebody knocked on the door, and then it opened. Herbia came in. She saw the girl and then looked quickly at Mike.

"The Genrul," she said. "He says yes."

Herbia looked at the girl with bitter, outraged eyes. How could she have lowered herself to converse with white trash?

The old man was standing in the main parlor in front of the fireplace, of green Italian marble, most suitable to a peasant hut. The General was warming his thin, tightly trousered behind. He looked at Mike with no expression—just a slight upward contortion of the lips, like a plaster smile. He had a high beak of a nose, like a turtle's, and quiet blue eyes.

"Mr. Michael Allen," the General said. Mike couldn't tell whether there was a trace of irony. It should have been pleasant, the voice, to go with the plaster smile. Maybe it was.

"Yes," Michael said in the silence. "It's a pleasure to meet you, sir," he went on, being careful not to let it sound like much of a pleasure. These old turkeys didn't like warmth; they liked respect. "A remarkable house," Michael said, glancing around briefly with a total lack of interest.

"It isn't mine," the General said. "I have not yet had the honor of meeting your father, sir," he said, "since he arrived in Cheyenne. I have been looking forward to a visit."

It was an art, lying in your teeth like that, Mike thought.

"He expressed the same feeling, sir," Mike said, feeling his way down this pitch dark corridor of spoofery. "He sent me to extend an invitation to dinner—dinner tonight, in fact—with his apologies for the late notice. The fact is, we only knew of your presence here this afternoon, and we have to leave Cheyenne this evening—and so we do hope you can find it possible to accept. Would eight o'clock be too early?"

"Please accept my thanks, young man," the General said, "and tender my regrets to your father. Perhaps some other time. It has been a pleasure, sir."

The General's smile increased, which was a signal to depart.

Herbia cleared her throat meekly.

"He will be very sorry, sir," Mike said. "May I ask you a favor?"

The General's eyes opened a little wider, and a look of innocence or incredulity appeared in them.

"My father was hoping to ask you this later on," Mike said. "As that won't be possible, permit me the liberty of bringing up the subject of business now."

How had the General's eyes become so cold, with all that scientific detachment?

"Certainly," the General said.

Mike stood silent. Nothing would come. The General waited with a face like a dead Indian's. He was used to waiting.

The door opened behind Mike; he heard the faint rustle of satin.

The old man's face softened, and the small, habitual smile actually became a smile.

"Mr. Allen is asking me a favor, Clara," the General said.

"Is that so?" the girl asked in a nice voice. "I thought he was praying."

Mike looked at her. "It's simply this," he said. "My father wants an extension on his option." He looked at the General. "He wants a month. Our cattle are coming along in proper order, and he will be able to make his payments. But he wants a little more margin of time. I simply wanted to ask you—don't give it to him."

"What?" the General asked.

"Don't give him an extension."

"Why not?" the General asked. "The odd thing is, I hadn't the slightest intention of doing so. I have obtained money enough to carry on and I don't have to sell, now. I hope your father does miss his date. The only reason I ever sold him an option in the first place was because he talked such immense sums, and I was—well—never mind! I hope he fails absolutely."

"I hope so too," Mike said. "He wouldn't like Montana." He looked at the girl. "Why don't you?"

"So many suitors—all impossible. They're so pitiful, all either like little boys —or drunk." She picked a piece of candy out of a silver dish on a small table by the fireplace. "They idealize women so. Why? Heaven only knows."

"Clara," the General said.

"It's a free country, Father," she said. "I can speak plainly before Mr. Allen. He's a plain-spoken person himself, aren't you—Michael?" She smiled at him and he had a slight attack of vertigo.

"Frankly, I hope your father *does* make his option. I want to go back to New Jersey. Most of the time in Montana, I sew. I embroider horse cloths for Daddy. Don't I, Daddy? Have a piece of chocolate, Mr.—What did you say your name was?"

"Michael Horsecloth."

"What?" the General asked.

"Give Mr. Allen an extension, Daddy," Clara said.

"I won't," the General said. "He has eight days in which to make his first payment."

"Could you tell me one thing, General?" Mike asked.

"What?"

"Why is it that my father wants your ranch?"

"Well, I will say this much. He is pursuing an illusion. I knew your father well at one time. If you will forgive my saying so, he is a man of illusions. For instance, he always thought the Civil War was a personal issue between the two of us. Believe me," he added, "I am not criticizing him. He was a valiant man."

"And this whole Montana venture is another illusion?"

"He has his. I have mine. The pursuit of illusion is a favorite human occupation. No doubt you have yours." He glanced at his daughter with a look of mild malevolence. "Perhaps that the possession of a mere woman will make you happy." He smiled. "That is a very popular illusion."

"Really," Clara said. "Don't mind Father," she said to Mike. "He is just playing with you."

"Not at all," the General said. "I am most serious. We all live in a fog, Mr. Allen. Those who think they have the clearest sight are the most deluded. Only the ones who admit they are lost are wise."

"Rubbish," Clara said. "He's perfectly happy, Mr. Allen."

"My daughter has the characteristically feminine illusion that saying something is so will make it actually exist."

"You've been talking too much with Lydia Kuykendahl," Clara said. "Mrs. Kuykendahl has the unfortunate gift of making Father feel as though he were wise. Have a piece of chocolate, Mr. Allen—I mean, Mr. Horsecloth."

"I wish I could," Mike said. "But really I must get back."

"Why don't you stay to dinner?" Clara asked.

"Yes," the General said. "Why not stay to dinner? Lydia is out gossiping, and old Kuyk is out gambling somewhere, and we will have a nice, private little philosophical discussion. We will call it a seminar in the Pursuit of Illusion, guaranteed by the Constitution of our beloved country."

"I have to go back. My father has a lot of business."

"Duty," the General said. "The only solution. The surrender of the will to the impositions of somebody even more stupid than oneself. We're having some quail. Do stay."

"I wish I could," Mike said, holding out his hand.

"You know," the General said, taking it, "I had the illusion that I would detest any relative of Buford's. And I find myself inviting you to dinner. How we blunder about in our private little fogs! And there's no cure for it, is there? Come," the General said, "I can tell by your face you'd like to stay—surrender, my boy, surrender! Say something, Clara."

"Surrender," Clara said, smiling at him. She was challenging him in a peculiar way. Mike felt a slight giddiness.

"All right," he said. "I surrender." It was a silly kind of thing to say, and do, like stepping off the roof of a three-story building just to prove you weren't a coward; but there was more to it than that—a kind of flash between them, as though she had summed up all their latent and potential hostilities, the little bothersome male-female conflicts that would confuse the issue, and had thrown them in his face, to have it all out at once. That's when he had stepped off the edge, with that faint feeling—when he gave up instead of stringing it out. He wouldn't have done it with anybody else, least of all Nancy Berry—he wouldn't have dared to. And thinking that, he realized with a shock that he simply did not trust his beloved Nancy.

Clara was different. But behind all that nerve, that monstrous affront to the laws of courtship and flirtation, there was something else. She looked like a queen, but on a closer look, he could detect a small girl dressed up in adult clothing. And then he realized that, of course, the old man and his daughter were both lonely. That was why they liked him.

They lived in the wilds of Montana, and he was quite a change with his clean shave, flashing white teeth, and button shoes, plus Southern accent.

He saw a look pass over her face that was the equivalent of a colorless blush

—she became more lovely, and yet retreated, smiling just a little, turning her face away from him. She was pleased at her victory, but what was more, he had touched her. More appalling yet, she had touched him. He looked at her half-averted face, feeling peculiarly happy.

"He surrenders," the General said, smiling in his pale Indian way. "Herbia, go tell one of the boys in the stable to ride down to the Elk Horn and tell Mr. Allen, Senior, thanks very much but no, thanks. We have kidnaped his son."

"Yassuh. You ain't going."

"Advise Mr. Allen that his son is staying to dinner."

"Yassuh." Herbia was obviously miserable. She slunk out, kicking her heavy petticoats before her.

"Poor Herbia," Clara said. "She's obsessed with the thought that I can't take care of myself."

"The most deluded of us all," the General said, looking at Mike.

If there was something in the Montroses' status of poor relations, in Kuykendahl's monstrous cottage, the servants didn't show it. The light in the dining room was splendid. The pale candles dripped and fluttered in the chandelier, making the girl's face seem to come and go, like an illusion or a dream. It was extremely difficult at times for Mike not to gawk—but he did his best to maintain a facade of pleasant detachment which allowed him to look at her almost as much as he wanted.

"To subsist, one must be rude," the General said, more or less to himself, and drank off his Chablis. "Fill it up," he said to the footman, who was no laggard anyway. "It is a profound mistake, politically speaking, ever to accept a delicate sentiment or a gentle gesture with anything like courtesy. Must be sure to trample on it in the sight of everybody."

"Dear Daddy," Clara said, picking up a bit of quail with her fork. "Mr. Shoestrap will think you are a cynic."

"So he will," the General said, lifting his wine-glass. "I am overdoing it on purpose, my dear. He is obviously too nice for this poor world, and I am trying to tan him in a vicarious spleen, so to speak, before some woman gets the best of him. He looks as though he'd decay rather easily, don't you think, my dear?"

Clara looked at Mike. Mike's head was beginning to have a rather tight, swollen feeling from the wine, as though he were a good deal more than all there.

"I think he's very nice," Clara said objectively.

"How do you think he would stand up in Montana?" the General asked, pushing his dessert aside. "Can you rope a steer, young man?"

"Without any false modesty," Mike said, looking at Clara, "I can say I am an expert."

"Break a horse?"

"Certainly. The very worst."

"Well, take my advice and stop it," the General said. "You can always hire some fool to get his bones broken for you. Why do it yourself? Dear children, will you excuse me?" he asked, rising. "I feel rather giddy, and I think I will go to bed. Such a delightful evening, Mike, with old Kuyk's wine. I furnished the quail, I'll have you know." He wandered out of the room.

"I have to go too," Mike said quietly. "I'm sorry."

"Do you really?" she asked, rising. How did she do it? At one moment, she was sitting there, erect, swayed forward just a little, and the next, she had risen and was standing, looking at him sadly.

"I wish I didn't," Mike said. "I'd much rather stay here."

"Then why don't you?"

"Such a tangle of business."

"Such a busy young man. I hope you'll make lots of money. Will you?"

"I doubt it," he said, smiling. "Mostly, I'm just working for my father."

"Why?" she asked.

He looked at her blankly for a long moment. It was a simple question. In succession he thought of a lot of answers, none of which was the real one. Then he said, "Because he's more or less helpless, really. And I love him. That's all."

She looked back at him. "I should think, if you love him, he must really be a very nice man. In spite of what Father says. Father must be—prejudiced."

Mike shook his head. "No, he isn't a nice man. He's a headache. Sitting here tonight, I wish I could get out of it—his cockeyed life. It's a terrible thing always trying to get the world by the tail. It's a terrible strain."

"Listen to the wind," she said, and he stopped thinking. The wind was coming over the thatch overhead, from the west.

"I wish I could," he said. "Maybe I can—later."

Then, deliberately, she came up and kissed him, for a moment, and then stood back.

He looked at her in astonishment. "Why did you do that?" He began to blush.

"Because I like you—and I may not see you again. Is that too honest for a woman?"

He watched her, beginning to smile, and the blush died. "No," he said.

"A simple answer from an honest man," she said. "Most men are such fools. As soon as they look at a woman, they start acting. In one way or another."

He looked down at her face, calm and lovely, "Just like a General's daughter." The lightness in his head was gone. "I won't forget you," he said.

They stood looking at each other, and suddenly all his plans, those set and stodgy patterns, divided down the middle and he looked beyond them. What was there, really, to keep him from going to Montana and even from getting a job with the General?

Why should he go back to the hotel? Back to Texas? All that was like some cockeyed nightmare, his father's hallucinations and his own brittle little dreams. Who was Nancy Berry? He could barely recall her face; but then, compunction brought the effort. He was committed there, he had told her he was coming back, and she had said that she would wait. It was practically arranged. Honor was a hard, wooden master in a loose world. He sobered down.

He opened the front door and they stood on Kuykendahl's steps.

How little time there was for anything! Here, on these steps, he was allowed two minutes, when a thousand things hammered at him to be solved. What could he do? He stood there helpless.

"Michael," she said, "you seem to be decaying, right in front of me. Please don't try to solve all the problems tonight."

He looked up at her. She was right, of course. He looked at her eyes plainly, openly. Why think anything? A fat lot of good thought did, or words, or any of the other civilities.

"Good night," he said, looking into her eyes. And then the knowledge of it came up in him, all the way to the top of his head—the simple fact that he was beginning to fall in love with her. He kissed her, a little longer than a friend.

It wasn't much of a kiss, but it said a great deal to both of them. Then it was over, and she was standing there again, as she had been before.

"Michael," she said, "please don't say a word. Go away now, Michael. Please go away."

"I—I—"

"Please, not a single word, Michael—you'll say something noble. You'll start acting, like all the others, and I don't want you to. Please go away."

"All right," he said. "Good-by."

"Good-by, good-by," she said, and he turned and walked away down the long path to the street. He looked back once. She was gone.

9

Cheyenne
A Private Dining Room
at the Elk Horn
Same Day—8:00 P.M.

Buford stood in the ornately paneled room, facing one of Kuykendahl's colored people.

"Yassuh," the boy said. "That's what Mr. Allen he's doing. Eating with the General. The General he sends his regrets."

Buford's hand glided into his pants pocket and came out with a five-dollar gold piece. He tossed it smoothly down the length of the damask-covered table and the boy caught it, ducking expertly and gliding from the room.

The headwaiter stood there with his card under his arm looking like a band-master who had just heard that his band had been lost at sea.

"Get out of here," Buford said civilly, not looking at him—looking instead at the four candles on their tall silver sticks in the middle of the table, surrounding the roses. Buford's sensibilities ran along certain obvious, well-established lines. Nothing pleased him as much as red roses, silver candlesticks, and white linen; the picture was standard, inevitable, and unalterable.

"The dinner, sir?" the captain asked, sucking his stomach in, rising slightly on his toes and trying to look menacing.

"Serve it," Buford said, fingering another gold piece in his pocket.

"Here, sir? For one?" It was ludicrous, one old man eating dinner for three in a private dining room. Mr. Allen stood there with his white beard shining genteelly in the candlelight.

"Get the hell out of here," Buford said quietly. "Send me in a bottle of bourbon." He sat down at the table.

"Yes, sir," the captain said, and bowed, and withdrew.

Buford sat eating olives and looking at the wall across the room. The place was like a warm, soft tomb, the ceiling and the paneling dark, gleaming faintly in the light. The candles made no sound, the flames were still as ice.

"Bastard," Buford said, just to hear something.

The door opened. It was another colored boy with the oysters.

"Bring it all in," Buford said quietly. "Then go away somewhere and leave me alone."

"It'll get cold, boss."

"Who cares?" Buford said, skinning the meat off an olive pit. He spat the seed out on the carpet.

"Yassuh," the boy said, his eyes glistening.

They came and went, amiable colored boys of all ages, while Buford looked at nothing. A bottle sat before him. Mr. Holt's pheasants gradually cooled.

What difference does it make? Buford thought, looking about at the waste. He took a stiff drink. Uptown, wherever Mike was, he would be eating with the General and his daughter, enjoying himself, and it was no doubt better. There was no use feeling offended. Why be offended? He hadn't even wanted Montrose to come.

No, but he might have liked seeing young Clara again. A young, immature version of her mother. Or was that fair? Well, in any case, why expect her to be like the other Clara?

He took four big swallows from the bottle and ate two oysters. He sat there looking at nothing, listening to the silence.

Ah, to be young, Buford thought, the whiskey tightening in his head. To be a fool again, to see nothing, to play the fool, to throw it all away. To be young again, and not to know that everything was dust but love. Not the sentimental crap that went with the German valse bands and violins, not the jolly stuff of housewives, but the disease, hardly recognizable by the name, that lived like a slow fouling of the bone, an endless desolation of the heart.

Suppose she weren't dead, after all? Suppose his Clara had not died at all, as he had been told? What they said, that she was lying in the ground up there in Warhorse now, and had been for eleven years, might not be true. It might be just Montrose's lie, to put him off. She might have left Montrose for some reason. She might, she might.

He took another drink. Death was the thing nobody could overcome. That was the end of everything, the unanswerable, senseless eclipse of all one's reasons, of all the arguments and justifications, of the self-excusings, the apologies, the pleadings, the hopings. What had he, Buford, done to her, that could ever equal death? No drunkenness, no shouting, no offensiveness; no boastings, no vain accusings, could have done what death had done to her; all these things he could have undone; all his stupidities, in time, could have been paid for, and he could have got her back, even after she married Montrose. He could have outlived Montrose, but he could not outlive death.

He kept seeing her there, or an image of her, vague and tenuous, sitting across the flowers from him, and he sat with his fists clenched on the edge of the white table, feeling the rage which he had felt at the news of her death rise again in his chest, bottled up and suffocating. He had heard it in a saloon, and he had sat in the saloon and after a while the horrible rage had burst out and he had flung the bottle against the backbar, smashing what he could, as though the mirror were death. And always that preposterous vain rage in his chest, that bursting uncomprehending sense of affront, of indignation and outrage. Death was not in it at all. He had planned very well how to get her back, how to undo all the damage he had done, to show her again his real love for her, beneath all the stupidities. And then she had been taken out by death like a stranger, and all his hope and rage and grief were useless.

You might really be there, he said in his heart, his wordless mind making these words to the shape of her, there across the flowers. *We might be here, old, yes, through with all that stuff of passion. We could have had all these years, if I had not been such a fool.*

She sat there smiling at him—not a delusion, for he knew what he imagined —and the dark room closed in around them, warm, compact, like a comfortable tomb.

But why worry about that now? she said. *Here we are, you and I.*

I never knew, he said, *how much I loved you until I had driven you away. Oh, why was I such a fool, my dear?*

But it doesn't matter, Buford. We're here, now.

If I had known what it would be like, all these years without you—not seeing you, not hearing you, not even knowing where you were—do you think, in my pride, I would have offended you?

She sat there, smiling.

You know I couldn't help it, don't you? That I was born a fool. God forgive my pride. God forgive me for hurting you.

He sat looking at his vision. But it said nothing. It had nothing to say. He kept her there, so delicately turned out in her white dress, as she had been one night when they had all gone down to the Palm Garden and danced, long ago, before the war. She said nothing, and vaguely smiled.

The image of her vanished and he looked at the dark wall, clearly. There was no use in illusions, they were poor stuff, and wore thin. Clara was dead, she had been dead for years. But what did it matter, when everything else had died too? Nearly everything he had ever loved was a corpse: his father, the whole South, and all those towering dreams of his own capabilities, which he had once believed in as though he were God. He himself was nothing but a potential corpse, with barely enough power left to carry out one more coup, and maybe not that.

In the end, one had to be satisfied with what one could get, and if that were no more than a woman's grave, a piece of earth, far off in some God-forgotten corner of the continent, why, then, a man had to be content with that, for even a grave was something real, some relic of what had been, and any solid relic was better than the rubbish of memories and dreams that time and age wore down into a finally unrecognizable litter.

And if, there in Warhorse, there was no more of her than her bones, and those invisible; still, that much was her, it was not nothing, and he could live out the last ten years, or whatever was left, at least possessing that much. How little a man asked, at the very end.

He got up, his bottle in one hand, and the plate of oysters in the other, and left the private dining room with its banquet, rotting in spotless splendor.

Upstairs he got undressed and brushed and combed his beard and washed and smoothed himself until he felt relaxed and comfortable again, and then, in his beautiful billowing nightshirt, he got his little suitcase and climbed into his big, smooth bed, with his bottle on one side and the oysters on the other.

He opened the little locked suitcase and took a large portrait daguerreotype in a heavy silver frame from a little nest of letters, neatly tied in packets.

He sat and looked at it, and then he looked away.

Outside it was very quiet, and he lay there with a moth beating about the lamp mantle, looking at Clara's face with a faint smile; not thinking, hardly remembering, but simply feeling what he had felt for her long before, and which he still felt.

He put down the picture and picked up a letter.

After she had married Montrose, he had not seen her until 1864, when she had been living in the camp attached to the prison. And after the war, he had not seen her again, only knowing that she was in Montana. But he had forgotten all those years of bitterness and sadness; and as he lay now, alone in the hotel room, he remembered only her—her voice, so sweet; her breath, to which he had listened with such delight; her movements; and he lay now with eyes shut, remembering how he had once sat, with eyes closed, listening to her movements, the small rustle of her dress—blind, yet knowing, foreseeing what she would do, what she would say, as though he had some intuitive gift of understanding her; as though his love actually contained her whole soul.

How was it possible that she could have died, and gone from the earth, and that he would never see her again?

It was not possible. Some day, when he was free of all the mortal complications of his life, he would see her again in some fashion.

She had gone to Montana. And in that strange, far northern country, she had lived, and each tree, each mountain, had reflected something of her, and something of her—a radiance perhaps—had remained in the stones where she had passed; and in that country, he could follow where she had gone, and the stones and the trees would tell him that she had been there; and perhaps, there, he would find her in some sense. She was there. That was the last place she had been. If he were to find her again in any sense, it would be there, on Montrose's ranch.

And he could do it. Buford closed and locked the suitcase again. He had a

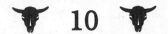

million dollars coming up the trail. He was a cinch to make Montrose's option. And from then on he would have peace and a home—a home where all that mattered to him, the little that was left, was waiting for him now.

10

The Elk Horn Hotel
Buford's Bedroom—10:00 P.M.

An hour later Mike opened the door and looked at his father. Buford was propped up in bed on four massive white pillows.

Buford smiled with only a slight blear. "I'll keep for days," he said hoarsely, speaking with care. He was at the carefully spoken stage, where he made perfect sense but had to run at reduced speed.

"I hope you got the General's message," Mike said.

"Silly old bastard," Buford said, taking a sip out of his bottle. "I knew he wouldn't come. Have an oyster, my boy. You may take one." He shoved the plate at Mike. Some of the ice-water slopped onto the spread. "Call the maid," Buford said.

"Don't be so finicky," Mike said. "Why did you send me up there for nothing, if you knew he wouldn't come?"

"I wanted you to meet the girl. Clara."

"Oh, you know her?"

"Why, of course I know her. I've known her for years. When I was in Montrose's prison, she was just about two years old. Beautiful girl, Mike. I want you to marry her."

"You're drunk."

"What of it? I can still think circles around you and that potty old bastard Montrose." He snickered, snuffling to himself at some private thought. "She liked you, didn't she?"

"Yes. Why not?"

"If I can't make my option on time, my boy, you're going to marry her immediately."

"Sure, sure."

"Bed," Buford said. "Beautiful, wonderful bed. Everything good is done in bed. Kings made. Thrones united. Quarrels settled. Ranches sewed up."

"You're through, Dad. We'd better pack up and go home."

"Shut up," Buford said with sudden cold sobriety. "You get Morton—you remember our long-connected sucker. And McCullough, the second buyer. You start out tonight and go on down on a cattle train. Make 'em let you off where the line hits the South Platte—you know where the Lodgepole Creek joins in. You ride southeast forty miles or so and you hit the trail. You can pick up Tucker. The way I figure, Tucker is about eighty miles south of Ogalalla. You cut his trail before he gets forty miles closer to Ogalalla. That'll keep you out of Keith County. If Dickson's agent—" His words died off till he was mumbling to himself. "Ergo," he burst out again, "he won't have jurisdiction, in any case. Well, you sell Morton his cattle and get his money, and then take McCullough and ride south and sell the second herd. You take it from there."

"Sounds like you heard something new."

The old man waved a hand at the bureau and took another drink. "Another wire from Streeter. The dirty little scut."

Mike picked up the yellow telegram:

Long says you defaulted a suit by Dickson. Dickson's agent met Long on trail and has attachments on all your cattle. In view of this and various complications I herewith tender my resignation as your agent but understanding your financial position and appreciating our past friendship I relinquish all claims to commissions and fees now outstanding. Streeter.

Mike laid the paper on the marble bureau top.

Buford raised the bottle. "No more agent."

"I told you I didn't believe we'd make it." Mike's voice was shaking. "I told you it was too good to be true. Another steamboat."

"Don't disturb my peace of mind. Go get Morton and get started." The old man's speech was beginning to blur.

"What are you going to do? Die in bed?"

"I'm going to Ogalalla to thrash Long and hoodwink the authorities—if I can."

"My God—more fraud? Why didn't you tell me about Dickson's suit? And why in God's name did you default it?"

"He would have won it anyway," the old man said languidly. "I didn't default it, son. I never got the summons. Your mother wired me after the judgment. Deputy claimed I refused the summons. Swore it. I never saw it." He smiled. "Dickson had won by that time—he had all my notes. Just go on and get Morton, boy. We'll get something out of the mess yet. I was just hoping—just hoping I could sell them cattle before Dickson could attach them."

"You haven't got any conscience at all, have you? Nothing bothers you, does it?"

"Nothing," Buford said, closing his large handsome eyes, "except starvation. And defeat."

Mike said nothing.

"Get going, sonny."

"Suppose I said I was through?"

His father looked at him. "Would you?" he asked quietly. "You know if you don't take Morton down there and sell that herd, I'm sunk. I'm too old to ride a hundred miles without stopping. Anyway, Dickson won all that money off me by cheating at cards. I know right now, without being told, how Dickson got all my notes. That's why Long is so sore, because he sold my notes for peanuts to Dickson, and now he sees Dickson is going to collect at par. Damn Long anyway, can't a man be a simple business competitor without stabbing me in the back?"

Sudden fury rose in Buford's face, swelling the veins and turning it red. He half rose in bed. Then, without a word, he sank back and lay breathing a little fast.

"I'll kill that Long. That lousy bastard, selling me down the river to that—"

He stopped himself and lay quiet, staring at nothing. He turned suddenly to Mike. "What does it matter to you, stealing what? We're all a pack of thieves, by God! Dickson most of all. What's thievery among thieves? It's past all accounting. And as for you and your priggy little notions, what would you do if you didn't thieve with me? Do you think there is anything honest to do in the world? What else can you do if you're not a preacher or a priest? Why didn't you become a priest, the way your mother wanted you to? Either that or sell fertilizer." He took a long, hard pull at the bottle.

Mike looked at him. All he noticed was the babble, the froth of words coming out of the old man. He was helpless—holed up in bed with a bottle.

"Or are you with the others?" Buford said. "Are you going to sell me down the river too?"

"Hell, no," Mike said. "I don't suppose I can. I suppose you'll drag me right down with you."

"What do you mean, down?" Buford said. "Where I am is up."

"As long as you didn't steal 'em, I'll sell 'em," Mike said.

The old man smiled. "That's the boy. I knew you wouldn't let me down. *Caveat Emptor!* Troop, charge, ho! I'll go to Ogalalla. Oh, God, God help us all."

Mike shut the door and went to his own room for his guns and his boots. Evidently the time had passed for button shoes.

11

Ogalalla, Nebraska
July 9—4:00 P.M.

In the evening the foremen and the men from the herds which were bedded down south of the river would come into town and get drunk and gamble, and this went on for weeks sometimes until a foreman and his men got paid off, after the herd was brought up and the old man got the cash.

So all summer long the plains south of the little board town between the Platte and the U.P. would be dotted with cattle, herd after herd as far as you could see.

There were flowers in the grass early in the season, and along the river the cowboys would go swimming and wash out their clothes, and when they weren't riding night guard or getting drunk in Ogalalla, or when they were trying to save their money for back home, they would sit around the fires and tell lies and maybe do a little singing, or listening to somebody else sing. And in the daytime they would play mumblety-peg, with its eternal complications and contortions.

The biggest thing about it all was not the sky, or the plains, or the vast herds of cattle, or even the big slow river—it was the wind. The wind came out of the west, a thousand miles high and five thousand miles wide, and it never quit for more than a few hours at a time.

It blew away the blowflies and the deer flies and the horseflies, and sometimes it nearly blew away the horses too. It swept under the barroom door and sent the dust in little whirls, and it sucked the cigar smoke out of a rich man's mouth before he could inhale it, and blew the Bull Durham out of the poor man's cigarette paper before he could roll it. A pretty girl would come out from St. Paul to dance in the dance hall and in a week her lips were all cracked and peeling, dried out like buffalo bones.

Down by the railroad, where the buffalo bones were stacked higher than a man's head, waiting for shipment, the wind sighed in the gray piles, moaning in the honeycombed stacks.

The wind blew Nebraska all over the nation, hell, west, and crossways. A man could spit in the street in Ogalalla on Tuesday, and by Friday it would be in New York.

In the late afternoon, around four, they would hear the U.P. train—the regular passenger, coming down the long grade from Cheyenne, 160 miles away—long before the train would come in sight, the sound carried ahead for miles on the wind.

Gunfire was louder to windward, and a man shouting upwind was hard put. All night long, when the wind was bad, the flapping and banging of loose signs and shutters would keep the drummers awake, and every stranger. Then the men would go in the saloons, and the women in their back parlors, and everything human, hidden away from the wind, would get warmer and more close, and all would stand around drinking and smiling, and voices would boom out louder, as though in triumph at the victory of the human race over the universe. And all the time that they sang and blustered in the saloons, outside the big wind, that started in the entrails of the stars, would reach and boom and play with the roofs and rip off the shingles and rattle and ting and bang the shutters, while out on the plains, in the sod huts, some of the women, to whom the stars had come too close, knelt in the moonlight and bayed like hounds.

Late in the afternoon of July 9, Buford stepped carefully down from the U.P. passenger car, carrying only his small, locked suitcase, and faced the monumental piles of the bones of the dead giants of the plains.

The wind blew his silky beard eastward, and the brim of his hat flopped up. Down the slope from the tracks to the South Platte, the town lay gaunt and rattling, bone-gray clapboard mixed in with new yellow pine.

He felt the old gun stuck in his pants, its long muzzle uncomfortable in his groin, and started across the wide street toward the livery stable.

There were three horses tied outside the big door, and they all had Long's brand. Buford smiled.

"If it ain't my luck," he said, walking in. They had a fourth horse with a neck sling on, being shod.

Four wide, slow smiles. "Hello, Pappy," one tall one said. "Figured you'd be along. The old man's hotter'n hell."

"Screw the old man," Buford said. "Mr. Smith, I want a horse."

"He's waiting for you," a third one said. "He says if you got the goddam guts to come here, he'll kill you."

Buford laughed. "Go down to whatever saloon he's boarding at and tell him I've come down here to beat him like a six-year-old boy. Tell him that. Tell him I'm going to make him cry like a baby. Where is he?"

"The Paradise," the short one said.

The horse in the sling was shaking all over with fear, eyes rolled back. The smith touched a hot shoe to the hoof. Blue smoke boiled up, stinking.

"That's a hell of a way to fit a shoe," Buford said.

"Yeah?" the smith said. "Who are you to come into this town and start telling me what to do?"

"Any damn fool knows better than to burn a shoe on. Any damn fool can take the time to hammer it to a fit. Any damn fool, I guess, but Long's smith."

The smith stood up slowly and looked at Buford.

"Screw you all," Buford said. "You think that old bastard boss of yours can say things about an Allen, and you can sit there grinning like a bunch of crap-eating cats. I'll whip the whole damn cheap outfit of you right into the gutter. Now get going and tell your old woman of a boss to hire himself a bed, because he's going to need one."

The four stood looking at him quietly, and the smith too.

Without a word, the short one went to the door and swung up on one of the three horses, and left.

"I want a horse," Buford said to the smith. "A good heavy horse sixteen hands high. Seventeen. Good and heavy."

"I ain't got such a horse," the smith said. "I ain't got no horse at all."

"You mean to tell me," Buford said, "you can stand there and lie to me, and turn away my trade, just because I bawled you out properly for burning a horse that way? You ought to be ashamed of yourself. You should have been bawled out long ago. Any man with any self-respect would have told you off. That's a cruel, lazy way to fit a shoe, and nobody but a sloppy bum would do it. Now, by God, start running your business like a man and hire me a horse."

The smith stood with his face red. The others stood silent, stiff, their eyes lowered.

"You know I'm right, don't you?" Buford said, looking straight at the smith.

The smith blinked. "Yes," he said, "I know you're right." He turned and looked at the three hands leaning against the wall. They stopped smiling. "If one of you says one goddam word, I'll bust his head with these here tongs." He turned and walked back into the shadows of the big barn.

Buford smiled at the three. "Bums," he said quietly. "Sheep-lovers."

"You better watch yourself, Allen," the tall one said. "We ain't going to take much more."

"Trash," Buford said. "Country trash. Knifers. Back-country knifers. A bunch of skinny, underbred, cold-blooded plain trash. Start something, you trash."

The forge glowed quietly. The wind howled in the rafters. Buford laughed. "That's it," he said. "That's it. My back ain't turned—better wait."

The smith brought back a horse. It was a big, raw mountain of a horse, seventeen hands high, with a head on it like a stump. It came along jazzing around, snorting, head in the air like a wild goose, little red eyes peering down like mice out of a belfry.

"Crazy," the smith said. "But it's what you asked for, and I don't mind if he kills you."

"I notice you got a saddle on him without any help," Buford said. "I guess I can sit on it."

"He don't buck," the smith said. "He's just a damn fool. Last week he went straight through a solid board fence and never even felt it. Shied at a bit of paper. He ain't mean. He's just plain dumb and careless. Crazy."

"That's the kind of horse I like," Buford said. "Now I want to buy a couple of light buggy springs. You got any such?"

"I have. Four bits apiece."

"Bring me two. About a yard long and an inch wide. Light ones."

The smith went back in the barn and came out with a couple of springs. Buford stuck them under his arm and pulled out a twenty-dollar bill. "What's the name of this horse? He looks a lot like Long."

"We call him Old Iron Ass," the smith said. "Have a good time."

Buford neck-reined the jag-boned mountain of a horse away from the barn. He touched him once with his heels and the horse rolled forward into a long, easy lope, ponderous and smooth as water. Buford reined him up and down beside the railroad twice, and then trotted down the slope toward the main street, where the dust was blowing harder than ever.

In Rooney's saloon there was plenty of noise, the stamp of boots and laughter, and a steady roar of conversation. Buford went up the wobbling stairs, tripped on an empty bottle, and went down the long second-story hall to the front of the building. He knocked on No. 47.

"Who is it?" a man's voice complained.

"Buford. Open up, Streeter."

There was a long silence.

Then: "Go away, Buford. You got my wire."

"Open up, Streeter," Buford said.

Bedsprings creaked. Then the door opened, and a short man with a large paunch stood back, holding it.

"Streeter, you are a heartless wretch."

The other blinked, twice, as though thinking this over. He had long gray hair brushed down smoothly, and the impress of his hat made a perfect shelf in it, all the way around. His eyes were dark, and drooped sadly at the outside corners. Still, the general effect was one of resigned dignity.

"I don't accept your goddam resignation," Buford said quietly in a small, nasty voice. "You hurt me, Streeter. You hurt me deeply. It's all right for these cheap bastards like Long to call me a thief, these picayune cattle buyers and scrambling cheats. But for you—for you—"

Streeter looked at him, dark eyes protesting sadly. "I did not call you any-thing, Buford. Why deny the facts? Why—why try to? Everybody knows it, everybody but me. Here I am, your agent, doing business in your name, assum-ing—assuming everything. And all of a sudden it appears you are not only broke but you have a million-dollar lawsuit on top of, of—on top, I say. And they— and they—are calling me a dirty crook—a crook, Buford, a crook." There was genuine grief in the dark eyes. "How could you, how could you? Your own friend. How could you? Lie to the others, Buford—but not, but not to me—not to me."

Buford raised the springs and slammed them against the board wall. Streeter's eyes opened wide.

"For the last damn time, Streeter, I am not lying to anybody! How could you believe it?"

He pulled his two hands down over his face and his beard, dragging them. His face was old and lined, sad and mournful, his big, handsome eyes drooped almost exactly like Streeter's.

"It's my enemies. Long, Dickson. They tried to ruin my credit. I was going to pay every cent. Can I count on you?" Buford asked humbly. "Your word, against my enemies. Say that you'll vouch for me against my enemies. Against this son of a bitch that's been spreading lies."

"Long?"

"Him and the other one too, the fellow that's got the attachments."

"The attachments. Oh, dear. You mean—what?"

"Vouch for me. With the sheriff. Bailey is such a damn gullible fool, he'll believe anything Dickson's man says."

"What? Oh, you mean this attachment fellow will come, and will come to see Bailey?"

"Well, what the hell else? He's got to have the law to enforce it all, doesn't he? If he ain't got the local law, why, screw his attachments."

Streeter's sad eyes twinkled at something in the distance. "Why, how per-fectly true."

"And he got them by a fraud. A lie. I know those damn process servers down in Texas. You can buy them for two dollars a day, they'll swear anything. For two bucks they'll swear they served a summons on George the Third."

Streeter hummed.

Buford said, "Besides, if Dickson gets all those cattle, he's stealing your com-mission. What's three per cent of a million dollars, Streeter, old friend?"

A look of anger lighted Streeter's sad, resigned face. "The dirty thieves," he said with a jaded rancor. "My poor friend—of course, of course, I will vouch for you with Bailey."

Buford smiled, his white beard spreading. His big, handsome eyes were full of light and kindness. "Streeter, I knew you wouldn't let me down, old friend. And I won't let you down either. I have many devices—many plans, Streeter. Always another plan, my friend."

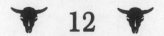

12

Ogalalla
Rooney's Hotel—Same Day
6:00 P.M.

Buford left No. 47 and went down the long, dark hall to the steps.

The wind was still blowing, creaking the rafters overhead, but downstairs it was quiet. Buford paused at the head of the stairs and listened.

There was still talking, below, but it was much softer. He sniffed the fragrance coming up the stair well on the draft—a delicate conflux of Old Bull, sweat, whiskey, and horse manure.

He went down, with a caution that looked much like dignity.

Somebody below called. "He's acoming!" and all the talking died. Buford stood still, halfway down.

Then a long fellow with a fresh, red, scrawny face and tobacco-yellow cavalry mustaches appeared, smiling, at the foot of the steps.

"Bless us all to hell," the tall individual said. "It's Buford. Buford, I heard you was looking for a tussle, so I come here instead of waiting. Let's have a drink for old times' sake, before I mop up the floor with your hide."

Buford went on down, slowly, smiling gently.

The doors to the dining room and the saloon were crowded with men, waiting quietly. Nobody wore guns, except hide-outs like Buford's, and nobody knew who had those except the men that wore them. There was no gun on Long that Buford could see, but that didn't mean anything. There might have been a dozen guns in that crowd.

"What do you know about mopping, trash?" Buford asked. "You was brought up on mud floors, weren't you?"

Long's smile looked pained.

"I never robbed nobody, though," Long said.

"And I never sold out a friend the way you sold my note to Dickson—my worst enemy."

Long flushed and lost his smile.

"I heard from my agent," Buford went on, "that you've been calling me a thief. Ruining my character."

There had been a kind of suppressed enjoyment in the crowd, an anticipation of something more or less amusing, if bloody. The merriment had gone now.

"Your character," Long said, his red face hostile. His little black eyes snapped. "You owed me two thousand dollars, Allen. You ain't got a dime now, and you ran out on everybody at home. Hear that, you all?" he shouted at the crowd. "Everybody knows it."

"You damn chicken-hearted pimp, you sold my note for nothing. I was going to pay you and I am still going to pay you. Like this." Buford spat straight into Long's face.

Long gasped. His face turned bright red and his right hand dived into his pants pocket. It got stuck, hauling the derringer out, and Buford, smiling with joy, swung one of the springs and caught Long across the side of the neck with it. Long went down with his hand still in his pocket.

Somebody burst out laughing, and then everybody began to laugh. The front door opened and on a burst of wind and dirt, a small, compact man with a black beard and bright, hard eyes came in. He had a wide black belt with a big gun hanging from it. He pulled that out and stood there with his black bowler hat on straight, and looked at Long, and then at Buford.

"I'm Sheriff Bailey," he said. "What's wrong?"

Long was sitting up, swearing horribly in a low voice. The little gun was still stuck in the pocket of his tight pants, and he didn't have sense enough to let go so he could get his hand out.

Bailey went over and stuck his gun under Long's sharp, red nose. "Give me that, sonny," Bailey said matter-of-factly, "or I'll break your head."

Long looked at Bailey's gun. He sat there glaring at Buford, and then slowly got up. He got the two-shot gun out and gave it up.

"Now, listen," Bailey said. "This is a peaceful town. If you want to kill each other, get the hell across the river."

"He's a back-shooting son of a bitch," Buford said. "I'd never make it across the river. Here, Long," he said, and threw one of the springs at him. "You was in the cavalry too, as I recall. Go outside and get on your horse and I'll saber-whip you. A little contest," he said to Bailey, "a sporting event solely. No malice aforethought. Surely you can't boggle at a little workout with the sword?"

They began laughing again, and Buford laughed too.

"You got any guns?" Bailey asked, his hard, bright eyes unchanging.

"Who, me?" Buford asked. "If I was armed, don't you think I would have shot this skunk just now, in self-defense? Here I was, with nothing but these pieces of iron, helpless, with him pulling at that boudoir cannon."

"The hell with all that," Bailey said, without change. He looked like a bull terrier on the end of a chain, eyes fixed and intent. "Answer my question, yes or no. Have you got any guns?"

"Why, yes, Mr. Bailey, of course I have," Buford said politely, smiling, and pulling his old Colt out of his pants. "Did you think I'd be crazy enough to come into this town without a gun?"

"No," Bailey said. "That's why I asked you." He took the gun and stuck it down his own pants.

Long was looking at the spring on the floor. He picked it up and worked it with his wrist, and a slow smile started. He looked up at Buford. "A damn good idea, you old sack of bull. I ain't had my hands on a saber for fifteen years. Come on."

He headed for the door, and the crowd followed.

Outside, Buford mounted Old Iron Ass and rode him down the street. He stopped and turned, holding his spring on his shoulder, and saw Long riding his nag down the other way. Long turned and faced him, and Buford could tell by the way Long's horse turned that he was a cutting horse, and fast.

The sun was going down, and the red light shone straight and flat down the wide, dusty street. A piece of paper whipped by on the wind, and Old Iron Ass let out a snort and jumped a yard. Buford said, "Sit still, you son of a bitch," and held the black mountain of meat down tight.

"Lord God Almighty," Buford said in the wind, "I ain't done this for a coon's age. God Almighty, let me whip that bastard good and hold my arm up, my God, because I'm old. Look at 'em! They're like a pack of dogs, waiting for him to slap me out of this saddle, God, and I'm alone—there ain't a man here that's my friend. Lord Jesus Christ, help me to best my enemies, and flog the bastard in the dust."

He saw Long lean forward, and he too leaned forward, giving his horse the rein. He kept the big bulk down to a neat, collected canter, though the brute was fighting the bit all the way, and he kept the spring trailing behind him, half raised, balanced.

He saw Long coming at him, Long with the spring in the air, ready for a chop, Long all set to do or die, and immediately Buford had a vision of Long's iron sliding down his, and that hard blade crashing into his knuckles. The son-of-a-bitch springs had no guards, of course.

All this time he was rolling forward on the old locomotive of a horse, and as Long raised the saber, coming full up on him, his eyes wide and glaring. Buford leaned far to the off side and swung Old Iron Ass to Long's left, passing on the wrong side.

Long let out a yell and went on, shouting curses and calling Buford a damned, dirty cheat and a coward. That was all right with Buford—Long had lost his initiative, and now he'd be on the watch for tricks—defensive.

Old Iron Ass was no cutting horse; he lumbered on down the street twenty-five yards before Buford, throwing all his weight to the off side again and ramming the old boat in the flank with his heel, forced him around in a circle so tight the horse almost went down on his knees. Long was sitting up there, faced around, shouting curses and waving his spring. Buford gave Old Iron Ass hell on the rump with his own saber. The crowd, lined along the walks, was watching intently.

Buford bore down on Long, and Long saw him coming. He put the spurs to his nag. He came at Buford not with that dangerous rush, but with a kind of wide-open caution, not knowing, now, what to expect, and he wasn't coming fast enough. Buford came in on him hacking, and beat Long's iron down, getting in a few heavy blows on the shoulder and back as Long wheeled, but he couldn't work fast enough to do it again, and Long was no fool. They sat there, the horses scared out of their wits, rearing and shoving, with the iron ringing, smashing at each other.

Buford's arm was aching and the sweat was pouring into his eyes. He could see Long's iron, a black yard swinging down out of the sky, and wished to God for a straight sword. He knocked the blow down, and he saw that Long knew he was tiring, because Long was smiling and he had a nasty light in his eyes.

Old Iron Ass was going crazy, and getting too hard to manage. In his heart Buford cursed his tiring body and his aching arm. His shoulder was going dead from fatigue, burning like fire, and there wasn't a damn thing he could do about it. That was what he got for sitting in hotels while Long worked his butt to the bone in the saddle. He couldn't keep it up, and Long could.

Buford got his last chance when the knot-headed horses wheeled away at the same time. He had Long broadside for a moment, a moment that hung forever in front of him, and Buford hauled off and whapped Old Iron Ass on the butt with the spring as hard as he could.

Old Iron Ass let out a shriek and charged, head on, straight into Long and Long's horse, and went right on over them without batting an eye. Long went down in a sprawl of thrashing legs and stirrups, and Buford, hauling Old Iron Ass around, was on him before he could get up.

Long didn't have a chance. Buford danced his horse for fair, knowing that it wouldn't step on Long, and from above, grinning through his tangled white beard, he beat down on Long, beating his iron out of his hand, and then beating him over the shoulders with the flat of his spring. Long put his arms over his head and tried to dodge, but Buford kept right on top of him, slamming away while Long howled like a dog.

"You son of a bitch," Buford shouted. "I'll teach you to black my name." He slammed him on the head. Long fell headlong in the dust and lay quiet.

The crowd was silent. Buford rode Old Iron Ass down the street, along one gutter, close to the crowd, carrying his spring, and shouted out, "Now get this, you people. My name is Allen and I stick by my word. This man called me a liar. Any man that blacks my name again is going to get beat like a dog, just like that."

The crowd along the boardwalk drew back as he rode by, trailing the iron spring. His hat was gone, and his white hair stood out in the wind, and his beard, dirty and full of sweat, straggled down from his chin. With the red sunlight through that white hair, riding that black mountain of a red-eyed horse, and trailing that curve of black steel so close, nobody felt like saying anything back.

Except one man, who had ridden down the street and stopped in the middle, beyond where Long lay. He sat his horse, ganted and matted with dried sweat, and smiled as Buford rode toward him. There were four riders in the row behind him.

"A nice job," Spence said as Buford rode up. "I just got here. I believe every word you say, Mr. Allen. I know you will pay back every cent. I don't know what with, but I honor your intentions." He pulled a sheaf of blue-backed papers out of his breast pocket.

"These are attachments on your herds. I just rode the hardest sixty miles I ever rode in my life, but I'm going to get the sheriff now and ride back. Would you care to come along?"

Buford, with the sweat drying on his face, and his shirt clammy on his back in the cold wind, sat quiet in the saddle. He tried to say something and couldn't.

The iron spring in his hand was too heavy, and he dropped it. He sat quiet, just trying to hold his head up.

Bailey rode up and said, "You gentlemen will have to check your guns. Town law."

"Why, of course, sir," Spence said. "In your office? We're leaving town again, though, sheriff," he went on. "We have papers to attach some cattle coming up the trail and I want your help." He blinked. He was having a hard time keeping his eyes open. The four men behind him sat stiff, their faces thin, their eyes red, almost asleep in the saddle.

"Now, boys," Buford said, "and I say boys because I know we're all going to be friends, why don't we take all this to Rooney's, out of the wind? There's no rush now. Everything can be settled legally. I need a wash and a few drinks. I reckon you could use the same, couldn't you, Mr. Spence? And your men?"

Spence looked at him steadily. "Do you mean that you're going to accept our papers, Mr. Allen?"

"Why, sir," Buford said, "that all depends on the nature of the papers, doesn't it? Naturally I'll have to have a look at them. Come along, out of the wind."

He went on up the street, not looking back.

The others rode after him.

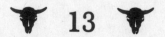 13

Ogalalla
Rooney's Hotel
Room 47—7:30 P.M.

The four of them sat in Streeter's room with the last light of the red sun slanting through the dirty front window.

"Thanks for feeding my men," Spence said, sawing his knife into a large, rare T-bone which was half buried in two pounds of baked beans, canned tomatoes, and piccalilli. There were two open bottles of Old Croak on the table, and four water glasses half full, and two spare bottles on the floor, one on each side of Buford's chair.

Streeter sat on the edge of the bed nibbling a large dill pickle, and the sheriff sat calmly working through another steak.

"Good men," Buford said, faking diligently at his dinner. He was too busy thinking to do anything but drink. "Tough men. Especially that bird with the crooked nose. A man like that would walk straight through a brick wall if you told him."

"Forrest," Spence said, munching. "Isaac Forrest. Eyes like a hawk."

"Good name, Isaac. Now Isaac was an obedient boy. And Abraham! Do you remember Abraham? How God told him to cut off Isaac's head, and Abraham took him and was all ready to do it? Of course God supplied him with a ram, to save him from it—but Abraham would have done it. A good man, Abraham."

"Abraham who? Who are you talking about; who is this Abraham?" Streeter asked through a mouthful of pickle.

Buford looked at him with a large, serene blue eye. "Haven't you ever read the Bible, my old friend? I'd read the Bible twice by the time I was fourteen. My daddy was a minister of the Gospel. Didn't you know that? Came from Tennessee."

"Oh," Streeter said. "The Bible. Excuse me."

"Reminds me of your man Tucker," Spence said. "Tucker and Forrest would make a good pair in a fight. I couldn't get anywhere with your man Tucker. He claimed he couldn't read." He took his bluebacked legal sheets out of his pocket and laid them on the table. "I don't mean to be rude, Buford—you don't mind if I call you Buford?—but time is flying, and—"

"*Tempus fugit,*" Streeter said, taking a drink from a tumbler.

"Shut up, Ed," Buford said calmly.

"Is he getting drunk?" Bailey asked.

"Hell, no," Streeter said, putting down his glass. "I'm getting sober. What you think? I was drinking for nothing?"

"Charming fellow," Spence said, as though Streeter were about four miles away on the end of a pin. "Point is, Buford, your good man Tucker is now about fifty miles from here. I saw him noon yesterday, and he was making twenty miles a day. Soon as I finish this fine steak of yours, I want to go back and take over that herd, and shunt 'em up to Cheyenne. But I can't get them away from Tucker without your okay—or the sheriff. If I leave in an hour, you understand, I can get to them by morning, even if I go in a buggy, which I intend. I want your cooperation, and I want it quick."

"I ought to be down on the street," Bailey said. "New herds come in today. Always got some new young fellers on the crews that want to shoot Yankees."

"Have another drink, sheriff," Buford said. "Take your mind off those Yankees."

"I can't," Bailey said. "One's aplenty."

"Leave a deputy," Spence said. "I want you to ride back with me and enforce these attachments—that is, if Buford won't sign a quitclaim himself, right here." He smiled. "Now."

Buford poured himself a refill. "Relax," he said. "What's your first name, my good friend?"

"Will."

"Will Spence," Buford said, with extraordinary satisfaction. "A fine name, a fine name."

"Will Spence what?" Streeter said, eating another pickle. He looked mischievous, his drooping eyes twinkling with some secret anticipation. "Chop off Abraham's head?"

"Ed, can't you for the God's sake stay sober?" Buford asked. "I need your advice."

"You don't need anybody's advice, Buford," Spence said. "You know Noonan,

I'm sure. Do you admit that this is his signature?" He waved a paper in front of Buford's face.

"I acknowledge nothing except the time of day," Buford said, and lifted a forkful of beans.

"Those papers look legal to me," Bailey said. "It says right here, the Twenty-Second District Court, and that's a county seal, ain't it?"

"District seal," Spence said. "They're legal, all right. Ogalalla is county seat of Keith County, so Tucker's in your jurisdiction by now."

"Bailey," Streeter said, "you can't do this to our friend Buford. Buford is our old pal. Old, real old."

"Mr. Streeter," Bailey said politely, his black, hard eyes as sharp and expressionless as ever, "why don't you lay off that stuff? You know it's bad for you."

"Hulp," Streeter said. He beamed around at everybody. "This *is* my room, isn't it? Number four-sheven? Never saw it going around like this before."

"Is he a competent witness?" Spence asked Bailey. "Can he witness Buford's signature?"

"Anybody that can sit up is a competent witness in Keith County," Bailey said.

"Have you boys met before?" Buford asked. "I thought you were strangers, but I seem to detect a strange intimacy, or a singular singleness of purpose and mind. Anyway, I'll sign nothing. Will, why do you work so hard for Dickson? Why not work for me? You won't have to ride another sixty miles in a goddam buggy, for one thing."

Spence smiled at him. "You tempt me," he said. "I'd give a thousand dollars for a week in bed. What's your proposition?"

"I'll give you ten thousand dollars to deliver those attachments to me now. Across the table."

Spence shook his head.

"Twenty-five thousand."

"You haven't got it."

"I will have damn soon."

Spence shook his head.

Buford said, his voice getting lower, "Fifty thousand."

"You owe Dickson, altogether, damn near a million. Why would I sell him out for fifty thousand? I could take that one herd myself and sell it for a hundred thousand and they'd call it cheap."

"Is Dickson paying you anything like fifty thousand? At any time?"

"No, he gives me a nice salary, Bufe, and a commission on certain deals. I'm happy. I ain't rich, but I'm happy."

"In God's name, why? I'll give you a hundred thousand."

"I think this is bribery," Bailey said.

"*Cogito ergo non sum*," Streeter said, taking a quick one out of a bottle.

"I want no bribery around here, gentlemen," Bailey said.

"This ain't bribery, sheriff," Buford said. "This is a game of Mongolian fantan."

"A hundred thousand ain't enough," Spence said, taking a deep gulp of Old Croak. "You'd have to kill Dickson."

"My God, another Isaac."

"Not exactly. But Dickson doesn't like welshers and double-crossers. You ought to know him well enough to know what would happen to me."

"You look well able to take care of yourself."

"Not with Dickson. Nobody can stay awake all the time, and nobody has eyes in the back of his head. That's one thing about Dickson. He'll even things with a welsher if it costs him every cent he's got. He forgets everything else."

"You wouldn't speak so open in San Antonio, would you, Will?" Buford asked.

"No, and I wouldn't say it here either, except I know Bailey'll never get to San Antonio because he won't live that long, and Streeter won't because he's too—My God, look at him."

Streeter was sitting on the edge of the bed, turning yellow.

"It's those goddam pickles," Buford said. "Ed, for the God's sake, go to the window."

Streeter moaned faintly. He kept blinking his eyes and peering around.

"I'm willing to make a little compensation, though," Spence said. "If you sign those quitclaim deeds without any more fuss, I'll give you ten thousand cash, now. That's all."

Buford looked at the deeds—there were five of them—and slowly picked them up. He seemed to sink into deep thought.

"Streeter—" Bailey began.

There was a succession of hollow knocks as Streeter rolled off the bed and hit the floor, one loose bone after the other.

"Out," Bailey said. "How many drinks did he have?"

"Let's go," Spence said. "Come on, Bailey. My principal will pay your fee and plenty more for traveling. What's your fee?"

"Fifty dollars to ride that far."

"We'll allow you a thousand bucks for traveling expenses."

"That's too much," Bailey said.

"How do you know? You may get yourself shot up on this junket. That is, if Buford's son is doing what I think he's doing. I suddenly just wised up to what this little party is all about." Spence stood up.

"Now, now," Buford said. "Where's a pen? Who's got a pen? And what's your hurry?"

"Sheriff," Spence said, "be a friend and run down for a pen and a bottle of ink. Maybe Buford's softening up."

Bailey had a parting shot and left, wobbling slightly.

"Now, have a drink, Will," Buford said, "now, sit down, and have a drink. Don't go rushing off mad at me. After all, ten thousand's better than nothing, ain't it? And what did you mean, what my son is doing?" He looked old and bewildered. He picked up one of the spare bottles on the floor and poured some into Spence's glass.

"All this goddam stalling," Spence said. "The light just dawned. Feeding my men. What? Arsenic?" He laughed gently and sat looking at Streeter. "How could he get that drunk on four drinks, Buford?" He looked at Buford with twinkling eyes. Streeter was snoring jerkily. His face was green.

"What do you mean about my son?" Buford said, old and bewildered. He looked down at Streeter. "Silly ass. Never could hold it."

"I'll bet you a thousand your son is on his way down with your customers now, isn't he? He left Cheyenne last night to sell the herd and you came here to stall me. And every goddam minute you hold me here shooting off my mouth, your son's got that much more time to beat me to that herd."

Buford laughed sadly. "If only I'd thought of that. You overestimate me, Will, my boy. What a play that would have been! Selling those cattle right out from under your nose."

Spence said nothing.

"Have a drink," Buford said amiably. "After all, we can still be friends, can't we?"

Bailey came back into the room with a pen and a bottle of ink. "Rooney says be careful with his ink. He ain't got no more." He set them down on the table.

Spence pushed them across to the old man. "Go ahead, Buford, sign. Hurry up."

Buford picked up the pen. He dipped it in the ink, his hand shaking. He spattered ink on the table, and redipped it. He sat looking at the deeds, and at the pen, and slowly tears began to roll down his cheeks into his beard. He covered his eyes with his hands, dropping the pen, and wept. "For God's sake, can't you have pity on an old man?" he cried.

Spence laughed. In the midst of his laughter, while Buford was weeping desperately into his hands, he swapped glasses with him.

"Sign, Bufie," he said, laughing. "Cut out the horse crap."

"For ten thousand? Ten lousy, measly thousand?" Buford quavered. There was mud in his beard as he raised his face, from where the tears had soaked into the dust. He looked old and bedraggled, utterly washed up.

Spence pulled out a fat wallet and showed the bills in it.

"Then let's be friends," Buford said. "Let's drink on it." He raised his glass. "All of it, and smash the glasses."

"A pleasure," Spence said, and lifted his. They drank, and threw the tumblers against the neighboring wall.

Sniffing, Buford signed three of the deeds. He put his hand to his head, and then shook it. He signed the other two. He sat there, blotting the ink with the tail of his shirt.

"Well?" Spence asked. "Hand them over."

"Another little drink," Buford said. His old eyes were keen as a fox's behind the rheum of his tears. He watched Spence with an expression of amiable timidity, pleading. He poured Spence's glass full.

"Well, what the hell are you waiting for?" Bailey said. "Give him the papers."

Buford put his hand to his eyes, and then looked at his hand, and blinked slowly three times. "Son of a bitch," he said softly.

Spence burst into a roar of laughter. He cut it off short and stood there grinning at Buford.

Buford suddenly sat forward, erect on the edge of his chair, and grabbed the edge of the table. He swayed.

"You damned old fool," Spence said, "why didn't you set that bottle down on the other side of your chair, where that silly bastard Streeter couldn't reach it? You might have known he'd foul you up. How could any man pass out that quick on four drinks, if it wasn't doped all to hell? This ought to teach you one thing—you can't outsmart me and Dickson. You can't possibly win."

Buford glared up at him, holding on to the table.

He half rose. "You son of a bitch," he said.

Spence moved.

Buford grabbed just in time, a split second before Spence's hands got to the deeds. He tore them savagely between his hands, and grabbed wildly, reeling, for the attachments. Spence seized the papers, and Buford lunged at him, fighting for them like an old lion, his beard wild and his clouding eyes wild with fury. He staggered into the table and Spence shook him off. Panting, Spence backed to the door, stuffing the papers in his pockets. "Come on!" he shouted to Bailey. He opened the door.

"Come back!" Buford shouted.

"I ought to throw him in the can," Bailey said.

"Come on," Spence said, "he'll pass out in a minute."

He and Bailey ran. Buford grabbed two bottles and staggered after them into the hall.

"You sons of bitches!" he roared. "You rotten thieves!" He staggered over to the stair well. The others were hurrying down the stairs. Buford hurled a bottle down the stair well at them. It smashed, spattering whiskey all over.

"Damn you to hell!" Buford screamed. "I'll win! You can't, you can't beat— me!" He ran to the head of the stairs and hurled the other bottle. The swing carried him forward. With a cry, he fell, and tumbled down the stairs.

He caught himself and crouched panting for breath.

A face came up the stairs, and he squinted at it.

"My old friend," Long said bitterly. There was blood from a cut on his cheek, and the whole side of his face was a swollen, black bruise. "My old friend Buford."

Buford went limp; helpless, he slipped down the stairs. Long laughed. "He's drunk, boys!" he shouted. He grabbed one of Buford's feet and dragged him the rest of the way down.

Buford lay quiet, paralyzed, staring blindly up at Long and Long's men, fading into a swirling mist.

He heard their voices, from far away.

"Drag him out in the gutter, boys," Long said joyously. "Let the horses water on him awhile. Let him lie in the dung. I'll show him who wins."

Fury rose in Buford as hands grabbed him and lifted him up. Dark closed in. In his ancient rage he wept, and even as he wept he slept.

☗ 14 ☗

The Plains 30 Miles North
of Frenchman's Creek
July 10—9:00 P.M.

There were ten men in the group riding along the next morning: Mike; Morton, who had contracted for the first herd; McCullough, who was buying the second; and seven of Morton's hands.

They were moving along at a good fast trot paralleling the broad trail of dust where the herds had gone ahead, and McCullough was still trying to post.

"Stand up in your stirrups," Mike said.

"Don't try to tell me how to ride a horse," McCullough said, his desperate, hopeless exasperation rising feebly over his exhaustion. "It's these damn saddles. Where in hell are we?"

Up ahead there was dust in the air, lying like a golden cloud. For once, the wind was quiet.

"There's a herd about four miles ahead," Mike said. He was beginning to smell the dust in the air.

"Our herd?" Morton asked. He was a hard rider, careless, stiff, and rough, and his horse was sweating all over, yellow foam beginning to churn in the heating sun. The rest of the horses were plenty tired out, kept up in that steady trot; they had been going that way all night with only two breaks.

"Our herd?" Morton asked again. Tall, thin, his black eyes gazing ahead with happy expectancy, like an eager cadaver. Stiff as an arrow, he'd pound that horse down to the knees and never even notice, until it rolled over dead.

"Reckon," Mike said.

"Reckon!" McCullough said. "I'm through. I quit."

"You can't quit," Mike said. "You said you'd do this for me."

"I was drunk," McCullough said.

"Well, have another drink," Morton said. "Good for you, Mac. Wear that pot of yours down a little."

Morton pulled a bottle out of a saddlebag. A twenty-dollar bill fell out and floated back in the dust. "I'll be damned," he said. "Package must have bust."

"Ain't you going to get it?" one of the hands asked, riding along behind.

"Ah, the hell with it," Morton said. "Here, Mac, have a drink. Do you good." He held the bottle out.

"Leave him alone," Mike said. "One more drink and he'll fall out of the saddle."

"That's what I mean. Good for him," Morton said. "Teach him how to ride."

"Can't we stop this for a goddam minute?" McCullough asked, panting. He

528

had a bad stitch, and the pain was screwing up one side of his face. "What's all the goddam hurry?"

"No," Mike said. "Only three more miles, Mac. I'll knock fifteen cents off your price. That make you feel any better?"

McCullough twisted, and looked at the loaded saddlebags, bouncing along behind him.

"No, by God," Mac panted.

One of Morton's men came up at a lope and held the twenty-dollar bill out to Morton between two fingers. Morton took it, grinning. "Lee, you fall out by the side here with Mr. McCullough and ride him after us at a walk. You coming back down here anyway, ain't you, Mike?"

"Yes. Mac's herd is about a day down the trail. We'll ride back down for it after you get yours."

"Like hell we will," Mac said. "I'm going straight into Ogalalla. You leave me here alone with all this money? Like hell."

"It's fifty miles to Ogalalla," Mike said. "You'll never make it on that horse. You stick with me and buy your herd tomorrow, Mac, like you promised."

"You and your damn liquor," Mac panted.

There were seven riders behind them, eating the dust of the owners. They weren't amused by McCullough. He was nothing but a damn responsibility. They rode easy in the saddle, faces stiff with dust and sweat, fatigue showing in their eyes, but complacent in the face of a mild hardship.

"I'll take my money on to Ogalalla. Screw you and your cows."

"Two more miles," Mike said.

"How do you know it's the right herd?"

"Got to be," Mike said. "Foreman back there said so, didn't he? Got to be my herd."

He rode with a set face, and every rise of the pony was like salt in a burn on his buttocks. The saddle was too short for him, hired out of a livery, and the cantle pinched his behind. He rode forward, squatting on his crotch and standing, as he had been doing all night, ever since they put the horses down from the cattle car at Lodgepole Creek and crossed the South Platte in the dark. He kept thinking of that twenty-dollar bill floating away in the dust. There was about $160,000 in those saddlebags of Morton's, and more in McCullough's, since McCullough's contract was for $59 a head instead of $55.

"You and your goddam option," McCullough shouted, pain turning into rage. "I don't believe you got an option on any goddam ranch. It's some kind of a trick, just to get me down here with my money." McCullough was about to cry, and Morton looked at him sideways, enjoying it all.

They all lifted their noses. There was cow dung in the air, like snuff, bright in the nostrils. Then they came into the low-hanging dust, and it got thicker. The low bawl of the herd rose in their ears like the sound of water, and then they saw it, a dense, complex mass of dark under the dust, like a viscous liquid, churning and bubbling, flowing north slowly under its own smoke.

They were all lined out, now, through with their morning graze, and moving forward at a steady, bobbing walk, heads going up and down like pump handles. Stink, bawl, and dust.

Mike came up on the drag riders, and waved. The two men, recognizing him, waved back and yelled. The lame, the halt, the feeble, and the blind strung out behind for half a mile, and the drag men were letting the worst just fall out altogether, to be picked up by the next herd.

"It's ours," Mike said. He forgot the chafe, and sat up straighter, his face and his mind brightening.

He put the horse into a lope, and Morton followed him. The rest came on at a jog.

He and Morton came up on Tucker, and Tucker grinned. He stuck out a hard paw and shook Mike's hand, and then Morton's.

"We're going to tally out here," Mike said. "Right now."

They got the herd in a slow mill, stationed two tally men, facing each other across the trail, and let the herd slip through in dribbles, singles, and clots of two, three, and four cows coming through at a time. They tallied with knots on thongs, ten cows to a knot. The booze was making Morton sleepy and happy. He and McCullough, who had come up and been helped off by two of Morton's hands, were sitting on the ground with their moneybags, knocking off the bottle in a leisurely way, watching the tally.

Tucker beckoned Mike away from them. He pointed east. "See that rider?"

Mike looked. The rider was a speck of black on the yellow grass.

"Spence's man," Tucker said. "You remember Spence—Dickson's boy."

"I know all about it."

"Well, Spence left here yesterday noon. If he rode like hell, he'll be back here with the sheriff of this county in a couple of hours. If he run a remuda with him and killed a few horses—he might be here now."

"Tucker," Mike said, "just mosey down to the herd and tell the boys to start shoving them through a little faster. Just a little. And another thing." He sat quiet, as Tucker waited, his cigarette dead in his big mouth. "If Spence comes —there'll be trouble. And he's got the law on his side."

"Not God, though," Tucker said. "As long as he ain't got God on his side, I don't give a damn how much law he's got."

"I don't want our boys hurt," Mike said. "I want them back home with their money."

Half an hour later Tucker looked eastward at the horizon. "See there, Mike."

There was a low feather of dust lying away across the edge of the sky.

"After you pay your crew off," Mike said, "I want you to go south and tell the boys on the other herds to turn the cattle over to Spence. No shooting. We can't fight the law, and I've run out of tricks."

"Ain't you giving up awful easy?"

"I've run out of buyers. You see the fat slob in the check suit, lying on the blanket down there? He's my last buyer. I was going to take him south. But it's too late now."

The herd was through and the tally men were riding up the slope toward Morton and McCullough.

The smoke on the east plain was bigger now, and Mike could see where it was growing, nosing along the earth.

"Won't be any more time to talk, Tucker," Mike said. "Somewhere in the

Indian country there's two more herds. Three thousand head each. The old man's taking them to Montana—his own private outfit. Spence doesn't know about them."

Down on the blanket, Morton was going over the tally strings, checking them on a piece of paper. Mike's tally men came up with his strings and sat waiting. Down below, Tucker's men were keeping the herd in a big, slow mill.

"The thing is," Mike said, "the old man's lost his butt."

Tucker said nothing.

"We're going to try to save him those two herds. He's got to eat. Colby is driving them. You take over. You take them west and get lost, and keep on going north. You keep going, Tucker, because it's getting later in the year, and they're still south of Dodge. We got to get them on winter range in Montana before the snow starts—they got to be fat. So push the hell out of them. On up the Oregon trail. Take them over the Bridger cutoff."

"You got that winter range lined out? Where is it?"

"A place called Warhorse. Hell, I'll see you again before you get that far. I'll give you an extra two thousand, and you buy new rifles and plenty of cartridges, and don't let anybody take those cows away from you. Stay off the trail."

"Better sell 'em," Tucker said. "You got too much stacked against you."

"I thought of that. But where?"

"Dodge, of course."

"Spence has put the word out all over. There isn't a buyer on the whole trail that would touch those cattle, knowing about those attachments. Get me a fresh horse, and drive your remuda out somewhere and lose it. We don't want to leave any fresh horses around for Spence."

Tucker winked, and wheeled his horse down the slope.

Mike glanced at the eastward dust. There was a tiny black knot at the head of the stream, men and horses, indistinguishable.

He got down on his knees on the blanket by Morton and Morton said, "I got 2,906. What do you get?" There was plenty of booze on the air around that blanket, but Morton's eyes were as hard and black as a squaw's.

"2,908," Mike said. He was afraid his voice would shake with impatience, and he deliberately threw this into the settlement to foul it up. It was normal to have some kind of difference.

"Split the difference?" Morton asked. "Or do you want a recount?"

"I want a recount," Mike said, trying to keep his voice calm. Anything to keep Morton from noticing Spence coming, and holding up the payment.

"Oh, hell," Morton said, "don't be a hardnose, Mike. You mean we got to go through all that again for two lousy cows? What's two lousy cows?"

"A hundred and ten dollars," Mike said firmly and quietly. "I demand a recount. Or take my figure."

"Son of a bitch," Morton said. A recount would run more than 1,600 pounds of beef off that herd, even if it was only water. "I'll take your lousy figure. Do you do this all the time?" He scratched on a paper with a pencil. "Now how much do I owe you? I figure $159,940."

"You take my figure, I'll take yours," Mike said. "Count out the money, friend."

So they counted out the money, which came to 79 packets of a hundred bills each, and 97 loose ones. "Now if you'll kindly sign this bill of sale," Morton said, and Mike did, and it was done.

Tucker came up with a big roan and Mike strapped Morton's saddlebags on behind the saddle. There was a rifle in the scabbard. He pulled it out and checked the loading. Westward, there was a fan of dust in the air, where Tucker's boys were scattering the horse herd.

"I'd be obliged for a remount," Morton said, eyeing the big horse.

"Why, you bet," Mike said. "Tucker, you send a man up the line and see if he can bring our remuda back. You reckon your boys can handle the herd till we get you some fresh horses, Morton?" Mike asked in a kindly way. "Tucker, you take Morton's men and relieve ours, and help them get the herd lined out again."

"Northwest," Morton said, grinning at his cows. "Cheyenne way. Who the hell is that?" He was blinking at the east. There were men and riders now, clear in the sun.

"Looks like a posse," Mike said. "Maybe hunting some crook or other. Cow thief, maybe."

"Well, damn them, they better not run into my herd," Morton said. "I can't take no stampede now, with all my horses shot. Let's ride out and warn 'em off, Mike."

"Let's not," Mike said. "They've seen us. They're heading here."

He bent down and counted out Tucker's paymoney, gave it to him, and then began stacking the bundles of bills in the crook of his arm, like kindling. He stuffed it into the saddlebags deliberately, showing no haste.

He mounted and sat waiting, his eyes on the advancing riders. He recognized Spence at a distance, and saw a star flash on Bailey's chest. Behind them were Spence's five riders.

"The law," Morton said. "You guessed right."

Behind them, Tucker laughed. He had ridden up with his men. "Damn good guessers, all the Allens. Well, Mike, think we might as well mosey along?"

"Nope," Mike said. "We'll have to talk this one out, Tucker." He gently took his Colt by the butt and pulled it loose in his holster.

Spence and the others were coming through the grass, and Spence was grinning, with his blue-backed papers in his hand. They stopped, and their horses drooped, blowing hard and wet with sweat.

"All right, Mr. Tucker," Spence said, his smile brilliant, happy as a lark, "this is the end of your goddam trail. Here's the sheriff and here's the papers, and the sooner you get your ass out of Keith County, the better it'll be for you."

"Just a minute, sir," Tucker said. "Just as soon as I get leave from the teacher, me and the girls'll leave." He laughed. Nobody else did.

Mike got an amiable smile on his face as Spence looked at him. "Who are these gentlemen?" he asked, waving a hand at Morton and McCullough.

"Don't know," Mike said. "Never saw them before in my life."

"What the hell?" Morton said. "What the hell is this about? Are you arresting somebody?" he asked Spence. He blinked his bloodshot eyes.

"I'm attaching this herd, that's all," Spence said. "It belongs to me."

"In a pig's hind end it belongs to you," Morton said, rearing up in his saddle. "Is this trouble?" He looked at Spence and at his men, and at the law in front of him, and waved a long arm in the air, circling it. Four of his riders came up from the herd.

"Who the hell are you?" Morton asked Bailey. Morton looked about six stories tall, and his red eyes glared."

"I'm the sheriff of Keith County."

"Well, puke on Keith County!" Morton bawled. "I own these here cows, and if you lay a rope on one I'll see you all in hell. I just paid Mike Allen here for 'em and they're mine. Here's the goddam bill of sale."

Spence quit smiling. He looked at Mike and then back at Morton. "You've been screwed, my friend. Mr. Allen here never had title to these cows. They belong to me by court order, and if you don't believe it, here's the order."

He shoved the tattered sheets at Morton, and Morton took them and gazed in bewilderment at the seal and all the close writing, both in Spanish and English. He handed them back and looked at Mike.

"Well, I'll be a son of a bitch," Morton said quietly. "So that's why all the rush. You and your option. Give me back my money." His eyes turned cold and his face menacing. He was leaning forward in the saddle.

Tucker said, "Mike, I think it's time for us to fall back on Atlanta."

"Which the hell way is Atlanta?"

"Just follow me," Tucker said and, jamming in his spurs, he drew his Colt and, screaming like a Comanche, charged his horse straight into Sheriff Bailey. Mike and the others piled right in on top of him, firing into the air.

Bailey, his horse, and Spence went down and with Tucker firing his cannon over their heads, Spence's men turned in a panic. Tucker's party went on through and scattered screaming away down the slope toward the herd.

Morton and Morton's men began firing at them, and then, as Mike swung down the herd, Morton stopped shooting and shouted. "Stop, you bastards!" he bawled in agony. "Don't do it!"

"Caveat Emptor!" Mike shouted. "Charge!"

They ran through the herd, firing, and back, breaking it into five terrified separate stampedes.

They pulled up in the clear and watched Morton's 2,908 cattle split in all directions, bawling in a crazy panic. In a little while the thunder died, and in the cover of the storms of dust, Mike and the rest headed north. They heard shouting behind them.

Mike swung his horse east, up toward a long, slow rise, into the sun. A mile farther, he stopped and looked back. Dust lay like smoke over a battle. Out of it, three small figures appeared, and headed toward him. They saw him and stopped at eight hundred yards. He saw the tiny puffs of rifle smoke, and then the bullets snapped over his head, and one struck the dust twenty yards short.

On his fresh horse he turned and headed north, toward Ogalalla, at a steady trot, all that was left of Buford's million bouncing lightly behind him.

One of the three riders followed him at the same steady trot. Mike pulled his rifle and stopped. He took a long hold on the rider and dropped one on him, and he saw the dust spit up where the bullet skipped on the ground, six feet to the rider's lee. After that, the other kept his distance.

Mike tried to shake him, but the other's horse was fresh. Mike remembered the single guard that Spence had left on Tucker. He slowed, and they rode that way, at a steady trot, about four hundred yards apart, all the way to Ogalalla, saving their ammunition.

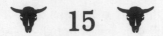

15

Ogalalla
Rooney's Hotel—Room 47
July 10—9:00 P.M.

The lid was on in Ogalalla, with Bailey's deputy sitting on it. He'd go up politely to the newcomers and ask for their guns, and if they didn't co-operate, he'd pull his own and club them over the head, which was both surprising and humane.

Mike gave his up without a word and then went on to Rooney's.

The old man was lying on a blanket on the floor in No. 47. He was sick, his face slack and his eyes full of red veins on yellow white. He coughed and spat a lot in a china cuspidor and his hands shook all the time. Mike, with the saddle-bags hanging from his arm, stood and watched him set down a bowl of bean soup on the floor and try to get up, and his heart turned in him. Buford looked ten years older.

"What the hell happened to you?" he asked quietly. He went to the front window. Spence's man was across the street, plain in the lamplight. He had no gun that Mike could see.

He turned back and looked at his father. The old man's clothes were covered with mud and gutter filth, bits of manure and straw clinging to the cloth, his beard stained with horse urine and more mud. His hair was matted with it.

"It was Long," Streeter said. He was lying on the bed, and though he was a lot cleaner than Buford, he didn't look any healthier. "Your father fed me and himself a Mickey Finn, yes, my boy, a Mickey, a true, real, honest Mickey. Then Long dragged him out and kept him lying in the gutter all night, down under the hitchrail."

"I am happy to say," Buford said in a hoarse voice, his throat full of phlegm, "that most of the time I was unconscious. Have you got a gun, my boy? I owe Long a call before we go."

"No. We're getting out of town as fast as we can."

"Not before I kill Long." Buford dipped his spoon into the soup and lifted it toward his mouth, and immediately shook all the soup over himself, out of the spoon.

He swore, and tried it again, this time holding the spoon with both hands. He got the soup down and held it down. "Filthy stuff. Surely God did not invent the bean. I'm just trying to get the strength to kill him. That's all."

"You better get the strength to get on your feet first," Mike said. "We got to get out of here. One of Spence's men followed me in. He'll get help. Spence himself'll be back here as soon as he can catch a horse. There's a train down at the station, loading cows. I saw it as I came in. It'll pull out pretty damn quick, and we're going to be on it."

"Have you got a gun?" the old man repeated.

"For God's sake, forget Long." Mike dropped the saddlebags and unstrapped one of them. "Put your mind on this. If you want to keep it, we've got to leave —now."

Buford looked at the packs of bills. "How much?" he asked dully.

"About a hundred and fifty-five thousand. I paid the boys. Tucker's going down the trail warning the other herds to give up. I'm going back to Cheyenne to pay the hotel bill."

"You would. How about the other four herds?"

"Not a chance."

Buford's fists clenched. "How about McCullough's money. Didn't you sell him the second herd?"

"There wasn't time. I was just lucky to get Morton's money."

"Can't we beat Spence down the trail and sell off the others?" the old man cried.

"There's Spence and all his men between us and those herds, Dad. Write them off." He went to the window.

"Streeter, haven't you got any kind of small gun?" Buford asked.

"Get out," Streeter said. "I've had enough trouble. Get your damn problems out of my room. I don't want any shooting."

"Pay him something, Mike," Buford said. "He's got some commission coming."

"I don't want your dirty money," Streeter said. "All I want is peace and quiet, yes, peace. Take your stolen money and get out of here. Yes, out."

Mike looked down at the old man, still ladling soup into his mouth, shaking half of it on his beard, where it blended slowly with the mud and the manure. "Is it?" Mike asked.

"Is it the hell what?" the old man snarled, showing a little life for the first time.

"Is it stolen?" Mike shouted, suddenly exasperated beyond words, fatigue, dirt, sweat, and failure flooding over him like a wave of solid sewage.

"No!" the old man roared, and they subsided.

"That train," Streeter said. "Go on. I don't want your bodies on my hands. I've had enough, yes, enough trouble. Take your dirty money and go."

"I'm trying to go, you whining little shyster," Buford snarled. "My dirty money, he says, when he sees the end of it. Yes, we'll go. Just as soon as I finish this delicious bean soup." He slurped another spoonful, a little more deftly. "Go down and buy a ham off Rooney, boy. A ham keeps well. I'll need it on the way to Omaha. A good ham will—" He suddenly leaned sideways and threw up into the cuspidor.

Streeter moaned.

"Son of a bitch," the old man said. "If I only had a drink, I could keep it down. Son, get me a drink." He staggered to his feet and stood swaying. "The hell with a drink. Son, give me that goddam bowl."

Mike handed it to him, and he drank the rest of it, one swallow after another, and threw the bowl against the wall.

"I'll make that damn stuff stay down if I have to whip myself with a belt," he said. "Give me a thousand dollars."

The old man threw the money on the bed. "Clean up the mess, you sniveling little bastard," he said to Streeter, "and there's something for your goddam trouble." He went to the corner of the room and got his little locked suitcase.

They went out into the hall, the old man holding on to Mike's arm, and Mike carrying the saddlebags. They stood in the gloomy hall, looking out the end window at the man waiting below.

A train whistle hooted mournfully from somewhere.

"Let's go," Mike said. "If he's got a friend covering the back, we'll have to go out the side window."

They moved slowly down the hall. "I'll go back down there to San Antonio and cut Dickson's throat," the old man mumbled savagely. "I'll get every damn cent back out of him. Listen, Mike. You pay the damn hotel bill in Cheyenne and come after me. I'll wait for you at the Planters' in St. Louis. Bring my bags down with you."

"I'd better ride a way with you," Mike said.

There was no watcher at the back; evidently Spence's man didn't expect them to move so fast, or else he was covering both doors by turns. He might show up at any moment. They went out of the back yard, through the dark bulks of crates and barrels, hurrying as fast as they could.

The moon was out. They kept to the shadows, the old man moving at a slow, weak walk. He leaned on Mike's arm at every step, and still he mumbled.

"Has Spence's man caught on?" Buford whispered.

"Not yet," Mike said, looking behind. "Can't you go any faster? If Streeter should happen to turn the lamp out in that room, he'll know we've gone."

The old man was panting heavily, sweat running down his face. "Maybe he won't wise up," he breathed.

Ahead of them the gray mountains of buffalo bones rose beside the tracks. Up the line, the engine and cars were backing out of a siding onto the main line.

Mike guided his father in among the bone piles, and they moved slowly through them, surrounded by the maze of dead and motionless skeletons.

The train came slowly down the main line and pulled up by the station. The cars were full of cattle. At the end of the train, ahead of the caboose, were empties for some consignment down the line. In the caboose, somebody was singing.

For a moment Mike had the feeling he was lost in a maze, among the piles of bones. There were countless thousands of them, patiently collected from the plains, waiting for shipment by the carload—all that was left of the great northern buffalo herd. Who would have thought, ten years ago, that they could come to this? These mountains of death? He looked at his father's bent shoulders ahead of him. It was all the same, the endless herds and the immense delusions. In the end, they were all dreams and vanished in the air.

Mike followed his father into one of the empties. Alone in the moonlight, slatted by the bars of the car, they rolled out of town, eastward; silent, without arms. The son sat propped against the end of the car, his father's head on his lap, and he looked down at the old, tired face while the old man slept.

And he wept, alone in the rattling, empty car, his tears slow, without any sound, running down his cheeks, and from his chin falling silently into the dung in his father's hair.

PART TWO

On the Train Between
Seguin and San Antonio
11:00 A.M.—July 31, 1882

The train pulled out of Seguin, rattling across the Guadalupe River bridge, and headed across country for San Antonio.

"Listen," Buford said, trying to keep his voice down, "for the last time, Mike, give me those saddlebags. I know Montrose'll say yes. I know it. I know it. Right now there's an answer waiting for me at the Menger."

Mike looked bitterly through the window at the countryside, passing at a sedate pace. The train rolled and bucked like a drunken cow.

"You're living on dreams," Mike said. "Montrose was through when I talked to him in Cheyenne. You were through when you didn't make the option date. I don't care how many wires you sent him from St. Louis, he's through, and so are you. Take my advice—"

"Take your advice," Buford said bitterly. "The chick tells the hen."

"Take my advice," Mike went on. "You pay Terman the hundred thousand you owe him for those two herds Tucker is trailing now, the ones you're stealing, and sell those herds, and you've got some working capital. I'll just take the other forty thousand, or whatever's left, and that will give *me* some working capital. I'm going to marry Nancy Berry with that money, and that's that."

The old man bit his lip, his eyes screwing up with his agony. Mike was almost sitting on the saddlebags, crammed against the side of the swaying car. The old man's hands twitched futilely.

He was wearing a Panama hat, now, and was back in condition, except that he was thinner and there were heavy shadows under his eyes. His beard was fine and silky again, and he was wearing a pair of onyx cuff links, set, with simple dignity, in platinum.

He was wearing these black cuff links, he would have said, in mourning for the emerald ones, and he had made up his mind that he would wear them until he got the emerald ones back, along with Long's head, or whoever it was that had stolen them in Ogalalla.

"For the last time, son," the old man said gently, "won't you listen to reason? We're going to get home in an hour. I offered Montrose the whole hundred and fifty thousand, and I got to have it. I got to wire it to him immediately. Then you and I will go north and drive those herds up there to Warhorse. Won't we?" He smiled painfully at his son. "Won't we?" he coaxed.

He saw his son's eyes open wide, startled, and followed their look. His heart gave two heavy thumps, missed two beats, and then started in again at a fast pace.

Spence was standing at the end of the car, looking down the swaying aisle. Spence was smiling his eternal smile. Behind him were two other men, and these men wore stars.

Buford and Mike sat paralyzed.

Spence came down the aisle, holding to the seat backs to keep himself from being thrown. His smile was almost melting.

"My," he said, "am I glad to see you, Mr. Allen. And Mike!" He stood there in the aisle, holding tight to the seat back. Behind him the two officers stood with feet apart, braced. "We've been waiting, Bufie old pal. You have no idea how we've been waiting. I assure you, no mother ever waited for her son as Dickson and I have been waiting for you. Not a train has gone through Seguin without one of Dickson's boys on it, and an officer or two. Where is it?"

Buford smiled. His tongue wouldn't work. The wheels pounded furiously. Nobody in the car was paying any attention. It was useless to start shouting. *Murder! Police!* with the two policemen standing right there.

In the silence, Spence's smile flagged. Out of his pocket came two papers. "One for you, Buford," he said, handing them out, "and one for you, Mike. Warrants for your arrest. Now, where's the money? The hundred and fifty-five thousand?"

Buford threw his warrant on the floor. "Go to hell," he said.

"All right, I'll go to hell, and you go to jail," Spence answered. "I don't care. Did you think you could get away with it? Why, the first thing Bailey did when we got back to Ogalalla was get two warrants out on you for everything he could think of—cow stealing, fraud, assault with a deadly weapon—a few others. However, if you hand over the money, all will be clear. Restitution is all that is wanted."

"Screw you," Buford said. "You talk about restitution."

Spence stopped smiling.

"Arrest them," he said to the two officers. "Handcuffs. They're dangerous."

One of the officers pulled a pair of cuffs from his hip pocket.

"You think I don't mean it?" Spence asked, his face blank. "Where's the money? Hand it over and I'll tear these warrants up."

"You put a hand on me," Buford said nastily, "and I'll have you hanged. We ain't in Bexar County yet, and those two courthouse monkeys haven't got any right to anything until we are. Screw your warrants."

Spence blinked. The officers looked at each other.

"In other words, all you're doing now is plain robbery," Buford said. "Train robbery. Until we hit the next creek, we're in Guadalupe County and you can go climb a tree. Isn't that right, sonny?" he asked one of the officers.

The officer looked foolish.

"How far is it to the creek?" Spence asked him quickly.

"About three miles, I reckon."

"Pardon me," Mike said, "I have to go to the toilet." He stood up, with the saddlebags on his left arm. "My toilet articles," he said to Spence. "Would you mind moving the hell out of my way?"

Spence's mouth tightened.

"Come on," Spence said to the officers, "keep close to him. I don't know what he's up to, but I want him nabbed when we get past the creek."

"I have to go to the toilet, too," Buford said.

He got up and trod heavily on the officers' feet, swaying and falling onto them as the train pitched. "Pardon me," he said. The three of them went down in a heap. The officers swore.

Mike walked quickly away down the aisle.

"Get off of me!" one of the officers shouted, struggling.

"Excuse me," Buford said, struggling feebly to get up. He accidentally stuck his finger into one of their eyes. "I'm so sorry," he said, kneeling on the other man's groin. "I'm such a clumsy old fellow," Buford said sadly.

The officer with the outraged groin let out a howl and lunged to his feet, spilling Buford. The other one stood swaying, with one hand over his eye, weeping copiously.

Spence was right on Mike's heels. Mike reached the door in the end of the car and opened it. Dust, dirt, cinders, and smoke blew in, and he staggered out on the puny platform.

"Where are you going?" Spence shouted. "The can's back there, inside."

"Afraid to try it, on this train," Mike shouted. "Might miss!" Taking a deep breath, he leaped straight out from the platform toward the flying countryside, saddlebags and all. He promptly disappeared.

Spence let out a roar of rage, pulled a gun, and stood there helpless. There was nothing to shoot at, except Texas.

With a burst of bedlam, the train rushed over the creek, and Spence rushed back into the car. Everybody was huddled around the wounded officers, trying to comfort them. Buford was sitting handcuffed to the seat, smiling quietly.

Spence stood in the aisle and cursed steadily at the officers of the law.

"Take these things off me," Buford said complacently.

"I'll throw you in prison!" Spence shouted. "You'll never get out!"

"Don't be silly," Buford said. "You know very well Dickson will want to talk to me as soon as we get into San Antonio, and he's the last man on earth to want anybody dragged into the Little House with handcuffs on. Kindly remove them, before you anger your employer. You should save your bluster and threats, my good fellow, for lesser men than I. Besides, I am a friend of Police Commissioner Berry."

"Take them off," Spence shouted at the officers.

The two officers bent with their keys and unlocked the cuffs, trying to inflict as many minor abrasions and lacerations on Buford's wrists, in the brief time allowed them by the performance of their duties, as they possibly could.

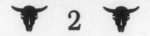

At Keppelbauer's House—
3:00 P.M.

Young Keppelbauer stood by his window with a glass of whiskey in his hand. He looked exactly the same as he had in Dickson's house the night he got his deadline, except that his eye was no longer placid, nor his chin whiskers neatly combed. His paunch was still firm, but his cheeks needed a shave, and the bags under his eyes were the color of old liver.

He had been jailed once on an assault complaint falsely sworn by three of Dickson's men. He was now out on Dickson's bail.

Keppelbauer had not been to his office for four days. Midnight tonight was his deadline.

He had been hiding at home, watching a man out the front window who was watching his house. There was another man down in front of his office on Houston Street. It seemed that there were men watching him everywhere he went.

He wrapped up a loaf of bread and some cheese in a spare suit, and tied this with a string. There was no reason for using the suit as a wrapping, but he was not thinking clearly any more. He forgot to take any water.

He harnessed the last horse (he had sold all the others) to his buggy and, with the man watching, started down Navarro Street toward Houston, as though he were going to his office.

On Houston he turned west, and kept on going. He kept on right out of town, at a trot, and when he hit the country, he whipped his horse into a gallop.

An hour later, his horse was fagging out. He heard hoofs behind him and lashed the horse harder. Isaac Forrest and another man rode up beside him. Isaac Forrest shouted for him to stop.

Keppelbauer did not stop. He kept whipping his horse. Forrest's partner grabbed the reins at the bit and pulled the horse down. It stood there, drooping and gasping for breath, legs shaking, almost dead. Keppelbauer, with a white face, sat and stared straight before him with his bread and his cheese beside him.

"Don't you know," Isaac Forrest said, "there is nothing you can do?"

Keppelbauer's mouth twitched.

"Today's the thirty-first. Why try to run away? Didn't we catch you before? On the train?"

"I can't get the money," Keppelbauer said.

"Turn your rig around," Isaac said. His eyes were not unkind—they were just indifferent. Wide and bright like an eagle's, with that hard jut of nose between.

Keppelbauer's hands tightened on the reins.

"No!" he shouted, and slashing at the horse, leaned forward as though to force the buggy on. The horse lunged ahead, and the other man jumped his horse and grabbed the bridle. The buggy stopped short.

Keppelbauer, his face set, white and full of terror, kept beating with his whip, and the horse reared and shook violently.

Isaac Forrest picked up his quirt and with a heavy swing brought it down across Keppelbauer's thighs. Keppelbauer let out a piercing shriek, dropped his whip, and sat there dumbfounded.

"Now turn around," Isaac said again.

Keppelbauer let out another scream of fury and pain to which this time was added surprise and outrage.

Isaac Forrest swung again.

Keppelbauer didn't have the breath to scream. He sat panting, gasping, almost unable to breathe, rocking in his seat, his face the color of paper ash.

"Turn it around," Isaac said, like a teacher, gently and patiently.

Keppelbauer dashed from the seat, leaping to the ground. He stumbled, picked himself up, and ran into the brush beside the road.

Isaac Forrest was after him, on top of him, his horse cutting Keppelbauer back as though he were a cow. The whip went up and came down, and went up and came down, on Keppelbauer's back, and Keppelbauer fell in the dusty road, back by his buggy, and whimpered like a dog.

"Don't you know by now there's nothing you can do?" Forrest said. The whip rose and fell. Keppelbauer writhed in the dirt, his smartly cut sack coat no longer neatly creased and businesslike.

"Nothing," Forrest said. "Turn your rig around."

Keppelbauer got up and staggered to his buggy.

"Nothing," Forrest said. He struck again.

Keppelbauer staggered and caught the edge of the dashboard.

"Nothing."

The whip rose and fell once more, and Keppelbauer sagged, clinging feebly.

"You won't go to the police, because they'll just jail you again on the same warrant, won't they?"

"Yes," Keppelbauer whispered. He climbed weakly up into the seat. He sat there, his head bowed. His eyes were shut and he was crying, his hands over his face.

"And they'll just turn you loose on our bail, when we want you, won't they?" Isaac said, like a patient teacher.

"Yes," Keppelbauer whispered.

"And there's nothing you can do," Forrest said. "Is there?"

The whip whistled, and slashed through the material of the buggy top beside Keppelbauer's ear. Keppelbauer shrank in terror.

"No," he said, barely making the words. "Nothing."

"We'll see you at the Little House at twelve."

"Yes," Keppelbauer whispered.

"Because there's nothing you can do, is there?"

"No, nothing," Keppelbauer said, sitting there. "Nothing. Please, just don't hit me again. Please!"

Isaac Forrest hung his quirt back on his saddle horn and rode away.

Slowly Keppelbauer drove back to his house, and went inside, and sat again in the living room, watching the man who was again across the street, and who was, again, watching the house, as quietly as before.

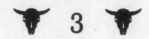

3

The Little House
Dickson's Office—5:00 P.M.

There was a catbird singing outside Dickson's office window. The garden lay lush and green down toward the little green river—an English garden, with Canterbury bells, foxglove, geranium, daisies, St. Johnswort, and bluebells.

Near the House there was a garden of roses. Dickson had them trained under gauze so that they grew with longer stems and richer colors. Everywhere in the Little House there were dozens of roses—red, pink, or white—in silver or crystal vases. He would allow no gold—nothing but silver or crystal was to go with the gray-and-white interior.

Somebody knocked on the office door and opened it. Spence stuck his head in. "We got the old man. The young one jumped off the train."

"That's fine," Dickson said. "You idiot. Well, put some of the boys out around the Menger. Isaac will do nicely. Did you get the money all right?"

"No. Mike had it."

Dickson's face turned just faintly pink.

"We'll get it," Spence said quickly. "Don't worry."

"I never worry, my boy. Bring Buford in."

Buford came in and looked around. "Lovely," he said. "Smells like a woman." He looked at Dickson. "A visitor, I presume. Not you, that is."

Dickson's mouth tightened and pinched. "Let's be pleasant, Buford. After all, we were friends for many months—"

"I see no need to be pleasant," Buford said. "You lied about me behind my back. You cheated my friends. You robbed me of almost all my money. You have ruined me. I see no need to be pleasant."

"Very well," Dickson said, sitting down behind his desk. "Let's be unpleasant. I give you until twelve midnight, this very night, to hand over the rest of the money you owe me."

"The rest. What do I owe you? You took my herds. What else do you want?"

"You owe me exactly $114,000, as the balance of the $300,000 of our private debt, not covered by the profits from your cattle. My dear Buford, I know you haven't got a dime except the $160,000 you got for that one herd. You owe me that too."

"$159,940," Spence said. "According to the buyer."

"So, altogether, you owe me $274,000, in cash. I am going to be generous," Dickson said. "I'll settle everything for that $160,000, Buford—if you'll tell me where those last two herds are."

"What herds?" Buford said.

"Terman's cattle."

"Never heard of them. Never heard of Terman, for that matter."

"Dear me," Dickson said, pulling open a drawer of his desk. "Must I prove everything? Is there no one I can trust?" He laid a piece of paper on the desk. "Promissory note by you to Terman. I bought it from Terman just last week. Let's grow up, Buford. You're surrounded. I have attachments on those two herds, now, and I want to know where they are."

Buford looked at the note, lying on the desk. He stood silent, wilting, and slowly his face lowered, clouding, the wrinkles in his forehead getting deeper and the lines around his eyes getting darker. "So he sold me out too," Buford said quietly.

"They were all cowards," Dickson said. "I, on the other hand, had perfect confidence in you, Buford. I still have. I know you'll pay me."

"It's not even a fair offer," Buford said heavily. "Those herds of Terman's are worth almost $400,000 and you want to settle, as you say, for $160,000, and the herds too. Such generosity."

In the silence the catbird sang, his voice trilling and warbling as the first gray of dusk rose from the river.

"Suppose I said," Buford said quietly, looking out of the window, "that I would pay you the $160,000 and you let me keep the herds. I have an option on a ranch, you see, in Montana. I offered the owner a down payment of $150,000. I could sell one of those herds and make that, and have the other left for stock. You see," he said looking down in a way that was almost benign, "you aren't leaving me any future, Dickson. What will I do? Drive a hack? It would kill me. I'm old. You're leaving me without a cent. Suppose I offer you everything but the two herds. I will give you all the cash Mike has."

"Why should I?" Dickson asked.

"I'm an old man," Buford said humbly. "Just leave me enough for another start." He stood there, gentle, old, meek, his handsome eyes smiling appealingly.

"Quit acting," Dickson said. "How many more herds have you got up your sleeve, Buford? You, who claimed you'd never heard of Terman. You're so full of tricks you bulge. You have a couple of million stowed away somewhere in a sack. I know your kind."

Buford stood quiet, his expression unchanged. "I'm not acting," he said. "God help me, I have acted. I have lied and pretended. I am not acting now, Dickson. I am begging. Look at me. How can you refuse an old man this? How little it is, to leave to an old man—an old fool."

Dickson looked up quietly. "Magnificent," he said. "Buford, you're tearing my heart. I love you."

"Then you won't?"

"No."

Buford looked down at him quietly. Then a kind of veil came down in his eyes, concealing, and he looked away. He licked his lips once, and stood quiet.

"Midnight," Dickson said. "You're over a barrel, Buford. I need the money, and I need it quick."

Buford cleared his throat. "There is one more possibility. I will give you everything, all the money and both herds, if you will buy that ranch and give me the job as manager. Just a job, for my old age. That's all I ask. You can take all the profits."

"What kind of profits?"

"I will guarantee you twenty per cent a year on your investment. A hundred thousand a year, with one herd. That is conservative."

"It's just crazy."

"They're making that now in Wyoming and Montana. On cattle for which they paid sixty dollars a head. These cost you thirty-five. I'd call it twenty-eight per cent. The market's going up. It's been going up for six years."

"I need my money fast," Dickson said, looking out at the garden. "I want to go back to England soon. With your money and these two herds I can just about make my goal. You see, Buford, you've delayed me six months. I can't forgive you that."

Buford's hands clenched and he looked down.

"Midnight," Dickson said. "I want the cash here, and a map showing the general trail of the cattle, and your son will ride north with Spence to locate them."

Buford stood looking at the floor.

"Don't look so hurt, Buford. Don't look so broken. You'll look fine on a hack, driving it around town. Think of all your friends, who'll hire you! 'Poor old fellow,' they'll say. But you'll do all right. You're only fifty-eight. I know it's just the beard that makes you look so venerable."

Buford looked up at him slowly, his face haggard.

"How can you say such a thing? Are you mocking me? Isn't it enough to break me, without mocking me?"

Dickson sat back in his chair and laughed. "Buford," he said, "you are delightful. Why couldn't we have been friends? You're much too good to be true."

A shadow passed across Buford's face. He was sagging. "Why do you say such things?"

"Because I know them. You're fifty-eight, and healthy as an ox. Your beard turned white in the military prison in—New Jersey. Is it New Jersey? Is there such a place as New Jersey? In February, 1864. Brace up, old boy, you've got decades ahead of you. Driving a hack."

Buford said nothing. He moved toward the door with a kind of shuffle.

"Midnight, old boy," Dickson called after him.

Buford suddenly turned back. "Mr. Dickson," he said, with all the mildness and humility of helpless old age, "you referred to a goal. I admire a man who has a goal. What is your goal, if I may ask?"

Dickson smiled. "Four million dollars. A paltry thing, but enough for a modest living."

"Let me commend your modesty," Buford said, and shuffled out.

The Menger Hotel—5:45 P.M.

They welcomed Buford home to the Menger with the same genuine hospitality they had always shown—not excessively, but sincerely—which was the reason he had sold his house long ago, and taken to living in the hotel with Mrs. Allen. Why not? He could go sit in the patio with its old alamo tree and drink beer in the evening, hearing the remote thumping of the waltz bands over along the river, from the Casino and the Palm Garden.

"Do you have a wire for me?" Buford asked the clerk on duty. His fingernails rattled on the desk top in an insistent, repeated rhythm.

"No, sir."

The fingernails stopped. "Are you sure? Couldn't it have been mislaid?"

"Let me send over to the telegraph office, Mr. Allen," the clerk said, smiling. He snapped his fingers and one of the boys came scampering up.

"Is Mrs. Allen in or out?" Buford asked, moving his cigar into the corner of his mouth. He never smoked more than an inch of any cigar, to keep the smoke from yellowing his mustache.

The clerk turned around and said, "Why, sir, I assumed you knew. Mrs. Allen left the hotel a month ago. About a week after you went north, Mr. Allen."

"She what?" Buford looked at the clerk in silence. "What do you mean, left? Checked out?"

"She rented a little house on Laredo Street, sir," the clerk said, "just between Paseo and Presidio."

Laredo Street, Buford thought. He threw his cigar into a palm pot. *Is she trying to shame me? Is that her way of criticizing extravagance, as she calls it? Living in some little Spanish flea trap? With some of those Mexicans of hers? Trying to make a fool of me?*

"The other side of the Creek?" Buford asked, shocked, "My God," he said to the clerk. "No wife. No telegram. Let me know when Mike comes. Right away."

"Yes, sir. What's the matter, Mr. Allen? You look ill."

"Nothing."

"Where will you be?"

He didn't know where he was going. "I?" He paused. He had a vague notion of going to see Berry. "Laredo Street. My God. Colonel Berry, too. Yes."

He walked out and stood on the curb outside, looking at the gutter. His left knee was shaking, and he felt weak and sick.

"Good afternoon, Mr. Allen," a man said behind him.

Buford looked around.

"Isaac Forrest," the man said, smiling. "Ogalalla. You fed me in Rooney's."

Buford's eyes narrowed. "Yes. I remember."

"We have a mutual friend. Thomas Dickson. He sent me to—to see that you were comfortable." Buford looked at him without speaking. For some reason, Isaac Forrest looked much bigger and taller on foot, in a derby hat, than he had on a horse.

"My orders," Isaac Forrest said, blinking his round bright eyes rapidly, "are to stay here and wait for your son. Do you see that man, over by the Market House?" He pointed a heavy, knobby finger across the Plaza. "He has been sent to follow you and see that you come to no harm. And Mr. Dickson told me especially to remind you about midnight. That was his word. Midnight."

Buford looked up at the high, hooked nose and the round eyes. In one instant he saw in them an absolute, implacable decision, and before it he quailed. The striking thing about Forrest's eyes, and what they showed, was a total lack of thought, of prudence, of hesitation. He was a man of total obedience, a soldier.

Buford's clothes suddenly became cold and damp, clinging to him. Some kind of bug seemed to be crawling between his shoulder blades.

"Indeed, indeed," he said in a confused way, looking around. Forrest backed a step, turned, and strolled off down the sidewalk. Buford was acutely conscious of the man across the Plaza.

He was suddenly sick with despair. He was caught, there was no way out. He looked away from the fellow, up, toward the sky. Birds were flying about in the trees. He stood and listened, escaping for a moment, just as he had stood in this same spot when he was four and five years old, and many times since, watching the ancestors of these same birds. For a moment he felt secure.

How beautiful his city appeared to him! With its little birds, the children of the towers and the gutters, flitting and darting in the evening sky.

Midnight.

The single word stabbed through him like fire. Where had it come from? The word faded away.

What could happen to him in San Antonio? Nothing. Nothing could harm him in the least. How could it? And then the truth broke through his careful web of delusions, and he saw with perfect clarity the dreadful certainty: there would be no telegram from Montrose, and he could not escape from Dickson unless—it was barely possible—he could bribe Dickson's men.

But where was Mike? Where was the money? If there were only someone left he could borrow from—borrow one more last time, scrape San Antonio to the very bone, so to speak, take all he could get, and run—

It wasn't lost yet. If only he could get to Warhorse and wave that cash under Montrose's nose, Montrose would change his mind. That was it. All was not lost, not yet.

He looked behind him. The little man was waiting.

And then it came to him, like the first gleam of rationality after a long delirium, quiet and clear. Colonel Berry might lend him the cash. Why hadn't he thought of Berry before? If Mike was going to marry Nancy Berry that made them practically related. He racked his brains. Why wouldn't Berry lend him the money? He could offer Terman's herds as security, as he had the bills of sale in his pocket this minute. And then—and then—

A gleam of positive hope brightened Buford's mind. It was all going to be wonderful again. And suddenly, like a final proof, it dawned on him why he had never borrowed money from Berry before, and why his credit ought to be good at Berry's bank. It was simply because he never had borrowed cash anywhere. All his debts were in accounts for real goods, cattle, supplies, horses, wagons, etc. He had never borrowed cash because he had never needed actual cash, in his business.

Oh, my God, Buford thought, *if only Berry will lend me $300,000.*

The bells of the Cathedral, and of St. Joseph's down by Blum Street, began to ring. Six o'clock. *Six,* he thought.

The bells stopped ringing, and the heavy tone lay in the ear like an almost inaudible droning.

Midnight.

The word struck through his mind like a saber, and he sank floundering into a pool of black fear, in silent agony. He had to get out, he had to get out—the words hammered through his mind. And what if Berry refused him? Where was Mike and the money? He had to have that $159,000 for bribes. And where was Mike?

He looked behind him. The little man was still there, apparently without a care in the world.

5

Colonel Berry's Bank
on Houston Street—6:00 P.M.

Colonel Berry, sitting in his office, listened to the telephone ring, with something like malevolent enjoyment at the thought that it was wearing itself out. He let it ring until it stopped. He hated the thing.

The head bookkeeper knocked neatly on Berry's frosted-glass partition door.

"Yes, yes," Berry said in a husky voice, between a drawl and a groan. He was sitting at his plain, clean desk with his head leaning on his hand.

Outside, they were finishing up the general ledger for the day, and in a little while they would be gone.

The bookkeeper put his head in. "Buford Allen is here to see you," he said.

The Colonel sat tapping with one of his dried, emaciated fingers. He had a momentary stab of fear, for some unknown reason, since he couldn't possibly feel guilty about anything, and then a feeling of alert interest. He smiled slightly, his lined, pale face showing this merely by a rearrangement of wrinkles, a shifting of its papery crevasses.

Buford—that healthy fool. What kind of peace was there in this world, anyway? As soon as a man got some money piled up, just as soon as his undoubted genius in the quartermaster corps had finally been turned loose in the free market, he began to feel his belly falling out from under him.

What kind of a world was it, where no sooner were you through with your service than your own body began to give way? Was there any reason, any reward, in this? Any justice? If the government was going to give him a pension, why didn't they give him a new stomach, too? That would have been justice.

His stool had been black for two days, and last night he had vomited a red so bright and brilliant that it could only be described as splendid. And it hurt. Yes, it hurt, all the time, and worse and worse, gnawing hideously, exactly as though some small, blind, stupid animal were inside him, gnawing continually. Why? Why? What had he ever done to deserve this?

"Have Mr. Allen wait," he said, hating Mr. Allen inexplicably.

The bookkeeper nodded and pulled his head back.

"How deep was the grave?" the Colonel asked a vague shadow sitting in the corner, which the bookkeeper hadn't even noticed. It was the old Mexican the Colonel had hired to follow Dickson. "How many feet deep?" He had been sitting there like a lizard, so still that he looked simply like a heap of clothing thrown on the chair. In the office it was fairly cool, and as long as he sat still, the old Mexican's smell was hardly noticeable, not much worse than that of an old boarding-house hall runner. When he was moving around outside in the sun, it was like fourteen buck goats fighting in a Mexican shoe factory.

"How many feet deep, Io?"

Io held up three fingers.

"Just below Berg's Mill? Where they went that night?"

"Sss," Io said, almost a whisper, just the sibilant of the word "Si" hissing in the dusk, out of the corner. He sat there, his old brown hands folded on his stomach, across a filthy white shirt that had blue stripes running up and down.

"But you didn't see them bury the boy there. You didn't see Dickson actually putting anybody in the grave, or the Negro digging it?"

Io's heavy, square head, set on his shoulders without benefit of neck, moved from side to side like an owl's.

"But that's where they pulled the boat up, isn't it?" the Colonel said. He had to do all the talking, he had found out. "You saw them pull the boat up there, and go ashore—Dickson and the Negro, carrying the body. Then, yesterday, you found this grave under the brush."

Io said nothing. He had reported all this a week ago. Let the old Americano rehearse it in his mind.

"Did you find any tracks around the grave?"

"Sss."

The Colonel looked at him. The fact was, Io would make a first-rate witness. "Dickson's tracks? The Negro's?"

"Sss."

"You are well known around San Antonio as a hunter and tracker? You make your living that way?"

"Sss."

"And you will swear that the boy—what's his name—Hugh Buss, the young boy got in the boat, and they carried him out into the brush, after you followed them in the other boat, down there below Berg's Mill. And now you have found the boy's body, and he was stabbed. Well, that's all I need. But you will swear?"

Io looked very faintly troubled. *"Otro,"* he whispered and grunted at the same time, his voice heavy in his chest.

"Another? You mean besides the boy?"

"Sss," Io sighed, much relieved at the Colonel's neat perception.

"Who?"

Io shrugged.

"What did he look like? American? Mexican? Fair? Dark? Thin face? Fat face?"

Io held up five brown fingers.

"You found five graves?"

"Sss." Io suddenly yawned, his mouth opening very wide and his white teeth gleaming.

"My God," Colonel Berry said to himself.

"Un cemeterio secreto," Io said, suddenly breaking all bounds.

The Colonel put his hands up to his head and held them there. It was as though he had had a glimpse into some subterranean world, as though he had suddenly, with a great gift, seen a soul all the way to its bottom, and he shut his eyes to it. It had occurred to him, just once, that knowledge of one murder by Dickson would be a handy thing to have, in reserve. There was always the remote danger of blackmail by Dickson—the Colonel had always admitted the risks of his weaknesses. But the five brown fingers raised suddenly out of the shadows—

He turned away and swallowed. "The girl. Haven't you found her yet?"

"Sss."

The Colonel whirled around. "Well, why didn't you tell me?" he cried. "Where is she?"

Io drew a deep breath and sat forward. He was getting ready for a speech. He said, speaking clearly, in a rather cultivated voice, "Laredo Street. She is in the big white house with the green shutters."

The Colonel looked at him with a faint, kindly smile. "Thank God," he said. In the dark, two tears formed in his eyes. He brushed them away with the back of his hand. "Thank God. Io, isn't she pretty? Is she well?"

Io said nothing.

"What a charming girl. How did she get into a life like that? So sweet. She was always so nice, so kind. She wasn't like the others."

"Sss."

"Is she well? Does she seem—" He started to say "happy," and stopped. "Is she in good health?"

Io sighed deeply and shook his head.

"What do you mean?"

"Dead."

"What?" the Colonel asked faintly.

Io looked down and said nothing. There was no use repeating what he knew the Colonel had heard.

The Colonel stood up and shouted. "What? What? You damned liar, what? You lie! Stand up! Stand up! Damn you, why should you lie?"

Outside in the office, everything stopped. Everybody stood still, frozen.

Io stood up slowly. "I am not a liar." The Colonel stood there shaking, his mouth pinched as though he wanted to speak, or was trying to keep himself from doing so. His head shook on his neck, and his lips trembled. "Sit down," he whispered. "I beg your pardon. Sit down."

Io sat down with dignity.

"Dead," the Colonel whispered. "My God, dead." For a moment he covered his face with his two hands. "But why she?" he asked plaintively. "Why she? Why did it have to be she?" He sat looking at the picture on the wall, of the old-time officers in their fading group.

Io put one finger to his throat, or at least under his chin, where he would have had a throat if he had had any neck; he opened his mouth and made a loud sound like somebody throwing up.

The Colonel looked at him miserably.

"She was choke," Io said.

"What?"

Io put his finger to his throat again, stuck out his tongue, and waggled his head, again making that noise.

"For God's sake, stop that," the Colonel said, his voice shaking with anger. "How the hell do you know? If she was—was killed in town, I'd have heard. What about the police? The police?" He started to call Io a liar again, but thought better of it, and so repeated, "The police? The police?" as though his insistence meant something. "Do they know?"

Io put his forefinger to his head, looked as wise as he could, and tapped.

"They suspect?"

"Sss."

"Where is she? Where is she?" He kept repeating everything because, like a man in pain, who has to moan, he had to make some sound, any sound, just to ease the pain.

"The White House on Laredo Street. With the green shutters."

"Who did it?" the Colonel asked.

"In the street, I listened. I am following Dickson as you say. One night—two nights ago. She is upstairs. I hear Dickson. Talk, talk, talk. She screams, words, words. He says, 'Shut up, shut up, shut up.' She screams, mad, mad, mad." Io raised his eyes, whistled sadly, and sighed profoundly. "A little while. Then— out she comes—the window. But no screaming." He put his finger to his throat, stuck out his tongue, and again made that noise.

The Colonel shut his eyes. He squeezed them. He opened them wide. "Get me the police," he said to nobody.

He stood up. "Get me the police!" he shouted.

He turned around and hit the bell on his desk as hard as he could.

The head bookkeeper came running in.

"Get me the police!" the Colonel shouted.

Already the shouts were having their effect on him, and he felt better, and also weaker.

The head bookkeeper ran.

The Colonel stood shaking. "Follow Dickson," he said to Io. "Wherever he goes. Don't lose sight of him. I'm going to dig up those graves. I'm going to arrest him, tonight. And I'll hang him. Hang him. Hang him."

"Sss," Io said, and rose, moving smoothly and easily. He moved like water, without effort, much more Aztec than Spanish. He made a small, courteous bow, in the country way, and then took a silent, Indian departure.

The assistant head bookkeeper came to the door and said, "Mr. Buford Allen is here to see you, sir," and immediately Buford Allen, smiling broadly, pushed past him and went up to the desk with his hand out.

There were tears in the Colonel's eyes, tears of sorrow and frustration and of solid physical pain, but Buford could not see that. "What do you want?" the Colonel cried out.

Buford stood, his smile gone, his mouth open. His hand dropped to his side. "Why, why," he said, and looked around vacantly, not knowing what he had wanted.

"Get out," the Colonel cried, trying to control his voice. It was too much, all of a sudden. "Get out of here, Buford! You have cost me thousands of dollars." This was not true, but the Colonel was saying it anyway, because here was a man who had cost many others thousands of dollars, a wretch who should be hanged. "I have lost thousands of dollars. Thousands, thousands. I don't want to see you again, there is nothing, absolutely nothing, I can do for you." And even when he said this, he was sorry for it, seeing Buford's face, the blankness, the lostness. But it was too late to change. "So go! Go on, get out!"

Buford's face was dead white. He stood speechless, looking at Berry. Then he turned and walked out, moving unsteadily, bumping the door frame as he passed.

Colonel Berry sat down with his head in his hands, and waited for the police. Vaguely he knew that the police could do no good. They would just hang somebody. The police never brought anybody back to life.

He listened to the sounds of revelry rise in the town around him, from the two Plazas up Houston Street. The fox gnawed steadily in his stomach. There was no way to stop it. What would happen? What was next? How little there was left, in any case, even if, by some miracle, they could stop the fox. If it wasn't the fox, it would be something else just as certain, a little later.

Nobody ever lived forever, everybody died of something. This notion, which he had known so long, but until now had never realized at all, stood clearly before him. Why? Why? What was it all for? If this was the way it ended, what was the use of beginning at all? What had been accomplished, in between? It was all some kind of stupid, insane joke. You had a cold and deceitful little daughter, and you found, incredibly, a little girl in some chance house, who was really a kind of daughter, who for some incredible reason was a little fond of you—or was it all an illusion?—actually did have some sweetness, some affection. And then she died. Why? Why? Why that particular one?

A key rattled in the front door. He looked up. It was the head bookkeeper and the tall lean man with him was Cash, a lieutenant of the city police.

The Colonel said to Lieutenant Cash, "I want Thomas Dickson arrested tonight. On five counts of murder. You had a suspicious death in a house on Laredo, didn't you?"

"Yes, sir," Cash said to the commissioner. "One of the girls. It's Dickson's house."

"I think Dickson did that one too. Put a watch on that house, Cash."

"They're having a party there tonight, sir," Cash said. "Colonel Berry, this party is an open flaunting of the law. I know damn well the girl was murdered—"

"I can prove it," the Colonel said.

"Then let me use that for an excuse to bust a few heads, for once."

The Colonel said nothing for a long moment. "I'll meet you there at—when's the party?"

"Make it nine, sir." Cash left.

What could you do, the Colonel thought, in the end, but fight? Reason had no answer, at least for him. He would fight the fox as long as he could, he would fight it to the end, and even when he knew it would win, he would buckle down and hold on and continue to fight it, holding his breath against the moans, until the very end. What else could you do? It would get him—the darkness would come, and fighting did no good. And yet there was nothing to do but fight. Just hold on, and never give an inch.

He sat there waiting, his wrinkled mouth quiet and his jaw still.

6

Mary Allen's House—6:30 P.M.

Buford wandered down Houston Street from Berry's bank, heading west in a mental fog. There was only one place where he could go, one place where he was not an outcast, and he headed there without conscious intention, simply by instinct, like a drunk. He angled across the crowded Plaza to Dolorosa and then came back up Laredo to his wife's number. He knocked on the street gate. There was no answer.

Down Laredo Street, the big white house with green shutters had come to life. For some reason, all the shutters were open—an incredible thing, really—and light was streaming out from them in wide golden bands, breaking through the deepening evening. Lights and music. The music was a waltz, and he saw that a party was going on. Laughter came out, the laughter of women, high and sparkling; and deeper, that of men. In front of the house five carriages were drawn up, and saddled horses were hitched to the posts along the curb. The rest of the block was, as usual, in its Spanish way, dead quiet and totally deserted.

There was still no answer—but this was the right house. Buford pushed open the gate and went into the little garden, and closed the gate behind him. The moon was just coming up, and its light shot across the roofs across the street, lighting the front door of the little house before him. He looked around. It was a garden no longer—the place was piled with old furniture, chairs, stoves, tables, bureaus, commodes, all of it broken, with legs missing, rungs unglued, doors hanging by twisted hinges. On one side of the yard there was an open shed, with a carpenter's bench in it and some partly mended chairs.

He went up to the door and knocked. After a moment it opened.

He could see his wife in the doorway.

"Si?" Mary said.

The moonlight shone full on her handsome face. Then she saw his beard.

"Why, Buford!" she said, her voice—still so young—full of pleasure, surprise, and oddly, a little shyness. "Why, Buford, dear—come in, come in."

She stood back, and he went in. She closed the door behind him. He stood there, looking at her in the light from the kerosene table lamp, and they looked at each other in silence for a moment. He felt her warmth, which was her love, and there rose in him the discomfort of the memory of all his injustice to her, so that he was happy to see her, and didn't want to see her, at the same time.

He didn't kiss her, and she didn't expect it.

"Still the same Mary," was all he said.

"I?" she asked. "Why should I change? It has only been three months since you left."

"Yes. But everything else—it seems like such a long time." He looked around with a somewhat dazed expression. "What a place, Mary. I don't understand."

It was a large, square room with adobe walls, hand-plastered. There was a crucifix over the door, and another on the wall before him. There was a small statue of the Virgin by a little bed in the corner, and a single candle to one side, and a rosary.

"You really live here?" he asked. He had meant to upbraid her, to scold her, but as always happened, when he was actually in her presence, he could not.

The floor was dirt, packed hard and almost shiny with sweeping. On tables along the wall there were great heaps of clothing. Then he noticed, against the back wall, two small cribs. He had thought at first they were merely two crates —but now he noticed a movement in one of them, and recognized them for what they were.

He went over and looked down inside one of them. There was a tiny baby in it, well bundled up, sleeping on its back. It was sweating. He very gently took off one of the blankets. The crucifix was directly over the babies.

Mary was standing looking at them. "I have three more," she said, and nodded at the rear door.

"Where did you get them?"

She sat down at the sewing table. "People leave them."

"Here?"

"Everywhere. In the gutters. On the sidewalk."

"But what are you doing? Trying to start a new family or something?"

"No, oh, no," she said, rather sadly. "I keep them. We try to find families for them, or the sisters take them. But, you see, now that I live here, I find more than the sisters do."

She nodded toward the piles of sewing. "I have five Mexican girls now, sewing for me. You see if they know how to do anything at all, they can make a little living, and the sisters help them. They bring in the work from all over town. Mostly old clothes, mending—but sometimes seamstress work. Two of my girls are quite clever."

All Buford could see was cockroaches, scuttling along the base of the wall.

"It's a fad. It can't last. I know the women who go for this sort of thing—they all pitch in—but wait till your girls make a few mistakes, they'll get sick of it. The pious ones'll quit you."

"Of course, you're right," she said. "I know exactly how fickle human beings are." She smiled at him.

He felt the blood falling away out of his head and heart.

"But you see, if our 'ladies' fail us, the Archbishop will give us help—and, of course, we expect things to be a little difficult."

"Why did you leave the Menger?" he asked.

"Because I was embarrassed."

"Why should you be embarrassed?" he asked, his fist tightening. "We lived there for years, didn't we? And all of a sudden you left. Why? It almost looks like a separation."

Her eyes, blue and gentle in her handsome face, had a very open, luminous look. They were the eyes of a child, but very thoughtful, and at times very shrewd. "I was thinking of the bill. There I was, living on Mr. Menger, with the bill going on, knowing you had not paid it—"

"But I would have!"

"Would you? Why, Buford, I wired you myself that news about the suit. You surely don't pretend you have any money!"

"I have a hundred and fifty thousand dollars," he said.

"Is there nobody that has a claim to it?"

"Not a just claim," he said, with a confusion that angered him more than ever.

"So it's not really yours, is it?" she asked. "That is what I meant, Buford. That is the way I began to feel in Menger's—there I was going, every morning, down to Mass at St. Joseph's, and then I would go back to Menger's for breakfast, and contribute to a debt which I doubt very much could be paid. Buford, Buford. Don't look offended! All our lives, you have been living on debts. Debts and schemes, Buford. The only change is that the debts have got bigger and bigger, and the schemes to go with them. Why don't you face it, Buford? You're at the very end. You know, when a man's friends insist that he sign notes against his word, he is at the very end. Buford, why don't you let it all go? I watched you take the blanket off the baby then because it was too hot. Why don't you help me here? You could mend the furniture we get. Why not do something for somebody else, for a change, instead of always for yourself?"

They sat in silence, he looking at the cockroaches.

Then she went on: "So every morning I would go to Mass and Holy Communion, and in my heart it grew greater and greater, a kind of reproach, as though He were saying, 'Why do you continue taking what is not yours?' As though He said, 'You love Me, but don't you see that justice must come before love, before charity?' I thought, you can't keep taking Menger's food and lodging, knowing he won't be paid. No matter how fond he is of you, he will suffer all the same, losing that money; no matter how generous he is, he is in a business."

She looked down at her sewing. "So I left Menger's."

He was sitting up straight, his own face red. "That's preposterous. Absolutely preposterous. This is what this continual religion does for you. How can you get so crazy? Was it those priests? Your spiritual directors?" he asked, biting the words "spiritual directors" with a kind of sarcasm.

She glanced up quickly. "How pleasant it is," she said, her great, bright eyes looking right into him, "to see you so sensitive. Thank God you still have a conscience. It makes me happy, Buford. It only proves I was not a fool to fall in love with you—that my judgment was right, after all. Poor Buford." She smiled at him, and his anger, or what he tried to make into anger, turned into confusion again.

"Why don't you just give up? Why pretend? For some reason, you have always thought it necessary to live up to a certain preconceived notion, level, or whatever you call it. You never once have actually been what you actually were, or allowed me to be what I actually was. Always the grand lady! That was my role. But I was never grand; and that's why you hated me, I suppose. And even now I suppose it shocks you to have it known by me, that you hated me, at times—it goes against the pretense. You always insisted that I know nothing about Clara, and nothing about you—as though I could help it—as though I were some kind of a fool. Well, perhaps I was a fool to marry you, Buford. But I was not deceived. You still love her. I don't blame you! But I will never go to Montana with you."

"What? How can you say that?" he cried out. "After all I've gone through— My God, if you knew, right now, what I'm going through!"

"I can imagine your difficulties," she said, "and I already know all your arguments. The ranch in Montana is to be our last home—away from our creditors, with me there to take care of you, as I have always done, and Clara's grave there, also, for you to potter about and put flowers on. What a perfect picture of you! Forgive me, it is so comic: your tummy well filled, somebody else's money in the bank, and a woman to worship who can no longer be anything but virtuous. Forgive me! I suppose I do resent it, Buford. But how I tried not to! All those years."

"Clara has nothing to do with it," he said. "Are you telling me you are leaving me?" He was quite sober, quite matter-of-fact.

"No. You will be leaving me. I have a life here. I was born here. But I am telling you more than that, Buford. What is up there for you? Nothing. A strange country, without friends. You think it will solve all your problems. It won't. Oh, Buford, if only you would be humble! You could get a job at Menger's. What a wonderful desk clerk you would make! So affable, so charming, so tactful."

"Why are you mocking me? Why are you trying to hurt me?"

"I'm not, Buford. You're too old to start over in a strange country with nothing but the memories of a dead woman. It all comes from the devil—illusions and dreams. You will die alone, Buford, alone in the dark, without a friend. And without God."

"I don't know why you're saying this," Buford said quietly. "I have to go north. I have to push this thing through."

"Where are your emerald cuff links?" she asked suddenly.

"Stolen," he said. "In Ogalalla."

"You see, Buford," she said, "everything is going, little by little. I want you to live decently. There's nothing wrong in being poor, Buford. You and I could be happily poor, here."

"Poor!" he said, standing up. "I was poor once. My father starved to death. It took him four years to do it, but he starved to death, trying to feed us. A minister of the Gospel, living on handouts, riding a circuit for a forest-full of scrimping bastards. A meek and humble man, a man God must have loved indeed." A sudden fury shot up into his eyes. "Poor! I've been poorer than the dogs in the gutter. I know what that is, I loved my father, and I watched him die."

"That wasn't His fault."

"His? You mean God's? Who's blaming God? I'm only thinking of the people, the damned, mean, grasping, mealymouthed hypocrites always talking about charity, and handing him a skinny old hen and half a dozen pullet eggs on Sunday, for him to feed us with, and thinking they were serving God. Their God was the devil. Damn them all!" He started to shout and suddenly saw the babies, and checked himself.

He looked at his wife. "That's why I hate their souls. Poor! I'll make them poor, I'll grind their faces in the dust."

"And where are they now," she asked quietly, "the ones who starved your father, that you will grind in the dust?"

"You know where they are," he said. "They're dead." The anger died.

He looked at his wife, and the cockroaches. "But I won't be poor. Never. Never. Never."

He turned and went out of her house, and out of her garden, full of its broken and mended furniture.

He stood in the street, alone, facing the risen moon. The noise of the dancers, singing and hilariously shouting, came up the street from the big house. He stood there in a daze. Where was Mike? All he could do now was bribe Dickson's men.

His follower came slowly up the sidewalk. He was a short man, and had to look up to Buford, who was not tall himself. He said, "Listen, Pop, I don't mind following you around, but when are you going to eat? I'm getting awful hungry.

"I know everybody in that house," his follower went on. "Let's go on down the street and go in. They got a hell of a spread. Turkeys, hams, beef—you should see it; all kinds of booze. What say?"

Buford said nothing. The music grew louder. Why not? He had to eat. He couldn't lose this fellow. He couldn't go back to the Menger to wait for Mike. But Mike would come to see his mother, and this party was close by.

"Why not?" Buford said wearily, and walked down the sidewalk with the other. When Mike came, the two of them would bribe this little fellow—maybe tie him up and throw him over a wall somewhere.

A man stepped out of a carriage in front of them. He had a gun in his hand. "Step in, Buford," Spence said, motioning with the gun. "We'll wait here for Mike."

Buford said, his voice low with shock and fear, "He doesn't know where I am."

"No," Spence said, "but he'll come by and see his mother, won't he? Isn't he a good boy? Get in."

Buford climbed in.

Dickson, sitting inside, smiled gently. "Quite a little party, Buford," he said. "Do you know Mr. Keppelbauer? Keppelbauer, if you will stop moaning and sniveling for a moment, I would like to introduce you to somebody. A fool like yourself, let us say. Exactly." He climbed over Buford and got out of the carriage. "I'll just stroll to the Menger and see if Mike's shown up, eh? Ta-ta, boys."

7

Degen's Brewery—7:00 P.M.

Mike came into town on a farmer's horse, for which he had paid double. It was dark, and the moon was just coming up as he rode slowly up Blum Street from the east, toward the Menger. He got off the horse at the door of Degen's Brewery, which was just behind the Menger, down Blum Street, and knocked on the door.

Old Adolf Dallmeyer let him in. Adolf had a policeman's nightstick. He was eating his supper, liverwurst-and-rye sandwiches with pickles, and a big stein of Degen's best.

"Vell, vell, Mike," Adolf said, backing away from the door and letting Mike in. "What is this? A horse you on her highvay drags?"

"I fell off a train," Mike said. "Mind if I leave something here for a while?"

"Mind? Who, me? Vy should I mind? Leave anything. What? Your horse, is it?" He laughed a big, deep haw, haw, haw, and rubbed his stomach.

Mike had the saddlebags in his hand. All the way down from Cheyenne, through Pueblo and Dodge, over to Kansas City, he had never opened those bags, never changed the money into a suitcase, never thought of it, until he had paid his father's bill in St. Louis. He looked around for a place to hide it.

The brewery, with a single lamp high on one damp wall, looked like a cavern with its big barrels and mash vats. The place was warm and cozy, full of slopped water from the barrel-washing department, and the rich smell of the mash and the hops was everywhere.

"You take them," Mike said, handing Adolf the saddlebags. "Keep 'em for me awhile."

"Sure, sure," Adolf said, and slung them neatly behind his big chair under the lamp. "A beer, Mike?"

"No time," Mike said. He smiled. "Going to see my girl."

"Haw, haw, haw," Adolf laughed, patting his stomach.

Mike got back on his horse and rode up around to the front door of Menger's.

Isaac Forrest was leaning against the wall beside the front steps.

"Hello, sonny," Isaac said. "Been waiting."

"I hope I haven't been too long," Mike said.

"Where is it?"

"Where is what?" Mike asked, and walked past him, up the steps.

"The money," Isaac said, following him into the lobby.

"Is my father in?" Mike asked at the desk.

"He left a message he'd be at your mother's," the clerk said politely. He looked at the clipboard. "Mrs. Allen is staying in a house on Laredo." He wrote the address for Mike.

"Are the bags upstairs?"

"Yes, sir."

Mike started for the stairway.

"Just a minute," Isaac said, putting his hand on Mike's arm. Mike stopped.

"There's a warrant out for your arrest," Isaac said in a low, serious voice. "Don't give me the runaround, boy, or I'll have you chucked in the can. Where's the money? The boss has given your old man till midnight to kick through. It's up to you, sonny. So give."

Mike looked down at the hand on his arm, and carefully spat on it.

Isaac snatched his hand away and stood there, his eyes snapping. He wiped his hand on the side of his pants. "After I get the money," Isaac said. "Business before pleasure."

"I haven't got the money," Mike said. "A man in Baton Rouge has it. I bought two cassowaries with it. They died. I ate them."

He turned and walked up the stairs.

Isaac stood in the middle of the lobby with his big fists clenched. The clerk looked at him warily. Tommy Dickson, who had been sitting peacefully under a palm tree, got up and walked over to Isaac.

"Well done, Isaac," Tommy said, patting him gently on the shoulder. "You naughty kitten, go find your mitten, or else you'll have no pie. Evidently he's

going to see his mother, as I thought. Just follow him around town. Sooner or later he'll lead you right to the money, wherever he left it."

Dickson sauntered out, swinging his cane jauntily.

8

Colonel Berry's House—7:15 P.M.

Nancy Berry put her hand over the mouthpiece of her father's home phone, that splendid toy of which she was so proud.

"Oh, dear," she said. "Daddy, it's Mike Allen. He's back in town. I thought he might be killed."

"How interesting," the Colonel said. He was sitting in the parlor, drinking a double bourbon and water, waiting for the fox to go to sleep.

"But what will I do?" Nancy cried.

"Do what you usually do when you get tired of them," the Colonel said. "Put your foot in the middle of his face and push. Hard."

"How can you say such a thing?" Nancy quavered, her hand still over the phone. "Oh, Daddy." She tried to sound sorrowful and aggrieved. But somehow the thought of putting her foot in the middle of Mike's face was so funny that she laughed. While she was still laughing, she took her hand off the phone so Mike could hear it. He would wonder why she was laughing. A girl had to keep them wondering.

"Oh, Mike darling. Oh, how nice that you're back!"

Mike said something.

"Tonight? Now?" she asked, with pretty dismay. "But Daddy's going out. There won't be anybody here—except just me."

Mike said something.

Suddenly all the charm and mirth vanished from Nancy Berry's face. She looked a little angry, and then, as Mike talked on, a little bored, and finally she smiled a smile of contempt. "Very well, darling," she finally cooed, "since I promised all that, come on over—in an hour." She put the telephone carefully together again and left it hanging on the wall.

"I thought you said Lieutenant Milford was coming over this evening," the Colonel said.

"Jimmie Milford?" she asked. "Oh, Daddy, don't be so quaint. Captain Barnes is coming over, not that little old Jimmie. That little old Jimmie Milford? Why, he's so silly. He threatened to shoot himself. Anyway, I want Mike to meet Captain Barnes. It should be amusing."

"One of them actually did shoot himself, didn't he?" the Colonel asked.

"You mean that little old Tommy Bragg? Oh, gracious, Daddy, you can't think he did that over me, do you?"

"I don't think anything," the Colonel said. "There is a point in life beyond which it does not pay to think."

She looked at him, wondering what he meant, or if he was just drunk. He sat there, bitterly enduring her. There was nothing he could do about it. It took all his self-control to keep from remembering her as a baby, as a little girl, in those times when she was so tiny, sweet, and happy. Maybe later, when she was gone, when she had carried her little whirl of private vice into somebody else's jurisdiction, was married, and had moved from the sphere of fornication into that of adultery, he would feel safe to remember those happy days. But he could not afford to now.

Her sweet, low, husky voice went on, talking about Mike, sticking him full of pins. A smelly cowhand, was the gist of it. The Colonel sat and drank. When he had finished, he got up and stood straight and still, looking at his daughter.

How pretty she was! Standing there in that evening dress. Her pale-gold hair, her blue eyes, her delicately pointed chin, her vivacious smile. It had taken a long time for his hatred of her conduct to kill his love for her.

Somebody knocked on the front door.

"Another sheep to the slaughter," the Colonel said. "What a carnage."

"What's that, Daddy?" she asked.

"Nothing," he said. "I'll run along. I suppose you'll be sending the servants home early. As usual."

"Why not?" she asked gaily. "Poor things, they need a rest."

"I should think they would," the Colonel said, and went out.

"Where are you going, Daddy?" she cried, running after him, affection on her face like icing on a cake. "If I need you?" She always said that. The six-year-old innocent.

"To a party," he said. "They're having a dance in a whorehouse down on Laredo Street." He said this with profound pleasure. It was the first time in his life he had ever used that word in the presence of a woman. With interest, he watched the lies coming and going on her face, nymphic glee chasing girlish wonder. "I'm going down there with Lieutenant Cash and get drunk."

At the door moments later the young captain, turning upon the spit of her charm, himself, in turn, turned upon her the full force and beam of his own winning smile, telling her with his eyes that he adored her, while the old houseman, wheezing and snuffling, took his cap.

"You may go, Joseph," Nancy said. This rather regal form of address she used on the servants in front of Northern men, who wouldn't understand if she spoke to old Uncle Joe as one of the family.

Joe sighed, "Yazzum," and chuffing and wheezing painfully, padded slowly away down the hall in his old split shoes, which had large holes cut out of the sides of the uppers, to make room for his bunions.

"Darling," the captain said, opening his arms. "Darling." What he lacked in vocabulary he made up in expressiveness.

"Not yet!" she whispered, her finger on her lips, looking at him from the side

of her eye. "Let's go out in the garden. It's so lovely in the moonlight!" What she meant was that they could both lie to each other better if they couldn't see each other quite so well.

9

Colonel Berry's House—8:30 P.M.

All the way across town in the carriage, Mike had been thinking about Nancy Berry. The two dozen red roses which he had bought, and which he held carefully suspended by the stems, filled the musty old box with their sweet scent.

He was not rich, he thought, but at least he had about forty thousand dollars, which was enough to start his own business. His father could pay for the two herds which were now going north secretly, and use them to start himself again, while Mike took what was left of the $160,000 and made his own way.

With Nancy. At least, that had been the plan—the "understanding."

Was there ever a girl like Nancy? A gay little girl, a flirt, in a way, but so tender, so delicate, so charming, with her little pointed chin and her golden hair.

The picture, for some reason, lacked life. His habitual response to it, of tender affection, was sluggish. He prodded it, and remembered Clara Montrosc. What was the matter with him? He had been in love with Nancy Berry for eight long years. He must be tired, that was all. Clara was just a friend. He loved Nancy. Yes, he loved Nancy. Maybe he didn't like her much, but he loved her. He sat suddenly astounded at this thought. How, indeed, could he have thought it? But he had. Was he crazy?

The carriage pulled up in front of the Colonel's house, and he got out and told the driver to wait. He was going to take Nancy for a ride, if the old Colonel would permit it. The thought of Nancy's forwardness—that innocent excess of desire, which seemed to him to be such an evidence of her love for him—crossed his mind, and he shut it away immediately. That was a problem that would soon be solved decently, and happily.

Nobody answered Mike's knock.

He knocked again, just a little longer.

He waited. He remembered Sister Margaret Mary, long ago cautioning the boys at St. Mary's College to say two Our Fathers before knocking the second time. He said two Our Fathers.

Then he knocked again, just a little louder.

There was a light on in the parlor, but there was not a sound in the whole house.

He stood there, surprise turning into a kind of unbelieving dismay. She had said she would be in, and for him to come over in an hour. Well, he was here, wasn't he? And where was she?

He began to be a little alarmed. The house was so still.

He went to the parlor window and looked in. There was nobody in the room.

He stood in the night, listening to the insects and the treefrogs, trying to think of what could have happened.

The silence of the house began to oppress him, and suddenly his whole attitude changed from the rather dizzy one of expectant excitement to a clear alertness, without any emotion at all, exactly as though he were again facing Spence on the trail north.

It was just barely possible that something was wrong. Still carrying the roses, he went quietly along the side of the house, looking at the windows, and at the second story.

In the rear there was the usual lawn, running down to the river, cut off from the neighboring houses and yards by hedges of oleander and mock orange. The moon was bright, his button shoes sank in the smooth grass, and the crickets hardly paused as he passed, so full were they of moonlight and the heat of summer.

He came around the back of the house, and there, in a kind of bower, across the lawn, where a lace vine grew, he saw his beloved Nancy in the arms of an army officer, who was kissing her. Then he noticed that one of Nancy's shoulders was bared, something he had never seen before.

Almost at the same time, Nancy saw him—almost, in fact, as though she had been waiting for him—and cried, "Oh! Oh! A man!"

The captain sprang to his feet, his hair and his wits in great dishevelment. He saw Mike. "You, there! Stand where you are."

Mike said nothing, and stood where he was.

"Who are you?" the captain demanded, jerking down his tunic and straightening himself out while trying to speak in a tone of military authority.

Mike moved slowly toward them, carrying the roses. "My name is Allen," he said. "I hope you will—I, that is—I had an engagement this evening with—" His head was swimming. He could hardly see.

"Why, Mike," she said, from the bower, "what an awful thing—Why, you know I told you I didn't want to see you again. How could you have come here, uninvited, when I told you—"

"You don't want him here, Miss Nancy?" the captain asked, whirling around.

"Now, Mike," Nancy said, "please don't make any trouble."

"I'm not making any trouble," Mike said. "I'm just standing here."

"Get out," the captain said. "I order you to get off this place at once. If you don't, I shall have the pleasure—"

"What?" Mike turned slowly and looked at him. "What did you say?" he asked dully.

The captain took two steps toward Mike, pulled back his fist, and hit Mike on the right cheekbone. Mike fell down. He sat there shaking his head.

"Stand up, sir," the captain said, "and fight like a man."

"Listen," Mike said, his head clearing, "I don't feel like fighting." He got up slowly and stood shaking his head again.

The captain swung once more, and Mike moved to the side with an expression of fatigue. "Please," Mike said, "I told you once I don't feel like fighting. Not at all. Can't you wait till some other time? Really, this all—"

The captain swung again. His tunic was binding him so that he puffed.

"Oh, for God's sake," Mike said. "You damn fool."

He sank one in the captain's stomach. The captain bent over, and Mike hit him in the side of the jaw. The captain had a head like iron. Mike had to hit him four times before he collapsed. When the captain finally lay out on the turf, he relaxed and started breathing again. Mike nursed his knuckles. He felt dizzy.

He turned and looked at Nancy. She was sitting in the bower, her face pale and pinched, without expression.

"Get out," she said sharply. "You are not a gentleman. Get out, you smelly cattle driver."

Mike stood looking at her. He couldn't believe it. He couldn't believe any of it. He stood there like a cow in a slaughterhouse, that has been hit once on the head, but not quite hard enough.

"Who is this man?" he finally asked. "I don't understand. I thought—Then you don't—Who is this man? Are you engaged?"

She laughed in a low, throaty voice. "Get out!" she said. "You idiot. Engaged! Get away, with your dirty cows! Go away! Go away! Do you think I ever cared anything about you?"

"With your dress half off," he said. "What's this?" It sank in, little by little. The harsh voice, the white, pinched face, the hate behind the words, and the words themselves. No matter how dumb he was, it had to sink in sometime.

"I knew there was some competition," he said, his voice trembling. "But— Do you know what you looked like? You and that man? You looked like a piece of raw meat with a big fat blowfly on top of it."

He whipped her across the face with the roses, paper and all. Petals flew.

"You dirty little tramp." She sat there, stunned.

He whipped her again, and the petals showered on the lawn. "You damn, dirty little bitch."

His eyes suddenly filled with tears, not for her, not for love, not for dreams, but simply from humiliation, from the feeling of filth, at being in contact with what he could now perceive. He saw himself with a dull certainty, for what he had been—a fathead. For the first time in his life he saw with absolute clarity that there was a distinct difference between what might actually be and what he wished to be, and that nothing in heaven and earth could make what he wished to be out of what was, if it wasn't that by nature.

He looked at the roses, still in his hand. He started to throw them down, and couldn't. They had done nothing. Why should he associate them with this little tart? They represented love—well, there was nothing wrong with love, and nothing wrong with roses. So why throw them down? The only thing wrong was his own fat head.

Without looking again at Nancy, who was now sitting there rigid with fright, he took the roses down to the river and, taking off the paper, threw them far out into the water. He watched them float away in the moonlight until they were gone, and then came back.

He stood in front of the paralyzed girl, who now was sure he was crazy, and was waiting for the worst, and said, "Please accept my apologies for my conduct."

His voice was quiet, cold, and heavy, as it had never been before. His face was heavier too, and it had a wholly new expression of profound reserve. He spoke with complete gravity and calm.

"Good-by," he said. "I am sorry, from the bottom of my heart, for having hurt you, in any way."

He looked at the captain, still lying peacefully on the turf. He stooped over and straightened the captain out a little, so that he looked a little more dignified. He sighed deeply.

He turned and walked away, back to the carriage.

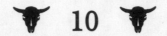

10

Mary Allen's House—9:00 P.M.

"Have you seen Nancy Berry?" his mother asked.

"Yes, I saw her," Mike said.

He sat looking at his mother, and she sat looking at him, smiling quietly.

The heavy lines of his face softened and he smiled at her. He was sitting on the same chair his father had used. The sound of the dance band came up the street. There was something cold about his smile, something too reserved.

"What's the matter, Mike?"

"Nothing," he said.

"I hope—you mustn't mind if I say this—I hope you won't allow one experience to make you bitter. In fact," she said, looking at his face, "I know you won't."

"That's right," he said. The dance band in the big house down the street swung along, and a shriek of laughter rose and subsided.

"Marriage depends on making a sensible choice," she said. "Love is no substitute for character."

"Yes," he said, seeing through her, and seeing what she had not meant him to see, her life with Buford. After a moment he said, "Father still wants that ranch. He can't possibly get it. But he's still scheming."

"Yes. He told me."

"What is the matter with him? Why that one ranch in Montana, of all places? There's something between him and Montrose. But what?"

"I suppose I'd better tell you. Only I don't want you to be angry with him,

Mike." She sighed. "You mustn't expect people to be noble—or even good. Buford—hasn't much character. Don't be angry with weak people, Mike."

"What's he done now? Anything new?"

"No, no. Do you know anything about a Clara Montrose?" she asked.

For some reason, he blushed. "Yes. I met her in Cheyenne. How did he know her?"

"That's the daughter. I mean her mother. Her mother was named Clara too. She and your father were engaged, here in San Antonio. That was in 1855—six years before the war." Her thread snarled. She straightened it.

"She lived here with her father." She sat quiet, not sewing. Then she said, with difficulty, "He was in love with her then. He's always been in love with her. I'm quite sure he's in love with her now. That's why he wants Montrose's ranch."

"That's crazy," Mike said. "What's the ranch got to do with a woman?"

"Because she died there. He isn't crazy, Mike. He just—he simply has never been able to get over loving that one woman. And I know he has tried. You see, he was always so impulsive, and he didn't have much head, for all his scheming. Your father isn't really a schemer, although he appears to be. I admired him so much—I haven't the slightest idea why, now. I suppose I thought he was so brave and dashing.

"He was engaged to her that spring, in 1855. He used to get drunk and ride his horses through town, scaring everybody. Buford was so wild that summer. He would get into fights and many people were afraid of him. My father said he hoped somebody would shoot him.

"And do you know, that was when I began to love Buford, I suppose, because I saw that everybody was against him—and I thought I understood him. San Antonio was such a little town then, Mike—everybody knew everybody.

"And I suppose he used to go up there to her house drunk—or half drunk. I don't know what happened. I really don't. But I suppose if I had been Clara, I would have done the same thing. After all, an engagement is supposed to be a happy time, and certainly she couldn't have been very happy. So that fall she broke their engagement, and Buford stopped drinking—not right away, but pretty soon. And he started courting her all over again, but of course it was too late.

"And besides, Montrose had come to town by then, and he was courting Clara too, and he was so distinguished—and so different from Buford." She stopped and thought, her eyes far away.

"Your father had a good deal of money then; he was trading in cotton with the English. He was more handsome than ever—such fine clothes! He bought those emerald cuff links then. And he started coming to our house more often, and he had stopped drinking, and I thought it was I who had made him stop. You see, I was nineteen, and so wise. Clara was engaged to Lieutenant Montrose. Your father and I were engaged that same year, and he used to take me to so many parties, and we had such a good time, and I really got to know Clara quite well.

"Everywhere we went, there was Clara, with Montrose, and I didn't notice it then, but I see why now.

"Actually, I saw the next year. Because when Clara married Montrose that next June, in 1857, and they went away on their trip, Buford and I—"

She stopped for a long time. Her face lost the remembering look, and became present. She said, rather stiffly, "Buford and I were married that summer. And when Montrose was transferred north somewhere, then Buford and I stopped going to all the parties and the picnics, and I began to understand."

She said, after a moment, "I want you to go north with him again, and take care of him. I know you don't want to go. But I am sure no good will come of this venture. Will you?"

He looked at her. "Why not? I'll leave my money with you—what I figure is my share. He can lose the rest."

"That's a good idea. He never let me save anything. Mike, don't be like Buford. Be humble, see the truth, and don't expect anything except what you deserve. Work hard, save your money, and try to be kind to the weak. Try to be like St. Joseph. Be a good man."

"All right," he said. "I'll try." He added, "The only trouble is, taking care of Dad, it's kind of hard to be good, sometimes."

"Well, you won't have too much longer. He's coming to the end of his rope. If he doesn't change, he'll crash. He's headed for a fall, Mike. Please try to help him."

"I'd better find him," Mike said, standing up. "Where did you say he was going when he left here?"

"He didn't say. But try the Menger. He always used to end up there."

Out in the street, Lt. Cash was staring at the lights of the big white house with a look of bleak hatred. Colonel Berry stood beside him, humped over, smoking a cigar. Four cops leaned against the wall, smoking cigars and talking. Somebody had brought out sandwiches and beer, and Lt. Cash had increased his popularity by knocking the tray into the gutter.

"Look at 'em, Colonel," he said. "God, how I hate their guts. I know what it all is, it's just Dickson's way of mocking the public. A murder in one of his whorehouses, so he produces a dance. Let me at 'em."

"How are you coming with the five graves I told you about?"

"They're digging at them now, Colonel. We'll know in a little while. Come on, let me at this. Just let me and my boys at this."

The Colonel said, "It's just barely possible those graves are innocent—Mexicans or somebody. We'll have to wait. I can't close down this place just because it's a whorehouse. You know that."

"I'd burn it to the ground," Cash said. He was a strict Presbyterian, and the open flaunting of the law infuriated him.

The Colonel thought a long while. "I guess you'd better have them take the girl's body back to the morgue. I guess we'd better have the autopsy. The doctor says that's the only way we can prove she was strangled before she fell out the window."

The thought of this was the one thing that was like a hot iron in the Colonel's mind.

Cash stood there fuming, chewing his mustache, his tall, lean figure tense and stooped. A buggy drove up.

"What did you find, doctor?" the Colonel asked as a little man jumped out of the buggy. The doctor shook his head.

"Colonel," he said, "three of them were stabbed through, one of them was shot in the head. The other was so far gone I couldn't—"

"That's enough," the Colonel said. "Lieutenant Cash, I want you to get a warrant immediately for the arrest of Thomas Dickson for these six murders. I have a witness."

Suddenly he closed his eyes and stopped talking, because of the tears that came out of nowhere. The dance music from the house across the street had been working on him all evening. He had looked back on his delusions, remembering the little girl, of whom he had been so fond, who had seemed to him, in his age, so gentle, so meek, and even affectionate, in her way; and he had known them indeed to have been delusions, nothing but the wishes of his heart, his loneliness; and this had made the bitterness of her death even more bitter.

Underneath the heavy tears a flame of rage lit up, of hatred and revenge. "Go get 'em, Cash," he said. "Clean 'em out. Every damn one. And use your nightsticks."

A laugh came out of Cash's lean, hard mouth, harsh and joyful. "Come on, boys! Let's clean it out! Let's go!"

In a tight, sober group, grinning, the policemen ran across the street, toward the front door.

Somebody shouted the magic cry of "Cops!" and immediately panic spread and flying bodies jammed the door. Windows crashed, and men and women fled screaming out of the house and down the street, some still singing and laughing, scattering in all directions.

Cash came out and stood sweating by the Colonel.

"Cinch bugs," Cash said, laughing heartily. "Look at 'em," he cried with delight at the fleeing men and women. "Just like kicking a bed in a country hotel. Watch 'em run!"

Inside, the cops were cleaning up. The wagon had come clanging, then a second, and they were bundling the wounded and the drunk and the unconscious in, packing them in like tamales in a pot.

"Never mind them," the Colonel said. "Get going. I want Dickson in the jail tonight."

Cash ran to his horse.

Down the street, Dickson was sitting quietly in his carriage.

Buford sat glumly in the corner, beside Spence. Dickson saw Mike coming down the street, and he pointed and nudged Spence.

Spence got out and pulled a gun. One of the police wagons clanged past, and then the other, and the hubbub quieted.

Mike slowed up, seeing the gun.

"Get in there," Spence said.

"I've got to find my father," Mike said.

"He's in there already. Get in. We're going to have a talk."

"The time has come," Dickson said politely, "to settle our accounts. Your father refuses to give up the money. There's only one alternative."

Mike got in. His father looked at him without expression. "Don't give them a cent, Mike. They're bluffing."

In the other corner Keppelbauer sat with his face in his hands. His sack suit was still covered with the dust of his falls under Forrest's whip. Sweat ran into his chin whiskers.

"Drive on," Dickson said, slamming the door.

The driver slapped the reins, and they moved from the light to the darkness.

The Colonel stood alone with the last of the carriages rolling away down the street. The lights of the house still burned brilliantly, but now there was total silence.

The Colonel's Mexican came by, trotting quietly on an unshod mule.

"Io!" the Colonel cried. "Where is Dickson?"

Io pointed down the street at the last of the carriages, which was turning the corner into Dolorosa. "There he goes. Didn't you know he was there all the time?"

The Colonel looked around for help. The street was empty and silent. He ran and got his horse. He trotted on down the street after Io, who was riding a safe distance behind the carriage.

The Colonel felt suddenly for a gun. He had none. He kept on, keeping well behind Io, so that the shod hoofs of his own horse would not be heard by the driver of the carriage, far up ahead.

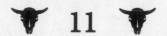 **11**

The Country West of Town
Same Night—11:00 P.M.

"You can run if you like," Dickson said. "However, you won't get far."

"This is a very poor joke," Buford said. His voice shook.

"I assure you, it is no joke," Dickson said. His voice was tight and strained.

They were standing in a triangle, back to back—Keppelbauer, Buford, and Mike. They were handcuffed together.

Buford's Panama hat shone white in the moonlight. The countryside was quite clear—mesquite and brush silver-tipped, shadows black and unmoving. There was no wind.

They were nowhere. It was just a small clearing in the brush west of town, four miles out and well off the road.

The carriage was silver-topped in the moonlight, and the horses moved gently, clinking their harness and bits. There were five riders sitting their horses quietly in a rough circle around the three men, at a distance of about ten yards. Dickson and Spence were on foot, facing the three men in the middle of the clearing.

How had they ever got this far? Mike thought, with a kind of stupefied wonder. He was deathly afraid—fear like pitch darkness inside him. First he had got into the carriage. What else could he have done? Spence had had the gun, and he had submitted, because Buford was inside. He couldn't run, with Buford in there, and Spence armed like that.

They had driven out of town, fast, with these five horsemen around the coach. Nobody had said anything. But what could he have done then? Shout? Who would have heard him?

Should he have jumped out into the road? But how could he, leaving his father in there? So he had submitted to one thing after another, believing somehow that nothing much could happen in the end. Even the handcuffs he had taken, because his father could not have fought and run.

And so here they were now, handcuffed together in the moonlight, and he could not believe what Dickson was saying. How could it have gone this far? Half an hour ago he had been walking down the street—and here he was, helpless.

It wasn't a joke, but it was a threat. That was all it was—a threat; they were simply trying to scare the Allens into giving up the money. But in that case, why was Keppelbauer there?

"Welshers," Dickson said, as though answering him. "Welshers. Wretched, rotten suckers. You play, you think you can bluff out of anything. Why should I let you go? To spread the news that Dickson is a soft touch? You're through. Through. And the world is better off without you. Cover their eyes, Spence."

And Spence was walking around them. Keppelbauer was whimpering like a dog. He sounded like a lonesome little puppy, out in the cold, lost.

"This is absurd," Buford said. "It is preposterous and insulting. Do you think you are dealing with children, Dickson? Do you think for an instant you can frighten us into doing anything?"

"It's long past that," Dickson said quietly. Spence appeared in front of Mike holding a white bandage in his hands. Mike saw the bandage coming up, and right then he knew that this was more than a threat. He swung his foot and kicked at Spence's groin. Spence turned, and Mike's foot caught him in the thigh. Mike tried to get him again. The handcuffs yanked and tore and the three men staggered together. Keppelbauer fell down, crying.

Then Spence's fists were pounding Mike in the face, and he could see Spence's teeth glinting in a fixed smile, as the fists showered into him. He staggered, dizzy, and fell.

After a moment, he found himself on his knees, the bandage over his eyes. Keppelbauer was crying loudly, and Buford was cursing Spence and Dickson.

"How unresigned," Dickson said from far away. "One should try to die with dignity, at least."

In Mike there was nothing but sick horror at the suddenness of it. Dickson really meant it, and he was helpless, and so that was that. But it was the suddenness, the unpreparedness, that was horrible, the horrible knowledge of time lost, of things he would never now do. He became aware of a tooth rolling around in his mouth, and tasted sweet blood. He spat out the tooth and got slowly to his feet.

His father was still cursing, in a voice incredibly slow and cold and full of hatred—cursing not as swearing, but as calling down the solemn curses of God on their heads, damning them into the pits of hell. His voice went on, solemnly, low and rough, deliberately and with terrible, anguished sincerity.

"You see," Dickson said, "you people always think you can get away with it. Well, you can't."

It was incredible, and yet it was true.

"Wait," Mike said.

"I did wait," Dickson said. "Gentlemen, ride away. Ride away. You know I require privacy."

Horses' hoofs shoved sand. Mike could hear the grating and the crunching of gravel, and the squeaking of leather, fading away. How many were left?

"Mr. Keppelbauer is leaving San Antonio," Dickson said. "He is a bankrupt and he is running out on his creditors. Let's say so, anyway. To Venezuela. At least that will be the rumor. And the Allens—let's see—another trip—what does it matter? Bankrupts, too. They ran away to California—or is it Montana? —completely disappeared. Who cares? People are always doing it."

Suddenly Mike felt like laughing, and then this feeling turned into nausea. It was all quite unreal. And yet the fear was bigger than ever, a black cloud growing inside of him that would reach his mind, in a moment, and swamp it. What was coming? What was this silence? What was coming out of the silence?

"Dickson, Dickson, where are you?" he asked.

His father was whispering to himself.

"Here I am," Dickson said. He was off to the right somewhere, quite close.

Keppelbauer suddenly gave a sharp cry of pain and surprise, and stopped as suddenly, and fell. Mike felt his dead weight, dragging down on his left arm.

"Poor fellow," Dickson said, quite close. "And now you, my dear old friend. Why didn't you give me the money on time, Buford? It was a small thing, after all."

"I'll tell you where the money is," Mike said quickly. "You'll never find it if you kill us. I'll tell you, only just don't hurt my father."

"No." Dickson's voice was tight.

"Let us loose," Mike said, speaking as quickly as he could. "Take us back. I'll take you directly to the money."

"No!" Dickson said. "Damn you, do you think this is easy? Do you think I like to come out here? No! I gave you the chance—"

"You'll never find the money," Mike said. "You'll never find the herds. Think of the herds—$400,000. Half a million altogether."

"Don't do it," Spence said from somewhere. "Don't. Get the money. The money. Money, money, money. Dickson, get the money. Half a million. He's right."

Mike heard whispering somewhere, sharp hissing through the dark.

And then Spence said, "No, no, they're not. They didn't see you. They can't swear to anything. You can let them loose."

Feet crunched in the sand. There was a clicking sound and tugging at Mike's left arm, and he knew it was the padlock key. Suddenly the weight of Keppelbauer's body was gone, and then there was panting and grunting.

There was silence for a long moment. He heard the trunk of the carriage slam.

A hand seized Mike's arm, and the key slid and caught. The handcuff came off. The bandage fell down.

Spence was kicking dirt and sand over something on the ground. Keppelbauer was gone.

Dickson was stretching himself in the moonlight, like a cat, yawning as though he had just got out of bed after a long sleep. "Ah, what a beautiful evening," he said. "What a lovely drive we have had in the country! Come along, gentlemen, let's go back to the city, shall we? We'll pick up the money, and then we'll have a little talk." There was silence.

Dickson looked at Mike and his father with a smile. "Let's have no further foolishness, my friends. As for Keppelbauer—do you see him? There are seven of us who will swear we never came here at all."

Buford was shaking. Mike could hear his teeth rattling. Buford suddenly sat down on the ground, and Mike knelt and held his old body up.

"Give him a drink," Dickson said. Spence brought a bottle from the carriage.

They got Buford on his feet and he stood there, licking his lips, looking around with a terrible fatigue.

"The carriage," Dickson said pleasantly, gesturing with his cane.

Mike followed his father into the carriage. The carriage swung forward, and the horsemen closed around it, traveling as before, a guard.

"And where are we going, Mike?" Dickson asked brightly.

"Degen's Brewery," Mike said.

12

Degen's Brewery—Midnight

They came back into town on Houston, down around the Cathedral, and up West Crockett toward the Little House. As they crossed Navarro, Dickson, looking ahead across the bridge, saw three men standing across the street from the Little House, plain in the bright light coming from the doors.

"Police," he said to Spence, and Spence sat forward a little. "Didn't you pay off on time?"

Spence didn't answer. He stuck his head out of a window and said to the driver, "Keep going, don't stop. Drive right past." He turned to Forrest, who was riding alongside with the five other men and said, "Ride right on past, Ike. Looks like trouble." Forrest smiled and glanced quickly around at the other riders. He gathered himself in the saddle, sucking his guts up and grinning.

Spence sat back. He and Dickson looked at the police through the window as they passed. The police were just standing there, one leaning against a wall, the other two against the lamp post.

"Most peculiar," Dickson said. "If I thought it would do any good, I would feel outraged. God knows we pay enough not to be bothered."

"It isn't that," Spence said, gnawing at a few bristles from his mustache. "Something's got fouled up with that girl—Joanne."

Dickson sat tense, perfectly quiet. "Absurd."

"It isn't absurd. It couldn't be anything else."

"It is something else," Dickson said. "I ought to go in the back door and find out."

"Get the money first," Spence said. "Forrest can go back and ask some of the boys."

"Is there, by any chance, anybody following us?" Dickson asked.

Spence turned quickly and looked out the back. There wasn't much traffic left that late at night, but there was enough to keep him from noticing Io, slopping along on his mule. The Colonel was too far back.

They went on past toward Alamo Plaza. "Send one of the men back," Spence said to Forrest out of the window. "Find out why the police are hanging around."

He sat back, and the carriage went on across the Plaza, on down Crockett Street, around the block along Nacogdoches, and then up Blum Street toward the Plaza again, slowing in front of the brewery door.

Dickson looked around the dark street. There were lights from the Plaza, but the carriage sat in a bank of darkness. Music came from the bands along the river, faintly through the summer night.

"Let's get out of sight," Dickson said. Spence poked a gun in Mike's ribs. "Get us in there," Spence said in a hard, low voice. "Don't try a break, mister. If there's going to be trouble, you'll catch it first."

Mike knocked at the door.

"Who is it?" the big watchman asked from inside.

"It's me, Mike. Let me in, Adolf."

"Oh, you, mine friend."

The big door slid back, and Adolf looked at the men behind Mike—Spence, Dickson, Forrest, and the other four.

"Vat is dis, Mike?" he asked. "I can't sell no beer now."

"We won't be a minute," Mike said. "Where's the saddlebags?"

A horse was coming up Blum Street, going hard. The rider pulled up in front of the brewery, and they all turned. It was the man Forrest had sent back to the Little House. He swung down and ran up to Dickson. "It's you they're looking for," he said. "Cash has a warrant out for you—for murder."

Dickson's mouth set in a pinched line.

"And I passed Colonel Berry," the man said. "He's coming along Nacogdoches Street. It sure as hell looks like he was following us."

Dickson glanced quickly down Blum Street. It was empty. "Get inside the brewery, everybody," he said. "You drive that carriage out of here," he ordered the driver. "And you keep your damn mouth shut, boy, or I'll cut your damn head off. Now drive like the devil—hurry! Forrest, you and your men get up the street and cover this door."

He turned and went quickly through the big doorway. Spence followed with his gun, herding Mike and Buford in after Dickson. He shoved the heavy door shut behind them. They heard Forrest and his men clatter away outside.

"Murder," Adolf breathed heavily, his eyes wide on Dickson. He half-raised his nightstick. "You?" It was too much for him. He was paid to manhandle breakers-in, not figure things out. While he was standing there trying desperately to think, Spence slipped around behind him and before Mike could lift a hand, yell, or move a foot, he had slugged Adolf across the back of the head with the pistol barrel. Adolf went down like a wet hide and lay in ponderous sleep on the black flags.

"I hope to God I didn't kill him," Spence said, looking down at him.

"What's the difference?" Dickson said. "One more won't matter." He turned and looked at Mike and Buford. His thin face with its high, fine nose was dead pale in the light of the single lantern. "After all I've paid, they wouldn't get out a warrant without evidence." He barely managed a smile. "Be careful, please. No noise. We're all on thin ice."

"Where's the money?" Spence asked in that hard, tight voice. "Get it quick, so we can get out of here."

Mike pointed to the saddlebags lying under Adolf's chair. Spence smiled quickly and, stooping, scooped them up.

"Count it," Dickson said quietly.

"Let's get out of here," Spence said, his beautiful white teeth released in a smile at last, shining in the lantern light. With the money in his hand, he seemed to swell again with self-confidence.

"Do as I say," Dickson said. Dickson's voice was sleepy and dull, and he looked tired rather than afraid.

"There's a way out the front, through the hotel kitchen."

A spot of red showed on Dickson's cheek, and his chin lifted a little. "You take my orders."

Spence held his eye for a moment; then lifting his eyebrows he looked away, patiently smiling.

"There's always time to run," Dickson said. "Only fools run because they're afraid. Count the money."

"It'll take too long," Spence said quietly.

"We've got all night," Dickson said with his icy stubbornness. "We're dealing with fools, Spence," he said, waving generally toward the Allens. "They may still be holding out. I'll hold the gun."

The sound of many horses came up the street. Spence stopped with the first strap unbuckled in his hands. Dickson stood with the gun on Mike and his father. They all listened. Voices came through the big, solid door, at first faintly, and then clearly. The horsemen stopped up the block.

"You, driver," Colonel Berry said outside, his voice faint. "Are you Thomas Dickson's man?"

"Get on with it," Dickson whispered, his eyes bright and his face alive once more. Spence undid the other strap.

Dickson turned and went, smiling, over to Mike and his father. Mike looked at the gun, pointed steadily at his stomach. He could try it, he could gamble. It wasn't more than five feet away. But he would have to take one step; he would have to bend his knees to jump, and that would be enough of a signal. Dickson had made sure to leave room for just that much warning.

Dickson smiled at him, reading his mind. "Don't try it. After all, while there's life there's hope, eh? Anything's better than being dead—and you know it, don't you." It wasn't a question; and Mike did know it, now.

Buford said nothing. He sat down suddenly in Adolf's chair and put his face in his hands.

"Before they break in here," Dickson whispered, "Forrest will battle them. I think we're quite safe."

The noise up the block, of talking, the blowing of horses, Berry swearing at the coachman, grew slowly. Inside, behind the massive door, there was no sound except the quick whisper of the banknotes as Spence counted, licking his thumb and not being very careful.

Colonel Berry had picked up the three men as he passed the Little House. They were all mounted in a minute, and he sent one for Lt. Cash and reinforcements. Hardly losing a stride, the Colonel and the two remaining men followed Io, hurrying a little to keep him in sight as he went down Crockett Street across the Alamo Plaza.

Up ahead, Berry saw Io stop, lighted by the moon at his back, at the corner of Blum Street. They caught up with him, and the Colonel, dismounting, looked around the corner.

"The same carriage?" the Colonel asked. The carriage, having left the brewery door, was pulling up toward the corner by the Menger Hotel.

Io hissed at him softly, and pointed a finger at something in the roadway. It was a dark black spot in the moonlit dust, about the size of a dime, but shaped like a tear. "Sangre."

"Keppelbauer," the Colonel said. "They put the body in the back. I could see that much. It's leaking. That's all we need. Come on. Hey, there!" he shouted up the block after the carriage. "Pull over there! Police!" The carriage stopped.

They remounted and went up Blum Street toward the carriage, which had pulled up just short of the corner of the Plaza, thirty yards away from the brewery door.

The colored driver was sitting in a huddle on top, his hands over his eyes. The carriage was empty.

Berry looked up the street toward the Plaza. There were half a dozen horses in front of the Gallagher building, but that wasn't unusual—late gamblers in the San Antonio Club, upstairs.

The Colonel saw Lt. Cash and four men gallop into the Plaza from South Alamo Street. He shouted. They didn't hear him, and rode on north beyond the Menger.

"You, driver," Colonel Berry said, "are you Thomas Dickson's man?"

The Negro, face buried in his hands, sighed deeply.

"Answer me," the Colonel said sharply.

"Oh, my Gawd," the driver said, his voice shuddering.

"He is, he is, you can see that," one of the police said.

"Open the trunk," Berry ordered. The clatter of Cash's horsemen dimmed, and then rose again, searching up and down the streets. Berry swore. He should have left a guide. At the rear of the carriage two cops worked at the straps and then opened the back.

"Lord Jesus," one of them said, holding a match. Keppelbauer lay there, his round face in a faint gauze of spiderwebs. Spiderwebs and dust covered his neat sack suit. The suit was black with blood.

"Run through, just like the others," Berry said.

Cash's people rounded the corner into Blum Street and Berry shouted again. Cash galloped up and slid off. He ran over to the trunk.

"Well," he cried, looking around, "where are the son of a bitches? This is enough, ain't it, Colonel? By God, they must be in the hotel. Old Allen lives there. Allen's as thick as thieves with Dickson, always has been."

"They killed Keppelbauer," Berry said.

"The two of them? Who?"

"They all drove out west of town. I don't know just what they did. I had to stay out of sight. But the two Allens and Dickson and the rest of Dickson's people were out there, and by God, Keppelbauer's dead, isn't he?"

"That makes them all accessories."

"Not old Allen," one of the cops said. "Old Buford wouldn't harm a flea."

"Oh, is that so?" Cash snapped. "Well, get the hell in the hotel and find him, if he's so damned innocent."

"He owed Dickson a lot of money," Berry said. "Get that driver down here."

"Oh, my Gawd," the driver said.

"Get down here, you," Cash shouted.

"Oh, my Jesus," the driver moaned, rocking. "Ah don't know nothing, boss."

"You know enough to keep your mouth shut, and that's plenty," Cash shouted. "Get down here. You want to hang? Get him off of there, boys."

Two cops grabbed and dragged him down.

"Oh, dear Lawd," the driver moaned, crouching in the street. He squatted down and put his hands over his ears, and rocked back and forth, crying, "Oh, Lawd."

"The son of a bitch knows," Cash said, wrath twisting his whole face. "Where did they go?" he shouted, stooping down beside the driver's head.

"Oh, Lawd," the driver cried more loudly, holding his hands over his ears. Cash stood upright. "Take that man's hands," he said to the two cops, "and hold them away from his ears."

The driver let out a quavering howl as the cops grabbed him.

"Now, now, now, boss, now, now, boss, now, boss," he cried twisting his head, the whites of his eyes flashing in the moonlight. "Now, boss, I ain't nothing but a pore old colored man, ah ain' done nothin'."

"You lying son of a bitch," Cash said. "You were driving this hack when they killed a man." He moved closer. "You helped in a murder. Where's your boss? You tell me and I'll let you go, boy."

"Oh, Jesus," the driver moaned. "He'd kill me, he'll cut off mah head."

"By God," Cash cried, "I'll hang you till your eyes pop out. You want the birds picking your eyeballs out, boy? I'm going to hang your boss Dickson, boy. You tell me where he is, and I'll let you go. You'll be safe."

The driver burst into tears, wriggling around, held by the two cops. "He said he'd cut off mah head," he cried. "He'll do it too, boss."

"Get me a rope, somebody," Cash said in a brisk, sharp voice. "I'll hang the son of a bitch right now."

The driver fell to his knees. "Awright, awright, boss."

There were five shots, crackling on top of each other like a string of firecrackers. The red sparks of gun muzzles jumped in the dark, from the corner by Alamo Street, two more down at the other end of the block from the corner at Nacogdoches.

One of the cops said, "Oh," and fell against the carriage. His knees gave and he fell in the street, blood coming out of his neck.

"Son of a bitch," Cash said, drawing, and began firing at the corner of Alamo Street.

"Get in the carriage!" Berry shouted. The fire was pouring at them from both ends of the block, the bullets smacking through the wooden walls of the carriage body. One of the horses screamed and jumped, shot in the rump, and Berry scrambled up onto the seat, grabbing the reins.

The cops huddled behind the carriage, firing under the belly of it. Berry crouched in the driver's seat, shouting.

"Hold your fire, you damn fools," he shouted. "We haven't got any more loads. Get in the carriage and we'll make a run for it. Cash, get up here with me. I'm going to drive at the ones by the Plaza. Boys, get set. Wipe 'em out, by God. Kill 'em all. The hell with arrests."

He grabbed the whip out of the socket and swung at the horses, holding his gun between his knees. The horses lunged ahead and the carriage rolled heavily forward into the fire from up the block.

Cash shot into the fire, damping it, and they saw the men, now in the shadow, three of them in the street.

The Colonel fired at them, aiming as well as he could from the rolling carriage as he bore down on them. The bright-orange flames winked and the street roared with the gunfire, pounding back and forth between the buildings. The police inside the carriage were firing out the windows.

"If they kill the horses, get out and charge 'em," Berry shouted at Cash as they bore down on the five men. He saw one of Forrest's people fall, and then another. The others were running for their horses. He fired again.

The Colonel felt young. It was like the first skirmish he had ever been in, with a small band of Comanches on the Nueces River, as a lieutenant, in the days when he had thought of musketry only as a military formality. He was cool, the winking of the muzzle blasts meant nothing, he wasn't thinking of death, of the odds and the chances, any more than he had thought of them that day forty-five years before, and he crouched not in fear, but simply because it was the sensible thing to do.

His ulcer did not enter his mind, nor his daughter, nor anything, except the cool, fast action-thinking of a fighter, completely taken up with the thing happening at the instant, the job right now. It was a good enough feeling for an old soldier, to be fighting—he knew his tools.

So he died, with his enemies scattering before him like sparrows. One of Forrest's parting shots went through his left eye. The carriage stopped, the horses floundering in their tangled harness, and Cash held the old man up.

Cash felt a fume of terrible anger rise in him like the smoke out of hell; he wanted to stand up and swear, to curse his men, to reach out after the murderers and seize them. But he sat there, and the anger died away. Was that all it came to? A man you respected, a man you loved, a boss you worked for and sweated for and obeyed exactly, suddenly gone, leaving this limp, warm carcass.

A bit of knowledge flowed into Cash's head, as cool as moonlight. In the end, there was nothing but the job; it was the job that lasted. In the end, everyone died, all friends, all lovers, every man everywhere, and all affection passed away. Nothing remained but simple duty and the God who alone made it a duty and not just a dirty farce.

Cash said to his men, "The Colonel is dead. Go back to the station, Tom, and get out the whole force to cover the roads. Get on the telegraph and wire Houston and Austin and El Paso." His voice was cool, for once.

"They're gone," said the man who was named Tom. "You know how it is. If a man's got a horse, he can lose himself forever, fifteen miles out of town."

Cash sat quiet. "Do it anyway."

"We've lost 'em, Ben. Might as well face it. Better print up a reader," Tom said. "They won't hit a town till they get out of Texas. Dodge? Who cares, in Dodge? They got more'n they can handle right there in Ford County. But I'll wire 'em, Ben. Just you say which towns. Which way will they go? K.C.? San Francisco?"

Cash sat quiet. Dickson and his men had got clean away, except for the two dead. There was no use wiring. And as for the readers, who cared? West of the Mississippi, murder was much too common to attract much attention.

"Send out the readers, Tom," Cash said quietly. "We'll hear from Dickson some day. We can wait." Waiting, he thought, was the main power of the law, and if he never got Dickson and his people, he knew God would, who would outwait them all; and that was some consolation to set against the hard, hot pain of the Colonel's death.

13

Degen's Brewery—2:30 A.M.

Inside the brewery they heard the shooting and the shouting, the slamming of the fast battle, the clatter of hoofs and the slow silence, coming back again. Shooting wasn't unusual in San Antonio.

"What'll we do?" Spence whispered.

"Wait," Dickson said, taking the rebuckled saddlebags and putting them under his chair, from which he had turned out Buford. "Forrest will be back when the police have gone. We'll get horses and leave town. You'd better hit the watchman, Spence. He's coming around again."

Spence looked at Mike and Buford, standing together across the wide flags. "What about them?" he said.

"Kill them," Dickson said.

Spence looked at them, studying.

Mike said, "My father's got two herds left, on the trail."

"That's right," Spence said.

"I remember," Dickson said. "I'm holding the notes on them. They're mine."

"They're worth about $400,000, delivered in Ogalalla," Mike said.

"I'm glad to hear it," Dickson said. "Where are they?"

Buford smiled a little. His face was coming back to life. "You'll never find them—without me."

"Maybe you've got enough money, Tommy," Spence said. "If we have to take these two out of here and go north after those herds—well, it might be easier not to. We could drop them in one of the mash vats—they wouldn't be found for a month."

"Delightful thought," Dickson said. "Think of all San Antonio quaffing the remains of the Allen family. Where can Forrest be? We have to leave before daylight. Where are those herds, Buford?"

The old man looked at Dickson heavily. "Do you think I'm crazy? If I tell you, you'd just kill us."

"And if you don't, I will," Dickson said. "So far I've never done away with anybody except for business reasons. But I am beginning to think that at times killing could be simply a dangerous pleasure. Didn't you ever feel like killing anyone? Haven't you ever been totally aggravated? You, Buford, have tried me dreadfully. The only trouble with killing people is that sheer quantity inevitably brings its own exposure, and there are always the police. Society is always so careful to preserve itself. One may well ask why. Surely being shot in the head is preferable to dying of cholera, or lying for years in bed soiling the sheets and making oneself a general nuisance to one's loved ones. I cannot imagine why people are in such a general rush to escape from death, when most of them make their lives so unbearable, all through their own stupidity. Take yourself, Buford. You'd be far better off dead. Where is that wretched Forrest? Spence, why don't you draw us all a beer, while we're waiting?"

"Do you want the herds?" Mike asked.

"Yes," Dickson said.

"Then you'll have to let us live long enough to find them for you."

"That's quite all right with me," Dickson said. "Please understand, my dear boy. I don't want you dead. There's nothing personal about it, really. Spence, I was not joking about that beer. I'm thirsty. Here, I'll hold the gun on them."

"All right," Buford said, rubbing his beard. "We'll find the herds for you."

Spence found a row of sampling steins on a shelf and they listened to the beer spurting from the taps. He came back with four of them, full.

"Buford's got a bunch of men with those herds," Spence said.

"Naturally," Dickson said. "We have a bunch of men too."

"How are you going to keep Buford from tying up with his men, and standing us off?"

"Don't be silly, Spence," Dickson said.

"I'm not being silly. We'll find the herds. Then the Allens will have at least a dozen men to help them, and they're all loyal. They always are to their bosses."

"Oh, God, virtue again," Dickson said. "Is there anything wrong with a pitched battle?"

"You can't fight around cattle," Spence said. He looked at Mike and smiled. "Mike taught me that. If you start shooting, the cattle stampede. So what will happen is that Buford will force us to trade with him. We can have him or the cattle, but not both."

"There's many a way to kill a cat," Dickson said, sipping his beer, and eyeing Buford. "How long will it take to find them?"

"Maybe a month."

"Then you're assured of a month of life. That should make you happy." He drank. "Let me see, you had an option on a ranch. You told me about it. Suppose you give me that option, Buford?"

"Oh, God," Buford said, and shut his eyes.

"It isn't any good," Mike said. "The date's gone."

"As I recall, you said you could buy it for $300,000. What's it worth?"

"I could have sold it in Cheyenne to some son of a bitching Englishman for half a million," Buford said.

"Then so could I," Dickson said.

Buford sat down on the steps leading to the upper level. Only one thought came to his mind through the fog of fatigue and spent fear and failure. Dickson couldn't be trusted. Nothing he said could be believed. The only thing he would respond to was money. He looked up at Dickson. Dickson's eyes were steady and cold.

"I want that ranch, Buford. The option. I had a certain goal—of money, you understand. With your cattle and this ranch, I can clear enough to go home. I could even sell the ranch in England—everybody's dying to get rich in the cattle business these days. Give me that option, Buford, and I may let you go."

It was a lie, Buford thought. He would never let him go, not now. He would kill him just as soon as he had sucked him dry. And Mike, too. There was only one possible escape—to find the herds, to join forces with Tucker, and then to fight a battle with Dickson and his forces. The only thing that would keep Dickson from killing him before he got help was the hope of getting money.

"Give me the option, Buford," Dickson said. "I suppose you have it on you."

One idea rose in Buford's mind: Escape. Everything depended on getting to Tucker.

"Spence, search him," Dickson said. "I'll hold the gun on Mike."

Buford looked up with a start. Spence was coming toward him. He stood up, angry blood rising to his head, and then he saw the gun on Mike and his heart stopped for a moment.

"Wait," he said quickly. "I'll give it to you." He took the option, in its envelope, out of his inside pocket and handed it to Spence. He smiled bitterly. "I hope you have more luck than I did with it."

"We'll be partners," Dickson said, reading the option. "So I can act in your name."

Buford watched his son's face as Mike looked steadily at the barrel of the gun. "Yes," he said.

"Spence, suppose we got half a million for that ranch, if Buford says it's worth $300,000? How would you like to go to England with me? We'd pay off Forrest and the others handsomely, and you and I could go. You could manage my estate. This last coup would do it."

"The option's no good," Spence said, handing it to Dickson. "Date's past over."

"I know a man in Chicago who knows a lot about changing figures."

Somebody tapped on the door. The four men froze.

"It's me, Forrest," a low voice said outside. Spence opened the door and Forrest came in. "I killed a police commissioner," he said, grinning. "The whole town's gone crazy. They'd lynch us all, boss, if they could."

"Did you get horses?" Dickson asked quietly.

"Hell, yes, and for these two buggers too. Stole them right off the rail down in front of Wolfram's. They're waiting down in the alley."

"All right, we'll be down directly. Go back and wait for us."

Spence shut the door behind Forrest, and Dickson faced Buford.

"Now, Buford, old man," Dickson said, "one last little thing. If I were in your shoes, I would try to play along until you got up to your herds, and then try to join forces with your driver's men. Then, if I were you, I'd stage a battle, and try to get free. Am I right?"

Buford's chest sank. He looked at Dickson, trying to keep his face from showing anything.

"Sensible idea," Dickson said. "You're quite convinced I'll kill you as soon as I get your cattle and your option. So I can expect some desperate measures as soon as you can try them."

"I don't know what you think," Buford said, "and I don't give a damn. All I know is that you can't get those cattle until I find them for you and tell my man to give them up. And if necessary I'll drive those cattle to the north pole before I give them up. I ain't going to get killed."

Dickson looked at him quietly. "Time will tell us everything. I can't keep you from joining Tucker, naturally, since he has the cattle now. But I can keep you quiet, my poor old friend. Spence, you are to take Mr. Michael Allen tonight and ride north by yourselves. Take two guards to relieve you. Forrest and his gang will go ahead with Buford. You keep Mike and Buford apart, and if either of them makes trouble, kill the other. Now, find the herds and sell them. Then go on to this town named Warhorse and wait there for me. I'm going to make a little trip to Chicago first. Everything clear?

"Now, Buford, you will go along with Forrest and find the cattle. And you'll keep the peace, understand? Because if you start a battle, Spence is to kill your son. They'll be in touch—Forrest and Spence. Do you understand?"

Buford looked at Dickson, his eyes full of hopeless hate.

"Michael will be our little hostage," Dickson said. "To keep you on your good behavior, my dear Buford. Run along, Spence. Take Michael with you. I'll deliver Buford to Forrest before I go."

Buford looked at his son, and then back to Dickson. "I want a private word with him," Buford said.

"Quite all right," Dickson said. "Climb those steps over there. We'll stay down here. But stay in sight, old man. I've got the gun on you."

Buford led Mike heavily up the steps, and in the dark confusion of vats and tanks, turned to face him.

"What are we going to do?" Mike whispered, looking at his father.

"Nothing," Buford said. His mouth shook weakly. "He's got us where the hair is short, boy. All we can do is play along."

"How long?" Mike asked.

"As long as we can, boy. Listen, they won't hurt you if I don't start anything. And I won't start anything. Listen, Mike, get this through your head. You'll get nervous, all by yourself, wondering about me. But keep this in your mind, always. Dickson can always be bought. He'll do anything for money. As long as we have the herd, he won't hurt me. He won't hurt me as long as Tucker and I are with the cattle, because we'll stampede 'em and he wants the money."

"He'll try to sell the cows in Ogalalla," Mike said.

"I know it," the old man whispered, his breath uneven and short. "That's where I've got to win. I've got to make them drive those cattle all the way to Warhorse. Listen, son. We neither of us can make a break until we're together again, understand? He won't kill me until I've given up the cows, and I've got to work it so I don't have to give 'em up till I'm with you again, understand? And I'll do it. Only, for God's sake, Mike, sit tight. Don't blow up. Wait. Trust me. Will you, for God's sake, just trust me? Tucker and I won't let them sell in Ogalalla. We'll make them drive on north. For the last time in our whole lives I ask you, Mike, please trust me. Will you?"

Mike looked at his father's haggard old face and smiled gently. "Sure, I'll trust you."

Buford took his son's head between his two hands and kissed him on the cheek. "Good-by, Mike, my dear old boy. I swear to God I'll get you out of this. We'll make it."

He turned and stumbled back over the pipes and buckets, and down the stone steps. Dickson took him by the arm and led him outside, and Spence and Mike were left alone.

"Come on," Spence said, smiling. Mike went down the steps.

"It's a long way from Frenchman's Creek," Spence said, his handsome teeth showing in his handsome smile. "But I've got you over a barrel this time, sonny. There won't be any tricks this time. Stand over there." He gestured with the gun to the wall. Mike moved back against it.

Spence knelt by Adolf and went through his pockets.

"Five bucks," Spence said finally, standing up and pocketing the money. "Not much, but then, every little bit helps, doesn't it? Get going, sonny," he said, waving the gun toward the door. "There's a long road ahead for us, and you'd better be goddam careful if you want to see your old man again. Move." He waved the gun again, smiling, and Mike moved.

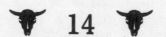

14

On the Trail, Headed Northwest
September 18–25

It was late in the season when Forrest's gang, with Buford under guard, neared Ogalalla six weeks later, still with no news of the two lost herds.

They would get a hard frost on the plains at night and wake up, teeth chattering, and huddle around the fire, murdering each other in their hearts, waiting for the coffee to boil up. Buford and Forrest and two others—a blond fellow named Sheffield and a black-haired one named Irving—kept one fire, and the rest of Forrest's men another.

The smoke from the cow chips stung their bleary eyes and made their dirty faces draw and crawl, and they would hunker there, some miserable, some getting meaner all the time, some wishing to God for a drink.

They hadn't found the herds, and it was beginning to look as though they wouldn't, and Forrest's face, as he looked at Buford nowadays, was losing its placid soldier's look and getting colder and harder. Buford looked right back at him across the dirty little fire. He was getting mean himself and he sometimes enjoyed the feeling.

They had hit the south Platte west of Ogalalla on the seventeenth, and all the men—there were ten in Forrest's party and two in Spence's, riding herd on Mike a day behind—had expected to go into town and kick hell out of somebody just to relieve their feelings. But Spence had ridden up from behind and put the lid on them. They were all too hot to show and nobody was to go into town. One man, a new hand under Forrest, agreed secretly with the others to go into town for whiskey, and he did; and when he got back Forrest beat him till he blubbered like a baby, lying on the ground with his nose pulped and his left ear half torn off. That's what soldier Forrest handed out for disobedience, under Spence's orders, and Spence watched it with a smile.

They dropped this poor wreck at some nester's, and went on across the river, following Buford's directions to go up the Oregon trail, and it was Spence's smile and his politicking art that made every man in the crew agree that the beaten man had got what he deserved.

They had Buford to hate, too. They all knew he was trying to find six thousand head of cattle, and the idea got around that he was trying to diddle somebody when he didn't. At first it was a joke, how the old man was diddling Forrest and even Dickson. In the Indian country they had begun to make bets each day, and by the time they hit the Kansas line, they had started a big pool on guessing how many days it would be when they hit the herds, and then at the Nebraska line they started another on how many weeks, which was not quite the same thing.

At Frenchman's Creek, where Tucker had diddled Spence last July, things started to go sour, and Spence's mood of suspicion traveled down through the men, and they began to watch Buford as though they were beginning to think about eating him.

They were all lousy by that time, partly because they camped dry a good deal and couldn't wash, and partly because most of them didn't like to wash, and when a non-washer was guarding Buford, he wouldn't go with Buford down to the creeks or holes, so Buford couldn't wash either. They changed the guard on him every four hours, just as though he were a prisoner of war. If he got a washing guard, it was at a dry camp.

They kept him riding all the time—no rest for the wicked, Forrest said. Every day he would ride out with his guard west, crossing trails, and circle back, and another team would ride northeast and circle back. Forrest sent out parties, gone for three days, cutting way west, a hundred miles, one time, and still they found nothing of a B A hair brand, which they were looking for. They didn't ride far to the east, because Buford had given orders to Tucker to take the herds west off the trail.

There was a rule, put down by Spence, that neither of the Allens was to be given any news of the other. Mike would ask about his father, a day ahead, and

Buford would ask about his son, a day behind. But as far as they were told, the other might as well have been dead.

By the time they started up the Platte on the Oregon trail, the bacon was maggoty and the weevils had all hatched out in the cornmeal, and Buford got the worst. He didn't mind much. He was so hungry from riding out constantly that he would have eaten grasshoppers. They would kill a straggler cow almost every evening, carrying nothing, leaving what was left from dinner for the coyotes, just like a pack of wolves.

They ran into other herds going north to the sweetgrass country, five hundred cows, a thousand cows, three hundred cows. Batches bought in Cheyenne or Ogalalla and being taken north over the Bozeman trail and the Oregon trail for fattening and breeding purposes. Nobody had seen any B A hair brand, and on the twenty-fourth of September, when they were nearing the west border of Nebraska and about to cross over into Wyoming, Buford was beginning to get a little desperate.

There were times when he thought he was crazy and the whole hunt a delusion. He would lie stiff in his sweat, full of saddle aches and pain, and begin to believe that he had relayed some other kind of order to Tucker. He knew perfectly well he had sent a map to Tucker, showing a change of route to the west, even setting up a rough schedule. And yet, had he? Maybe he just thought he had. Maybe he had dreamed up that map, to convince himself there was a herd somewhere. Maybe it was just his imagination, a delusion born of fear, something to keep himself from getting killed.

Day after day they nosed northward, riding hard, but not making much progress, because they were cutting trails back and forth all the time. Sooner or later, he would run out of days, there would be an end somewhere up by the Yellowstone. And what then? He could see Forrest looking at him one day, the last day, and what would Buford say?

Let's go back, he would say, and look again. We must have missed them by a hair, Forrest. Spence would be there too, for the showdown.

Let's go back, Spence. You know how easy it is to miss a herd of cattle.

No, Spence would say. No. There wasn't any herd, Buford. You were lying. And Spence would smile.

And there, at the end of nowhere, they would close in.

Your man Tucker sold you out, Buford, Spence would say. Your faithful Isaac.

He had heard Spence and Forrest planning things.

Spence said, "Old man Allen's got to be allowed to go up to this Tucker and tell him to turn over the herd. So we can't kill him. If we kill him now, Tucker will never hand over the herd. I know. I tried him once."

Forrest said, "Don't be a damn fool. Allen will never tell this Tucker that. Not if he gets that close."

Spence said, "I've got his son."

Forrest said, "The old man's a tough son of a bitch. Look at it square, Spence. He knows you want the herd. Killing the kid isn't going to get you the herd, is it? Hell, no. The old man will just make this Tucker fight, then."

Spence said, "I don't think so. The old man will cave in if I threaten about his son. He'll order Tucker off the herd."

Forrest said, "Bull turds. You got him figured for a coward. He ain't. He's a mean old son of a bitch and he's getting meaner and tougher all the time. I give him maggoty bacon to eat and he just looks back and chaws it up like he was saying, 'The same to you.' I say kill him now and battle it out with Tucker."

Spence answered, "We'll lose the cattle."

Forrest: "Not for long, if we win. Battle over, we can round 'em up again."

Spence: "If we win. We can't take a chance on losing, Forrest. Dickson doesn't like losers."

So for weeks Buford never knew when they were going to kill him, or if they would. Any day, the man riding herd behind him, on his big circles, might have orders to shoot him in the back and he'd never know when it was coming.

But Buford knew one thing. Much depended on just how they found the herds, if they ever did. They might locate the herd and ambush Tucker—kill him at three hundred yards. If the country was such that they could hold the cattle easily, they might risk a battle. If they came on them at night, with most of Tucker's riders sleeping, they might massacre the lot on the ground, and then be free to catch the stampeded cattle again.

On the twenty-fifth they were getting near Fort Fetterman, where the Bozeman trail left the Oregon and went northward. Buford and Irving were cutting to the west and they saw the long dust of a big herd and rode toward it, coming up toward the drag as usual so as not to scare the leaders. They cut into the trail it was leaving, and then, looking back, saw another dust about four miles south and three miles behind, about the same size, and a pain of hope shot through Buford's heart that almost made him sick. Irving saw it, too—two big herds about the same size, traveling fairly close together, but off the beaten track, and probably far enough off so that their dust couldn't be seen.

Irving closed up on him, drawing his gun as he always did until they saw the brand.

"Take it easy," Irving said. "If it's them, set your goddam horse, old man, or I'll plug you. If we spot the herd, we ride back pronto and report. That's orders and don't forget it."

They weren't going to let him get close enough to wise Tucker up, with only one of Forrest's men around. When he talked to Tucker, if ever, Forrest's whole gang would be there—they'd made sure of that. "Identify the herd," Forrest had said, "and then report back to me."

Buford rode up the trail with Irving's gun on him, eating the heavy dust. They began to pass stragglers, and his heart dropped. There were a few odd brands, pickups, stragglers from other herds gone by, but the mass of the lame were all branded a fancy cross on a box and a diamond around another box. It looked like some Englishman's brand, dreamed up in a hotel. They'd ask, now, if the foreman had seen a B A herd somewhere, sometime.

Irving put his gun away; they rode on at their constant jog-trot, cutting aside out of the herd, up past the bobbing, stinking cows through the fog of dust. The off swing rider showed ahead, vague through the glittering dust. This man turned around, hearing the quick chop of the ponies' hoofs, so different from the rumble of the cattle. Buford saw the face, and knew the man.

It was Tucker's cousin, a kid named Green. The kid kept riding in his station, but half-turned in the saddle, watching the old man come; and then the kid held up an arm and waved, and his white teeth showed through the haze of dust.

Irving was riding on Buford's near side, so his gun would be handy in case the old man tried something.

"Know him?"

"Sure I know him," Buford said, his heart pounding. Maybe it wasn't the Green kid, after all. He didn't dare look up. Maybe it was just another Texas hand that knew the old man by his beard. They all knew old Buford Allen with his free and easy drinks.

Buford glanced again at the fancy English brand bobbing along on the fifty cowhides he could see, and then looked at the kid again, and knew it was Green, and saw through it all at once. He felt like crying and swearing at the same time, and then he knew there wasn't time for either, that he had to do something fast. Tucker had just doubled the B back in a box, and doubled the A downward in another box. He'd done it to hide the herd, on his own initiative.

All Buford could do was wink at the kid with his right eye, the one Irving couldn't see.

"Hi, Mr. Allen," the Green kid called as they rode up.

Buford winked again. "Hi, kid," he said. "Who's your boss?"

The kid looked silly for a minute, and Buford winked again, and the kid saw it.

"Get him for me, will you? Just ride up ahead and tell him I want to talk to him."

Irving caught something in the air. The kid's grin was fixed now, unnatural-looking. He turned and loped his pony ahead and Irving looked at the old man.

"What the hell's up?" Irving asked, his hand on his gun. "Why did you send that kid off? This your goddam herd?"

"Of course it isn't," Buford shouted in a rage. All over, inside, he was jumping and seething with feelings and contrary emotions. "I just know that kid," he said, "and I know the foreman, and I know he'd rather ride back than have me barging up in front. He's that kind."

Irving looked at him with wide, comprehending eyes. His gun came out. "You're the boss, ain't you? I seen it in that kid's eyes and no foreman would ride back for no stranger, no bum like you look. Let's get out of here. Move. Move, by God, or I'll kill you."

Two men were coming back down through the dust, the kid and another, and two more behind, at an easy lope.

Irving moved in fast, pushing his horse close to Buford's.

"Go on and kill me," Buford said. "You'll live just about one minute, sonny."

"Drop them reins," Irving said, jamming the gun into Buford's kidneys.

Buford opened his left hand and the reins fell on the ground. The pony stopped stock-still, scared of stepping on them.

"They doctored the brand is all," Irving said quietly. "You probably knew it all the time. What the hell. I got this gun in your back, old man, and if you or them makes one bum move, you're through."

Buford saw Tucker's dirty black hat come out of the fog, and then Tucker's big grin with a dead cigarette hanging on it, and Tucker pulled up six feet away.

"Stay back," Irving called over the rumble of the cattle, and showed the gun.

Tucker's hand just started for his own and stopped. He raised his hands a little, just for peace, and then his eyes began to glance around, feeling for his own riders' positions, beyond the dust and the herd. The two other riders crowded up behind him and sat there too, looking at the gun, held steady on the old man's back.

They sat there and the drag went by, and presently there was one little calf limping along with its mother close by, and then they were gone, and there was nothing left but the amber sparkling dust and the stink, and the bawling rumble of the herd fading as silence grew.

Irving laughed a silly kind of courageous haw, and said, "Jesus, what a fast one. Get this, girls, I'll shoot the old goat at the first move."

Tucker sat placidly, his face a little peaked, watching his boss and Irving. The Green kid's face was working with a mixture of outrage and complete uncertainty.

Tucker said, "Do you mind if I take this butt out of my mouth?"

"Spit it out," Irving said.

"They got us over a barrel," Buford said to Tucker.

"Who?" Tucker asked.

"Dickson and Spence."

"I remember Spence."

"They got more than a dozen men. We've been looking for you for a month of Sundays."

"I suppose they got their goddam judgments again," Tucker said.

"No. But they're going to try to get the herd. And they got Mike over a barrel. Thank God you changed that brand, Tuck. It would have been a different story."

"What's different about it now?" Irving said. "We're going out of here. These gents are leaving us right now. I'm getting your reins and then we fade away."

"No," Buford said. "I'm not leaving."

"You'll leave or you'll die, by God," Irving said, jamming the gun.

"Go ahead and shoot," Buford said, sitting tight.

Irving looked at Tucker and Tucker's men, and they looked back.

"Send a man up toward the river, Tucker," Buford said. "He'll find Spence's outfit—all riders, no wagons. Tell them we found the herd and to come on over. We're staying here, Irving."

Irving looked back at Tucker.

"Go on," Tucker said quietly to Irving. "Shoot the old man. We got four guns here, and we're just waiting for you to get off that first shot. You'll get off just one, sonny. That's all."

Irving sat there looking like a calf trying to eat two pails of mash at once.

"We better just sit here," Tucker said soothingly, "until your friends get here. We won't shoot you as long as you got the boss covered, but you ain't going to shoot either, are you?"

"All right," Irving said, and sweat came out on his forehead. His face slacked off in a sick way and he blinked. "I'll wait."

Tucker sent off a man, and they listened to his horse's hoofs, hard across the ground, fading.

They sat in the bright sun, with the dead grass waving. The cow pies dropped by the herd sat and baked and stank and wild flies droned. The horses stamped and switched their tails.

"What we going to do, Buford?" Tucker said.

"Shut up," Irving said, jabbing Buford with the gun muzzle.

"You can't make me shut up," Buford said. "You can shoot me, but you can't shut me up."

"That's right, sonny," Tucker said placidly. "Shoot him if you want to. We're right here, waiting."

Irving said something that sounded like "Jesus" and sat there sweating. He was having a hard time and his arm was getting tired.

"Can I roll a cigarette, please," Tucker asked politely. "I'm dying for a smoke and I swear that I won't start nothing."

"No," Irving said. "Don't move. I'm getting nervous, so you be goddam careful."

Tucker said, "Boys, everybody just keep your hands high, will you? We don't want Nervous here to lose control of the situation. Buford, what's the story?"

Buford gave it to him.

Tucker said, "So what do we do?"

"Wait. But remember one thing, Tucker. The herd is what they want. As long as we got the herd, they won't do anything. We got to stay close to the herd, or they'll just blast us loose from the ground. They don't want to lose that herd, Tuck. Remember that always."

"Then let's go," Tucker said.

"No," Irving said. "We stay here."

"I'm going," Buford said. "I'm leaning over and getting those reins, and then I'm leaving, Irving. You ain't going to be very safe if you let me and that gun of yours get separated."

"You stay where you are," Irving said.

"Don't bluff, sonny," Tucker said. "You ain't dealing with kids. That one shot in there is all you got between you and hell, and you know it."

"Oh, Jesus," Irving said in an agony. "All right, you old son of a bitch, get going. Let one jump out of that horse, though, and by God, I'll plug you! I ain't fooling!" he shouted.

"I know you ain't," Buford said evenly. "I'll be good, don't worry. You goddam monkey, just wait till I get you off my back."

"Ride up ahead and get all the men you can," Tucker said to the Green kid. "Get all the riders off both herds except just enough to hold the points, and hurry back." The Green kid left at a dead run.

Buford rode after the herd at a fast walk, and the others rode well ahead of him, leaving Irving in control.

They made it to the herd just twenty minutes before Forrest and Spence caught up.

All Forrest's men were there, the full camp, and they pulled up to a walk forty yards behind Irving. They could see Tucker and his men, riding twisted in their saddles, ready for anything.

Forrest started to pull his gun, and Spence shouted sharply, "Don't!"

"Why the hell not?" Forrest said.

"We'll lose the cattle."

"We got the odds."

"What the hell of it? We can't kill 'em all," Spence said. "If there was four left, they'd keep the herds busted from now till doomsday. If any of you men," he shouted to the bunch behind him, "goes for a gun, I'll shoot the bastard myself."

"Well, what the hell are we going to do?" Forrest cried out over the din of the herd.

"Talk," Spence said. "Goddam it, I see it now. Goddam it, that fox Tucker changed the brands to hide the herds. And that fool Irving didn't wise up fast enough and the old man Allen did. Goddam the luck. Goddam it all to hell."

He started ahead at a walk, keeping forty yards behind Irving.

"What're we going to do?" Forrest asked again, bewilderment in his face.

"Talk," Spence said again. "We'll just have to wait till they're bedded down, that's all."

They rode that way for five more hours, down the long, hot afternoon, each side watching the other, Tucker's men riding backward with eyes like hawks. Nobody made a move, nobody smoked.

In the middle, Irving rode doggedly on Buford's near side, quartered behind him, his horse's withers almost touching the other's flanks.

I must be crazy, Buford thought, and then he didn't care. A gun in his back, he had the situation half under control. He wasn't underneath, for the first time since he had left Ogalalla so long ago.

They rode that way till sundown, till the big herd slowed onto the bed grounds that had been picked out, just south of Fort Fetterman, near the river.

Spence and Forrest made a camp by the river, a hundred yards from Tucker's chuck wagon, and while they were starting the fires, Spence rode quietly out into the open toward Buford and Irving, still sitting alone in the middle of nowhere. Tucker saw him coming and rode out to meet him.

They sat their horses, each about fifteen yards from Buford, and talked.

Spence said, evenly, "I've got your son, Buford. You've pulled a fast one on me. I admit it. But I've got Mike."

"And I've got the herd," Buford said. "You'll never get it until I give Tucker the order to pull out his men."

"I can see that," Spence said, his voice calm and level. "And when do you plan to do that? Why don't we do it now? I'll bring Mike up here tomorrow, and we can make the exchange right here. I don't want Mike, Buford. That was Dickson's idea."

"Don't pull that," Buford said. "You're all bastards."

"We can swap right here," Spence said. "Irving, put down that gun and get over by the fire."

Irving looked up in surprise, and so did Buford.

"I've got thirteen men," Spence said, "and your son and you aren't going anywhere with those cattle without me and my thirteen men. It's purely a question of when we swap, isn't it, Buford?"

Irving dropped his arm with a groan and turned his horse away into the dark. "Yes," Buford said.

"And you know you can't get Mike away from me," Spence said. "Any more than I can get the herd away from you." He smiled in the deep dusk. "So let's trade."

Buford was sitting there on his tired horse, looking northwest, up toward the Big Horns, and beyond them to where Warhorse would be.

"Come on," Spence said. "Let's trade, Buford, right here. You and Mike will be safe, and I'll have the herds, which you owe Dickson anyway. You can go home, and I'll sell the herds the way I'm supposed to."

Buford said nothing. He was thinking of Montrose's ranch and, deeper yet, of a certain place, perhaps under some tree, where there was a mystery he had not solved. Nobody else in all the world would understand it, how an old man would wander all that way to a woman's grave, as though it were a fire, a little warmth, in his old age.

He thought of giving up now, of getting Mike back. But he knew Mike would be safe as long as he controlled the herd. Mike could wait.

"It might be wise," Tucker said in the dark. "Nobody's been killed yet, Buford. It might be a wise thing to quit now, before somebody gets killed."

It was like climbing up one of those long talus slopes in the mountains, Buford thought, trying to reach the top. One struggled and slipped, but kept on struggling. A man had to, because at the bottom there was nothing but darkness —one of those god-awful canyons, cold as death, a trap.

"We're going ahead," he said quietly. "I'll trade you in Warhorse, Spence, maybe; we'll see what happens."

It had fallen into his hands, now, hadn't it? Buford thought. Who could say what might not happen, in the time ahead? A man was a fool to give up.

Spence said, his voice tightening, "Oblige me by trading now. What have you to gain?"

"We're going on north," Buford said quietly. "We'll take the Bridger cutoff and go on to Warhorse, and see how your boss Dickson is making out with getting that ranch."

Spence sat there in the dark. "There's your son, Allen," he said coldly.

"He's a good boy," Buford said. "He'll sit tight."

"Accidents can happen," Spence said in the dark.

"They'd better not," Buford said. "Not if you want these cattle. If Mike gets hurt in any way, we'll fight you, Spence, and to hell with the cattle. And even if you win, you'll never be able to collect 'em. Tucker and I'll shoot you down one by one, pick you off if we have to follow you for the next twenty years. Don't forget it."

Spence sat quiet, the heavy, quiet words still sounding like echoes in his mind.

"All right," Spence said patiently. He had felt like screaming for a moment, but even now he managed to smile, even though nobody could see it.

"Warhorse it is, then," he said. "God help you when Dickson gets hold of you again. I'll have to let him know about this."

"Just tell him," Buford said, "I'll trade in Warhorse."

Spence turned his horse away in the dark, and Tucker said, loudly and clearly, while Spence could still hear, "Greenie boy, we'll set a double guard around the chuck wagon. If anybody comes near in the night—shoot him and the hell with the cattle. We don't want to get murdered in our beds."

Buford sat in the dark, his eyes on Spence's distant campfires.

"They'll have riders all round us," Tucker said in the solid black. "They'll be watching us like a hawk, Buford, and the first slip, they'll be on us. If we let them get the drop, we're through. We'll have to stay out of canyons and such, and just travel as though they was Indians, because they'll murder us if they get a chance. I wish we had more men."

"We got enough," Buford said. "If we're careful."

He sat quiet in the dark, thinking one thought, over and over, like a kind of prayer he was sending down the trail, to Mike. How many miles away was he? Sitting with some stinking guard watching him, hunched over some lousy little fire?

Sit tight, Mike, he thought. *Sit tight, boy. With a few more breaks like this, we may make it out yet.*

That night Spence left Forrest to cover Buford, Tucker, and the herds, and rode on north, taking Mike with him, to Warhorse, where Dickson was waiting.

PART THREE

1

Warhorse, Montana
October 8, 1882—9:00 A.M.

In the upper room of the old stage station in the town of Warhorse, Montana, two weeks after Buford had found his two herds, Dickson stood looking at a large, clumsily drawn wall map of Montana Territory. He had taken the original from Buford. It showed the probable course of the two herds, and their location to date.

Harris came up the stairs and entered the room carrying a tea tray.

"Good morning, Harris. All rested after your trip?" Dickson said cheerily. "Toast right? Perfect!" He merrily spread some strawberry jam on a piece of toast and began munching. "What did you think of the United States of America, coming up on the train?" he asked.

"A remarkable country, sir," Harris said in his British voice, and poured Dickson a cup of tea.

"And how did you leave my mother?"

"Very well, sir. Since you asked her not to write you, she sent a verbal message. She has only fifteen hundred dollars left to live on."

"Oh, bother," Dickson said. "Well, she can apply for charity. Can't send her a dime with the police watching her. Did you take a boat down the river as I suggested?"

"Yes, sir, just as you suggested. At night."

More feet pounded up the stairs. Somebody knocked at the door.

"Come in, come in," Dickson called out in bright good humor.

Spence entered with Irving behind him. Irving was unshaven, dirty of face, and smelled powerfully of horse sweat and fresh manure.

"Why on earth don't you bathe before you come up here?" Dickson asked crossly.

"I just got in an hour ago," Irving said heavily.

"I thought you would want to hear his report right away," Spence put in.

"Go on," Dickson said, looking at the map. "Where's the herd? What's up?"

"They were just turning off the Oregon trail when I left," Irving said. "Three days ago. Forrest said to tell you he was right on schedule."

"Thirteen more days."

"Yes, if they don't run into trouble west of the Big Horns. There's a lot of small rivers to cross there."

599

"I'm figuring on the twentieth. He's got to hold to that date. Who're you going to send back, Spence?"

"Weaver's had a week's rest," Spence said, "he's due for a trip."

"I'll send a written message," Dickson said. "What about Tucker and old man Allen, Irving?" he asked.

Irving smiled slightly. "The old man's getting cocky. He's sassing Forrest night and day, hogs all the firewood and the best water places."

"He's a fool," Dickson said. "I suppose he thinks just because he outsmarted you when you found those herds together, he's got the upper hand. Well, let him dream. Does Forrest want anything? Guns, ammunition, more men? He can have anything but whiskey."

"Nothing," Irving said. "They're saving their cartridges, except for a little hunting. Don't you worry about Forrest."

"Fine, fine," Dickson said. "All right, Irving, run along and, for heaven's sake, do take a bath. And don't get drunk. And stay out of the town saloons. You can go, Harris. Leave the tea things."

Irving grinned and left, Harris following him.

"Things are coming to a head, Spence," Dickson said. He pulled Buford's option out of his pocket and looked at the date. It was a new one: October 9. It was a delicate piece of forgery, indeed a matter of pride to its author in Chicago, whom Dickson had visited on his way north.

"The judge will rule on this tomorrow," Dickson said. "I've got the town sewed up. But we can't have any slips. I've got two suckers down in Denver— an Englishman for $500,000 and a Scotsman for $450,000. We can't afford to miss."

He looked at Spence. "I gather Montrose wouldn't even talk to the Allen boy when I sent him up to dicker. What do people say? Does anybody believe old Montrose? Anybody at all?"

Spence looked at the hooked rug on the floor for a long moment. "I'm afraid," he said, "when it comes to actually throwing Montrose off his place, he'll find too many friends. Even if they believe that date, and think Montrose is just trying to welsh out of his option—later they may remember it and have doubts."

Dickson smiled. "About what I thought. So we've got to have a clincher. Montrose has to become a scoundrel. We've got to make him thoroughly untrustworthy in the eyes of the town. It has occurred to me that he might murder somebody—or better yet, fall under suspicion of it. Remember that plan we made for killing Vickers? Nasty little fellow anyway—much better off dead if he only knew it. It's a bit daring, Spence old man—I know what you're thinking— but we need something dramatic. Shall we use Sheffield—to do the job?"

Spence shrugged. "He's due for a turn."

"He's been getting a little cocky, hasn't he? Maybe it's time to remind him of a few things. Tell you what, you get Sheffield and meet me down by the pigpen in half an hour. I'm going to talk to our little ward Michael. I have a little plan for him, too. Come along."

They went downstairs together.

"Good morning, good morning, Humboldt!" Dickson cried, stepping lightly through the big downstairs barroom. "Go along, Spence," he said.

Humboldt was sitting in front of the fire, drinking a weak grog.

"Good morning, Mr. Dickson," he answered. "I've put the boys hard to work digging that barbecue pit, and the fire will be going soon." This was a pure lie. He had just waked up, with a terrible hang-over.

"Leave all that to Harris, my dear fellow," Dickson said, marching briskly by, and went out the back door. Humboldt was a political investment.

With the Northern Pacific railroad having gone through town, and building west—the work trains went up and down every day—the stage station was deserted of trade, except as a local saloon, and the owner, Humboldt, had been delighted to sell out cheap, especially as Dickson kept him on as barman and general caretaker.

Dickson had made the station house a charming place, with American furnishings, a bit of bright paint and varnish, and a good deal of copper, brass, and Revere silver, as well as hooked rugs and other products of primitive native crafts.

The stage station was located on the main street (the only one, in fact) of Warhorse, in what was left of a grove of cottonwoods. The whole town lay along a large creek which joined the Yellowstone River four miles south of town, and the stage station, around which the town had grown, was a natural center.

There were a number of saloons besides the bar in the station, one general hardware and dry-goods house, one feed and grain house, one livery-and-wheelwright combination, a small bank, and a building which contained the offices of two lawyers, one of whom was the county judge.

The county court and the town marshal's office were in the same building, and both used the same log jail in the rear. There was one small church, a schoolhouse, and a new building which was to house the new library.

Dickson's rear yard was quite large, the bare earth running sixty yards down to the creek, spotted with cottonwood trunks gnawed by horses customarily tied to them. Along the creek lay a big corral, and the old barn which had been used for the relay stock for the stages, and next to this was the pigpen and a small henhouse.

The pale autumn sun, sharp in the frosty Montana air, was warm and gold on the yellowing cottonwood leaves. Wood smoke made a pleasant, spicy odor, and the men digging the barbecue pit were joking together, their voices clear in the bright air.

The tables for today's barbecue, an affair to which Dickson had invited practically everybody in town, had been set up the day before, bright new pine planks, their oozing sap covered with newspapers. Everywhere there were evidences of a lively social life, which Dickson loved, although the place now was so nearly deserted.

The stage station had, in fact, become a kind of men's "clubroom" with card tables and billiard table (although Dickson was not now running any professional games). The walls had been decorated with old arms, Indian weapons and trophies, and some good heads of game.

What Dickson had done was to introduce the pleasures of an easygoing country house or hunting lodge into a town which had known nothing but hardship and barrenness. People came and went freely through it, always welcome, and Dickson was always the open, genial, pleasant, and cheerful fellow who had plenty of money and knew what to do with it.

He had bought a large organ for the church, and he went there regularly and sang loudly, at least for the five Sundays he had been steadily in town.

Everybody knew his business. He was an Englishman who, like many other Englishmen, was investing his money in cattle. He had an option on General Montrose's ranch, and he had six thousand head of cattle coming up the Bozeman trail, due to arrive about October 20. They also knew that Montrose did not intend to sell, despite the option, and little by little Dickson had brought them to believe that Montrose was trying to lie out of his contractual obligations.

In five weeks Dickson had made himself better liked than Montrose had in thirteen years, for Montrose was a cold, reserved old fellow, inclined to be harsh and critical in public, and never sociable.

The general opinion was that Montrose was a typical old army crab who seemed to think he was better than everybody else combined.

Dickson, on the other hand, simply assumed that everybody was just as good as he. He just ignored all differences. He never, for instance, kept wine off his table just because the people in Warhorse held wine drinking in contempt.

The fact was, he educated the people, and they naturally enjoyed the process, since they weren't aware of it. The men of Warhorse now almost enjoyed drinking brandy in the evening at the Station House.

Dickson had accomplished all this in six short weeks by being breezy and friendly and persistently aggressive in being generous. In Dickson's company they all felt gay and above themselves.

And, of course, behind all this charm there was money. How could anyone possibly criticize a man who believed in the public good and gave a library to the town, and a beautiful organ to the church, and yet did it so casually?

Everything that Dickson did had been deliberate, or at least conscious, except one thing. There was one factor which was working on him of which he was quite unaware.

This was the fact that it was fall. It was the first autumn Dickson had seen since he had left England, and he loved it; and this love, which was a reflection of his love for England and Lamont, colored his whole feeling, his whole attitude, in an entirely unconscious way.

As the leaves began to turn, and the nights to grow more chill, and as the boughs of the aspens became bare, Dickson had even begun to dream of keeping Montrose's place as an investment, in exactly the way many Englishmen were dreaming. Instead of selling it he could very well live in England and keep this for a summer hunting place.

It was the color of the leaves that moved him most—a thing which he never realized, and which was therefore all the more potent. Warhorse, because it was autumn now, reminded him of England and Lamont; the chill of autumn, the hard frost of morning, the clarity of the air, this was England again, as he had not seen it for years—or almost England.

For all his years away from England had been spent in the tropics or in the semitropics, in Jamaica or in San Antonio, or New Orleans or Cuba. So he looked now at the yellowing leaves and sniffed the wood smoke and, rubbing his reddening hands briskly, he felt an old love stirring.

▼ 2 ▼

Behind the Station House
Same Morning

Mike Allen was walking up and down between two of the cottonwood trees, his hands in his pockets, moving with a rough restlessness. He had been under guard, living in the barn, for a week. Beyond him, sitting at one of the new picnic tables, was one of Dickson's men, holding a steaming cup of coffee between his hands. Farther down the gentle incline toward the creek, the man named Vickers was leaning against the pigpen looking at the swine.

"Ah," Dickson said, strolling up to Mike, "our Damon and Pythias, as usual!"

Mike stopped pacing.

"What is it today?" Mike asked. "Horseshoes again? Or mumblety peg? Aren't people beginning to wonder just what I am supposed to be doing? Don't they ever ask who I am, and what my name is, and why I am followed around by Stringer or somebody? Isn't there any gossip?"

"Not so loudly, my boy. As far as I know, nobody in Warhorse finds you at all interesting. But be careful, or I may have to lock you up in the house—voices carry remarkably in this delightful mountain air."

Vickers was coming up from the pigpen, hobbling hurriedly on bowed, spindly legs, his small, angular body moving with nervous energy, almost twitching. He looked from side to side, his blue eyes darting everywhere as though on the watch.

"Hey, hey," he said, coming up. "What goes on? Good morning, Mr. Dickson, good morning. Mrs. Vickers sent her very best. Say, did you know the old sow was blind? I was poking her with your stick, and I saw her eyes—plumb poked out, Mr. Dickson."

"An accident," Dickson said. "An unfortunate error on my part. I was simply scratching at her snout, and—well, she made a false move. False moves are always expensive. Eh, Mike?"

Vickers' manner changed to acute wariness as he eyed Mike, and then in an instant his expression became sad. "Today's the day, Mr. Dickson. My note. It's due. My God, what will I do? Eh? You know if Montrose didn't keep robbing me, I'd have plenty of money."

"My dear fellow, you know I have always had complete faith in you. No one understands better than I the difficulties of having bad neighbors. Now, Joe, you run along up to the bank and entertain Mr. Curtis a few minutes, will you?

It's nearly ten, and he'll be there. I'll be along and perhaps we'll work something out."

"You know he'd take my ranch, don't you?" Vickers said. "I couldn't help thinking—Eh?" He blinked quickly, pale blue eyes beseeching, promising, and doubting all at once.

Dickson laughed gently. "Why worry, Joe?"

A pale smile broke out on Vickers' face. The wiry stubble on his chin spread and seemed less dark. He licked his lips and nodded. He spat, with sudden force, and started off again, grinning now to himself.

"Charming fellow," Dickson said. "Now, to you, dear boy," he began afresh, turning to Mike. "Come along, let's walk down to the pigpen while we talk over a little job for you."

Mike sat still, looking up at Dickson with remote coldness.

"What is it now?"

"Another visit to the Montroses."

"They wouldn't even see me."

"Oh, yes, they will. It's quite obvious the girl is fond of you."

Mike looked wretched. "There's no use talking about it," he said. "They told me not to come back again."

"You think she is disgusted with you, through with you," Dickson said. "But let me tell you, it is quite different. Love in a woman is like a flower—"

"Shut up. Keep your filthy mouth shut. What do you know about love, you lousy bastard?"

Dickson turned white, and then two round red spots appeared on his cheekbones, like pats of rouge. They stood facing each other for a moment, and then Dickson took a breath. He had a little difficulty controlling his voice, which he could not wholly keep from shaking.

"Listen to me, you wretched yearling bull, you hulking backwoods oaf. There comes a time when nothing, not even common sense, will restrain me. I have put up with you and that stupid old fool of a father of yours for the sake of the money he owes me. But there will come a time when I can endure no more, and I shall turn loose on you and on your miserable, wretched little group. I shall turn loose, I shall strike you all, I shall thrash you bloody in the dust—" His upper lip was lifted and his white teeth showed; his eyes sparkled with sheer vicious fury. Then he stopped himself.

They stood in silence, and then looked away from each other. Dickson took three paces away and then three paces back.

He lifted his eyebrows. He looked about at the yellow leaves. "A lovely day," he said. His voice still shook. He looked around again. "A sparkle in the air, a chill."

He said, "Have a care, my boy. Remember, I too have my animal to control. Now, let us discuss these matters civilly. Shall we?"

Mike looked at him. It was the first time he had ever seen Dickson angry, and it was as though, between two delicate, parted curtains, he had seen a lean, pale wolf ravening, a naked, hairless blue-skinned wolf with pink eyes, held by a slender golden chain.

"As I was saying," Dickson went on, trying stubbornly to keep a light tone in his voice, "love in a woman blossoms like a flower, and don't think I am being personal about a lady who so obviously has your approval. I am merely making an objective remark.

"And just as nothing can keep a flower from blooming—not wind, nor storm, nor worm—so nothing can prevent a woman's love, once she has conceived it. She can hate you, think you a wretched coward, a villain, she can despise you— and yet, how unhappily! For she still loves you.

"Well, so, if I may be permitted this quite impersonal observation. Miss Montrose despises you, and yet I think you can still go out and talk to her and her father without being shot through the head. Something I cannot say for myself. Come along. Don't balk! If you won't come quietly, I'll have you dragged bodily, my boy."

He strolled on down toward the pigpen, Mike following. "At any rate, you are going out there, this very morning, and offer the good General a cool $75,000 for his ranch. It is his last chance. I shall take it by legal force tomorrow."

"Suppose I tell everybody that option date is forged, instead."

"My dear boy, that's just what Montrose is saying. Poor fellow! If only he could prove it! But of course he can't and neither can you, because, of course, he really did give Buford an extension."

"That's a lie," Mike said.

"Philanthropists never lie," Dickson said. "Ask anybody. The town doesn't want to believe I'm a liar. And why on earth should they believe you, if they won't believe the General himself? Anyway, if Montrose sells the ranch to me today, we shall save a lot of trouble. Surely he will appreciate my courtesy."

"I can't think why not," Mike said.

"Oh, come, let's not be sarcastic," Dickson said. "Good morning, Joanne," Dickson said, leaning on the pigpen fence and addressing the old blind sow. She stiffened with alarm at the sound of his voice.

"What's wrong, Joanne, darling?" he asked. "Why don't you speak to me?"

The sow in the mire grunted and turned swiftly toward the teasing voice, her teeth showing in a snarl. Her eyes were empty, the little lids fallen in, the short blond eyelashes sticking out all awry.

Leaning on the fence was a six-foot pole with a sharp prod in the end of it.

"Why, Joanne, darling," Dickson said sweetly, "don't you love me any more? I think we will eat you today at the barbecue."

Dickson picked up the prod and reached in. The pigs stampeded in panic. Dickson jabbed one of them in the rear and it jumped three feet, sprawling on another. Dickson laughed heartily, and wiped his eyes with a big, snowy handkerchief. "See how they run," he said. "Silly beasts. Don't they know they can't get away?" He jabbed another.

"Well, trot along out there, my boy, and make your offer. If Montrose has any sense, he'll take it."

"I thought you offered him $100,000 and he refused on principle."

"Oh, dear, why be so dense, Mike? This $75,000 is your offer, Mike. If he accepts your offer, I shall not press my option, and you shall transfer the deed to me. The whole point is simply, through you, to give Montrose a chance to get out in such a way that he won't lose face openly by having to submit to me."

Dickson poked another of the pigs. They stood trembling against the other side of the pen, which was too small for them. They were all quite thin, worn down by constant teasing. Suddenly one of them charged, with the speed of lightning, against the fence in front of Dickson, and fell, champing its jaws furiously, into the mud. Dickson stepped back, his eyes alight. "Savage little beasts, aren't they? Don't they know they can do nothing? That one over there —the fattest one. I will name him Keppelbauer. Here, Keppelbauer, boy— come here!"

Mike looked sick. "All right," he said, and walked slowly away.

Dickson reached over the fence and deftly jabbed out one of Keppelbauer's eyes.

As he leaned the stick back against the fence, Spence and Sheffield came around the other end of the barn from the bunkhouse, walking slowly together, talking.

"I told him the plan about Vickers," Spence said.

Sheffield looked at his boss without particular interest. "Suppose I do it? It's a hell of a risk."

"Aren't you paid well?" Dickson asked easily and pleasantly. "I haven't bought the police here, no. But the country's wide open. You're safe."

"It ain't only being safe," Sheffield said. "It's just that it's a big job, that's all."

"No bigger than Roarty or Madison, or that fellow in New Orleans," Dickson said, with the same smile.

Sheffield's eyes dodged, and he colored slightly.

"What was his name?" Dickson asked lightly. "I've forgotten. But, of course, the New Orleans police haven't. They could find it somewhere."

Sheffield's color grew bright. "What are you trying?" he cried suddenly.

"What are you?" Dickson asked calmly.

They looked at each other for a moment, and Sheffield's eyes dodged again.

"I have fifteen men now," Dickson said. "I've picked you, personally, to give an opportunity to. What are you trying to do? Hit me for a raise, just because this is particularly important, urgent—and there isn't much time? Is that it, Sheffield?"

Sheffield glanced at Spence, and his eyes ducked even more quickly. "No."

"Are you becoming unreliable?" Dickson asked, moving a step closer. "Having ideas of your own?"

Sheffield shifted away slightly. "No. No, not that, Mr. Dickson."

"When I bailed you out of that jail in Baton Rouge you liked my proposition, didn't you? Enough to jump the bail? You owe me two thousand dollars on that count, my dear Sheffield, and if I may say so, you owe the Baton Rouge authorities around fifteen years on a manslaughter charge, if you haven't forgotten. I assure you I haven't."

"Listen, I didn't mean anything," Sheffield said. "I was just kind of nervous, that's all."

"Nervous?" Dickson asked, moving another step forward. "Don't you trust me? Don't you have confidence in my ability to take care of you? What do you mean, nervous?"

Sheffield shook his head sharply. "I don't mean nervous. I didn't mean that."

"Afraid?" Spence said. "Are you afraid, Sheffield?"

"Hell, no."

"You like your pay? The regular five-hundred-dollar bonus?"

"Hell, yes."

"You want to talk to Forrest about it? The soldier? A private talk?"

"No. I like Forrest. I don't want to talk to him."

Dickson stepped close. "Listen, don't think, Sheffield. You're well off. Lots of money. Easy work. A man like myself to take care of you. Don't make the mistake of thinking, eh? Let me do all the thinking, eh?"

"Yes. All right, Mr. Dickson. All right. Jesus, what did I open my mouth for?"

"Then go saddle some horses for yourself and Spence. Spence will explain everything as you go along.

"Here's what's going to happen, Spence," Dickson said as Sheffield hurried away. "You know how Vickers has always accused Montrose of stealing his cattle. This afternoon Sheffield will shoot Vickers, and it will look as though Montrose did it or one of Montrose's men—as though Vickers had caught them red-handed. Do it just as we planned it before. And just because Vickers is a damned old fool and has been accusing Montrose of stealing his cattle, half the people in town will believe the setup. Then tomorrow Judge Frank can rule my option is good in court and that Montrose forfeits, and turn the ranch over to me. And then who's going to believe it if Montrose keeps on saying I forged the date? He'll have enough trouble talking himself out of a suspicion of murder. Do you think that will do it?"

"The only thing is," Spence said slowly, "you might push Montrose too far. Killing somebody is always a big thing. It scares people. Do you think we really have to do it? Is it really necessary?"

Dickson smiled pleasantly, his handsome, aristocratic face full of charm and affection.

"My dear Spence," he said in a gentle voice. "To make sure of getting this ranch, I'd do a lot more. What's one little man? Are you a Christian or something? Vickers is just sixty-eight cents' worth of blood and bone as far as I'm concerned.

"I want Montrose to do all his shouting about whether or not he's a murderer —not about fraudulent option dates. And why shouldn't we arrange this insurance? For the sake of sixty-eight cents' worth of blood and bone that moves and squeaks and sounds like a man? When I was a boy, we used to catch mice in flour barrels and chop them up with butcher knives, on the run. It was jolly sport. A pity killing Vickers has to be so secretive, so mechanical."

He looked at Spence with twinkling eyes. Spence's face was troubled. "Calm yourself, dear boy. There's nothing cheaper than human life. The supply is so much greater than the demand. Now, run along, Spence. I'm going to the bunkhouse to prepare the boys for coming events. And remember, the main thing—I want Mrs. Vickers to see the brand on Sheffield's horse—don't forget."

"Ta-ta, Joanne." Dickson waved to the pig, and strolled away.

3

The Railroad Station
Same Morning

In all his years of being on the dodge, since he had fled from Jamaica, one of Dickson's greatest problems had been the safekeeping of his growing fortune.

Above all else, his fortune had to be in some form which would allow him immediate flight, for he knew that for him, calamity was instant. He had always foreseen, and discounted, the collapse of his small criminal empires through some human error of his own; he was far too clever to believe that he could frustrate the law forever at any one place, and was content to enrich himself at a succession of places for limited times, being quite happy with losing all the battles with society, as long as he ultimately won the war.

But this implied a succession of escapes; and hence his fortune had to be highly portable. He could not bank it; the police could easily stop his credit. He could not hide it, as he might easily find himself barred from a particular part of the country. He could not carry it as currency, which was too bulky, and also liable to depreciation; nor as gold, which was too heavy. His solution was not very satisfactory, but he could devise nothing better.

Dickson had a large suitcase in his room, upstairs, locked in the closet. The closet had two locks. In this suitcase there was a great deal of money, but only a minor part of it was in cash.

A good part of the three and a half million dollars was in English notes, some of it in French bills, and some in Russian rubles; most of the cash was in U.S. Federal gold notes. This was for current and emergency use.

But the bulk of Dickson's fortune was in diamonds. Thus, while most of the suitcase was filled with ribbon-tied packages of paper notes, the greater part of his money was contained in seven canvas sacks, lined with velvet, in which were smaller packets of diamonds, each packet in tissue. He could have carried most of his wealth in his pockets if he had been forced to do so. None of his diamonds was very remarkable, none of them large. But they were all first-class stones, all perfectly cut; each of them would bring a full price and could be sold without any question anywhere in the world.

Out of the suitcase Dickson now took three hundred separate bills and put them in a large envelope.

He ran down the stairs and out onto the main street. Harris had his horse ready for him, and he swung up easily. He went down the street toward the railroad station at a nice trot, posting elegantly on his English saddle.

People stopped and stared.

Dickson swung down at the yellow railroad station, almost the newest building in Warhorse. The agent doubled on the telegraph key, and he was working at it now, his face blank and absent as he wrote down a message.

There was nobody else in the office. Dickson waited. The big railroad clock ticked on the wall—brand-new, shiny brass pendulum swinging jauntily. A brand-new pot-bellied stove sat confidently in the middle of the waiting-room.

The key stopped rattling.

"Good morning, good morning, Lee, old boy," Dickson said gaily, leaning on the counter. "How's our little woodpecker?"

Lee turned around on his swivel stool. He slowly pushed back his green eyeshade and looked at Dickson. He had a quiet, pasty face which looked stone-cold, and a wide mouth with thin lips. He looked at Dickson now, his face a perfect, observant blank. This masklike quality meant little. Actually, he was a family-loving, warm-hearted man, and Dickson knew he was. He had a young wife and two small daughters, and they had just moved into Warhorse with very little money. The railroad was paying them mostly in prospects, with which it was paying nearly everybody at that time. The blank face concealed worry about the future. Lee had the habit of worry, a small vice which seemed to him to be founded on prudence and foresight, but which actually had its source in timidity. His mouth barely twitched, a movement which Dickson took as a warm smile.

"I heard our books had arrived, John," Dickson said. "Thought I'd look in." Lee was the kind of man who was reassured by being called by his first name. Also, he liked the "our" books, as though Warhorse were just one big family.

"They did," Lee said. "Over there." He nodded his head an inch toward a pile of boxes in the corner.

"Mrs. Frisby said she's going to send a man down late this morning. Coming to the barbecue, I suppose? Don't forget to bring the girls—everybody's going to be there." Dickson laid a small envelope and a piece of paper on the counter.

Lee saw them and blinked. He looked afraid.

He came over to the counter, picked up the envelope delicately, and looked inside.

"What now?" he asked in a low, husky voice, looking quietly at Dickson.

"Nothing much. Just sign the receipt, John."

Lee signed the other piece of paper. "What am I going to tell the old lady? I haven't told her anything yet. I've been thinking and thinking. How am I ever going to spend the money without her knowing it? How am I going to explain it all?"

He glanced out the window to see if anybody was near.

"When the time comes to build your house, just pull a surprise on her," Dickson said. "Say you had it saved up from years ago. She'll think you're a smart man. They always respect you more if they think you've put one over on them. Just take your envelope, Lee, old boy."

Lee slipped the envelope into his pocket.

Dickson gave him a folded paper. "Here's a phony message from the police in San Antonio. An answer to the one Montrose tried to send. He'll be in today, I think. Give it to him."

"He's been in every day," Lee said, and took the sheet of paper. He read it.

General Lucius Montrose Warhorse Montana
Regarding your inquiry September fifteen this office re Thomas Dickson
subject is prominent citizen this city very highly regarded in all quarters
known for civic activity no charges of any kind have ever been made
against him and he has highest local reputation personally vouch for him
as gentleman of highest character
Benjamin Cash Asst Chief Police San Antonio Texas

The impassive, pale face did not move. Lee nodded. He glanced out of the window again.

"I want that copy back," Dickson said. "No sense in leaving my autograph around."

He leaned forward across the counter, a little closer to Lee. "You see, my dear fellow, we have to understand each other. Always remember, no matter what you might be tempted to do, I have your receipts. So, far, for three thousand dollars."

Dickson smiled. "Did you by any chance, actually send the General's wire asking information about me? I mean, the motive of curiosity must have made it very tempting."

"No," Lee said. "I didn't send it. I gave it to you, didn't I?"

"Yes, you did," Dickson said, and knew that Lee was lying. He smiled. "The reason why I told you not to send his wire was because if the police down there got any inquiries about me from here, naturally they'd assume I was here, wouldn't they? And they would most naturally wire the local sheriff, wouldn't they? You see, if I am exposed here, you will be too. That's why I told you not to send it, even to satisfy your private curiosity. Much too dangerous."

He watched the skin of Lee's face turn a shade paler.

"The important thing is to let me know of any messages, John," Dickson said patiently. "I can handle anything—answer anything. But if they don't get any answer in San Antonio, they may start using the mails, and then we're through. We can't control the mails, can we?" He smiled.

Dickson took his receipt and put it carefully into his wallet. "See you at the barbecue," he said. He reached a hand toward Lee and, with one forefinger, very gently tapped the back of Lee's hand, which was lying beside the phony message from San Antonio. "Don't make the mistake of taking me for a fool," he said, in a quite ungenial voice.

Lee looked up slowly into Dickson's eyes and dropped his own quickly again. "No," he said. "I won't, Mr. Dickson."

Dickson strode jauntily back to his horse.

Lee went to his sending desk and from the bottom drawer took out a cigar box. He opened it and took out a message, which was still in rough copy, as he had taken it down from the key.

It read:

General Lucius Montrose Warhorse Montana
In answer your wire September fifteen you are advised that Thomas Dick-
son is notorious character wanted urgently by this office on six charges of
murder in first degree he is professional gambler also wanted for extortion
and on numerous other counts if you have knowledge of his whereabouts
we request you advise your local authorities to arrest on our charges and
we will mail warrants and requests for extradition immediately upon your
advice by wire here he is probably accompanied by William Spence and
Isaac Forrest both wanted as accomplices and on other charges and per-
haps by others known to us urge you to use caution in dealing with these
men as all are dangerous will greatly appreciate any help you can extend
us in apprehending these individuals
Benjamin Cash Asst Chief of Police San Antonio Texas

Lee heard the hoofs of Dickson's horse trotting away up the main street. He
sat at his desk and wiped his cold face with both hands. There was a light dew
of sweat on it, in spite of the chill air.

He went to his key and sent this message:

Benjamin Cash Asst Chief of Police San Antonio Texas
Sorry cannot assist you as Dickson and others left here two weeks ago were
last seen in Dakota Territory near Deadwood and thought to be heading
east will advise you if I receive any further information
Lucius Montrose

Then Lee took out a pen and wrote on a telegraph form: *Dear Sheriff Bolt:*
In case I am killed, this will explain why. I am sorry I ever got mixed up in this.
His pen scratched and spat. His hand was shaking. *I was a damn fool but I*
needed the money. Lee stopped and thought. It wasn't true that he had needed
the money. He had only thought he had needed the money. But it was too late
to change the wording, just as it was too late to change the deed. *I am in too*
deep in this to come out clean, but this is so you will know the truth. The money
is in the bottom right-hand drawer of my desk in a cigar box. I haven't even
been able to spend it. The pen dug in with a bitter incisiveness on the last
words. The peculiar thing about the note was that it explained nothing, even
when he took the rough message describing Dickson and put it in an envelope
with his note.

He addressed the note: *To Sheriff Bolt. In case of my death. John Lee.* He
put the sealed envelope into his inside pocket and sat quiet. It felt like a bomb,
and at the same time, it was warm and comforting. But the thought of giving it
to Bolt made the blood drain out of Lee's head and hands and feet, leaving him
feeling hollow. He sat helpless, trying to get up the courage to do what he had
to do.

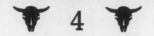

4

Curtis's Bank
Same Morning—9:45 A.M.

Joe Curtis, the banker of Warhorse, had one assistant, who did all the work. It was a good thing this young man, named Lewin, liked banking and figures, because business in Warhorse had picked up a great deal with the coming of the railroad, and he had plenty of both.

The savings deposits had taken great jumps, but nothing in comparison to the commercial loans. The fact was, as Lewin had pointed out twice to big, fat Joe Curtis, if a depositor like Red Timmons, who ran 10,000 head of cattle, pulled out his money, it would be very dangerous indeed. If not disastrous.

"If we need cash, call somebody," Joe Curtis said.

"We can't. You know as well as I everybody's up to the hilt. Who the hell can you call, when the money's all in nails and boards? There won't be any income from all this expansion for another year, Joe."

Joe lolled back in his chair, which tilted and swung in all directions. He had a heavy black mustache and heavy black hair, and his eyebrows shelved out in great tufts. He was heavy with fat of a rather loose kind, and his voice had a harsh, rattling quality associated with the constant quaffing of bourbon.

"For God's sake, Lew," he said, clearing his throat and shooting a load at the spittoon, "do you want to be a goddam clerk all your life, or a banker? The railroad won't let us down."

"Listen," Lew said. "If we don't collect a couple of those short-term notes like Vickers' before Saturday, we can't meet the railroad payroll, and if that happens, everybody in town will come yelling for his money, and we're sunk."

Beads of sweat crept out on Joe's forehead and rolled down into his bushy eyebrows. "Hush, Lew," he said. "Hush. Those are forbidden thoughts. You've got to keep your mind healthy, son. Healthy."

"Healthy like being drunk all day. No thanks. Take a tip, Joe—try a few forbidden thoughts once in a while, it keeps a body sane. We got too much out on loans. For one thing, we'd better foreclose on Vickers. We can sell that ranch fast, it's all flat land, first class, and plenty of water."

"Dickson is backing Vickers. For some damn reason they're friends. I can't foreclose the little bastard."

"Foreclose and sell it to Dickson. That'll give us some cash. Besides, it's right next to Montrose, and Dickson wants that. It's perfect."

"Do you think it's possibly true that Montrose is stealing from Vickers? Or having his men do it? Maybe the old boy is really doing it."

"Who cares?" Lew asked. "All I care about is the deposits. I have to look the damn balance sheet in the face every day, and it makes me sick."

Curtis heard boot heels coming quickly along the board sidewalk. He wheeled around in his chair. "Here comes Vickers now."

"Shall I let him in?" Lew asked.

"Hell, no, let him wait. It ain't ten yet and I don't know what to do with him, anyway."

"Renew his note?"

"Well, we need the money, don't we?"

Vickers knocked on the door, timidly and urgently.

Joe Curtis sat still. Lew waited.

Vickers hobbled rapidly back to the saloon, cussing to himself. Then Lewin saw Dickson trotting up the street.

"Bet you five he's coming here," Lewin said. "He knows Vickers' note is up. You really want to put his money in the kitty—I mean, the deposits?"

"He won't leave town. The General'll sell."

"How do you know?"

"I just know."

"You mean you got the Judge to go for that option, is that it?"

"There ain't nothing wrong with that option," Curtis said.

"Montrose says the date was changed. He says the date was July fifteenth, and it's been changed by somebody."

Joe Curtis spat in the cuspidor. "Montrose is a contrary, nasty, mean, stuck-up old bastard that keeps his money in his sock. He's just lying to throw us off, 'cause he doesn't want to sell. Changed his mind."

"You mean you'd rather have Dickson around town than Montrose," Lewin said, his face committing nothing.

"Well, wouldn't you?" Joe asked, his big voice rattling. "Dickson is a friendly man, for one thing. He's forward. Look at this library. And I believe his option is good, and I'm going to back him up, and so is the Judge."

"How do you know?"

Joe spat. "Well, I was playing cards with Dickson and the Judge last night. Just a little private game, down at the Station House. The Judge told me when we was riding home. He told me he thought Montrose was just trying to lie out of his contract, that's all."

Lewin looked at his boss. "The Judge's account is down to seventy-five dollars. He's taken out three thousand in the last four weeks. His savings, I mean."

"So what?" Curtis asked coldly.

"Don't get sore. Just look facts in the face," Lewin said.

"Everybody knows Dickson lost two thousand to the Judge. Are you implying the Judge is in the hole? Why, everybody knows the Judge won two thousand bucks off Dickson."

"Sure. And how much has he lost since? If he hasn't been losing, what's he been doing with his account? He hasn't bought anything around town. He hasn't sent it anywhere. So who's got the Judge's money?"

"What's that got to do with the price of beans?" Joe asked.

"You know damn well what it's got to do with the price of beans," Lewin said.

Joe leaned forward. "Go on, I want you to say it out loud. What's that got to do with the Judge's decision on the option?"

Lewin said nothing.

"Go on, tell me," Joe said. "Put up or shut up. Are you slandering two good men—the Judge and Dickson both?"

Lewin looked at his boss with a faint spark of fright. "Now, don't get sore, now, Joe," he said. "I'm just trying to work for you. You're putting a lot of chips on Dickson, and you don't really know anything about him. What about that wire the General sent to San Antonio last month—the one he says he will show everybody?"

"Well, what about it?"

Lewin said nothing.

"More dust kicked up by the General in a tantrum," Joe said. "He's just sore 'cause he's got to sell his ranch, is all. Just sore and slandering. Don't be a slanderer, Lew."

Lew's mouth closed tightly.

"Lew, you know as well as I do," Joe Curtis said, noting the closing in of Lewin's mind, and turning gentle, "that Warhorse is going to grow big by big thinking and by big people. We want people like Dickson here. If it comes to a choice between Montrose and Dickson, we'll take Dickson. Montrose was the first man in this country, and if it was left to him, there'd be nothing today but him and the Indians, this very day. Dickson is a happy, cheerful man with plenty of money and business sense. We can gamble on Dickson. I'm sure of it." There was a prophetic light in his eyes.

"All right," Lewin said. "You're the boss. Thank God I don't own any stock in this bank." He stood up.

Outside, Dickson swung down from his horse, and Vickers came hobbling back along the walk from the saloon.

Joe Curtis stood up as Dickson came in, followed by Vickers.

"Good morning, there, Joe old boy!" Dickson cried out cheerily, and extended a hand.

"Good morning, there, Tommy old son," Curtis boomed in his rattling voice, pumping Dickson's hand up and down with heavy warmth. "Sit down, son, sit down. Vickers, find a seat, will you?" he said, as though suggesting that Vickers could find one out in the shed behind the bank. "What's on your mind, Tommy? Anything I can do for you?"

"Well, Joe," Dickson said, letting his lean, neat length down into a chair against the partition, "our friend Vickers here tells me he's in a tight, as we say out here in God's country. That right? Note's up. Six thousand, he says. So I thought I'd come in here and"—he pulled out his wallet—"just take up Vickers' note for him, and make it a personal matter between him and myself. All right, Vickers?" he asked, beaming. "All right, Joe?" he asked again, turning and beaming at Curtis. He pulled out six neat, clean thousand-dollar bills, and laid them on the desk.

Curtis beamed broadly.

"Now just charge my account for the interest, will you, Joe? And sometime you just stick that old note in the mail to me. All right?"

"Well, I should say so," Joe said in a low, warm voice, exactly like an old Southern mammy crooning over a hurt pickaninny. He picked up the six bills with dear love and tender affection.

"Kind of figured," Dickson said, using the subjectless verb in true Western fashion, "Vickers and I would work together when I take over the General's place tomorrow."

"Yes, by golly, it is tomorrow," Joe said. He pulled out a drawer and took out Buford's old option. "That's right, so it says, right here. October ninth. No getting around that." He lifted his heavy, smiling face and winked lightly at Dickson. "Is there?"

Dickson pulled out his big envelope and laid it in front of Curtis. "Three hundred thousand dollars. Set it up in escrow, Joe. That takes up the option without any question."

Joe Curtis looked in the envelope and shut his mouth. He saw the denomination and riffled a finger over the packets. He half-shut his eyes, to keep them from bugging.

"Surely does, Tommy," he said in a slightly weak voice. He wondered for a moment if he should not call Tommy "Mr. Dickson" from now on, and immediately revolted at the servile idea. "I don't mind saying, Tommy, Warhorse is mighty proud to have a man like you in its midst. Mighty proud."

Vickers blinked and smiled, looking with childish happiness first at Curtis and then at Dickson.

"Come along," Dickson said, taking his arm. "We'll just ride out and look your place over. Especially your fence line. We'll probably take that down altogether, eh? We'll pool our cattle and we can operate more cheaply that way. So long, Joe! See you down at the barbecue this afternoon! Bring the missus and the kids!"

They went out, the long and the short, the short hopping and dancing, as happy and excited as a child.

Joe Curtis sank down into his swivel chair with a deep sigh and dragged a bottle out of his desk.

"Lew," he called, and Lewin came in.

"Did you hear all that, Lew?" Curtis asked benignly, taking the money out of the big envelope and showing it. "Never mind putting this in escrow, boy. Put her right on deposit. I'm going out and make some more seven-per-cent loans."

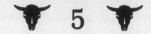
Montrose's Ranch
Same Day—2:00 P.M.

Montrose's ranch lay back between two great spurs of the Warhorse Mountains, fenced only at the lower end where the hay land lay flattening out down toward the Yellowstone.

Warhorse Creek, which started high in the mountains above Montrose's place, ran down through it for twelve miles to the fence along Vickers' place, and then another nine miles to the town.

As Mike, followed by Irving, rode up the ruts toward the mountains, he could see small scattered bunches of Montrose's cattle, dotted over the steepening country. They left the hay land, and the grass thinned, and as he climbed along the road beside the rushing creek, he could see easily enough why Montrose ran only a thousand head while everybody was saying he should run four.

Four miles farther, Mike caught a glimpse of the summer headquarters, far up the canyon. They had passed the winter house, down on the flats, to which Montrose had not yet returned, and the road began to get into rough upland, by-passing boulders and running over exposed gravel. They were entering the big head canyon, which narrowed as it rose toward the far blue peaks, covered with black forest.

The summer house was in clear view, far up. It was built of logs with a tin roof laid over planking.

Mike stopped at a new gate across the road. It hadn't been there the last time he had been up. He got down and opened it, and they went through. On the upper side of the road, there was a kind of barricade or small fort built of rocks. There was nobody in it.

They rode up before the big log house and swung down. There was no one around.

"You wait here," Mike said. "I won't be long."

"Take your time," Irving said, rolling a cigarette and sitting down against the house. "There ain't but one way out of this canyon."

Mike went up the wide plank steps and crossed the creaking porch. He knocked at the big plank door.

The big door opened and Herbia looked out at him. She gave a kind of hiss, her heavy lips drawing back a little, and seemed to shrink.

"You ain't wanted here," she said. "Get out."

"Herbia, tell the General I want to see him."

"You get out," Herbia said, her voice rising. "You ain't going to trouble the General no more. Miss Clara said if you came you wasn't—"

"Herbia," the General said from behind the door.

Herbia dropped her eyes and moved back. The door opened wider and the

General stood there, dressed in the same tight black coat and smart trousers which he had worn in Cheyenne. At this range, though, Mike could see the shine on the seams and the threadbare edge of the coat cuffs. The General was wearing a gun and he had his coat tail tucked up inside the gun butt, leaving it handy.

"Get out," the General said in a voice like an icicle. "I drove you off once. This time I'll shoot you off."

"General," Mike said, "I am not armed, I'm bringing a message. I ask you to believe I have no part in this business. I've come up here to try to help as much as I can. I ask you to believe me."

"I have been subjected to too much trickery," the General said. "You are a tool of Dickson's. You came here the first time pretending to be our friend, and we found your offer was just a lie. Why come here again? Do you think we are fools?"

"I'm a prisoner," Mike said to the General. "I have been for two months. A hostage. I told you that before. Why don't you believe it? I want to help, but I can only do so much."

"It's a trick. I do not dare believe it is anything else," the General said. A look of indecision and confusion, momentary weakness, crossed his face. "Deception, everything has been deception, from the beginning."

"Wait a minute, Father," Clara said from inside the room. "It's a little too much to believe that this is a trick. Surely not everyone is a master of lies. If Mr. Allen did not want to help us, as he says, why would he come up here again? Surely he knows that if we threw him out once, we can do it again." Her voice was hardly bitter, very much controlled.

"What is it you have to say, then?" the General asked. "Say it, and go. We're leaving for the party—Mr. Dickson's great social event—to try to improve our social standing. I'm afraid it's a little too late."

"Do you mind if I come in?" Mike said, gesturing in Irving's direction.

"Such secrecy," the General said. "Come in, then. I suppose I shall have to endure it. My daughter insists on politics. Let this be part of politics." The General looked almost sick with disgust, and then suddenly a look of surprise crossed his face as he stepped back. He said, in an almost civil voice, "You know, I cannot understand your patience under insults. God knows I have insulted you enough to keep you away from here. Why do you keep coming back?"

He stepped back out of the doorway. Mike went in, taking off his hat. Herbia shut the door, and the gloom of the big room closed in on them.

"The truth is, I am simply ashamed," Mike said. "I can't afford to feel insulted, General. Nearly everything you say is true."

"And I might say, I am ashamed *for* you," the General said. "You are a most peculiar mixture of humility and asininity, if I may say so. You come up here apparently abject, offering to help. How on earth can you help, with that armed dog at your heels, if I may ask? I cannot follow your line of reasoning. You remind me, in fact, of a puppy on a string. Now what is it, please? What is the message?"

Mike looked at Clara. She looked back, directly, for a moment, and then dropped her eyes. Mike had the feeling, for a moment, that the General, Dickson, the whole mess was a game—that the only real thing in the whole business was the instantaneous feeling that came over him, when they looked at each other, of—of what? He knew that she was happy when he came, and he knew that she knew exactly what he was feeling. It was as though each of them were suddenly looking through a hole in the dense wall of their accustomed human reservations and amenities, straight into the eyes of a perfectly charming friend who understood everything, and with whom there was little use for words. It made him happy just to be here, and it made her happy, and the peculiar thing was that it was making the General happy, in spite of everything. That was why the horrible mess in which they were all involved seemed for a moment quite unreal. That was why the General had suddenly begun to abuse him—because he liked him, in spite of himself.

"Dickson told me to offer you $75,000 for your ranch. In my name."

"Bosh. That is merely insulting."

"I know it. But I want to offer the balance in my own notes. I want you to give me title to the ranch, and I will fight Dickson."

"What kind of chicanery is this? What on earth good are your notes?"

"The point is," Mike said, laboring on, "that if my father and I—" Why was it always so difficult to talk to the General? The same thing had happened in Cheyenne, the feeling of dreadful mental labor, to outline his plans clearly. Then it occurred to Mike that he only had this difficulty when he was being specious, or trying to be clever. It was difficult to be a fool with General Montrose, and easy to be sensible. It was as simple as that.

"Your father and you," the General said. "You mean, you two would take over my problem with Dickson, and fight shoulder to shoulder, sparing my daughter and myself, while accomplishing what Buford still wants to do—rob me. You would defeat Dickson, operate the ranch successfully, and pay off your notes to me, while I lived in Mt. Holly. How extremely noble in conception, if I may say so. Didn't I tell you once we all had our illusions? Yours seems to be that it is possible to be virtuous simply by having good intentions. Why, it seems to me that you and your father are responsible for this whole incredible mess. You've come up here into a peaceful country like a swarm of locusts, you and your father and that wretched creature Dickson. You and your father have loosed a horde of villains on us all, simply from your father's incredible greed and your incredible weakness.

"That fellow Dickson is now in the process of actually trying to force me out of my simple rights. What in God's name are we coming to? Why, he has bewitched the entire community. He has turned all their heads. And you are with him. That is the fact you cannot deny. You are actually enjoying his hospitality.

"If you were to come here and endure our privations with us, the calumnies of people we once called friends, I would be more inclined to believe your protestations of friendship. And yet, I do believe your protestations, but what else are they? As I said, you are exactly like a puppy on a string. You can take your incredible offer and go to hell with it."

"Father," Clara said, "I am getting tired of all this ranting. I am simply tired." She sighed heavily. "I can't help feeling there is something good behind Mr. Allen's feeble moves."

"Ranting?" the General asked. "Have I been ranting? Herbia, do get me some coffee, will you? Bring Mr. Allen a cup of coffee."

His face suddenly became tired. "This wretched business," he said, looking almost vaguely around. "It's the ruin of everything. I feel myself slipping, and I cannot understand why. All of a sudden, this filthy fellow Dickson is upon us, and how did it all happen? He is ruining me among my friends, and they believe him. Those incredible accusations of that poor fellow Vickers. It's simply fantastic. The whole world is slowly turning upside down."

"Dickson's bought them," Mike said.

"He's bought you too," Clara said.

"No," Mike said. "All I can do is wait. Don't you understand? I can't do anything until my father gets here. The only thing I can do is persuade him to give it all up and clear out, and I can't do that until he comes."

Herbia came in with the coffee cups on a tray. " 'Scuse me, General," Herbia said, "You'll be mad if I don't tell you. There ain't no more of that."

"Of what?"

"Coffee, suh. No more hardly nothin'. Flouah. Beans. Hawss radish. How'se ah goan laht the fah 'thout no matches?"

"Never mind, Herbia," Clara said. "We're going to get everything this afternoon."

The General turned to Mike. "Even if you could make the ranch pay well enough to pay off your notes, you would still have to beat off that devil Dickson, and how could you do that even as well as I? So what do I have to gain by your offer? Surely the ranch is in better hands than in those of men who have already proven themselves unable to cope with this Dickson. Your father—poor, greedy, muddling fellow—and you, a young man of decent inclinations and not half brains enough to implement them—what on earth could you do that I cannot do? My God, Mr. Allen, how can you sit there and endure what I say?"

Clara's cheeks were faintly pink. There was a light in her eyes, a subdued glow. She could not escape Mike's look. It did not embarrass her, but it made her feel far too beautiful.

"Because I want to help you."

The General smiled thinly. "Would you fight for me? Against your father? If it came to that?"

Mike looked at him astounded. "Why? Believe me, all my father wants is to get free from Dickson."

"Are you sure? He could get free easily enough, by giving up those herds you told me about. Are you sure he isn't planning still to get my ranch?"

"How? How would he do that?"

"How do I know?" the General asked. "You said he had a dozen men, with this man Tucker. He could do a lot with a dozen men—fight Dickson himself, for instance. Or me. To get the ranch."

The blood drained slowly out of Mike's head. "He couldn't be such a fool. He learned his lesson in San Antonio."

The General shook his head. "In all his life, Buford has never learned a lesson. I told you he was pursuing an illusion, didn't I? He lives on hope—on dreams. And he always bounces back. Wait and see, my boy. As for you, you're going to have to learn to go your own way—alone. Honor and justice at times require one to step squarely on the faces of his friends, and even of his own father. I say again, you are a puppy on a string, sir, and I give you one simple, all-inclusive counsel: Grow up."

The General stood back from the table, and Mike knew he was through. He rose slowly and wearily. "Thank you for the coffee," he said.

"You may also tell Dickson that he will never get my property by any means. I do not say, even over my dead body, as he shall be the one who dies, not I. I suppose you noticed the new gate, and my rather neat little sentry box."

Mike said, "Do you mean to tell me you are getting ready for an invasion?"

"What else? I am not a general for nothing. I can read that fop's mind like a map. Tomorrow he will try to get a judgment against me and he will succeed simply because Judge Frank owes him money. Frank owes everybody money. He is an habitual moocher. Dickson will try to evict me, and I shall resist, and I assure you it will take at least a troop of cavalry to get me out of here." He held the door open.

Mike did not get another look at Clara. He crossed the porch and went down to his horse.

Irving got up. For a moment, Mike had an almost irresistible desire to smash him in the face, gun and all. With a bitterness that burned like alkali in the mouth, he kept the impulse down and mounted his horse. They rode out without speaking.

Mike knew he would never have a better chance to get away than now. Irving was quartered to his rear; but Irving wasn't wary. Mike's long weeks of patience and good behavior had put all his guards to sleep. If he could get away from Irving—

The future opened up in Mike's mind, and he saw how little chance he had, even if he did get away. He had no way of killing Irving. Even if he was able to get away, Irving would reach Warhorse as soon as he hit the Yellowstone, and Dickson would put ten men on his trail.

And where would he go? They'd know he would have gone to his father. What else could he do, except try to warn Tucker and the rest, and start the battle now? And if they lost the battle, he and his father would both be dead, and Montrose left at Dickson's mercy.

It was a hopeless situation. But Mike knew that nothing ever worked out as any man foresaw it, ever. Things happened—accidents, lucky breaks. A man had to try, to give the breaks a chance to happen. A man had to do something. He had found out that night in San Antonio that nothing was worse than simply accepting what the enemy made you do.

Mike's horse didn't have much nerve, it was a decent, good-natured animal out of the livery. What he needed was a wild one, an easy shier, a cat. But he did the best he could. He hauled back on the reins and rammed in his spurs at the same time, rearing his horse and wheeling it toward Irving, trying to throw it on Irving's mount. Mike's horse was slow, but Irving's wasn't. It dodged backward away from the forefeet pawing over it, almost throwing Irving over its neck, and Mike brought his horse down and wheeled away down the road, beating with his heels, leaning low over the horn, as Irving fought to get his own horse under control again.

Mike was fifty yards down the road when the first shot whipped over him. He glanced back. Irving was off his horse, standing, holding his hand-gun at aim, steadying it by holding his right wrist in his left hand.

The second shot hit Mike's horse in the rump, and the third hit it in the spine. The horse dropped, throwing Mike over its head, and they plowed down the road together through the dust.

Irving stood there, seventy-five yards away, smiling quietly. Mike sat there in the dirt, listening to the horse scream.

Irving remounted, and trotted up. He shot Mike's horse through the head and it stopped screaming.

Irving put his gun away and picked his quirt off the horn. "Get up, you simple bastard," he said to Mike. Mike slowly stood up. His shirt sleeves were torn out where he had landed in the gravel, and the torn skin of his arms burned like acid.

Irving pushed his horse forward and brought the quirt down through the air, lashing across Mike's shoulder. Mike's vision turned black with the pain and he staggered backward.

"March," Irving said, pushing forward with the horse. The quirt came down again, and Mike staggered forward down the road.

"You'd better learn, you son of a bitch," Irving said with quiet fury. The quirt lashes whistled and Mike's back ached, his hands rising in the air. He seemed to dance a few steps, and broke into a trot.

"You damned, dumb son of a bitch," Irving said quietly through his teeth. "You'll learn. By God, you'll learn. Pulling a thing like that on me. I might have lost my job."

It was some time before Irving's temper sank again, and by that time Mike could hardly see at all. He staggered forward down the long, dusty road in the burning sun, his hat gone, blood collecting slowly in the burning welts on his back.

It hadn't been any use. He hadn't thought it was going to work. But a man had to try. Sometimes things broke right.

And sometimes they didn't.

6

Vickers' Ranch—2:00 P.M.

Nine miles down the creek from Montrose's ranch, Mrs. Vickers sat in her house, wiping the tears from her eyes.

For the first time in five years, she was perfectly happy. Her husband and Dickson had arrived with the joyful news about the note being taken up, and for an hour after they left together in the direction of the fence line, she wandered about the house in a dream.

At first she dreamed of curtains, new curtains on the windows, and then she began to dream of new windows, and then she began to dream of a small, but very neat clapboard house, painted white, with green shutters, just like the one she had left in Indiana. It was then that she felt as though an immense weight had been lifted from her back—she literally stood up and breathed more freely for the first time in years.

When Dickson and Vickers came back, she was brewing a pot of fresh coffee. She felt the tension in the two men; then she noticed the big round ball of fresh hide which her husband was carrying.

"Got him, Martha," was all Vickers said. "Got him. Look." He unrolled the hide on the ground in front of the house. "Look there," he said, pointing to the raw burn of new branding-iron marks. "Took a shot at us, he did."

"Who?" she asked.

"Montrose."

"Probably not Montrose himself," Dickson said from his horse. "Probably one of his men. Looked about the size of Fred Hand."

"Don't matter," Vickers said shortly. "Look," he said to his wife, pointing a dirty finger at the big, sprawled brand. His meaning was plain enough. The old scar of V, with a bar under it, had been altered to that of an M by the addition of two legs to the V. "Doctored my brand and took a shot at us, too. There was two of 'em. Gitcher dress on," he said. "I'll take this to the party. I'll show them all. We'll see who was the liar."

Dickson smiled at Mrs. Vickers and took off his hat. "I'll ride along," he said. "See you later."

Vickers rolled up the hide and put it in the wagon. He hitched up the wagon while his old lady ran inside and "got her dress on," a phrase which included everything from washing her feet to dabbing a touch of flour on her tanned cheeks.

After he had hitched the horses, Vickers went inside and sat down with a cup of coffee.

Suddenly a thought jumped up before him, and he sat quiet, his confidence

622

draining, fear beginning to shrink him again. He remembered that all his accusations against Montrose were actually lies. He had been lying so long and so
consistently that he had built up an actual belief in his stories. But now, as he
sat alone, the belief broke.

He barely moved. He was afraid. This sudden proof, this hide which he had
skinned off his own cow, now had the effect of unnerving him. Could it be
really true that Montrose was robbing him? He sat in numb confusion, knowing
in his heart that the idea of Montrose thieving was absurd. Something was false.
But surely not the evidence of the hide? Then what was it? He faced a gray
cloud of mental paralysis. He either could not think at all, at this moment, or
the thought he faced was too terrible to entertain, and hid itself behind a
curtain of wool. In all the five years he had run stock on this place, he had
never had a single good reason to suspect Montrose; yet this in itself had in
some way seemed to him all the more reason to suspect Montrose of villainy,
for surely his calves did disappear.

He was, in fact, too lazy to ride his own range, and therefore many of the
calves were weaned without a brand. These were mavericked by anybody who
had the nerve to do it. The fact was that the whole idea of Montrose robbing
him had been conceived in Vickers' head for the purpose of detracting from the
General's superiority as well as excusing his own laziness.

The very lack of proof was an asset, in a peculiar way, because people had
never seriously believed Vickers' hints, insinuations, and secret accusations, and
this meant that Vickers could repeat them endlessly, which was what he wanted
to do. His purpose was not to see justice done but to escape it himself.

In his heart he knew that this hide was an incredible thing, not real at all. He
knew vaguely that it did not mean what it purported to mean—he knew that
this event had a hidden significance. But he did not know what this hidden
meaning was. He suddenly gave up, under the pressure of fear and indecision.
He would take the hide to the party. Let the others decide what was the matter,
if anything really was.

His wife came out of the bedroom in her one good dress. She had a smile
which was quite beautiful, of which she was unaware. She looked like a young
girl, as she had looked when she was fifteen, in her first real dress—excited,
timid, eager, but brave, for the first time adventuring into a social world where
anything romantic and exciting might happen.

"Pretty," Vickers said, and she turned pink with pleasure.

They went out and got into their wagon, Vickers chewing his front teeth
incisively, looking boldly and clearly ahead, and also from side to side.

They drove down the road.

Half a mile farther, Mrs. Vickers was startled out of her dreams into a
stunned blankness by a shot close to the road.

She turned her head toward the noise, and saw her husband falling forward
onto the dashboard. The horses, panicked, plunged into their collars. She saw
the man with a smoking rifle and a red neckerchief over his face.

She also saw the Montrose horse brand on the horse's shoulder, as the rider
turned and quirted the horse away.

Then the wagon horses were flying down the road, and her husband was lying in a heap at her feet, rolling and jolting with the roll and rattle of the wagon as it hit the potholes.

She stopped the horses. She sat there looking at her husband. There were two holes—all she could see was a trickle of black blood—one on each side of his head, small and somehow obscene, hideous and final.

A few birds came back to rest.

The horse flicked a fly off its ear.

She began to scream.

7

The Barbecue
The Station House—3:00 P.M.

It was understood in Warhorse that the Montroses had not been invited to the party that afternoon.

General Montrose had indeed been invited, but quite privately.

Therefore, when the General drove up beside the Station House in his buggy, with Clara sitting beside him, and followed by the small retinue of his four hands, there was a general hush that went like a wave of wind over the throng, and the temperature dropped a few degrees as eyebrows rose and looks were exchanged.

The four Montrose hands who had accompanied the buggy rode off down the street, obviously toward one of the saloons. It was well known that the General encouraged drunkenness and gambling on his ranch.

At this first big party of Dickson's everyone had begun by feeling wonderful and had progressed upward. The roast pig was delicious, and so was the beef, and the steak sauce, made by Harris, was something fascinatingly exotic.

There was beer, there was bourbon, and there was wine, and the ladies delighted themselves in exchanging guesses as to what local maiden would end by snaring this remarkable man, while the husbands exercised their newly acquired wine lingo, sagely judging this wine and that as they passed from bottle to bottle.

They were on their best behavior, they had come dressed in their finest, but the jealousy and hatred which the ladies had concealed beneath their complimentary remarks on each other's new silks and feathers soon dissolved in a general animosity toward the cause of dear Mr. Dickson's difficulties, which bolstered up the general feeling of self-satisfaction.

The arrival of the General put a stop to all this geniality. Mr. Dickson showed some confusion and surprise, but he recovered himself and hurried forward like a true gentleman, hand extended and with a most hospitable smile on his face.

General Montrose had been primed by his daughter. He had been forced into this, and he was doing his best not to show it. But as he helped his daughter down from the buggy, and saw Dickson hurrying forward with hand extended, all his resolutions and discipline of mind dissolved in a mixture of fear and bewilderment. It was incredible that this proven enemy was actually going to shake his hand. But what was he to do?

Clara, even while she was stepping down, read all this in his face, and as Dickson came up, she managed to turn her ankle and give enough of a cry to concentrate all the General's concern on her welfare rather than his own.

With a flutter of concern, Dickson caught Clara's other elbow, and with pretty gratitude she batted her eyes at him, at the same time inwardly shuddering.

"I am so happy that you could come, General," Dickson said.

The General managed to smile. "We feel especially honored," Clara said, her voice incredibly sweet in her father's unbelieving ears. How could she do it? he wondered. But somehow she infected him also with a feeling that it was possible to utter complete nonsense with the greatest ease.

"Let us hope," Dickson said, contributing abundantly to the nonsense, "that all our differences will be ironed out. I know, I am sure, that they are merely the results of misunderstandings."

"Indeed, indeed," the General said in such a voice that the words could be taken as affirmation or complete disbelief with equal ease. "Why, Dickson, I see that you know everybody. Look, Clara, all our friends." He gazed over the crowd.

It reminded Montrose of truce meetings between the commanders of hostile forces, during which everyone treated everyone with the most perfect courtesy, rendering compliments and tributes to valor, serving drinks and food if available. The day before, each had been desperately plotting the other's destruction, and both would have been profoundly moved with gratitude if the other had been smashed to bits by a stray cannonball—but here they were, soft-soaping each other like two rival mothers at a spelling bee.

The General accepted a bourbon and water, and he actually tried a sip. He had sworn he would simply carry a drink around until they left, but would eat or drink nothing of Dickson's. He and his daughter slowly walked through the crowd of chattering ladies and sedately conversing gentlemen, who were wandering around the tables and sitting in groups.

Nobody noticed as Mrs. Vickers drove up beside the General's buggy and sat there. Dickson saw her first, because he was expecting her. He saw the two legs, in gray trousers and black boots, hanging down from the side, the toes dirty and dusty where they had brushed the bumps.

Mrs. Curtis, spreading caviar determinedly on a cracker, saw Dickson's look and followed it with a jerk of her ostrich-plumed hat.

She said, "Why, why, what's that?" And other ladies looked, and then others. All of them, unbelieving, saw the feet and the legs, hanging down.

One by one, voices shut off in the middle of words as eyes saw looks, and followed. The thought of *drunk* flashed by and went, impossible because of the way Mrs. Vickers was sitting there. Without thinking, they knew she would never have come there with a drunken husband. And there was the wrong kind of pain in her face—not worry, not shame, but a gaunt, stretched look that was far different.

With what breath she had in her lungs, Mrs. Vickers screamed; and then she bent over, huddling in the seat, her hands over her face, rocking, moaning uncontrollably.

Dickson was the first one to move. He ran up the yard to her, mounted the wagon to help her down. Other men ran, and then a few women. They got her down from the wagon and carried her to one of the benches. They poured whiskey into her throat, which almost strangled her. She stood staring about at the crowd of worried faces and clung to Dickson.

"Mr. Dickson!" was the first thing she said, and they saw how she clung to him, her poor yellow hands dragging and clutching. She leaned her head against his chest and closed her eyes.

There was a crowd of men around the wagon, looking at Vickers' body.

"They killed him," she said.

"Who?" one of the men asked. Dickson said nothing.

"Montrose. I saw the horse." She told all this as though it were a secret, a little story, which she was telling to her father. And even though the others asked the questions, she addressed only Dickson, her voice low and intimate, as though the others were not there.

They heard her answer, and they sat and stood absolutely still, shocked out of thought.

Montrose heard it. He stood quiet with his daughter.

Down at the wagon, men were spreading out the hide. They came back up, dragging it through the dust.

"What's this?" one of them asked. "Mrs. Vickers, there was a hide in the wagon. A blotched brand." The speaker looked at Montrose once. "What does it mean? Somebody ran a Montrose M over the Vickers V, you can see it easy."

"The hide," she said. "Yes, that was it. They came back with the hide. Mr. Dickson, you remember."

Dickson said nothing.

A cold wind came over the yard, and they noticed that the sun had gone down behind the Station House roof.

"Won't you tell us?" one of the women asked. Many of the women, their faces drugged with shock, were fumbling to put on their veils and shawls. It was over, the party was all over. Where had it gone? Many of them were half drunk, and the shock of Mrs. Vickers' screams and the sight of the body had left them stupefied.

The Sheriff came up, walking quickly on his short legs, abrupt in movement. He had taken one look into the wagon with his sharp black eyes, his square, grizzled head turning quickly like a bird's, and seen enough.

He sat down next to Mrs. Vickers, his blunt, square hands on the knees of his shiny black trousers, and said, alert and at the same time trying to be gentle, "The hide, Mrs. Vickers. What is the hide?"

"They found it out on the fence line," Mrs. Vickers said, almost sleepily. It was easy to rest there on Mr. Dickson's shoulder.

"Montrose forged the brand," she said. "My husband said so."

The Sheriff looked up at the General, who was standing with Clara, apart from the crowd. "You'd better come over here, General Montrose." The General advanced slowly, and Clara followed. The women and men drew back to let them pass, farther than they need have drawn.

"My husband said it was him branding the cow," Mrs. Vickers said from far away.

"The General himself?" the Sheriff asked.

The General's mouth was tight. He was trying to contain himself.

"I don't know."

"This is—This is—" The General started to say "absurd," but murder was not absurd. He thought of "outrageous" and the Sheriff said, "General, please wait."

"A man shot him," Mrs. Vickers said. "I didn't see his face. He had a red handkerchief. But I saw the brand on the horse. Yes, I saw that." She burst into tears. "I know that one—just like the hide. Montrose's horse, it was Montrose's horse. Oh, my God, my God," she wept, and kept on crying, "My God, my God," over and over.

By now half the men and nearly all the women had left. Only the most sober remained. They looked at Montrose all at once, their eyes steady, wide, and waiting.

The General said, "Why, why, surely—surely you don't believe—Sheriff Bolt, surely this is some trickery—" He shot a look at Dickson. "It is not true. I deny every implication. Why, I was up in my headquarters all day. I have witnesses. It is simply—simply—fantastic."

The Sheriff looked at him alertly, a small, square, troubled bird. "I rule out now a personal accusation. Nobody accuses you personally, General. But—a man, one of your men—" Immediately there obtruded on his mind the possibility of collusion between the General and one of his men, and he shut it out.

"Mr. Dickson," the Sheriff said, "why does she keep on addressing you?"

"Because I befriended her husband, I suppose."

"Is that all? There's nothing more?"

"I must say I was a witness to the branding," Dickson said, with a troubled look. "Vickers and I rode down his line this morning. You know, I took up his note at the bank and we were discussing some plans. We saw two men at work over a cow—in fact, one of them shot at us. But I have no idea who it was. No idea at all. They turned and ran. We went up to the cow. It was tied. Vickers took off the hide for evidence."

"Where is the Judge?" the Sheriff asked.

"He's home," somebody said. "Sick."

"Somebody get him," Bolt said.

"I'll go," Curtis offered, and waddled toward his horse.

The Sheriff sat still. He detested the presence of these people. It was no longer their business. And yet if he moved the proceedings away from here, he would have to ask the General to come to his office and that would imply an accusation, the shadow of an arrest, and he did not want to imply this.

So he said, "Didn't you see the face of the man at all, Mrs. Vickers?"

"My God, my God," she said rolling her head wearily. "No, no."

"But you saw the brand on the horse."

"Yes," she whispered.

"Someone should take care of her," Dickson said. "Would one of you ladies be good enough to take her to your home?"

Two of the women helped Mrs. Vickers away.

The General was left with a large group of men. They stood silent, and a change came over them, now that all the women except Clara were gone—a quickening of eye and a sobering and hardening of mood.

"I would like to say now—" the General began. "I want to—I deny every charge. The whole thing—this whole thing—"

"What charge?" a man asked quickly. "There's been no charge." This with a gleam of eye, as though he had said something very astute.

"Why, by God," the General said, his own eye glinting, "you know what I mean, and there had better be no charge out of this. It's all a pack of lies!"

"Lies?" the same man said. "By Mrs. Vickers? Is she in any condition to lie?"

"What about that hide?" another asked. "Is that hide a lie? Vickers has been saying for years you were stealing his cattle. Look there, at your brand on it."

"Are you accusing me?" the General asked, his face turning pink, as he took a step forward.

"Father," Clara said from behind him.

He turned quickly. "Get in the buggy."

"Father, please," she said.

"Get in the buggy."

She turned and went.

"Let's have it out here and now," the General said, "and enough of stabbing in the back and tattling behind doors."

"Have what out?" another voice asked. The eyes were watching him, all except Dickson's and the Sheriff's. Dickson sat there, his face remote, saying nothing. The Sheriff listened.

"Tomorrow it is to be decided by our local judge," the General said, "whether I shall keep my ranch or whether I shall be forced to give it up on the basis of an option agreement which I claim is not valid. Why is it so apropos that I am today accused of murder?"

"Nobody has accused you of that," Sheriff Bolt said without looking up. "Don't exaggerate."

"Don't mince words," the General said.

The Sheriff winced. Why did the General have to make himself unpopular? After all, the Sheriff was in the position of authority here, and should be respected; and Bolt did not want respect for himself, either, but simply for his office. "I am not mincing words," he said stubbornly. "I have not made a charge. All we have is a fact. We have a murder. Somebody murdered Vickers. The murderer was riding a Montrose horse."

"And I say that somebody might be anybody who stole a horse to make it look like me or one of my men."

"And what enemy do you have who might do this?" Bolt asked quietly.

"Any man who might forge an option in order to force me out of my rights, and who might want to turn public opinion against me."

"And who do you mean?" Bolt asked gently.

The General looked down at Dickson.

Joe Curtis rode up, bulging over his fat mare, with another man. The other was a lean, shrewd-mouthed old gentleman with wet eyes and a red mouth.

"I mean Dickson," the General said. "I know, I swear by God, that either he forged that option or else he knows it was forged by someone else. It is not the true date."

"And so you accuse me," Dickson said, smiling faintly, "of killing Vickers. What, if I may ask, is the connection?"

The General stared blankly at him. What, exactly, was the connection? He was excited, he was upset, he could not find it. His mind was suddenly a total blank. Someone laughed, and then another, and his confusion became worse. And yet he had thought of the reason, just a moment ago.

"It seems to me," Dickson said very gently, patiently, without the slightest animosity, "that you are overeager to accuse someone else of a crime. Do you accuse me of it?" He remained sitting. He did not intend to make any attack on Montrose, even to the extent of physically standing up to him.

"Perhaps you have in mind," Dickson said in the same quiet, gentle voice, "that I helped out Vickers with his mortgage, and then murdered him so that I could obtain his ranch."

There were smiles and a few chuckles.

The General stood helpless. He could not think. Somewhere, behind this, there was a reason. Why couldn't he see it? He had seen it so clearly just a moment ago—the reason why Dickson had done this.

"Perhaps you feel that I am so evilly inclined," Dickson said smoothly, smiling just a little, "that the deed fits me too well to go wasting. After all, if I did forge that option, I might be capable of murdering a poor little man I had befriended. But why?"

The General could say nothing. He looked with miserable fatigue at his daughter, sitting in the buggy. Why had they come to this wretched party? Why were politics necessary?

"This accusation," he said, faltering for words because of a weakness that for some reason was undermining him, "this accusation of thieving from Vickers. It was always unfounded. You all know that. The very idea that I—" He stopped. "Do you make a charge, Sheriff? I thought I had reasonable friends here, with a sense of justice to which I could appeal. I shall have to turn to the law."

"General," Bolt said, "you know I can make no charge. There is no accused and not even a suspect. Somebody forged a brand and Vickers was bringing in the hide as proof. Somebody murdered Vickers. He rode a horse with your brand. I could hang the horse—if I could find it—for being an accomplice, and that's the end of it."

"Well, by God," the General said with a great flood of relief, "you are a fair man, Bolt."

"I, for one," the lean, wet-eyed man said from his horse, "would like to state another opinion." He glanced at Dickson and back. Everybody turned, and waited submissively.

"It is my opinion that the option is not forged," this man said.

"That's right, Judge," somebody said. "That's right. We all knew that."

"It is my opinion that it is a valid contract," the Judge said, licking his lips as though he had eaten a piece of candy.

"It occurs to me," the General said in a loud voice, "that you are prejudging a case which has not yet come to trial."

"I am not prejudging it," the Judge said in a mechanical voice. He looked quite ill, as though he were forcing himself to speak while nauseated, as though he had liver trouble, or a very bad hang-over. "I am merely stating an opinion. That does not become a judgment until tomorrow."

The General smiled bitterly.

"Will you appear?" the Judge asked.

"At what?" the General asked, contempt plain on his face.

"The suit. Mr. Dickson has brought suit. Tomorrow morning at nine o'clock."

"How can he have brought a suit, when the option date has not arrived, and I have not yet officially refused to comply?" the General asked.

"Nevertheless, he has brought it," the Judge said, like a gray mechanism.

"And what you have written, you have written. What kind of law is it that borrows so against the future, and assumes what does not even exist?" the General cried out. "By God, this stinks of your own affairs. Your damnable Honor! You always were a borrowing scoundrel, as I recall. Whose debts are you paying off now, may I ask? Whose debts?" He was shouting.

"Here, here," Bolt cried, standing up. "We can't have this."

"Contempt of court!" somebody cried out.

"Is this a court?" the General shouted. "Contempt of nothing! I say it man to man, I smell a stink of borrowing here, I know him to the bone, a conniving rat, a wretch—"

In his fury he was almost beside himself, his ancient cheeks pink, his eyes glittering.

"A pack of scurvy jades, trash, full of your wretched pomp, your civil judgments—I say to you, be damned."

"Be damned, is it!" one voice cried, while the others turned between fright and anger. "We'll see who's damned, by God! Get out, you damned old crow, you're not one of us, you never were."

"Will you respond?" the Judge asked quietly in his dead voice, his watery eyes looking at nothing, or perhaps a leaf upon the dust, his mouth firm and unflinching.

"To what?" the General asked, his voice shaking as his rage receded, letting in a trickle of fear. "Your wretched improper summons? Summons me at the proper time, you judge of nothing." He walked away, past the Judge, past Curtis, toward his buggy.

"Nevertheless," the Judge said, "I would suggest you stay in town overnight, as the trial will open at nine in the morning."

The General stopped, and turned back toward the crowd. "And where," he asked, his voice clear and unmoved, "would I stay, after thirteen years? Which one of you will have me overnight?"

Not one of them answered.

"Which one of you?" the General asked again. "Which man is still left uncorrupt enough to lend me his roof for one single night?"

They said nothing. In that crowd there were, in fact, six or seven who wished with all their souls that they might say something, might sing out, "I will!" But they did not; they were afraid of others around them.

"My friends," the General said. He no longer felt that trickle of fear, as he looked at them. "True friends! A wretched huddle of sheep. So much for politics." He turned on his heel and strode back to his buggy.

He picked up the reins and drove with Clara to the railroad station. He went in and asked abruptly, interrupting Lee at the sender, "Have you got an answer to my wire yet? About Dickson?"

Lee got up without answering, and handed him an envelope. General Montrose opened it with trembling fingers and read, and as he read, his anger and his excitement died. He finished, and his shoulders sagged. He looked once at Lee, hardly seeing him, and his face had become old, with the first signs of feebleness. He let the telegram fall to the floor, and turned and went out.

Lee looked after him. He wanted to cry out. He lifted one hand from the counter, and the cry was at his lips. But he could not. The buggy drove away, and Lee's hand fell. He looked at the paper on the floor, and then covered his face with his hands.

As the General drove up the main street again, his face bitter, he saw one of his men run out of one of the saloons, followed by the others, and then a pack of other men. They were fighting in the middle of the street, and horses tied near them danced and pawed. The Sheriff was running toward them, and other men.

"Already," the General said, whipping up the horse. "They've started already. Those are Dickson's men fighting ours. You see what's going to happen, Clara."

And then, suddenly, it came back to him—the connection between Dickson and the murder, the reason why Dickson would murder a man he had befriended. All Dickson was doing was making it possible to drive the General, without mercy, out of his holdings. He had cast suspicion, and he would feed suspicion, and the General saw the wisdom of this, for suspicion was more dangerous even than a charge, since it could not be answered in court. The suspicion that he, General Montrose, was a murderer, or the boss of murderers, would make almost any act of Dickson's justifiable. For now Dickson could do anything to Montrose and his men and get away with it.

The men had stopped fighting, driven apart by the Sheriff and other townsmen. The General's men had mounted their horses. The General got out of his buggy and, taking his foreman, marched into the one hardware store.

"Give me all the 30-30 cartridges and forty-five Colts that you've got," he said to the clerk.

"I haven't got a one," the other said.

The General flushed. "Then this is the first time in thirteen years you've run out."

"That's true, General," the other said simply. "I was bought clean out this morning. Mr. Dickson bought every cartridge in the store, and it'll be a month before I get another shipment. Why don't you ask Mr. Dickson? I asked him what I'd do with my customers, if they came in; he said, just send them to him."

The General very slowly smiled. His wrinkles were deeper, as though his flesh were shrinking. His eyes had lost their boldness and their light. He was getting back the look he had had in the war, a look of quiet shrewdness and patience. The bombast, the wrath, the ire, all that pap for the peacetime garrisons, was gone.

"Thank you very much," the General said gently and humbly. "When the opportunity arrives, I will call on Mr. Dickson and get what I need."

8

The Station House
October 9—8:00 A.M.

At eight o'clock the next morning, an hour before the hearing was to begin, Dickson was lying in bed in the Station House. He had sent the word about, the previous evening, that he was ill—nervously ill, he let it be known—and the dear ladies, with a most pitiful rush of compassion, attributed this, as he had intended them to do, to the coarse attacks of General Montrose at the barbecue.

There was not a wife in town who had not become enraged at the dinner table, when told of the insufferable calumnies broadsided by the General at the community as a whole. "Huddle of sheep" was the thing that stung worst.

The next morning some of the more gentle ladies brought Dickson some delicious broth and homemade crackers for breakfast, inquired about his health, and noted, with much cooing, the volume of Keats which Dickson had laid, face down, on the bed cover. They asked him to read them a poem, and in his most elegiac voice, somewhat faint, to be sure, he read them "La Belle Dame Sans Merci."

" 'And there we slumbered on the moss' "—*How daring,* the ladies thought, *to read this in mixed company!*—" 'and there I dreamed, ah woe betide, the latest dream I ever dreamed on the cold hill side.' " Ah, how they longed to comfort this noble young man, as each of them was sure that she alone could do it.

" 'I saw pale kings, and princes too, pale warriors, deathpale were they all; who cried—"La Belle Dame Sans Merci hath thee in thrall!" ' "

He ended his reading here, as the rest of the poem was just so much morbid rubbish, as far as politics was concerned.

The dear ladies left in a body, cackling like excited hens.

He was so handsome in bed!

The Keats had kept everything on a high level, and it was all so deliciously depressing—the poor, dear young man might die because of that vicious beast, the General. There was a furious hiss of horrified whispering all over town. Could it possibly be true that Montrose had been behind that brutal murder?

Mrs. Judge Frank took the trouble to drop in at court, where the Judge was busy brushing his black robes (it was, in fact, the very robe in which he had been graduated from a small college in Kentucky) and admire his astuteness in favoring Dickson.

As for the $2,500 which the Judge owed Dickson for private gambling losses, that had never been mentioned by Dickson. The Judge knew it never would be. How wonderful it was to deal with well-bred people!

Seven of the dear ladies trooped into the courtroom and settled themselves, bringing out their crocheting and knitting. They had been visiting the sick.

Oh, how sweet it was to be charitable to the sick! Especially when they read poetry, and, above all, did not moan, stink, and complain.

By this time Dickson had recovered enough to ride over to the preacher's house, where Mrs. Vickers had stayed the night.

"But you see, Mrs. Vickers," Dickson said gently, settling down with a cup of hot tea which the minister's wife had given him, "we want to do you justice, my dear. Are you sure you can't remember which one it was?"

"But I didn't see. He had a handkerchief over his face."

They were alone in the front parlor.

"Yes, of course, but surely you must have had a glimpse of his eyes. Were they brown, like Fred Hand's? You know Fred Hand, the biggest of Montrose's men. Surely you've seen him dozens of times in town here. You remember his brown eyes? He has a kind of square forehead, with wrinkles going across. Remember?" He sipped his tea, smiling and waiting.

Mrs. Vickers sat thinking, her eyes vacant.

"You remember the man's eyes," Dickson went on gently. "They are round, and smiling—like Fred Hand's. You remember, but of course they would not have smiled while he was shooting. It was a big man, wasn't it?"

"Yes," Mrs. Vickers said, "he was a big man. And he did, yes, he did have brown eyes. Yes, I remember." She remembered nothing of the kind, because she had seen nothing of the kind. In the fury of that moment after the shot, all she had seen was smoke, a blotch of red where the handkerchief had been, across the rider's face, and the brand on the shoulder of the horse. That was all.

But she remembered from other times, Fred's eyes, and the wrinkles, and as she thought, the two images became merged in one image, so that the clarity of the true image of the murderer was lost, forever confused with that of Fred Hand. It had happened, as Dickson knew it would happen—as he was making it happen, like a painter, painting one image over another.

"His hands, as he held the rifle," Dickson went on gently. "You remember Fred's, how big and rough they are. Just the hands for a mean man, a rough man. You remember his ring? That big silver ring with the turquoise in it? The blue-green stone. Perhaps he was wearing that—perhaps you remember it now."

Mrs. Vickers sat trying to remember.

"On his left hand," Dickson said. "The hand that was out in front, holding the barrel of the rifle. Not the hand that pulled the trigger—the other hand, the one nearest you. Do you see the ring?"

"Yes," she said. "Was it? It might have been. I don't remember."

"A blue stone, in silver—blue-green. In the sun, it might have showed. Or perhaps you only saw the silver, not the stone."

"Yes, he might have been wearing a silver ring. Yes, he might have. Oh, dear. Did he? No—no, I don't—But did he?" She put her hand to her forehead. She had imagined a ring on that hand, and now she could not get the ring off the hand, she could not remember it as it had been actually—quite bare. But because the image was now there, she began to see it as the remembered image, and she said, "Yes, he might have been wearing a ring. In fact, I think now I did see something. Yes. But not the stone."

"And he was a big man," Dickson said, passing over this point easily, to something obvious.

"Oh, yes, very big, like Hand."

"You see, it could only have been one of those five men, riding a Montrose horse."

"Yes," she nodded. That was quite clear.

"And he was a big man, so he was either Fred or the General. All Montrose's other men are small. Remember?"

Her eyes lighted, and she raised her eyebrows in surprise. Why, yes, she suddenly realized with pleasure at the thought, that was true. It had to be true. "Yes," she said, "the other three are shorter men. But it wasn't the General."

"No, it wouldn't have been the General," Dickson said, "because the General's daughter says he was up at the house. So who must it have been?"

"Why," she said, again with that pleasure she found in making a logical deduction, "it must have been Fred Hand. It couldn't have been anybody else, could it?"

He left her with this thought. He knew she was imagining Hand's face, and trying it on the face of that mysterious rider, perfecting his forgery for him.

"It was him, I am sure of it," Mrs. Vickers said. "Oh, why didn't I realize it before? It must have been him!" Her voice rose, and grief re-entered. "Oh, how could he have done it! Why? Why?"

Dickson led Mrs. Vickers out the front door, toward the Sheriff's office.

9

The Station House
October 9—8:30 A.M.

On his return from Montrose's headquarters, Mike had been moved from the barn quarters to an empty room on the second floor of the Station House, and he had been kept there, with the door locked and with a guard to watch him.

The room had one window facing the main street, and another facing the rear yard, and he had been able to see the party, and hear some of what the General had said when he was shouting, but he did not know what was happening, and nobody had told him. He did not know that Vickers had been murdered. He had seen Clara walking about during the party, but he had been afraid to wave to her.

It seemed to Mike that Dickson was quietly getting ready for a final battle. At first, Dickson had had only two men in Warhorse, Spence and Irving. Irving had ridden back to the herd, and had been replaced not by one man, but by two. One of these had in turn acted as a courier, and the other had simply stayed in Warhorse. As the herd drew nearer, Dickson had little by little weakened the party of men riding under Forrest, and added these men to his force in Warhorse. The closer Buford got to Warhorse, the less need there was for a strong party to keep him from making off with the cattle. Dickson could reduce that guard to all but two men, or even one, and that would be enough, when Buford was only two days' drive away, for Buford could not possibly escape with the herd when he was that close.

This meant that Dickson would have almost the whole of his pack in Warhorse on the day that Buford arrived—a strong, rested force of well-armed men, ready to take on Buford and Tucker, with their trail-weary crew, who had been riding fagged-out horses. Meanwhile, Dickson was keeping his growing force of men out of sight down in the barn quarters, and would not allow more than three at a time to go out on the main street, or into the saloons.

Sitting on his rope bed by the window, Mike saw the General come into town, this time with a wagon, and without Clara, and ride with his four men up the street. He saw the Sheriff come out of his office and talk to the General, and watched them talk in a gathering crowd for five minutes. Mrs. Vickers and Dickson were mixed in it for some reason.

The General turned to Fred Hand, the big man in the rear, and spoke to him. Mike saw Fred Hand get off his horse and follow the Sheriff into his office next to the county court, and he attached no significance to this. All he could surmise from the crowd was that they were holding the option hearing. The guard would tell him nothing.

He sat with his guard, drinking coffee and playing cards. There was nothing to do but wait. He had seen them lug the cases of ammunition up to his prison room the day before, and assumed Dickson had brought it into town. He had no way of knowing that it was the town's whole supply. Spence had objected to storing the ammunition with the prisoner as being too risky. But Dickson pointed out that the ammunition was useless to Mike, who had no weapons, and it saved a guard. Dickson had no doubt that Montrose would steal the cartridges if he could. There was a case of 30-30 and one of .45 besides twenty-five pounds of Ffg black powder in one keg and ten pounds in cannisters.

Mrs. Vickers accused Fred Hand in the street, in a cool, steady voice, and the Sheriff adjourned to his office to get away from the crowd. Mrs. Vickers looked at the turquoise ring on Fred's finger, and her eyes lighted exactly as though she had seen it before, on that dreadful occasion.

"The ring," she said. "I saw it."

"Are you sure?" Sheriff Bolt asked, sitting back easily in his chair. He always made a point of looking sleepy at such a moment, it kept people relaxed. He wasn't afraid of Fred Hand, who was a big, easy-going and good-natured fellow, powerful and amiable.

"Yes," Mrs. Vickers said. "I'm sure."

Her manner impressed Bolt. If she had said, "Of course I'm sure," or "Why, certainly, what do you think?" he would have retained a doubt of her sincerity. But her simplicity, her calm, her actual subjective certitude, had a deep effect.

He looked at Hand, and at the General. "How about it?"

"Couldn't be," one of the General's other men said. "Fred was with me all afternoon yesterday, brushing the horses and such, until we went down with the General."

Dickson looked at the other men. "Is that true?"

"Well, whatya think?" one of them asked angrily, as though Dickson's question had been an insult. "Of course it's true."

"You saw them? You saw them together all that time?" Dickson asked.

"Why, yes, of course," the man said, reddening. "How about it, Joe?" He turned to the other hands.

They agreed unanimously. It was this which increased the shadow of doubt in Bolt's mind. None of the General's men had meant to lie, but they had lied. The first one was telling the truth, but the others were lying. Bolt didn't know why.

Dickson did. Dickson had known that the second man had been offended when he had asked him to confirm the first man's alibi—as Dickson had intended that he be offended. To his simple country mind, the question had seemed like an accusation of lying, and he had followed up the second question with another angry affirmation, just because he wasn't going to "let some son-of-a-bitch Englishman make a liar out of him." But this, in fact, was what Dickson had actually done. On a ranch the size of Montrose's, all of his four hands couldn't possibly have been within sight of each other in the middle of a working day, and everybody knew it.

Montrose's men stood there, looking at Bolt, realizing that their unanimity had had the wrong effect. But to retract would have weakened their position still further. So they stood there, angry and stubborn, looking at Bolt. This was what Dickson had wanted—an appearance of collusion.

"But that can't be," Mrs. Vickers said, in the same calm voice. "Because I saw him."

"What about it, General?"

"Well, what about it?" the General asked back. He had been watching Dickson, and he knew he had a war on his hands. If fear of the Lord was the beginning of wisdom, fear of the enemy was the beginning of strategy, and the first rule of strategy was not to commit yourself unless you had the advantage. His damn-fool employees had committed themselves in a bucket. Let the Sheriff answer his own questions from now on.

Bolt sighed. Everybody was lying. It didn't matter; there were whole counties in Montana where nobody had ever been hanged for murder, because of alibiing relatives. Nobody would ever hang Fred Hand.

"Well," Bolt said, "he has been accused, General, and that makes it a legal matter. I can't let him go."

"You can't convict him, either."

"I ain't even going to try to," Bolt said. "But there's got to be a trial."

"All right," the General said. "Throw him in jail. How about it, Fred? Could you stand a few days in the clink?"

"How's the food?" Fred asked.

"Not bad," Bolt said. "I eat it sometimes."

Dickson was happy. He knew he could never convince Bolt by himself that the General was a thief or that Hand was a murderer. He didn't even want to. What he wanted to do was to stir up emotions and suspicions, particularly in the women, and the women could ride rough on their husbands until it was a domestic necessity to concur. Again, it would not be crime or vice that would get rid of the General, but the sanctity of the marriage bond.

The General took off his hat and bowed respectfully to Mrs. Vickers. He left the office without looking at Dickson and, followed by his men, went into the court next door.

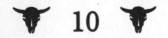

▼ 10 ▼

Courtroom Same Day—9:00 A.M.

Judge Frank came into the courtroom and sat down amid the usual gabble, and everybody stirred and resettled themselves. The doors were opened and people kept coming in, scuttling as though they were late for church.

"We have here an option agreement between one Buford Allen and you, General Montrose, by which he contracts to buy, and you contract to sell, your ranch property upon the payment of $300,000 on or before October 9, 1882. It is today October 9, 1882. I have here a record of deposit by Thomas Dickson, acting as agent for and partner of Buford Allen, of $300,000. The court would like to know, Mr. Dickson, is it your intention to buy this property in accordance with the agreement?"

"It is," Dickson said, standing up and smiling pleasantly.

"General Montrose," Judge Frank said, "is it your—"

"No," the General said. "Decidedly not."

"Do not interrupt the court," Judge Frank said. He was doing beautifully. Mrs. Frank beamed at him with approval and love.

"General Montrose," Judge Frank began again, with that smooth, mechanical order of thought which sounded so dead to the ear, "is it your intention to sell your ranch in accordance with the agreement?"

"No."

The Judge shuffled some papers. The mechanism had hit something. Then he recalled what he had planned.

"Mr. Dickson, do you claim that this is a breach of contract?"

"I do," Mr. Dickson said. "I ask that the court enforce the contract with a judgment giving me this property."

"The court," Judge Frank said, "sees no reason why this contract should not be enforced. General Montrose, do you have any answer?"

"The date on that contract is a forgery," the General said. "I do not accuse anyone of anything. I state the simple fact that it is a forgery. I state that the original date was July fifteenth. I state moreover that that date was passed by and the option right forfeited by Buford Allen. I have here three telegrams from Buford Allen asking for an extension of that date, and I offer them in substantiation of my claim. You will note that Buford Allen asks for an extension to September fifteenth. If the true date of the contract was October ninth, why would he ask for an extension to September fifteenth? You will see that the telegram was sent from St. Louis." He marched up to the bench and laid the papers before the Judge and retired to his former position.

The Judge looked at the telegrams. He was obviously nonplused.

The General asked, "How do you explain that, Your Honor?" He could not help a smile, and this was his undoing.

Judge Frank felt himself stimulated by this prick of scorn, and he said, "I accept these telegrams in evidence but I must point out that they do not refer to any particular agreement. They request a general extension until September fifteenth. An extension of what, may I ask?" He looked up.

The General's face turned pink. "Of the option in question."

"That is not stated here," the Judge said. "Nothing is specified in these telegrams. There is no evidence that these telegrams refer specifically to this particular option. They might refer to some other contract entirely outside our knowledge." He smiled and pushed the telegrams to one side.

"Holy God," the General said, "how many contracts would I have, I would like to know?"

The ladies looked at each other with profound shock. What had burst from the General as a genuine prayer, they took as sheer blasphemy.

"That, I would not know," the Judge said, smiling mechanically with his firm mouth. He blinked his wet eyes twice.

"What kind of flummery is this?" the General cried.

"I warn the General against this sort of language," the Judge said. "Another outburst, and I shall hand down a substantial fine for contempt."

The General turned from pink to red, but he kept his mouth shut.

"I take it," the Judge went on smoothly, "that the General means these telegrams to substantiate his assertion that the contract has been forged. Is that so, General?"

"You bet your damn—" The General stopped himself. "Yes."

"Then we have a question actually of whether the contract date is forged. These telegrams, because of their lack of specification, do not constitute proof, or indicate anything at all. They may suggest something, but we cannot render a judgment on the basis of suggestion." He smirked. "Mr. Curtis, you have carefully examined this contract?"

Joe Curtis stood up. He cleared his throat and coughed, looked around for a spittoon, and found nothing. He swallowed. "I have," he said solemnly.

"Have you found any evidence of tampering?"

"No, I have not."

"Mr. Lewin, have you examined this contract?"

Lewin stood up. "Yes, I have."

"Have you found any evidence of tampering?"

"No, I have not." He sat down.

"Are these men experts?" the General asked. "I say, let the whole thing go to Helena for judgment."

"The time will come when you may appeal," the Judge said. "But not until I have rendered my verdict. These men are experts in that as bankers they are accustomed to inspect signatures and other writing for validity. I should say they are experts."

"Well, by God," the General said, "since I do not owe them any money, I feel perfectly free to say that I shouldn't say they are anything of the kind!"

"You are entitled to your opinion, but that is hardly evidence. I judge that this contract is valid. Furthermore, there is no reason in evidence why it should not be carried out. I therefore order you, General Montrose, to surrender your title to your property in exchange for the money on deposit in Mr. Curtis's bank."

"By God, you are too hasty," the General said. "Get Buford Allen here. Let him testify as to that date! Mr. Dickson, where is Buford Allen? I have heard he is driving your cattle here. How far away is he? How soon can he be reached?"

Dickson had not thought of this. He hastily sorted out the lies possible in the situation and said, with an appearance of ease, "The fact is, I am not sure how far away he is."

"That has nothing to do with the case in any event," Judge Frank said.

"And why not?" the General barked. "It seems to me most essential."

"Why, Mr. Allen's testimony could not gainsay the testimony of experts, could it? If he were to say that these telegrams referred to this contract, and that it had been forged, he would be asserting the incompetence of our present witnesses."

For a moment the General stood dumbfounded. "Did I hear you rightly?" he asked finally. "Are you asserting that an actual party to the contract is not a reliable witness to it?"

Judge Frank blushed to the ears.

"The fact of the matter is, if Your Honor will allow me to speak," Dickson said hurriedly, "the fact is that Buford Allen told me that this contract, which you now have, is actually a new contract granted by General Montrose in answer to Mr. Allen's request for an extension." This story had occurred to Dickson as a flash of inspiration. He knew it was good instinctively. It was beautiful.

"That's a damned lie!" Montrose shouted, his face a deep red. "I never granted a second contract."

Dickson looked at the floor and said nothing.

"It is you who are lying," the General cried. "You or Allen, I don't know which."

A murmur of protest rose in the courtroom. The General was being uncivilized. Dickson stood silent, looking at the floor.

The Judge banged on the bench. "I warned you once, General."

"Where is Michael Allen?" the General asked. "He has been living with Dickson. Surely he can give an account of this matter."

"I don't know where he is," Dickson said. "He left town last night. I presume to see his father."

"I demand that his father be subpoenaed," the General said.

"I ask," Dickson said in a humble, quiet voice, "that Your Honor render a judgment on the basis of this evidence, rather than prolong the affair. Mr. Allen is my partner in this matter. I think I can be taken reliably as his spokesman, without subjection to insult."

Judge Frank sat behind his bench and thought. At least, he appeared to be thinking. He looked at the faces of the men he knew, at Dickson, Lewin, Curtis, and all the others. He looked at the faces of their wives, and of his wife. He knew what they were thinking, he could feel it. He could feel easily enough when he was approved by his peers, and when he wasn't.

He knew, furthermore, that nothing in the world would make him more popular, nor more quickly bring the forgiveness of his social lapses and sins, than to follow the judgment of the audience.

"In rendering this judgment," he said, "I have to take into consideration a number of factors. First, we have the testimony of experts that this is a valid contract, and, on this basis, I must rule that it must be fulfilled. Second, we have certain other evidence that this may not be a valid contract, but this evidence needs substantiation which cannot at once be made available."

He paused. During this pause, he was thinking: *Why should Buford Allen testify differently from Dickson? They are partners. Therefore, I can assume that Allen will, back up Dickson, and even if this comes to appeal on the basis of new evidence, I shall be in the end confirmed in my judgment. All I have to do is find some justification for excluding that evidence now, which is plausible enough to please the court of appeals in Helena.*

He said aloud, "In the meantime, we have an urgent reason why this judgment should be made now, rather than have the case continued until we can reach Mr. Allen, and that is the expected arrival of the cattle belonging to the plaintiff, an investment which will suffer damage if it is not taken care of properly, care which requires possession of the ranch in dispute. Now, it might be contended that any damage to the cattle could be taken care of in a separate suit. But in considering the general welfare of those involved, and the values at stake, it seems to the court that judgment should be rendered for the plaintiff. For the plaintiff should not be required to undergo certain damage as the result of continuing the case, while the evidence at hand is for him, simply because the defendant makes a claim to have at his disposal certain evidence which in any case would not be in itself wholly conclusive, and which could not be expected to bear the defendant out.

"Therefore the court orders that the defendant comply with the conditions of the contract, and transfer title to the plaintiff this day, and that he make available to the plaintiff all the property, and all access to it, and use thereof." Judge Frank knew the end of his hour had come, and he hated to see it. "Mr. Dickson, have you ready a deed describing this property?"

"I have," Dickson said, pulling a fat packet of papers out of his inside pocket. "It is a transcript of the county record as far as the description goes."

"Have you examined this deed, Mr. Curtis?"

"I have," Joe Curtis rumbled.

"It is an adequate deed?" the Judge asked, pursuing the silly rubrics to the very end.

"It is," Joe Curtis said.

At this point, Sheriff Bolt, watching the General's face, saw what was coming, and he prudently left the court.

The General said, "I refuse to comply with your judgment, and I shall take this whole matter immediately to Helena. Furthermore, I shall bring a charge of malfeasance and incompetence against you, Mr. Frank. I desire to put Mr. Allen on the stand and force the truth from him. You should continue this case, and you are—"

Frank smashed his gavel on the bench. A tear rolled down his cheek and he dashed it away. He felt no grief—it was simply that the ducts of his tear glands, which drained into his nasal passages, were chronically swollen by horse dander, and would not drain. Nevertheless, he gave the impression of being stricken with grief, and the courtroom rumbled with sympathy.

"Sheriff Bolt!" the Judge cried. "Where is Sheriff Bolt? I fine you herewith one thousand dollars for contempt of court, General Montrose. You shall not leave this court without paying it or going to jail. Where is Sheriff Bolt?"

"If I submitted to this court," the General shouted over the uproar of voices, "I should soon find myself without a head. I shall leave it when I damn well please." His three men got up from their places and stood there. None of them was armed, but nobody moved to stop them.

"Sheriff Bolt!" Judge Frank cried out. "Find him!"

The General turned and walked toward the door. His men followed him.

"Stop him!" the Judge cried.

The General and his men disappeared.

Mr. Dickson said, "I should like to ask the Judge to appoint a deputy in the absence of the Sheriff—Mr. William Spence, a reliable, honest, and efficient man whom I can personally recommend for what duty you require."

"Thank God, yes," Judge Frank said. "By all means, Mr. Spence, you are hereby appointed."

"I also ask Your Honor for an order of eviction, which will empower the Sheriff to oust General Montrose from his holdings. His attitude of hostility makes such action necessary."

The Judge faltered.

Three men came back, leading Sheriff Bolt. Joe Curtis, Lewin, and others crowded around the bench where Dickson was standing. There was an atmosphere of relief and excitement, and their expressions were happy and victorious, and at the same time surprised. The thing had been done, the issue raised, and whether all had been good or not, the General had been told off.

"Sheriff," the Judge said, keeping safely on his bench (not for physical safety, but simply to preserve his official status), "Mr. Dickson wants an order to evict the General. In view of my judgment, it seems to me entirely appropriate."

Sheriff Bolt looked at Spence and Dickson. Spence was smiling pleasantly, and Dickson looked sober and rather regretful at all this.

"The General won't evict," the Sheriff said. "I heard him, out there in the street. He said he'd fight till either him or us was laid out dead."

"He can't talk like that," Curtis said. He looked at Bolt as though he were lying. Immediately the thought flashed from eye to eye that the Sheriff was trying to get out of an unpleasant duty.

"The law must be carried out," Judge Frank said.

Bolt looked up quietly. "That's perfectly true, but there's ways and ways of doing it. The law ain't designed to get people killed. The law is to protect the peace. If I go up there and the old man shoots anybody, it makes him a murderer. I don't want that. There's got to be some better way, some way that don't force anybody into doing anything worse than what's been done. Things are dirty enough now." For some reason he looked at Dickson.

"Very well," Dickson said, giving in easily where he could, as he always did. "I am not a hard man, God knows. You all know that. I don't mean the General any harm."

"Of course," Curtis murmured, patting Dickson on the shoulder. "We know that, Tommy. We're for you."

"So let him stay until he gets ready to move out," Dickson said. "But give me the legal ability to use the place. I mean, let me use the conveyances and the stock, which I will need. Give me a judgment against the personal property on the place, and the ability to attach it and enter. Surely that will cause no trouble. Spence will see to it that no trouble is caused."

"Spence is your new deputy," the Judge informed Bolt. Bolt looked at Spence without expression.

"I will give you a general attachment on all his personal property," the Judge said. "God knows I do not want to precipitate some kind of battle with the General. Maybe in time he will see reason."

"How much time are you giving him?" Bolt asked.

"My herd will be here the twentieth," Dickson said. "I would like to have Montrose gone by then."

"We'll give him until the nineteenth," Judge Frank said. "That gives him ten days."

Bolt said nothing.

Spence said, "Your Honor, I would like to have two more men as deputies. Montrose may try to sell some of the stock. We will have to have men to watch the fence line. There's no telling what he might do to damage the property—or make off with it."

"By God, that's right," Curtis said. "I wouldn't put nothing past the old bastard, after what he said today. Give Spence enough men to do the job, Judge."

Judge Frank asked, "Who do you want? Give me their names, and I'll include them in the same order."

"Isaac Forrest," Spence said. "Joe Irving. Robert Sheffield."

"Do I know these men?" Bolt asked. "I don't know them by name, at any rate."

"They are all my men," Dickson said.

"It seems to me the town should be represented," Bolt said. "This seems to me to make it a party affair."

"They have worked under me," Spence said. "Since they are only temporary deputies, why not let them be my men? They will do the job more efficiently."

"That's right, they're temporary," Bolt said, grabbing at this straw. He knew he couldn't oppose Dickson and Spence. He knew he was adrift as soon as he saw that the Judge had appointed a deputy without consulting him. "How long is temporary?"

"Oh, two weeks," Dickson said, again giving easily where it didn't matter.

"All right," Bolt said. "Come on. I'll give you your stars, and you will be entitled to wear arms. But I warn you—I shall hold you accountable."

Spence said nothing, and followed him like a lamb.

Spence got Irving and Sheffield and gave them their stars and told them what to do. The General was up the street with his men, and they were loading their wagon full of groceries, staples of all kinds, an immense supply. They had armed themselves out of the wagon.

The General rode off, alone, down to the railroad station. He went inside and sent a wire to Helena, asking for military help and a proclamation of martial law. While he was inside, Spence took his horse and rode back up the street with it. He put it in the Station House barn.

When the General came out, he saw his horse gone and, in a confusion of bewilderment and rage, hurried on foot back up the street.

He found his men in one of the saloons, having a drink on completion of their job of loading the wagon, and he ordered them outside.

The wagon was gone, with its load of supplies.

The General and his men stood looking up and down the street. Their personal horses were gone, all three of them, as well as the one Fred Hand had used, which they had been leading.

The General saw the Sheriff coming down the street with Spence.

"Sheriff, where is my wagon?" the General said. "Somebody has stolen our wagon and all our horses. Is this some kind of silly practical joke?"

"No," Bolt said heavily. "It ain't a joke, General, it's damn serious. The court ordered us to attach all your personal property. And I might as well warn you, you're to be evicted in ten days." He stopped and looked at the guns on the hips of Montrose and his men. "General, I see you have armed yourself. I trust you will not start any trouble in this town." He knew perfectly well he couldn't get the guns away from those four men, and so he didn't ask for them. "I would be obliged if you would leave this town at once, and don't come back until you're peaceful."

The General looked down at him, and at Spence and the other two deputies behind him. "I don't choose to start a fight," the General said. "But I want at least decent treatment. I want our personal horses back, and my wagon."

"General," Bolt said doggedly, "they were taken on a court order. They are the property of Mr. Dickson now. Take my advice, and don't leave nothing around loose. The only things we can't take are the things you actually got in your hands. Do you understand?"

"But I need the supplies," the General said, his voice rising. "Keep the wagon, but give me the supplies."

"No," Dickson said, coming up, "not the supplies, General. And I might as well warn you, your account at the bank has just been blocked pending a settlement of this affair, and the stores have been warned about it, so you have no credit in town."

"Are you trying to starve me out?" the General cried.

"General," Dickson said, smiling gently, "I am only trying to get my property. My money is waiting in the bank for you, any time you wish to pick it up and leave. All you have to do is ask for it. Three hundred thousand dollars."

The General flushed. "That I shall never do," he said. "This is far beyond a matter of price or value. I shall never give up what is rightfully mine, or give in to thieves and—for all I know—worse." He turned and started to walk down the street.

"Wait," Bolt said. "I'll lend you a horse." He looked angrily at Dickson, and Dickson realized he had tripped up on something. He didn't know what it was, exactly (actually it was the feeling among these men that to take another's horse was the worst thing you could do to him, legally or not) but he knew he had to put it right. "I'll give you the wagon," he said. "Spence, hurry and get the General's wagon."

Spence ran.

"I'm not a hard man," Dickson said. "I have no intention of being mean about things."

Spence came back with the wagon, at a trot.

"Where are the supplies?" the General asked.

"I said I would give you the wagon," Dickson said. "But not the supplies."

The General smiled bitterly. He climbed onto the wagon seat, and his men got into the back. He drove off without another word.

Bolt was left alone in the street. He wandered slowly back to his office. Words kept repeating in his head. Thieves and worse; thieves and worse.

He was fundamentally a simple man, and he could no longer follow this affair through all its legal windings. All he knew was that the General, a man after his own heart, was being jimmied out of his property,by a set of people whom Bolt did not actually know at all. Who were they? They had been in Warhorse only five weeks or so.

Bolt was different from most of the people in Warhorse. He was somewhat seclusive, like the General, by nature, but he also had a political reason for being so. As Sheriff, he had to maintain respect, and he could not cultivate anyone too intimately, or permit obligations to grow up. He had to keep himself somewhat aloof. For this reason, he knew nothing of the associations of Dickson with everybody else, and he did not share their enthusiasm for Dickson, simply because he had not been subjected to Dickson's influence.

Somebody came in his office door. Bolt looked up from where he was sitting. It was John Lee.

Lee took an envelope out of his pocket and handed it to the Sheriff.

Bolt thought it was a telegram, and started to open it. Lee saw this, and said, "Don't. Don't open it," and left the office as suddenly as he had come.

Bolt looked at the writing on the face of the envelope: *To be opened only in case of my death. John Lee.*

He tried to read through the envelope. He couldn't. He slipped it into the top drawer of his roll-top desk. What crime had Lee done? For of course, people never left this kind of envelope with policemen unless they had committed some crime, or were involved in one. If the fool would only tell him, it could be solved. But that was it—they were all fools, the kind who were ashamed, but not ashamed enough.

At that moment, Dickson was down in the telegraph office, waiting for Lee. When Lee came in, Dickson asked what the General had been doing in there, and Lee told him. He handed Dickson the General's message to Helena, and Dickson took one look at it and tore it to shreds.

Lee said, "I told you a lie, Mr. Dickson."

Dickson said, "I know you did."

"I know all about you," Lee said. "I got the answer from San Antonio."

Dickson waited. It didn't look like blackmail. Lee didn't have the right expression for blackmail. Lee was afraid, his white face weak and stiff.

"I just wanted to tell you, Mr. Dickson," Lee said in a low, weak voice, forcing himself to speak, "that I gave that information to Sheriff Bolt."

"Yes," Dickson said. "Sealed in an envelope. To be opened only in case of your death."

Lee's heavy-lidded eyes opened a little wider.

"Poor boy," Dickson said, smiling. "Did you think I meant you harm? Haven't I paid you well? You're worth a lot of money to me, John. Why should I hurt you?"

Lee's lower lip trembled, and then he wiped at it with his hand. "Why?" he asked. "Ain't I the only one that knows?"

Dickson said nothing. "Perhaps you were wise, John. Anyway, let's be friends." He smiled engagingly. "You don't tell on me, and I won't tell on you."

"Yes," Lee said, leaning against the counter, and looking sick to his stomach. "I guess that's right."

He watched Dickson go without hatred. He was too sick with fear to hate anything, even himself.

That night Dickson sent a rider for Buford Allen, who was at that time presumably crossing the Bad River and going down it to the upper waters of the Big Horn—about 220 miles away. It would take three days to reach him, riding hard, and when the rider got there, Buford would probably be at the crossing of the Big Horn, south of Norwood Creek—that is, if the cattle could be pushed that fast through that country. They could make it back to Warhorse in something over two days. If all went well, Dickson figured, Buford should be in Warhorse by the 15th or 16th, which would give him four days before the herd arrived.

While Dickson had counted on the General's sense of principle to save him his $300,000, he was not quite prepared to push things to an outright war, and he would gladly settle with Montrose for $75,000. He thought that Buford might be able to persuade the General where Mike had failed. In any case, the effort would look well.

He had another reason also, which was that he wanted Buford publicly to state that the option was not forged. It was the only weakness in his case, and he wanted it removed.

And lastly, he wanted to divide Buford from Tucker. Tucker was a strong hand, but like all the Isaacs of history, he was not much use without his boss.

Everything was going simply beautifully.

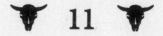

11

The Last Days of Warhorse
October 10–17

During the next six days, while he was waiting for Buford, Dickson did a number of things to improve his position. Indignation was not enough. What he needed in the hearts of Warhorse was fear.

So the night of October 11, the day after Vickers' funeral, he ordered Forrest, Spence, and Irving to take their horses and ropes and break Fred Hand out of jail.

Spence and Forrest, in the dark, called each other by the names of the

General's men, and since they did this in whispers, poor Hand could not know that the names were false.

They yanked the barred window out of the frame, and left a horse—one of the horses taken from the General—and of course Fred Hand climbed out, since there is no consideration to a man in jail which is greater than immediate freedom.

If he had refused to run, he would have served the General well, and done Dickson immense damage, but he did not refuse. He climbed eagerly out, jumped on the horse, and dashed away.

Spence, Forrest, and Irving, seeing him pounding out of town, immediately set to work shooting it up. In fifteen minutes—just the time needed for Bolt to wake up, get out of bed and get his clothes on, and wake the neighbors—they had smashed every store window along one whole side of the street and thrown the window displays into the gutter, broken into the hardware store and stolen four rifles, and smashed all the showcases and dumped the shelves in five other stores. They worked fast and efficiently.

Bolt appeared on the scene and fired at them in the dark—there was only starlight and the first sliver of a new moon—and they fired back, and would gladly have killed him if they could.

Two other men arrived with rifles and added to the shooting, and then three more, and by that time the three vandals decided it was time to escape, so they galloped out of town on the Montrose road and, four hours later, came back into town from the other direction, crossing the creek just before dawn and sneaking their fagged-out horses into Dickson's barn unseen.

The next morning, October 12, a town meeting was held in the courtroom, and it was decided to send Bolt up to the General's headquarters to ask for the surrender of the three men (three had been seen in the dark) as well as that of Hand. In the court there was no oratory. The owners of the wrecked stores had come down at dawn and counted up their damage in silence, and they remained in silence. Dickson welcomed this with a sigh of relief, for he knew that this silence in the men and women meant that they were seriously thinking.

They were adjusting to a new conception, which was that the General, instead of being merely a bore, a crank, and finally a senile recalcitrant, had become a positive danger to them all. A couple of them suggested that the General had gone mad. Others thought merely that he could not control the scoundrels he employed. Others ridiculed this, and said it had been an act of vengeance for the seizing of his horses.

But whatever they said, their tone had changed. There was no emotion except bitterness, and under that there was a deep undercurrent of uneasiness. Bolt returned and said he had been met by a shot from the stone fort at the new gate.

The General had denied his accusations. He said that he had fired Fred Hand on his return, as he would not harbor him, since harboring a man who broke jail while awaiting trial would injure his own position. He denied that his men had broken Hand out of jail in the first place, and that they had left the ranch that night at all.

This was greeted with the most bitter derision as a barefaced lie. The General at least could have admitted what he had done. In every heart in Warhorse, that next day, there was an ache for revenge that spread to their backs. That night, all the store owners slept in their stores with loaded shotguns, and Curtis sat in his bank with two cowhands he had borrowed from one of the ranchers. Nothing happened, and this increased their anger, for by now they positively wanted revenge, and had almost hoped Montrose would try another raid.

The worst thing had been the shooting at night. Nobody had been hurt. But it was plain, now, that the General was out for blood, and was taking the offensive. It began to be rumored that he had never been a general at all; that he had been a Confederate general in disguise; that he had been running a rustling business on a grand scale; that his daughter was entertaining all the men in the mountains, etc., etc. Nobody again asserted he was mad, as this would have made him inculpable, and so robbed them of retaliation.

Dickson knew that sooner or later they would begin blaming him, if they didn't get their hands on Montrose—for, after all, it was Dickson who had, by his purchase of the ranch, brought all this on the town. So on the morning of October 14 Dickson sent Spence and Forrest and four other men (by this time his gang had grown to seven) up to the General's ranch and they tore down ten miles of fence in one afternoon simply by roping the fence posts and pulling them down, ten rods at a time. The General evidently saw the dust, or had a patrol out, for at three o'clock in the afternoon he and his three remaining men opened fire on Spence's party, wounding one of them. Spence answered this with rifle fire, and then with a charge, but Montrose was well placed and drove them off with hot fire, wounding another.

The two wounded men were taken back to Warhorse and the ladies fought to nurse them.

Bolt went again to the General the morning of the fifteenth, and was stopped at the old fence line. The guard was a stranger to him, and the General, to whom he had been taken by another stranger, informed him that he had hired two gunfighters to protect his interests.

The General pointed out that the Judge should have continued the case, knowing there was additional evidence, that his ruling was illegal, and therefore any action upon it was illegal.

Bolt answered by saying simply that there existed a state of war which had to be suppressed somehow, and if the General did not surrender and get out, he would be driven out, even if killing was necessary.

The General simply refused to go.

Bolt asked him if he intended to take on the whole town and county of Warhorse?

The General calmly replied: Yes.

There was nobody in Warhorse equal to this decision. They could not match it. But their silence burst out in a bitter rage when Bolt told them, and then Dickson knew he was free to do what he chose.

The first thing he did—the next day, the morning of the sixteenth—was to run off a hundred and fifty of Montrose's cows and donate them (everybody agreed they were his property) to the town of Warhorse to be sold for cash to cover the damages, and to insure any more that might occur. He got away with these cattle with nothing worse than a few shots from Montrose's patrol—a lone man who was riding the line and could not possibly stand off Spence's party nor get to the General in time.

This act greatly heartened the people of Warhorse, and they turned to Dickson as a leader. Bolt, clearly, was incompetent—all he could do was talk.

Judge Frank issued the order to evict the General, dating it the 16th instead of the 19th, and Dickson nobly said that he would hold off, and protect the people of Warhorse, while giving the General the last possible chance to get out. He made it clear that on the nineteenth he would take his men and advance into the General's territory and lay siege to the headquarters. He was trying to avoid a battle with the General, partly for political effect and partly because he might suffer so much damage in forces that he could not easily cope with Tucker, which would soon be necessary.

That night he had Spence kill one of the townsmen, the hardware-store owner, by the simple method of shooting him through a window. Spence then set fire to the house, and to the one next door, by throwing burning tar on the roofs, and in the ensuing shooting—wild as usual—he and his men escaped, after killing a Montrose horse which they had stolen and leaving it for evidence. Thereafter, the people went to bed at dark, or nailed blankets over the windows.

Some of them came to Dickson and begged him to go and kill Montrose. The fear which Dickson needed was blossoming nicely.

By this time, October 17, everybody, including Bolt, had forgotten the original issue.

The last thing in the world they wanted was interference by the military and a declaration of martial law. When Bolt suggested this, they denounced him openly as a coward, incompetent, and even feeble-minded. They wanted revenge—not safety.

On the night of the 17th, Buford arrived, his horse a wreck, and he not much better. The herd was then crossing the Clark Fork of the Yellowstone sixty miles away, and it was due to arrive the evening of the 20th, right on schedule.

 **12**

The Station House
October 18—8:00 P.M.

The silver of the moon had widened during the week, and Buford got a general idea of Warhorse as he rode up the main street behind Dickson's rider, followed by the packhorse.

He had come because Dickson still held Mike hostage, but he was full of confidence. Tucker held the herd, and had his orders.

Buford could see nothing of the damage done to the stores; the broken and gutted windows were hidden deep in black shadows. There was hard frost in this valley, and his feet and hands ached and tingled with the cold.

They got down in front of the Station House, and Buford limped after the rider on his numb feet. Dickson's man went in ahead of him, and the heat of the big room poured into Buford like whiskey. Then he saw Dickson, standing on the other side of the big flaming hearth.

"Welcome," Dickson said. "You look magnificent, Buford. A wayward Santa Claus."

"Keep your stupid wit to yourself," Buford said. "I'm hungry. I've ridden my butt off because you wanted to see me. Now what the hell is it?"

"Troubles," Dickson said. "Harris," he called toward the kitchen. "Troubles, Buford. Final complications. The General is pigheaded. He won't leave."

"That's your business," Buford said. The heat was making him more tired than ever. He stood there, feeling unwilling to sit down in Dickson's house. And yet, where else was there to go?

"True," Dickson said. "But I need help. You once mentioned a job on this ranch—as manager. If you help me, Buford, I'll offer you the job and twenty-five per cent of the business. I'll be quite frank. You have control over those cattle. I can't get them against your will. If I try to take them by force, you'll stampede them, and I'll never get them rounded up again. A pity cattle are so nervous! They never get used to gunfire, it seems. Well, Buford, I'm willing to compromise with you all down the line—for your help. How about it?"

Buford said nothing. He just stood there, his beard gray with trail dust, his face brown with wind and sun, his cheeks flat, almost gaunt. "Where's Mike?"

"Harris, get Mr. Allen some supper. Everything of the best. And hurry it up, too. Come in, Buford, you can't stand there all night. Come and sit down by the fire. Have some supper, and then I'll show you your room."

"Where's Mike?"

"I think he's upstairs, in bed."

"Didn't he know I was coming?"

"No, he didn't. I have nine men here now, Buford," Dickson said. "By to-morrow I shall have eleven. I trust the herd is on time? It'll be here the twentieth? The day after tomorrow?"

"Yes," Buford said. "Let's get it straight, Dickson. My man Tucker has orders to start the shooting the same day he fails to get a written message from me. You don't think I came here unprotected, do you? He will break up the herd and start a war on you. Understand?"

"I understand perfectly. It could be quite a battle. But who ever wins a battle? We can both win if we cooperate, Buford. Come and sit down. I really do need your help."

Harris came in with a tray. He had half a rib roast, bread and butter, and part of a cold chicken, with a bottle of wine.

Dickson sliced beef and began making Buford a sandwich.

"I need a man of military experience," he said, busily cutting. "Do try that wine, Buford. It was horribly shaken up coming across the country on those dreadful roadbeds, but it's recovered remarkably well. General Montrose insists on being defeated bodily. Like all men of excessive principle, he is hidebound in strategy, and will not retreat. I can't say I am sorry for his nobility of soul; it saves me a tremendous lot of chasing him about over those ghastly mountains. He has entrenched himself with a force of four men and his daughter. They are nearly out of ammunition. But still, he can hurt us. I need your military gifts. Your rank was major, was it not? At the time of Appomattox? Remarkable word, Appomattox. Sounds quite Aztec."

"At the time of Appomattox, my rank was mud, like everybody else's."

"You have an excellent opportunity to beat General Montrose, Buford. I want you to do it. Our position is perfectly legal." He finished the sandwich and offered it to Buford. Buford took it.

"You want me to drive him out of his place?" Buford asked, and stuffed part of the sandwich into his mouth.

"Not exactly. As I said, I have nine men. I want you to go with Mike tomorrow and try to reason with Montrose, and get him to give up. After all, nobody likes bloodshed, do they? But if he won't surrender, you're to give him an ultimatum. If he doesn't surrender, we will attack at noon the day after tomorrow." He carefully explained the situation to Buford, while Buford ate.

As he listened, Buford began to smile. Dickson watched him relax.

"I thought you'd feel better about things," Dickson said, "when you found out why I sent for you."

Buford looked at Dickson. Evidently Dickson was finding himself a little out of his element—at least he was losing control of the situation enough to ask for help. The tables were slowly turning. If they turned far enough—if he got enough breaks—Buford might even be able to take Montrose's ranch and then turn on Dickson and vanquish him. This seemed vaguely feasible because Dickson seemed so meek and friendly, smiling and making that sandwich.

"I'll think it over," Buford said. "Where's Mike?"

"Right at the top of those stairs," Dickson said. "See you in the morning."

Dickson waited until the door to Mike's room had closed behind Buford, and then turned to Irving, who had been waiting. "Keep a watch down here," he said. "I'm going to let them wear arms tomorrow—but don't let them get away from you. If they try, just kill them."

"What about Tucker and his gang?" Irving asked. "We can't—"

"Suppose you were Tucker?" Dickson said. "Suppose you received a message from Buford that all was well? Suppose you thought the writing might be forged? Copied? What would you do? You can't be certain, you understand. Would you start the battle and lose all your boss's cattle? Or would you wait until you made sure?"

"I guess I'd send a rider up here to make sure," Irving said.

"Certainly you would," Dickson said. "And that would be too late. That's why Buford's arrangement with Tucker is foolish. He thinks Tucker is protecting him, but it won't work out that way. I'm going to keep Buford under guard from now on. Tomorrow you'll send one of the men to Tucker with a message from Buford—a fake one—that everything's all right. Even if Tucker's suspicious about the writing—who cares if he is? He won't just leave those cattle alone with Forrest; he'll send a man here to see for himself. And that's all the time we need. So you just do as I say, Irving, and don't worry about Tucker."

* * *

When Judge Frank and Mr. Curtis arrived at nine o'clock to play Boston, Dickson told them of the arrival of his partner, and how his partner would not stand for any more delay. Dickson had pleaded with him, so Dickson said, for patience, but Allen would not hear of it. Allen demanded immediate surrender by the General, and had sworn that he would go up and wipe the General out. He was going up tomorrow to deliver an ultimatum. There was nothing Dickson could do to stop him. Allen was a rather rude fellow, and had not cared to meet Mr. Curtis and the Judge. He had gone upstairs to bed, half drunk.

A feeling of comfortable friendliness enveloped their lively game. Dickson had not needed to explain anything. As the day for Montrose's eviction had neared, Curtis and Frank, in spite of their hatred for Montrose and the murders committed by his men, had begun to feel at heart a sense of bewilderment. The situation was really bigger than their powers, although they would not admit that.

"And the option?" Frank asked. "Will your partner swear to the validity of the option?"

"Oh of course," Dickson said. "That goes without saying."

The Judge and Curtis settled back in their chairs with a deep sense of relief. They were safe. Whatever the Governor might do, upon investigation, if worse came to worst and Montrose and his people were slaughtered, the people of Warhorse would be exonerated completely.

"It's murder," Mike said, after his father had finished telling him about Dickson's plan. A wind had risen in the night, and ice-cold air sifted in around the windows, through the walls.

Buford didn't even hear him. He sat by the little stove in the middle of the room, baking, a bottle of whiskey, which Harris had brought with his things, on the floor beside him.

"It couldn't be more perfect," Buford said, smiling to himself. "It's come at last. Two whole years, Mike, I waited in that damned prison camp. He used to come down there through the camp on his big horse and inspect us. General Montrose and his aides and staff. Inspecting the Flower of the South for lice. There we stood shivering at attention, and he—a two-bit quartermaster general —inspected us for lice. They never got rid of the rats, and all winter long the floors were either mud soup or ice, but every month on the dot he would come down and try to find a louse. And of course he did. But he made it such a crime."

"So now you're going to murder him because you had lice and he had none," Mike said from the bed. "He beat the hell out of you in the war, so now you're going up there with a pack of cutthroats and kill him."

"What?" Buford asked. "What did you say?"

"I said, it is murder," Mike repeated quietly.

Buford's face turned red. "It's a legal eviction. Dickson got a judgment!"

"How?" Mike asked quietly.

"Who cares!" Buford cried. "The court's the law here, isn't it?"

"You know damn well your option expired. Montrose says Dickson forged a new date."

"What does Dickson say about it?" Buford challenged.

"He says Montrose sent you a new option."

"Well, maybe the hell he did! And Dickson waylaid it. Maybe it came to San Antonio after we left. It must be good or the court wouldn't approve it."

"Maybe Dickson bought the court," Mike said.

"Why do you argue?" Buford asked. "The whole town is behind Dickson. He's told me. Montrose's men murdered a man here in town. They wrecked the stores. They burned two houses. Maybe Dickson is a son of a bitch, but Montrose is worse. Let Dickson and me beat hell out of Montrose, and then I'll beat hell out of Dickson alone."

"But you're not going up there," Mike said, "and neither am I."

Buford turned and looked at him. "I don't think I can force you, Mike. But I want you. Dickson needs our help. This is our chance. With a decent break, we can get the ranch for ourselves; we can fight Dickson when Tucker comes. That's all I want—this last chance."

"I'm sick of what you want," Mike said. "All our lives we've been in trouble because of things you wanted. Mother wanted me to keep you out of trouble. What good have I been? None. What can I do? Nothing. But I won't work against the General."

"The General," Buford cried. "You sound as though you like the old bastard."

"I do," Mike said. "He's a true gentleman, and that's more than you ever were."

Buford's face twitched. He blinked at his son, and a sudden sense of grief welled up in Mike as he looked at his father's face. "I'm sorry," he said.

Buford took a breath that sounded like a gasp for air. "Yes, but you're right," he said, short of breath, forcing the words as though he had been hit in the stomach. "I never was a gentleman. You're perfectly right." He looked around vaguely, pain in his face. "Mike, what else am I to do?"

"Quit," Mike said. "Leave with me, tonight. We can break out of here, run away."

"Where?" Buford asked, looking around. It seemed to him that the windows were unnaturally dark.

"Back home," Mike said, but his voice was flat. Buford wasn't even listening. "No, we can't do that either. We've brought this on the General, we've got to help him. It's our fault, all our fault. We'll have to help him out. We can go over to him. We'll warn Tucker and go to the General's."

Buford was silent. He was thinking of a place of darkness, not listening to his son. He was thinking of his own father, long ago, preaching in the woods of East Texas, at the little meetings he had held on his circuit, sometimes in a tent, sometimes in a barn, sometimes under the trees. "And there shall be weeping and gnashing of teeth," he had said, and something about casting into the outer darkness.

To be cast into the outer darkness—that was the end of all ends, the vast, final, terrible perishing, the irrevocable oblivion—and yet not oblivion, for there was weeping and gnashing of teeth.

When Mike talked of leaving, this was what Buford saw—outer darkness staring him in the face. He had faced it handcuffed to Keppelbauer that night, and many nights after on the trail. Where was there to go? Suppose he did quit, as Mike said. He would have nothing, no money, no friends, no home. What was he to do? Desert this last promise, the prospect of a ranch, a final home? A place where the woman he loved was buried—a place to live, safe with many cattle, with plenty to eat and nothing to fear. How could he desert this?

And how could this be wrong, when it was so perfectly fitting and proper? For here now, too, he would bring an old enemy to his knees.

In all sincerity, Buford weighed it as well as he could. It seemed to him that his case was perfectly just, and yet, under the bottom of his heart, there was a pit of darkness, an abyss into which he could not look, a profound questioning of all his reasons, of his most basic justifications. How could he look into that? For that would be to question his own soul, his whole life. To question that would be to cast himself up like a leaf in the wind, at the mercy of an unknown judge. For Buford's most profound assumption, the thought which from childhood had been the premise of every judgment, was simply that money was the best thing in the world, the greatest possible good. Of all the people who had listened to his father, there was probably no one who had learned less than Buford. The only thing Buford had learned from his father was that if you were poor, you starved.

So Buford knew he had to go on. There was nothing else to do. How could he turn back? And yet there was something now which dragged at his bones, a dreadful fatigue, which was new to him.

That was it—he was tired, he was old, and he was thin. The fat of his years had gone, and the passions which had lived on the fat had shriveled as his belly had shriveled, and all the justifications of passion were dried and gray.

And yet he had to go on, tomorrow, up to Montrose's.

A flicker of his old resentment rose, and with it a slight sense of pleasure. There would be triumph in that, at least.

With that thought, Buford sighed and thought he was at peace.

And yet, underneath, something, somebody within him was crying out, out of darkness, protesting in anguish. It was himself, the secret part of his mind that knew there was a truth to be faced, but which it was perdition to face, which it were better to die than face.

And he thought this was bodily fatigue.

♈ 13 ♈

Montrose's Ranch—October 19

In the morning they went up toward the mountains, the old man at the lead, followed by his son, and then by the nine fighters, all silent. A match flamed here, a horse grunted there, someone coughed, but nobody talked in the cold.

They were heavy with arms, each bearing a pistol and a rifle and a belt full of ammunition.

The ground was hard with frost, just barely warming under the thin morning sun, and there was a fringe of ice along the shadowed bank of the creek as they splashed through, passing Vickers' place.

In the rear of the band rode Spence and Forrest, with orders to kill Buford and Mike if anything went wrong.

Buford had forgotten the thoughts of the night before. Now it was morning, and the air was bright and hard as steel. All Buford needed was a saber heavy at his side, and he would have felt happy.

He saw the new gate and the stone fort. A small puff of white smoke appeared in front of the little fort, and a bullet cracked high over their heads, like a whip snapping.

Buford held up his hand, halting his band, and went forward with Mike, holding up a white handkerchief.

The two of them waited for an hour in the increasing sun, the horses stamping with flies, until the General came down with his other men in answer to a gun signal.

The General had taken his time as a matter of policy, but he was most civil as he let Buford and Mike through the gate, and closed it, and left his four men in the fort. They kept two of Forrest's men under their guns, as hostages.

The General took them into his house cordially enough. He invited them to sit down, and they did so. They sat in silence, looking at each other, the bright sun cutting into the gloomy darkness of the big room, while Herbia went, on orders, and got coffee.

"It's not much good," the General said, when Herbia came back with the steaming cups. He was slightly amused by the ambassadors, who didn't seem to know what to do. Didn't they realize that every worthy war conference should take on the aspect of a ladies' tea party? "We've been brewing the same pot of grounds for almost two weeks. But it is all I have to offer."

He smiled at Buford, inviting conversation, but Buford seemed to be confused and ill at ease in Montrose's actual presence.

"How strange to see you under arms again, Buford," the General said.

Buford sipped his coffee as politely as he could, still finding nothing to say.

"I confess I find a certain pleasure in a state of war," the General said easily. "A pity we never had the pleasure of meeting on the field, isn't it? I expect your memories of me are very bitter; it must be most humiliating to be a prisoner of war; although God knows I did my best to see that you people were kept well fed and decently clean. Cleaner than in the field, at least." He drank some of his own coffee. It tasted like a very weak dilution of church ashes, hemlock, wolfbane, and bat droppings, but it was attaining a certain respectability of its own, purely by virtue of its age.

"It was humiliating to us both, in different ways, I suppose," the General went on, filling the heavy silence. "I resented it so when they took me off the line and put me in charge of that prison camp, Buford."

Buford colored slightly. He felt increasingly uncomfortable.

"No doubt you gentlemen have some final offer for me," General Montrose went on, smiling steadily. There sat the Allens, their faces increasingly dull, apparently unable to swing into the subject matter. "Perhaps I should let you make it. Or perhaps I can save you the trouble. You wish my surrender. I reply I shall not. You then give me an ultimatum"—Buford blushed—"I must be gone by a certain time, or you will attack, well supplied with legal formalities and ammunition. What is your deadline, Buford? When waging war, it is best to get on with it."

"I am instructed to give you until noon tomorrow," Buford said woodenly.

"How well put. You are instructed. The typical military evasion of responsibility. Nobody knows anything but the chief of staff, and he won't be back till Wednesday. You are greedy, Buford. Very greedy." It was suddenly becoming impossible to remain civil in front of that stiff, pink face of Buford's. "I tremble at the magnitude of your gall."

"If you prefer," Buford said, "I will fight you personally with any weapon you may choose."

"And make an affair of honor out of an affair that has no honor, is that it? What a wealth of choice your virtues afford you, Buford. Leave the room," he said suddenly to Mike, his eyes flaming. "I wish to tell your father a few things in private."

"Let me tell you, Buford," Montrose said as the door closed, "that I shall never give up. You know that, and I suppose it affords you pleasure, to get what you regard as revenge. But what am I to say to you? You can win. Yes, certainly, you will win. The best I can promise you is a dreadful damage, and believe me, when you come up that canyon, I will do you as much damage as I can, before you slaughter us. But I shall not permit you to take a false satisfaction in your victory. You are going to know the truth. For you are a fool, Buford.

"You are a blind food, and you are quite capable of going ahead and committing the most atrocious crimes with a perfect blandness of conscience. There are some criminals who know and enjoy their malice, like Dickson, and there are others who commit everything with a most genuine sense of virtue. How well I know you, you wretched little soul. You are transparent because you are simple, and you are simple because you are ignorant. You are a creature of the woods, with simple thoughts."

Buford's face was red, but he made no move. He sat there with his mouth slightly open, looking steadily at the General. The General went on, talking in a fast, low voice, which seemed to be amused at times, and at others, shaking with rage, yet always subdued.

"How satisfying to an empty soul it must be, to revenge its rotten little pride in just this way. It was pride that got you into the war—but never mind all that. But I suppose it is Clara, most of all, isn't it? That's where your pride hurts the worst. That is the reason, isn't it? Because she is buried out there on the hill. I suppose all these years you have hated me for taking her away from you, for I suppose you have lied about that as well as everything else. That was what you said the last time you came up there drunk, wasn't it? After we were married. That you would get her back, that I had deceived her and lied about you.

"What need was there to lie about you, when you were making a public fool and nuisance out of yourself? But you lied to yourself then, and of course you have lied about it ever since. As though she loved you! As though any woman could long love such a rude, uncontrollable savage.

"But if you think that you shall come here and lord it over my place after killing me, you who covet the bones of my wife like some dirty little maggot, remember when I tell you that she detested your memory, that she despised you for humiliating her by your conduct, and that you caused her nothing but sorrow and grief when you were engaged, and nothing but unease forever after, because she believed you might hurt me—even though I knew you were too much of a coward to do so.

"And if she never visited you in prison, know now it was not because I prevented her, as you accused me, but simply because she did not want to see you. Do you understand? You fool, she loved you once, better than she ever loved me, but you ruined that. It was I who made her happy, it was I she loved in the end."

The General's eyes were weary and wretched. Buford sat in a lump, his face empty.

"I spit upon your dirty little soul, Buford. You come up here like a swine out of nowhere, nothing but a rampant snout, to devour me and gobble up all that I have. What are you but a grunting pig? Full of desire and appetite, always snouting around after some new bit of garbage, scheming how to crowd out your brothers at the trough? What have you ever done but fill yourself with things? What did you ever give to anybody else but trouble? Even to your own poor son, who can't help loving you. Why are you alive? Why did God create such a wretched mimic of a man? A true swine, grunting with benign lusts and witless sentiments, with not a ghost of honor. Now get out of here, you wretched little comic, and go tell that swineherd Dickson, your master, I shall slaughter as many of you as I can and as God wills. And if you win, and live, I command you now to remember everything I have said, and know that if in heaven she looks down and sees you maundering about her grave, she will spit upon you with the angels. For you are purely of the devil, and there is nothing good about you at all. Now get out."

The General stood up.

Buford rose and stood still, his face empty and flat. How should he stand it? For what the General did not know was that Buford knew that all he had said was true, and had always known it. All his feeble roofs came tumbling in, and there was nothing left on him but dirty rags.

The General turned and left the room.

"So I am saying good-by," Clara said, standing on the edge of the little canyon, looking up at Mike. "I am not condemning anyone. What is the good of that? All these things happen, and God knows who can sort it all out, the good from the bad—only God himself, I suppose. But I am saying good-by, because—" What was there left that she could say? She had come out of the house to say good-by, and all the reasons for all the good-bys there ever were could not prevent the parting.

He looked down at her. "I love you," he said. Down across the rushing creek a horse in the corral stamped. "I always have loved you, since the first day I saw you when I was sitting on that porch in Cheyenne."

A cold wind came down from the mountaintops, which were covered now with gray mist.

"A funny kind of love, wasn't it?" she said. "It was there all the time, but it never got anywhere. I was waiting, all those months, hoping you would come. And then you did come. And now it's over. That's a funny kind of ending, isn't it?" She wanted to cry; she knew he was going, but she didn't want him to; so she kept on talking.

"I used to think if things worked out that far, they'd work out all the way, but that isn't so, is it? I suppose all over the world there are thousands of people like us. Things end, they fail, people starve, people are killed, and who ever thinks they will starve to death or be murdered? But they are. And love doesn't always have a happy ending, though I thought it must because it is so lovely. The funny thing is, we are starving now, almost, up here. All the game has gone down the mountain. It is going to snow. There isn't much left to hunt. And we're almost out of ammunition." She knew it sounded odd to keep on saying things were "funny" and yet that was the only way she could express them, and make them speakable at all.

"Well, listen," he said, "I just want to tell you this isn't the end." He looked down at her quietly. "I can't go on with this. I don't know what's going to happen, but I can't fight your father. Do you mind if I call you Clara?" He had never called her anything, as far as he could remember. He had carefully avoided being forward or verbally intimate, and yet it had always seemed silly to call her Miss Montrose, for some reason; so he had called her nothing.

"Yes," she said. "Call me by my name. Go on. I want you to finish what you were saying. All of it."

"I said I loved you." They stood looking at each other. The cold wind sighed in the firs, and the creek talked below.

"I love you, too, Mike."

He put out his arms, and she came into them, and he held her for a moment, not tightly, simply sheltering her, feeling the wind on his back, and her, warm inside his arms.

"I won't let you down," he said. "I've got a kind of plan. I need a derringer. Have you got one? And the buggy."

"My father has a derringer under his pillow," she said. "Don't you want something bigger?"

"No. I've got to have something I can hide."

"I'll get it. He won't miss it until tonight."

"I'm coming back tonight, Clara. I'll take the buggy down to bring the ammunition in, and I'll be back tonight."

She ran for the house.

He ran down the path that led to the corrals, across the creek.

Buford Allen came out of the big log house and stood on the porch. His eyes were dry and sunken. The cold wind flicked his beard. His cheeks were hollow and lined. He listened to the cold winter wind and listened to the words of the General, quite clear in his mind. High above him, as he lifted his beard and looked at the mountains, the dark peaks towered like judgments, hiding in the mist. A scatter of snow fell.

He had never seen anything so cold, nor so great, nor so powerful. The longer he lived, the smaller he got, it seemed to him. His enemy had already won the victory. Was there nothing in the end but to become small, to return, at first a child, then dumb, then deaf, then blind, to nothing?

Everywhere the snow grew, like the dancing of a million tiny spirits, and then it began to die, leaving a fine white powder in the crannies of the blown ground.

Within himself he felt the first faint stir of anger and resentment at the General's words, and he stood there in the freezing air, regarding these sparks with contempt and derision, because he could see that they were the beginnings of illusion, the beginnings of lies, erecting themselves again in his own defense, like snow building and obscuring the towering mountain. It was as though there were two people in him, one swiftly recovering his position with lies, the other regarding this artificer with derision.

He was a swine. All his life he had been a swine. He had the heart of a swine. He saw himself with a snout, in swill, or scheming how to get more swill. It was all he had ever done.

But if he was a swine, what were the others? Were not all men, then, swine? And if they were, what else was there to be?

He suddenly saw his father's face, the wide, white brow, the eyes, big like Buford's, but different—open, understanding, and smiling. What did he seem to be saying, patient and loving as he preached, he who had starved because he had no time to hunt? Nothing. The face, smiling, faded.

"Come on," Mike said from somewhere.

Buford looked down from the porch. Mike was sitting in the General's buggy. "We've got to go," he said. "Dickson's waiting for an answer."

Dickson. Suddenly Buford felt sick. All the strength drained out of his back and he felt like falling down the steps onto the ground. Dickson. All his bones ached.

He went slowly down the steps and climbed into the buggy. "Tie my horse behind," he said in a low voice to his son. "I'm getting too old to ride."

14

The Station House
October 19—At Night

All that day the sky darkened. There was no wind, and the cold grew, and everywhere in Warhorse there was the sound of axes and handsaws as the people hurried to finish up a last bit of woodcutting.

Mike and his father sat in the upstairs room. They had come up from the buggy to thaw out, and when Mike had started to go back to take care of the horse, he had found the door locked. That had been at two o'clock. Mike had spent the whole four hours since in needling the old man, who was sitting again by the stove.

The whiskey bottle, so thoughtfully provided by Dickson the night before, was gone. There was nothing to do, nothing to eat, and nothing to drink.

"Warhorse," Mike said. "So this is what we've got, after all these months." He too was waiting for Dickson to come and hear their report, but with a different purpose. The derringer was warm in his pocket. "Last July you were eating oysters in Cheyenne, remember? You almost had your hands on a million dollars. And now you're in a little room, locked in like a tramp in a jail, without a dime. Waiting for a pimp to decide what to do with you. Do you still think you can outsmart the world? Do you?"

In desperation Buford put his hands over his ears and leaned his elbows on his knees. It had been going on for hours. The words came through his hands. Even when he put his fingers directly into his ears, they came through. There was nothing bitter in Mike's words, no resentment, nothing but simple fact.

"All your life you've been trying to get rich. Not just well off, not just comfortable, the way most men do, but rich—stinking rich. Why?"

The old man pressed harder.

"Do you want to lord it over everybody else? Is that it?"

Buford lowered his head still farther and groaned. "Leave me alone," he said. "For God's sake, leave me alone," he said. "Is this why I had a son? So he could shame me in my old age?"

"The same old steamboat," Mike said. "Only this time, you're going to sink with it. You know that, don't you? Dickson will kill us both, just to get us out of the way."

"You're a coward. You're a silly little coward, Mike. He won't kill us." Buford dropped his hands and sat up. "That's what's the matter with you."

"I know Dickson. I've watched him twelve hours a day. He'll kill us both without a thought. Do you remember Keppelbauer? He would have killed us that night, except for our money. He would have killed us the next day, if it hadn't been for the herd. But tomorrow he'll have the herd, and we have nothing left that he can get. He's a devil. And you're a fool. When a devil gets hold of a fool, who wins?"

"You lie!" the old man shouted. His eyes roamed around the room, seeking for some escape from the constant sting of the quiet words. "I've got ten men and Tucker. I can beat Dickson any day."

"Locked up in this room?"

"I'll get out. I'll get a horse."

"Try the door. The horses are all in the barn, down by the bunkhouse. Try."

Buford rubbed his face miserably. "Tucker's got my orders. I haven't been able to send him a message today. He'll come tomorrow. He'll know something's wrong."

"Did you tell Dickson about this message-sending plan?"

"Of course I told him," Buford said. "To warn him."

"Well, if you told Dickson, he sure as hell has figured out some way to outsmart you by now. Tucker'll never show up. Or if he does, it will be too damned late. Don't you know Dickson is smarter than you by now? Smarter than all of us put together?"

Buford got up suddenly and ran to the corner where the firewood was stacked. He grabbed up a piece and turned on his son. "Shut up," he said in a lower voice. "I can't stand any more. If you don't shut up, I'll beat you, I swear it. I haven't beaten you for fifteen years, but I can do it again."

"Go ahead," Mike said. "Why don't you kill me? That would put you in good with Dickson, and maybe he'd give you Montrose's ranch after all."

Buford moaned and turned away. He dropped the piece of wood on the floor and sat down again, covering his ears.

"What about Montrose?" Mike asked. "Haven't you got any feeling at all for him? You've brought all this on him, absolute ruin. He can't possibly escape. Wouldn't you feel better fighting for him? After all, if we're going to get killed in this business, we might at least get killed trying to make things right."

Buford sat still, trying to ignore the voice.

"Why not admit it's our fault," Mike said. "You started it, and I kept you going. So why not admit it? Why not do what Mom's always talking about? A little penance for our sins. A lot of penance for our sins. They used to teach us that at St. Mary's. We'd have to pay for everything wrong we did, even if we got forgiven. So let's pay. You know something? If we went up there and helped old Montrose fight off Dickson—even if we get killed, which we probably would, it might keep us out of hell."

The old man made no move.

Snow began to fall. Mike could see the hard little pellets, coming down dry and tiny, bouncing off the window sill into the growing dark. It must be about seven o'clock.

"There ain't no hell," Buford said, remembering his father in the tents and barns, and all the hell-fire sermons he had heard and hated.

"You can't prove it. Suppose there is? Suppose it's a hundred-to-one shot. A thousand-to-one shot. For God's sake, do something decent for somebody else for once in your life."

"Didn't I give you the Remington pistols?" Buford suddenly shouted, at his wit's end.

"No," Mike said.

"I did, I did, I swear I did."

"No, you didn't," Mike said quietly. "You said you were going to, and I guess you dreamed it up that you did. But you never actually did."

"Oh, Jesus," the old man said, and put his hands over his face.

Mike shut up. His throat ached with talking. He'd done all he could. There wasn't anything left he could say, he'd said everything twice.

He felt the derringer in his pocket.

Mike went to the window. The horse and buggy were still below, there in the street. There wasn't a single reason in the world why Dickson's people had left that horse out there in this cold, but they had. Maybe because it was in front of the house, and the hands kept to the back.

Feet came evenly up the stairs, a key turned in the lock. The door was kicked open. Harris came in with a big tray. The smell of hot food filled the room.

"Well, well, Harris," Buford said, with feeble warmth, the light of fakery arising in his old eyes.

Mike looked at his father distantly.

In the end, what could a man do? As he had thought in Cheyenne, Mike thought now, a man couldn't just kick his old father in the teeth. It was true, children had to overlook the faults of their parents when they grew old, and help them when they needed help.

But there was a limit, and he had passed it long ago. No child ever had the right to condone or excuse or help a parent in sins and follies. His father wouldn't come. He was still lost in some delusion, he couldn't see the truth of what he was doing, and he couldn't be stopped. So, standing there by the window, watching Harris serve the food from the serving dishes to the plates, watching his father's face, he said good-by in his heart. There was no good crying about it. The older you got the less crying you did.

Dickson came into the room—he had come up the stairs without a creak, like a cat—and watched Harris finish serving.

"Eat! Eat!" Dickson said. "Come on, Mike, a man needs food before the battle, and tomorrow we fight. Tomorrow you lead our forces."

Mike looked at him and said, "A good idea."

Harris went out, and Dickson closed the door. "I just thought I'd come up and go over our plans, gentlemen. I suppose Montrose refused to budge."

Buford nodded. "Absolutely."

All Buford did was nod and listen, as though approving what Dickson proposed. The main body was to go up the main road and engage Montrose in a fight at the stone fort, and two men were to go up each side of the canyon and take them from the rear. However it developed, whether the fight was at the fort or at the house, there was to be no open assault by Buford, and no retreat by Montrose. The whole plan was based on Montrose's tendency to stick and fight a pitched battle. Wherever it happened he was simply to be surrounded and kept under slow fire until either killed or forced to surrender for lack of food and water. If he fought from the house, he was to be burned out. He was not to be permitted to surrender, but was to be shot on giving himself up. Dickson was quite carried away by the prospect.

Buford balked at the idea of murdering Montrose after his surrender, and Dickson allowed this change.

It didn't matter to Dickson. The only reason he was up here at all, talking to these fools and disclosing his intentions, was simply to make sure that Buford and his son got out in front, where they could be easily dispatched by Forrest at the beginning of the fight. Why not accede to Buford's scruples? By the time the General gave up, Buford would be dead, so the General could be murdered without hurting anybody's feelings. And, of course, Buford, dead, would take the blame for all the violence and, as a corpse, would hardly care.

"That's a fine plan," Mike said. "An excellent plan. But I'm going to change it." He put his hand into his pocket and casually took out the derringer.

Dickson saw it, and he turned pale, his face stiffening. "How careless of me," he said in a cold voice. "I might have known something like this would happen, with a woman mixed up in it. You were always unstable, Mike."

"Keep your mouth shut," Mike said. He spoke in a quiet, steady voice, not wasting an ounce of energy. "Please understand me, Dickson; if I did nothing but kill you now, I would do a tremendous good. If I killed you now, I would put an end to this whole thing, but your people would get me and my father for it, so I'd better wait for a better chance. But remember, I will do so with pleasure, if you make a single sound. Do you understand?"

Dickson looked at the two barrels of the derringer, and then at Mike's calm eyes.

"I understand perfectly," Dickson said.

Buford simply sat and stared, his mouth full and open.

"Now, listen," Mike said. "We are going down the stairs, with you just in front of me. You will be carrying the case of rifle cartridges, and I will be carrying the other. I warn you now that if you make a single sound or a single sign to the guard, I will kill you on the spot. Do you understand?"

"Yes. I understand perfectly."

"You will go out the front door in front of me. You will put your case in the buggy, and take the reins. I will put mine in, and get up beside you. You will then drive the buggy out of town on Montrose's road. And don't forget, at any time, I shall be most pleased to kill you. My only difficulty is that scruple about murder."

"The Christian ethic," Dickson said, "prevails again." He was getting used to the gun, and cheered up. "I advise you to kill me, my dear boy. If I ever get back, I shall make it hard indeed upon your old father. I take it you are joining Montrose with all our ammunition. For that alone, I would have all his teeth pulled out with a pair of pliers."

"You take it, and you have got it. You can do with my father whatever you please. Whatever you do, he's got it coming."

"What's that?" Buford asked.

"I'm fooling, Buford," Dickson said. "Just fooling."

"Will you come along with me?" Mike asked Buford politely. "I don't intend to argue that matter any more. Make your choice."

"You're a fool," Buford said, his face turning red. One fact in this crisis stood out in his mind. He might lose the ranch. All scruples and pangs of sentimental conscience had vanished in this pinch. In his heart, he hoped Mike would kill Dickson out on the road. "I am not coming," Buford said.

"He's just a boy, Buford," Dickson said. "He'll get over all this. I'll forgive him. Best be patient. Best be calm."

"Get up, Dickson," Mike said. "Do what I told you to do."

Quietly and obediently, Dickson went and lifted one case of cartridges. Mike took the other and managed to get it up on his hip. Dickson opened the door and went down the stairs. Mike followed him, keeping as close as he could so as to keep the guard from seeing the derringer.

Sheffield was on duty. He watched them without a move, Dickson in front leading the way out the door, Mike following with the other case. There was no sound, no movement on Dickson's part, that Mike could see, but he knew Dickson had made some signal, probably with his eyes, because he could see Sheffield stiffen and sit forward slightly.

The snow was falling steadily, still the fine, blizzard pellets, almost ice, granular underfoot. In the dim light from the Station House windows, Mike saw Dickson climb into the buggy, and he followed.

"We have no lights," Dickson said with some satisfaction.

"You get the horse on the Montrose road," Mike said. "He knows his way home."

Dickson flapped the reins gracefully and they went off down the street.

Two hours later the snow eased and stopped. The night was perfectly still, but no longer perfectly black.

A fat slice of moon appeared, and suddenly the whole country was almost blazing with its cool, serene light, glittering on the icy snow. At the same time, the air became sharper, colder, and tiny sounds became audible—the very distant barking of a dog and coyotes, coming through the creaking of the buggy wheels.

Then he heard Sheffield, far behind.

"Pull off the road," Mike said. "He can see us now, and he's probably got a rifle. I'll have to ambush him." They were going along the creek. "Hide the buggy behind those willows," Mike said.

He got out of the hidden buggy. "Lie down on the floor there," he said, and Dickson obeyed.

Mike waited with the derringer. The faint sound of hoofs came nearer. He kept in the trees until the rider came into view, keeping the gun on Dickson's prone body until Sheffield was almost abreast. Then he swung the gun and, taking as careful aim as he could in the moonlight, he fired.

Sheffield stood up in the saddle. The horse bolted from under him, and he fell into the road. Mike leaped on him and held the gun against his forehead. Sheffield was dead. The bullet had hit him in the ear, eighteen inches above the point of aim. It was just so much luck he had been hit at all, as Mike knew it would be, with that little gun, but he was hit and that was that.

He took Sheffield's arms and his mackinaw and laid them by the wheel of the buggy.

"Get out," Mike said. "I am going to enjoy myself, for a change. Perhaps it is my memories of Joanne and Keppelbauer, and the rest of those pigs. It is probably that I am part swine myself, Mr. Dickson. But I am going to mark you, permanently.

"Before I do, get something straight. The General and I are going to fight you, and keep on fighting you. You're depending on him to get cornered. But I'm going to change his mind. You won't catch us in any house, or any fort. There won't be any siege. We'll let you have the place, and pick you off one by one from the trees. Do you understand? In other words, you're getting a war, not a battle. And more than that, if you try to run Tucker's herd in there, we'll run it out again. We'll run you and your damned cows to rags. It's you who'll be burned out of your houses and shot as you come out of your doors—not us. Because as soon as I get to the General, I'm going to make him put you on the defensive. And as soon as I get the warrants from San Antonio, you'll be hanged. What ever made you think you could win, in the end?"

In the snow he beat Dickson, hammering him until he was helpless. Dickson was no fist-fighter. He made a few aimless swings, and collapsed.

Mike picked him up, and with one precise and well-balanced blow, smashed his nose flat on his face.

Dickson lay in the road, his blood black on the moonlit snow.

"It's only about ten miles back to town. If you get up on your feet before you freeze to death, you can make it by dawn."

He turned and went back to the buggy. As he drove it back onto the road, he stopped for a moment and looked down at Dickson, who was sitting up, his nose still bleeding. It would never be aquiline again.

"I'd hate to see you freeze before I got the chance to shoot you in a fight," Mike said. He threw down the mackinaw, and drove off toward the mountains.

Dickson sat there in the powdery snow, his nose hurting as nothing had ever hurt him before. The cold was freezing it. He got up and put on the mackinaw. He stripped the jacket and the shirt off Sheffield's body, and held the shirt over his face. Looking down at the body of the servant who had failed him, he was overcome with fury. He kicked the corpse as hard as he could, kicking the head this way and that, and if he had had any kind of a knife, he would have mutilated it.

Panting, he staggered off down the road toward town, moaning slightly with the pain of his nose and his beaten body. He hurried as fast as he could. Certain changes would have to be made, quickly.

🐃 15 🐃

Buford's Prison—Same Night

Buford had gone to the door, which Mike and Dickson had left open. He had stood there, his mind empty, and watched Sheffield come quickly up the stairs, gun drawn, and close the door in his face.

He sat down on the bed where Mike had been, and listened to the silence, and then to the wheels of the buggy creaking away. The stove glowed hotly in the middle of the room, its heat fiercely penetrating the air for about six feet on each side, where it died against the solid wall of freezing air.

For a long time Buford sat there, thinking of nothing, looking at nothing, and then, very slowly, like the trickle of icy rage melting, loneliness crept in and he sat silent, wondering at it.

Where was Mike? He looked around. It was a senseless question, he knew quite well where Mike was, just then. But he looked around and asked it, because suddenly Mike had gone in a new way, and for the first time in his life Buford realized that Mike had never really left him before and that he had never been lonely.

And now the presence was removed, the Mike who had been holding his elbow for years, who had never let him stumble—unimportant Mike, amusing Mike, the slightly contemptible Mike; for, of course, he had abused him in a casual way, and nobody can help feeling contempt for people they can abuse, even when they love them.

Mike was gone, not sent but departed of his own will. Mike had left him.

He looked around the four walls, freezing in the icy air. Where were they, that he had never seen them before? As he was for the first time alone, for the first time he began to feel something new, a slight fear of the world itself. Suddenly the world was smaller, sharper and clearer, and these walls, which he had simply taken for granted, now took on a strange aspect, as though slightly threatening. He was lonely and he didn't know it, because he had never been lonely before. He was surrounded by the world, and there was no fellow at his back.

Mike, Mike, he kept saying over and over inside himself, the unspoken, inaudible spiritual word repeating like a cry, as though in him there were a soul, stranger to himself, groping in a dark place, crying the name of a friend who had gone. *Mike, Mike;* crying down the unseen corridors of an interior world where all the true things finally happened, not confusedly as with the broken and accidental images of the outside world, but simply and completely. *Mike, Mike;* crying backward through all the lost years, and he could not remember a

666

time where there had not been Mike, somewhere nearby, following, listening, serving.

Now and then a heavy billow of wind, coming out of nothing, smote the house, and it creaked. Trees popped with the frost, and the fire in the stove shook and fell, sighing and spitting. The red was darker, and Buford got up and added more wood to it.

He stood in the middle of the room, listening. For what? To the silence. It was a new silence, a death, there was nothing but silence and the cracking of the trees. Silence was nothing, and into it the heart spent out, and died.

And Buford began to weep, partly with loneliness, with age, with weakness and fatigue, and partly from simple self-pity; but mostly because of shame and remorse, as he looked back on all those dead years, and remembered all the things he had not given his son, and all the things he had not done for him, in his pride and his vanity and his self-centeredness. The son was always a shadow, following faithfully and with devotion. Not a face full of love and gratitude, with eyes shining, clear and well-remembered, but a shadow.

And there was nothing that could be done now. It was all too late. All the times for giving had passed and Mike was gone.

He was gone indeed, and if he had died, the going could not have been more complete.

He remembered him suddenly, in short blue pants and a white shirt, getting into a rowboat on the river—he must have been about four years old, or five—scrambling into the boat with four other boys, shouting and laughing, and starting away down the green water toward St. Mary's, where they tied up the boats every day, and went to school.

He remembered the tiny body when Mike had been born, and how Mary had held it, and loved her one baby, smiling. And always, wherever he had gone, there had been Mike, following along, slowly growing bigger and bigger, joked with, and yet hardly noticed, talked to, and yet never heard, a kind of smaller shadow. Little by little, a bigger and bigger shadow, which gradually had begun to hold him up.

Buford sagged, sitting alone like an old bag of potatoes on the edge of the rope bed. Mike was gone, Mike had gone.

He got up in a sudden fury and seized a piece of firewood and, in simple tantrum, flung the chunk against the wall. It shook the wall, bark flew from the chunk, and it fell with a heavy thumping; and afterward, there was the same silence and the same cold, and he stood again, listening to nothing.

All kinds of things suddenly beset the old man, shame, a vision of himself hopelessly entangled in the final ends of his own shameful weaving, a sudden vision of the future opening before him and closed out again by panic, a shaking of anger, a weakness of despair.

He slipped off the bed and sat on the floor, resting his head on the edge of the bedframe, his eyes shut. A vast whirl of things flew up, like leaves in the winter wind, visions of things past, of dreams and plans, of money lost, money sought.

The cold crept up through his buttocks, and his bones ached. He let them ache, and damned them. There was nothing to get now, with which to glut himself, no hope left; he had nothing left but the stinking corpse he had tried to fill up, a rotten, feeble existence which he had once vaunted and adored. What was this, sitting on the floor? Just garbage, fit for hogs, and he was nothing but a mockery for thieves and swindlers to laugh at.

He fell on the floor and put his forehead on the dirty boards, and said, *God help me. My God, I will not get up, I will die here on the floor, unless you help me.*

And then he remembered his little suitcase, very clearly.

He got up. *What? What?* He asked himself in surprise. He was going to do something, but he hardly knew what it was.

He went straight over to the little suitcase. He was still surprised. He did not know what he was going to do, and yet he also did know, before he did it, and he did it with quiet purpose. He moved with extraordinary ease, without fatigue, with a smoothness and certainty which he had not felt for years, and picked up the suitcase.

He set it down on the bed and opened the door of the stove. He opened the suitcase, and without any emotion whatever, with just a simple, clear purpose, he put the picture in the fire, and the letters, one bundle after another, until the suitcase was empty. Then he closed the suitcase and set it on the floor.

He watched the picture and the letters burn up and crumble, and closed the stove door.

And then he knew he had to follow Mike; all the clouds of illusion parted and he saw what was really at stake, with a sober, simple common sense—not a few thousand animals, a piece of the earth, or money, but something much simpler.

He looked down at an internal vision of a great black chasm at his feet, the edge of murder. If he went forward he would fall into nothing, darkness forever, crumbling, dissolving, hating himself forever, utterly ruined. What he had been about to do could not be repaired, and ruining Montrose would not have been a means, it would have been an end. And he himself would have been lost in the dark, where cattle and money whirled like dust, with all the other vanished illusions. The thing that was at stake was simply himself, his innermost being.

He walked to the door and tried to open it. It was locked. He shook it. He threw himself at it frantically, trying to smash it with his shoulder.

Outside, a voice said, "If you don't stop doing that, I'll come in there and beat you over the head, old man." It was Irving.

Buford knelt by the door and held his head in his hands.

▼ 16 ▼

The Station House
October 20—6:30 A.M.

My dear General Montrose, Dickson wrote on his very best rag paper, as he sat exhausted in the big room of the Station House, barely able to move the pen with his still-numb hands. *I have come to realize the impossibility of pressing our present situation* (what he meant was "inadvisability" but he decided to throw the General a bone or two) *and I would like to meet with you in the presence of the citizens of Warhorse to try to make some kind of settlement of our difficulties.*

Surely we both must realize by now that to pursue our present course must end in disaster for all concerned, and that neither of us can expect to gain. May I suggest, nay, entreat, that you and Mr. Michael Allen come to town this afternoon for a public or private discussion of our difficulties. I will arrange a meeting with the town leaders for four o'clock.

As to what may be proposed, I am of completely open mind. I have not permitted myself to formulate any demands, but continue to hold in first esteem the needs of the public welfare, with the single purpose of preventing bloodshed. Most sincerely, Thomas Dickson.

He stopped shaking with the cold, and sleep was fogging his mind, together with the pain of his broken nose. He had staggered into town at six o'clock, and the town doctor had come and stuck padded bits of shingle up his nostrils in an attempt to straighten and raise the wreckage of that once-classic feature, and he had become slightly habituated to the intense ache.

It was now half past six. Dickson sealed the letter and handed it to Spence. "You waste any damn time, Spence," he said, by way of godspeed, "and I'll cut off your silly ears." Spence went.

Moving with legs of lead, Dickson followed him and watched him gallop off down the street with the letter. Dickson felt as though he were about to drop through the floor, and doubted if he could make it to his bed; but it would be noon before the General got the letter, and he would be able to cope with the situation again by that time. Dickson started to shut the door, and then saw something which drove all the fatigue straight out of him, and left him cold with alarm.

Lee was sitting on the steps of the Sheriff's office, his head in his hands. From the position, from the very fact that he was sitting there, alone in the dark of dawn, waiting under the morning star at the Sheriff's place of official business rather than going to his house, Dickson knew everything. The fool had gone noble and was going to confess. And like all the amateurs there ever were, he was bungling it.

In a fury that almost blinded him—there was a limit to what a man could stand in twenty-four hours—Dickson frantically searched the room for a pistol, found none, and ran to the kitchen for a knife.

He ran out of the house holding it under his coat. He slowed to a walk as his panic faded—there was nobody around to see anything.

As he approached Lee, sitting huddled on the snowy steps, apparently in a stupor of self-abnegation, Dickson managed to smile.

"Up early, John," he said, coming up. "How about a cup of coffee, old man?"

Lee looked up at him with eyes dull with shock.

"I—I—" He looked around. "Oh, my God."

"A damned shame I was awake so early," Dickson said. "For you, that is. Come along, dear boy." He was trying desperately to keep on smiling. "Come along and we'll think things over." He showed the knife and glanced hurriedly around. There was still nobody about, but there was no telling when the miserable rodents would come out of their holes.

Lee looked at the knife. "You wouldn't dare," he said, and the dullness of his eyes cleared a little with a kind of shivering confidence. "You wouldn't dare. You know he has that letter."

"My dear boy," Dickson said, hardly able to withstand the impulse to whip off one of the fool's ears, out of sheer spite. "I know very well Bolt has the letter. I searched his office last week and I couldn't find it. But I shall never harm you. I merely want you to come in out of the cold, John."

"No," Lee said, "you don't dare kill me, and I won't go with you."

"Listen to me, my dear boy," Dickson said, moving up close, his bloodshot eyes glaring on each side of his swollen nose, which was now a pitiful blue, "I am reaching the point where I would kill you for the sheer fun of it. If you force me, I will knife you to death here in the street and burn the Sheriff's office and get your silly letter that way. I shall then break a window in the bank, and swear I caught you trying to rob it. The silly asses will give me a medal for killing you. Now, come along."

Lee stood up, his face wretched, his confidence gone.

"Never fear," Dickson said. "I won't harm you—until I get that letter." He put the edge of the knife suddenly across Lee's bare throat, and pressed the edge against the skin. Lee made a peculiar choking sound, like the squawk of a chicken seized from a roost at night.

"Walk," Dickson commanded, and put the point of the knife in Lee's side.

Lee walked. Together they went back toward the Station House, Dickson's left arm around Lee's shoulder in the most companionable manner, his right hand holding the knife against Lee's ribs.

He drove Lee up the stairs to Buford's room and locked them in together. Then he sent Irving for Forrest.

When Forrest came, Dickson was standing in front of the fire, trying to keep his eyes open in order to keep from falling.

"Forrest, there is a change of plan. Mike Allen got away last night. He killed Sheffield. He might be coming into town this afternoon for a peace talk. You take two men out and wait on Montrose's road for them, and when they come, if they come, kill them. Take shovels with you. I want them buried right there. No bodies, no questions.

"Now, send two other men to wait on the road south out of town. They might come that way for some reason. Not likely, but possible. And three men to the north road. I want all Montrose's people ambushed and dead before anybody sees them. If they happen to come in any other way, I'll be waiting for them with two parties, one in the hardware, one in the library. Send two men to each of those places now, Forrest. And don't fail. If any of them get by, or get away—" He moved up close to Forrest, his eyes glaring, and Forrest instinctively backed away from the ferocity he saw in those two eyes.

He turned and, wobbling on his spent legs, headed for his bed.

17

Buford's Prison
October 20—7:00 A.M.

Buford and John Lee were standing behind their door, listening. Dickson's words, though somewhat distant, were clear enough.

Lee and Buford looked at each other.

"One of us had better get out of here," Lee said. "One of us has got to warn the General."

Buford looked at his little suitcase and rubbed his cold hands together. There was not much wood left, and he was saving it. His hands trembled. In the growing morning light, hungry and still tired, he felt older than ever. "Maybe Montrose won't come down," Buford said. "Surely they're not fools enough to trust Dickson."

"Aren't you a fool?" Lee asked.

"What?"

"If you weren't a fool," Lee said, "you wouldn't be here, locked in. The whole town's fools. I'm a fool. Why shouldn't they be fools? We're all used to believing people. Dickson made us all believe him. Fools."

"And how did you get in here?" Buford asked, rubbing his trembling hands continually. "What was your particular folly?"

"I sold my soul," Lee said. "For three thousand dollars."

"Is that all?" Buford smiled, a wintry, old man's smile. "Have you got the money, my boy?"

"Yes, God help me, I've still got the money," Lee said, looking far off through the window with sad, half-closed eyes.

"Then I'm the biggest fool here," Buford said, "because I sold mine for a million, and I haven't got a damned dime. But I don't think Mike's a fool. He ran out, last night. A good boy."

He looked at the little suitcase, and suddenly gave it a kick, sending it bouncing across the dirty floor. "A good boy." He walked around the room restlessly, grinning in his old man's way.

"If I could get out," Lee said, "I could tell the Sheriff. I wish I had let him kill me in the street. It would have been better. The Sheriff would have found out." He told Buford about the letter he had given to Bolt.

"Maybe I could tie those blankets together and get down from the window."

"There's another window below," Buford said. "You'd go down your blanket and the guard would see you. You think they haven't thought of that? The only chance you have is to jump and run like hell. It's fifteen feet down there. You might break a leg. But you might not, either."

"You see," Lee said, "if it hadn't been for me, none of this would have happened. I thought I was poor. I thought I had to have more money."

"You did?" Buford said. "Isn't that funny. All my life, I've been thinking I was poor. It's the great American crime, being poor. We both had the same thought, and now look at us. Pigs in a pen." He snickered. "Two skinny swine. Have you got a knife?"

"No. What are you going to do?"

"I was going to try to cut the lock out of that door. No good jumping out of the window and breaking a leg. If we had a knife, we could start to work and cut the lock out of that door and get out."

"How long do you think we've got to warn them?" Lee asked. He was standing at the window.

"Afternoon. Maybe three o'clock. They couldn't get a message and get down here any sooner. One of us has got to jump," Buford said. "Go on. From what you say about that letter, you're worth more dead than alive anyway. Nobody knows me. If Dickson shot me, who'd care?"

Lee sat there on the bed. "Yes," he said feebly.

"It's only fifteen feet," Buford said. "I fell out of a barn once. Only broke my arm. You're young."

Lee sat still, hunched on the bed. "He'll kill me."

"You deserve killing," Buford said. "Go on and jump."

"My two little daughters," Lee said. "Who's going to take care of them?"

"Go on and jump, son. It'll do you a world of good. Teach you how unimportant you are."

Lee looked at him miserably.

Heavy feet came up the stairs, the door was unlocked, and Irving came in with a shotgun in one hand.

"Party's going to begin soon," Irving said, slamming the door and setting a chair against it. He sat down with the shotgun across his knees and smiled broadly. "Boss said to me, if they make a sound, just shoot off their goddam heads. Never mind the goddam noise, he says. Just blast away, and I'll say it was the ammunition caught fire in the stove." Irving's grin widened mightily.

"Why all the blasphemy?" Buford asked. "Kindly keep your damn dirty mouth shut while in here with your betters."

The grin fell like a wet towel.

"The first rule of them all is not to use the name of God in vain, you dumb-looking son of a bitch," Buford said. "He didn't say anything about just plain vulgarity, so I can call you a dumb son of a bitch as long as I want."

"Why you damned old crow, I'll—"

"Shut up," Buford screeched in sudden fury. "You big damn slob of a back-woods farmer, put down that gun and fight me." He grabbed up a chunk of wood and shook it at Irving. "I'll beat in your head, you flea-ridden bastard." He was shaking with rage and frustration.

Suddenly Irving burst into a roar of laughter. He laughed out one long breath, and then Dickson's voice said from down the stairs, "Kindly shut up. All of you. Immediately."

Silence fell.

After a while, Lee got up slowly and wandered over to the window.

"Get away from there," Irving whispered harshly. "Boss says no shouting at the people. Get back on the bed or I'll blow your—" He glanced at Buford. "I'll blow your damn lousy guts out," he finished.

"You're learning, stupid," Buford said quietly, with a gentle, infuriating smile. "The fear of the Lord is the beginning of wisdom. For such a clod-faced bas-tard as you, you're pretty smart.

"When I was a boy," Buford said quietly to Lee, "the first time I dived, I just ran and held my nose and shut my eyes. It was noisy and sloppy, but it got me in the water."

Lee dropped his head. "Yes," he said. "I know. Just don't badger me. I know."

Irving spat on the floor.

It was then noon.

At three o'clock Buford heard Tucker's voice in the street and jumped to his feet. Irving raised the shotgun at him. He stood silent. Dickson was talking to Tucker in the street below.

Dickson said pleasantly, "Why, they went hunting, Tucker, old man. Jolly good to have you here; fine thing, right on schedule."

"Never mind all that," Tucker said. "You send a man and bring Buford back. In a hell of a hurry, too, buster."

"I will," Dickson said. "And Buford and I will ride down there. Just as soon as they come back. I know Buford'll want to look at the cattle."

"I got twelve men," Tucker said. "I'm ready for anything, Dickson. Buford had better show up quick and Mike with him. You understand?"

"Don't worry," Dickson said. "We'll be there. I'll send somebody out to find him right now. Where are you camped?"

"Half a mile south, down on that big meadow by the creek. Hell, you can't miss six thousand head of cattle. And you'd better not fail."

Tucker turned his horse and loped off down the street.

At four o'clock, Dickson came up the stairs and knocked on the door. Irving got up and opened it. Dickson, not entering, said, "I just got a message, Irving. Montrose'll be down at seven o'clock. Come on. I need you in the hardware store. I'll keep a watch on these two from downstairs."

They went out and locked the door.

"Seven," Buford said. "We got till five, Lee."

"You heard him," Lee said. "He said he was going to keep a watch from downstairs. Whoever jumps is going to get killed right there in the street."

"Why don't you ever learn?" Buford asked. "If you're going to do it, do it now. Every time you wait, something happens, like Irving coming up here, and then it's too late. I'll give you till six to jump, and then I'll do it. I can't do much good, nobody knows me. But at least I'll try."

"All right," Lee said wretchedly. "All right. Just leave me alone, will you? I'll do it."

18

Buford's Prison—Dusk

At about six o'clock, with the last streaks of the bleak winter sunlight coming through the window, Lee stood up straight from the bed and cried out, "Oh, Christ, oh, Christ!"

He let out another cry, without words, just a wail of hopeless beseeching, and ran to the window. He had intended to make it a heroic dive evidently, but as he neared it, he quailed. He jerked up the lower sash and put his leg over the sill, and then, holding to the sill with both hands, put the other over. He let himself down outside as far as he could, and then shouted, "Bolt! Bolt!"

It was the worst possible time of day for him to have done this, just as six-thirty in the morning had been the worst possible time for him to confess to Bolt in the first place. Almost everybody in Warhorse was home eating supper. There was one woman walking down the street. She stopped and looked at Lee hanging from the window. Her mouth opened and she screamed timidly, and ran for her life.

Lee dropped. He cried out sharply.

Buford ran to the window.

"Bolt! Bolt!" Lee shouted, trying to raise his wail of pain to some volume. He was hobbling away up the street, hunching along, dragging one foot, hopping on the good one, and then, with cries of pain, dragging the other. He fell and began scuttling on all fours. There was nobody in the street at all.

A door slammed below Buford. He saw Dickson come out with a rifle. Dickson raised the rifle. The shot cracked in the empty street and Lee fell on his face. He rolled over and lay there, twenty yards from Bolt's office, and rolled back and forth. Dickson aimed carefully again, and fired. Lee lay still. His upraised hands flopped down onto the roadway.

Bolt came running around a corner out of an alley. He had a sandwich in one hand, and a pistol in the other. He stood looking at Lee, and then at Dickson. Dickson ran up the street toward him, carrying the rifle.

"The damned thief!" Dickson shouted. "Sheriff, arrest him!"

The Sheriff did not move. Dickson reached the body. He looked up from it to Bolt, and as the two looked at each other, the Sheriff's eyes expressing nothing, Dickson's rifle came up and covered him. Bolt had been totally perplexed by the spectacle of the dead Lee and Dickson with the rifle. He didn't like Dickson, but that didn't mean anything. It was only when he looked at Dickson's eyes that he realized something completely foul was in the air, and then it was too late.

"Drop that pistol," Dickson said.

Bolt looked at the black end of the rifle bore. There was nothing he could do. He knew perfectly well, from Dickson's eyes, that he would shoot, and he wondered why he didn't. He dropped his gun.

Bolt remembered the letter. Suddenly a dogged anger came up in him. He looked once at Dickson, and then turned his back on Dickson and walked back to his office, his sandwich still in his hand. Dickson ran after him.

As Dickson ran into the office, Bolt was opening the letter.

"Drop that!" Dickson shouted desperately.

Bolt read on. When he was finished, he put the telegram in his pocket.

"Give me that," Dickson said.

"No," Bolt said. He didn't understand why Dickson didn't shoot him, and he was waiting for the bullet.

Dickson looked around desperately. In one blow, his edifice of lies had fallen. He was known. And yet it had been so sudden that he was still caught in the lying. He still had the habit of depending on lies. The problem was to get the Sheriff out of sight.

Bolt made a sudden dive for him. Dickson shot wildly and, dodging, evaded Bolt, and as Bolt fell and slid on the floor, Dickson clubbed him on the back of the head.

Bolt lay moving feebly and groaning. Dickson got the telegram out of his pocket.

"Get up or I'll kill you," Dickson said, prodding with the rifle. "Walk. To the Station House."

The Sheriff got up and staggered out of the office, Dickson behind him.

Bolt walked straight ahead.

"Hurry," Dickson said, his voice shaking. His one hope was to cover things up. Killing the Sheriff was one thing that he could not distort.

Dickson forced him into the Station House and up the stairs to Buford's room. He slammed the door on them and locked it.

He stood on the stairs where they could hear him mumbling. "My God, my God," he kept saying. Then he ran down the stairs shouting for Harris. It had occurred to Dickson in that moment that the worst might come to the worst. A wise man always kept a line of retreat open. A saddled horse was worth a million dollars at certain times.

Buford and Bolt looked at each other.

"You're the Sheriff?" Buford asked. "Montrose is coming into town. That bastard is ambushing him."

"Why didn't he kill me? I caught him red-handed in a murder. Jesus, now I see everything. Jesus, what fools we've been."

"You ain't any bigger fool than me," Buford said. "I've been trying to get out of this room all day, and I just saw the answer right in front of my face. Look there by the wall."

The last flare of sun died, and the shadows began to creep up the street. Men were calling to each other, asking questions about Lee's body lying in the street.

"There ain't a damn one of them knows the truth but me," Bolt said. "If Montrose comes into town, they'll gang up on him. Jesus, what a pack of fools."

"Get out of my way," Buford said, and set the chair against the door. "I guess the ball has opened."

He opened three one-pound cans of black powder and set them on the seat of the chair against the door and then poured loose powder out of a fourth around them. He brought four heavy pieces of wood from the woodpile and stacked them over the powder, to direct the force of the blast against the panel.

"For God's sake," Bolt said, "for God's sake."

"Upend that bed and lie down behind it," Buford said. "Open the windows to let out the blast."

"You'll blow the whole place up," Bolt cried.

"What of it?" Buford answered, busily smashing out the windows. "If I had a little more powder, I'd blow up the whole goddam town."

He went to the fire, shoveled out a panful of coals, and carried them to the chair by the door. He dropped the coals into the wood, and ran.

Mike and Montrose, with their four men and a small wagon loaded with hay, came into Warhorse through back lots. They had left the road outside of town as a precaution against ambush. The wagon bumped and heaved over stumps and rocks, but it got through. They were carrying eight one-gallon cans of kerosene and had two torches, unlighted—sticks wrapped with old cloth, wired on, and soaked in the oil. They were all heavily armed, carrying two pistols apiece and one rifle each.

"Here's the orders," Montrose said as they dismounted in the dusk. "Mike, you go down to the south end of town and ride up the main street and draw their fire as we planned. I'll wager there's eight of them in town now, and that means you two boys will have to work fast. Remember, they'll be in a crowd somewhere, waiting for the showdown, because Dickson will have to figure we might have got through, or scared off, or might even bring the attack on him. So he'll have posted his men somewhere to meet us, on the chance. We've got to find out where, in order to work our plan, and all we can do is draw their fire. Mike, don't ride down that street too damn fast. You've got to give them a chance to shoot at you. Keep low, and don't give them time to aim, and you'll get through all right.

"You two boys," the General said to the gun fighters, "keep in the alleys till you see where the gunfire is coming from, after Mike rides through. Run around to the back and fire the back entrance of their place and when they get burned out the front, Joe and I and Mike will catch them coming out into the street. Joe will have the hay burning in the street to give us light to shoot by. We'll cut down the odds right away.

"We'll kill as many as we can, and meet in the church and then run for the woods. You got it? The object is not to fight a battle, but to hit and run. Reduce the odds. Tomorrow we can hit them again. But now's our big chance. So long, boys."

He turned his horse and headed up the street toward the north end of town.

The two gun fighters and Montrose's third hand went off into the dark, carrying their cans of kerosene and torches. Joe headed the wagon south, Mike riding alongside.

In the Station House, Buford and the Sheriff lay behind the bed, holding on to themselves.

Just as Buford was getting ready to get up and dump some more coals on the powder, the place blew up.

All they knew was a terrible blast, and then they found themselves coming out of a stupor into a blinding, whirling hell of sulfur smoke and heat. Buford saw a flame through the smoke. The twenty-five-pound keg had gone off, too, from the concussion. The door was blown out. The room was burning.

They staggered up and pawed through the smoke to the door.

The Sheriff kicked the burning wreckage of paneling out of the way and half-fell down the stairs. He ran out shouting. Buford tried to kick out the fire, and then ran down after him.

He saw the weapons on the wall and grabbed down an old saber. The remains of the burning paneling fell down the stairs behind him, coals and embers rolling across the room. He dashed for the door.

At the south end of the street, Mike pulled up and sat in the shadow of a house. Joe drove the hay wagon out into the roadway. He had the lantern in his hand.

"So long, boy," Mike said as Joe slapped the reins.

"So long, son," Joe said, and the wagon creaked off.

Up the street there was the roar of the explosion. The flash shot out from the second story of the Station House, and then the dark jumped back again. Joe's horse reared. Joe beat it down and raised his rifle, ready.

"Go on," Mike said. "Never mind all that. Follow the orders."

Joe slapped the horse up again, and Mike sat forward in the saddle. The one problem he had was whether to run straight up the street, or to identify himself in some way.

He began to say his prayers. They all came back out of nowhere at once, all the ones he had learned as a child, in school, from his mother.

The smell of black powder came down the street, and then he saw his father, walking unsteadily toward him in the gloom of the winter evening. The old man's clothes were smoking, and his face and arms were black with burned powder. The flames shot out of the Station House roof and the red light glowed around on the trees.

"Dad," Mike shouted, and spurred his horse out into the road.

"Jesus, son, get out of here," Buford said, stumbling up. "They're all laying for you and Montrose."

"Where?" Mike asked.

"I don't know."

"I've got to draw their fire so my boys can locate them," Mike said. "Then they'll take them from the rear."

"Mike, wait. Tucker's camped south of town. I'm going to get him. Don't ride down that street, boy. You'll be killed for sure. Oh, God, where's a horse?"

"I can't wait," Mike said, pointing at Joe's wagon, trundling up the street toward the church at the north end of town. "It's too late to change the plans now."

Hoofs were beating up the street from the direction of the railroad station.

"It's the other ambush," Buford said. "Give me one of those guns, boy; I got to get me a horse."

Three riders came up the road, and at the same time, light streamed down the street, and they saw the wagon load of hay go up in flame. The loose horse ran up the street, dragging tugs and lines, and they saw Joe scuttling for an alley. The bright flame spread everywhere, towering fifteen feet. Mike handed his father a pistol.

The three riders came on fast, the flame-light shining on bits and leather, and Buford fired. Mike put two shots into them. They slowed up, panic-stricken from the gunfire in their faces. Two of them turned and ran back down the road, and Buford had the bridle of the third, and was shooting straight into the rider's face. The rider toppled out of the saddle, and Buford climbed up. He sat there for a moment, waving his saber at his son, laughing, with the red flame firing his white beard and hair. He turned the horse and beat it into a run with the flat of the saber.

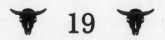

▼ 19 ▼

In the Town—Evening

Mike bent over his horse's neck and put it into an easy lope, keeping it well gathered up and rolling. He headed for the burning wagon, keeping to the right, and forty yards from it he let out a yell that sounded all the way to the church. He put his spurs to the horse and let it out, and it lunged forward, passing the burning Station House at a dead run.

At the same time, gunfire burst from one of the dark buildings and bullets snapped above and behind him. He spurred the horse into a second line of fire, a second volley pouring at him, and as he passed, the horse died on its feet, shot in the neck.

Falling, it slid on its breast for fifteen yards, sending Mike flying through the air another ten beyond. Mike scrambled up and ran on with the bullets snapping at his heels.

He made the door of the church just as the ambush party from the north road galloped into town. They saw him dash into the building, and opened fire. Montrose was lying on the floor in the doorway. He opened fire on the three men in the party, and they broke and ran for cover, smashing into the two closest stores. They began to fire back into the church doorway, and Mike dragged one of the heavy benches into the doorway for cover.

"Take a window and keep moving," the General said, rising and running to one of the small panes on each side of the door.

Some men were coming from the hardware store, and then flames began to jump up from the back of the library. There was shooting down the street, from behind the buildings.

"They'll be coming out," the General said. "Where in hell is Joe?" He was ignoring the firing from the two nearest stores.

A man ran out of the hardware, and then another, into the light of the burning wagon. Then two out of the library.

"Take the hardware," the General said, and fired. Mike shot at the first one on his side of the wagon. A man on each side dropped into the street. The others stood still, turning, looking for the firing. Mike and the General fired again. The General's man dropped and began crawling away, and Mike's ran down an alley.

A bullet from the near stores smacked through the wall and caught the General in the leg. He fell to the floor and cursed.

Somebody came in the back of the church. "It's me!" Joe hollered. "The bastards chased me all the way here; they're in the woods, two of them. Mike, you hold that door, I'll cover this one."

The firing fell off, except in the rear, where a rifle kept up steadily.

Mike moved over to the General's window. "Damn the luck," the General groaned, "we can't run now. They'll rush us."

"You bleeding much?"

"Hell, no. It's not much of a hole." The General dragged himself to the doorway.

Suddenly a long flame poured up the side of the church, showing in through the side window.

"They're all around us," the General said. "They'll burn us out."

The firing began again from the near stores, hard and steady, and Mike saw men running out of the doors under cover of it, heading for the sides of the church.

"They'll be shooting in through the windows," the General said. "You run, Mike. I'll kill a few."

Four stores, besides the library and the hardware, were burning now, as well as the church and the Station House. The street was brighter than day and hot as summer.

Down the street men and women were hurrying with buckets and washtubs, trying to save the rest of the stores. The sparks were flying high, coals falling on all the roofs.

The rush started, men pouring in on the front door from both sides. The General was firing fast into the huddle. The rush fell back, and then it came on again. Mike slammed the doors shut and shot the bolt.

Outside some of Dickson's men were shooting in through the walls. Mike and the General dropped to the floor. The gang in the street had got a beam from somewhere, and they began to ram into the doors. At the second blow, the end of the beam came through the panel, and Mike fired through the hole, driving them away from the ram.

From down the street a hammer of hoofs grew, and outside, the crowd of men began to shout, and the firing rose hotter, but it was away from the church. Mike ran to one of the windows. Dickson's men were flying from the porch and Tucker's gang was whirling and wheeling in the street, men jumping and running for cover, firing as they ran, Tucker in the middle, shouting. Tucker with a pistol charged his horse straight into one of the bunches of men beside the church, and back through it. Mike saw his father run his horse back past the church, his old saber raised, his teeth grinning in his beard.

The Sheriff and Lewin joined Tucker's men, who were dismounting and running for cover. Curtis was down the street running out of the bank with boxes of papers. Back under one of the store porches, well protected, Dickson was shouting at his men, firing a pistol. He shot Tucker out of his saddle, and Tucker rolled and ran out of the way of the loose horses. The horses ran down the street, neighing in panic, and the firefighting citizens scattered before them, and came back, shrieking and weeping and shouting and cursing each other while the flames roared steadily.

Out in back, Buford ran his horse through the brush and the trees, where the two rifles were spitting at the back door of the church. He ran down one of the men, breaking his arm with the saber, and the other rose out of the brush and ran for safety. Buford ran the horse straight over him, wheeled, and rode back to the church. He ran inside.

The old man was crazy with delight, his eyes danced. "Oh, Jesus!" he shouted. "Come on, Mike, get the General out of here before he gets fried."

He grabbed the General under the arms, and Mike took him by the feet, and they ran out of the door and down the steps, into the shadows behind one of the stores.

Buford looked up and saw Dickson down the street, in the act of shooting at one of Tucker's men. Buford fired and ran toward him, and Dickson turned.

Dickson fired back at Buford, and Buford ran on, shooting. Dickson's gun snapped empty. At twenty feet he hurled the empty pistol at Buford. It caught the old man square in the forehead and he went down, stunned. Dickson ran away toward the Station House. He saw Spence run into the Station House ahead of him.

In the Station House, the whole bar was burning, and the smoke was too thick for Dickson to stand upright. He ran in, panting, and got a fresh gun from his office.

The fire was climbing up the banisters and eating already at the treads. Smoke poured up the well and through the open bedroom doorway.

He heard Spence cursing furiously above the roar and snapping of the fire.

Dickson leaped up the burning stairs and into the bedroom. Spence was just coming out of the closet, his clothes scorched and his eyes streaming from the smoke and heat. The locks had been shot out. He held the suitcase in both arms. One end of it was badly burned and partly burned bills were slipping out. He held a gun awkwardly in his right hand.

"Where are you going with that?" Dickson asked sharply.

Spence said nothing for a moment. The two men stood staring at each other.

"I thought," Spence said, "things were going wrong. I thought I'd better—"

"You thought you'd beat me to it," Dickson said. "You lying son of a bitch, I should have known what you were waiting for."

Spence dropped the suitcase and raised his gun at the same time, but Dickson fired first. He fired again, and Spence dropped where he stood, his hands over his belly, groaning. His hair caught fire from the smoking cracks in the floor and he screamed. Dickson stooped and tried to beat the flames of the suitcase out with his hands. He grabbed it up and ran. The whole room was on fire.

A small shower of money fell out on the staircase, and at that instant, Dickson's hair also caught fire. He, too, screamed.

He turned and ran down the stairway, holding the burning suitcase under one arm, beating at his burning head with the other. Halfway down, his leg went through a burned tread and he tumbled the rest of the way down, wrenching his knee badly, the suitcase rolling ahead of him out into the big room.

In the middle of the room, the suitcase fell open and the money poured out, bundles tumbling over each other, burned ribbons breaking, bills sliding in heaps. Dickson made it to the suitcase, his burned, bald, red head oozing water, and his face twisted in a grimace of agony.

He grabbed up the little sacks of diamonds, stuffing them frantically into his pockets. It was almost impossible to breathe with the heat and smoke scorching his lungs. He had to crawl close to the floor.

A ceiling joist fell behind him. He jumped up and ran for the back door, and just as he reached it, another beam fell flaming before him, and he fell over it.

He scrambled to the burning doorway, then got out into the air. He ran on down the slope toward the barn, where Harris had saddled three horses. Half blinded by the smoke and heat, he ran into one of the cottonwood trees, and stood there peering around, his clothes smoking and glowing like tinder. He stumbled on into the dark, away from the fire.

Buford burst into the burning barroom of the Station House just as Dickson went out the back. He charged in, his arms over his head, jumping over the fallen beam, and saw the suitcase standing in the middle of the floor with the burning money around it.

With a cry of horror he fell on his hands and knees, choking with smoke, his eyes streaming, and frantically clutched for the bills. He grabbed handfuls of money and stuffed bills wildly into his pockets; more handfuls he stuffed into the front of his shirt, burning himself in frantic haste. His fingers burned from the flaming bills, and he uttered shriek after shriek of pain, and yet still he fought to get more and more.

He stood up finally, clutching money to his breast like leaves, burning francs, pounds, dollars, rubles, every kind in fringes of flame, charred and uncharred, the bills dribbling from his arms in showers.

He staggered forward. Beams crashed about him. In a burst of panic he ran for the back door. The whole second floor came down behind him, and he fell on his face outside in the open air, the money flying in all directions. He got to his knees, trying to beat out his flaming clothes and the flaming money at the same time.

He heard a shot. Down the slope, Dickson stood in the dark with the flaming house at his back, his burned, bald head making him cry out. His knee buckled under him as the panic of the fire left him, the wrench too bad to stand. He sat down on the ground twenty feet from the corral fence, the pistol in one hand, his handkerchief in the other, barely sixty yards from the waiting horses.

"Harris!" he shouted, looking wildly about. The streams of tears from the smoke and burns were slacking a little. He saw Harris's vague shape climbing the fence.

Harris ran up and stood over him, the red of the fire flickering on his black face, pink on the whites of his eyes.

"Where's the money?" Harris asked.

Dickson saw the knife in his hand and swung the pistol toward him. At the same time, Harris swung down the knife, driving at Dickson's chest. The knife caught Dickson in the shoulder as he dodged, and Dickson shot Harris square in the face. Harris fell without a sound and Dickson struggled to his feet. He limped toward the fence.

Down the slope, Buford saw Dickson stagger toward the corral fence, and then he saw the horses beyond it.

With a hoarse shout, Buford got up, raising his gun. Dickson was awkwardly climbing the fence. He turned at Buford's shout, saw him outlined against the fire of the house, and, standing with his feet on one pole, his knees balancing him against the top rail, he fired back.

The bullet cracked past Buford's head, and Buford rubbed the smoke tears out of his eyes. He aimed with all the coolness he could manage, and squeezed off carefully.

Dickson cried out sharply. For a moment he stood there, and then he fell backward, arms whirling to save himself, on the other side of the fence.

Buford ran after him, gun ready, bills falling out of his clothing as he hurried.

From beyond the corral fence a scream rose, a single, throat-tearing shriek of agony and fear, rising straight into the night. Buford stopped, frozen with horror at the sound.

It rose again, dizzying Buford for a moment, and then he ran forward again.

Dickson lay on his back in the pigpen. In his panic, his eyes still smarting, and bewildered by the dark after the fire, Dickson had climbed the wrong part of the fence. He lay on his back thrashing and kicking wildly while the pigs attacked him, squealing and grunting with fury.

Buford in a panic of terrible haste fired through the fence. He killed one pig, and then another, and then the gun snapped empty. He threw the gun furiously at the nearest pig, and looked around desperately for something to drive them off with. He found Dickson's spiked stick, and jabbed futilely at the nearest pig with it, but it paid it no attention.

The horrible screams of despair, agony, and fear rose more and more weakly and finally ceased, as Buford, numb with horror, helplessly watched. It was too much for him. He fell to his knees, exhaustion overtaking him as the screams died. There was no sound left now but the snuffling and grunting of the pigs as they rummaged and gorged. Buford covered his face with his hands, and still he could see it, the horrible, mangled wreckage of what had been Dickson.

He vomited, kneeling there with Dickson's money sticking out of his pockets and out of his shirt, money he had owed, stolen, and fought over. And there was the man he had shot, whom he had tried to kill, and now, suddenly, all the hatred, misery, fear, and desperation Dickson had caused him was gone, wiped out in an instant, gone in the horror of what had happened to his enemy.

He knelt there, padded with Dickson's money, stupefied under the shock of his death, and he remembered his father's face for the second time. Suddenly the money felt like a great load of the most disgusting filth, as though there were toads and leeches clinging to him, sucking his blood, and it seemed to him that all these bills were covered with other people's blood and crimes.

He began to pull it out of his pockets and let it fall to the ground, shaking it free of his fingers. He pulled the stinking bills out of his shirt until he was free of it all, and it lay in the dirt beside the mire of the pigpen.

He could see his father talking to the people now, his mouth forming inaudible words. He was talking about love, and Buford remembered it now. He had always been talking about love, that was all. Telling the people about love, about the love of God for them, and the love they should have had for each other.

That was all he had ever talked about, and he had died of it, starved because he was too busy preaching on the circuit to stop and hunt. That was all he had said, what Buford had never wanted to hear: that love was all any man could ever get, and ever give. That there was nothing else to be had, in the end; that love was everything, and that all the rest was shadows.

Buford stood up. He opened his eyes and looked at his enemy in the slime— hardly even a man any longer, a poor, pitiful shape of bloody bones, helpless in the mire, slowly sinking, as the beasts gnawed and crunched, slowly disappearing, with all Dickson's fortune, in eighteen inches of muck.

Buford went down to the creek and, sitting on the edge, washed his hands in the icy water. He took off his shoes, and washed his feet, and then washed his face and his beard, and then his bare chest, and when he was through with that, he wandered quietly back along the barn, no longer even hearing the pigs, not even noticing the money. He stopped by the barn and looked at the fire. The heat of it spread all the way to the creek, making the winter night comfortable, and he listened. He noticed that it was snowing again, the tiny flakes coming down soft this time, and slow.

Up in the town, the shooting had died. Dickson's men had scattered with a pounding of hoofs, flying like dark bats in all directions.

Women, weeping and some of them hysterical, men talking in a daze, wandered about as though lost. The whole town had burned, except the houses off the main street. There was nothing left of Warhorse except two long lines of hot coals and naked chimneys, stoves standing alone or overturned. As it snowed, the people instinctively held their hands out to the warm coals of their possessions even while they cursed and wailed.

Buford stood alone and watched them, from within the shadows of the cottonwood trees. He quietly regarded one simple fact: All this ruin, desolation, and death was one man's fault.

His.

20

Montrose's House
October 23—Noon

The one thing he had come to Warhorse to find, Buford thought, he had not even seen: Clara Montrose's grave. He sat at the long table in the main room of the General's house, drinking a cup of fresh coffee. He was going to leave now, and he could not go without seeing it, and yet he couldn't even ask where it was. Not any more.

"Three thousand head go to you, General," he said. "For God's sake, sell them and give the money to the people in Warhorse. Just to keep them off my trail. Tucker told me how bad the feeling is."

Buford looked at his son, sitting on the other side of the table, and at Clara beside him. He pulled two bills of sale out of his pocket. "The other three thousand go to Mike and Clara. I won't want any cows in San Antonio. Give me two dollars, Mike." He shoved the bills of sale across the table. "I'll take two bucks, and two horses as well, and I'll ask you to pay off Tucker when he gets well, and all our men. You and Clara keep the rest, with my blessing."

"You'd better wait until we can sell part of the herds," Mike said. "You can't go home broke."

"I don't want any of the dirty money," Buford said. He had seen it burning by the handful, like leaves. He sat remembering Dickson's death, and the smell of the mire of the pigpen, and the feel of the money in his hands.

Mike rolled two silver dollars across the table. Buford got up and stood looking at Mike and Clara. "Come and see your mother. After you get married."

Mike nodded.

"I wish—I wish—" Buford said, looking down at Mike. "I wish that all these years—when we were together—I could have been—"

He stopped. How could he say it? The past was all gone and it could never be changed now. It was lost for good.

He went over to Mike and kissed him on the cheek. He turned and went out on the porch, with his two dollars clinking in his pants.

Mike came out after him, because he did not want to sit there, the way he felt.

He watched the old man go down the steps, and then followed him. He held the old man's horse while he mounted. "Dad. Don't think I ever looked down on you. I never did, I never will. If you want me—I'll always be here."

The old man looked at him, and Mike saw his smile. "I know, Mike," he said. "I always loved you, too."

He turned his horse and went away down the road, with the packhorse following.

He rode on down the canyon, letting his horse amble, loose-jointed, the packhorse moseying along behind.

He sat slumped in the saddle, his knees open, and as he looked down at the greasy, cracked old reins in his left hand, and at the worn leather of the pommel, and felt the loneliness beside him where Mike had been for so long, he wanted to stop and die.

To move on, into that gaunt world before him, so wide, so empty, made him cringe inside himself, huddling back. It was a motion that made no sense, this aimless drifting forward into nothing.

Buford, helplessly gripped by the terrible fatigue in himself, the exhaustion in the face of his futile future, pulled up the gray horse and sat there, his eyes shut. He was out of sight of the house, and the brave front he had made, the erectness of spine he had maintained, all crumbled. Out of sight, need he be brave? Everything in him, his heart, his memories, his habits of cheerfulness and optimism, cried out to go back up the road, to stay with his people, to see his grandchildren. And yet it was impossible. He had destroyed their town.

Where was her grave? Surely there was one good thing left, surely he would feel again the happiness of her presence, in some way. He could hear her voice in his mind now, and feel the lift, the happy peacefulness it had always given him.

He picked up the reins and the gray horse wandered on down the ruts. Trees and granite passed, and as he emerged from the wall of the mountains, the growing distance behind him made a quieting of all his feelings. The sky, limited till now to a wide V between the mountain spurs beside him, opened out, and the whole expanse of the country lay before him.

A dry, cold wind, bitter off the snow, blew down the canyon, and whirling around the granite escarpments above him, beat at him in gusts. Far below him the icy water of the creek washed and rattled over the boulders, and there was nothing around him but cold, silence, and loneliness.

Home! Home! he thought. *If I could go home, if I had a home—if there were one place in the whole world where there was a fire waiting, and food, and a roof which was mine; where there was even a dog to wag his tail at me and pant a welcome; how much I would give for that much of peace, a simple place, somewhere in this hideous wilderness.*

Suddenly he saw, off to his left, on a brow of the mountain which bore three pine trees, a little fence enclosing a square of ground about twenty feet to the side. Immediately he knew what it was, and pulled up.

He sat looking at it, forgetting everything he had been thinking and feeling. A kind of hope, a distinct sensation of love, came up in him, like new life.

That was it, that was the thing he had come so far to get.

He almost laughed to himself—destitute, on a charity horse, beaten, broke, and futureless, he was seeing for the first time what had brought him to this end.

He left the road and guided the gray over to the little fence. The bare, dead grass waved in the chill wind, the ungrazed stalks rising high and shining in the sun out of the inch of snow that was already melting. There was a plain headboard on the one grave. That was all.

Clara Montrose.

He got down from the gray and went over to the headboard, feeling that remarkable alertness and expectation.

Under the pine trees, the deep bed of needles had caught the snow, and the grave was quite bare. Somebody had hoed it, during the summer, to keep the weeds off.

There it was. What else had he expected? A simple, bare, clean grave, quite smooth on top, about six feet long, as usual; no different from any other grave.

He knelt down beside it, not out of any reverence, but simply to be closer to it, to see it in more detail.

What was there? The icy wind cut down off the cliffs through the pines. A patch of bright sun struck down on the bare ground. No sound, but the soft breathing of the air in the pine needles above him.

All the bright expectancy, the actual, physical emotion of love burned in him, like a light held through a long night.

What had he expected?

He put his hands down on the earth of the grave and brushed the dirt. There was nothing—just damp earth, a few twigs and needles. A momentary seizure of anguish came over his mind and lifted like a hand again. A voice in him cried out, *Are you there? Are you there?* exactly as to a living person—as though she herself had been waiting, somehow alive, for all of death, in that place.

Why don't you answer?

How many years he had dreamed of this, the comfort, the happiness of being with her, in some mysterious sense, as though he and she could talk across death in some mysterious, but quite real fashion.

And he had never once questioned his dreams! Not once. Always there had been the illusion of the possibility of somehow feeling her presence again, in some way.

And there was nothing here but dirt. And down below, just bones. The bones of a body that she had left. Not a thousand miles below, or a thousand feet, not at some extravagant distance which would have left him the seed of another illusion—but merely six poor feet below, so close, indeed, that it was horrible.

And that was death—a simple departure. Oh, how the earth stared back at him, that blank, bare space of dirt, with what cold vacancy. He dug his fingers into the dirt, scratching it, as though indeed it did conceal something, some-where; but there was nothing in his hands but dirt, the same simple black stuff that he could have found anywhere. He dug them in again, and held his dirty hands up in front of him, and there he knelt, with nothing in his hands but dirt, as he had knelt by the place where Dickson died, with nothing in his hands but burned paper, a uselessness of filth.

He stood up, his mind vacant and quiet. The wind blew about him, clean and fresh. He looked down at the grave again—it was still vacant. It meant nothing to him. And then he looked out across all that vast country, seeing it from high on the mountain; it, too, was empty. He imagined all the trails that he had followed, leading him to this place—the years of the war, the years after, years of struggle, by one means or another, to gain this one point, eventually, to be, as he thought, with her.

And all wasted. All of it gone, with nothing to show, and he was here at last, and it was nothing, nothing at all. And there had never been anything.

He had loved something, surely. The love was real enough. But if a man could love something that didn't even exist—And then he realized that what he had loved had really existed—the illusion had existed, that was all. The love was real enough. And yet, if it was real, why was it so lost? Why had he come all this way for nothing?

The hostility of the country bore down on him, like the chill of the wind. It would stand no loitering. There was no welcome on this earth for any man; wind and cold and hunger would drive him on from place to place as long as he could move, and in the end the silent, savage, relentless indifference of his enemy, the world, would drive the very soul out of his body.

And yet he loved.

He went, blown on by the wind. He picked up the reins of his horse, and led it and the pack animal back to the road. He stood there, unable to summon up the will even to climb back on the horse. He stood by the gray, the reins in his hands, head bowed, and slowly, because there was no other living thing at all, he leaned his forehead on the neck of the horse.

And then he realized with perfect simplicity that of course the peculiar qual-ity of his own life was actually to be loving something; and then he saw, for the first time in his life, that everybody else was busy loving something, even Dick-son—whether it was money, or card games, or women, or horseraces, or cats, or antique furniture, they were all blundering around after the objects of their various loves.

Then he thought, *It was not even Clara that I loved. There was nothing actually in her that I loved, but something about her that I thought was there—something I read into her, just as I imagined that there was something in Mary that I loved, only that was not quite so great an illusion. Clara simply suggested something to me that was lovable; it was not herself, for she was not particularly good, or intelligent, and so on. And no doubt that was why I got drunk—because I knew in my heart it was an illusion.*

Ah, yes, he thought, *I wanted the illusion.* And then he saw the truth of it—that he wanted to love, but he had never found anything good enough to love except an illusion. And if this was so, then why did anybody love anything? Why had God put it in his heart, why did it exist at all, for what purpose?

He began to think that he saw the answer. But the actual thought that came into his mind was quite different. It came suddenly, as a realization that he had no friends in San Antonio, and no future. He couldn't start in business again there, for everybody who had trusted him had lost money on him. True, he owed nobody, since they had all settled with Dickson for his notes, and Dickson had died. But still, they would not receive him again.

Suppose I go back? he thought.

Why shouldn't people despise me?

Isn't it just?

Don't I see the justice of it in myself? Is there anything else that I have a right to, except being despised? For if I did all these evil things, then surely there can be no relief for me, until I have paid. And how can I pay now, except just to bow my head and take it? Surely, if I give up, if I bow, God will have mercy.

Why had he thought of that? Buford looked around quickly. He was not in the habit of such thoughts; and yet it had seemed most reasonable to him, and the idea of God's mercy had even brought tears to his eyes. But why was he thinking such things now? Well, what else? In the end, when everything else was lost, there was nothing left but God. In the end, all the vanquished turned to God, when the rods of fortune had beat them flat.

If I go home, Buford thought, looking up, looking far away, *if I go home and endure their spite, and their contempt, and their scorn, and endure the worst of all, their damnable kindness, I will have done the just thing.*

But he did not think of justice as an idea, he did not really think consciously at all. It was an ache in his bones, as though the marrow of his bones themselves ached and cried out for justice.

He began to think of another dream, and he watched it carefully, to see if it was an illusion. It was simply to live at peace, not attempting great things, not living over chasms, not inducing others to risk themselves; but simply to live in peace. And this meant to live fairly. And if he, for instance, heard of anyone who needed help, to help him, and so keep the scales balanced.

His heart began to brighten. He climbed laboriously back on the gray, and clucked to it, and they ambled on down the road.

He did not look back toward that grave. He was thinking new thoughts, jumping ahead again, dreaming dreams. Who could tell what might happen? (when he had labored through the penance he had just begun)—Mary had five Mexican seamstresses. Without a doubt the pious ladies of San Antonio could be eased out of—or rather, persuaded to donate—sewing machines, used, or perhaps even new.

Your Excellency, he began, addressing the Archbishop in his imagination, *don't you see what this means? Production of cheap dresses for the poor, by the poor—very modest profits, so much for the other diocesan charities, so much for myself as manager—Good God, Your Excellency, a man must live, and a little to put by—ten sewing machines, your Excellency! It's all for the poor—am I not poor? And if, as St. Paul said, a servant is worthy of his hire, am I not your servant? And if, like Zaccheus, I give half of what I get to the poor, if I get more, will not the poor profit as much as I? Your Excellency, think of it! Twenty sewing machines!*

So he rode down, his white beard shining in the sun, his old eyes bright and alert, sparkling with thoughts and imaginations, ruminating plans and dreaming of rewards—but of a strange kind, for these rewards would be just.

The icy wind blew after him, blowing up dust and dirt over his back, but he rode along unaware of it, his mind turned inward. The wind tugged at his coat, flapping the tears in his clothing, tugging his beard, but he paid no attention.

The sun would burn him, the ice freeze him, the devils would rage and ridicule him. And why not? For he was nothing, now, but an animated old crate of bones, a burden of garbage, a comic, foolish, futile, weak, and pompous creature—still half drunk with pride, still full of illusions, stumbling, as a billion other human beings had stumbled, through the last contortions of a precarious existence.

But he was on the way, and he had a talisman. If he kept it, nothing could touch him or impair him or cause him, in the end, to be lost in that terrible darkness which he so much feared. Because, in his heart, in the midst of all the flapping wreckage of his life, there was, now, the beginning of a love, at last, of justice.

About the Editor

MARC JAFFE began reading western pulps as a teenager, moved on to the slicks with some of his favorite writers, and began his long publishing career as Western and Mystery Editor at the New American Library. He was Louis L'Amour's editor while Editorial Director at Bantam Books during the Sixties and Seventies, and included such others as Will Henry, Dan Cushman, and W.R. Cox among his friends and authors. For Bantam, he acquired the Wagons West series from Lyle Kenyon Engel's Book Creations, Inc., which has over 20,000,000 copies in print. Mr. Jaffe, a longtime associate member of the Western Writers of America, has had his own imprint, Marc Jaffe Books, at the Houghton Mifflin Company since 1987, and says, "I will not retire until I bring another A.B. Guthrie to the house." He lives on a tree farm in Berlin, New York, with his wife and two children.